THE POWER OF ONE

Bryce Courtenay was born in South Africa but has spent the greater part of his adult life in Australia. He lives in Sydney and is a creative director at George Patterson advertising agency. He also writes a weekly column in the *Australian*. *The Power of One* was his first novel. The sequel, *Tandia*, was published in 1991.

By the same author
available from Mandarin Paperbacks

Tandia

BRYCE COURTENAY

THE POWER OF ONE

MANDARIN

A Mandarin Paperback

THE POWER OF ONE

First published in Great Britain 1989
by William Heinemann Ltd
First published in paperback 1990
Reprinted 1990 (five times), 1991 (four times), 1992 (five times)
This edition published 1992
by Mandarin Paperbacks
an imprint of Reed Consumer Books Limited
Michelin House, 81 Fulham Road, London SW3 6RB
and Auckland, Melbourne, Singapore and Toronto

Reprinted 1992 (three times), 1993 (five times)

Copyright © Bryce Courtenay 1989

A CIP catalogue record for this title
is available from the British Library
ISBN 0 7493 1221 1

ACKNOWLEDGEMENT

I must begin with my wife Benita who went without a husband for the year
this book took to write. Others who helped with advice, legwork, research
and the million chores that go into making a book happen are Adam
Courtenay, my second son, who as a young journalist became, with Peter
Keeble, my continuity readers. I am indebted to them both. Other names
that tumble out easily because they were generous with their help are: Alex
Hamill and Owen Denmeade, Linda Van Niekerk, 'Chig' Chignall, Siân
Powell, Jill Hickson, Tony Lun, Ken Cato, Joe Loewy, Annette Dupree,
Laura Longrigg and Kate Medina. I thank you all.

Printed and bound in Great Britain
by Cox & Wyman Ltd, Reading, Berks

For Maude Jasmine Greer and Enda Murphy.
Here is the book I promised you so long ago.

ONE

This is what happened.

Before my life started properly, I was doing the usual mewling and sucking, which in my case occurred on a pair of huge, soft black breasts. In the African tradition I continued to suckle for my first two and a half years after which my Zulu wet nurse became my nanny. She was a person made for laughter, warmth and softness and she would clasp me to her breasts and stroke my golden curls with a hand so large it seemed to contain my whole head. My hurts were soothed with a song about a brave young warrior hunting a lion and a women's song about doing the washing down on the big rock beside the river where, at sunset, the baboons would come out of the hills to drink.

My life proper started at the age of five when my mother had her nervous breakdown. I was torn from my lovely black nanny with her big white smile and sent to boarding school.

Then began a time of yellow wedges of pumpkin, burnt black and bitter at the edges; mashed potato with glassy lumps; meat aproned with gristle in grey gravy; diced carrots; warm, wet, flatulent cabbage; beds that wet themselves in the morning; and an entirely new sensation called loneliness.

I was the youngest child in the school by two years, and I spoke only English, the infected tongue that had spread like a plague into the sacred land and contaminated the pure, sweet waters of Afrikanerdom.

The Boer War had created a great malevolence for the

English, for the *Rooineks*. It was a hate that had entered their bloodstream and pocked the hearts and minds of the next generation. To their barefoot sons, I was the first live example of the congenital hate they carried for my kind.

I spoke the language which had pronounced the sentences that had killed their grandfathers and sent their grand-mothers to the world's first concentration camps, where they died like flies from dysentery, malaria and black water fever. To the bitter Calvinist farmers, the sins of the fathers had been visited upon the sons, unto the third generation. I was infected.

I had had no previous warning that I was wicked and it came as a fearful surprise. I was blubbing to myself in the little kids' dormitory when suddenly I was dragged from under my horrid camphor-smelling blanket by two eleven-year-olds and taken to the seniors' dormitory, to stand trial before the council of war.

My trial, of course, was a travesty of justice. But then what could I expect? I had been caught deep behind enemy lines and everyone, even a five-year-old, knows this means the death sentence. I stood gibbering, unable to understand the language of the stentorian twelve-year-old judge, or the reason for the hilarity when sentence was passed. But I guessed the worst.

I wasn't quite sure what death was. I knew it was some-thing that happened on the farm in the slaughter house to pigs and goats and an occasional heifer. The squeal from the pigs was so awful that I knew it wasn't much of an experience, even for pigs.

And I knew something else for sure; death wasn't as good as life. Now death was about to happen to me before I could really get the hang of life. Trying hard to hold back my tears, I was dragged off.

It must have been a full moon that night because the shower room was bathed in blue light. The stark granite walls of the shower recesses stood sharply angled against the wet cement floor. I had never been in a shower room

2

before and this place resembled the slaughter house on the farm. It even smelt the same, of urine and blue carbolic soap, so I guessed this was where my death would take place.

My eyes were a bit swollen from crying but I could see where the meat hooks were supposed to hang. Each granite slab had a pipe protruding from the wall behind it with a knob on the end. They would suspend me from one of these and I would be dead, just like the pigs.

I was told to remove my pyjamas and to kneel inside the shower recess facing the wall. I looked directly down into the hole in the floor where all the blood would drain away.

I closed my eyes and said a silent, sobbing prayer. My prayer wasn't to God, but to my nanny. It seemed the more urgent thing to do. When she couldn't solve a problem for me she'd say, 'We must ask Inkosi-Inkosikazi, the great medicine man, he will know what to do.' Although we never actually called on the services of the great man it didn't seem to matter, it was comforting to know he was available when needed.

But it was too late to get a message through to Nanny, much less have her pass it on. I felt a sudden splash on my neck and then warm blood trickled over my trembling, naked body across the cold cement floor and into the drain. Funny, I didn't feel dead. But there you go. Who knows what dead feels like?

When the Judge and his council of war had all pissed on me, they left. After a while it got very quiet, just a drip, drip, drip from someplace overhead and a sniff from me that sounded as though it came from somewhere else.

As I had never seen a shower I didn't know how to turn one on and so had no way of washing myself. I had always been bathed by my nanny in a tin tub in front of the kitchen stove. I'd stand up and she'd soap me all over and Dee and Dum, the two kitchen maids who were twins, would giggle behind their hands when she soaped my little acorn. Sometimes it would just stand right up on its own and everyone

3

would have an extra good giggle. That's how I knew it was special. just how special I was soon to find out.

I tried to dry myself with my pyjamas, which were wet in patches from lying on the floor, and then I put them back on. I didn't bother to do up the buttons because my hands were shaking a lot. I wandered around that big dark place until I found the small kids' dormitory. There I crept under my blanket and came to the end of my first day in life.

I am unable to report that the second day of my life was much better than the first. Things started to go wrong from the moment I awoke. Kids surrounded my bed holding their noses and making loud groaning sounds. Let me tell you something, there was plenty to groan about. I smelt worse than a kaffir toilet, worse than the pigs at home. Worse even than both put together.

The kids scattered as a very large person with a smudge of dark hair above her lip entered. It was the same lady who had left me in the dormitory the previous evening. 'Good morning, Mevrou!' the kids chorused, each standing stiffly to attention at the foot of his bed.

The large person called Mevrou glared at me. '*Kom*,' she said in a fierce voice. Grabbing me by the ear she twisted me out of the stinking bed and led me back to the slaughter house. With her free hand she removed my unbuttoned pyjama jacket and pulled my pants down to my ankles. 'Step,' she barked.

I thought desperately, she's even bigger than Nanny. If she pisses on me I will surely drown. I stepped out of my pyjama pants, and releasing my ear she pushed me into the shower recess. There was a sudden hissing sound and needles of icy water drilled into me.

If you've never had a shower or even an unexpected icy-cold drenching, it's not too hard to believe that maybe this is death. I had my eyes tightly shut but the hail of water was remorseless, a thousand pricks at a time drilling into my skin. How could so much piss possibly come out of one person?

Death was cold as ice. Hell was supposed to be fire and brimstone and here I was freezing to death. It was very frightening, but like so much lately, quite the opposite to what I had been led to expect.

'When you go to boarding school you'll sleep in a big room with lots of little friends so you won't be afraid of the dark anymore.' How exciting it had all sounded.

The fierce hissing noise and the deluge of icy piss stopped suddenly. I opened my eyes to find no Mevrou. Instead, the Judge stood before me, his pyjama sleeve rolled up, his arm wet where he'd reached in to turn off the shower. Behind him stood the jury and all the smaller kids from my dormitory.

As the water cleared from my eyes I tried to smile gratefully. The Judge's wet arm shot out; grabbing me by the wrist he jerked me out of the granite recess. The jury formed a ring around me as I stood frightened, my hands cupped over my scrotum. My teeth chattering out of control, a weird, glassy syncopation inside my head. The Judge reached out again, and taking both my wrists in one large hand he pulled my hands away and pointed to my tiny acorn. 'Why you piss your bed, Rooinek?' he asked.

'Hey, look there is no hat on his snake!' someone yelled. They all crowded closer, delighted at this monstrous find.

'Pisskop! Pisskop!' one of the smaller kids shouted and in a moment all the small kids were chanting it.

'You hear, you a pisshead,' the Judge translated. 'Who cut the hat off your snake, Pisskop?'

I looked down to where he was pointing, my teeth changing into a quieter timpani. All looked perfectly normal to me, although the tip was a bright blue colour and had almost disappeared into its neat round collar of skin. I looked up at the Judge, confused.

The Judge dropped my arms and using both his hands parted his pyjama fly. His 'snake', monstrously large, hung level with my eyes and seemed to be made of a continuous sheath brought down to a point of ragged skin. A few stray

5

hairs grew at its base and, I must say, it wasn't much of a sight.

More serious trouble lay ahead of me for sure. I was a Rooinek and a pisskop. I spoke the wrong language. And now I was obviously made differently. But I was still alive, and in my book: where there's life, there's hope.

By the end of the first term I had reduced my persecution time to no more than an hour a day. I had the art of survival almost down pat. Except for one thing: I had become a chronic bed wetter.

It is impossible to be a perfect adapter if you leave a wet patch behind you every morning. My day would begin with a bed-wetting caning from Mevrou, after which I would make the tedious journey alone to the showers to wash my rubber sheet. When the blue carbolic soap was rubbed against the stiff cane bristles of the large wooden scrubbing brush I was made to use, fiercely stinging specks of soap would shoot up into my eyes. But I soon worked out that you didn't need the soap like Mevrou said, you could give the sheet a good go under the shower and it would be okay.

My morning routine did serve a useful purpose. I learned that crying is a luxury good adapters have to forgo. I soon had the school record for being thrashed. The Judge said so. It was the first time in my life that I owned something that wasn't a positive disadvantage to adaptation. I wasn't just a hated Rooinek and a pisskop, I was also a record holder. I can tell you it felt good.

The Judge ordered that I only be beaten up a little at a time. A punch here, a flat-hander there, and if I could stop being a pisskop he'd stop even that, although he added that, for a Rooinek, this was probably impossible. I must confess, I was inclined to agree. No amount of resolve on my part or saying prayers to Nanny or even to God seemed to have the least effect.

Maybe it had something to do with my defective acorn? I forced a hole in the side pockets of my shorts through which my forefinger and thumb would fit. I took secretly to pulling my foreskin and holding it over the tip of my acorn as long as I could in the hope that it would lose elasticity and render me normal. Alas, except for a sore acorn, nothing happened. I was doomed to be a pisshead for the rest of my life.

The end of the first term finally came. I was to return home for the May holidays: home to Nanny who would listen to my sadness and sleep on her mat at the foot of my bed so the bogey man couldn't get me. I also intended to enquire whether my mother had stopped breaking down so I would be allowed to stay home.

I rode home joyfully in the dicky-seat of Dr 'Henny' Boshoff's shiny new Chevrolet coupé. Dr Henny was a local hero who played fly-half for the Northern Transvaal rugby team. When the Judge saw who had come to pick me up, he shook me by the hand and promised things would be better next term.

It was Dr Henny who had first told me about the nervous breakdown, and he now confirmed that my mother was 'coming along nicely' but her nervous breakdown was still with her and she wouldn't be home just yet.

Sadly this put the kibosh on my chances of staying home and never leaving again until I was as old as my granpa, maybe not even then.

As we choofed along in the car, with me in the dicky-seat open to the wind and the sunshine, I was no longer a Rooinek and a pisskop but became a great chief. We passed through African villages where squawking chickens, pumping wings desperately, fled out of the way and yapping kaffir dogs, all ribs and snout and brindle markings, gave chase. Although only after my speeding throne had safely passed. As a great chief I was naturally above such common goings-on. Life was good. I can tell you for certain, life was very good.

Nanny wept tears that ran down her cheeks and splashed onto her huge, warm breasts. She kept rubbing her large, dark hand over my shaven head, moaning and groaning as she held me close. I had expected to do all the crying when I got home but there was no competing with her.

It was late summer. The days were filled with song as the field women picked cotton, working their way down the long rows, chatting and singing in perfect harmony while they plucked the fluffy white fibre heads from the sun-blackened cotton bolls.

Nanny sent a message to Inkosi-Inkosikazi to the effect that we urgently needed to see him on the matter of the child's night water. The message was put on the drums and in two days we heard that the great medicine man would call in a fortnight or so on his way to visit Modjadji, the great rain queen.

The whites of Nanny's eyes would grow big and her cheeks puff out as she talked about the greatness of Inkosi-Inkosikazi. 'He will dry your bed with one throw of the shin-bones of the great white ox,' she promised.

'Will he also grow skin over my acorn?' I demanded to know. She clutched me to her breast and her answer was lost in the heaving of her belly as she chortled all over me.

The problem of the night water was much discussed by the field women who pondered deeply that a matter so slight could bring the great one to visit. 'Surely a grass sleeping mat will dry in the morning sun? This is not a matter of proper concern for the greatest medicine man in Africa.'

It was all right for them, of course. They didn't have to go back to the Judge and Mevrou.

Almost two weeks to the day Inkosi-Inkosikazi arrived in his big, black Buick. The car was a symbol of his enormous power and wealth, even to the Boers, who despised him as the devil incarnate yet feared him with the superstition of all ignorant God-fearing men. None was prepared to pit the catechism of the Dutch Reformed Church against this aged black goblin.

All that day the field women brought gifts of food. By

late afternoon a small mountain of kaffir corn and mealies, gem squash, native spinach and water melons had grown under the big avocado tree next to the slaughter house. Bundles of dried tobacco leaf were stacked up beside it and, separated by two large grass *indaba* or meeting mats, lay six scrawny kaffir chickens. These were mostly tough old roosters, four-hour boilers, their legs tied and their wings clipped. They lay on their sides with their thin, featherless necks and bald heads caked with dust. Only an occasional 'sckwark!' and the sudden opening of a bright, beady eye showed that they were still alive, if not exactly kicking.

One especially scrawny old cock with mottled grey feathers looked very much like my granpa, except for his eyes. My granpa's eyes were pale blue and somewhat watery, eyes intended for gazing over soft English landscapes, whereas the old cock's were sharp as a bead of red light.

My granpa came down the steps and walked towards the big, black Buick. He stopped to kick one of the roosters, for he hated kaffir chickens almost as much as he hated Shangaans. His pride and joy were his one hundred black Orpington hens and six giant roosters. The presence of kaffir chickens in the farmyard, even though trussed and clipped, was like having half a dozen dirty old men present at a ballet class.

He greatly admired Inkosi-Inkosikazi who had once cured him of his gallstones. 'I took his foul, green muti and, by golly, the stones blasted out of me like a hail of buckshot! Never a trace of a gallstone since. If you ask me, the old monkey is the best damned doctor in the lowveld.'

We waited for Inkosi-Inkosikazi to alight from the Buick. The old medicine man, like Nanny, was a Zulu. It was said that he was the last son of the great Dingaan, the Zulu king who fought both the Boers and the British to a standstill. Two generations after the Boers had finally defeated his *impis* at the Battle of Blood River, they remained in awe of him.

9

Two years after that battle, Dingaan, fleeing from the combined forces of his half-brother Mpande and the Boers, had sought refuge among the Nyawo people on the summit of the great Lebombo mountains. On the night he was treacherously assassinated by Nyawo tribesmen he had been presented with a young virgin, and the seed of the second greatest of all the warrior kings was planted in her fourteen-year-old womb.

'Where I chose blood, this last of my sons will choose wisdom. You will call him Inkosi-Inkosikazi, he will be a man for all Africa,' Dingaan had told the frightened Nyawo maiden.

This made the small, wizened black man who was being helped from the rear of the Buick one hundred years old.

Inkosi-Inkosikazi was dressed in a mismatched suit, the jacket brown and shiny with age, the trousers blue pin-stripe. He wore a white shirt meant to go with a detachable starched collar, the collarless shirt was secured at the neck with a large gold and ivory collar stud. A mangy-looking leopard-skin cloak fell from his shoulders. As was the custom, he wore no shoes and the soles of his feet were splayed and cracked at the edges. In his right hand he carried a beautifully beaded fly switch, the symbol of an important chief.

I had never seen such an old man; his peppercorn hair was whiter than raw cotton, small tufts of snowy beard sprang from his chin and only three yellowed teeth remained in his mouth. He looked at us and his eyes burned sharp and clear, like the eyes of the old rooster.

Several of the women started keening and were quickly rebuked by the old man. 'Stupid *abafazi*! Death does not ride with me in my big motor, did you not hear the roar of its great belly?'

Silence fell as my granpa approached. He briefly welcomed Inkosi-Inkosikazi and granted him permission to stay overnight on the farm. The old man nodded, showing none of the customary obsequiousness expected from a Kaffir and my grandpa seemed to demand none. He simply shook the old man's bony claw and returned to his chair on the stoep.

Nanny, who had rubbed earth on her forehead like all the other women, finally spoke. 'Lord, the women have brought food and we have beer freshly fermented.'

Inkosi-Inkosikazi ignored her, which I thought was pretty brave of him, and ordered one of the women to untie the cockerels. Two women ran over and soon the chickens were loose. They continued to lie there, unsure of their freedom, until the old man raised his fly switch and waved it over them. With a sudden squawking and flapping of stunted wings all but one rose and dashed helter-skelter, their long legs rising high off the ground as they ran towards open territory. The old cock who looked like Granpa rose slowly, stretched his neck, flapped the bits of wing he had left, his head darting left and right, slightly cocked as though he were listening; then, calm as you like, he walked over to the heap of corn and started pecking away.

'Catch the feathered devils,' Inkosi-Inkosikazi suddenly commanded. He giggled, 'Catch an old man's dinner to-night.'

With squeals of delight the chickens were rounded up again. The ice had been broken as five of the women, each holding a chicken upside down by the legs, waited for the old man's instructions. Inkosi-Inkosikazi squatted down and with his finger traced a circle about two feet in diameter in the dust. He hopped around like an ancient chimpanzee completing five similar-sized circles, muttering to himself as he did so.

The incantations over, he signalled for one of the women to bring over a cockerel. Grabbing the old bird by its long scrawny neck and by both legs, he retraced the first circle on the ground, this time using the bird's beak as a marker. Then he laid the cockerel inside the circle where it lay unmoving, its eyes closed, a leg protruding from each wing.

He proceeded to do the same thing to the other five chickens until each lay in its own circle in front of the crowd. As each chicken was laid to rest there would be a gasp of amazement from the women. It was pretty low-grade magic but it served well enough to get things under way.

Inkosi-Inkosikazi moved over and squatted cross-legged in the centre of the indaba mats and beckoned that I should join him. It was the first time he'd acknowledged my presence and I clung fearfully to Nanny's skirts. She pushed me gently towards him and in a loud whisper said: 'You must go, it is a great honour, only a chief can sit with a chief on the meeting mat.'

He had the strong, distinctly sweet smell of African sweat, mixed with tobacco and very old man. After all I had been through in the smell department, it wasn't too bad, and I too sat cross-legged beside him with my eyes glued to the ground in front of me.

Inkosi-Inkosikazi leaned slightly towards me and spoke in Zulu. 'Tomorrow I will show you the trick of the chickens. It's not really magic, you know. These stupid Shangaans think it's magic but they don't deserve to know any better.'

'Thank you, sir,' I said softly. I was pleased at the notion of sharing a secret. Even if it was only a trick, it was a damned clever one which might confound the Judge and the jury if I could get my hands on a stray chicken at school. My confidence in his ability to change my status as a pisskop was growing by the minute.

Inkosi-Inkosikazi indicated to Nanny that she should begin the matter of the night water. Two women were quickly delegated to start the cooking fire and the rest of the field women settled down around the indaba mats, taking care not to touch even the tiniest part of the edge.

African stories are long, with every detail cherished, scooped up for telling a thousand times over. It was a great moment for Nanny as she stood alone in the rapidly fading twilight and told her story. She spoke in Shangaan so that all could share wide-eyed and groan and nod and sigh in the appropriate places.

The hugeness of Mevrou with her moustache they found amazing, the injustice of the Judge and jury they took in their stride, for they all knew how the white man passes sentences that have no relationship to what has been done. The pissing upon me by the Judge and jury had them rocking and moaning and holding their hands to their ears. Such an indignity was surely beyond even the white man?

In the sudden way of Africa it was dark now. A piece of green wood crackled sharply in the fire sending up a shower of sparks. The leaping flames lit Nanny's face; there was no doubt that they would remember this teller of a great story of misery and woe. Tears flowed copiously as she told of how death finally arrived in a shower of icy piss that jetted from the loins of the great, moustached angel of perdition.

I must admit I was hugely impressed, but when Nanny got to the part where my snake had no hat which, in my opinion, was the most important bit of the lot, they cupped their hands over their mouths and, between the tears, they started to giggle.

Nanny concluded by saying that the business of my night water was an evil spell brought upon me by the angel of death with the moustache like a man and waterfall loins, so that she could return each morning to feed her great beating sjambok on my frail child's flesh. Only a great medicine man such as Inkosi-Inkosikazi could defeat this evil spell.

The light from the fire showed the deeply shocked faces of the women as Nanny finally sat down, heaving with great sobs, knowing that such a tale had never been told before and that it might live forever, warped into a Shangaan legend.

I can tell you one thing, I was mighty impressed that any person, most of all me, could go through such a harrowing experience.

Inkosi-Inkosikazi rose, scratched his bum and yawned.

With the handle of his fly switch he prodded my weeping nanny. 'Get me some kaffir beer, woman,' he demanded.

Dee and Dum, the twin kitchen maids, served me my dinner, as Nanny was required to attend to the drinking and other needs of the scrawny old wizard. Both little girls were wide-eyed with the excitement of it all and told me I was the bravest person they had ever known.

By bedtime Nanny was at my side as usual, arriving with a large sweet potato, its tummy open with a spoon sticking out of the middle, tiny wisps of steam curling upwards, condensing on the handle. There is something about a sweet potato that cheers you up when you are low and celebrates with you when you are happy. Sweet potatoes baked in their jackets have a very large comfort factor built into them.

Nanny's excitement was still with her, she grabbed me and crushed me to her enormous bosom and laughed and told me how I had thrust greatness upon her with the coming of the old monkey who was, nevertheless, the greatest medicine man in all Africa; how the telling of the tale of the night water showed that a Zulu woman could be a teller of tales superior in every way to even the best told by the most eloquent Shangaan.

I pointed out that she had entirely missed the matter of my school record for canings. A large tear rolled down her cheek. 'In the matter of white man's punishment, the black people already understand that the body can be broken by a sjambok but never the spirit. We are the earth, that is why we are the colour of earth. In the end it is the earth who will win, every African knows this.'

Whatever all that was supposed to mean, it didn't answer my question. Nanny finally left me, but first she lit the paraffin lamp and turned it down low, but not so low that I wouldn't recognise the bogey man should he try to sneak into my room.

'Tonight Inkosi-Inkosikazi will visit in your dreams to find the way of your night water,' she said, tucking me in.

*

The morning after the night Inkosi-Inkosikazi went walkabout in my dreams, he summoned me to sit alone with him again on the meeting mat. From an old leather bag he produced the twelve magic shin-bones from the great white ox. Then, squatting on his haunches as he prepared to throw the bones, he commenced a deep, rumbling incantation that sounded like distant thunder.

The strange bone-yellowed dice which would solve my bed-wetting habit briefly clicked together in his hands and then fell onto the ground in front of him. Inkosi-Inkosikazi flicked at them with his forefinger, and as he did so, tiny rolls of thunder came from his throat. With a final grunt he gathered them up and tossed them back into his ancient leather satchel.

Inkosi-Inkosikazi's eyes, sharp pins of light in his incredibly wrinkled face, seemed to look right into me. 'I visited you in your dreams and we came to a place of three waterfalls and ten stones across the river. The shin-bones of the great white ox say I must take you back so that you can jump the three waterfalls and cross the river, stepping from stone to stone without falling into the rushing torrent. If you can do this then the unfortunate business of the night water will be over.'

I nodded, not knowing what to say. After all, five-year-old kids are pretty rotten at riddles. His face became even more simian as he chuckled, 'When you have learned this lesson I will show you the trick of the chicken sleep.'

I had seen the faint marks of last night's circles, but no chickens. I guessed that they had been consigned to the communal tummy. I only hope he doesn't use one of Granpa's black Orpingtons, what a kerfuffle that would be, I thought.

'Now, listen to me carefully, boy. Watch and listen. Watch and listen,' he repeated. 'When I tell you to close your eyes you will do so. Do you understand?'

Anxious to please him I shut my eyes tightly. 'Not now! Only when I tell you. Not tight, but as you do when your

15

eyes are heavy from the long day and it is time to sleep.'

I opened my eyes to see him crouched directly in front of me, his beautiful fly switch suspended slightly above my normal sightline. The fall of horsehair swayed gently before my eyes.

'Watch the tail of the horse.' My eyes followed the switch as it moved to and fro. 'It is time to close your eyes but not your ears. You must listen well for the roaring of water is great.'

A sudden roar of water filled my head and then I saw the three waterfalls. I was standing on an outcrop of rock directly above the highest one. Far below me the river rushed away, tumbling and boiling into a narrow gorge. Just before the water entered the gorge and churned white I noted the ten stepping stones, like ten anthracite teeth strung across its mouth.

Inkosi-Inkosikazi spoke to me, his voice soft, almost gentle. 'It is late, the bush doves, anticipating nightfall, are already silent. It is the time of day when the white waters roar most mightily as water does when it is cast in shadow.

'You are standing on a rock above the highest waterfall, a young warrior who has killed his first lion and is worthy now to fight in the legion of Dingaan, the great impi that destroys all before it. Worthy even to fight in the impi of Shaka, the greatest warrior king of all.

'You are wearing the skirt of lion tail as you face into the setting sun. Now the sun has passed beyond Zululand, even past the land of the Swazi and now it leaves the Shangaan and the royal kraal of Modjadji, the rain queen, to be cooled in the great, dark water beyond.

'You can see the moon rising over Africa and you are at peace with the night, unafraid of the great demon Skokijaan who comes to feed on the dark night, tearing its black flesh until, at last, it is finished and the new light comes to stir the sleeping herd boys and send them out to mind the lowing cattle.'

As I stood on the great rock waiting to jump, I could see the new moon rising, bright as a new florin above the thundering falls.

'You must take a deep breath and say the number three to yourself as you leap. Then, when you surface, you must take another breath and say the number two as you are washed across the rim of the second waterfall, then again a deep breath as you rise and are carried over the third. Now you must swim to the first stone, counting backwards from ten to one, counting each stone as you leap from it to the next to cross the rushing river.' The old medicine man paused long enough for me to work out the sequence he had given me. 'You must jump now, little warrior of the king.'

I took a deep breath and launched myself into the night. The cool air, mixed with spray, rushed past my face and then I hit the water below, sank briefly, rose to the surface and expelled the deep breath I had taken. With scarcely enough time to take a second breath I was swept over the second waterfall and then again I fell down the third roaring cascade to be plunged into a deep pool at the base of the third waterfall. I swam strongly and with great confidence to the first of the great stones glistening black and wet in the moonlight. Jumping from stone to stone I crossed the river, counting down from ten to one, then leaping to the pebbly beach on the far side.

Clear as an echo, his voice cut through the roar of the falls. 'We have crossed the night water to the other side and it is done, you must open your eyes now, little warrior.' Inkosi-Inkosikazi brought me back from the dreamtime and I looked around, a little surprised to see the familiar farmyard about me. 'When you need me you may come to the night country and I will be waiting. I will always be there in the place of the three waterfalls and the ten stones across the river.' Pointing to what appeared to be an empty mealie meal sack, he said: 'Bring me that chicken and I will show you the trick of the chicken sleep.'

I got up and walked over to the sack and opened it. Inside the sharp, beady red eye of the chicken that looked like Granpa blinked up at me. I dragged the sack over to where the previous circles he'd made in the dust had been and the old man rose and called over to me to draw a new circle in the dirt. Then he showed me how to hold the old rooster. This was done by securing the main body of the chicken under your right armpit like a set of bagpipes and grabbing it high up its neck with your left hand so that its featherless head is held between forefinger and thumb. Getting a good hold of its feet with your free hand, you dip the chicken towards the ground at an angle of forty-five degrees while squatting on the ground with the chicken's beak not quite touching the rim of the circle. The beak is then traced around the perimeter three times whereupon the bird is laid inside the circle.

The old man made me practise it three times. To my amazement and his amusement, the old rooster lay within the circle docile as a sow in warm mud. To bring the chicken back from wherever chickens go in such trying circumstances, all I needed to do was touch it and say in a gruff voice, 'Chicken sleep, chicken wake, if chicken not wake then chicken be ate!' Which is, I suppose, a pretty grim warning to a chicken.

I did not ask Inkosi-Inkosikazi how a Shangaan chicken could understand Zulu because you simply do not ask such questions of the greatest medicine man in all of Africa.

I was as yet unaware that this chicken was pretty exceptional, that the ability to understand a couple of African languages was probably not beyond him.

'The chicken trick is our bond. We are now brothers bound in this common knowledge and also the knowledge of the place in the dreamtime. Only you and I can do this trick or come to that place.'

I'm telling you something, it was pretty solemn stuff. With a yell across the farmyard the old man called for his driver who was asleep in the back of the Buick. Together we walked towards the big, black car.

'You may keep this chicken to practise on,' Inkosi-Inkosikazi said as he climbed into the back seat of the car.

As if from nowhere, the car was surrounded by field women who loaded up the trunk with the tributes they'd brought the previous day. Nanny handed the old man a small square of brightly coloured cloth into the corner of which were knotted several coins. Inkosi-Inkosikazi declined the offer of what was, for Nanny, two months' salary.

'It is a matter between me and the boy. This place is on my way to the Molototsi River where I go to see Modjadji, the rain queen.' He stuck his head out of the rear door window and gazed up into the sky. 'The rains have not come to Zululand, and in this matter her magic is greater than mine.'

The rains had been good north of the Drakensberg Mountains and now Nanny grew fearful as she asked for news of her people.

'The fields are ploughed three months and the seed maize is ready in the great seed pots, but the wind carries away the soil as we wait for the rains to come,' the old man sighed.

Nanny translated the news of the drought to the women. Drought is always news to be shared among the tribes. The women broke into a lament, doing a shuffling dance around the Buick and singing about the great one who brought the rains, gave barren women the sons they craved and cured the bite of snakes, even of the great black mamba.

Inkosi-Inkosikazi stuck his ancient head out of the window again and shook his fly switch impatiently. 'Be gone with you, you stupid old crows, sing for Modjadji the rain queen, this old rain maker has failed to squeeze a drop from the sky.'

With a roar from its mighty V8 engine, the big, black

automobile shot down the road, raising a cloud of dust behind it.

By the time the holidays were over Granpa Chook, for that was what I had called my chicken gift, and I were practically inseparable. Calling a chicken a 'chook' was a private joke my mother and I had shared. We had received a bunch of photos from a distant cousin in Australia one of which had shown a small boy not much older than me feeding the chickens. On the back of the photo was written: 'Young Lennie, feeding the chooks on the farm in Wagga Wagga.' We had called the two old drakes who always quacked around the farmyard together Wagga Wagga, and had started referring to Granpa's black Orpingtons as, 'the chooks'.

Granpa Chook was, I decided, a splendid name for the scraggy old rooster who came running the moment I appeared at the kitchen door. There was no doubt about it, that chicken had fallen for me. I don't mind admitting, I felt pretty powerfully attracted to him as well.

We practised the chicken trick for a couple of days but he got so smart that the moment I drew a circle in the dust he stepped into it and settled down politely. I think he was only trying to be co-operative, but it meant that I had lost all my power. Granpa Chook was the first living creature over which I held power and now this not-so-dumb cluck had found a way of getting back on even terms which was damned annoying if you ask me.

TWO

The holidays came to an end. My bed-wetting habit had, of course, been cured, but not my apprehension at the prospect of returning to boarding school. As for my hatless snake, I'd asked Inkosi-Inkosikazi about that and he'd hinted that we were similarly unique which was why we were so special. It was comforting at the time, but now I wasn't so sure.

Nanny and I had a good old weep on the last evening at home. She packed my khaki shorts and shirts and two pairs of pyjamas and a bright red jumper my mother had sent from the nervous breakdown place. We laughed and laughed, in between crying of course, because one sleeve was about ten inches shorter than the other. Nervous breakdowns probably do that sort of thing to people's knitting. By unpicking it at the shoulders Nanny made it into a nice red jumper.

We set out after breakfast in Granpa's old Model A Ford truck. On the way we picked up fat Mrs Vorster, the widow who owned the farm next door. Granpa spoke no Afrikaans and she no English so she thumped up and down in silence with her chins squashing onto her chest with every bump of the old truck.

I was delighted to be in the back with Nanny and Granpa Chook, who was concealed in the mealie sack where he lay so still you'd have sworn he was an empty sack. Nanny was going to town to send money to her family in Zululand to help with the terrible drought.

Granpa Chook's wing feathers had practically grown

again and by taking a run-up, his long legs pumping up and down, he could take off and land high up on a branch anytime he liked. I have to admit, while he was heavier, he wasn't any prettier. His long neck was still bare and his head still bald, his cock's comb was battered and hung like an empty scrotum to one side of his head. Compared to the black Orpingtons he was a mess.

We stopped at the school gates and Nanny handed me the suitcase and the bag with Granpa Chook playing possum. 'What have you got in the bag, son?' Granpa asked.

Before I could reply Nanny called from the back, 'It is only sweet potatoes, baas.'

The tears were as usual running down her cheeks and I wanted to rush back and hide myself in her big safe arms. With a bit of a backfire and a puff of blue exhaust smoke the truck lurched away and I was left standing at the gates. Ahead of me lay the dreaded Mevrou, the Judge and the jury and the beginning of the power of one, where I would learn that in each us there is a flame that must never be allowed to go out. That as long as it burns within us, we cannot be destroyed.

I released Granpa Chook from the sack and gave him a pat. Pisskop the Rooinek, possessor of a hatless snake, was back in town. But this time, for damn sure, he was not alone.

The playground was empty as we crossed it; Granpa Chook darted here and there after the tiny green grasshoppers that landed on its hot, dusty surface. They too seemed to be in enemy territory for not a blade of grass grew on the sun-baked square of earth. To make it across to safety they were forced to land frequently, exposing themselves to the dangers of a marauding Granpa Chook. Though the odds were rather better for them, there were hundreds of them and only one Granpa Chook, while it was the other way around with the two of us.

We seemed to have arrived early and so I made for my secret mango tree, which grew on the other side of the playground. Leaving my suitcase at its base, I climbed into its dark, comforting canopy of leaves. Granpa Chook, taking a run-up and flapping his wings furiously, flew up and perched on a branch beside me, swaying and wobbling and making a lot of unnecessary noise and fuss.

I carefully explained the situation to him. He just sat there and tossed his silly cock's comb and squawked a lot. I tried to impress on him that this was the big time, that things were different here to down on the farm. I must say that any chicken who could outsmart Inkosi-Inkosikazi's cooking pot and get the better of his magic circle had to be a real professional, so I didn't lecture him too much. Granpa Chook was a survivor; how fortunate I was to have him as my friend.

After a while we left the mango tree, and skirting the edge of the playground we made our way to the side of the hostel which contained the small kids' dormitory. It looked out onto a run-down citrus orchard of old, almost leafless grapefruit trees. Half a dozen cassia trees had seeded themselves over the years and their bright yellow blossom brought the dying orchard back to life. The ground was covered with khaki weed and black jack which reached to my shoulder. No one ever came here. It was the ideal place for Granpa Chook to stay while I reported to Mevrou.

Deep inside the orchard I set about making a small clearing amongst the rank-smelling weed and in the process unearthed a large white cutworm with a grey head and a yellow band around its neck. Granpa Chook thought all his Christmases had come at once, and with a sharp squawk he had the plump grub in his beak. You could see the progress of that worm as it made a bulge going down his long, naked neck.

The clearing complete, I drew a circle on the ground and he settled politely down into it. It still annoyed me a bit that he refused to go through the whole magic rigmarole, but what's the use, you can't go arguing with a chicken, can you?

I found Mevrou in the wash house folding blankets. She looked at me with distaste and pointed to a tin bucket which stood beside the mangle. 'Your rubber sheet is in that bucket, take it,' she said.

I tried not to sound scared. 'I . . . I am cured, Mevrou,' I stammered.

'Ha! Your *oupa*'s beating are better than mine then, ja?'

I stood with my head bowed, the way you were supposed to in the presence of Mevrou. 'No, Mevrou, your beatings are the best . . . better than my granpa's. It just happened, I just stopped doing it.'

'My sjambok will be lonely.' Mevrou always called the bamboo cane she carried her sjambok. She handed me a coarse towel and a blanket. 'You are too early, there is no lunch, the other children will be here not till this afternoon.' The blanket smelt of camphor balls and with the familiar smell the old fear returned and with it came doubt that perhaps I wasn't cured of my bed-wetting habit.

I dropped my blanket and towel off in the small kids' dormitory and returned to Granpa Chook. The absence of lunch didn't bother me. Nanny had packed two large sweet potatoes in my suitcase and I now planned to share one of these with Granpa Chook.

As I approached the abandoned orchard I could hear a fearful squawking coming from Granpa Chook. Suddenly he rose from above the weeds, his short wings beating the air. I lost sight of him again as he plunged back into the undergrowth. Up he came again, neck arched, legs stretched with talons wide. Down again, the weeds shaking wildly where he landed. This time he didn't come up and he had stopped squawking, though the khaki weed continued to shake where he'd disappeared. My heart beat wildly. Something had got Granpa Chook. A weasel or a feral cat? It was my fault, I'd left him helpless in the magic circle.

I stumbled blindly towards the tiny clearing where I'd left him, khaki weed and black jack lashing out at me, holding me back. Granpa Chook stood inside the circle;

held firmly in his beak was a three-foot grass snake. With a vigorous shake of his head and a snip of his powerful beak he removed the head from the snake and, to my astonishment, swallowed it. The snake's head went down in the same way as the fat cutworm had done. Unaware that the show was over, the snake's brilliant green body continued to wriggle wildly in the weeds.

The toughest damn chicken in the whole world tossed his head and gave me a beady wink. I could see he was pretty pleased with himself. I'll tell you something, I don't blame him, how can you go wrong with a friend like him at your side?

The snake had ceased to wriggle, and picking it up I hung it from a branch of a cassia tree growing only a few feet from the window nearest my bed in the little kids' dormitory. Now there were two hatless snakes in the world and I was involved with both of them.

The afternoon gradually filled with the cacophony of returning kids. I could hear them as they dumped their blankets and suitcases in the dormitory and rushed out to play. Granpa Chook and I spent the afternoon making his shelter from bits of corrugated iron I found among the weeds. He seemed to like his new home, scratching for worms where I'd pulled up the weeds. He would be safe and dry when it rained.

By the time the wash-up bell went at a quarter to five, I was a bit of a mess from all the weeding and building. I left Granpa Chook for the night scratching happily away in his new home and washed under a little-used tap on the side of the building facing the orchard. By the time the supper bell went the late afternoon sun had dried me and I was good as new. I waited until the last possible moment before slipping into the dining hall to take my place at the bottom table where the little kids sat.

Shortly after lights out that night I was summoned to appear before the Judge and the jury. It was a full moon again, just like the very first time. But also a moon like the one that rose above the waterfalls in the dreamtime when, as a young warrior, I had conquered my fears.

The Judge, seated cross-legged on a bed, was even bigger than I remembered. He wore only pyjama pants, and now sported a crude tattoo high up on his left arm. Cicatrisation wasn't new to me, African women do it to their faces all the time, though I had not seen a tattoo on white skin before. Reddish-pink skin still puckered along the edges of the crude blue lines which crossed at the centre like two headless snakes wriggling across each other.

Absently rubbing his tattoo, the Judge shook his head slowly as he looked at me. 'You are a fool, a *blêrrie* fool to have come back, Pisskop.' A small lump of snot in his left nostril pumped up and down as he breathed.

'You have marks like a Kaffir woman on your arm,' I heard myself saying.

The Judge's eyes seemed to pop out of his head. He snorted in amazement and the snolly-bomb shot out of his nostril and landed on my face. His hand followed a split second later. I felt an explosion in my head as I was knocked to the floor.

I got to my feet. Stars, just like in the comic books, were dancing in a red sky in front of my eyes and there was a ringing noise in my ears. But I wasn't crying. I cursed my stupidity, the holidays had blunted my sense of survival; adapt, blend, become part of the landscape, develop a camouflage, be a rock or a leaf or a stick insect, try in every way to be an Afrikaner. The jury was silent, struck dumb by my audacity. A warm trickle of blood ran from my nose, across my lips and down my chin.

The Judge grabbed me by the front of my pyjamas and pulled me up to his face, lifting me so that I stood on the very tips of my toes. 'This sign means death and destruction to all Rooineks. And you, Pisskop, are going to be the first.' He released me and I stumbled backwards but managed to stay on my feet.

'Yes, sir,' I said, my voice barely audible.

26

'This is a swastika, man! Do you know what that is?'

'N . . . no, sir.'

'God has sent us this sign from Adolf Hitler who will deliver the Afrikaner people from the hated English!'

I could see the jury was deeply impressed and I was too.

The Judge turned to address the jury, prodding at the swastika.

'We must all swear a blood oath to Adolf Hitler,' he said solemnly. The jury crowded around his bed, their eyes shining with excitement.

'I will swear too,' I said hopefully. The blood was still running from my nose and some had dripped to the floor.

'Don't be fuckin' stupid! Pisskop, you *are* the English.' The Judge stood upright on the bed and held his arm aloft at an angle, with his fingers straight and pointing to the ceiling. 'In the name of Adolf Hitler we will march every Rooinek bastard into the sea.'

I had never been to the sea but I knew it would be a long march all right. 'The blood oath! The blood oath!' the jury chanted.

'Come here, Pisskop,' the Judge commanded. I stepped over to his bed. 'Look up, man.' I looked up at him as he stood high above me on the bed. He wiped his forefinger under my nose and then he pushed me so that I sat down hard on the floor. He held up his finger, my blood on its tip shining in the moonlight.

'We will swear this oath with the blood of a Rooinek!' he announced solemnly. Two members of the jury lifted me to my feet while the others crowded around me, sticking their pudgy fingers into the blood running from my nose. The supply wasn't coming fast enough and one boy tweeked my nose to increase the flow.

This seemed to cause it to stop altogether, so that the last two members were forced to dab their fingers into the drops of blood on the floor.

The Judge, wiping the blood on his finger across the swastika, instructed the jury to do the same. Soon the swastika on his arm was almost totally concealed. 'Death to all Englishmen in South Africa, the fatherland,' the Judge cried, raising his arm once more.

'Death to all Englishmen in South Africa, the fatherland!' the jury chorused.

The Judge looked down at me. 'We won't kill you tonight, Pisskop. But when Hitler comes your days are numbered, you hear?'

'Yes, sir, when will that be, sir?' I asked.

'Soon!' He stepped from the bed, and placing his huge hand over the top of my head he turned me towards the dormitory door and gave me a swift kick up the bum which sent me sprawling headlong across the polished floor. I could smell the wax polish on the floorboards and then I got to my feet and ran.

Back in my own dormitory the little kids leapt out of bed, crowding around me, demanding to know what had happened. Too upset to mind my tongue, I sniffed out the story of the swastika and the blood oath and my threatened demise upon the arrival of Hitler.

An eight-year-old named Danie Coetzee shook his head solemnly.

'Pisskop, you are in deep shit, man,' he said.

'Who is this person called Adolf Hitler who is coming to get Pisskop?' a fellow we called 'Flap-lips' de Jaager asked.

It was apparent nobody knew the answer until Danie Coetzee said, 'He's probably the new headmaster.'

There had been some talk among the kids the previous term about the headmaster and his 'drinking problem'. I had wondered at the time what a drinking problem was. Obviously it was something pretty bad or the huge, morose man we all feared wouldn't be leaving.

One of the kids started to chant softly: 'Pisskop's in trouble . . . Pisskop's in trouble . . .' The others quickly took up the chant which grew louder and louder. I placed my hands over my ears to try to stop it.

'Still!' The dormitory rang to the command. Mevrou

stood at the doorway, her huge body filling the door frame.

'We was just talking, Mevrou,' Danie Coetzee said. As the oldest of the small kids he assumed the position of spokesman.

'You know that talking after lights out is verboten, Coetzee.'

Danie Coetzee was left standing at the end of my bed as the others tiptoed back to their beds. 'Ja, Mevrou. Sorry, Mevrou.' His voice sounded small and afraid.

'Bend over the bed, man,' Mevrou instructed. The cane cut through the air in a blur as she planted it into the seat of Coetzee's pyjamas. He let out a fearful yelp, and holding his bum with both hands hopped up and down. Without further ado, Mevrou left the dormitory.

For a moment there wasn't a sound and then Danie Coetzee, his voice on the edge of tears, blurted out, 'You will pay for this you *blêrrie* pisskop Rooinek!'

I waited until everyone was asleep and then crept quietly to the window. The full moon brought a soft sheen to the leaves of the grapefruit trees which seemed to shimmer in the ghosted light. Granpa Chook's headless snake made a silver loop in the moonlight, a beautiful and unexpected decoration on the branch of the cassia tree. 'I didn't cry. They'll never make me cry again!' I said to the moon. Then I returned to my bed. It was the loneliest moment that had ever been.

Granpa Chook's cover was blown the following morning. Like all kaffir chickens he was an early riser. Before even the six o'clock wake-up bell went, the whole dormitory had awakened to his raucous crowing. I awoke, startled out of a deep sleep, to see him perched on the window sill nearest my bed, his long scrawny neck stretched in a mighty rendition of cock-a-doodle-doooo! Then he cocked his head to one side, gave a tiny squawk and, from the window, flew onto my iron bed head. Stretching his long neck towards me, almost to the point of losing his balance, he gave my ear a gentle peck.

The kids raced from their beds to surround me. 'It's an old kaffir chicken come to visit Pisskop,' Flap-lips de Jaager yelled excitedly.

Granpa Chook, imperious on the bed head, fixed them with a beady stare. 'He is mine,' I said defiantly, 'he is my friend.'

Well! You should have heard them carry on. Danie Coetzee, temporarily forgetting his revenge for the caning the previous night, chortled: 'Don't be stupid, man, nobody has a kaffir chicken for a friend!'

'I do, he can do tricks and everything.'

'No he can't! He's a dumb kaffir chicken. Wait till the Judge hears about Pisskop's new friend,' Flap-lips de Jaager volunteered and everyone laughed.

The wake-up bell went, which meant Mevrou would arrive in a minute or two, and so we all scrambled back into bed to await her permission to get up. I barely had time to push Granpa Chook through the window into the orchard and climb back into bed when her huge form loomed through the door.

Mevrou paced the length of the dormitory, her sjambok hanging from a loop on the black leather belt of her dark blue uniform. She stopped as she reached my bed, whipped off the blanket and examined the dry mattress.

'Humph!' she snorted, dropping the blanket onto the floor. I jumped from my bed and stood beside it. She ignored me and turned slowly to address the dormitory. 'I am warning you, *kinders*, if I hear you talking after lights out again, my sjambok will also talk to all of you, you hear?'

'Ja, Mevrou,' we chorused.

Suddenly her eyes grew large and seemed almost to pop out of her head: 'Pisskop! There is chicken shit on your pillow!'

I looked down at my pillow in horror: deposited neatly between two lines of its mattress-ticking cover, Granpa Chook had left his green and white calling card.

'Explain, man!' Mevrou roared.

No explanation but the truth was possible. Shaking with terror I told her about Granpa Chook.

Mevrou glowered at me, and undoing the buckle of her leather belt she slipped the cane from it. 'Pisskop, I think you are sick in the head, like your poor mother. First you come here and you piss in your bed every night. Then you come back and you fill it with chicken shit!' She pointed to the end of the bed where Danie Coetzee had taken his medicine the previous night. 'Bend over,' she commanded.

She blasted me four strokes of the sjambok. Biting back the tears, I forced myself not to grab my bum by clamping my hands tightly between my thighs and hunching my shoulders. This also seemed to stop me shaking.

What a shit of a day already!

'Clean up your pillow and bring this devil's chicken to the kitchen door after breakfast, you hear?' At the door she turned and faced us: 'Go to the showers now,' she commanded.

Granpa Chook and I were in a terrible jam, all right. After breakfast I slipped out of the hostel to find him. He was still in the old orchard clucking and scratching around looking for worms. I produced a slice of bread which I'd saved at breakfast, and while breaking it up into bits small enough for him to swallow explained the latest disaster to him. So much for my resolution not to cry, I could feel the tears running down my cheeks.

After Granpa Chook had had his breakfast I picked him up and, fighting my way through the khaki weed and black jack, I took him to the edge of the orchard to a low corrugated iron fence which marked the hostel boundary. Standing on tiptoe I looked over the fence. My heart gave a leap; in the distance I could see three kaffir huts with smoke rising from a fire, for sure they'd keep kaffir chickens and Granpa Chook could board with them.

Considerably cheered I explained this new plan to Granpa Chook and then pushed him over the fence. There is a blurred distinction between imagination and reality in

31

a five-year-old child and the new plan, once imagined, was immediately achieved.

Granpa Chook, though, had other ideas. With an indignant squawk and a flap of his wings he was back on my side of the fence. We pantomimed for the next few minutes: over the fence I'd put him and back he'd come. Finally it became clear that the toughest damn chicken in the whole wide world had no intention of deserting his friend, even if his own life was at stake.

We waited at the kitchen door for about ten minutes before Mevrou appeared. 'So this is the chicken that shits in your bed, Pisskop?'

'It wasn't on purpose, Mevrou. He's very clean and very clever too.'

'Look who talks of clean! A chicken is a chicken. Who ever heard of a clever chicken?'

'Look, Mevrou, I'll show you.' I quickly drew a circle in the dust and Granpa Chook immediately hopped into it and settled down as though he were laying an egg, which he couldn't, of course. 'He'll stay in that circle until I say to come out,' I said.

For a moment Mevrou looked impressed and then she suddenly scowled. 'This is just some dumb thing kaffir chickens do that white chickens don't,' she said smugly.

'No, Mevrou!' I begged. 'He can do lots of other things too!'

I made Granpa Chook hop around the perimeter of the circle on one leg going 'Squawk' with every hop. I showed her how he would fly onto my shoulder and, at my command, peck my ear.

This last trick signalled the end of Mevrou's patience. 'Your hair will be full of lice, you stupid boy!' she screamed. Just inside the kitchen door stood a butcher's block with a large cleaver resting on it. 'Give me that filthy, lice-ridden, bed-shitting, kaffir chicken!' she yelled, grabbing the cleaver.

Two cockroaches resting under the cleaver on the block

raced up the back of Mevrou's hand. She let out an almighty scream, dropping the cleaver and frantically flapping both arms. One cockroach dropped to the floor, while the other ran up her arm and disappeared down her bodice.

With a delighted squawk, Granpa Chook came charging into the kitchen and scooped up the cockroach frantically crossing the kitchen floor. Mevrou was waving her arms, her bosoms jiggling up and down. She made little gasping noises as though she was struggling to get a scream out as she danced from one foot to the other in extreme agitation. The second cockroach fell from under her skirt and made for a crack in the polished cement floor. But Granpa Chook was too fast for it and had it in a trice.

Mevrou had turned a deep crimson and her head seemed to vibrate from the shock. 'It's oright, Mevrou, the other one fell out and Granpa Chook got it,' I said, pointing to Granpa Chook strutting around looking very pleased with himself.

I rushed to fetch a kitchen chair and Mevrou plopped down into it like an overripe watermelon. Taking a dish-cloth from a drying rack beside the huge black wood-burning stove, I began to fan her the way I had seen Nanny do when my mother had one of her turns.

I became aware of a dripping sound coming from under the rattan seat of the chair and realised in alarm that Mevrou had pissed her pants. I think she must have been too upset to notice it herself. I wondered how many strokes pissing your pants would earn in her book. When she had recovered somewhat she pointed a trembling finger at Granpa Chook.

'You are right, Pisskop. That is a good chicken. He can stay. But he has to earn his keep,' she gasped. Then she seemed to become aware of what had happened beneath the chair. 'Go now,' she said, and grabbing the cloth from my hand she pointed to the door.

And that's how Granpa Chook came to do kitchen duty. Every day after breakfast he checked every last corner in the hostel kitchen for creepy-crawlies of every description. The toughest damn chicken in the world had survived, he had beaten the executor by adapting perfectly and we were safely together again.

The weeks and then a couple of months went by. I had become slave to the Judge. In return for being at his constant beck and call, I was more or less left to my own devices. The odd cuff behind the head or a rude push from an older kid was about all I had to endure. Things were pretty good, really. If the Judge needed me he would simply put two fingers to his mouth and give one of his piercing whistles and Granpa Chook and I would come running.

Granpa Chook was now under the protection of Mevrou, although he still needed to be constantly on the alert. Farm kids just can't help chucking stones at kaffir chickens. He would cluck around the playground during lessons, hunting for grubs. The moment the recess bell went he would come charging over to my classroom, skidding to a halt in the dust, cackling his anxiety to be with me again.

No class existed for my age and so I had been placed with the seven-year-old kids, all of whom were still learning to read. I had been reading in English for at least a year so that the switch to reading Afrikaans wasn't difficult, and I was soon the best in the class. Yet I quickly realised that survival means never being best at anything except being best at nothing, and I soon learned to minimise my reading skills, appearing to pause and stumble over words which were perfectly clear to me.

Mediocrity is the best camouflage known to man. Our teacher, Miss du Plessis, wasn't anxious for a five-year-old Rooinek to shine in a class of knot-headed Boers. She was happy enough to put my poor results down to my inability to grasp the subtlety of the Afrikaans language as well as being the youngest in class, whereas I already spoke Zulu and Shangaan and, like most small kids, found learning a new language simple enough.

It became increasingly hard for the other kids to think of me as being different when no visible or audible differences separated us. Except, of course, for my hatless snake; but even this, like a kid with a birthmark or a little finger missing, started to go unnoticed. I was becoming the perfect stick insect.

And then on September 3rd, 1939, Neville Chamberlain finally and sadly concluded that Herr Hitler was not a gentleman, not to be trusted and not open to negotiation. That Britain, having let Czechoslovakia down thoroughly, couldn't face the embarrassment of doing the same thing to Poland and so found it necessary to declare war on Germany. The new headmaster had arrived.

At lunch in the hostel dining hall, the old headmaster with the drinking problem addressed us. He stood, swaying slightly, both hands holding the edge of the table. Then, picking up a knife, he thumped it on the table with the handle. 'Silence!' he roared. Whereupon Miss du Plessis, lips pursed, rose quickly and left through the swinging doors. The old headmaster seemed not to notice, dropping the knife onto the table he started to talk in a very loud voice, as though he were addressing hundreds of people: 'Today, England has declared war on Germany!' He paused to gauge the effect of his words on us. There was no reaction except for a low murmur from where the senior boys sat. 'Do you know what this means, man?' Not waiting for an answer he continued, 'It means freedom! Freedom and liberty for our beloved fatherland! Adolf Hitler will destroy the cursed English and remove the yoke of oppression placed on the Afrikaner nation by these *uitlanders* who burn down homes and imprison Boer woman and children in concentration camps where twenty-six thousand died of starvation, dysentery and black-water fever!'

The headmaster made it sound as though it was all happening at that very moment in South Africa. I suddenly realised that this was what had really happened to my mother. She had been mistaken for a Boer woman and put in a concentration camp.

The headmaster took a couple of steps back from the table and then lurched forward again, his spit-flecked mouth worked silently, as though he were trying to say something but it wouldn't come out. Instead he raised his arm in the same way the Judge had done in the dormitory. 'Heil Hitler!' he blurted out at last.

Just then the doors burst open and Mevrou entered the dining room; through the briefly open doors we could see Miss du Plessis standing in the hallway biting her knuckles. Mevrou marched up to the headmaster, and taking him firmly by the elbow she led him quickly from the dining hall.

'Heil Hitler!' he shouted back at us as he passed through the swing doors.

We sat there bewildered. Then the Judge jumped to his feet and stepped up onto the bench on his side of the top table. He rolled the sleeve of his shirt up over the top of his shoulder so we could all see the crude blue crossed and angled lines of his swastika tattoo.

'Adolf Hitler is the King of Germany and God has sent him to take South Africa back from the English and give it to us.' He jabbed at the swastika on his arm. 'This is his sign . . . the swastika, the swastika will make us free again.' His right hand shot up in the same salute the headmaster had given moments before. 'Heil Hitler!' he cried.

We all jumped to our feet and, thrusting our arms out in the manner of his own, yelled, 'Heil Hitler!'

It was all very exciting. To think that this man, Adolf Hitler, who was going to save us all from the accursed English, was going to be our new headmaster!

Then, slowly at first, the words of the Judge on the first night back at school began to form in my mind, gathered momentum, and then roared into my consciousness.

'Don't be stupid! Pisskop, you *are* the fuckin' English!'

The long march to the sea had begun.

Flap-lips de Jaager at our table just kept on shouting 'Heil Hitler' and soon everyone was chanting it louder and louder. A piercing whistle from the Judge finally stopped them.

'Some of us have sworn a blood oath to Adolf Hitler and the time has now come to march the Rooineks into the sea. After school we will meet behind the shit houses for a council of war!'

I don't suppose any of us had much idea of where the sea was supposed to be, somewhere across the Lebombo Mountains and probably over the Limpopo River. Whichever direction, it was a long, long way away. The long march to the sea would be a pretty serious undertaking and I could understand why it would take some planning.

The dining room buzzed with excitement and the Judge held up his hand to silence us. Then he pointed directly at me. 'Pisskop, you are our first prisoner of war!' He brought his fingers together and raised his arm higher. 'Heil Hitler!' he shouted.

We all jumped up again, but the two kids on either side of me pushed me back into my seat. 'Heil Hitler!' the rest of dining hall chorused back.

It was the most exciting day in the school's history, although my own prospects looked pretty bleak. What was certain was that Granpa Chook and I were living on borrowed time and needed to make some pretty urgent escape plans. I was in despair. Even if I did know how to get home, which I didn't, how far could a little kid and a chicken travel without being spotted by the enemy?

That afternoon in class Miss du Plessis, who seemed even more upset than usual, rapped my knuckles sharply on two occasions with her eighteen-inch ruler. In the end she grew totally exasperated when, deep into my escape plans, I simply didn't hear her ask what three times four came to.

'*Domkop*! You will have to stay in after school!' The idea was impossible. Granpa Chook and I had to escape before the council of war met behind the shit houses.

'Please, miss! I'm sorry, miss. It won't happen again, miss,' I begged. In a desperate attempt to make amends I blew my camouflage. I recited the nine times table, then the ten, eleven and twelve. I had carefully concealed my knowledge of anything beyond the four times table and, what's more, we hadn't even reached the eleven and twelve times tables in class. The effect was profound. By the time I had almost completed the twelve times table, which I'd learned from the back of the Judge's arithmetic book, Miss du Plessis was consumed by anger.

'Twelve times twelve is, ah . . . one hundred and . . . er, forty-four,' I announced, my voice faltering as I perceived the extent of her indignation.

'You wicked, rotten, lying, cheating child!' she screamed, raising her steel-edged ruler. The blows rained down on me though, in her agitation, her aim was wild and I took most of them on my arms and shoulders. One swipe got through my guard and the thin metal strip in the ruler sliced into the top of my ear. I dropped my guard and grabbed at my ear which was stinging like billy-o. The warm blood started to run through my fingers and down my arm.

The sight of the blood snapped Miss du Plessis out of her frenzy. She looked down at me and brought her hand to her mouth. Then she screamed and fell dead at my feet.

The shock of seeing Miss du Plessis drop dead at my feet was so great that I was unable to move. The blood dripped from my ear onto her spotless white blouse until a crimson blot the size of my fist stained the area just above her heart.

'Cripes! You've broken her heart and killed her,' I heard Flap-lips de Jaager say as he ran from the classroom. All the others followed, screaming as they fought each other to vacate the scene of the crime. I just stood there, unable to think, the blood leaking from my head.

I was unaware of anyone entering the room until a huge hand lifted me and hurled me across the classroom where I landed against the wall. I was too stunned to hurt and sat there propped up by the wall like a discarded rag doll. Mr Stoffel, the master who taught the Judge's class, was on his knees bending over Miss du Plessis and shaking her by the shoulder. His eyes grew wide as he observed the blood on her blouse. 'Shit, he's killed her!' I heard him say.

Just then Miss du Plessis opened her eyes and sat up like Lazarus. Then she looked down and saw her bloodstained blouse and with a soft sigh she passed out again. Mr Stoffel slapped her cheeks and she opened her eyes and sat up. 'Oh, oh, what have I done!' she sobbed.

Quite suddenly the classroom grew very still and dark, like a cloud passing over the sun. I could dimly see Mr Stoffel coming towards me, his long, hairy arms flapping at his sides as though in slow motion, his shape wavy at the edges. I tried to cover my face but my arms refused to lift from my lap.

'Look what happens when you forget your camouflage, Pisskop,' I observed to myself. Then I must have passed out.

I awoke in my bed in the small kids' dormitory, but before I'd opened my eyes I could smell Mevrou at my side. She must have seen the flicker of my eyelids. 'Are you awake, Pisskop?' she asked, not unkindly.

'Ja, Mevrou.' I was back in the real world and I quickly gathered my mental camouflage about me. My head was swathed in a thick crêpe bandage and I was wearing my pyjamas. My head didn't hurt a bit but my shoulder ached where I'd landed against the wall.

'Now listen to me, Pisskop.' There was a note of urgency in Mevrou's voice. 'When the doctor comes you must tell him you fell out of a tree, you hear?'

'Ja, Mevrou.'

'What tree did you fall out of, Pisskop?' she asked.

'There was no tree, Mevrou.' I had fallen at once for the trick.

'Domkop!' she shouted. 'Wash out your ears. What did I just tell you, man?'

'It was the mango tree, the big one next to the playground,' I corrected.

'Ja, that's good, the mango tree.' She rose from the chair beside my bed. 'You have a good memory when you try, Pisskop. Remember to tell the doctor when he comes.'

No sooner had she left than I leapt from the bed and ran to the window where I whistled for Granpa Chook. In a few moments he appeared, clucking and beady-eyed as ever as he came to rest on the window sill beside me.

'Granpa Chook, we're in a lot of trouble,' I told him and explained about the arrival any day now of Adolf Hitler who was coming to march us into the sea. 'Can you swim?' I asked him. Granpa Chook was so amazing that it wouldn't have surprised me if he turned out to be the only chicken in the world who could swim.

'Squawk!' he replied, which could have meant he could or he couldn't, who's to say? Granpa Chook wasn't always easy to understand.

We could hear voices coming towards the dormitory so I quickly pushed Granpa Chook back into the orchard and jumped into bed.

To my joy Mevrou entered with Dr Henny. He sat on my bed and unwound the bandage around my head. 'What's the matter, son? You look pretty done in.'

Even if Dr Henny wasn't a Rooinek I knew he was on my side, and I longed to burst into tears and tell him all my troubles. But I had already blown my camouflage once that day with near disastrous results. A bandaged ear and a sore shoulder weren't too bad a result for having been unforgivably stupid. Next time I might not be so lucky. Choking back the tears I told him how I had fallen from the big old mango tree next to the playground.

I must have laid it on a bit thick because he turned to Mevrou and in Afrikaans he said: 'Hmm, except for the cut between the ear and the skull there are no contusions or abrasions, are you quite sure this child fell from a tree?'

'The other children saw it happen, Doctor. There is no

doubt.' Mevrou said this with such conviction that I began to wonder myself. I realised that Dr Henny's line of questioning could only mean trouble for me.

'It's true, sir. That's what happened, I fell out of the tree and hurt my shoulder against the wall.'

Dr Henny didn't seem to notice that I'd replied in Afrikaans. 'The wall? What wall?'

Fear showed for a moment in Mevrou's eyes but she quickly recovered. 'The child doesn't speak Afrikaans very well, he means the ground.'

'Ja, the ground,' I added, my camouflage damn nearly blown sky high.

Dr Henny looked puzzled. 'Okay, let's look at your shoulder, then.' He rotated my shoulder clockwise. 'That hurt? Tell me when it hurts.' I shook my head. He moved it the opposite way with the same result. Then he lifted it upwards and I winced. 'That's sore, hey?' I nodded. 'Well it's not dislocated anyway.' He checked my heart and chest and my back with his stethoscope which was cold against my skin. 'Seems fine. We'll just put in a couple of little stitches and you'll be right as rain,' he said in English.

'Can I go home please?'

'No need for that, old son. You'll be brand new tomorrow.' He dug into his bag and produced a yellow sucker. 'Here, this will make you feel better, you get stuck into that while I fix up these stitches.'

He must have seen the look on my face. 'Ja, it's going to hurt a bit, but you're not going to cry on me now, are you?'

'He's a brave boy, Doctor,' Mevrou said, relaxed now that the truth had remained concealed.

'Well done,' Henny said, dabbing my stiches with mercurochrome, 'no need for a bandage, we'll be back in a week to remove the stitches.' He turned to Mevrou, 'Let me know if he complains of backache.' He took a second sucker from his bag and handed it to me. 'That's for being extra brave.'

'Thank you, sir. Doctor Henny, are you English?' I asked, taking the second sucker.

41

His expression changed and I could see that he was upset. 'We are all South Africans, son. Don't let anyone tell you otherwise.' He spoke with a quiet vehemence, then repeated: 'Don't let anyone ever tell you anything else!'

I had certainly had better days, but a two-sucker day doesn't come along very often so it wasn't all bad.

Despite my prisoner of war status, the kids were pretty good for the next few days. My stitches made me a hero in the small kids' dormitory and even Maatie de Jaager kept his loose mouth buttoned for a change.

We had a new teacher, Mrs Gerber, who turned out to be the wife of the Government vet who had once come out to the farm to check Granpa's black Orpingtons for Newcastle's disease. Mrs Gerber wasn't tetchy and I don't think she even knew I was a Rooinek. She wasn't a real teacher so she was quite nice.

There was a rumour going around that Miss du Plessis had suffered a nervous breakdown. I knew of course that I was to blame and it struck me with dismay that I had probably been the direct cause of my mother's nervous breakdown as well. I must be a nervous breakdown type of person. First my mother, now Miss du Plessis and, while I hadn't given Mevrou one yet, I had caused her to piss in her pants, which was probably the next best thing.

Granpa Chook and I discussed our predicament at some length but were unable to reach a useful conclusion. After all, Granpa Chook was a kaffir chicken and they don't have such a good life. One minute you're walking along scratching about and the next you're dinner for a jackal or a python, or bubbling away in a three-legged cast-iron cooking pot. Granpa Chook, a proven survivor, worked on the principle that if anything bad could happen it would. A five-year-old isn't much of a pessimist, though we agreed that one thing was for sure, something pretty bad was bound to happen.

THREE

The night after I had my stitches out I was summoned to appear before the Judge and jury.

The Judge had been quite nice to me over the past week and, because of my sore shoulder, hadn't required that I carry his books to school each day. In fact, because Miss du Plessis was generally disliked, I'd become a bit of a hero.

But Rooineks in this part of the world are not designed to be permanent heroes. I knew it would soon come to an end: when the stitches were out, my temporary reprieve would be over. So, here I was again, being marched straight into another calamity.

'Stand to attention, prisoner Pisskop,' the Judge snarled.

I drew myself up, my arms ramrods at my side. 'Bring your stupid legs together, man!' one of the jury shouted.

'Name?'

I looked confused, everyone knew my name?

'What is your name, Pisskop?' the Judge asked again.

'Pisskop?' I ventured, still not certain what he meant.

'What does your name mean?'

Again I looked querulous. 'That I piss my bed?'

'Ja, and chickens shit in it as well! What is a Rooinek?'

'I am English.'

'Yes I know, man! But how do you know you're a Rooinek?'

'I . . . I just know, sir.'

The Judge shook his head and gave a deep sigh. 'Come here. Come closer, man.'

I stepped forward to stand directly in front of where he

sat cross-legged on his bed. The Judge's arm came up and my hand flew up to protect my face, but instead of hitting me he pulled at the cord of my pyjama pants which collapsed round my ankles.

'Your blêrrie snake has no hat on its head, domkop! That's how you know you're English! Understand?'

'Yes, sir.' I bent down to pull my pyjama pants back up.

'Don't!' I jumped back to attention. 'What am I, Pisskop?' the Judge demanded.

'A Boer, sir?'

'Yes, and what is a Boer?'

'An Afrikaner, sir.'

'Yes, of course . . . but what else?'

'A Boer has a hat on his snake.' Why, when He has made all white people look alike, had God given the English snakes without a hat? It seemed terribly unfair. My camouflage was perfect except for this one little thing.

'Tonight you will learn to march. We must get you ready for your march into the sea.' The Judge pointed to the corridor between the beds and gave me a push. I tripped over my pyjama pants and fell to the floor. One of the jury reached down and pulled the pants away from my ankles. I rose bare-arsed and looked uncertainly at the Judge. 'March!' he commanded pointing down the corridor between the beds once more. I started to march, swinging my arms high. '*Links, regs, links, regs, halt!*' he bawled. Then again: 'Left, right, left, right, halt! Which is your left foot, prisoner Pisskop?' I had no idea but pointed to a foot. 'Domkop! Don't you even know your left from your right?'

'No, sir,' I said, feeling stupid. But I did now, the left side was where my shoulder hurt.

'Every day after school you will march around the playground for five thousand steps, you hear?' I nodded. 'You will count backwards from five thousand until you get to number one.'

I couldn't believe my luck, no one had laid a hand on

me. I retrieved my pyjama pants and scurried back along the dark passage to my dormitory.

Being a prisoner of war and learning how to march wasn't such a bad thing. I had nothing to do after school anyway. But I must admit, counting backwards from five thousand isn't much of a way to pass the time. It's impossible anyway, your thoughts wander and before you know it you're all jumbled up and have to start all over again. I learned to mumble a number if anyone came close, but mostly I did the Judge's homework in my head. Carrying his books from school, I would memorise his arithmetic lesson and then I would work the equations out in my head as I marched along. If things got a bit complicated, I'd make sure nobody was looking and I'd work out a more complex sum using a stick in the dirt. It got so I couldn't wait to see what he'd done in class each day.

The Judge was an awful domkop. In the mornings carrying his books to school I'd check his homework. It was always a mess and mostly all wrong. I began to despair for him and for myself as well, you see, he could only leave the school if the work he did during the year gave him a pass mark. So far, he didn't have a hope. If he failed I'd have him for another year. That is, if Hitler hadn't come by then to march me away.

Escape seemed impossible, so I'd have to think of something else. Over a period of several marching afternoons a plan began to form. The something else, when it finally emerged, was breathtakingly simple though fraught with danger. For the next two days I thought of little else. If I blew my camouflage and helped the Judge with his homework so that he would pass, would he not be forced to spare Granpa Chook and me if Adolf Hitler arrived before the end of term?

I must say I was worried. Every time I had blown my camouflage disaster had followed. Finally, after a long talk with Granpa Chook, we agreed it was a chance worth taking.

After breakfast the following morning, when I was folding the Judge's blanket and arranging his towel over his bed rail, I broached the subject. He was sitting on a bed licking his pencil and trying to do some last-minute arithmetic.

'Can I help you, sir?' My heart thumped like a donkey engine, though I was surprised how steady my voice sounded.

'Push off, Pisskop. Can't you see I'm busy, man.' The Judge was doing the fractions I'd done in my head the previous afternoon and getting them hopelessly wrong.

Gulping down my fear I said, 'What happens if you don't pass at the end of the year?' The Judge looked at me, I could see the thought wasn't new to him. He reached out and grabbed me by the shirtfront.

'If I don't pass, I'll kill you first and then I'll run away!'

I took my courage in both hands. 'I . . . I can help you, sir,' I stammered.

The Judge released me and went back to chewing his pencil, his brow furrowed as he squinted at the page of equations. He appeared not to have heard me. I pointed to the equation he'd just completed. 'That's wrong. The answer is seven-ninths.' I moved my finger quickly. 'Four-fifths, six-eighths, nine-tenths, five-sevenths . . .' I paused as he grabbed my hand and looked up at me, open-mouthed.

'Where did you learn to do this, man?'

I shrugged, 'It's just easy for me, that's all.' I hoped he couldn't sense how scared I was.

A look of cunning came into his eyes. He released my hand and handed me the book and the pencil. 'Just write the answers very softly and I'll copy them, you hear?'

The camouflage was intact and I'd moved up into the next evolutionary stage. From knowing to hide my brains I had now learned to use them. Granpa Chook and I were one step further away from the sea.

But I had already experienced the consequences of revealing too much too soon. I knew if a domkop like the Judge

46

went from bottom to the top of his class overnight, Mr Stoffel would soon smell a rat. Telling the Judge he was a duffer was more than my life was worth. Besides, I was beginning to understand how manipulation can be an important weapon in the armoury of the small and weak.

'We have a problem,' I said to the Judge.

'What problem, man? I don't see a problem. You just write in the answers very soft, that's all.'

'Judge, you're a very clever fellow.'

'Ja, that's right. So?'

'So arithmetic doesn't interest you, does it? I mean, if it did you could do it,' I snapped my fingers, 'just like that!'

'Ja, if I wanted to I could. Only little kids like you are interested in all that shit!'

I could see this conclusion pleased him and I grew bolder. 'So you can't just get ten out of ten today when yesterday you only got two sums right out of ten. Mr Stoffel will know there's some monkey business going on.'

The Judge looked worried. 'You mean, you're not going to help me?'

'Of course I am. But you will get better a little bit each week and you'll tell Mr Stoffel that you suddenly got the hang of doing sums.'

The Judge looked relieved and then grinned slyly. '*Jy is 'n slimmetjie*, Pisskop,' he said.

The Judge had called me clever. Me! Pisskop! Rooinek and possessor of a hatless snake! It was the greatest compliment of my life and I was beside myself with pride.

But before the Judge could notice the effect of his words on me, I quickly resumed my obsequious manner. The thrill of the compliment had almost caused me to forget my other anxiety.

'What will happen if Adolf Hitler comes before the end of term?' I asked, my heart beating overtime.

The Judge looked at me blankly, then suddenly grinned, understanding the reason for my question. 'Okay, man, you got me there. I will say nothing until I've passed at the end of the year.' He shook his head and gave me a look not entirely without sympathy. 'I'm sorry, Pisskop, after that I will have to tell him about you. You must be punished for killing twenty-six thousand Boer women and children. You and your stupid kaffir chicken are dead meat when he comes. But I'll tell you something, I give you my word as a Boer, if I pass in sums, I swear on a stack of Bibles not to tell Adolf Hitler until next term.'

The Judge, his brow furrowed as though he were doing the calculations himself, started to copy over the answers I had written in his exercise book.

I had won: my plan had worked. I could hardly believe my ears. Granpa Chook and I were safe for the remainder of the term.

The Judge had come to the end of his copying. I had never seen him quite so happy, not even when he was Heil Hitlering all over the place. I saw my opportunity and, taking a sharp inward breath, said quickly, 'It will be difficult to march every afternoon and still do your homework, sir.'

The inside of my head filled with a zinging sound. Had I gone too far? I'd won the battle and here I was risking all on a minor skirmish. Marching around wasn't so bad. Quite fun really. What if he realised I used the time to do his homework anyway?

The Judge sniffed and wiped his nose on the back of his hand. 'Orright, no more marching. But you do my homework, you hear? If I catch you and that kaffir chicken messing around, you'll do twice as much marching as before. You are both prisoners of war and you better not forget it, man.'

Victory was mine a second time. My first conscious efforts at manipulation had been successful. It was a heady feeling as Granpa Chook and I followed the Judge to school that morning.

*

One thing is certain in life. Just when things are going well, soon after they are certain to go wrong. It's just the way things are meant to be.

Mrs Gerber told us that day in class, there had been an outbreak of Newcastle's disease on a chicken farm near Merensky Dam. Her husband, the vet, had left to visit all the surrounding farms.

Even the youngest kids know what havoc a disease of any kind can cause with poultry or livestock. Of course, rinderpest and foot-and-mouth disease amongst the cattle were the worst, but every farm keeps at least fifty chickens for eggs, so Mrs Gerber's news was met with consternation. My mother had once said that if my granpa lost all his black Orpingtons it would break his heart.

It was pretty depressing to think of my mother with her nervous breakdown in an English concentration camp knitting jumpers with funny sleeves. Knitting away with all the Boer mothers and children as she waited to starve to death or die of black water fever. Meanwhile, back on the farm, there was poor old Granpa slowly dying of a broken heart. That was, if Adolf Hitler didn't arrive first. If he did, I knew Granpa wouldn't even have the strength to make escape plans or drive the Model A and then what would become of me?

Maybe I could live with Nanny in Zululand? This thought cheered me up a lot. Adolf Hitler would never look for a small English person in the middle of Zululand. Inkosi-Inkosikazi would hide me with a magic spell and they wouldn't have a hope. As for Granpa Chook, Adolf Hitler would never be able to tell an English-speaking chicken apart from all the other kaffir chickens. I decided right there and then, when I got back to the farm I would put this excellent plan to Nanny.

From what we could gather from the Judge, who was allowed to listen to the news on Mr Stoffel's wireless on Saturday nights, the war was going pretty badly for the English. Adolf Hitler had taken Poland, which I took to be a place somewhere in South Africa, like Zululand, but where the Po tribe lived. The Judge made it sound as though Adolf Hitler could be expected any day now in our neck of the woods.

I had no idea that South Africa was on England's side, from where I sat the English were most definitely the local enemy. While I knew myself to be English, I regarded this as my misfortune, like being born into a poor and degenerate family.

Most of my information came from the regular war councils the Judge held behind the school shit houses. All the senior hostel boys were stormtroopers and Danie Coetzee, as head of the small kids' dormitory, was also allowed to attend. As the official prisoners of war, Granpa Chook and I were dragged along for the purposes of interrogation and torture.

I was blindfolded and tied to the trunk of a jacaranda tree with a rope around my chest and waist, leaving my arms and legs free. This was because two of the main tortures required my hands to be free.

Most torture sessions began with the iron bar which was known as 'Chinese torture' after the make of the Judge's big, cheap pocket watch, one of his most treasured possessions. I was required to hold the bar out in front of me while he timed each session, so that I would have to hold the bar up longer than the previous time before dropping it. My times were duly recorded by a kid called Boetie Van der Merwe, who was known in the Nazi Party as Stormtrooper, Timekeeper and Tallyman.

Van der Merwe was very proud of his job and would remind me at every opportunity of the minimum time allocated for the next Chinese torture session. If I failed to best my previous time I got a severe cuff from the Judge and the six stormtroopers whose turn it was to beat me up.

The second main torture which required my hands be free was referred to as 'shooting practice'. Every stormtrooper carried a catapult as his deadly weapon. Farm kids all have catapults for shooting birds and grow very skilled at using them. While they were not allowed to be worn openly, all the senior boys had one stashed away and they would wear these around their necks at Nazi Party meetings.

For shooting practice I was required to stretch my arms out on either side of me with my palms open and turned upwards. An empty jam tin was placed on either hand and each of the stormtroopers was allowed two shots to try to knock the tins down. The six best results for the day earned the right to beat me up on the next occasion it became necessary. As usual, Boetie Van der Merwe was the tally-man.

I must say this for those Nazis, while they hit the tins from twenty feet often enough, only once did I collect a stone which thudded into the butt of my hand. Lucky it was my left hand as I was unable to use it for several days.

Granpa Chook would fly up onto a branch of the jacaranda where he would keep a beady eye on the proceedings. He was known to the Nazi Party as Prisoner of War Kaffir Chicken Rooinek. There isn't too much interrogation and torture you can do to a chicken. As Mevrou's leading kitchen insect exterminator, Granpa Chook was pretty safe. Tough as the Judge was, he wasn't willing to take Mevrou on.

He would look up at Granpa Chook and say menacingly, 'Your time will come, Prisoner of War Kaffir Chicken Rooinek, don't think we've forgotten about you, you hear?'

I was constantly fearful for Granpa Chook but there wasn't much I could do about it. Like me, he was a prisoner of war. Together we just had to hope for the best and try to muddle through. Besides, Granpa Chook had it easy up there in the jacaranda tree while I was the one who suffered at ground level.

The Nazi Party sessions were held twice a week. Although they would leave me trembling for hours afterwards, the physical damage wasn't too bad. I only got hit if I dropped the iron bar too soon and in one or two other conditions, like when the Judge got very excited or I failed to answer one of his ranting questions fast enough for his liking.

'What is your mother, Pisskop?'

'A whore, sir!' I had no idea what a whore was, but I knew it was the answer he wanted.

'Who does she sleep with?'

'Kaffirs, sir.'

'Ag sis man! Dirty, stinking Kaffirs!' the rest of the Nazis would chorus, groaning and sticking their tongues out and clasping their hands to their throats pretending to vomit.

Even the smallest farm kid knows about animal sex, though it never occurred to me that humans performed the same function. I would wonder why this particular answer was so insulting. After all, Nanny had slept with me on her sleeping mat at the foot of my bed all my life and to the Nazis she was a Kaffir.

'What are you, Pisskop?'

'A piece of shit!' I would respond.

'Not shit! Dog shit!' they would all chorus back.

You can get used to anything, I discovered. They expected me to make the mistake so that they could all pantomime back. Halfway through the interrogation I would be blindfolded. Then, often in the middle of an interrogation, someone would throw a bucket of water over me. Knowing it might come but not knowing when meant that I would get an awful shock. The imagination is always the best torturer.

Or they would release half a dozen red ants down my trousers and watch me frantically trying to find them as the ants bit painfully into my scrotum and the soft inner parts of my legs. If I tore my blindfold away it would mean a double clout from every member of the Party. I soon learnt that a red ant tends to bite only once if you leave it alone. But, let me tell you something, that one bite isn't a very nice experience.

If some new trick, like the red ants, worked, they would congratulate each other loudly and yell with laughter as my legs pumped up and down and my hands searched frantically in my khaki shorts to rid myself of the marauding ants.

The Judge encouraged new insults and tortures, but he ruled out any torture that left obvious bruises. For instance, Chinese burns were allowed but pinching was out. As the last term wore on, their limited minds ran out of ideas and as I knew all the answers to all the dumb questions and had admitted to everything they accused me of while happily accepting all their insults, the proceedings quietened down a lot. I have found in life that everything, no matter how bad, comes to an end.

One thing got to all of them more than anything else. They couldn't make me cry. Even the Judge, with all the fear he could provoke, could not make me cry. I suspect they even began to admire me a bit. Many of them had little brothers of my age at home and they knew how easy it is for a five-year-old to cry. In fact I had turned six but nobody had told me, so in my head I was still five.

Not being able to cry was the hardest part for me as well. Crying can be a good camouflage. In truth, my willpower had very little to do with my resolve never to cry, I had learned a special trick and, in the process, had somehow lost the knack of turning on the tap.

What they didn't know was that behind the blindfold I had learned to be in two places at once. I could easily answer their stupid questions, while with another part of my mind I would visit Inkosi-Inkosikazi. Down there in the night country I was safe from the stormtroopers who were unable to harm me or make me cry.

As they tied the dirty piece of rag over my eyes, I would take three deep breaths. Immediately I would hear Inkosi-Inkosikazi's voice, soft as distant thunder: 'You are standing on the rock above the highest waterfall, a young warrior who has killed his first lion and is thus worthy to fight in the impi of Shaka, the greatest warrior king of all.'

I stood in the moonlight on the rock above the three waterfalls. Far below I could see the ten stones wet and glistening and the white water as it crashed through the narrow gorge beyond. I knew then that the person on the outside was only a shell, a presence to be seen and provoked. Inside was the real me, where my tears joined the tears of all the sad people to form the three waterfalls in the night country.

The last term of the year had come to an end, only one more day remained, just one more interrogation, then freedom.

The Judge had pleased Mr Stoffel with his efforts in the final term and his poor performance earlier in the year had been forgotten. He was top of his class by the time term ended. Mr Stoffel would hold him up as an example and I think he also liked to take a bit of the credit. The Judge had been considered a hopeless case and now he was the star performer. The Judge showed me his report card which said, in black and white, that he had passed. He had come to accept his brilliance and expected the compliments of his fellow Party members. Not only was he tough but he was also smart, it was a most satisfactory situation.

Therefore I had no reason to expect anything but a light going over at the last interrogation and torture session before the Judge would disappear from my life forever. After all he owed me something, and as Adolf Hitler, despite his smashing victory at a place called Dunkirk, hadn't arrived yet he hadn't been compromised one bit.

Prisoners of War Pisskop and Kaffir Chicken Rooinek were marched off to the jacaranda tree for the last time under the Nazi leadership of the Judge. This time I was blindfolded immediately as I was tied to the tree in the usual manner. I could hear Granpa Chook squawking away in the branches above me. I was about to visit the night country when the Judge's voice rang out harshly.

'This is the last time, English bastard!'

With a sudden certainty I knew today would be different. That, in his mind, the Judge owed me nothing. The bad times were back. I tried to get down to the safety of the

54

night country, but the fear rose in me like a Vesuvius spewing vomit and I was unable to detach myself from it.

'Today, Englishman, you eat shit.' His use of the word 'Englishman' rather than the familiar, almost friendly Rooinek added greatly to his menace.

'Hold your hands out in front of you.' I could hear him sniff as I held my hands out in front of me, palms upwards. He grabbed my arms about the wrists and held them so tightly I couldn't move them. 'Bring it here, Stormtrooper Van der Merwe,' I heard him say.

A soft object was dropped first into one hand and then into the other. 'Close your hands, bastard,' the Judge commanded.

The pain in my wrists was almost unbearable. Slowly I closed my hands. 'Take his blindfold off,' the Judge commanded again. The rest of the Nazis had grown very quiet and one of them unknotted the blindfold. I blinked at the sudden light. My nose as well as my eyes had been covered by the blindfold and even before I'd looked down a terrible smell rose up at me. My hands were sticky and I opened them to see that they contained two squashed human turds.

The Judge released my wrists. 'Now, lick your fingers,' he demanded.

I stood with my hands held out in front of me, not knowing what to do.

'I am going to count to three, if you haven't licked your fingers I'm going to knock your blêrrie head off, you shit house!' The Judge stood pop-eyed in front of me and I could see he was trembling.

I was too deeply shocked to react. I think I would have eaten the shit when the message finally made it through my disconnected brain. But at that moment all the wires were fusing.

'*Een ... twee ... drie!*' he counted. The Judge reached three and I remained with my hands held out in front of me, quaking with terror. He made a gurgling sort of animal sound deep in his throat, then, grabbing my wrists, he forced my hands into my mouth. My teeth were clamped shut in fear, and the shit was rubbed all over my lips and teeth and the rest of my face. Some of it must have got onto the Judge's hand because he released my wrists and wiped it through my closely cropped hair.

Then he grabbed the tree trunk about two feet above my head, his body straddled over mine. First he tried to shake the tree. Then he began beating at it with his clenched fists. Suddenly he threw his head back so that he was looking directly upwards into the tree.

'Heil Hitler!' he screamed.

In the tree high above the Judge Granpa Chook's anus opened, and from it dropped a perfect bomb of green and white chicken shit straight into the Judge's open mouth.

Granpa Chook had waited until the last day of term to give his opinion of the Nazi Party. As usual it was short, accurate and to the point.

The Judge spat furiously, bent double, racing round in circles clutching his throat and stomach, hawking and spitting and then finally throwing up. He raced for the tap and filled his mouth and spat out about six times. Then he stuck his index finger into his mouth like a toothbrush and rubbed his teeth and gums, took more water and spat and spat.

'Run, Granpa Chook! Run, man, run!' I screamed up into the tree.

But Granpa Chook had done enough running for one old kaffir chicken. Sitting squawking up there amongst the purple jacaranda blossom he sounded as though he was laughing his scraggy old head off.

'Please run, Granpa Chook, please, please run! The bastard will kill you!' I screamed, oblivious to the shit on my face and in my hair.

Granpa Chook hopped onto a lower branch and then, to my horror, flew onto my shoulder and gave my ear one of his famous Granpa Chook kisses. I grabbed him, intending to throw him on his way, but as I lifted him from my shoulder there was an explosion of feathers in my face. Granpa Chook let out a fearful squawk as he was blasted from my hands and fell to the ground. The Judge stood a few feet away, his empty catapult dangling in his left hand.

'Run, Granpa Chook, run for your life!' I pleaded.

Granpa Chook tried to get up from where he had landed but the stone from the Judge's powerful catapult had broken his ribcage. He made several more attempts, each time falling back onto his wing. I think he knew it was useless. After a while he just sat there, looked up at me and said, 'Squawk!'

Danie Coetzee ran over and grabbed Granpa Chook. I managed to kick him once, but then he held Granpa Chook triumphantly upside down by his legs. Granpa Chook beat his wings furiously, the pain must have been terrible. Quite suddenly he stopped and I thought he must be dead. But then I saw his bright, beady eye trying to find me from his upside down position.

'No blêrrie kaffir chicken shits on me! Hang him up by the legs next to Pisskop,' the Judge commanded. He was still doing little dry spits and wiping his mouth on the back of his hand. Two stormtroopers slung a piece of rope over a branch and Granpa Chook soon hung upside down just beyond my reach and at about the level of my head.

'Please, sir. I will do anything! Anything you ever ask! Anything you want! Please don't kill Granpa Chook!'

The Judge, his eyes cruel, bent down and looked into my face. 'Now we'll see who'll cry,' he grinned.

I was seized by panic. 'Kill me!' I begged. 'Please kill me. But don't kill Granpa Chook!'

The Judge butted me on the forehead with the heel of his hand and my head slammed against the trunk of the jacaranda, leaving me dazed. 'Ag, shit!' he exclaimed, some of the shit on my face had rubbed off onto his hand. Then he wiped his hand in my hair once again.

'You're shit and your fuckin' kaffir chicken is shit. Did

you see what he did to me? Me, Jaapie Botha! That fuckin' chicken shit in my mouth!'

Still dazed, I tried another desperate tack. 'I'll tell Mevrou!' I shouted, trying to sound threatening.

'*Mevrou kan gaan kak!*' (Mevrou can go to shit!) The Judge spat on the ground, this time with a proper, not a chicken-shit spit. He turned to the stormtroopers. 'Prisoner of War Kaffir Chicken Rooinek will be executed, two shots each!' He moved to take his place in the shooting line as the rest of the stormtroopers loaded up their catapults.

I sloughed the last of my camouflage. 'I'll tell Mr Stoffel about how I did your arithmetic for you!' I screamed at the Judge.

I heard the soft 'pfflifft' of his catapult at the same time as I felt the stone slam into my stomach. The pain was terrible, it seemed to be happening in slow motion as though the stone had a life of its own, gnawing at my gut, burning and squirming through my intestines and into my back. A vicious, determined, alive, eyeless thing. The shock to my system was enormous, my eyes bugged out of my head and my tongue poked out in involuntary surprise.

'Fire!' A series of dull plops tore into the fragile bones of Granpa Chook's breast. The first stones had set the rope swinging, but the stormtroopers were expert shots and their second shots also tore into the funny old body of that upside-down chicken. Spots of blood dropped into the dry dust and among the fallen jacaranda blossoms, the rope swinging so that no two drops landed in the same place. Granpa Chook, the toughest damn chicken in the whole world, was dead.

A tiny feather drifted towards me, it was one of the soft downy ones which grew at the very top of Granpa Chook's scrawny legs. It stuck to a piece of shit in my face. The Judge walked over and untied the rope from around my waist and I dropped to my haunches at his feet. He placed his bare foot on my shoulder.

'What are you, Englishman?'

'Dog shit, sir.'

'Look at me when you say it!' he barked.

Slowly I looked up at the giant with his foot resting on my shoulder. High above him I could see a milky moon hanging in the afternoon sky. We had got so close, Granpa Chook and I had got so close to making it through to the end, just a few more hours.

I spat at him, 'You're dog shit! Your ma is a whore!'

He pushed violently downwards with his foot, sending me sprawling. Then he let out a howl, a mixture of anger and anguish. 'Why don't you cry, you fucking bastard!' he sobbed and started to kick blindly at me.

The stormtroopers rushed to restrain him, pulling him from me. The Judge allowed himself to be led away and we were left alone behind the shit houses under a white moon set in a flawless blue sky.

I untied the broken body of Granpa Chook and we sat under the jacaranda tree and I stroked his bloody feathers. No more gentle African dawn folding back the night, no more early cock-a-doodle-doo to tell me you are there, my loved and faithful chicken friend. Who will peck my ear? Who will be my friend? I sobbed and sobbed and sobbed. The great drought was over, the inside man was out, the rains had come to Zululand.

After a long, long while, when the crying was all out of me and the loneliness bird had entered to build a nest of stones in the hollow place inside of me, I carried Granpa Chook to the orchard and laid him in the place I had made for him to keep him from the rain. Then I climbed through the window into the dormitory to fetch my new red jumper, the one my mother had knitted in the concentration camp and Nanny had fixed.

I gathered as many rocks as I could find and then I pulled my red jumper over Granpa Chook's body, his wings poked out of the arm holes and his long neck stuck out of the head part and his feet poked out of the bottom.

He looked the best I'd ever seen him. I took the jam tin

I had used for his water and, in about five minutes, I'd collected twenty little green grasshoppers, which are the very best chicken scoff there is. I placed the tin beside his body so that he'd have a special treat on the way to heaven. Finally I covered his body with the stones.

South Africa's first victim in the war against Adolf Hitler was safe at last.

I sat there on my haunches beside the pile of stones as the afternoon sun began to set. Now the sun was passing beyond Zululand, even past the land of the Swazi and now it leaves the Shangaan and the royal kraal of Modjadji, the rain queen, to be cooled in the great, dark water beyond.

The first bell for supper rang and I moved to the tap and began to wash the blood and shit from my hands and face and hair.

Deep inside me the loneliness bird sat on its crude stone nest and laid a large and very heavy stone egg.

The bell for supper sounded. The last supper. Everything comes to an end. Tomorrow I would be going home for Christmas and Nanny. Wonderful, soft, warm Nanny.

But life doesn't work that way. I, most of all, should have known this. At supper Boetie Van der Merwe told me Mevrou wanted to see me in the dispensary. 'If you tell about this afternoon, we'll kill you,' he hissed. I wasn't frightened, I knew a proper ending when I saw one.

Only hours remained before my liberation, nothing the Judge, Mevrou and, for the moment anyway, Adolf Hitler could do would alter that. Soon I would be returning to my quiet backwater.

I didn't know then that what seemed like the end was only the beginning. All children are flotsam driven by the ebb and flow of adult lives. Unbeknownst to me the tide had turned and I was being swept out to sea.

FOUR

At the end of supper, after Mr Stoffel had read the Bible lesson and concluded evening prayers, I waited for Mevrou outside the dispensary. She arrived a short time later. 'Kom!' Mevrou said as she brushed past me. I entered and waited with my hands behind my back, my head bowed in the customary manner.

'Why is there blood on your shirt, Pisskop?'

I looked down at my shirt which was stained with Granpa Chook's blood and a biggish spot where the stone had torn into me.

Mevrou sighed and sat down heavily on a bentwood chair painted the same light green as the dispensary walls. 'Take off your shirt,' she commanded.

I hurriedly removed my shirt and Mevrou made a cursory examination of my stomach. 'Ag, is that all?' She prodded at the wound the stone had made and I flinched involuntarily.

'Please, Mevrou, I fell on a rock.' Mevrou removed the cork from a large bottle of iodine and upended it onto a wad of cotton wool.

'Yes, I can see that.' She dabbed at my wound and the iodine stung like billy-o and I winced and hopped up and down in dismay, wringing my hands to stop the burning pain. 'Come, that's not enough.' She upended the bottle once again and dabbed hard at my tummy. This time I knew what to expect and, gritting my teeth and closing my eyes tightly, I managed to hold back most of the pain. 'You can't go getting blood poisoning on the train,' she said, tossing the wad on the table. She retrieved the cork and pushed it back into the bottle.

'What train, Mevrou?' I asked, confused.

'Your oupa called long distance on the telephone from a *dorp* in the Eastern Transvaal called Barberton. You are not going back to the farm. He says Newcastle's disease has made him kill all his chickens and he has sold the farm to a Mevrou Vorster.'

'What's my granpa doing in this town called Barberton, Mevrou?'

My head was swimming, my whole world was coming apart at the seams. If Granpa had sold the farm to fat Mrs Vorster and was making telephone calls from some strange town in the Eastern Transvaal, where was Nanny? Without Granpa Chook and Nanny, life was not possible.

'I'm not a mind reader. Maybe he got work in this place.' She reached into her bag and held up an envelope. 'In here is the ticket. Tomorrow night you will catch the train to Barberton. Two days and two nights. I will take you to the train.' She dismissed me with a wave of the envelope.

I turned to go, and as I reached the door Mevrou called me back. 'You can't take the chicken, you hear?' She looked at me smugly. 'South African Railways won't let you take a kaffir chicken, not even in the goods van.' She seemed pleased with this thought. 'I will take the chicken, he will earn his keep even if he is only a kaffir chicken.'

'He is dead, Mevrou. A dog ate him today.' I managed somehow to keep the tears out of my voice.

'That is a shame, he was good in the kitchen.' She rose from her chair with a sigh, fanning herself with the letter. 'I'm telling you, man, a kaffir chicken is no different from a kaffir. Just when you think you can trust them, they go and let you down.'

I had never owned a pair of shoes. At that time, in the Northern Transvaal, a farm kid only got boots if he had rich parents or if he had turned thirteen. That's when the

Old Testament says a boy becomes a man. A pair of khaki shorts, a shirt and a jumper when it was cold was all you got. Underpants hadn't been invented. Even if they had been, Boer kids wouldn't have worn them. More expense for what?

The day after Granpa Chook's funeral was the last day of term. Everyone was up and packed long before breakfast. After breakfast Mevrou summoned me to the dispensary to tell me that after lunch we would be going into town to buy a pair of tackies for me at Harry Crown's shop.

'What are tackies, Mevrou?'

'Domkop! Tackies are shoes only made of canvas with rubber bottoms. Don't you know anything? Make sure you have clean feet or we will be shamed in front of the Jew.'

From my secret mango tree, I watched the kids leave the hostel. Parents arrived in old pick-up trucks and mule carts. Some kids left on donkeys brought to the school by a farm servant. I watched as the Judge left in a mule cart. He made the black servant sit on the tailboard, then he jumped up into the driver's seat, took up the reins and the whip and set off at a furious pace, whipping at the mules and making the whip crack like a rifle shot. I breathed a huge sigh of relief. As my mother used to say, 'Good riddance of bad rubbish.'

Finally everyone had gone and I climbed down from the mango tree and crossed the school playground. It wasn't the same without Granpa Chook. The sun felt the same. The little green grasshoppers still couldn't make it across the playground in one hit. The day moon, made of skimmed milk, still hung in the cloudless morning sky. But it wasn't ever going to be the same again. I saved the need to grieve for a later time. I had enough on my mind with the prospect of going to town to buy a pair of shoes and catching the train. I'd never owned a pair of shoes and I'd never been on a train, never even seen a real train. Two nevers in one day is enough to fill anyone's mind.

After a lunch of bread and jam with a mug of sweet tea,

I hurried to meet Mevrou in the dispensary, stopping only long enough to give my feet and legs a good scrub like Mevrou said. The same shower which had been dripping that first night when I thought I was in a slaughter house was still sounding drip, drip, drip, like a metronome. Funny how little kids can get things mixed up like that. It all seemed such a long time ago; I sure had been a baby then.

I had been waiting at the dispensary a few minutes when Mevrou arrived. She was wearing a shapeless floral cotton dress and a funny old black straw hat with two cherries on it. A third wire stem stuck up where a cherry had once been. In her town clothes she looked not unlike fat old Mrs Vorster, except younger and with a moustache.

The town I knew to be about two miles from the school. 'Maybe we could visit the railway station as well as Harry Crown's shop?' I suggested tentatively.

'It is enough that I do this for you, Pisskop. What do you want? Blood from a stone? Tonight I must do it all over again for you. There is nothing at the station to see, only sleeping Kaffirs waiting for the train.'

For the remainder of the journey we said nothing. Mevrou walked three paces ahead of me all the way to town. Her huge shape sort of rocked along, stopping every once in a while to catch her breath. The early afternoon sun beat down on us. By the time we arrived Mevrou was very hot and bothered and her special smell was worse than ever.

Harry Crown's shop was closed and nothing much seemed to be happening in the main street. Mevrou took a large red *doek* from her basket and proceeded to wipe her face. 'Everyone is still having their lunch, we must wait,' she explained. With great effort she climbed the five steps up to the stoep of the shop and sat down on a bench beside the padlocked door. 'Go and find a tap and wash your feet,' she panted.

I crossed the street to the garage which had a sign which read Atlantic Service Station. It had two pumps outside a small office and workshop bay. Just inside the bay was a tap. The whole place smelt of oil and grease. I washed my feet and walked back across the road on my heels so as not to dirty my feet. Half a dozen Africans were asleep at the far end of the verandah where there was a second entrance to the shop. Above this entrance was written 'Blacks only'. I wondered briefly why whites were not allowed to enter.

Flies, flying heavy in the heat, settled on sleeping eyes and every now and again a desultory black hand would come up and brush at them, its owner seemingly still asleep.

One black man with his left eye missing remained awake and sat with his back against the shop wall. His cupped hands and mouth concealed a Jew's harp which twanged an urgent rhythm.

'The Jew is late, who does he think he is?' Mevrou said impatiently. She half turned and addressed the African playing the Jew's harp. 'Hey, Kaffir! Where is the baas?'

The black man jumped to his feet, removing the tiny harp and placing it in the pocket of his ragged pants. He said nothing, not understanding Afrikaans.

'Do you work here?' I asked him in Shangaan.

'No, small baas, I also, I am waiting. The big baas for the shop will be here soon I think. When the hooter goes for the saw mill he will surely come.'

'He doesn't work for Mr Crown, Mevrou.'

Just then a hooter sounded. We were familiar with the saw mill hooter, which blew at one o'clock and again at two.

Almost on the dot a big, black Chevrolet drove up and parked outside the shop. It was the most beautiful car I had ever seen. I had never imagined a motor car could be as shiny and powerful. The man inside it revved the engine before he cut the ignition and it roared as though alive. Obviously being a Jew was a very profitable business. Maybe I could be one when I grew up.

Harry Crown was a fat man in his late fifties. He wore his trousers high so that his entire tummy and most of his chest were covered with trouser top, held up by a pair of bright red braces. His white open-neck cotton shirt seemed to extend no more than eight inches from his collar before it was swallowed by his trousers. He was almost completely bald and when he smiled he showed two gold front teeth.

'A thousand apologies, Mevrou. Have you been waiting long?' he said, making a fuss of unlocking the padlocked doors to the shop.

'Ag, it was nothing. Not even a few minutes,' Mevrou said, all smiles for the fat, bald man.

In the part boarded off for white customers, two large ceiling fans whirred softly overhead and the shop was dark and cool. Mevrou heaved herself gratefully onto a chair beside the counter and Harry Crown poured her a cup of coffee from a pot he removed from a small hotplate on a shelf behind the counter.

'What can I do for you, Mevrou?' he asked, then turning to me he bowed slightly. 'And for you, Mister?' he said solemnly.

I was not used to jocularity so, not knowing what to do, I dropped my eyes to avoid his gaze.

Observing my shyness he turned from me to a large glass jar on the counter and from it produced a raspberry sucker, its ruby head wrapped in Cellophane. He held the sucker out for me to take. I looked at Mevrou who took a polite sip from her coffee cup and then nodded. I took the delicious prize and put it into my shirt pocket.

'Thank you, Meneer,' I said softly.

'Ag, eat it now, boy. When we have finished business you can have another one.' He paused. 'A green one maybe, huh?' He turned to Mevrou. 'I have had this shop for thirty years and I can tell you with God's certainty that children like raspberry first and green second. If I know nothing for certain in this life, of this one thing I am sure.' He snapped his braces with his thumbs and gave a loud, happy snort.

I had never met a man who laughed and carried on like this and I felt intimidated, so I left the raspberry sucker in my pocket where I hoped it was safe.

'What is your name, boy?' Harry Crown asked.

'Pisskop, sir,' I replied.

Harry Crown's shiny bald head jerked back and he looked down at me in consternation. 'Pisskop? Pisskop! This is a name for a nice boy?' he asked in alarm. 'Who calls you this name?'

Mevrou interrupted sharply. 'Never mind his name, what have you got in tackies? The boy must have some tackies. He is going on the train alone tonight to his oupa in Barberton.'

Turning momentarily to acknowledge he had heard her, Harry Crown turned back to me and gave a low whistle. 'Barberton eh? That is in the lowveld in the Eastern Transvaal. Easy two days away in the train, a long journey alone for a small boy.' He had moved around from behind the counter and was looking at my feet. 'We have nothing so small, Mevrou. I don't have much call for tackies. The Boere round here don't play much tennis.' He chortled loudly at his own joke, which was completely lost on Mevrou and me.

'Show me what you got, Mr Crown. His oupa did not send enough money for boots, only tackies.'

'It makes no difference, boots, smoots, tackies, smackies, the boy's foot is too small.' He moved back behind the counter where he pulled a battered cardboard box from the shelf. From it he withdrew a pair of dark brown canvas shoes.

'Let the boy try them,' Mevrou said.

'It is useless, Mevrou. These tackies are four sizes too big for him. It is a miracle I have these, but they are too big already.'

'The boy will grow,' Mevrou said, a trifle impatiently.

'Ja certainly, Mevrou. Maybe in five or six years they will fit him like a glove. In the meantime they will fit him like the clown in a circus.' He slapped his stomach. 'Very amusing,' he said to himself in English.

'We will try them on. With newspaper we can fix them.'

'Mevrou, with the whole *Zoutpansberg Gazette* we couldn't stuff these tackies to fit. He has very small feet for a Boer child.'

'He is not a Boer child. He is a Rooinek!' Mevrou said, suddenly angry. She put the cup of coffee down on the counter, and leaning over grabbed the tackies and turned to me. 'Put your foot up here on my lap, child,' she ordered.

The first tackie slipped around my foot without touching the sides. With my heel on Mevrou's lap the canvas shoe seemed to reach almost up to my chin.

Mevrou pulled the laces tightly until the eyelets overlapped. 'Now the other one,' she said.

I stood there, rooted to the floor, not daring to move and not knowing what to do next. The tackies seemed to extend twice the distance of my feet.

'Walk, child,' Mevrou commanded.

I took a tentative step forward and the left tackie stayed behind on the floor, though I managed to drag the right one forward by not lifting my foot.

'Bring some paper.' Mevrou cunningly fashioned two little boats from strips of newspaper. She then put the paper boats in the tackies and instructed me to insert my feet into them and tied the laces. This time they fitted snug as a bug in a rug. Though I must say they felt very strange and when I walked they made a phlifft-floft sound where the tackies bent at the end of my toes.

I had never felt as grand in all my life. 'We will take them,' Mevrou announced triumphantly. She reached into her handbag for her purse.

Harry Crown sighed. 'Those tackies are no good, Mevrou.'

If Mevrou had had her sjambok she would have made fat old Harry Crown bend over the counter and she would have given him six of the best.

'How much?' she said curtly, her lips pursed.

'Half a crown, for you only two shillings,' Harry Crown

said, adjusting the price automatically, his heart obviously not in the sale.

I tugged at the end of a lace and to my relief the bow collapsed. I did the same for the second tackie then slipped ever so carefully out of the newspaper boats and handed the tackies to Harry Crown.

'You poor little bugger,' he said in English. He slipped the tackies back into the soft brown cardboard box and when he saw Mevrou wasn't looking, quickly put two green and two red suckers into the box and handed it to me. 'I wish you health to wear them,' Harry Crown said in English. Speaking out of the corner of his mouth he added, 'Can she understand English?'

Not daring to reply, I shook my head almost imperceptibly, indicating no.

'Inside is for the journey, green and red, the best! Believe me, I know. So long, Peekay.' He patted me on the shoulder. His eyes widened and drawing up to his full height, his hands clasped over his belly, gold teeth flashing, he grinned. 'Maybe the tackies don't fit, but I think your new name fits perfect. Peekay! Ja, that is a nice name for a brave person who is travelling by himself to the lowveld to meet his granpa.'

Mevrou, who was practically snorting with rage, threw two shillings on the counter and marched out of the shop. I followed along with the precious box of loot under my arm. At the door I turned to say goodbye to Harry Crown.

'Goodbye, sir!' I said in English. The two English words sounded strangely out of place, like a language newly learned.

Mevrou turned furiously. Grabbing me by the ear, she hissed, 'Do not talk to that . . . that dirty Jew in the accursed language. You will hear from my sjambok when we get home!'

'Ouch! You have my sore ear, Mevrou.' I knew immediately she'd feel guilty grabbing me by my recently damaged ear, even though it was completely healed.

Mevrou let go of my ear as though it were a red-hot poker. You've got to be quick on your feet in this world if you want to survive. Though, once you know the rules, it is not too hard to play the game.

Mevrou stormed ahead and I fell some five paces behind her. After I'd given her what I hoped was enough guilt for her to withdraw the promised thrashing, I dropped back another fifteen paces and took the raspberry sucker out of my pocket. Taking off the Cellophane wrapper I licked the tiny bits of crimson sugar crystal which had stuck to it before throwing it away. I then settled down to suck my way back to the hostel.

I was right about the sjambok, which was not mentioned on our return. I spent the remainder of the afternoon putting more stones on Granpa Chook's grave and making a border around the pile of rocks with white pebbles which took ages to collect from all around the place. I must say, the toughest damn chicken in the whole world had a very impressive grave, a stone cairn which would probably last forever, hidden by successive generations of khaki weed and black jack.

The cook boy had packed me a big brown paper bag of sandwiches for the train journey. We left the hostel about five o'clock to catch the seven o'clock train. My suitcase, though large, contained very few things. Two shirts, two pairs of khaki shorts, my pyjamas, the four suckers which I'd hidden in a pair of shorts and my new tackies with the paper boats in them. There was plenty of room for the sandwiches. While the suitcase banged against my knees, it wasn't really heavy and besides, with all the iron bar torture sessions, my muscles were pretty big. Mevrou was completely puffed out from making two trips into town in one day, and with the suitcase banging against my knees it took us almost an hour to get to the station.

The station turned out to be a raised platform about thirty yards long upon which sat a building with two doors facing the railway line. On one door Station Master was written and to the right of this door was a window. Above the window it read Tickets. On the remaining door it said Waiting Room. Outside the station master's office there were three truck tyres painted white and in the middle of these grew red cannas, their long, flat leaves dusty and shredded with the blooms equally torn and bedraggled looking. Mevrou seemed to know the station master. He opened the locked waiting room for us and brought her a cup of coffee in a big white cup with SAR monogrammed on it.

'Don't worry, Hoppie Groenewald is the guard on this train, he will take good care of the boy.' He turned to acknowledge me for the first time. 'He is champion of the railways, you know. That Hoppie,' the station master grinned at the thought, 'he laughs all the time, but if you get into a fight, I'm telling you, man, you better pray he's on your side!'

I wondered what a champion of the railways was, but I clearly understood, and greatly liked, the idea of having someone on my side who was good in a fight. My life seemed to be made for trouble and it would make a nice change to have a champion of the railways beside me when the next lot hit, as was bound to happen.

Sometimes the slightest things change the directions of our lives, the merest breath of a circumstance, a random moment that connects like a meteorite striking the earth. Lives have swivelled and changed direction on the strength of a chance remark. Hoppie Groenewald was to prove to be a passing mentor who would set the next seventeen years of my life on an irrevocable course. He would do so in little more than a day and a night.

'The boy is a Rooinek and also too small to fight yet,' Mevrou said, as though it were only a matter of time before my bad English blood would turn nasty. She produced a ticket from an envelope and inserted a large safety pin into the hole at one end. 'Come here, child.' She pinned the ticket to my shirt pocket. 'Listen carefully to me now, man, this ticket will take you to Barberton but your oupa only sent enough money for one breakfast and one lunch and one supper on the train. Tonight you eat only one sandwich, you hear?' I nodded. 'Tomorrow for breakfast another one and for lunch the last one. Then you can eat on the train. Do you understand now?'

'Ja, Mevrou, for the next three meals I eat the sandwiches.'

'No, man! That's not what I said. For tonight and for breakfast tomorrow and lunch tomorrow. And also eat the meat first because the jam will keep the bread soft for tomorrow. Do you hear?'

'Ja, Mevrou.'

She took out a small square of white cloth about the size of a lady's hanky and placed it on her lap. In the centre she placed a shilling.

'Watch carefully now, Pisskop. I am putting this shilling in here and tying it so.' She brought the two opposite corners together and tied them over the shilling and then did the same with the remaining two. She took a second large safety pin from her handbag, then, pushing the doek with the shilling into the pocket of my khaki shorts, she pinned it to the lining.

'Now listen good. It is for an emergency. Only if you have to can you use some of it. But you must tie up the change like I just showed you and put it back in your pocket with the safety pin. If you don't need it you must give it to your oupa, it is his change.'

The station master entered and told us that the train was on time and we had five minutes.

'Quick, man, get your tackies,' Mevrou said, giving me a push towards the suitcase.

I was seized by a sudden panic. What if I opened my suitcase and she saw my suckers? I placed the case flat on the floor and opened it so the lid was between Mevrou and me, preventing her from seeing inside. Just as well, a green sucker had worked out of its hiding place in my shorts and my heart went thump. Phew! I removed the tackies and quickly snapped the case shut. I slipped each foot carefully into a paper boat and Mevrou tied the laces. I tried desperately to memorise how she did this but wasn't sure I had the idea.

'Please, Mevrou, will you teach me how to tie the laces so I can take my tackies off in the train?'

Mevrou looked up, alarmed. 'You must not take your tackies off until you get to Barberton. If you lose them your oupa will think I stole the money he sent. You keep them on, do you hear me now?'

The train could be heard a long way off and we left the waiting room to watch it coming in. Real walking in my tackies was difficult and very different from the three or four tentative steps I had taken in Harry Crown's shop. I stumbled several times as I went phlifft-floft, phlifft-floft from the waiting room to the edge of the platform. Bits of newspaper crept up past my ankles and I had to stop and press them back in.

With a deafening choof of steam, immediately followed by two short sharp hisses and a screeching sound of metal rubbing on metal, the huge train pulled into the station, and carriage after carriage of black people went by. They were laughing and sticking their heads out of windows and having themselves a proper good time. Finally the last two carriages and the goods van came to a halt neatly lined up with the platform. The two end carriages read South African Railways First Class and Second Class respectively. I had seen pictures of trains of course, and sometimes at night as I lay in the small kids' dormitory I had heard a train whistle carried in the wind, the beautiful sound of going to faraway places away from the hostel, Mevrou, the Judge and his Nazi stormtroopers. But I must say I wasn't prepared for anything quite as big and black and blustering with steam, smoke, fire, brass pipes and hissing pistons.

Africans appeared as if from nowhere. They carried bundles on their heads which they handed up through the

73

third-class carriage windows to the passengers inside and then climbed aboard laughing with the excitement of it all. From inside the carriages came song and more laughter and a great deal of shouting and good-natured banter. I knew at once that I would like trains.

The guard leapt down onto the platform carrying a canvas bag with Mail stamped on the outside. He handed it to the station master who gave him an identical bag in return.

The station master introduced the guard to Mevrou. 'This is Hoppie Groenewald, he is guard and conductor until you get to Gravelotte. He will look after the boy.'

Hoppie Groenewald grinned down at me and tipped his navy blue guard's cap to Mevrou. 'No worries, Mevrou, I will look after him until Gravelotte. Then I will hand him over to Pik Botha who will take him through to Kaapmuiden.' He opened the door of the second-class carriage and put my suitcase into the train and indicated that I should enter. The three steps up into the carriage were fairly high and I put my tackied foot on the bottom step. As I put my weight on the step the toe of the tacky buckled and I fell on my bum on the platform. Wearing shoes was a much trickier business than I had first supposed. A bit distressed, I wondered how adults seemed to manage so easily. I tried to get up but the tackies were too big and I couldn't get a proper grip on the loose gravel which covered the platform.

'Get up, man!' Mevrou said, visibly annoyed. She shook her head, 'For God's sake! Even now you make trouble for me.'

Hoppie Groenewald put the canvas mail bag on the platform, and bending down he grabbed me under the armpits and hoisted me high into the air and through the door to land inside the carriage.

'No worries, little brother, I too have fallen up those *verdomde* steps many a time. I, who am a guard and soon to be a conductor, and who should know better.'

He retrieved the mail bag and put it next to my suitcase. Then he hopped up the steps without even looking and unhooked a neatly rolled green flag from above the door of the carriage. He unfurled the flag and absently pulled at a chain attached to a button on his navy serge waistcoat and withdrew a large silver whistle from his fob pocket.

'Watch the Kaffirs get a fright,' he said with a grin. He showed me how to hold onto the handrail inside the door and lean out of the carriage so I could see down the full length of the train to the third-class carriages. He then jumped back onto the platform and began to wave the flag, giving a long blast on his whistle.

You should have seen the kerfuffle. Africans who had left the train to stretch their legs or have a pee scrambled frantically to get through the doors of the carriages as the train began slowly to move, laughing and yelling and climbing on top of each other. Hoppie Groenewald gave two more short blasts on his whistle and hopped aboard the train.

'Goodbye, Mevrou. Thank you,' I shouted, waving at her.

'Keep your tackies on, you hear!' Mevrou shouted back.

It was a dry-eyed farewell on both sides. I ardently hoped the Rooinek and Mevrou would never have to see each other again.

Hoppie Groenewald closed the carriage door as the train began to gather momentum. He quickly refurled the flag and clicked it back into its holder next to a red one above the door. Then he picked up my suitcase and opened the door to the nearest compartment.

The train was moving along smoothly now and I enjoyed the comforting, predictable clackity clack, clackity clack of the carriage wheels.

The empty compartment had two bright green leather seats facing each other, each seat big enough for three adults. A small table, which I was later to discover turned into a wash basin, was positioned between the two windows. The rest of the compartment seemed to be panelled in highly varnished wood and immediately above each green leather seat was a glass frame about ten inches high running the length of the seats. Inside the frames were lots of photographs. It was all very posh. Before it got completely dark, Hoppie Groenewald turned on the compartment lights and all seemed very cosy ... just like the beginning of a proper adventure.

'It's all yours until we get to Tzaneen. After that who knows. No worries, Hoppie will take good care of you.' He looked down at my tackies, bits of newspaper were sticking out of the sides and up past my ankles.

'The old cow can't get you now, take them off,' the guard said. I tugged the canvas shoes off. My feet were hot and uncomfortable and had turned black from the newsprint rubbing off on them. It felt delicious to squiggle my toes again. Hoppie Groenewald stuck his hand out. 'Shake a paw. You know my name but I haven't had the pleasure.'

I'd already thought about what Harry Crown had said and had decided to take his advice and call myself Peekay. 'Peekay,' I said tentatively. I pronounced it in English, the way Harry Crown had, so it sounded like a proper name.

I suddenly felt new and clean. Nobody ever again would know that I had been called Pisskop. Granpa Chook was dead and so was Pisskop. The first two South African casualties in the Second World War.

'All the best, Peekay. We will be pals.' He took his cap off and put it on my head. I wondered if he was a Nazi. He didn't seem to know I was English, so why tempt fate?

'Thank you for taking care of me, Mr Groenewald,' I said politely and handed him back his cap.

'Ag man, just call me Hoppie.' He grinned as he replaced his cap.

Hoppie left to check the tickets in the African carriages but promised he would return soon.

It was almost totally dark outside, as I sat alone in a lighted room, flying through the African night, lickity-clack, lickity-clack. I had defeated the Judge and his Nazi storm-troopers, survived Mevrou and I had grown up and changed my name, lickity-clack, lickity-clack.

Opening my suitcase I took out one of Harry Crown's green suckers. Carefully removing the Cellophane wrapper I licked the bits of green sugar that had stuck to it. The faint taste of lime transferred to my tongue, sweet promise of the main event when I began on the sucker itself.

Harry Crown was right, of course the green ones were a very close second to the raspberry. I examined the photographs above the seats, sepia-toned pictures of a flat mountain with a streak of white cloud resting just above it. The caption underneath read, 'World famous Table Mountain wearing its renowned tablecloth'. All there was was a big white cloud above it but I couldn't see a renowned tablecloth. Another showed a big city seen from the air with the caption, 'Cape Town, home of the famous Cape Doctor'. I wondered what the doctor had done to be famous and rich enough to own a big town for his home. He must have been richer even than Harry Crown. Years later I discovered that the Cape Doctor was a wind which blew in early spring to clean out the flu germs and general accumulated nasties that had gathered during the winter. Another photograph of Table Mountain was captioned 'Truly one of the world's natural wonders'. The last picture showed a big white house and it said, 'Groot Constantia's famed and spacious cellars, the home of superb wine'.

'Well,' I thought, 'this will be a pretty good journey if we visit all those places!' I decided I'd ask Hoppie about them when he came back.

Hoppie returned after what seemed ages but probably wasn't very long. On a train, with the darkness galloping past, time seemed to disappear, the lickity-clack of the wheels on the track gobbled up the minutes.

He plonked himself wearily on the seat opposite me. 'Sis, man, those Kaffirs stink!' he declared then gave me a big grin and a light playful punch to the point of my chin.

'When we get to Tzaneen in an hour we'll have some dinner. We stop for forty-five minutes to take on coal and water and there's a café across the road from the station. From Tzaneen I'm only the guard and another conductor takes over. What's your favourite food, Peekay?'

'Sweet potatoes,' I answered.

'Sweet potatoes, maybe and maybe not, I've never asked for sweet potatoes at that café. How about a mixed grill. A two-bob special, heh?'

'I've only got a shilling and it's for emergencies. Is a mixed grill an emergency?' I asked.

Hoppie laughed. 'For me it is. Tonight I'm paying, old mate. The mixed grills are on me.'

I didn't want to ask him what a grill was and how it was mixed so I asked him about the pictures on the wall. 'When are we going to see Table-Mountain-one-of-the-natural-wonders-of-the-world?'

'Huh, come again?'

I pointed to the picture above his head. 'When do we go there?'

Hoppie turned around to look at the picture, but he didn't laugh when he worked out what I was talking about. 'It's just stupid pictures showing where South African Railways go, but we are not going there, Peekay.' He started to study all the pictures as if he'd noticed them for the first time.

'I almost went to Cape Town last year to fight in the finals but I was beaten in the Northern Transvaal championships. Split decision but the referee gave it to the fighter from Pretoria. I'm telling you, man, I beat the bastard fair and square. It was close, I've got to admit that, but I knew all the time I had him on points.'

I listened, astonished. What on earth was he talking about?

Hoppie looked me straight in the eyes. 'You're almost looking at the railways boxing champion of the Transvaal, you know.' He brought his finger and thumb together in front of my face. 'That close and I would of been in the National Railway Boxing Championships in Cape Town.'

'What's a boxing champion?' I asked.

It was Hoppie's turn to look astonished. 'What a domkop you are, Peekay. Don't you know what boxing is?'

'No, sir.' I dropped my eyes, ashamed of my ignorance.

Hoppie Groenewald put his hand under my chin and lifted my head up. 'It's nothing to be ashamed of. There comes a time in everything when you don't know something.' He grinned. 'Okay, man, settle down, make yourself at home, we're in for a long talk.'

'Wait a minute, Hoppie,' I said excitedly. I clicked open my suitcase. 'Green or red?' I asked, taking out a sucker of each colour. I had decided that I would have one sucker in the morning and one at night, that way they would last me the whole journey. But a friend like this doesn't come along every day and I hadn't heard a good story since Nanny.

'You choose first, Peekay. What's your favourite?'

'No, you choose, Hoppie. You're the one who is going to tell the story so you get first choice,' I said with great generosity.

'Green,' he said. 'I like green, my mother had green eyes.' He took the green sucker and I put the raspberry one back and clicked the suitcase shut.

'I've just had one,' I said, grateful that I had two of the best raspberry ones left for the next two days.

'We will share then,' he said, 'you lick first because I'm going to be too busy doing the talking.' He watched me as I unwrapped the Cellophane and licked it clean. 'When I was your age I used to do the same.' He looked at his watch. 'One hour to Tzaneen, just about time for a boxing lecture and maybe even a demonstration.'

I settled back happily into the corner of the large green leather seat and proceeded to lick the sucker. One and a half suckers in less than an hour was an all-time happiness and having a real friend was another. What an adventure this was turning out to be.

'Boxing is the greatest sport in the world,' Hoppie began, 'even greater than rugby.' He looked up, ready to defend this last statement if necessary, but saw that I was prepared to accept his premise. 'The art of self-defence is the greatest art of all and boxing is the greatest art of self-defence. Take me, a natural welterweight, there isn't any man I have to be afraid of, not even a big animal like a front-row forward. I'm fast and I can hit hard and in a street fight a little bloke like me can take on any big gorilla.' He jabbed once or twice into the air in front of him to demonstrate his lightning speed.

'How little can beat how big?' I asked, getting excited.

'Big as anything, man. If you've got the speed to move and can throw a big punch as you're moving away. Timing, speed and footwork, in boxing they are everything. To be a welterweight is perfect. Not too big to be slow, not too small to lack a punch. A welterweight is the perfect fighter, I'm telling you for sure, man!' Hoppie's eyes were shining with conviction.

I stood up on the seat and lifted my hand about another eight inches above my head. Which, of course, was about the height of the Judge. 'A little kid like me and a big kid, big as this?'

Hoppie paused for a moment; he seemed to be thinking. 'Ja, now you see with small kids it's a bit different. Small kids don't have the punch. Maybe they're fast enough to stay out of the way, but one stray punch from a big gorilla and it's all over, man. Kids are best to fight in their own division.' He looked at me. 'Who you want to fight, hey? What big kid gave you a bad time? Just you tell me, Peekay, and he'll have to reckon with Hoppie Groenewald. I'm telling you, man, nobody hurts a friend of mine.'

'Just some boys at school,' I replied, delighted that even though this was the wrong place and time, I now had someone strong in the world who was on my side. I wanted to tell him about the Judge and his Nazi stormtroopers, but I wasn't prepared to go the whole way, Hoppie Groenewald didn't know I was a Rooinek and he might think differently if he found out.

'Well, you just tell them next time they'll have to reckon with me,' Hoppie growled.

'It is all over now,' I said, handing him the sucker.

He took the sucker and started to lick it absently. 'Peekay, take my advice. When you get to Barberton, find someone who can teach you to box.' He looked at me, squinting slightly. 'I can see you could be a good boxer, your arms are strong for a little bloke. Hey, stand up again, let me see your legs.'

I stood up on the seat. 'Not bad, Peekay, nice light legs, you could have speed. With a boxer speed is everything. Hit and move. Hit and move, one two one, a left and a left again and a right.' He was sparring in the air, throwing lightning punches at an invisible foe. It was scary and exciting at the same time.

'Wait here,' he said suddenly and left the compartment. He returned in a couple of minutes carrying a pair of funny-looking leather gloves.

'These are boxing gloves, Peekay. These are the equalisers, when you can use them well you need fear no man. In the goods van I have a speedball, tomorrow I will show you how to use it.' He slipped the huge gloves over my hands which disappeared into the gloves halfway up to my elbows. 'Feels good, hey?' he said, tying the laces.

My hands in the gloves were just as lost as my feet had felt in the tackies when Mevrou first made me put them on. Only this was different. The gloves felt like old friends, big yes, and very clumsy, but not strangers.

'C'mon kid, hit me,' Hoppie said, sticking out his jaw. I took a jab at him and his head moved away so my glove simply whizzed through the air. 'Again, hit me again.' I pulled my arm back and let go with a terrible punch which landed flush on his chin. Hoppie fell back into the leather seat opposite me, groaning and holding his jaw. 'Holy macaroni! You're a killer. A natural-born fighter. You sure planted one on me, man.' He sat up rubbing his jaw and I began to laugh. 'That's the way, little *boetie*, I was beginning to wonder if you knew how to laugh,' he said with a big grin.

And then I started to cry, not blubbing, just tears that wouldn't stop rolling down my cheeks. Hoppie Groenewald picked me up and put me on his lap and I put my arms with the boxing gloves around his neck and buried my head in his blue serge waistcoat. The heavy chain that held the whistle was cool against my face.

'Sometimes it is good to cry,' he said softly. 'Sometimes you fight better when you've had a good cry. Now tell old Hoppie what's the matter.'

I couldn't tell him of course. It was a dumb thing to cry like that, but it was as far as I prepared to go. I got off his lap. 'It's nothing, honest,' I said going to sit on my side of the compartment.

Hoppie picked up the sucker which he'd put on the table before we had started to spar and held it out to me. 'You finish it. It will spoil my appetite for my mixed grill. You're still going to have a mixed grill with me, aren't you? I mean, I'm paying and all that.'

I reached for the sucker but the gloves were still on my hands and we laughed together at the joke. He pulled the gloves off and handed it to me.

'No worries, Peekay. When you grow up you'll be the best damn welterweight in South Africa and nobody . . . and I mean no-bod-ee, will give Kid Peekay any crapola. I'm telling you, man.'

When we reached Tzaneen Hoppie pulled down a bunk concealed in the wall above my head which, to my amazement, turned out to be a proper bed with blankets and sheets. From a slot behind the bunk he took out a pillow with a pillow slip, and a small towel. He then put my suitcase on the bed to reserve it, in case other folk came into the compartment at Tzaneen.

Taking me by the hand, we crossed the station platform

which looked much like the one from which we had left, only the platform was longer and the buildings bigger. Opposite the station was a lighted building with a big glass window on which Railway Café was written. Inside were lots of little tables and chairs. Several people were seated, eating and drinking coffee. There seemed to be a lot of smoke in the room.

A pretty young lady behind the counter looked up as we entered and gave Hoppie a big smile. 'Well, well, look who's here. If it isn't Kid Louis, champion of the railways,' she announced. An older woman came out of the back. Wiping her hands on her apron, she came up to Hoppie and he gave her a big hug.

'Your cheeky daughter is already giving me a hard time, *ounooi*,' Hoppie said. 'She needs to go three rounds in the ring with Hoppie Groenewald and then we'll see who's laughing.' He was grinning from ear to ear.

'So when's your next fight, champ?' the lady behind the counter asked.

'Tomorrow night at the railway club in Gravelotte, a light-heavy from the mines. It's the big time for me at last.' Hoppie smiled.

The pretty young lady giggled. 'Put two bob on the other bloke for me.' One or two of the other customers also laughed, but in a good-natured way. The older woman was clearing a table for us and fussing around Hoppie. He turned towards me, and taking my hand held my arm aloft. 'Hello everyone, I want you to meet Kid Peekay, the next welterweight contender,' he said, keeping his voice serious. I dropped my eyes, not knowing what to do.

'Enough of your nonsense, Hoppie Groenewald. Come sit now or you will not be fed before the train leaves,' the older woman fussed.

The pretty young woman smiled at me. 'How would the contender like a strawberry milkshake?' she asked.

I looked at Hoppie. 'What's a milkshake, please, Hoppie?'

'A milkshake is heaven,' he said. 'Make that two, you lazy frump.' He turned to the older woman who was still fussing about. 'Two super-duper mixed grills please, *ounooi*. Me and my partner here are starving.'

Hoppie was right again, a strawberry milkshake is heaven. When the mixed grill arrived I couldn't believe my own eyes. Chop, steak, sausage, bacon, liver, chips, a fried egg and tomato. What a blow-out! I had never eaten a meal as grand and was quite unable to finish it. Hoppie helped himself to the remaining food on my plate, although I slurped the milkshake, in its aluminium shaker, right down to the last gurgling drop.

The pretty lady came over and sat with us and Hoppie seemed to like her a lot. Her name was Anna and her lips were very shiny and red. The clock above the counter read ten o'clock. It was set into a picture of a beautiful lady in a long white nightdress that clung to her body. She too had very red lips and was smoking a cigarette; the smoke from the cigarette curled up on to the face of the clock where it turned into running writing. The running writing said 'C to C for satisfaction.' I had never been up as late as this before and my eyelids felt as though they were made of lead.

The next thing I remembered was Hoppie tucking me into my bunk between the nice clean, cool sheets and the pillow that smelt of starch. 'Sleep sweet, old mate,' I heard him say.

The last thing I remembered before I fell asleep again was the deep, comforting feeling of my hands in the boxing gloves. 'The equalisers,' Hoppie had called them. Peekay had found the equalisers.

FIVE

I woke up early and lay in my bunk listening to the lickity-clack of the rails. Outside in the dawn light lay the grey savannah grasslands; an occasional baobab stood hugely sentinel against the smudged blue sky with the darker blue of the Murchison range just beginning to break out of the flat horizon. The door of the compartment slid open and Hoppie, dressed only in his white shirt and pants with his braces looped and hanging from his waist, came in carrying a steaming mug of coffee.

'Did you sleep good, Peekay?' He handed me the mug of coffee.

'Ja, thanks, Hoppie. I'm sorry I couldn't stay awake.'

'No worries, little boetie, there comes a time for all of us when you can't get up out of your corner.'

I didn't understand the boxing parlance but it didn't seem to matter. To my amazement Hoppie then lifted the top of the small compartment table to reveal a wash basin underneath. He turned on the taps and hot water came out of one and cold out of the other. He kept running his fingers through the water until he said the temperature was 'just right'.

'When you've had your coffee you can have a nice wash and then I'll take you to breakfast,' he said.

'It's okay, Hoppie, I have my breakfast in my suitcase,' I said hastily.

Hoppie looked at me with a grin. 'Humph, this I got to see. In your suitcase you have a stove and a frying pan and butter and eggs and bacon and sausages and tomato and toast and jam and coffee?' He gave a low whistle. 'That's a magic suitcase you've got there, Peekay.'

'Mevrou gave me sandwiches for the first three meals because my oupa didn't send enough money. Only last night we had a mixed grill when I should have eaten the meat one,' I said in a hectic tumbling out of words.

Hoppie stood for a moment looking out of the carriage window, he seemed to be talking to himself. 'Sandwiches, eh? I hate sandwiches. By now the bread is all turned up in the corners and the jam has come through the middle of the bread. I bet it's peach jam. They always have blêrrie peach jam.' He turned to address me directly, 'Where are these sandwiches?' I pointed to my suitcase on the seat below my bunk. He stooped down and clicked it open and from the case removed the brown paper package tied with coarse string.

'As your manager, it is my solemn duty to inspect your breakfast. Fighters have to be very careful about the things they eat, you know.' He unwrapped the parcel, splotches of grease had stained the brown paper. He was right, the bread had curled up at the corners. He removed the slice of bread uppermost on the first sandwich and sniffed the thin brown slices of meat, then he replaced the slice. He dug down to the bottom two sandwiches; the jam had oozed through the middle of the brown bread while the outside edges had curled inwards dry and hard.

'Peach!' Hoppie said triumphantly. 'Always peach!' He looked up at me, his eyes expressionless. 'I have sad news for you, Peekay. These sandwiches have died a horrible death, most likely from a disease they caught in an institution. We must get rid of them immediately before we catch it ourselves.' With that, he slid down the window of the compartment and hurled the sandwiches into the passing landscape. 'First-class fighters eat first-class food. Hurry up and have a wash, Peekay, I'm starving and breakfast comes with the compliments of South African Railways.'

I flung the blanket and sheet back to get down from my

bunk and looked down at my headless snake in horror. Hoppie had removed my pants before putting me to bed. My heart pounded. Maybe it had been dark and he hadn't noticed I was a Rooinek. If he found out, everything was spoiled, just when I was having the greatest adventure of my life.

'C'mon, Peekay, we haven't got all day you know.' Hoppie pulled his braces over his shoulders.

'I am still full from the mixed grill last night, Hoppie, I can't eat another thing, man.' I quickly pulled the blanket back over me.

'Hey, you're talking to me, man, Hoppie Groenewald. Who you trying to bluff?' He took a step nearer to the bunk and ripped the blanket and sheet off me in one swift movement. My hatless snake was exposed, not six inches from his face. I cupped my hands over it but it was too late, I knew that he knew.

'I'm not the next welterweight contender, Mr Groene-wald, I'm just a verdomde Rooinek,' I said, my voice breaking as I fought to hold back my tears. It always happens, just when things are perfect, down comes the retribution.

Hoppie stood quietly in front of me, saying nothing until his silence forced me to raise my downcast eyes and look at him. His eyes were sad, he shook his head as he spoke. 'That's why you're going to be the next champ, Peekay, you've got the reason.' He paused and smiled. 'I didn't tell you before, man. You know that bloke who beat me for the title in Pretoria? Well he was English, a Rooinek like you. He had this left hook, every time it connected it was like a goods train had shunted into me.' Hoppie brought his arms up and lifted me out of the bunk and put me gently down beside the wash basin. 'But I think you're going to be even better than him, little boetie. C'mon wash up and let's go eat, man.'

I can tell you things were looking up all right. Hoppie took me through to the dining car which had a snowy tablecloth on every table, silver knives and forks and starched linen napkins folded to look like dunces' caps. Even the coffee came in a silver pot with SAR in running writing on one side and SAS done the same way on the other. A man dressed not unlike Hoppie, but without a cap and with a napkin draped across his arm, said good morning and showed us to a small table. He asked Hoppie if it was true that the light-heavy whom he was to fight that night had a total of twenty-seven fights with seventeen knockouts to his credit . . . a real brawler?

Hoppie said you couldn't believe everything you heard, especially in a railway dining car. That it was the first he'd heard of it. Then he shrugged his shoulders and grinned. 'First he's got to catch me, man.' He asked him about something called odds and the man said two to one on the big bloke. Hoppie laughed and gave the man ten bob and the man wrote something in a small book.

The man left and soon returned with toast and two huge plates of bacon and eggs and sausages and tomato, just the way Hoppie said it would happen. I decided that when I grew up the railways were most definitely for me.

'Are you frightened about tonight?' I asked Hoppie. Although I couldn't imagine him being frightened of anything, I wanted him to know I was on his side. He had told me how it was with a light-heavy, and it was obvious the man he was going to fight was to him just as big as the Judge was to me.

Hoppie looked at me for a moment and then washed the sausage he was chewing down with a gulp of coffee. 'It's good to be a little frightened. It's good to respect your opponent. It keeps you sharp. In the fight game, the head rules the heart. But in the end the heart is the boss,' he said, tapping his heart with the handle of his fork. I noticed he held his fork in the wrong hand and he later explained: a left-handed fighter is called a southpaw. 'Being a southpaw helps when you're fighting a big gorilla like the guy tonight. Everything is coming at him the wrong way round. It cuts down his reach, you can get in closer. A straight left becomes a right jab and that leaves him open for a left hook.'

Hoppie might as well have been speaking Chinese, but it didn't matter: like the feel of my hands in the gloves, the language felt right. A right cross, a left hook, a jab, an uppercut, a straight left. The words and the terms had a direction, they meant business. A set of words that could be turned into action. 'You work it like a piston, with me it's the right, you keep it coming all night into the face until you close his eye, then he tries to defend what he can't see and in goes the left, pow, pow, pow all night until the other eye starts to close. Then whammo! The left uppercut. In a southpaw that's where the knock-out lives.'

'Do you think I can do it, Hoppie?' I was desperate for his confidence in me.

'Piece sa cake, Peekay. I already told you, man. You're a natural.' Hoppie's words were like seed pods with wings. They flew straight out of his mouth and into my head where they germinated in the rich, fertile, receptive soil of my mind.

The remainder of the morning was taken up with Hoppie writing up some books in the guard's van where he had a bunk, table and wash basin and a cupboard all to himself. Attached to a hook in the ceiling was a thing he called a speedball, for sharpening your punching. I was too short to reach it but Hoppie punched it so fast he made it almost disappear. I was beginning to like the whole idea of this boxing business.

Hoppie explained that at Gravelotte the train had to take on antimony from the mines. There would be a nine-hour stop before the train left for Kaapmuiden at eleven o'clock that night. 'No worries, little boetie. You will be my guest at the fight and then I will put you back on the train.'

At lunch my eyes nearly popped out of my head. We sat down at the same table as before and the man who had been at breakfast, whose name turned out to be Gert, brought Hoppie a huge steak and me a little one.

'Compliments of the cook, Hoppie. The cook's got his whole week's pay down on an odds-on bet with four miners. He says it's rump steak, red in the middle to make you a mean bugger.' Gert laughed. 'I reckon his wife is going to be the mean bugger if you don't win.'

Hoppie squinted up at Gert. 'I get my head knocked in, the cook loses his money, but the man who keeps the book always wins, eh Gert?'

Gert looked indignant. 'Not always, Hoppie. I dropped a bundle when you lost to that blêrrie Rooinek in Pretoria.'

'My heart bleeds for you, man, fifteen fights, fourteen wins and you've always given my opponents the better odds. Christ, I've made you rich!' Hoppie said and began to tuck into his steak.

At breakfast we had been in too early to see many other passengers, but at lunch the dining compartment was full and everyone was talking about the fight. Gert was moving from table to table, and in between serving was taking ten-shilling and pound notes from passengers and writing it down in his book.

Hoppie looked up at me, the handle of his fork resting on the table with a piece of red meat spiked on the end. 'You a betting man, Peekay?'

I looked at him confused. 'What's a betting man, Hoppie?'

Hoppie laughed. 'Mostly a blêrrie fool, little boetie.' Then he explained about betting. He signalled for Gert to come over. 'What odds will you give the next welterweight contender?' he asked, pointing to me.

Gert asked me how much I had.

'One shilling,' I said nervously.

'Ten to one,' Gert said, 'that's the best I can do.'

'Is this an emergency?' I asked, fearful for Granpa's shilling.

'At ten to one? I'll say so!' Hoppie answered.

It took positively ages to get the safety pin inside my pocket loose and then to undo the doek Granpa's shilling had been tied into. I handed Gert the shilling and he wrote something down again in his little book. Hoppie saw the anxiety on my face. It wasn't really my shilling and he knew it.

'Sometimes in life doing what we shouldn't do is the emergency, Peekay,' he said.

We arrived in Gravelotte at two-thirty on the dot. The heat of the day was at its most intense and the vapoured light shimmered along the railway tracks. Hoppie said the temperature was one hundred and eight degrees and tonight would be a sweat bath. There were lots of rails in what Hoppie called the shunting yards and our train was moved off the main track into a siding.

'This is where I got my shunting ticket. When the ore comes in from Consolidated Murchison and you got to put together a train in this kind of heat, I'm telling you, Peekay, you know you're alive, man,' Hoppie said, pointing to a little shunting engine moving ore trucks around.

We crossed the tracks and walked through the railway workshops where they were working on a train. The men stopped and talked to Hoppie and wished him luck and said they'd be there tonight, no way they were going to work overtime. The temperature inside the corrugated-iron workshops seemed worse than outside and most of the men wore only khaki shorts and boots, their bodies shining from grease and sweat. Hoppie called them 'Grease Monkeys' and said they were the salt of the earth.

We arrived at the railway mess where Hoppie lived. We had a shower and Hoppie opened a brown envelope which a mess servant brought to him when we arrived. He read the letter inside for a long time and then, without a word, put it into the top drawer of the small dressing table in his room. He said it was best to keep my old clothes on because we would have another shower before the fight and I could put a clean shirt and pants on then.

'We are going shopping, little boetie, and then to the railway club to meet my seconds and have a good look over the big gorilla I'm fighting tonight. Bring your tackies, Peekay, I have an idea.'

We set off with my tackies under my arm. The main street was only a few hundred yards from the mess and there didn't seem to be too much happening. Every time a truck passed it sent up a cloud of dust, and by the time we got to the shop Hoppie was looking for I could taste the dust in my mouth and my eyes were smarting. It sure was hot.

The shop we entered had written above the door, G. Patel & Son, General Merchants. On its verandah were bags of mealie meal and red beans and bundles of pickaxes, a complete plough and a dozen four-gallon tins of Vacuum Oil paraffin. Inside it was dark and hot and there was a peculiar smell quite unlike anything I had previously experienced.

'It smells funny in here, Hoppie.'

'It's coolie stuff they burn, man, it's called incense.'

A young woman dressed in bright swirls of almost diaphanous cloth came out of the back of the shop. She was a mid-brown colour, her straight black hair was parted in the middle and a long plait hung over her shoulder almost to her waist. Her eyes were large and dark and very beautiful. On the centre of her forehead was painted a red dot.

Hoppie nudged me with his elbow. 'Give me your tackies, Peekay,' he whispered. I handed him the two brown canvas shoes which had endured no more than twenty or so steps and showed no sign of wear.

'Good afternoon, Meneer, I can help you please?' she said to Hoppie.

Hoppie did not return her greeting and I could tell from the way he looked at her that she was somehow not equal. I thought only Kaffirs were not equal, so it came as quite a surprise that this beautiful lady was not also. 'Tackies, you got tackies?' he demanded.

The lady looked down at the tackies Hoppie was holding. 'Only white and black, not brown like this.'

'You got a size for the boy?' Hoppie said curtly. The lady leaned over and looked at my feet and went to the other end of the counter. She brought a whole lot of tackies tied together in a bundle back with her. She unpicked a pair and handed them to Hoppie, who said, 'Try them on, Peekay. Make sure they fit, you hear?'

I slipped into the tackies which were white and looked splendid. They fitted perfectly. 'Tie the laces,' Hoppie instructed.

'I can't, Hoppie. Mevrou didn't show me how.' The beautiful dark lady came around the counter, went down on her haunches and started to tie the laces. Her coal black hair was oiled and the path down the centre of her head was straight as an arrow. When she had finished tying the laces she tested the front of the tackies with the ball of her thumb, pressing down onto my toes, then she looked up at me and smiled. I couldn't believe my own eyes, she had a diamond set into the middle of one tooth!

She turned to look up at Hoppie. 'They fit good,' she said.

Hoppie waited until she was back behind the counter. 'Okay, now we make a swap. Those tackies for these tackies.' He placed my old tackies in front of her.

The lady stood looking at Harry Crown's tackies and then shook her head slowly. 'I cannot do this,' she said quietly.

Hoppie leaned his elbows on the counter so he was looking directly into her eyes. His back was straight, his jaw jutted out and his head was held high, his whole body seemed to be threatening her. He allowed his silence to take effect, forcing her to speak again.

'These are not the same, where did you buy these tackies?' She picked up one and examined the sole, then she turned towards the door behind the counter and said something in a strange language. In a few moments we were joined by a man with the same straight black hair and brown skin but dressed in a shirt and pants just like everyone else. The lady handed the tacky to the man, speaking again in the strange language. He seemed much older than she, old enough to be her father. The man turned to Hoppie.

'We cannot make a change, this tacky is not the same. See here is the brand, made in China.' He tapped the sole of the tacky with his forefinger. Then he walked over to the bundle on the counter and pulled one tacky loose from the pile. 'See, by golly, here is altogether another brand and not from China, this time made in Japan. That is a different place you see, this is a different tacky. You did not buy this tacky from Patel & Son. You must pay me three shilling.'

Hoppie appeared not to have heard, and leaning over the counter he tapped the man on the shoulder. 'Outside it says Patel & Son, this is your daughter but where is your son, Patel?'

Patel's face lost its aggrieved look. 'My son is very-very clever. A very-very clever student who is studying at University of Bombay. Every month we are sending him money and he is sending us letters. Soon he will be returning BA and we will be most overjoyed on his returnings.'

'Sixpence and these tackies, Patel. I can't be fairer than that, man,' Hoppie said emphatically. Patel bent and twisted the tacky in his hand, a sour look appearing on his face.

'One shilling,' he said suddenly.

'Sixpence,' Hoppie said again. Patel shook his head.

'Too much I am losing,' he said.

Hoppie looked at him. 'Patel, this is my last and final offer and only if the boy gets a *bansela*, I'll give you another tickey, take it or leave it, man!' Patel shook his head and clucked his tongue and finally nodded. Hoppie took the ninepence out of his pocket and put it on the counter. The beautiful lady held out a yellow sucker.

'Here is your bansela,' she said with a smile and I caught another glimpse of the diamond. I thanked her for the sucker, wondering what yellow tasted like. I still had one red one and with this one I would have two for the fight tonight.

'Thank you, Hoppie,' I said, looking down proudly at my new white tackies. I can tell you they looked good and I could walk in them just like that.

'Better take them off, Peekay. If you're going to be in my corner tonight we don't want you wearing dirty tackies, man,' Hoppie said with a grin. I took the tackies off and Hoppie tied the laces in a knot and hung them around my neck. I turned to thank Patel. He seemed to have become very excited and was pointing to Hoppie.

'Meneer Kid Louis, I am very-very honoured to meet you! All week, my golly, I am hearing about you and the fisticuffs business. This morning only, the telephone from my brother in Mica and my brother in Letsitele is ringing for placing a wager. My goodness gracious, now I am meeting the person myself!'

Hoppie laughed. 'Bet the ninepence you rooked out of me on me and it will pay for your son's education, Patel.'

'No, no, we are doing much, much better. Ten pounds we are wagering on Kid Louis.'

'Holy shit! Ten pounds! That's twice as much as I win if I win.'

Patel proffered the ninepence he had been holding. 'Please take it back, Meneer Kid Louis, it will bring very-very bad luck if I am keeping this money.'

Hoppie shrugged and pointed to me. 'Give it to the next welterweight contender.'

'You are a boxer also?'

I nodded gravely, in my head it seemed almost true. Patel dug into his pocket and produced a handful of change, he dropped the ninepence amongst the coins and selected a shilling. 'Here is for you a shilling,' he said fearfully. Turning to Hoppie he said: 'Please, you must be fighting very-very hard tonight.'

Hoppie grinned at him. 'You don't know what you just did, Patel, but it is a very good omen.'

'Thank you, Mr Patel,' I said, my hand closing around

95

the silver coin. Granpa's change was safe again and I must say it was a load off my mind.

As we left the shop Hoppie gave me a bump with his elbow. 'You're a funny little bugger, Peekay. You don't call a blêrrie coolie "Mister". A coolie is not a kaffir because he is clever and he will cheat you any time he can. But a coolie is still not a white man!'

'That lady had a diamond in her tooth, Hoppie.'

'Yeah, the bastards have got lots of money all right. You never see a poor *charah*. Behind the shop is probably a big V8 Pontiac.'

'What if she swallows it?'

'What?'

'The diamond . . . if it comes loose or something?'

Hoppie laughed. 'They'd be sifting through kak for days!'

We stopped at a café and Hoppie bought two bottles of red stuff. The old lady behind the counter took them out of an ice box, opened them, popped a sort of pipe only made of paper into the tops and handed them to us. I watched to see how Hoppie did it and then I did it too. Tiny bubbles ran up the bottle and went up my nose and it tasted wonderful. On the side were the words American Cream Soda. The stuff was like a raspberry sucker only different. It was the first bottled soft drink I had ever tasted.

We arrived at the railway club just before five o'clock. The club manager, who came onto the verandah to meet us, said the temperature was still in the high nineties, the rains were overdue and there was already severe drought in the Kruger National Park at the far end of the Murchison range.

The club was cool with polished red cement floors and large ceiling fans. The manager told us the boys from the mine had already arrived and the railway boys, including Hoppie's seconds, were with them in the billiard room having a few beers. Hoppie took my hand and we followed the manager into the billiard room.

The room contained three large tables covered in green

stuff on which were lots of pretty coloured balls. Men with long sticks were knocking the balls together all over the place. In the far corner some twenty or so men were seated at a long table covered in aeroplane cloth on which were lots of brown bottles. They all stopped talking as we walked in. Two of them put down their glasses, rose from the table and came towards us smiling. Hoppie shook them by the hand and seemed very happy to see them. He turned to me and said: 'Peekay, this is Nels and Bokkie. Nels, Bokkie, this is Peekay, the next welterweight contender.' Both men grinned and said hello and I said hello back. We walked over to the group of men who had remained sitting around the long table.

Bokkie cleared his throat and put his hand on Hoppie's shoulder. He was a big man with a huge round tummy, and a very red face with a flat nose that appeared to have been broken several times. I noticed that Hoppie was staring at a man who was sitting at the table with a jug of beer in front of him. The man was looking straight back at Hoppie, and their eyes were locked together for a long time. Hoppie was still holding my hand and although his grip didn't seem to increase I could feel the sudden tension. At last the man grinned and dropped his eyes and reached out for his glass.

'Gentlemen,' Bokkie said, 'this is Kid Louis, the next welterweight champion of the South African Railways.' The men at the side of the table nearest to us all cheered and whistled, and a man on the other side of the table stood up and pointed to the man Hoppie and I had been staring at.

'This is Jackhammer Smit. Stand up, Jackhammer, where's your manners, man?' he grinned. The miners surrounding Jackhammer whistled and cheered just as the railway men had done a moment before. Jackhammer rose slowly to his feet. He was a giant of a man with his head completely shaved. Hoppie's grip tightened around my fingers momentarily and then relaxed again. 'This is one big gorilla, Peekay,' he said out of the corner of his mouth. Jackhammer took a couple of steps towards us. His heavy eyebrows were like dark awnings above coal-black eyes. A growth of several days made a bluish stubble over his chin and gave him a permanently angry look. His nose was almost as flat as Bokkie's and one ear looked mashed.

Hoppie stuck his hand out but the big man didn't take it. The men all fell silent. Jackhammer Smit put his hands on his hips, and tilting his head back slightly he looked down at Hoppie and me with eyes of anthracite and doom. Then he turned back to the miners. 'Which of the two midgets do I fight?' The miners broke up and beat the surface of the table and whistled. Jackhammer Smit turned back to face us. 'Kid Louis, huh? Tell me, man, what's a Boer fighter doing with a Kaffir name? Shit man, you should be ashamed of yourself. Kid Louis? I don't usually fight kids and I don't fight *Kaffirboeties*, but tonight I'm going to make an exception.' He laughed. 'You the exception, railway man. Every time I hit you you're going to think a bloody train shunted into you!' He turned and grinned at the seated miners who shouted and cheered again, then he walked the two steps back to his chair where he slumped down and took a deep drink from the jug of beer.

Hoppie was breathing hard beside me but quickly calmed down as the men turned to see his reaction to Jackhammer's taunts. He grinned and shrugged his shoulders. 'All I can say is, I'm lucky I'm not fighting your mouth, which is a super heavyweight.'

Jackhammer exploded and sprayed beer all over the railway men who were seated opposite him. 'Come, Peekay, let's get going, man,' Hoppie said moving towards the door to the cheers, whistles and claps of the railway men.

Bokkie and Nels followed quickly. Hoppie turned at the door. 'Keep him sober, gentlemen, I don't want people to think I beat him 'cause he was drunk!'

Jackhammer Smit half rose in his chair as if to come after us. 'You fucking midget, I'll kill you!' he shouted.

'You done good,' Bokkie said, 'it will take the bastard two rounds just to get over his anger.' He then told Hoppie to get some rest, that they'd pick us up at the mess at seven-fifteen to drive to the rugby field where the ring had been set up. 'People are coming from all over the district and from Letsitele and Mica and even as far as Hoedspruit and Tzaneen. I'm telling you, man, there's big money on this fight, those miners like a bet.'

'No worries,' Hoppie said. 'See you at quarter past seven.'

We walked the short distance to the railway mess. The sun had not yet set over the Murchison range and the day baked on, hot as ever. 'If it stays hot then that changes the odds.' Hoppie squinted up into a sky the colour of pewter, his hand cupped above his eyebrow. 'I think it's going to be a bastard of a night, Peekay. A real Gravelotte night, hot as hell.'

When we got to the mess Hoppie told me his plan. 'First we have a shower, then we lie down, but here's the plan, Peekay, every ten minutes you bring me a mug of water. Even if I say "no more", even if I beg you, you still bring me a glass every ten minutes, you understand?'

'Ja, Hoppie, I understand,' I replied, pleased that I was playing a part in getting him ready. Hoppie took his railway timekeeper from one of the fob pockets of his blue serge waistcoat hanging up behind the door.

'Every ten minutes, you hear! And you make me drink it, okay little boetie?'

'I promise, Hoppie,' I said solemnly as he began to undress for his shower.

The window of Hoppie's room was wide open and a ceiling fan moved slowly above us. Hoppie lay on the bed wearing only an old pair of khaki shorts. I sat on the cool cement floor with my back against the wall, the big railway timekeeper in my hands. In almost no time at all Hoppie's body was wet with perspiration and after a while even the sheet was wet. Every ten minutes I went through to the bathroom and brought him a mug of water. After five mugfuls Hoppie turned to me, still on the bed resting on his elbow.

'It's an old trick I read about in *Ring* magazine. Joe Louis was fighting Jack Sharkey. Anyway, it was hot as hell, just like tonight. Joe's manager made him drink water all afternoon just like us. To cut a long story short, by the eighth round the fight was still pretty even. Then Sharkey started to run out of steam in the tremendous heat. You see, Peekay, the fight was in the open just like tonight and these huge lights were burning down into the ring, the temperature was over one hundred degrees. In a fifteen-round fight a man can lose two pints of water just sweating and if he can't get it back, I'm telling you, man, he is in big trouble. I dunno just how it works but you can store water up just like a camel sort of, that's what Joe did and he's the heavyweight champion of the world now.'

'What did Mr Jackhammer mean when he said you were a kaffir lover, Hoppie?'

'Ag, man, take no notice of that big gorilla, Peekay. He's just trying to put me off my stride for tonight. You see Joe Louis is a black man. Not a Kaffir like our Kaffirs, black yes, but not stupid and dirty and ignorant. He is what you call a negro, that's different, man. He's sort of a white man with a black skin, black on the top, white underneath. But that big gorilla is too stupid to know the difference.'

It was all very complicated, beautiful ladies with skin like honey who were not as good as us and black men who were white men underneath and as good as us. The world sure was a complicated place where people were concerned.

'I've got a nanny just like Joe Louis,' I said to Hoppie as I rose to get his sixth mug of water.

Hoppie laughed. 'In that case I'm glad I'm not fighting your nanny tonight, Peekay.'

After a while Hoppie rose from the bed and went to a small dresser and returned with a mouth organ. For a while we sat there and he played *Boeremusiek* on the mouth organ. He was very good and the tappy country music seemed to cheer him up.

'A mouth organ is a man's best friend, Peekay. You can slip it in your pocket and when you're sad it will make you happy. When you're happy it can make you want to dance. If you have a mouth organ in your pocket you'll never starve for company or a good meal. You should try it, it's a certain cure for loneliness.'

Just then we heard the sound of a piece of steel being hit against another. 'Time for your dinner,' Hoppie said, slipping on a pair of shoes without socks and putting on an old shirt.

Dinner at the railway mess was pretty good. I had roast beef and mashed potatoes and beans and tinned peaches and custard. Hoppie had nothing except another glass of water. Other diners crowded round our table and wished Hoppie luck and joked a bit and he introduced me to some of them as the next contender. They all told him they had their money on him and how Jackhammer Smit was weak down below. They almost all said things like, 'Box him, Hoppie. Stay away from him, wear him out. They say he's carrying a lot of flab, go for the belly, man. You can hit him all night in the head, but his belly is his weakness.' When they had left Hoppie said they were nice blokes but if he listened to them he'd be a dead man.

'You know why he's called Jackhammer, Peekay?'

'What's a jackhammer, Hoppie?'

'A jackhammer is used in the mines to drill into rock, it weighs one hundred and thirty pounds. Two Kaffirs work a jackhammer, one holds the end and the other the middle as they drill into the sides of a mine shaft. I'm telling you, it's blêrrie hard work for two big Kaffirs. Well, Smit is called Jackhammer because, if he wants, he can hold a jackhammer in place on his own pushing against it with his stomach and holding it in both hands. What do you think that would do to his stomach muscles? I'm telling you, hitting that big gorilla in the solar plexus all night would be like fighting a brick wall.'

'I know,' I said excitedly, 'you keep it coming all night into the face until you close his eye, then he tries to defend against what he can't see and in goes the left, pow, pow, pow until the other eye starts to close. Then whammo!'

Hoppie rose from the table and looked down at me in surprise. 'Where did you hear that?' he exclaimed.

'You told me, Hoppie. It's right, isn't it? That's what you're going to do, isn't it?'

'Shhhhh . . . you'll tell everyone my fight plan, Peekay! My, my, you're the clever one,' he said as I followed him from the dining hall.

'You didn't say what happened to Jack Sharkey?'

'Who?'

'In the heat when Joe Louis fought him and drank all the water?'

'Oh, Joe knocked him out, I forget what round.'

Bokkie and Nels picked us up in a one-ton truck which had South African Railways, Gravelotte painted on the door. Nels and I sat in the back and Hoppie sat in the front with Bokkie. In the back with me was a small suitcase Hoppie had packed with his boxing boots and red pants made of a lovely shiny material and a blue dressing gown. Hoppie was very proud of his gown and he had held it up to show me the 'Kid Louis' embroidered in running writing on the back.

'You know the lady in the café in Tzaneen, the young one?'

'The pretty one?' I asked, knowing all along whom he meant.

'Ja, she's really pretty, isn't she? Well, she done this with her own hands.'

'Is she your *nooi*? Are you going to marry her, Hoppie?'

'Ag man, with the war and all that, who knows.' He had

walked over to the dressing table and taken the brown envelope from the top drawer. He tapped the corner of the envelope into the palm of his open hand. 'These are my call-up papers. They were waiting for me when we got in today. I have to go and fight in the war, Peekay. A man can't go asking someone to marry him and then go off to a war, it's not fair.'

I was stunned. How could Hoppie be as nice as he was and fight for Adolf Hitler? If he had got his call-up papers that must mean that Adolf Hitler had arrived and Hoppie would join the Judge in the army that was going to march all the Rooineks, including me, into the sea.

'Has Hitler arrived already?' I asked in a fearful voice.

'No, thank God,' Hoppie said absently, 'we're going to have to fight the bastard before he gets here.' He looked up and must have seen the distress on my face. 'What's the matter, little boetie?'

I told Hoppie about Hitler coming and marching all the Rooineks right over the Lebombo mountains into the sea and how happy all the Afrikaners would be because the Rooineks had killed twenty-six thousand women and children with black water fever and dysentery.

Hoppie came over to me and, kneeling down so that his head was almost the same height as my own, he clasped me to his chest. 'You poor little bastard.' He held me tight and safe. Then he took me by the shoulders and held me at arm's length, looking me straight in the eyes. 'I'm not going to say the English haven't got a lot to answer for, Peekay, because they have, but that's past history, man. You can't go feeding your hate on the past, it's not natural. Hitler is a bad, bad man and we've got to go and fight him so you can grow up and be welterweight champion of the world. But first we've got to go and fight the big gorilla who called me a Kaffir lover. I tell you what, we'll use Jackhammer Smit as a warm-up for that bastard Hitler. Okay by you?'

We had a good laugh and he told me to hurry up and

put my tackies on and he'd show me how to tie the laces like a fighter.

The sudden sound of a motor horn outside made Hoppie jump up. He put the dressing gown in the suitcase with his other things. 'Let's go, champ, that's Bokkie and Nels.'

'Wait a minute, Hoppie. I nearly forgot my suckers.' I hurriedly retrieved them from my suitcase.

SIX

The rugby field was on the edge of town, down a dusty road. By the time we arrived I could taste the dust in my mouth. We parked the ute with all the other cars and trucks under a stand of large old blue gums, their palomino trunks shredded with strips of grey bark. In the centre of the football field the men from the railway workshop had built a boxing ring that stood about four feet from the ground. The miners, who were responsible for the electrics, had rigged two huge lights on wire which stretched from four poles, each one set into the ground some ten feet from each corner of the ring.

Huge tin shades were fitted over the lights and in the gathering dusk the light spilled down so that it was like daylight in the ring. Hundreds of moths and flying insects spun and danced about the lights, tiny planets orbiting erratically around two brilliant artificial suns. The stands, which were really a series of stepped or tiered benches each about twenty feet long and twelve high, were arranged in a large circle around the ring. It meant everyone had a ringside seat. There looked to be about two thousand men packing the stands, while underneath them, looking through the legs of the seated whites, the Africans stood or crouched, trying to get a view of the ring as best they could.

Bokkie and Nels led us to a large tent, on the side flaps of which was stencilled Property of Murchison Consolidated Mines Limited. We entered to find Jackhammer Smit, his seconds and four other men, three of them ordinary size and one of them not much bigger than me. Hoppie whispered that they were the judges and that, 'the dwarf is the referee'. I was fascinated by the tiny little man with the large bald head. 'He may look silly, man. But take it from me, he knows his onions,' Hoppie confided.

Jackhammer Smit had already changed into black shiny boxing shorts and soft black boxing boots. In the confines of the tent, lit by two hurricane lamps which cast a bluish light, he seemed bigger than ever. As we'd entered he'd turned to talk to one of his seconds. My heart sank, Hoppie was right, I had seen his stomach muscles as he had turned, they looked like plaited rope and his shoulders seemed to loom over the smaller men.

'This is one big sonofabitch, Peekay,' Hoppie said. 'Moses was still blubbing in the bullrushes the last time he weighed in as a light-heavy.' He clipped open his small suitcase, and taking off his shorts and shirt he quickly slipped on a jock strap. He looked tough, tightly put together, good knotting around the shoulders and tapered to the waist, his legs slight but strong. He slipped on his shiny red shorts and sat down on the grass of the tent floor to put on his socks and boxing boots.

Jackhammer Smit now stood in the opposite corner of the tent facing us, with the light behind him. He looked black and huge and he kept banging his right fist into the palm of his left hand. It was like a metronome, a solid, regular smacking sound that seemed to fill the tent.

The referee, who only came halfway up Jackhammer Smit's legs, called the two boxers together. I wondered if all dwarfs had such deep voices. He asked them if they wanted to glove up in the tent or in the ring.

'In the ring,' Hoppie said quickly.

'What's blêrrie wrong with right here, man?' Jackhammer shot back.

'It's all part of the show, brother,' Hoppie said with a grin, 'some of the folk have come a long way.'

'Ja, man, to see a short fight. Putting on the blêrrie gloves is going to take longer than the fucking fight.'

'Now, boys, take it easy.' The referee pointed to a fairly large cardboard box. 'Them's the gloves, ten-ounce Everlasts from Solly Goldman's gym in Jo'burg, specially sent, man,' he said with obvious pride.

Bokkie walked over to the box and took the two pairs of gloves out, and moving over to Smit's seconds he offered both sets to them. They each took a pair, examined and kneaded them between their knees before making a choice. The gloves were shiny black; they caught the light from the hurricane lamp and, even empty, they looked full of action.

Bokkie held the gloves out for Hoppie to inspect. 'Nice gloves, not too light,' he said softly.

'No worries.' Hoppie put a towel around his neck and then slipped into his dressing gown. Bokkie slung the gloves around Hoppie's neck. 'Let's kick the dust,' Hoppie said, moving towards the open tent flap.

Suddenly Jackhammer barked, 'What you say, Groenewald, okay by you, winner takes all?'

Hoppie turned slowly to look at the big man. 'I wouldn't do that to you, Smit, what would you do for hospital expenses?' He took my hand.

'That kid of yours is gunna to be a fucking orphan by the time I'm through with you t'night, you nigger lover,' Jackhammer yelled at Hoppie's departing back.

Hoppie squeezed my hand and laughed softly. 'I reckon that was worth at least another two rounds, Peekay.' Pausing in the dark outside the tent, he took me by the shoulders. 'Never forget, Peekay, sometimes, very occasionally, you do your best boxing with your mouth.'

A small corridor intersected the stands on either side of the brilliantly lit ring by which the patrons and the fighters entered. It at once became obvious that one semicircle contained only miners while the other only railway men, while smiling, excited African faces under the stands peered through gaps between the legs of the whites. I had never been at a large gathering of people before and the tension in the crowd was quite frightening. I held onto Nels' hand tightly as he took me to the top tier of a stand and handed me over into the care of Big Hettie.

Big Hettie seemed to be the only lady at the fight. She was the cook at the railway mess and Hoppie had introduced us earlier at dinner. Big Hettie had given me a second helping of peaches with custard and Hoppie had said that I had better eat it even if I was full because Big Hettie was a genuine heavyweight who could take on two drunken railwaymen with one arm behind her back.

Big Hettie patted the place beside her. 'Come sit here, Peekay. You and me is in this together. If that big baboon hurts Kid Louis we'll go in and finish off the big bugger ourselves,' she said, rocking with laughter.

Hoppie was seated on a small stool in the corner of the ring with Bokkie standing over him bandaging his hands. When Jackhammer Smit entered, he didn't look up. Jackhammer paused in the middle of the ring and cocked two fingers in Hoppie's direction, much to the delight of the miners who were cheering him like mad.

'Ho, ho, ho, have we got a fight on our hands!' Big Hettie said gleefully. Then she rose from her seat and in a voice that carried right over the ring she yelled, 'I'll give you two fingers, you big baboon, right up the arse!'

It was almost totally dark. The sound of a woman's voice was unexpected and for a split second the stands were hushed and then both sides convulsed with laughter.

Big Hettie sat down again. Reaching into a large basket at her side she brought out a half-jack of brandy. She popped the cork from the slim, flat bottle and took a long swig, grimacing as she withdrew it from her lips as though it was really nasty *muti*. 'That will fix the big ape,' she said, thumping the cork back into the half-jack with the flat of her hand.

The fighters had both been gloved up and while Hoppie remained seated on the tiny stool, Jackhammer Smit continued to stand, looking big and hard as a mountain. While my faith and my love was invested in my beloved friend,

I'd been around long enough to know the realities of big versus small. Big, it seemed to me, always finished on top and my heart was filled with fear for my new-found friend.

'My God! Look at that sparrow fart!' Big Hettie exclaimed, pointing to the tiny referee. 'How the devil is he going to keep them men apart?'

'Hoppie says he knows his onions, Mevrou Hettie,' I ventured.

Jackhammer Smit began to shuffle around the ring throwing imaginary punches. He seemed to be increasing in size by the minute, while Hoppie, seated on his stool, looked like a small frog crouched in the corner of the ring. Nels was putting Vaseline over Hoppie's eyebrows while Bokkie seemed to be giving him some last-minute instructions.

The tiny referee said something and the seconds left the ring and the fighters moved to the centre. The crowd grew suddenly still. Standing between the two men with his head thrown right back, the referee looked up at them and said something. They both nodded and touched gloves lightly and then turned and walked back to their corners. The crowd began to cheer like mad. The referee held his hands up, turning slowly in a circle to hush the crowd, his head only just showing above the top rope of the ring. Soon a three-quarter moon, on the wane, would rise over the Murchison range, though as yet the night was matt black with only a sharp square of brilliant light etching out the ring with the three men in it. It was as though the two fighters and the dwarf stood alone, watched by an audience of a million stars.

The referee addressed the stilled crowd, his surprisingly deep voice carrying easily to where we sat. '*Dames en Here*, tonight we are witnessing the great biblical drama of David and Goliath.' He paused for his words to take effect.

'Weeping Jesus! Sparrow Fart's going to give us a Bible lesson,' Big Hettie hissed at no one in particular. She took a quick swig from the half-jack as the referee continued.

'Will history repeat itself? Will David once again defeat

Goliath?' The railwaymen went wild and the miners hissed and booed. The referee held his hands up for silence. 'Or will Goliath have his revenge?' The miners cheered like mad and this time it was the railway men who booed and hissed.

The little man held up his hands again and the audience calmed down.

'Introducing in the blue corner, weighing two hundred and five pounds and hailing from Murchison Consolidated Mines, the ex-light-heavyweight champion of the Northern Transvaal, Jackhammer Smit. Twenty-two fights, eleven knockouts, eleven losses on points, a fighter with an even stevens record in the ring. Ladies and gentlemen, put your hands together for Jackhammer Smit!' The miners cheered and whistled.

'What's eleven losses on points mean, Mevrou Hettie?' I asked urgently.

'It means he's a pug, a one-punch Johnny, a slugger,' she said, taking another swig and wiping the top of the bottle with the palm of her hand. 'It means he's no boxer.'

The referee turned to indicate Hoppie who raised his hands to acknowledge the crowd. 'In the red corner, weighing one hundred and forty-five pounds, from Gravelotte, Kid Louis of the South African Railways, Northern Transvaal welterweight champion and the recent losing contender for the Transvaal title; fifteen fights, fourteen wins, eight knockouts, one loss.' He cleared his throat before continuing, 'Let me remind you that the fighter he narrowly lost to on points in Pretoria went on to win the South African title in Cape Town.' He raised his voice slightly. 'Let's hear it for the one and only Kid Louis!' It was our turn to cheer until the referee orchestrated us back to silence. Hoppie had once again calmly seated himself on the tiny stool, while Jackhammer Smit was snorting and throwing punches at an imaginary opponent soon to become Hoppie.

'This is a fifteen-round contest, may the best man win.' The referee had already assumed the authority of the fight and he didn't look small any more. It was clear the crowd accepted him. He moved to the edge of the ring where the light spilled sufficiently to show three men seated at a small table. 'Ready, judges?' They nodded and he turned to the two fighters. 'At the sound of the bell come out fighting, gentlemen.'

Out of the darkness the bell sounded for round one.

Hoppie jumped from the stool as Nels pulled it out of the ring and Jackhammer Smit stormed towards him. In the oppressive heat the air was as still as a dead man's breath and the big boxer's torso was already glistening with sweat. I had earlier unwrapped my first sucker, as usual licking the clear Cellophane clean. It was the yellow one the beautiful Indian lady with the diamond in her tooth had given me, and the wrapper tasted vaguely of pineapple, only even sweeter than a real pineapple.

Hoppie danced around the big man and Jackhammer Smit let go two left jabs and a right uppercut, all of which missed Hoppie by a mile. He followed with a straight left which Hoppie caught neatly in his glove as he was going away. Hoppie feinted to the right as Jackhammer tried to catch him with two left jabs, then he stepped in under the last jab and peppered Jackhammer's face with a two-handed attack. Two left, then two stabbing rights to the head. The blows were lightning fast; Hoppie had moved out of reach by the time Jackhammer Smit could bring his gloves back into position in front of his face. Hoppie continued to back-pedal most of the time, making Smit chase him around the ring. Occasionally he darted in with a flurry of blows to the head and then danced out of range again. Jackhammer came doggedly after him, trying to get set for a big punch, but Hoppie was content to land a quick left and a right and then move quickly out of harm's way. The first round saw him land a dozen good punches, most of them just above Jackhammer's left eye, while the big man only managed a long straight left that caught Hoppie on the shoulder as the welterweight was moving away.

It was clear that Jackhammer Smit was having trouble

with the southpaw and was showing his frustration. The bell went for the end of the first round and the fighters returned to their corners. This time, like Hoppie, Jackhammer sat down, breathing heavily. He drank deeply, straight from a bottle of water one of his seconds held up to his mouth. The other second sponged him, dried him and smeared Vaseline above his left eye.

Hoppie looked composed, breathing lightly. He drank from a bottle with a tiny bent pipe coming out of it, rinsing his mouth and spitting the water back into a bucket Bokkie held for him. Nels was massaging his shoulders and Hoppie was nodding his head at something Bokkie was saying.

'Is Hoppie winning, Mevrou Hettie?' I asked anxiously.

'It's early times yet, Peekay. In the early rounds the Kid will be too fast for the big guy, but one thing's for sure, Hoppie's punches are too short to hurt Smit.'

The bell went for round two, a round much the same as round one except that Jackhammer Smit landed three punches to Hoppie's head, all of them glancing blows, but each time the miners went wild. After the second round a red blotch began to appear above Jackhammer's left eye. The next three rounds saw Hoppie leading Smit all around the ring making him throw punches that nearly always missed and then darting in with a quick flurry of blows before bouncing back out of harm's way.

The bell went for the sixth round and Jackhammer shuffled to the centre of the ring, his gloves rotating slowly in front of his chest. He was getting the hang of the southpaw and was going to make Hoppie take the fight to where he stood rooted to the centre of the ring.

Jackhammer dropped his gloves, leaving his head a clear target, knowing he could take anything Hoppie dished out. Hoppie was forced to move in close enough for Smit to hit him in the gut and around the kidneys. In this way Hoppie had to take a couple of vicious blows to the body every time he moved in to hit the spot above Jackhammer's left eye. Jackhammer gave a grunt as he drove a left or a right into Hoppie's body and the crowd responded as one man with an exclamation of pain. By the end of the sixth Jackhammer's left eye was almost closed but deep red welts showed on Hoppie's ribs where Jackhammer had caught him. Both men were breathing hard as they returned to their corners.

'It's not looking good for the Kid. The big ape has found his mark and he's going to wear him down with body punches. You could of fooled me, he got more brains than I would have given him credit for,' Big Hettie said. She didn't show any emotion, appraising the progress of the fight as though she were simply an informed, though disinterested bystander.

'Don't let him have brains, Mevrou Hettie. Brains is one thing you've got to have to win,' I said in anguish. Big Hettie was fanning herself with a brightly coloured Chinese paper fan, the perspiration running down the sides of her face and neck. 'He hits awful hard, Peekay,' she said absently.

The bell went for the seventh and Jackhammer shuffled back to the centre of the ring. The heat was plainly telling on him and his gloves were held even lower than before. This left enough of his body exposed for Hoppie to hit him at long range, getting a lot more power behind his punches. The left eye was closed and Hoppie was beginning to work on the right, jabbing straight lefts right on the button every time. Near the end of the round he attempted a right-cross to Jackhammer's jaw just as the big man had moved back slightly to throw a punch. Hoppie missed with the right and was thrown slightly off balance as Smit followed through with an uppercut that caught the smaller man under the heart. You could hear his grunt as the punch landed and Hoppie's legs buckled under him as he toppled to the canvas.

'Oh, shit! One-punch Johnny has found the punch. Goliath wins in seven,' Big Hettie said in dismay as the miners went wild. The tiny referee was standing over Hoppie and yelling at Jackhammer Smit to get into a neutral corner, but the big man just stood there his chest heaving, waiting for Hoppie to rise so that he could finish him off. The referee wouldn't start the count and precious seconds passed as the big man stood belligerently over the fallen welterweight. Jackhammer's seconds were screaming at him to move away and when finally he did so a good thirty seconds had passed.

The referee started to put in the count. Hoppie rose onto one knee and waited until the count of eight before rising and getting to his feet. The referee signalled for the fight to continue and Jackhammer Smit lumbered across the ring to finish Hoppie off. The almost forty-second respite had been enough to stave off disaster and Hoppie simply kept out of harm's way as Jackhammer, energy leaking out of him with every assault, kept charging at him like an angry bull. The bell went just as Hoppie landed a hard left uppercut to Jackhammer's eye when the big man tried another desperate charge.

'Dammit, Peekay! That was lucky. Thank the Lord Jesus, Sparrow Fart knows the blêrrie rules, the Kid was out for a ten count for sure.' Big Hettie removed a dishtowel that covered the basket and mopped her face and bosom. 'Smit's just another stupid Boer after all. All balls and no brains. Hoppie can thank his lucky stars for that.'

In all the excitement I had bitten the sucker clean off its stick and crunched it to bits, shortening its life by at least half an hour. I ran my tongue around the inside of my mouth, seeking the last of the pineappley taste. It could be a long time before another one came my way. Big Hettie took a Thermos flask from the basket and, using the silver lid which was shaped like a cup, poured it full of hot, sweet, milky coffee and handed it to me. Then she opened a large cake tin and handed me a huge slice of chocolate cake. My eyes nearly stood out on stalks, this was going to be a night to remember all right. If Hoppie, beloved Hoppie, could just keep away from the big gorilla. The way he danced around the big man, seeming only to get out of the way of a punch at the last second, reminded me of how Granpa Chook used to dodge when stones were thrown at him. I only hoped that Hoppie had the same survival instinct. For an instant I grew sad. In the end even Granpa Chook's highly developed sense of survival couldn't save him, the big gorilla finally got him.

The eighth round saw another change in the fight. Jackhammer Smit had chased Hoppie too hard and too long. The gorilla's great strength had been sapped by the heat and he was down to barely a shuffle, both eyes nearly closed. Hoppie was hitting him almost at will and Jackhammer pulled the smaller man into a clinch whenever he could, causing the tiny referee to stand on the tips of his toes and pull at his massive arms, yelling 'Break!' at the top of his voice.

The ninth and the tenth rounds were much of the same but Hoppie didn't seem to have the punch to put Jackhammer away. Early in the eleventh Smit managed to get Hoppie into yet another clinch, leaning heavily on the smaller man. As the referee moved in to break them up, Jackhammer Smit stepped backwards into him, sending the tiny referee arse over tip to the floor. Still holding Hoppie, Smit head-butted him viciously. On the railway side of the ring we saw the incident clearly, but all the miners, like the ref, saw was Hoppie's legs buckle and the welterweight crash to the floor as Jackhammer Smit broke out of the clinch.

This time Smit moved quickly to the neutral corner and the referee, bouncing to his feet like a rubber ball, started to count Hoppie out.

Pandemonium broke loose. The railwaymen, shouting 'Foul!' began to come down from the stands shaking their fists. At the count of six the bell went for the end of the round and Bokkie and Nels rushed into the ring to help a dazed and wobbly Hoppie to his corner.

A score of railwaymen had reached the ring and were shouting abuse at Jackhammer. The miners were yelling and coming down from their stands and, I'm telling you, the whole scene was a proper kerfuffle.

Jackhammer sat in his corner vomiting into a bucket and Bokkie and Nels were frantically trying to bring Hoppie round, holding a small bottle under his nose. I had begun to cry and Big Hettie drew me into her bosom while hurling abuse at Jackhammer Smit. 'You bastard, you dirty bastard, come into my kitchen tomorrow and I'll de-knacker you, you sonofabitch!' she screamed.

I could hear her heart going boom, boom, boom and the smell of brandy on her breath was overpowering. I can tell you, I stopped crying quick smart, her arm was pinning me to her heaving bosom so tightly that I was beginning to feel faint. Thank God she released me so she could stand up and shake her fist.

Several fights had started around the base of the ring and the judges' table had been overturned. The referee stood in the centre of the ring, his hands raised, his head shining like a beacon. He didn't move and this seemed to have a calming effect on the crowd. Others rushed in to stop the ringside brawling, pulling their mates away. Not until there was complete silence did the referee indicate that both fighters should come to the centre of the ring. Hoppie, meanwhile, seemed fully recovered while Jackhammer, huge chest still heaving and both eyes puffed-up slits, looked a mess. The referee took Hoppie's arm and raised it as high as he was able. 'Kid Louis on a foul in the eleventh,' he shouted.

The railwaymen went wild with excitement while the miners started to come down from their stands again. 'Shit, it's going to be one-for-one-and-all,' Big Hettie said.

Hoppie jerked his arm away and started an animated argument with the ref, pointing his glove at the near-blind Jackhammer. Finally the referee held his hands up for silence. 'The fight goes on!' he shouted and both boxers moved back to their corners. The bell began to clang repeatedly and in a short while the ringside fighting stopped and the men, walking backwards still shaking their fists at each other, returned to their seats.

'That Hoppie Groenewald is mad as a meat axe,' Big Hettie declared. 'He had the blêrrie fight won and he wants to start all over again!' She wiped away a tear with the dishcloth. 'Jesus, Peekay, he has guts, that one is a real Irishman!'

Ten minutes passed before the bell went for round twelve, by which time Hoppie was good as gold and Jackhammer's seconds, in between his bouts of vomiting, had managed to half open his left eye. The closed lids of his right eye extended beyond his brow so that he was forced to hunt Hoppie with only half a left eye.

It was no contest. Hoppie darted in and slammed two quick left jabs straight into the half-open eye and closed it again. The rest of the round was a shambles, with Jackhammer simply covering his face with his gloves and Hoppie boring into his body. The years behind a jackhammer were counting and Jackhammer Smit simply leaned on the ropes and took everything Hoppie could throw at him. He grunted as Hoppie ripped a blow under his heart and Jackhammer opened his gloves in a reflex action. Hoppie saw the opening and moved in with a perfect left uppercut that landed flush on Jackhammer's jaw. The big man sank to the canvas just as the bell went for the end of the round.

Hoppie's shoulders sagged as he walked back to his corner. It was clear to us all that he was exhausted, fighting more by instinct than by conscious will. Jackhammer's seconds climbed into the ring and helped him to his feet, leading the almost blind fighter to his corner.

'Sweet Jesus, they gotta throw in the towel!' Big Hettie said in elation. 'Hoppie's got it on a TKO.' My heart was pounding fiercely. It seemed certain now that small could beat big, all it took was brains and skill and heart and a plan. A perfect plan.

But we were wrong. The bell went for the thirteenth and Jackhammer Smit rose slowly to his feet, half-dragging himself into the centre of the ring. Hoppie, too exhausted to gain much from the rest between rounds, was also clearly spent. He hadn't expected Jackhammer Smit to come out for the thirteenth and his extreme fatigue sapped his will to continue. It was as though both moved towards the other in a dream. Hoppie landed a straight left into Jackhammer's face, starting his nose bleeding again. He followed this with several more blows to the head but his punches lacked strength and Jackhammer, unable to reply, his pride keeping him on his feet, absorbed the extra punishment. He managed to get Hoppie into a clinch, leaning hard on the smaller man in an attempt to sap what strength was left. When the referee shouted at the two men to break he pushed at Hoppie and at the same time hit him with a round arm blow to the head that carried absolutely no authority as a punch. To our consternation and the tremendous surprise of the miners, Hoppie went down. He rose instantly to one knee, his right hand on the deck to steady him. Jackhammer, sensing from the roar of the crowd that his opponent was down, dropped his gloves and moved forward. Through his bloodied fog he may not have seen the punch coming at him. The left from Hoppie came all the way from the deck with the full weight of his body to drive the blow straight to the point of Jackhammer Smit's jaw. The giant wobbled for a split second then crashed unconscious to the canvas.

'Timber!' Big Hettie screamed as the crowd went berserk. I had just witnessed the final move in a perfectly wrought plan where small defeats big. First with the head and then with the heart. To the very end Hoppie had been thinking. I had learned the most important rule in winning . . . keep thinking.

For a moment Hoppie stood over the unconscious body of his opponent, then he brought his glove up in an unmistakable salute to Jackhammer Smit. He moved slowly to a neutral corner and the referee commenced to count. At the count of ten Jackhammer Smit still hadn't moved. Hoppie moved over to his corner and then, turning to us, he held his arms up in victory. His legs were wobbling as Nels pushed the stool into the corner for him to sit down.

In my excitement I was jumping up and down and yelling my head off. It was the greatest moment of my life. I had hope. I had witnessed small triumph over big. I was not powerless. Big Hettie grabbed me and held me high above her head. In the bright moonlight we must have stood out clearly. Hoppie stood up unsteadily and, grinning, he waved one glove in our direction.

Jackhammer had been helped to his feet by his seconds and was standing in the centre of the ring supported by them as the referee called Hoppie over. Holding Hoppie's hand up in victory he shouted, 'The good book tells the truth, little David has done it again! The winner by a knockout in the thirteenth round, Kid Louis!' The railwaymen cheered their heads off and the miners clapped sportingly and people started to leave the stands.

As the boxers left the ring, Jackhammer still supported by his seconds, Gert, the waiter who took bets in the dining car on the train, entered the ring and began to settle bets. It had been a tremendous fight and even the miners seemed happy enough and would stay for the *braaivleis* and *tiekie-draai* afterwards.

It took four big railwaymen to get Big Hettie down from the top of the stand where we had been sitting. She had finished one half-jack of brandy and was well into the next and so was in no state to make it to the bottom on her own.

'We showed 'em. Our boy sure socked the bejesus out of the big Palooka! Jaysus, Peekay, what a fight, heh? A darlin' boy with the heart of a lion.' Big Hettie was speaking in a soft accented English, which came as a surprise. 'Oops!' she said as she nearly missed her step and fell heavily against two of her helpers who were laughing almost fit to burst.

We walked over to the ring where Gert was paying out. Big Hettie had one hand resting on my shoulder as though

I were a sort of human walking stick. 'I always speak the Irish tongue when I've had toomush brandy. Me darlin' father, God rest his soul, he used to say, "M'dear, only the Irish tongue is made smooth enough fer a dacent drinkin' man when he's had a few." And he was right, you cannot get properly sozzled speaking the verdomde taal!'

I said nothing. Hoppie must have told Big Hettie I was a Rooinek, but I wasn't taking any chances and my camouflage remained intact. I saw no point in letting her know there was an enemy or even a friend in her midst.

At the ringside the men were lining up to be paid. As we drew closer Big Hettie, reverting back to Afrikaans, shouted at Gert, 'You good for nothing *skelm*! Where's my fiver?' Speaking Afrikaans seemed to have an immediate sobering effect on her. She moved imperiously to the head of the queue where Gert took five one-pound notes from his satchel and handed them down to her.

'Thank you for your business, Hettie,' Gert said politely.

Big Hettie squinted up at him, 'And don't you forget our little business either, my boy. Three cases of Crown Lager for the mess tomorrow night. Bring them early so I can put them on ice.'

'You said only two,' Gert whined.

'The Afrikaner in me said two, but it was such a good fight, the Irish in me says three. You won big anyway, the odds were against Hoppie Groenewald winning.'

'Scheesh! I didn't win so big, there was a last-minute rush to bet on Hoppie.'

'Pig's arse! You won't eat steak till next Christmas if it isn't three cases for my boys.' By this time Big Hettie seemed completely sober.

'A man might as well not make book with you around, Hettie.' Gert grinned and turned back to his other customers.

Hoppie came out of the tent just as we reached it and was immediately surrounded by railwaymen. He looked perfect, except for a large piece of sticking plaster over his left eye where Jackhammer Smit had butted him. Well, not absolutely perfect, in the light you could see his right eye was swollen and was turning a deep purple colour.

Bokkie and Nels were with him. Neither could stop talking and throwing punches in the air and replaying the fight. I was too small to see Hoppie as more and more railwaymen crowded around him. Big Hettie grabbed me and lofted me into the air. 'Make way for the next contender,' I heard Hoppie shout. Hands grabbed hold of me and carried me over the heads of the men to where he stood.

Hoppie pulled me close to him and put his hand around my shoulder. 'We showed the big gorilla, heh, Peekay?'

'Ja, Hoppie.' I was suddenly a bit tearful. 'Small can beat big if you have a plan.'

Hoppie laughed. 'I'm telling you, man, I nearly thought the plan wasn't going to work tonight.'

'I'll never forget, first with the head and then with the heart.' I hugged him around the top of the legs. Hoppie rubbed his hand through my hair. The last time someone had done this, it was to rub shit into my head. Now it felt warm and safe.

It was almost three hours before the train was due to leave and most of the crowd had stayed behind to meet their wives after the fight at the tiekiedraai dance. Miners and railwaymen, as well as the passengers travelling on, all mixed together, the animosity during the fight forgotten. Only the Africans went home because they didn't have passes and wouldn't have been allowed to stay anyway.

With a slice of Big Hettie's chocolate cake already in me I could scarcely manage two sausages and a chop. I even left some meat on the chop which I gave to a passing dog, who must have thought it was Christmas because, from then on, she stayed with me. She was a nice old bitch, although she looked a bit worn out from having puppies and her teats hung almost to the ground. She walked slowly, like old bitches do, and after a while I felt we'd always known each other. One ear was torn and her left eye drooped, probably from a fight or something. She was a nice yellow colour with a brown patch on her bum.

It had been a long day and I was beginning to feel tired. I'd never been up this late when I was happy. Hoppie found me and the dog sitting against a big gum tree nodding off. Picking me up, he carried me to the utility. I was too tired to notice if the old yellow bitch followed us.

Big Hettie was sitting in the back of the truck, her huge body almost filling it. She had a fresh half-jack and was using it to conduct herself in song, 'When Irish eyes are smilin' sure it's like the mornin' breeeeze!' I was amazed at her raucous sound. I had never before encountered a woman who couldn't sing.

'Shhh! Hettie, the next contender wants to sleep,' Hoppie said.

Big Hettie stopped, the brandy bottle poised mid-stroke. 'Me darlin' boy, come and give Hettie a big kiss.' It was the last thing I remember. Big Hettie was speaking Irish again. I guess she must have gone back to being drunk.

SEVEN

I woke at dawn to the by now familiar lickity-clack of the carriage wheels. From the colour of the light coming through the compartment window I could see it was the time Granpa Chook would come to the dormitory window and crow his silly old neck off. I supposed he had conditioned me to waking at first light.

The light which fled past the compartment window was still soft with a greyish tint; soon the sun would come and polish it till it shone. The landscape had changed in a subtle way. Yesterday's rolling grassland was now broken by an occasional koppie, rocky outcrops with clumps of dark green bush, each no more than a hundred feet high. Flat-topped fever trees were more frequent and in the far distance a sharp line of mountains brushed the horizon in a wet, watercolour purple. We were coming into the true lowveld.

I sat up and became aware of a note pinned to the front of my shirt. I undid the safety pin to find a piece of paper with a ten-shilling note attached to it. I was a bit stunned. I'd never handled a banknote and it was difficult to imagine it belonged to me. If one sucker cost a penny, I could buy one hundred and twenty suckers with this ten shillings. On the piece of paper was a carefully printed note from Hoppie.

Dear Peekay,

Here is the money you won. We sure showed that big gorilla who was the boss. Small can beat big. But remember, you have to have a plan — like when I hit Jackhammer

*Smit the knock-out punch when he thought I was down
for the count. Ha, ha. Remember always, first with the
head and then with the heart. Without both, I'm telling
you, plans are useless!*

*Remember, you are the next contender. Good luck, little
boetie.*

Your friend in boxing and always,

Hoppie Groenewald

*PS Say always to yourself, First with the head and then
with the heart, that's how a man stays ahead from the
start. H. G.*

I was distressed at having left the best friend after Granpa
Chook and Nanny that I had ever had, without so much
as a goodbye. Hoppie had passed briefly through my life,
like a train passing in the night, I had known him a little
over twenty-four hours, yet he had managed to change my
life. He had given me the power of one, one idea, one heart,
one mind, one plan, one determination. Hoppie had sensed
my need to grow, my need to be assured that the world
around me had not been specially arranged to bring about
my undoing. He gave me a defence system and with it he
gave me hope.

In the early morning the lickity-clack of the carriage
wheels sounded sharper and louder as though racing
towards the light. It was only by concentrating hard that I
could hear the cadence of someone breathing, first an
inhalation, deep and mournful, then complete silence for a
few moments and then a powerful whistling sound as a
great volume of air was exhaled. At first I thought it might
be a part of the train. After all, I was not much of an expert
on trains.

But then I began to suspect that the whistling sound had
something to do with the smell in the compartment. It was

so severe I had to cover my nose with my sheet. Holding my nose, I peered over the edge of the bunk. In the bunk below me lay Big Hettie still fully dressed. She was heaving in her sleep like a beached sperm whale. With every intake of air her bosom and stomach rose almost to touch the bottom of my bunk. Wow! Kapow! What a stink! Her arm was stretched out with her hand planted firmly on the carpet, acting as a prop to prevent her from tumbling to the floor.

On the bunk directly opposite her was a smallish suitcase and a very large square wicker picnic hamper. Big Hettie and I had the compartment to ourselves. Which was just as well as Big Hettie's brandy breath filled it and I knew that if I remained in my bunk I was done for. I moved to the bottom of my bunk and managed to push the compartment window down. Sitting as close to the window as possible I gulped at the fresh air flying past. Then, withdrawing my head when my nose was almost frozen, I removed the doek from my pocket and carefully folding Hoppie's note and the ten-shilling banknote together I tied them into the corner with Granpa's shilling. Then I pinned the doek back into my pocket, feeling dangerously rich.

Dangling from my bunk I managed to swing clear of Big Hettie's body to land with a soft thud on the floor. My heart beat wildly at the thought of waking her up, but it soon became apparent that she was pretty fast asleep. The door to the compartment was open just a crack, and using both hands I slid it open just enough to squeeze through into the corridor. The corridor window almost directly opposite was half-open, and by standing on my toes I could get my nose into the fresh air.

I stood there watching the early morning folding back. It can be very cold in the lowveld before the sun rises and without a blanket I soon began to shiver. I tried to ignore the cold, concentrating on the lickity-clack of the carriage wheels. I became aware that the lickity-clack was talking to me: *Mix-the-head with-the-heart you're-ahead from-*

the-start. Mix-the-head with-the-heart you're-ahead from-the-start the wheels chanted until my head began to pound with the rhythm. It was becoming the plan I would follow for the remainder of my life; it was to become the secret ingredient in the power of one.

It grew too cold to stand there in the corridor with the window open, so I made my way down to the end of the carriage and sat on the lavatory with the door closed. Then I felt like having a piss and I did that and pulled a lever at the side of the toilet and a trap door at the bottom of the toilet bowl opened directly onto the tracks. The noise of the wheels rose up at me and you could see a blur of gravel and a flash of sleepers as the train whizzed over them. I stood there with my hand on the lever; since the episode with the Judge I had thought a bit about shit. At the hostel we did it in tins which would be taken away every week and empty ones that smelt of disinfectant put in their place. I often wondered where they took all the stuff. At least now I knew what the railways did with theirs.

It grew too cold even in the lavatory and so I made my way back to the compartment. As I slid back the door, I saw that a calamity had befallen Big Hettie. The arm that had propped her up all night had finally collapsed and she lay with the top half of her massive body on the floor while her legs remained on the bunk. The skirt of her dress had ridden up to cover her face. With each intake of breath, it was sucked tightly against her face and with every exhalation it billowed out like the collar on a frill-necked lizard. Her huge legs, bluish-white and laced with varicose veins, stuck out of an enormous pair of shiny pink bloomers, the elastic ends of which reached down to just above her knees. She appeared to be carrying most of her weight on her neck and shoulders, and I observed that her face was growing increasingly flushed and tiny bubbles were forming at the corners of her mouth. I tried to wake her by shaking her as hard as I could. 'Wake up, Mevrou Hettie,' I begged, but she just grunted and inhaled, was silent and exhaled with a whistle of stale air and a short snort which brought on the bubbles. I soon realised that she couldn't remain half in and half out of the bunk in such a topsy-turvy position, but lifting her back onto it was plainly beyond me.

I climbed over her body and onto her bunk. Using all my strength and by propping my legs against the walls of the compartment, I managed to push both her legs off the bunk so that they landed on the compartment floor with a great plop I was sure would wake her. Her huge body now filled every inch of floor space between the bunks as neatly as if she had been canned in a sardine factory in Portugal, but she did not wake. The bright red colour soon left her face and while she continued to whistle she did not snort, which I took as a good sign. Soon even the bubbles stopped.

I climbed onto her tummy and managed to pull a blanket off her bunk. I pulled her dress down and covered her with the blanket and, with some difficulty, managed to get a cushion under her head. She gave a soft sigh and then let go a huge burp which was damn nearly the end of me. Boy, did she stink!

The blanket wasn't big enough to cover her entirely. It fell like a small blue tent, covering her bosom and tummy and reaching to the top of her legs. The Big Hettie tent was pitched right in the middle of the compartment, inhaling and exhaling and whistling away.

I wrapped myself in the remaining blanket and sat with my nose at the open compartment window. There was simply nothing else I could think to do. The sun was coming up over the distant Lebombo mountains and the African veld sparkled as though it were contained in a crystal goblet.

There was a sudden rattle at the door and a single sharp word, 'Conductor!' Whereupon the door slid open to reveal a slight man in a navy serge uniform just like Hoppie's. Only this man looked very neat and his boots shone like a mirror. Around the edge of the elliptical blue and white enamel badge on his cap it read, South African Railways – Suid Afrikaanse Spoorweë, but unlike Hoppie's which had the word Guard written across the centre, this badge read, Conductor. I don't suppose it is important to know what a badge says, but when you're small and on your own, you've got to gather all the information you can, as fast as you can. Good camouflage depends on this.

The man at the compartment door wore a thin black moustache which looked as though it had been drawn on with a school crayon. His bleak expression suggested someone already soured by the burdens of life. He looked down at the Big Hettie tent with her head only inches from his polished boots.

'What's going on here, man?' he demanded.

'Mevrou Hettie fell off the bunk, Meneer,' I answered in a frightened voice.

'Why me? Why always me? Why always Pik Botha? Why not somebody else? What have I ever done to anyone?' He looked directly at me. 'Does she belong to you?' he asked in an accusing voice. Before I was able to reply he put a finger and thumb to his furrowed brow and with a wince corrected himself. 'No, of course not. That is Big Hettie.' He gasped as the realisation hit him fully. 'My God! Big Hettie is on my train!' He sounded as if he were about to cry. 'What am I going to do, man!' he wailed.

'I, I don't know, Meneer. She was just here when I woke up.'

Pik Botha sniffed, jerking his head back. 'Well, I'm telling you now, man, she can't stay like this!' He looked down in distaste at the slumbering woman, then stuck his hand into the compartment, leaning slightly over Big Hettie. 'Where's your ticket? Give it here, boy,' he said.

'I have it here, Meneer.' I hurriedly fumbled with the safety pin where Hoppie had pinned my ticket to the clean shirt I had changed into for the fight.

'Bring it here, man, I can't climb over this dead cow to get it.' I crawled along the bunk and, by stretching out my arm as far as I could, managed to reach his hand.

'This ticket is not clipped,' he said accusingly. 'You got

on this train who knows where? I'm not a mind reader, this ticket is not clipped, man!'

'I didn't know I had to give it to be clipped, Meneer,' I said, suddenly fearful.

'It's that verdomde Hoppie Groenewald! He did this on purpose to make work for me. Not clipping tickets is an offence. Just because he is going into the army he thinks he can go around not clipping tickets. Who does he think he is, man? What do you think would happen if we all went around not clipping tickets?'

'Please, Meneer, Hoppie clipped everybody's ticket. He only forgot mine, that's the honest truth, honest!' I pleaded, frantic that Hoppie would get into trouble on my behalf.

'Humph! It wouldn't surprise me to find that that one lets dirty Kaffirs ride for nothing and then does bad things to their women. He is not a married man, you know. First I lose one pound ten shilling betting on that big ape from the mines and now that one who calls himself after a nigger boxer goes around not clipping people's tickets.' He paused and cleared his throat. 'I'm afraid it is my duty to report this,' he said, his lips drawn thinly so that his crayon moustache stretched in a dead straight line across his upper lip.

'Please, Meneer, he hates Kaffirs just like you. Please don't report him.'

'It's all right for you. You're his friend, you'll say anything.' He paused as though thinking. 'Orright, I'm a fair man, you can ask anybody about that. But mark my word. Next time that Hoppie Groenewald is going to be in a lot of trouble or my name is not Pik Botha.' He withdrew a pair of clippers from his waistcoat pocket and clipped my ticket.

'Thank you, Meneer Botha, you are a very kind man.'

'Too kind for my own good, boy! If you help others all you get is a kick in the face. But I am a born-again Christian and not a vengeful type. The Bible says, "Vengeance is mine, sayeth the Lord", but sometimes, I'm telling you,' he nudged Big Hettie with the toe of his shiny boot, 'the cross the Lord expects me to carry is very heavy, man.' He gave Big Hettie several more quick nudges with his boot. 'Wake up you old cow! This compartment is the property of the South African Railways and it says in the rules, no passenger shall decamp on the floor of the carriages. Wake up! You are officially breaking the rules lying there like a dead cow.'

Snort, sigh, breath in, silence, breath out, whistle, snort, was all he got back.

'Come, boy, I will take you to breakfast, your ticket says you get breakfast.'

Breakfast was another feast of bacon and eggs with toast, jam and coffee. It was too early for the other passengers and a waiter called Hennie Venter served us. He was pleased as punch with himself because he had won five pounds on the fight. Forgetting what he had said to me about losing one pound ten, Pik Botha proceeded to give him a long lecture on the sin of fighting and the even greater evil of gambling. He ended by asking Hennie if he was ashamed and ready to repent.

Hennie put down a plate of fresh toast covered with a linen napkin to keep it warm. 'No, Meneer Botha, gambling is only a sin if you lose because you didn't back your own kind, but bet on the other side.' He lifted the silver coffee pot and commenced to fill the conductor's cup.

'Hmmph! He's only a grade two railwayman and look how cheeky he is already, young people don't know their place any more. Bring more coffee, man, can't you see this pot is cold?' Pik Botha cried.

We returned to the compartment to find Big Hettie still whistling and snorting away. Pik Botha, a little mellowed from breakfast, did not prod her with the toe of his shiny boot. 'She's not a true Afrikaner, you know. Her father was an Irishman who was too fond of the bottle, drink is a sin that is passed on. The Bible says the sins of the fathers shall be passed unto the third and fourth generation.' Now he gave Big Hettie a nudge. 'Here lies a good example of God's terrible vengeance.'

'Balls!' Big Hettie said suddenly, opening one eye and looking backwards up at us. 'Pig's arse! You are a miserable Bible-bashing, two-faced bastard, Pik Botha. You probably already had a good look up my dress heh? Get me up, you self-righteous little shit! Get me up at once!'

'I did not! How could I? A person would have to climb over you to get such a look, and you have also a blanket over you,' Pik Botha whined.

'Mother-of-Jesus! My head hurts. I must have water, my mouth tastes like the splashboard of an Indian lavatory in the mango season.'

'Thou shalt not take the name of the Lord thy God in vain,' Pik Botha spluttered.

Big Hettie ignored him. 'I must have a glass of water, Peekay, or I shall die.'

'I will have to climb over you, Mevrou Hettie. The glass and the wash basin are on the other side.'

'Climb over, darling. Take also the blanket off me, I am burning up.' I climbed over Big Hettie, and when I got to the empty bunk I pulled the blanket off her. Crawling to the end of the bunk, I removed a glass from the chrome metal loop where it rested on the wall, and lifting the lid off the washbasin I half filled the glass with water. I had to sit on Hettie's chest to give it to her and she drank greedily. She had three half-glasses full before she'd had enough. 'Thank you, darling,' she smiled, 'you've saved my life for sure.'

'The wages of sin is death!' Pik Botha spat out.

Half turning her head towards him, Big Hettie said, 'Oh my God, to think I may die on the floor of a second-class compartment of the South African Railways under the incompetent management of that snivelling arsehole, Pik Botha.' She paused for a moment. 'Who, by the way, calls himself a man and then bets against his fellow railwayman in boxing matches!'

'It's a free world! How was I to know that big ape had a glass jaw?' he protested in his whining voice.

'Glass jaw! What do you mean, glass jaw? Glass jaw my arse! Hoppie Groenewald knocked him out fair and square!' Big Hettie's face had turned purple with indignation and her head bobbed up and down on the pillow. 'Oh, oh, my head, get me a wet towel, Peekay, I think it's going to explode.'

I scrambled over to the basin, and removing the hand towel from where it was hanging at the side of the basin, I rinsed it in cold water.

'Wring it out well, you hear,' Pik Botha shouted, 'I can't have wet towels. These towels are the property of South African Railways and you are supposed to use them for drying yourself, not for wetting yourself.'

'Ja, Meneer Botha,' I replied. I was suddenly grateful for the Judge's iron-bar torture because I was able to wring the small towel out quite well. I sat on Hettie's chest, and folding the wet towel to the right size I laid it across her forehead.

'Dankie, liefling,' she said. She half turned her head again to Pik Botha. 'So? Have you thought of a plan to get me up, domkop?'

'Please do not talk to me like this, Hettie. I am a grade one conductor with seventeen years' service in the railways. This whole train is under my command and all the people in it must do as I say. I demand more respect!' Pik Botha seemed on the verge of tears. 'I will have to get first inside the compartment and that is impossible without climbing over you.'

'Well take your boots off first.'

Pik Botha crouched down in the corridor and began to untie the laces of his boots. From where I sat I could see him pull off his boots and line them up against the outside wall of the compartment, toes pointing into the corridor.

He stretched his leg over Big Hettie's body in an attempt to reach the bunk without having to climb over her. His toes inside a well-darned black sock were wiggling like a pig's snout, trying to find the edge of the bunk. A larger man with longer legs might have made it, but Pik Botha's exploring big toe was well short of its mark. 'It's not possible, Hettie,' he said mournfully.

'Do it backwards, stupid! Come in backwards with your legs first.'

With his hands flat on the corridor floor, Pik Botha edged into the compartment backwards. He placed one foot on one of Big Hettie's breasts, then he followed with the other. He inched his way over her belly until he was obliged to put both his hands on her shoulders, his head only inches from her face. Big Hettie suddenly let go an enormous burp. The blast of foul air took all the strength out of Pik Botha's arms and he collapsed into the mountain of flesh below him.

Big Hettie let out a gasp. 'Excuse me!' she said, then she began to giggle, wobbling like a jelly mountain. 'Oh Christ! Oh Jesus! Ha . . . ha . . . ha, hee hee, hee, Lord have mercy, hee, hee . . . ha . . . ha . . . ha, are you trying to love me . . . hee, hee, or help me? Tee, hee, hee . . . ha . . . ha . . . ha . . . snort, ha . . . hee, hee, either way you're doing . . . hee . . . hee . . . a terrible job!' Big Hettie gave two more snorts and her head fell back onto the pillow exhausted. 'Oh, oh, I'm dying,' she moaned, and lifting the arm that pinned Pik Botha down she wiped away her tears. Sensing freedom, Pik Botha pushed off Big Hettie's shoulders with both hands and raised his torso. He managed to get his hands around the raised edge of the bunk on either side of Big Hettie, and inserted one foot between Big Hettie's calves while the other foot rested on the edge of the bunk.

Panting furiously he raised himself to a standing position. 'God will punish you for this. "He who plucks one hair from the head of a child of mine, it is as though he doeth this to me, thus sayeth the Lord".' Pik Botha was shaking his finger at Big Hettie and panting away like the old yellow bitch I had met the previous night.

'Keep your preaching for the next prayer meeting at the Apostolic Faith Mission, you miserable little shit house. Here, give me your hand.' Big Hettie stretched her arm out, offering her hand to Pik Botha. He shied away in alarm. 'Grab it dammit, man!'

'No damn fear, you'll only pull me back again,' Pik Botha said in terror.

'Do not flatter yourself, man. Use both hands, I can't stay like this all day unless you can cut a hole in the floor,' she threatened.

That was enough to spur him to action. He grabbed Big Hettie around the wrist with both hands while she grabbed onto his arm with her own hand. Grimacing with the effort, he started to pull. Big Hettie's freed shoulder wobbled a little in response but no other part moved. 'Pull, man!' she shouted, but soon it was obvious that nothing was going to happen. 'Give Tarzan here a hand, Peekay. Show him what a real man can do,' she said in some despair.

There wasn't any space to stand so I sat astride Big Hettie's hips, my feet not quite reaching the edge of the bunk on either side. The idea was to get Big Hettie's torso into an upright position, which might then enable us to get under her arms from the back to lift her up. I grabbed her around the wrists with both hands which failed to meet, but nevertheless gave me quite a good grip. Pik Botha was forced to bend over so that he could grab Big Hettie higher up her arm. 'Now get your backs into it, men. I'm going to count to three, on three give it all you've got, you hear? One, two, three!' We both pulled with all our might. After about five minutes of repeating such efforts she hadn't budged an inch.

'It's no use,' Pik Botha gasped. We were all beginning to realise that we were in a real pickle. The effort to co-operate had cost Big Hettie dearly and she lay there panting in a lather of sweat, her face as red as an old turkey cock's. Pik Botha stood with one foot still balanced on the edge of the bunk and the other inserted between Big Hettie's calves, wiping his sweaty hands on the shiny backside of his navy serge pants. He had taken off his jacket and thrown it on the top bunk. On his silver tie clip 'Witnessing for the Lord' was written. I wondered briefly what it meant.

'One last try. Just one more go. This time it will work for sure,' Big Hettie panted, her voice not sounding too hopeful. She made me clasp my hands together and she then grabbed me around both wrists, thus allowing Pik Botha to get a better two-handed grip around her wrists. He had also managed to get his bum up against the washbasin which gave him a much better pulling purchase.

'One, two, three. Pull!' Big Hettie commanded. We both pulled like mad, Pik Botha grunting with effort behind me. Big Hettie's way of holding me wasn't such a good idea, her hands were wet with perspiration and I could feel my own hands beginning to slip from her grasp. Suddenly they squeezed out like a wet pumpkin pip and I was catapulted violently backwards, the back of my head slamming hard into Pik Botha's crotch. He gave a loud scream and both his hands shot down between his legs.

Despite her discomfort, Big Hettie let out of scream of delight. 'You've knackered him, boy!' she roared. 'You've taken what was left of his manhood!' Her laughter filled the compartment, causing her great body to shake up and down.

'Coffee! Coffee! Early morning coffee!' It was Hennie Venter, the waiter from breakfast, doing the morning wake-up call. He paused at the open door of our compartment. 'Coffee?' he asked, starting to bring the tray down from his shoulder. His eyes widened in disbelief as he observed Big Hettie pumping up and down with laughter and Pik Botha moaning and clutching his genitals. He only just managed to lower the tray to the corridor floor before he burst into laughter. 'Pik Botha! You dirty old bastard! Sis, man! The door is not even closed.'

The sudden appearance of the waiter seemed to bring Big

Hettie around. 'Hennie Venter, not a moment too soon!' she declared.

Hennie, convulsed with laughter, appeared not to hear her. 'A cup of coffee, Mevrou?' he asked and then burst into renewed laughter.

They calmed down and with some difficulty Hennie Venter managed to pull the still groaning Pik Botha over Big Hettie's body and through the compartment door. He stood in the corridor almost doubled up, his face as white as a ghost. He winced, sucking the air through his brown teeth, as he bent down further to recover his boots.

I bundled up his coat and threw it over to Hennie Venter who draped it over the hapless Pik Botha's shoulder. With one hand carrying his boots and the other clutching his waterworks, he hobbled away down the corridor towards the guard's van.

Hennie Venter turned out to be the practical sort. He made me fetch a second pillow which he added to the first one to prop Big Hettie's head up as far as she could go. He even managed to get her to drink a cup of coffee by herself. He inspected the situation carefully and then announced that there was no way of lifting Big Hettie without first removing the lower bunks.

'Sorry, Hettie,' he said, shaking his head, 'we're going to have to wait until we get to Kaapmuiden.' He started to pour Hettie another cup of coffee.

'No damn fear!' she said quickly. 'Unless you want to cut a blêrrie hole in the floor.'

Hennie Venter scratched his head, giving Big Hettie a quizzical look. 'What the hell are you doing on this train, anyway?'

Big Hettie half turned to look backwards and up at him, her mouth in a pout of annoyance. 'Do you think for one moment that I would let this poor child travel all the way to Kaapmuiden on his own?' she asked.

Hennie Venter persisted. 'You were also a little drunk, maybe?'

'Pissed as a newt, drunk as a skunk,' she giggled. 'What a fight it was eh, Hennie?'

'You can say that again, Hettie,' Hennie said happily. 'I won two weeks' wages with a ten bob bet. *Magtig!* What a fighter that Hoppie Groenewald is. A real white man!'

Big Hettie looked up at me sheepishly. 'I came to look after you, Peekay.' She grinned suddenly. 'Anyway, man, let's make the most of a bad situation, heh? I always say, if you can't change things then you have to make sure you're riding on the front elephant and not walking with the poor people at the back. It's time for breakfast and I must say I'm starving.' She looked back at Hennie Venter. 'Off you go, you skelm, six sausages, six rashers of bacon, nice 'n' crisp mind, five hard-boiled eggs to constipate me and half a loaf of toast cut thick with lots of butter. No more coffee, you know what coffee does to a person, I'm going to have to cross my legs as it is. For Peekay, the same only half.'

'*Nee, nee,* Mevrou Hettie, I have already had breakfast,' I protested.

'Nonsense, child, you are no bigger than a sparrow. What will your mama say if I hand you over like this? We must feed you up and that's all there is to it.'

Hennie Venter left us to fetch breakfast and I imagined Big Hettie feeding me up in the next eight hours so that I arrived in Barberton as big, if not bigger than the Judge. There my granpa would be, looking around for a real skinny kid to get off the train, and there I'd be, big as the Judge. What a nasty shock he would get! 'I already ate a whole plate of things, Mevrou Hettie,' I said again.

'Never mind, Peekay, a little more never hurt. You've got to be like the Bushmen in the Kalahari desert, they eat as much as they can get in the good times till their bottoms stick out like their stomachs. Then when the bad times come they live off their own fat.' She chuckled softly, 'I reckon a person like me could go a whole year, or even more, living off their own fat, but you, my poor little blossom, I doubt if you'll get to Kaapmuiden.'

Hennie Venter returned with a large tray of food which he carefully balanced on Big Hettie's stomach. He left us to serve breakfast to the other passengers in the dining car, closing the door behind him and promising to return later.

The tray went up and down as Big Hettie breathed. She could only see what to take from a plate on a down breath, for on an up breath the tray raised above her eye level. I managed to eat one more sausage. Big Hettie didn't seem to notice and polished off my breakfast as well. Though when she finished she said, 'You'll never get to play rugby for the Springboks if you eat like a bird, Peekay.'

'That's okay, Mevrou Hettie,' I answered, 'I'm going to be a welterweight, which is not so big.'

She seemed amused. 'Just like that good for nothing, Hoppie Groenewald, huh? Well you could do worse, I suppose. Not a bad bone in his body that one. He could have made it big time but he doesn't hate. Not even kaffirs, which isn't natural.'

I was shocked. Hoppie hadn't said anything to me about the necessity of hate. Was this something he had neglected to tell me?

'How do you learn to hate, Mevrou Hettie?' I was fearful that it might prove to be something beyond the ability of a five-, really six-year-old. Perhaps that's why Hoppie hadn't mentioned this hate business. But hadn't he said I was a natural? If I was a natural, then I would be able to learn it for sure.

'The killer instinct, he hasn't got the killer instinct. You can tell when a fighter's got it. It's proper hate, like the Boere hate the Rooineks. It has to be blind hate like that, them or us, him or me, nothing less. Hoppie Groenewald just never learned to hate.'

'Then I will learn to hate also,' I said with conviction.

Big Hettie rocked with laughter. 'Plenty of time for that, Peekay. Better still to concentrate on love, there is already too much hate in this land of ours. This country has been starved of love too long.'

I wasn't listening, my mind was busy with the need to learn to hate. 'Didn't Hoppie hate Jackhammer Smit?'

'That was pride, Hoppie has plenty of that. And courage and even brains.' Big Hettie suddenly sensed my anxiety. 'Look here, man, maybe that's enough.' She chuckled softly, 'He sure out-foxed that big ape, Smit!'

I cast my mind back to when I had done the Judge's homework, just like that! I had no doubt I had brains. But during the torture sessions I hadn't shown any pride and precious little courage, although I had to admit to myself I wasn't at all sure what pride meant. Maybe I was fatally flawed? Only brains and nothing to go with them?

'How do you learn to have pride and courage, Mevrou Hettie?'

'My goodness me, we are full of questions, Peekay. Now let me see.' She thought for a few moments and then replied, 'Pride is holding your head up when everyone around you has theirs bowed. Courage is what makes you do it.' She looked up to see the confusion in my face. 'Never mind, Peekay, the understanding will come suddenly when you need it.'

I wasn't at all sure about that. Big Hettie's advice seemed downright stupid to me. I knew already that camouflage was the only way, that bowing your head with the rest was the best way to survive. Take the incident with Miss du Plessis, hadn't I raised my head then and she damn near cut it off? And Granpa Chook, if he hadn't shat in the Judge's mouth, we'd still be together. There were no two ways about it, when you stood out in the crowd, trouble was sure to follow.

Maybe there was something more to understand, the world of grown-ups seemed very complicated. I was good at remembering things, so I tucked Big Hettie's words away. Someday they might make sense.

Nanny was the only grown-up I knew who answered

questions properly and she wasn't really a grown-up because she was a nanny. When you asked her a thing she would answer with a story or a song and when she hadn't an answer she would say, 'That is a matter for later finding out.' She was always right, sooner or later the answer would come from somewhere. It seemed to me that white people grown-ups always had to have an answer on the spot. Like Pik Botha, they lived most of their lives being miserable and asking, 'Why me?' all the time. Nanny would say, 'Sadness has a season and will pass.' Then she would laugh and hug me and say, 'But it isn't the season for sadness yet.'

I kept wetting the towel for Big Hettie and got her two Aspro from her handbag. She told me to scrounge around because she might have some peppermints in there. I found half a packet, and she said, 'Give me a couple and try one yourself, Peekay.'

I took two large round white peppermints out of the pack and put them in her hand and popped a third into my mouth. At first nothing. Then, pow! I lasted about two good sucks and then spat the peppermint into my hand, it was like swallowing fire! I watched Big Hettie suck away happily. Talk about courage! But I must say those peppermints cleaned up her breath a treat.

Big Hettie and I just lay there, she on the floor and me on the bunk. She talked about her life, which seemed to have been quite a good one, but with some sadness also. Mostly she talked about men.

'Men, Peekay, are a good woman's downfall. Most of them are rotten but you've got to have them anyway. Without a man a woman's life is more rotten than with one. It's no use pretending you don't care, that you're stronger than a man. Because even if it is true, it means nothing except loneliness. Men are pigs who sleep with kaffir women and get drunk and beat you up. But a good beating never hurt and sometimes it's the only way those stupid men can show you they love you. It's stupid, heh?'

I tried to imagine a man beating up Big Hettie. 'My

granpa couldn't beat up a flea,' I said, trying to comfort her. Big Hettie stood six foot seven inches and weighed nobody knows how much. Even the Judge with all his stormtroopers couldn't get the better of her.

'Once I loved this little flyweight,' she continued. 'That's how I learned about boxing, Peekay. It was during the great depression and you couldn't find work nowhere, man. Me and that little flyweight, we used to travel all over the Transvaal and once to the Orange Free State to fight. There was never another flyweight to fight, the Boere like to see the bigger men and so he always had to fight way out of his division. A middleweight usually. If he was lucky he'd get a welterweight, but it didn't happen very often.

'That little flyweight of mine was game and he loved to fight, but you can't give away that much weight and he used to take some terrible poundings and nearly always lost. Afterwards I'd patch him up and he'd make me talk to him about the fight. Blow by blow, where he was good and where he went wrong. I'd tell him how he was always winning, which was true, he'd be a mile ahead on points and then the big ape he was fighting would catch him a lucky shot and put him away. And he used to look at me and say, "Next time, Hettie, you'll see, I'll win for sure."

'And then we would buy a bottle of cheap brandy and drive out of the town we were in and sit in the back of the Model T and get drunk. When he was drunk it was his turn to replay the fight, only he'd get it all mixed up in his head and he'd think he was still in the fight and I was his opponent and he'd beat the shit out of me. And I always let him, because he had to have some wins for his pride.

'Then when I had taken a beating and he had counted me out, we would drink some more and replay the fight again, which this time he won fair and square. We would then find some nice place behind some bushes and take our blankets and make love. I'm telling you, Peekay, most men can't get it up when they're drunk, but not my flyweight, he could go all night. What a man he was. They were good times. Oh, oh, such good times.'

Big Hettie's story worried me no end. Here it seemed big always beat small, except in a set-up. 'Hoppie was smaller than Jackhammer Smit and he beat him fair and square.' I said, somewhat defensively.

'Ja, that is true, Hoppie has brains. My flyweight had mashed potato for brains. But I loved that little fleabite until the day he died from taking on one big ape too many.' Big Hettie's eyes welled with tears. 'He was coming out for the sixth round when he staggered and fell, the crowd booed and booed, but he never faked anything in his life and I knew something terrible had happened. He had a brain haemorrhage, just like that. I carried him out of the hall in my arms and we sat on the grass outside in the fresh air with lots of stupid people in a circle looking down at us. But I didn't see any of them, just my darling little flyweight. And then he died right there in my arms.' Big Hettie was sobbing softly.

'Don't cry, Mevrou Hettie, please don't cry.' I quoted Nanny, 'Sadness has a season and will pass.'

She stopped sobbing after a while and dabbed at her eyes with the damp towel. 'He was the best. The very best of men.' She said it so softly I knew she was speaking to herself.

We talked about this and that deep into the hot morning. Big Hettie did most of the chatting as I had developed into a listener. Once I had been a regular chatterbox but school had changed all that. A person of my status was not expected to talk much, and besides, listening is a good camouflage. I soon discovered that it is also an art. You learn not simply to listen to what people say. It's what people don't say that is important. If you listen hard enough you can hear the most amazing things going on behind the speaker's voice. Quite often there is a regular conniption going on. It takes years to make a good translation of this secondary soundtrack and as a small child I could only define it as friendly or otherwise. For camouflage reasons this is often sufficient.

Around noon Hettie dozed off; this time her breathing was much better. Outside the compartment window the bushveld baked in the hot sun. The sunlight flattened the country in the foreground and smudged the horizon in a haze of heat. It is a time when the cicadas become so active that they fill the flat, hot space with a sound so constant it sings like silence in the brain. While I couldn't hear them for the clickity-clack of the carriage wheels I knew they were out there, brushing the heat into their green membraned wings, energising after the long sleep when their pupae lay buried in the dark earth, sometimes for years, until a conjunction of the moon and the right soil temperature creates the moment to emerge and once again fill the noon space.

In the heat the compartment seemed to float, lifting off the silver rails and moving through time and space. Through hours and days and weeks and years, off the blue planet, past the moon and the sun, into centuries and millenniums and aeons. Skirting planets, weaving through the stars. Coming finally to a black hole in space, further even than the mind can think, beyond even the curve of infinity and the silver cord which rings the cosmos. There I would remain safely hidden until I could grow up to be welterweight champion of the world.

'Are you asleep, Peekay?' I opened my eyes to see Big Hettie looking at me. 'A glass of water if you please.' She ran her tongue over her dry lips and removed the towel from her forehead. She handed me the towel and I gave her the glass of water which she gulped greedily. She handed the glass back and I refilled it. 'You're one in a thousand, Peekay,' she said gratefully.

I wet the towel, folded it and placed it over her head. 'One in maybe even a million,' she sighed. I could see she was restless and kept licking her lips. 'What's for lunch, do you think?'

'Meneer Venter hasn't been yet, Mevrou Hettie,' I answered.

'Ag man, I didn't mean that lunch. A person can't eat a train lunch. Breakfast is tolerable, lunch unbearable and dinner unthinkable. Open up my hamper, Peekay, and let a person hear what is inside.' She laughed. 'I'll tell you something, I wasn't concentrating too well when I packed it last night.'

I withdrew the slim bamboo rod threaded through the wicker and opened the large basket. Inside was enough food to feed an army. 'Tell me what we got in there, darling,' Big Hettie said anxiously.

'Two roasted chickens, nearly a full leg of mutton, some corned beef, three mangoes, lots of cold potatoes and sweet potatoes too, two oranges and there is also a big tin.'

'Thank the Lord I brought the tin,' Big Hettie said with obvious relief. 'Open it, Peekay. Quick, man, open the tin!' I was surprised at the urgency in her voice. I lifted the large round tin out of the hamper and, clamping it between my knees, struggled to remove the lid. It came away suddenly, sending me sprawling backwards on the bunk, and the tin slid over the edge of the bunk, spilling half of a large chocolate cake onto Big Hettie's stomach. In two swift movements her arm rose and fell, the edge of her hand sliced through the thick layer of deep brown chocolate icing rending the cake into two large pieces. She had started to pant and her eyes were glazed as she crammed her mouth full of cake. She grunted and snorted and even moaned as she demolished the first hunk and then reached greedily for the second. Her face was covered with chocolate icing. Stuffing the last bits into her mouth she sucked at her fingers as a small child might, two at a time. Then she plopped her thumb in and out of her mouth several times and ran her hand across her bosom, her fingers moving like a fat spider hunting for any cake she might have missed. She looked up at me and I dropped my gaze, ashamed and frightened, though at the same time I instinctively knew I was watching a sickness or a sadness or even both.

When she had finished Big Hettie was in a lather of sweat, the front of her dress soaked in perspiration, covered with cake crumbs and stained with chocolate icing. She used the damp towel to wipe her face and then lay there panting heavily, her eyes closed. I watched as tears ran down the side of her face, but she said nothing for a long while.

When she had recovered her breath she opened her eyes, which were red and looked puffy. 'I am sorry, Peekay. I am very, very sorry,' she said, her voice almost a whisper.

'It is nothing, Mevrou Hettie, it was only that you were hungry. Chocolate cake makes me feel like that all the time.'

'I'm sorry I ate all the cake, Peekay. But now you get first pick of everything!'

It had been a long time since I had been given first pick of anything and I laughed. 'There is enough for the whole train in here, Mevrou Hettie. I will have cold roast potatoes, after that sweet potatoes, they are my two favourites.'

'And maybe a nice piece of chicken, heh?'

Granpa Chook's death was still much too close to me. The prospect of eating one of his distant relatives, even if this chicken hadn't been a proper chicken person or even a kaffir chicken like Granpa Chook, was impossible to contemplate. Biting into a delicious golden potato, I shook my head.

'To be a welterweight you must eat properly, Peekay. Meat will make you strong. Some mutton perhaps?' she said coaxingly.

When pressed by my mother to have a second helping, my granpa used to say: 'A cow has eight stomachs but I, alas, have one. A cow must keep on chewing but I, my dear, am done.' I swallowed the potato and recited this to Big Hettie. It was bound, I felt, to cheer her up.

Instead she started to cry again.

'I'm sorry, Mevrou Hettie, I'm very sorry, I didn't mean

to make you cry again, it is only a silly thing my granpa says to my ma just to tease her.'

Big Hettie sniffed, blew her nose and wiped her eyes. A piece of chocolate icing from the cloth smeared on the bridge of her nose. 'It is not you, liefling. It's old Hettie. She's the one I'm crying for.' She smiled weakly through the tears. 'What the hell, Peekay, what do you say?' she sniffed. 'Might as well die eating as starving, pass me that leg of mutton, my good man!'

I handed her the leg of mutton, one half of which had been sliced away almost to the bone. Resting the big end on her chest, she commenced to happily tear away at the meat on the bone while I demolished a large sweet potato and a mango.

When she had finished the bone had been picked almost clean. To my surprise, she asked me to tear up one of the chickens and place the pieces on her stomach, also to put the slices of corned beef with it. She tore at the chicken as though she were starving, even crunching some of the softer bones. The chicken and the corned beef were soon demolished and with a soft sigh she wiped the grease and sweat from her face. Using the cake tin, I gathered up the chicken bones scattered over the area of her stomach and tipped them out of the window.

I then washed the mango from my face and hands, and set to work, soaking and squeezing out the only remaining towel. This I handed to Big Hettie and retrieved the old one which I washed with a bit of soap, rinsed and hung over the compartment window sill to dry. I had seen Dum and Dee, our kitchen maids, do the same thing with the wiping up cloths at home after dinner, so I knew I was doing it right. Only they used to hang the cloths from a small line at the side of the big black wood stove so the dry cloths always smelt a little of soup.

Big Hettie put the new cloth, wet as it was, over the front of her dress. 'It's so nice and cool and the heat of my body will soon dry it,' she said, but I knew it was an attempt to hide the chocolate and grease stains. I thought about having to wash Big Hettie's dress. It would take all day and would need a basin as big as a small dam.

There was a sudden rattle as the compartment door slid open and Hennie Venter appeared. 'I'm sorry I've been so long, Hettie, but Pik Botha says he can't walk and is sulking in the guard van and I have had to do conductor duty because Van Leemin the guard is drunk again. But also I have had to serve lunch,' he finished in an apologetic voice.

'What's for lunch?' Big Hettie asked.

Hennie seemed surprised at the question. 'Beef stew with mashed potato and peas like always.'

'Keep it! The boy and me would rather starve than eat that pig's swill,' she said haughtily.

'Banana custard for pudding today.' Hennie said enticingly.

'Ummph, and tastes like what comes out of a baby's bum,' Big Hettie said scornfully.

'Well, if you don't want any help I'll kick the dust.' Hennie looked over at the open hamper and winked at me. 'I'm sorry you two decided to starve, are you sure there is nothing I can do for you?'

'You can get me off this blêrrie floor, man!' Hettie said in a forlorn voice.

The waiter clucked his tongue sympathetically. 'Soon, Hettie. We get to Kaapmuiden in two hours. There they will know what to do.'

Hoppie had explained to me that from Kaapmuiden I would have to take the branch line to Barberton, a further three hours journey 'in a real little coffee pot', he had said. He had told me the story of a washerwoman with a huge pile of freshly ironed washing on her head who was walking along the railway line when the Barberton train drew up beside her. The driver had leaned out of the train and invited her to jump aboard into the kaffir carriage. 'No thank you, baas,' she had replied, 'today I am in a terrible big hurry.' It was a funny story when Hoppie told it, but I knew it wasn't true because no white train driver would ever think to offer a kaffir woman a ride in his train.

The afternoon was still and hot and it was nearly four o'clock when we arrived in Kaapmuiden. The train pulled slowly, shyly into the busy junction, the way trains do when they arrive in places where there are other trains. Kaapmuiden served as the rail link between the Northern and Southern Transvaal and the Mozambique seaport of Lourenço Marques and so was full of its own self-importance.

The station was all huff and puff, busier even than Gravelotte, with engines shunting, trucks banging, clanging and coupling on lines criss-crossing everywhere like neatly arranged spaghetti. Our train drew slowly into the main platform and with a final screech of metal on metal, drew to a standstill.

'What do I do now please, Mevrou Hettie?' I enquired nervously. I had put on my tackies, even though I knew I was to change trains and wouldn't arrive in Barberton until well into the evening. At the beginning of my journey the original over-sized tackies had been a banal signal of the end of the Judge, his stormtroopers, the hostel and Mevrou: a grotesque chapter in my life. Equally this second pair, fitted to my feet so perfectly by the beautiful Indian lady, seemed to symbolise the unknown. Sometimes we live a lifetime in two days. The two days between the first tackies and the snugly fitting ones I now wore were the beginning of the end of my small childhood, a bridge of time that would shape my life to come.

'We must wait here, Peekay. Hennie Venter will bring some men to help me and then I will put you on the train to Barberton. There is plenty of time, your train leaves at six o'clock.' Big Hettie was obviously in great discomfort and now that relief from her ordeal was at hand her great body had started to tremble with shock.

I watched from our compartment window as our carriage was uncoupled and, with much fuss, shunted into a small siding where a gang of men were waiting. Among them was Hennie Venter. As we came to a halt, he stuck his head through the open window.

'Nearly over, Hettie, we'll soon have you back on your feet,' he said cheerfully.

I passed all our stuff through the window and then, rather than clamber over Big Hettie again, I came through the window myself, jumping the short distance onto the siding. It was nice to be standing in the sun again. Two of the men climbed through the window onto one of the bunks. Using monkey wrenches, they managed to loosen the bolts attaching the bunk to the compartment wall. Then they slung ropes around both ends of the bunk, secured them to the one above and removed the bolts so the bunk was held suspended away from Big Hettie. Climbing onto the top bunk, they were able to lift the suspended one sufficiently for two men, crouching in the doorway of the compartment, to lift Big Hettie into a sitting position. The four men then tried to raise her to a standing position, but her weight was too much for them and she seemed unable to use her legs. Big Hettie was plainly in some distress and her face was very red. After a while it became plain that the whole ordeal was too much for her and she was too exhausted and too weak to stand up. She simply sat on the floor of the compartment, flushed and panting, her back propped up by a mound of pillows. A huge, sadly battered rag doll.

The men left to fetch a block and tackle. I returned to the compartment and sat on the bunk next to Big Hettie. Hennie Venter remained outside looking into the compartment, his arms resting on the window sill.

Big Hettie's breathing was becoming more laboured as she asked Hennie Venter to go to her hamper which now rested on the platform outside and take the remaining chicken and potatoes and fruit from it, pack them into the cake tin and put it into my suitcase. He nodded and left the window.

'It will be late before you get to Barberton, liefling. What will your oupa think of me if you have had no supper?' she panted, her hand clutching at her left breast.

I was too polite to tell Big Hettie that eating chicken was no longer my speciality. Instead I thanked her and then asked, 'Will you not be coming to the train like you said, Mevrou Hettie?'

She said nothing for a long while as though she were trying to gather up enough strength to speak without gasping. 'I think it is the final round coming up for me, Peekay. I have a terrible pain.' The colour had drained from her face and her lips had turned blue. Her left hand was kneading her left breast.

I scrambled over to the window. Hennie Venter had opened my suitcase and was putting the big cake tin into it. 'Meneer Venter! Come quick, Mevrou Hettie is sick!' I yelled.

I turned back to look at Big Hettie. Her voice was hardly more than a whisper. 'Hold my hand, Peekay,' she gasped. I moved back along the bunk and she took my hand into her own. Her grasp was weak, as though no strength remained in her.

'I don't think I can come out for the next round, liefling.' The words were sandwiched between sighs, quite different from the windy breathing of the morning.

Hennie Venter stuck his head through the window. 'Oh my God! I'll fetch the doctor.' I could hear his boots scrunching on the gravel as he started to run.

'Please don't die, Mevrou Hettie,' I begged, suddenly very afraid.

'Ag, Peekay, it has not been much of a life since my flyweight left me, it's not so much to give up.' She turned to look at me and a tear squeezed out of the corner of her eye and rolled in slow motion down her cheek. 'Peekay, you will be a great welterweight, I know it. You have pride and courage. Remember I told you about pride and courage?'

'Pride is holding your head up when everyone around

you has theirs bowed. Courage is what makes you do it,' I repeated, my lips trembling.

'You will be a great fighter, I know it,' she whispered. Big Hettie gave a little jerk and the pressure on my hand increased momentarily. Then her huge hand opened and she slid back into the pillows. For such a big, loud woman it was such a small, quiet death.

I started to cry. It wasn't a pain like Granpa Chook, it was a sadness. Even then I instinctively understood that the blithe spirit is rare among humans and that, for the period of an evening and a day, I had been with a part of the human condition at its best.

After a while I could hear the men returning with the block and tackle. They were laughing and chatting as men do when they are having a bit of a holiday from routine. Big Hettie could be moved now.

EIGHT

It was just after ten in the evening when the train puffed into Barberton station. The conductor woke me before we were due to arrive. My head was dizzy with sleep and mussed up with the events of the day.

Hennie had put me on the train, his mood a mixture of concern for me and the need to get back to the action, where he was such an important cog in the sad machinery of the day. 'You eat something, you hear. Here's a tickey to buy a cool drink,' he said handing me a tiny silver coin.

'I have money, Meneer Venter.'

But he insisted I take the threepenny bit. 'Go on, take it, take it, it is only a blêrrie tickey!' he blustered.

Fortunately he didn't have to hang around too long, we had only just made it to the Barberton train in time. As we departed with a great chuffing sound that seemed too big for the little coffee-pot engine, Hennie shouted: 'I will tell Hoppie Groenewald you behaved like a proper Boer, a real white man!'

I climbed down the steps of the carriage onto the gravel platform of Barberton station, struggling with my suitcase which had now become quite heavy with Big Hettie's tin. I had left its contents untouched, too tired and bewildered to eat. The platform was crowded with people hurrying up and down, heads jerking this way and that, greeting each other and generally carrying on the way people do when a train arrives. My granpa didn't seem to be amongst them. I decided to sit on my suitcase and wait, too tired to think of anything else I might do. I must have been crying without knowing it, maybe it was just from being tired or something. I had been in worse jams than this one, and I expected any moment that I would hear my nanny's big laugh followed by a series of tut-tuts as she swept me into her apron. That's when everything would be all right again.

A lady was approaching, although I could only see her dimly through my tears. She bent down beside me and crushed me to her bony bosom. 'My darling, my poor darling,' she wept, 'everything will be the same again, I promise.'

My mother was here! She was alive. Thin as ever, but not dead from dysentery and blackwater fever.

Yet I think we both knew, everything would never be the same again.

'Where is my nanny?' I asked, rubbing the tears from my eyes.

'Come darling, Pastor Mulvery is waiting in his car to take us home to your granpa. What a big boy you are now that you are six, much too big for a nanny!'

The hollow feeling inside me had begun to grow and I could hear the loneliness birds cackling away, their oily wings flapping gleefully as they sat on their dark stone nests.

Clearing her throat and reaching for my suitcase, my mother straightened up. 'Come darling, Pastor Mulvery is going to take us home to your grandfather.'

Her remark about my not needing a nanny now that I was six struck me so forcibly that it felt like one of the Judge's clouts across the mouth. My nanny, my darling beloved nanny was gone and I was six. The two pieces of information tumbled around in my head like two dogs tearing at each other as they fought, rolling over in the dust.

My mother had taken my hand and was leading me to a big grey Plymouth parked under a street lamp beside a peppercorn tree. A fat, balding man stepped out of the car as we approached. His top teeth jutted out at an angle, and peeped out from under his lip as though looking to see if the coast were clear so that they might escape. Pastor Mulvery seemed aware of this and he smiled in a quick flash so as not to allow his teeth to make a dash for it. He reached for my suitcase, taking it from my mother. 'Praise the Lord, sister, He has delivered the boy safely to His loved ones.' His voice was as soft and high-pitched as a woman's.

'Yes, praise His precious name,' my mother replied. I had never heard her talk like this before. It was quite obvious to me that the concentration camp must have had something to do with it. My finely tuned ear could hear all sorts of crazy bits and pieces going on behind her words.

Pastor Mulvery stuck his hand out. 'Welcome, son. The Lord has answered our prayers and brought you home safely.' I took his hand which was warm and slightly damp.

'Thank you, sir,' I said, my voice hardly above a whisper. It felt strange to be speaking in English. I climbed into the back seat of the car next to my mother. All the loneliness birds had become one big loneliness bird on a big stone nest and I could feel the heaviness of the stone egg as it hatched inside me.

Granpa Chook was dead, Hoppie had to go and fight Adolf Hitler and maybe he would never come back again, Big Hettie was dead and now my beloved nanny was gone. Like Pik Botha, my mother seemed to have entered into a very peculiar relationship with the Lord that was bound to create problems. My life was a mess.

We drove through the town which had street lights and tarred roads. It was late and only a few cars buzzed down the wide main street. We passed a square filled with big old flamboyant trees. The street was lined with shops one after the other, McClymonts, Gentleman's Outfitters, J. W. Winter, Chemist, The Savoy Café, Barberton Hardware Company. We turned up one street and passed a grand building called the Impala Hotel which had big wide steps and seemed to have lots of people in it. The sound of a concertina could be heard as Pastor Mulvery slowed the Plymouth down to a crawl.

'The devil is busy tonight, sister. We must pray for their souls, pray that they may see the glory that is Him and be granted everlasting life,' he said in his girlish voice.

My mother sighed. 'There is so much to be done before He comes again and takes us to His glory.' She turned to me. 'We have a lovely Sunday school at the Apostolic Faith Mission, you are not too young to meet the Lord, to be born again, my boy. The Lord has a special place in His heart for His precious children.'

'Hallelujah, praise His precious name, we go to meet Him!' Pastor Mulvery said.

'Can we meet Him tomorrow please? I am too tired tonight,' I asked.

They both laughed and I felt better. The laugh that rang from my mother was the old familiar one, the concentration camp hadn't stolen it. 'We're going straight home, darling, you must be completely exhausted,' she said gently.

I had almost dropped my camouflage, but now it was back again. Big Hettie had said Pik was a born-again Christian and also that he belonged to the Apostolic Faith Mission. Her tone had implied that both situations left a great deal to be desired. How had my mother come to this? Who was this strange man with escaping teeth? What was this new language and who exactly was the Lord?

I had seen my return to Granpa and to Nanny first as a means of urgent escape from Adolf Hitler and then, when Hoppie had calmed my fear of his imminent arrival, the continuation of my earlier life on the farm. Living in a small town hadn't meant anything to me. Living with silly old Granpa and beautiful Nanny had meant everything. My mother had been a nice part of a previous existence, though not an essential one; she was a frail and nervous woman and Nanny had taken up the caring, laughing, scolding and soothing role mothers play in other cultures. My mother suffered a lot from headaches. In the morning when I was required to do a reading lesson and had come to sit on the cool, polished red cement verandah next to her favourite bentwood rocking chair eager to show her my progress, she would often say: 'Not today, darling, I have a splitting headache.'

I would find Nanny and I would read my book to her and then she would bring a copy of *Outspan*, a magazine that used to come once a month and she would point to pictures that showed women doing things and I would read what it said about the pictures and translate them into Zulu. Her mouth would fall open and she would groan in amazement at the goings on. 'Oh, oh, oh, I think it is very hard to be a white woman,' she would sigh, clapping her hands.

I guessed that was why my mother was always getting splitting headaches, because she was a white woman and like Nanny said, it was a very hard thing to be.

We drew up beside a house which sat no more than twenty feet from the road. A low stone wall marked the front garden and steps led up to the stoep which ran the full width of the house. The place was only dimly lit by a distant street lamp so that further details were impossible to make out in the ghoulish darkness. Two squares of filtered orange light, each from a window in a separate part of the house, glowed through drawn curtains, shedding no real light but giving the house two eyes. The front door made a nose and the steps to it a mouth. Even in the dark it didn't seem to be an unfriendly sort of place. Behind the funny face would be my scraggy old granpa and he would tell about Nanny.

Pastor Mulvery said he wouldn't come in and he praised the Lord again for my delivery into the bosom of my loved ones and said that I would be a fine addition to the Lord's little congregation at the Apostolic Faith Mission Sunday school. My mother also praised His precious name and it was becoming very apparent to me that the Lord was a pretty important person around these parts.

We watched the red brake lights of the big Plymouth twinkle and then disappear down a dip in the road, for we seemed to be on the top of a rise. 'What a precious man,' my mother sighed.

Lugging my case in front of me with both hands I followed her up the dark steps. Her shoes made a hollow sound on the wooden verandah and the screen door squeaked loudly on its heavy snap-back hinges. She propped it open with the toe of her brown brogue and opened the front door. Sharp light spilled over us and down the front steps, grateful to escape the restrictions of the small square room.

This room, at least, was not much altered from the dark little parlour on the farm. The same heavy, overstuffed lounge and three high-backed armchairs in faded brocade, with polished arms and ball and claw legs of dark lacquered wood, the backs of the lounge and chairs scolloped by antimacassars, took up most of the room. The glass bookcase still contained the red and gold leather-bound set of the complete works of Charles Dickens and the two large blue and gold volumes of *The Invasion of the Crimea*. The old grandfather clock stood in a new position beside a door leading out of the room into another part of the house, and it was nice to see the steady old brass pendulum swinging away quietly in its glass-fronted cabinet. On one wall was my granpa's stuffed Kudu head, the horns of the giant antelope brushing the ceiling. Above and on either side of the glass bookcase hung two narrow oil paintings, one showing a scarlet and the other an almost identical yellow long-stemmed rose. Both pictures were framed in the same flat brown varnished frames and were the work of my grandmother who had died giving birth to my mother. The paintings had been rendered on sheets of tin and the paint had flecked in parts leaving dull pewter-coloured spots where the backgrounds of salmon and green had lifted. Alone on one wall was a hand-coloured steel engraving in a heavy walnut frame showing hundreds of Zulu dead and a handful of Welsh soldiers standing over them with bayonets fixed. They stood proud, looking towards heaven, each with a boot and putteed leg resting on the body of a near-naked savage. I had always thought how very clean and smart they still looked after having fought at close quarters with the Zulu hordes all night, each soldier seemingly responsible, if you counted the bodies and the soldiers in the picture, for the death of fifty-two Zulus. The caption under the painting, etched in a mechanical copperplate, read: The morning after the massacre. British honour is restored at Rorke's Drift, January, 1879. Brave men all.

The tired old zebra skin which, along with everything else, I had known all my life, covered the floor and the ball and claw legs of the lounge suite had been placed over the spots where they had worn the hair off the hide in their previous parlour existence. The only change in the room, for even the worn red velvet curtains had come along, was a small, round-shouldered wireless in brown bakelite which rested on the top of the bookcase where the gramophone had previously stood.

Perhaps only the outside of things had changed and the inside, like this room, largely remained the same. For a moment my spirits lifted. Just then my granpa walked into the room, tall and straight as a bluegum pole. His pipe was hooked over the brown tobacco stain on the corner of his bottom lip and he stood framed by the doorway, his baggy khaki pants tied up as ever with a piece of rope, his shirtsleeves rolled up to below the elbow on his collarless shirt. He looked unchanged. He took two puffs from his pipe so that the smoke whirled around his untidy mop of white hair and curled past his long nose. 'There's a good lad,' he said. His pale blue eyes shone wet, and he blinked quickly as he looked down at me. The smoke cleared around his head as he raised his arms slightly and spread his hands palms upwards as though to indicate the room and the house and the predicament all in one sad gesture of apology.

'Newcastle's disease, they had to kill all the Orpingtons,' he said.

'They killed Granpa Chook,' I said softly.

My mother put her hand on my shoulder and moved me past my granpa. 'That's right, darling, they killed all Granpa's chooks. Come along now, it's way past your bedtime.'

I hadn't meant to say anything about Granpa Chook. My granpa, after all, had never known him. It just came out. One chicken thing on top of another chicken thing. He had been enormously fond of those black Orpingtons. Even Nanny had said they must be Zulu birds because they stood so black and strong and the roosters were like elegantly feathered Zulu generals. She had never commented on Granpa Chook's motley appearance. While Nanny had never seen him at the height of his powers, like Inkosi-Inkosikazi she knew him to be different, an exception, a magic chicken of great power who had been conjured up by the old monkey to watch over me. Only on one occasion had she ventured the opinion that it was just like the old wizard to choose a lowly kaffir chicken and a Shangaan at that, when, to her mind, he could have dignified the relationship with one of Granpa's magnificent black Orpington roosters. If a chicken was to become home to the soul of a great warrior, why then could he not be an exemplary example of chickenhood? She had tut-tutted for a while and then, shaking her bandanna'd head, said: 'Who can know the way of a snake on a steep rock?' Whatever that was supposed to mean.

Nanny. Where was she now? Was she dead? Tomorrow I must speak urgently to my granpa. For, while grown-ups never talk to small kids about death, my granpa would tell me for sure. I would ask him when I returned his shilling to him in the morning.

I awakened early as always, and padded softly through the sleeping house to find myself in the kitchen. The black cast-iron stove was smaller than the one on the farm and, to my surprise, when I spit-licked my finger before dabbing it on one of the hot plates, it was cold. On the farm it had never been allowed to go out. The two little orphan kitchen maids Dee and Dum had slept on mats in the kitchen and it had been their job to stoke the embers back to life if the stove showed any signs of going out. This kitchen smelt vaguely of carbolic soap and disinfectant and I missed the warm smell of humans, coffee beans and the aroma of the huge old cast-iron soup pot which plopped and steamed on the back of the stove in a never-ending cycle of new soup bones added and old ones taken out. In the country food is a continuous preoccupation, not simply a pause to refuel. Country people know the sweat that goes into an ear of corn, a pail of milk, a churn of butter, bread warm from the oven and the eggs and bacon which sizzle in the breakfast frying pan. Food is hard earned and requires the proper degree of respect. This stove was bare but for the presence of a large blue and white speckled enamel kettle which looked new and temporary.

The doorway from the kitchen led out onto a wide back stoep which, unlike the front of the house, was level with the ground and looked out into a very large and well tended garden. The fragrance of hundreds of rose blossoms filled the crisp dawn air and I observed that stone terraces, planted with rose bushes, stretched up and away from me. Each terrace ended in a series of six steps and at the top of each set of steps an arbour of climbing roses bent over the pathway. Blossoms of white, pink, yellow and orange, each arboured trellis a different colour, cascaded to the ground in colourful loops. The path running up the centre of the garden looked like the sort of tunnel Alice might well have found in Wonderland. Six huge old trees, of kinds I had not see before, were planted one to each terrace. It was a well-settled garden and I wondered how it came to be Granpa's. Nothing on the farm had ever seemed to be well settled except the bits which had broken down forever.

I now saw that our house was situated a little way up a large hill, which accounted for the steps in the front and the terraces behind. Beyond a dark line of mulberry trees at the far end of the garden and a stone wall enclosure which stretched halfway across the last terrace, the hill of virgin rock and bush rose up steeply. It wasn't an unfriendly-looking hill and its slopes were dotted with aloe, each tall, shaggy plant carrying a candelabra of fiery, poker-like blossoms. A crown of rounded boulders clustered, like currants on a cupcake, at its very top.

As I walked up the path, I saw that each terrace carried beds of roses set into neatly trimmed lawns, though the last terrace was different. On one side it contained the stone wall enclosure too tall for me to see over; on the other it was planted with hundreds of freshly grafted rose stock behind which, acting as a windbreak, stood the line of mulberry trees.

Except for the strange and beautiful trees and whatever might lie behind the stone wall, no plants other than roses appeared to grow in this very tidy garden. Only the fences on either side testified to the sub-tropical climate. Quince and guava, lemon, orange, avocado, pawpaw, mango and pomegranate mixed with Pride of India, poinsettia, hibiscus and, covering a large dead tree, a brilliant shower of bougainvillaea. At the base of the trees grew hydrangea, agapanthus and red and pink canna. It was as though the local trees and plants had come to gawk at the elegant rose garden. They stood on the edges of the garden like colourful country hicks, jostling and pushing each other, too polite to intrude any further.

I decided to explore behind the stone wall a little later and ducked under the canopy of dark mulberry leaves. The ground under the trees had been completely shaded from the sun and was bare, slightly damp and covered with fallen fruit. As I walked the moist berries squashed underfoot, staining the skin between my toes a deep purple. I hadn't eaten since lunch with Big Hettie the previous day, and I began to feast hungrily on the luscious berries. The plumpest, purplest of them broke away from their tiny slender stalks at the slightest touch. Soon the palms of my hands were stained purple and my lips must have been the same from cramming the delicious berries into my mouth. Above me the birds, feeding on the berries, squabbled and chirped their heads off, the leaves and smaller branches shaking with their carry-on.

Emerging from the line of mulberry trees clear of the garden, the first of the aloe plants stood almost at my feet, its spikes of orange blossom tinged with yellow two feet above my head. In front of me, stretching upwards to the sky, the African hillside rose unchanged, while behind me, embroidered on its lap, tizzy and sentimental as a painting on a chocolate box, lay the rose garden.

Without thinking I had started to climb, skirting the rocks and the dark patches of scrub and thorn bush. In half an hour I had reached the summit and scrambling to the top of a huge, weather-rounded boulder I looked about. Behind me the hills tumbled on, accumulating height as they gathered momentum until, in the far distance, they became proper mountains. Far to my left an aerial cableway strung across the foothills into the mountains remained motionless, work had not yet started for the day. Below me, cradled in the foothills, lay the small town. It looked out across a vast and beautiful valley which stretched thirty miles over the lowveld to a slash of deep purple on the pale skyline, an escarpment which rose two thousand feet to the grasslands of the highveld.

It was the most beautiful place I had ever seen. The sun had just risen and was not yet warm enough to lap the dew from the grass, but it was sharp enough to polish the air. I could see the world below me but the world below could not see me. I had found my private place; how much better, it seemed to me, than the old mango tree beside the hostel playground. Above me, flying no higher than a small boy's kite, a sparrowhawk circled, searching the quilted back-yards below for a mother hen careless enough to let one of her plump chicks stray beyond hasty recovery to the safety of her broody undercarriage. Death, in a vortex of feathered air, was about to strike out of a sharp blue early morning sky.

Chimneys were beginning to smoke as domestic servants arrived from the black shanty town hidden behind a buttress of one of the foothills to make the white man's breakfast. The sound of roosters, spasmodic when I had started my climb, now gathered chorus and became more strident and urgent as they sensed the town start to wake. Part of the town was still in the shadow cast by the hills, but I could see it was criss-crossed with jacaranda-lined streets. My eyes followed a long line of purple which led beyond the houses clustered on the edge of the town to a square of dark buildings surrounded by a high wall perhaps a mile into the valley. The walls facing me stood some three storeys high and were studded with at least a hundred and fifty tiny dark windows all of the same size. The buildings, too, were built in a square around a centre quadrangle of hard, brown earth. On each corner of the outside wall was a neat little tower capped with a pyramid of corrugated iron which glinted in the early morning sun. I had never seen a prison, nor had I even imagined one, but there is a race memory in man which instinctively knows of these things. The architecture of misery has an unmistakable look and feel about it.

My granpa, who was an early riser, would be out and about soon and it took no more than twenty minutes to clamber down the hill, back under the green canopy of mulberry trees and into the rose garden. He was cutting away at the arbour on the third terrace, snipping and then pulling a long strand of roses from the overhang and dropping it on a heap on the pathway. He looked up as I approached down the corridor of roses.

'Morning, lad. Been exploring, have you?' He snipped at another string of roses and pulled it away from the trellis. 'Mrs Butt is an untidy old lady, if you let her have her way and don't trim her pretty locks, she's apt to get out of control,' he announced cheerfully. I said nothing. Much of what my granpa said was to himself and asking questions was no use. I was soon to learn the names of every rose in the garden and Mrs Butt, it turned out, was the name of this particular cascade of tiny pink roses.

I pulled the lining of my shorts' pocket inside out and carefully unclipped the large safety pin which held Mevrou's doek. Crouching on the ground at the old man's feet, I unknotted the grubby cloth to reveal Granpa's shilling, the threepenny bit Hennie had given me on my departure from Kaapmuiden and my folded ten-shilling note. I removed Granpa's shilling and once again knotted the cloth and pinned it back into the pocket lining of my trousers. 'This is your change from the tackies, Granpa,' I said, rising and holding the gleaming shilling out to him. He paused, holding the secateurs like a sword above his head. 'Here, take it, it's your shilling, isn't it,' I repeated. He reached down for the coin and dropped it into the pocket of his khaki trousers. 'There's a good lad, that will buy me tobacco for a week.' I thought he sounded quite pleased so I took a deep breath and came out with it.

'Granpa, where's Nanny?' He had moved back to the roses and now he turned slowly and looked down at me. Then he walked the few paces to the steps leading up to the terrace and slowly sat down on the top step.

'Sit down, lad.' He patted the space beside him on the step. I walked over and sat down beside him. He removed his pipe from his pocket, tapped it gently on the step below him and a plug of ash fell from the pipe. He blew through the pipe twice before taking his tobacco pouch from his pocket and refilling it. My granpa was not one for hurrying things so I waited with my hands cupped under my chin. Lighting a wax match on his thigh, he started at last to stoke up, puffing away at the pipe until the blue tobacco smoke swirled about his head. For a long time we sat there, my granpa looking out at nothing, his pipe making a gurgly noise when he drew on it, and me looking at the roof of the house which had once been painted but now only had patches of faded red clinging to the rusted corrugated iron. Coming up the hill in front of the house I could hear a truck, its low gear rasping in the struggle to get up the hill, then a pause as it reached the top and slipped into a higher gear, relieved the climb was over.

'Life is all beginnings and ends. Nothing stays the same, lad,' my granpa said at last. Then he puffed at his pipe and seemed to be examining his fingernails which were broken and dirty from gardening. 'Parting, losing the thing we love the most, that's the whole business of life, that's what it's mostly about.'

Shit, I know that already, I thought to myself. Then my heart sank. Was he trying to tell me Nanny was dead?

He was doing his looking-into-nothing trick again and his pipe had gone out. 'She was a soft and gentle woman. Africa was much too harsh a place for such a trembling little sparrow.' With this he struck another match and touched it to his pipe. Puff, puff, swirl, swirl, puff, puff, gurgle, but he did not continue. While it didn't sound a bit like big, fat Nanny, my granpa was always a bit vague about people and the sentiment seemed appropriate enough, so I waited patiently for him to continue. Taking his pipe from his mouth, he used it to indicate the rose garden around us. 'I built it and planned it for her, the roses, to a rosebud, were the ones which grew in her father's vicarage in her Yorkshire village, the trees too, elm and oak, spruce and walnut.' He replaced the pipe in his mouth, but it had gone out again and he had to light it a third time. This time he cupped his hands around the bowl and gave it a really good stoking up so that at one stage his head disappeared completely behind the clouds of blue smoke. I had already observed that my granpa could waste a great deal of time with his pipe when he didn't want to give my mother an answer or needed time to think. So I waited and thought it best to say nothing, though none of it made sense. Nanny, who discussed everything with me, had never once talked about the roses in the farm garden, and I knew for a fact that she came from a village in Zululand near the Tugela river. While she had often talked about the crops and the song of the wind in the green corn, of pumpkins ripening in the sun which were as big as a chief's beer pots, and of the sweet *tsamma* melons which grew wild near the banks of the river, she had never, even once, mentioned anything about roses to me.

After another long while of looking into nothing my granpa continued. 'When she died giving birth to your mother, I couldn't stay on here in her rose garden.' He looked down at me as though seeking my approval. 'Sometimes it's best just to walk away from your memories, just put one memory in front of the other and walk them right out of your head.'

I was beginning to realise that Nanny had nothing to do with my granpa's conversation.

'Her brother Richard had come out from England to try to cure his arthritis and decided to stay on. A grand lad, Richard, and a good rose man. In thirty years he hasn't changed a thing. When the roses grew old he replaced them with their own kind.' He pointed to a standard rose on the terrace below him. From it rose two perfect long-stemmed blossoms, the edges of their delicate orange petals tipped with red. 'I'll vouch that is the only Imperial Sunset left in Africa,' he said with deep satisfaction. He tapped the bowl of his pipe on the step until the smoking ash fell from it. Then, picking up the garden shears where they lay on the step below, he rose and turned to look about him. 'Now Dick's dead I've come home to her rose garden. The pain is gone but the roses, the sweet Yorkshire roses, not a day older, bloom forever on.'

They were the most words I could recall having come from my granpa in one sitting. While he hadn't answered my urgent questions about Nanny, I could see that he had said something out loud that must have been bouncing around in his head for a long time.

'There's a good lad, off you go and play now.' He moved

over to resume the tidying up of old Mrs Butt. I rose from the steps and started to walk towards the house. Smoke was coming from the chimney and breakfast couldn't be too far away. The clicking of the shears suddenly ceased. 'Lad!' he called after me. I turned to look at him, his shaggy old head was almost touching the canopy of roses covering the arbour. 'You must ask your mother about your nanny, it's got something to do with that damn fool religion she's caught up in.'

Imagine my delight when I walked into the kitchen to find our two little kitchen maids Dee and Dum. They saw me enter and with a squeal of pleasure rushed over to embrace me, each of them holding a hand and dancing me around the kitchen. 'You have grown. Your hair is still shaved. We must wash your clothes. Your mouth is stained from the fruit. You must eat. We will look after you now that Nanny has gone. Yes, yes, we will be your nanny, we have learned all the songs.' The two little girls were beside themselves with joy. It felt good, so very good to have them with me. While they had only been on the periphery of my life with Nanny, who had scolded them constantly and called them silly, empty-headed Shangaan girls but loved them anyway, I now realised how important they were to my past. They were continuity in a world that had been shattered and changed and was still changing. Now that my mother was following the Lord and could no longer be relied upon, my granpa and the two girls were my only constants.

'Me, Dum,' one of them said in English, tapping her chest with one hand while covering her mouth with the other to hide her giggle.

'Me, Dee,' the second one echoed, the whites of her eyes showing her delight as they lit up her small black face. They were identical twins and were reminding me of the names I had given them when I was much smaller. It had started as Tweedle Dum and Tweedle Dee and had simply become Dum and Dee. I laughed as they showed off their English.

The room smelt of fresh coffee and Dee moved over to a tall, brown enamel coffee pot on the back of the stove and Dum brought a mug and placed it on the table together with a hard rusk and then walked over to a coolbox on the stoep for a jug of milk. She returned with the milk and Dee poured the fresh coffee into the cup, both of them concentrating on their tasks, silent for the time being. Placing the pot back on the stove, Dee ladled two carefully measured spoons of sugar into the mug of steaming coffee, using the same spoon to stir it. It was a labour of love, an expression of their devotion. Dum brought me a *riempie* stool and placed it in the middle of the kitchen. I sat down and Dee placed the mug on the floor between my legs so that I could sit on the little rawhide chair and dunk the rock-hard rusk into it just the way I had always done on the farm. The two girls then sat on the polished cement floor in front of me, their legs tucked away under their skirts.

On the farm they had simply worn a single length of thin cotton cloth wrapped around their bodies and tied over one shoulder. Their wrists and ankles had been banded in bangles of copper and brass wire which jingled as they walked. Now these rings were gone and over their slim, pre-pubescent twelve-year-old bodies they wore identical sleeveless shifts of striped navy mattress cotton which reached almost to their ankles.

While I dunked and sipped at my coffee we chatted away in Shangaan. They asked me about the night water and I told them that Inkosi-Inkosikazi's magic had worked and the problem was solved. They clucked and sighed about this for a while and we then talked about the crops and about the men who came in a big truck and lit a huge bonfire and killed and burned all the black chickens. The smell of burning feathers and roasted chickens had lingered for three days, but no one was allowed to eat the meat. Such a waste had never been seen before. How my granpa had sat on the stoep at the farm for a day and a night, watching the fire die down to nothing, silently puffing at his pipe, leaving the food brought to him and letting the coffee beside him grow cold.

At last we reached silence, for the subject of Nanny had been standing on the edge of the conversation waiting to be introduced all along and they knew it could no longer be delayed.

'Where is she who is Nanny?' I asked at last, putting it in the formal manner so they could not avoid the question. Both girls lowered their heads and brought their hands up to cover their mouths.

'Ah, ah, ah!' they shook their heads slowly.

'Who forbids the answering?'

'We may not say,' Dee volunteered, and they both let out a miserable sigh.

'Is it the mistress?' I asked, already knowing the answer. Both looked up at me pleadingly, tears in their eyes.

'She is much changed since she has returned,' Dum said.

'She has made us take off our bangles of womanhood and these dresses make our bodies very hot,' Dee added with a sad little sniff. Both rose from the floor and moved over to the stove where they stood with their backs to me, sobbing.

'I will ask her myself,' I said, sounding more brave than I felt inside. 'At least tell me, is she who is Nanny alive?' They both turned to face me, relieved that there was something they could say without betraying my mother's instructions.

'She is alive!' they exclaimed together, their eyes wide. Using their knuckles to smudge away their tears they smiled at me, once again happy that they could bring me some good news.

'We will make hot water and wash you.' Dum reached down beside the stove for an empty four-gallon paraffin tin from which the top had been cut, the edges hammered flat and a wire handle added, to turn it into a container for hot water.

'See, the water comes to us along an iron snake which comes into the house,' Dee said, moving over to the sink and turning on the tap.

'I am too old to be washed by silly girls,' I said indignantly. 'Put on the water and I will bath myself.' Apart from wiping my face and hands with a damp flannel, my mother had let me climb into bed without washing, and I hadn't really washed since the shower with Hoppie at Gravelotte.

The girls showed me a small room leading off the back stoep in which stood an old tin bath. Carrying the four-gallon paraffin tin between them, they poured the scalding water into the bath. Then they fought over who should turn on the cold tap positioned over the tub. Dum won and Dee, pretending to sulk, left the bathroom. She returned shortly with a freshly washed shirt and pair of khaki shorts. I ordered them both to leave the room. Giggling their heads off, they bumped and jostled each other out of the small, dark bathroom.

That was a bath and a half, I can tell you. It soaked a lot of misery away. The thought that Nanny was still alive cheered me considerably and made the task of asking my mother about her a lot easier.

After breakfast my mother retired to her sewing room and several people turned up to see her. They were women from the town and I could hear her talking to them about clothes. When I questioned the maids about this, they said, 'The missus has become a maker of garments for other missus who come all the time to be fitted.' On the farm my mother had often been busy making things on her Singer machine, and had always made my granpa's and my clothes. Now she seemed to be doing it for other people as well.

Apart from a garden boy who came in to help my granpa, Dum and Dee were our only servants. They cleaned, scrubbed, polished, did the washing and prepared most of the food, though my mother did the cooking and the general bossing around like always. The maids slept in a small room built onto the garden shed behind the enclosed stone wall, which also housed the kitchen garden and an empty fowl run, the thought of chickens being too much for my granpa to contemplate.

At the time I was not concerned about how we lived, though later I was to realise that making enough to get by was a pretty precarious business in the little household. My granpa sold young rose trees and my mother worked all day and sometimes long into the night as a dressmaker. Between making dresses and serving the Lord she didn't have much time for anything else.

I whiled away the morning and after lunch gathered up enough courage to venture into my mother's sewing room. She had a new Singer machine with an electric foot treadle. It wasn't like the old one where you had to treadle it up and down to make it work. You simply put your foot on the little electric footrest and the sewing machine hummed away stitching happily. Dee had given me a cup of tea to take in to my mother and I had hardly spilled any by the time I handed it to her.

My mother had looked up and smiled as I entered. 'I was just thinking to myself, I would die for a cup of tea, and here you are,' she said as I gave her the cup. She poured the spilt tea in the saucer back into the cup and then took a sip, closing her eyes. 'Heaven, it's pure heaven, there's nothing like a good cup of tea.' She sounded just like she used to before she went away. For a moment I thought all the carry-on with Pastor Mulvery was exaggerated in my mind because I knew I had been very tired. I sat on one of the chairs and waited. 'Come in for a bit of a chat, have you? You must have so much to tell me about your school and the nice little friends you made.' She leaned over and kissed me on the top of the head. 'I tell you what. Tonight, after supper, when your grandfather listens to the wireless, we'll sit in the kitchen and have a good old chin-wag. You can tell me all about it. I'm dying to hear, really. Granpa tells me fat old Mevrou Vorster who we sold the farm to says you speak Afrikaans like a Boer. I suppose that's nice, dear, though thank goodness you won't need to talk it in this town. Dr Henny wrote to say you'd got into some sort of scrape with your ear. Is that all right now?' I nodded and she continued, 'I'm better now, quite better. The Lord reached down and touched me and I was healed. It is a glorious experience when you walk in the light of the Lord.' She stopped and took a sip from her cup.

'Mother, where is Nanny?' I asked, unable to contain myself any longer. There was a long pause and my mother took another sip and looked down into her lap.

Finally she looked up at me and said sweetly, 'Why, darling, your nanny has gone back to Zululand.'

'Did you send her there, Mother?' My voice was on the edge of tears.

'I prayed and the Lord told me, He guided me in my decision.' She put down her cup and fed a piece of material under the needle, brought the tension foot down onto it and, feeding the cloth skilfully through her fingers, zizzed away with the electric motor. Then, with a deep sigh, she stopped. Lifting the tension foot, she snipped the cotton thread and looked down at me. 'I tried to bring her to the Lord but she hardened her heart against Him.' She looked up at the ceiling as though asking for confirmation. 'I can't tell you the nights I spent on my knees asking for guidance.' She looked down at me again, and pursing her lips threw her head back. 'Your nanny would not remove her heathen charms and amulets and she insisted on wearing her bangles and ankle rings. I prayed and prayed and then the Lord sent me a sign I was looking for. Your grandfather told me about the visit of that awful old witchdoctor and that it had been at your nanny's instigation.' Her face grew angry, 'That disgusting, filthy, evil old man was tampering with the mind of my five-year-old son! God is not mocked! How could I let a black heathen woman riddled with superstition bring up my only son?' She picked up her cup and took a polite sip. 'Your nanny was possessed by the devil,' she said finally, satisfied the discussion was over.

I tried very hard not to cry. Inside me the loneliness birds were laying eggs thirteen to the dozen. Forcing back the tears, I got down from my chair and stood looking directly at my mother. 'The Lord is a shithead!' I shouted and rushed from the room.

I ran through the Alice in Wonderland tunnels and under the mulberry trees to the freedom of the hill, my sobs making it difficult to climb. At last I reached the safety of the large boulder and allowed myself a good bawl.

The fierce afternoon sun beat down, and below me the town baked in the heat. When was it all going to stop? Was life about losing the things we love the most, as my granpa had said? Couldn't things just stay the same for a little while until I grew up and understood the way they worked? Why did you have to wear camouflage all the time? The only person I had ever known who didn't need any camouflage was Nanny. She laughed and cried and wondered and loved and never told a thing the way it wasn't. I would write her a letter and send her my ten-shilling note, then she would know I loved her. Granpa would know how to do that.

As I sat on the rock high on my hill, and as the sun began to set over the bushveld, I grew up. Just like that. The loneliness birds stopped laying stone eggs, they rose from their stone nests and flapped away on their ugly wings and the eggs they left behind crumbled into dust. A fierce, howling wind came along and blew the dust away until I was empty inside.

I knew they would be back, but that, for the moment, I was alone. That I had permission from myself to love whomsoever I wished. The cords which bound me to the past had been severed. The emptiness was a new kind of loneliness, a free kind of loneliness. Not the kind which laid stone eggs deep inside of you until you filled up with heaviness and despair. I knew that when the bone-beaked birds returned I would be in control, master of loneliness and no longer its servant.

You may ask how a six-year-old could think like this. I can only answer that one did.

NINE

'It is a fine sunset, ja? Always here is the best place.' I looked behind me, and there was a tall, thin man, taller, much taller and perhaps even thinner than my granpa. He wore a battered old bush hat and his snowy hair hung down to the top of his shoulders. His face was clean shaven, wrinkled and deeply tanned, while his eyes were an intense blue and seemed too young for his face. He wore khaki overalls without a shirt and his arms and chest were also tanned. The legs of his overalls, beginning just below the knees, were swirled in puttees which wound down into socks rolled over the tops of a pair of stout hiking boots. Strapped to his back was a large canvas bag from which, rising three feet into the air directly behind his head, was a cactus, spines of long, dangerous thorns protruding from its dark green skin. Cupped in his left hand he held a curious-looking camera which appeared to be secured by a leather strap about his neck.

'You must excuse me, please, I have taken your picture. At other times I would not do such a thing. It is not polite. It was your expression. Ja, it is always the expression that is important. Without expression the human being is just a lump of meat. You have some problems I think, ja?'

At the sound of his voice I had stood up hastily and now faced him a little sheepishly, looking down at him from the rock, a good six feet higher than where he stood. He made a gesture at me and the rock and even at the sky beyond.

'I shall call it Boy on a Rock.' He paused and cocked his head slightly to one side. 'I think this is a good name. I have your permission, yes?' I nodded and he seemed pleased. Dropping the camera so that it hung around his neck, he extended his right hand up towards me. He was much too far away for our hands to meet but I stuck mine out too and we both shook the air in front of us. This seemed to be a perfectly satisfactory introduction. 'Von Vollensteen, Professor Von Vollensteen.' He withdrew his hand and gave me a stiff little bow from the waist.

'Peekay,' I said, withdrawing my hand at the same time as he dropped his. His friendliness was infectious and no hint of condescension showed in his manner. Best of all, I could hear nothing going on behind the scenes.

'Peekay? P-e-e-k-a-y, I like this name, it has a proper sound. I think a name like this would be good for a musician.' He squinted up at me, thinking, then took a sharp intake of breath as though he had reached an important decision. 'I think we can be friends, Peekay,' he said.

'Why aren't the thorns from that cactus sticking into your back?' The canvas bag was much too lightly constructed to protect him from the vicious three-inch thorns.

'Ha! This is a goot question, Peekay. I will give you one chance to think of the answer then you must pay a forfeit.'

'You first took off all the thorns on the part that's in the bag.'

'Ja, this is possible, also a very goot answer,' he shook his head slowly, 'but not true. Peekay, I am sorry to say you owe me a forfeit and then you must try again for the answer.' He stroked his chin. 'Now let me see . . . Ja! I know what we shall do. You must put your hands like so,' he placed his hands on his hips, 'at once we will stand on one leg and say, "No matter what has happened bad, today I'm finished from being sad. Absoloodle!" '

I stood on the rock, balanced on one leg with my hands on my hips, but each time I tried to say the words the laughter would bubble from me and I'd lose my balance. Soon we were both laughing fit to burst. Me on the rock and Professor Von Vollensteen dancing below me on the ground, slapping his thighs, the cactus clinging like a green papoose to his back. I could get the first part all right, but the 'Absoloodle!' at the end proved too much and I would topple, overcome by mirth.

Spent with laughter, Professor Von Vollensteen finally sat down, and taking a large red bandanna from the pocket of his overalls, wiped his eyes. 'My English is not so goot, ja?' He beckoned me to come down and sit beside him. 'Come, no more forfeiting, too dangerous, perhaps I die laughing next time. Come, Peekay, I will show you the secret.' He jerked his thumb over his shoulder indicating the cactus. 'But first you must introduce yourself to my prickly green friend who has a free ride on my back.'

I scrambled down from the rock and came to stand beside him. 'Peekay, this is *Euphorbia grandicornis*, he is a very shy cactus and very hard to find in these parts.'

'Hello,' I said to the cactus, not quite knowing what else to say.

'Goot, now you have been introduced you can see why Mr *Euphorbia grandicornis* does not scratch my back.' I walked behind him and looked into the canvas bag. Inside was a small collapsible shovel and the roots of the cactus were swaddled in hessian and tied with coarse string. The part of the bag resting on Professor Von Vollensteen's back was made of leather too thick for the long thorns to penetrate. 'Not so stupid, ha?' he said with a grin.

'Aaw! If you'd given me another chance I would've got it,' I said, immediately convincing myself that this was so.

'Ja, for sure! It is always easy to be a schmarty pantz when you know already the trick.'

'Honest, Mr Professor Von Vollensteen, I think I could've known the answer,' I protested, anxious now to impress him.

'Okay! Then I give you one chance more. A professor is not a mister but a mister can be a professor. Answer me that, Mister Schmarty Pantz?'

I sat down on a small rock trying to work this out, my

heart sank, for I knew almost immediately he had the better of me. I had simply thought his first name, like Peekay, was a little unusual. I had never heard of anyone called Professor, but then I was also the first Peekay I knew of, so who was I to judge?

'I give up, sir,' I said, feeling rather foolish. 'What is a professor?' He had removed the canvas bag from his back and once again held the camera cupped in his hands.

'Peekay, you are a genius my friend! Look what we find under this rock where you are sitting. This is *Aloe microsfigma*!' I rose from the rock and joined him on his knees looking underneath it. A small cluster of tiny spotted aloes, each not much bigger than a two-shilling piece grew in the grass at the base of the rock. Even at close quarters they would have been hard to see and to an untrained eye almost impossible. The old man brushed the grass out of the way, and lying flat on his tummy he focused the camera on the tiny succulents. Behind him the sunset bathed the plants in a red glow. 'The light is perfect but I must work quick.' His hands, fumbling with the camera, were shaking with excitement. Finally he clicked the shot and got slowly back to his knees. Removing a Joseph Rogers from the pocket of his overalls, he used the small knife to separate four of the aloes, leaving twice as many behind. He held the tiny plants in his hand for me to see. '*Wunderbar*, Peekay, small but so perfect, a good omen for our friendship.'

I must say I was not too impressed but I was glad that he was happy. 'You haven't said what a professor is.'

He wrapped the tiny aloes in his bandanna and placed them carefully into his canvas bag which he then slung back over his shoulders. 'Ja, I like that, you have good concentration, Peekay. What is a professor? That is a goot question.' He stood looking at the dying sun. 'A professor is a person who drinks too much whisky and once plays goot Beethoven and Brahms and Mozart and even sometimes when it was not serious, Chopin. Such a person who could command respect in Vienna, Leipzig, Warsaw and Budapest and also, ja, once in London.' His shoulders sagged visibly. 'A professor is also some person who can not anymore command respect from little girls who play not even schopstics goot.'

I could see his previous mood of elation had changed and there was a strange conversation going on in his head. But then, just as suddenly, his eyes regained their sparkle. 'A professor is a teacher, Peekay. I have the honour to be a teacher of music.' He put his hand on my shoulder. It was the first time he had touched me and the gesture was unthinking and friendly, like another kid might hold you when you are playing. 'You can call me Doc. You see I am also Doctor of Music, it is all the same thing. I am too old and you are too young for Mister this or Professor that. You and me will not hide behind such a small importance. Just Peekay and Doc. I think this is a goot plan?'

I nodded agreement, though I was too shy to say the word out loud. He seemed to sense my reluctance. 'What is my name, Peekay?' he asked casually.

'Doc,' I replied shyly. Hoppie was the only other adult with whom I had been on such familiar terms and I found it a little frightening.

'One hundred per cent! For this I give you eleven out of ten. Absoloodle!' he said and we both started to laugh.

The sun sets quickly in the bushveld and we hurried down the hill, small rocks rolling ahead of us as we raced to beat the dark. Below us the first lights were coming on, the chimneys were beginning to smoke as tired servants prepared supper for their white mistresses before washing the dishes and going home to the native location.

'So it is you who live now in the English rose garden,' Doc said when we reached the dark line of mulberry trees. 'Soon I will show you my cactus garden.' While it was too dark to see his face, I sensed his smile. 'We will meet again, my goot friend Peekay.' He touched me lightly and I watched his tall, shambling figure with the *Euphorbia grandicornis* sticking up beyond his head moving into the gathering darkness.

'Good night, Doc!' I said, and then on a whim shouted, '*Euphorbia grandicornis* and *Aloe microsfigma*!'

The old man turned in the dark, 'Magnificent, Peekay. Absoloodle!'

Euphorbia grandicornis, I rolled the name around in my head. Such a posh name for a silly old cactus with thorns. I wondered briefly how it might sound as a name for a fighter, but almost immediately rejected it. *Euphorbia grandicornis* was no name for the next welterweight champion of the world.

When I entered the kitchen, Dum and Dee averted their eyes and Dee said, 'The missus wants to see you, *Inkosikaan*.' She looked at me distressed. Dum walked over and reached out and touched me.

'We have put some food under your bed in the pot for night water,' she whispered and they clutched each other and whimpered in their anxiety that they might be discovered.

I knocked on the door of my mother's sewing room. 'Come in,' she said and looked up as I entered. Then she bent over her sewing machine and put her foot down on the motor and sewed away for quite a while.

Of course, she did not know she was dealing with a veteran of interrogation and punishment and since I had suddenly grown up on the hill, I was uncrackable. A real hard case.

After a while she stopped, and taking off her glasses she rubbed the top of her nose with her forefinger and thumb and gave a deep sigh. 'You have hurt me and you have hurt the Lord very deeply,' she said at last. 'Don't you know the Lord loves you?' She didn't wait for my answer. 'The gospel says, whosoever harms a hair upon the head of one of my little ones, harmeth me also.'

I had heard the same thing said by Pik Botha, which just about confirmed everything I thought about the Lord. Pik

Botha and my mother and Pastor Mulvery were all working for the same person.

My mother continued, 'When I had my quiet time with the Lord this afternoon, He spoke to me. You will not get a beating, but He is not mocked and you will go to your room at once without your supper.'

'Yes, Mother,' I said and turned to go.

'Just a moment! You have not apologised to me for your behaviour.' Her eyes were suddenly sharp with anger.

I hung my head just like I used to do with Mevrou. 'I'm sorry, Mother,' I said.

'Not sorry enough, if you ask me. Do you think it's easy for me trying to make ends meet? I'm not supposed to get tired. I'm only your mother, the dog's body about the place. All you care about is that black woman, that stinking black Zulu woman!' She suddenly lost her anger and her eyes filled with the tears of self-pity. Grabbing the dress she had been sewing she held it up to her eyes, her thin shoulders shaking, and began to sob. 'I don't think I can take much more, first your grandfather and then those two in the kitchen and now you!' She looked up at me, her pretty face distorted and ugly from crying. Then, with a sudden little wail, she once again buried her head in the dress and started to sob hysterically.

I felt enormously relieved. This was much more like my old mother. She was having one of her turns, and I knew exactly what to do. 'I'll make you a nice cup of tea and an Aspro and then you must have a good lie down,' I said and left the room.

Dum and Dee were delighted that I hadn't received a beating and hurriedly made me a pot of tea and then turned it around and around on the kitchen table to make it brew quickly. Dee handed me two Aspro from a big bottle kept in a cupboard above the sink and I put them in my pocket, for I was afraid that if I put them on the saucer I'd slop tea over them.

My mother was sitting at the machine unpicking stitches

as I entered the sewing room. Her eyes were red from crying but otherwise she seemed quite composed. I put the cup of tea down carefully on the table next to the machine and fished in my pocket for the Aspro which I placed next to the cup. 'Thank you,' she said in a tight voice, not looking up at me. 'Now go straight to your room, you may not come out until morning.'

It was light punishment, I had expected far worse. In the chamberpot Dum and Dee had left three cold sausages, two big roast potatoes and a couple of mandarins, a proper feast. There wasn't much else to do but go to sleep after that. It had been a long day and a very good one. The loneliness birds had flown away and I had grown up and made a new friend called Doc and had learned several new things. *Euphorbia grandicornis* was an ugly green cactus with long, dangerous looking thorns, *Aloe microsfigma* was a tiny, spotted aloe which liked to hide under rocks and a professor was a teacher who taught music. Also, there was a rose called Mrs Butt and another called Imperial Sunset.

Tomorrow I would write a letter to Nanny and send her my ten shillings. She would like that and she would know that somebody loved her. I fell asleep thinking about how big the hole would have to be to bury Big Hettie in, about Hoppie fighting Adolf Hitler, which would probably be an easier fight than the one against Jackhammer Smit, and how I was going to become welterweight champion of the world.

Two days later I was sitting on the front stoep watching army trucks passing the front door, for I had discovered that an army camp was being set up in the valley about three miles out of town. The big khaki Bedford, Chevrolet and Ford trucks, their backs covered with canvas tarpaulin canopies, had been passing for two days. Some contained soldiers who sat in the back carrying .303 rifles. But mostly they carried tents and timber and other things needed for building an army camp.

My granpa, when he heard the news on the wireless, had said it was typical of the army big-wigs, putting a military camp at the end of a branch line, which couldn't move troops out fast enough to anywhere, least of all to Lourenço Marques, where the Portuguese couldn't be relied on to maintain their neutrality for one moment.

My Adolf Hitler fears returned immediately. Lourenço Marques, I discovered, was no more than eighty miles away if they came through Swaziland. I was glad that my granpa had Nanny's address in Zululand and that I had sent her off a postal order for my ten shillings, my love in a letter and a photograph taken much earlier showing her holding me. If she couldn't get somebody to read the letter, she'd know it was from me and my original escape plan would still be intact.

I was also glad the army was so close at hand. Lourenço Marques, the nearest seaport, was obviously where Adolf Hitler planned to march all the Rooineks from these parts into the sea. Even an army at the end of a branch line was better than no army at all.

My mother added that Lourenço Marques was probably seething with German spies at this very moment, and they were probably using code words on Radio Lourenço Marques to relay messages to the Boer Nazis who were plotting to tear down the country from within. I thought about the Judge and Mr Stoffel and how they always listened to the wireless. When my granpa said that was a lot of poppycock, I was not so sure.

I thought about these things as I watched a convoy of one hundred and five army trucks go by, the biggest yet by far, so I didn't notice Doc coming up the hill until he almost reached the gate.

'Goot morning, Peekay.' He was dressed in a white linen suit and wore a panama hat, so that I hardly recognised him. He carried a string bag and a silver-handled walking stick and under one arm was a large manila envelope.

'Good morning, Doc,' I said, jumping to my feet. I found

it a little strange to say his name out loud, though in my head I'd said it a thousand times.

'I can come in, ja?' I hurried down the steps to open the gate. 'This is an official visit, Peekay, I have come to see your mother.'

I felt stupidly disappointed. I hadn't known he knew my mother. I followed him up the steps. 'You will introduce us please,' he said as we reached the verandah.

Unreasonably pleased that I was his first friend, I opened the front door and led him into the parlour. Visitors to the farm had been infrequent but the routine was unerring. First you sat people down and then you gave them coffee and cake. I asked Doc to sit down and he did so but not before he had stood in the centre of the zebra skin and slowly turned around taking the room in. When he reached the grandfather clock he paused and said, 'English, London, about 1680, a very good piece.' He took a gold Hunter from his fob pocket, and snapping it open examined it briefly. 'Four minutes a month,' he said, returning the watch to his pocket. I was amazed he should know how much our grandfather clock lost, for he was right. I thought perhaps my granpa had told him.

'Do you know my granpa?' I asked Doc.

'I have not yet had this pleasure but it will be okay, we are both men of thorns, with me the cactus, with him the rose. The English and the Germans are not so far apart. It will be all right, you will see.' He said this just as I was about to leave the room to get Dum and Dee to bring coffee and cake.

I was dumbfounded, Professor Von Vollensteen was a German! What should I do? My grandfather had gone to the library in town to change his books, that was one good thing anyway. You never knew what he might do coming face to face with a German, although even against Doc I didn't fancy his chances. I decided to say nothing to my mother, she might have a conniption on the spot.

Dum and Dee had somehow known we had a guest and

were putting out the tea things and half a canary cake on a plate. I could hear the sewing machine zizzing away as I walked over to the far side of the house to tell my mother she had a guest. I knocked before opening the door.

'There is someone to see you, Mother,' I shouted over the sound of the whirring machine. She stopped sewing and looked up.

'Tell her to come in, darling, it must be Mrs Cameron about her skirt.'

'It is Professor Von Vollensteen. He wants to see you,' I said in a low voice.

'Professor whom?' she asked, removing her glasses and looking directly at me.

'He is a teacher, a teacher of music,' I said urgently in an attempt to hide my confusion. She rose to her feet and patted her hair and reached for her bag. From it she took a compact and, looking into the tiny mirror on the inside flap of the bag, hurriedly powdered her nose.

'Well he can't teach music here, we haven't got that sort of money,' she said, putting the pad back into the compact and snapping it shut. I followed behind her, not at all sure of the reception Doc would get.

But my mother was country-bred and all visitors were treated courteously no matter what their purpose. Doc rose from the lounge as she entered and extended his hand. 'Madame,' he said, bowing slightly, 'Professor Karl Von Vollensteen.'

My mother extended her hand and Doc took it lightly and bowed over it bringing his heels together. 'Please sit down, professor, will you take coffee with us?' She reached no higher than his waist and when he sat down her head was level with his.

'You are very kind, madame. Today we have two things.' He reached into the string bag at his feet and produced a jam tin which held a small plant. The plant had only two leaves which stuck straight up out of the tin and were tinged with pink around the edges. They looked exactly like two light green rabbit ears. 'Allow me please to introduce *Kalanchoe thyrsiflora*, quite rare in these parts, often mistaken for a plant, but I assure you, madame, a true cactus.' Doc handed the jam tin to my mother who remarked that she couldn't possibly remember the name and laughed her nervous laugh. 'Ja, it is a difficult name but, if you wish, you may just call it Rabbit Ears,' Doc said charitably, though he somehow left the impression that the little cactus was demeaned by such a common name.

Dum and Dee entered, Dee carrying a tray with cups and cake and Dum carrying the china coffee pot we used for visitors. Dee set the tray on the traymobile and carefully wheeled it over to my mother who sent her back to fetch a knife for the cake. Dum, keeping her back straight and her arm rigid, bent her knees almost to the ground so she could put the coffee pot down on the traymobile without any possibility of spilling it. Dum, too, was sent back to the kitchen, for the coffee strainer.

'You can tell them a hundred times over, it's useless. I don't know what goes on inside their heads,' my mother sighed, putting the tiny plant on the shelf under the traymobile. I had been standing beside her chair and now she turned to me. 'Run along now.'

Doc looked up. 'With your permission, madame, I would like for Peekay to stay please?'

'Who?' my mother said.

'Your son, madame, I would much like him to stay.'

My mother turned to me. 'What on earth have you been telling the professor? Who is Peekay?'

'It's my new name. I, I haven't told you about it yet,' I said, flustered. My mother laughed, but I knew she was annoyed.

'Why, you have a perfectly good name, my dear.' She gave me a funny look, then turned to Doc. 'Of course he may stay, but I'm afraid our family never had much of an ear for music and lessons would be much too expensive.'

Without looking at Dee and Dum, who had re-entered

the room and now stood beside her, she held her hand out for the knife and strainer and dismissed them with an impatient flick of her head.

'I am most grateful, madame.' My mother lifted the coffee pot. 'Black only, no sugar,' Doc said, leaning forward in anticipation.

My mother poured his coffee. 'A nice piece of cake, professor?' Doc put his hand up in refusal. 'Thank you,' he said. It was a speech habit I was going to find hard to get used to, saying, 'Thank you,' when he meant, 'No thank you,' and clearly my mother misunderstood him for she placed a piece of the canary cake on a sideplate and handed it to him with his coffee. He accepted the cake without further protest.

Doc put the coffee and cake on the zebra hide between his legs and picked up the manila envelope. 'And so now we have the second thing.' His eyes sparkled as he handed the envelope to my mother.

'Goodness, what can it be?' she said, pulling out the tucked-in flap of the large brown envelope. She withdrew the largest photograph I had ever seen which, to my amazement, turned out to be me sitting on the rock on top of the hill. 'Goodness gracious!' My mother stared at it, momentarily lost for words. The photograph showed every detail, even the lichen on the rock, more clearly than any I had seen before. Shafts of sunlight shining through a silver-edged cloud seemed to be directed straight at the rock on which I sat. My body, half in shadow, appeared to be as one with the rock. I didn't know it at the time, but it was an extraordinary picture. At last my mother spoke. 'Wherever did you take this? It is so sad! Why did you take a picture of him when he was looking sad?'

Doc rubbed his chin, it was plainly not the comment he expected and he needed a moment to think about the answer. Ignoring the first question he leaned forward as he answered the second. 'Ja, this is so. Only one great picture shows a man when he smiles. Frans Hals, *Laughing*

Cavalier, early seventeenth century.' He pointed at the grandfather clock. 'Around that time they make this clock also. The smile, madame, is used by humans to hide the truth, the artist is only interested to reveal the truth.' He leaned back, clearly satisfied with his reply.

'Goodness, professor, all that is much to deep for simple country people like us. He's only a very little boy, you know? I prefer him to smile.'

'Of course! But sadness, like understanding, comes early in life for some. It is part of intelligence.'

My mother's back stiffened. 'You seem to know a lot about my son, professor. I can't imagine how, he has only been home from boarding school for three days.'

Doc clapped his hands gleefully. 'Boarding school! Ha, that explains I think everything. For a boy like this boarding school is a prison, ja?'

My mother was beginning to show her impatience, her fingers tapped steadily on the arms of the chair, a sure sign that things were not going well. 'We had no choice in the matter, professor. I was ill. One does the best one can under the circumstances.' She looked into her lap, her coffee untouched.

Doc suddenly seemed to realise that he had gone too far. 'Forgive me, madame.' He leaned forward. 'It is not said to make you angry. Your son is a gifted child. I don't know where, I don't know how. I only pray it is music. Today I have come to ask you, please madame, let me teach him?' He had spoken to my mother softly and with great charm and I could feel her relax as his voice stroked her ego.

'Humpf! I must say you seem to know more about him than his mother. I can't see how he is any different to any other child of his age,' she said huffily, though I could tell this was just a pretence and that she was secretly pleased by the compliment. My mother was a proud woman and didn't expect charity from anyone. 'It is out of the question. Piano lessons don't grow on trees, professor.'

'Ja, that is true. But, I think, maybe on cactus plants.'

Doc's deep blue eyes showed his amusement. 'For two years I have searched for the *Aloe microsfigma*, from here, zere, everywhere. Then, poof! Just by sitting on a rock, *Aloe microsfigma* comes. The boy is a genius. Absoloodle!'

'What ever can you be talking about, professor? What have you two been up to?' Whereas before she had been angry, now she was plainly charmed by him.

'Madame, we met on the mountain top with only the face of God above us, the picture will capture the moment forever,' he shrugged his scrawny shoulders. 'It was destiny, the new cactus man has come.'

My mother seemed unsure how to take this. 'I am a born-again Christian, professor, God's name is only used in praise in this house,' she said, mostly to cover her confusion but also as a caution to Doc not to assume an over-familiar manner with the Almighty.

'God and I have no quarrels, madame. The Almighty conceived the cactus plant. If God would choose a plant to represent him, I think he would choose of all plants the cactus. The cactus has all the blessings he tried, but mostly failed, to give to man. Let me tell you how. It has humility but it is not submissive. It grows where no other plant will grow. It does not complain when the sun bakes its back, or the wind tears it from the cliff or drowns it in the dry sand of the desert or when it is thirsty. When the rains come it stores water for the hard times to come. In good times and in bad it will still flower. It protects itself against danger, but it harms no other plant. It adapts perfectly to almost any environment. It has patience and enjoys solitude. In Mexico there is a cactus that flowers only once every hundred years and at night. This is saintliness of an extra-ordinary kind, would you not agree? The cactus has proper-ties that heal the wounds of men and from it come potions that can make man touch the face of God or stare into the mouth of hell. It is the plant of patience and solitude, love and madness, ugliness and beauty, toughness and gentleness. Of all plants surely God made the cactus in his own image? It has my enduring respect and is my passion.' He paused and pointed to the little green plant in the jam tin. '*Kalanchoe thyrsiflora*, such a shy little lady. Two years I search to find her, now she grows happily in my cactus garden where her big ears listen to all the gossip.'

'I'm sure that's all very nice, professor, but what does it all mean?' my mother said. I could see she was confused, not knowing whether, in the end, Doc had praised or blasphemed God.

'My eyes are not so goot. If the boy will come with me to collect cactus specimens, I will teach him music. It is a fine plan, ja? Cactus for Mozart!'

My mother looked pleased, as though a new thought had come into her head. 'His grandmother was very creative, an artist you know. But I don't know if there were any musicians in the family, perhaps Dad will know.' She pointed to the two rose pictures on either side of the bookcase. 'Her work,' she said modestly, 'she only ever painted roses.'

Doc did not turn to look at the pictures. 'When I came in I saw them already, very goot.'

The idea of a musician in the family was clearly to my mother's liking. The Boers are a naturally musical people and any excuse for a gathering brought out the concertinas and guitars and even an occasional violin. In my mother's eyes it was their sole redeeming feature. The idea of a son who played the piano, let alone classical music, was a social triumph of the sort she had never expected to come her way. Even in this largely English-speaking town, a classical piano player in the family was a social equaliser almost as good as money.

I was to learn that the Apostolic Faith Mission, who believed in being born again, baptism by immersion, the gift of speaking in tongues and faith healing, was deemed pretty low on the social scale. Barberton was not the sort of town which encouraged the crying out in prayer or sudden spontaneous religious combustion from the floor of a charismatic church. My mother was constantly fighting the need to remain loyal to the Lord and his religiously garrulous congregation while at the same time aspiring to the ranks of 'nice people'.

Old Pisskop at the piano promised to be the major instrument in balancing the family social scales. The bargain was struck just as Mrs Cameron arrived for her fitting. In return for trekking around the hills as Doc's constant companion, I would receive free piano lessons. I had to work very hard on my camouflage to contain my delight. While I had no concept of what it meant to be musical, from the very beginning pitch and harmony had been a part of my life with Nanny.

The long summer months were spent mostly with Doc, climbing the hills around Barberton. Often we would venture into the dark *kloofs* where the hills formed the deep creases at the start of the true mountains. These green, moist gullies of treefern and tall old yellow wood trees, the branches draped with beard lichen and the vines of wild grape, made a cool, dark contrast to the barren, sun-baked hills of aloe, thorn scrub, rock and coarse grass.

Occasionally, we saw a lone ironwood tree rising magnificently above the canopy. These relics had escaped the axes of the miners who had roamed these hills fifty years before in search of gold. The mountains were dotted with shafts sunk into the hills and mountainside, dark pits and passages supported by timber, which before it was consigned to the tunnels, may have stood for a thousand years.

Doc taught me the names of the flowering plants. The sugarbush with its splashy white blossoms. A patch of brilliant orange-red seen in the distance usually meant wild pomegranate. I learned to differentiate between species of tree fuchsia, to stop and crush the leaves of the camphor bush and breathe its beautiful aromatic smell. I recognised the pale yellow blossoms of wild gardenia and the blooms of the water alder. Monkey rope strung from tall trees draped with club moss was given names such as: traveller's joy, lemon capers, climbing saffron, milk rope and David's roots. Nothing escaped Doc's curiosity and he taught me the priceless lesson of identification. Soon trees and leaves, bush, vine and lichen began to assemble in my mind in a schematic order as he explained the nature of the ecosystems of bush and kloof and high mountain.

'Everything fits, Peekay. Nothing is unexplained. Nature is a chain reaction. One thing follows the other, everything is dependent on something else. The smallest is as important as the largest. See,' he would say, pointing to a tiny vine curled around a sapling, 'that is a stinkwood sapling which can grow thirty metres, but the vine will win and the tree will be choked to death long before it will ever see the sky.'

He would often use an analogy from nature. 'Ja, Peekay, always in life an idea starts small, it is only a sapling idea, but the vines will come and they will try to choke your idea so it cannot grow and it will die and you will never know you had a big idea, an idea so big it could have grown thirty metres through the dark canopy of leaves and touched the face of the sky.' He looked at me and continued, 'The vines are people who are afraid of originality, of new thinking; most people you encounter will be vines, when you are a young plant they are very dangerous.' His piercing blue eyes looked into mine. 'Always listen to yourself, Peekay. It is better to be wrong than simply to follow convention. If you are wrong, no matter, you have learned something and you will grow stronger. If you are right you have taken another step towards a fulfilling life.' He would sigh and squint at me. 'Experts, what did I tell you about experts, Peekay?'

'You can't always go by expert opinion. A chicken, if you ask a chicken, should be stuffed with grasshoppers, mealies and worms.' Even after repeating it a hundred times I still thought it was funny.

Or Doc would show me how a small lick of water trickling from a rock face would, drop by drop, gather round its wet apron fern and then scrub and later trees and vines until the kloof became an interdependent network of plant, insect, bird and animal life. 'Always you should go to the source, to the face of the rock, to the beginning. The more you know, the more you can control your destiny. Man is the only animal who can store knowledge outside his body. This has made him greater than the creatures around him. Everything has happened before, if you know what comes before then you know what happens now. Your brain, Peekay, has two functions; it is a place for original thought, but also it is a reference library, use it to tell you where to look and then you will have for yourself all the brains that have ever been.'

Doc never talked down. Much of what he said would take me years to understand, but I soaked it up nevertheless, storing it in my awkward young mind where it could mature and later come back to me. He taught me to read for meaning and information, to make margin notes and to follow these up with trips to the Barberton library where Mrs Boxall would give a great sigh when the two of us walked in. 'Here come the messpots!' She claimed she had to spend hours erasing the pencilled margin notes in the books we borrowed. Doc once insisted they made the books more valuable and Mrs Boxall arched an eyebrow, 'Written in German and in Kindergarten, Professor?'

Doc shrugged, looking up from his book and removing his gold-rimmed reading glasses. 'Kindergarten, that also is written in German, Madame Boxall.'

But I don't think Mrs Boxall really minded. The books on birds and insects and plants were seldom borrowed by anyone else and besides, as most of the books in the natural history section had once belonged to him, Doc adopted a proprietorial attitude towards the town library. Over the years his tiny cottage had become too small to contain them all and they had been bequeathed to the library which now acted, in Doc's mind anyway, as a bibliographical outpost to his cottage. Doc also taught me Latin roots so I was no longer forced to resort to memory alone and the botanical names of plants began to make sense to me.

We climbed the high *kranses* and the crags in search of cactus and succulents. Towards the end of summer, on the side of a mountain scarred by loose grey shale and tufts of coarse brown grass I stumbled on *Aloe brevifolia*, a tiny thorny aloe.

Doc was overjoyed. 'Gold! Absolute gold!' He jumped into the air and, upon landing, missed his footing on the shaley surface and fell arse over tip down the mountain, coming to a halt just short of a two-hundred-foot drop. He climbed gingerly back, hands bleeding from clutching at the sharp shale, a sheepish grin on his weather-beaten face. But the triumph of the rare find still showed in his excited eyes. '*brevifolia* in these parts, so high, impossible! You are a genius, Peekay. Absoloodle!'

It was the find of the summer and, to Doc, worth all the weary hours spent on the hills and in the mountains. We recorded the find with the camera and removed six of the tiny plants, leaving double that number clinging precariously to the inhospitable mountainside.

Like me, Doc was an early riser, so just after dawn all that summer he gave me piano lessons. 'In one year we will tell, but it is not so important. To love music is everything. First I will teach you to love music, after this slowly we shall learn to play.'

I was anxious to please Doc and worked hard, but I suspect he knew almost from the outset that I wouldn't prove an especially gifted musician. My progress, while superior to that of the small girls he was obliged to teach for a living, indicated a very modest talent. In the years that followed, it was enough to fool my mother and all the big-bosomed matriarchs who ruled the town's important families. At concerts which, I hasten to add, were not in my honour, I represented the cultured element and they would applaud me deliberately and loudly.

These occasions, which occurred in the spring and

autumn, made my mother very proud, though they also represented a compromise with the Lord. Concerts were the devil's work and very much against the Lord's teaching. They were just the sort of thing which, like money-lending, the Lord had clearly condemned when he castigated the Pharisees and Saducees in the temple of Jerusalem. She justified my participation and her attendance by pointing out, to herself mostly, that many of the great classical musicians wrote music for the church.

The Lord's will was equally explicit on drinking and smoking, the bioscope and dancing, except ballet. Ballet was another of the items cherished by the lavender-scented ladies from the town's upper-echelon families, and the ballet performance usually preceded my piano recital. Together they made up the cultural component of the twice-yearly concert. Chopin, by yours truly, and Tchaikovsky's Dance of the Swans by gramophone record, danced to by six-year-old neophytes in white tutus and duckbilled headdresses made of papier mâché.

We were the cultural meat in a popular sandwich otherwise liberally filled with amateur vaudeville acts, solo songs of an Irish nature, single or combined concertina, piano accordion and guitar renditions of well-known Afrikaans folk songs usually performed by the Afrikaner warders from the prison. To redress the racial balance, a Gilbert and Sullivan male quartet would generally follow. One English comic opera song was reckoned by the concert committee to equate roughly with a dozen Afrikaans folk songs no matter how pleasingly syncopated, harmonised, toe tappin' and hand clappin' they might prove to be.

The concert would always end with the All Saints Anglican church choir singing 'White Cliffs of Dover' with the audience joining in. To show the Rooinek majority where their unspoken loyalty lay the warders and their families would leave the town hall prior to the mass rendition of 'White Cliffs'. This would be accompanied by some booing and catcalls from less well-bred members of the remaining audience.

Germany had covertly helped the Boers during the Boer War. Apart from arms and ammunition sold for profit, she had donated food and medical supplies and had even sent medical orderlies and doctors to the harassed Boers who, due to the British scorched earth policy, were dying less from the aim of the British Lee-Metfords than from a land which could no longer feed them. To the Boers, Germany was an old and trusted friend in a country where a contract was a handshake and declared friendship a bond that continued beyond the grave. Anti-Semitism in the Dutch Reformed Church, where Jews were thought of as Christ-killers, had always existed and the concept of the superiority of some races over others was never for one moment in doubt. In this context, to many Boers Adolf Hitler was only doing his job and, to some minds, doing it damn well.

After the warders and other Nazi-sympathisers had walked out the remainder of the audience would stand up, lock arms and sing 'White Cliffs of Dover' at least twice to confirm doubly their love for a Britain facing her darkest hour. To bring the concert to a tearful close the concert party, with warders and other Afrikaners missing, would gather on the stage, each of us holding a long-stemmed rose delivered earlier by me as a sign of our family's inherent good breeding. With the misty-eyed audience fresh from the mawkishly sentimental journey to a country most of us would never see, we stood to rigid attention while a scratchy 78 r.p.m. rendered 'God Save the King'. Whereupon the cast hurled the long-stemmed roses into the audience.

My granpa, my mother and I then walked home, having politely refused the Mayor's invitation to the traditional post-concert party for the cast at the Phoenix Hotel. Worldly parties typified by one such as this, where drinking, smoking and dancing took place, were pretty high up on the Lord's banned list.

The next issue of the *Goldfields News* would report the

concert with the warder walkout splashed across the front page. Tongues wagged for days. Important people suggested the military be brought in to wipe out this nest of Nazi vipers or that the prison be moved to Nelspruit, an Afrikaans town forty miles away, where most of the prisoners probably came from in the first place.

My granpa, with his experience in fighting the Boers, had once been canvassed for his opinion by Mr Hankin, the editor of the *Goldfields News*. But they didn't print what he said. What he said was: 'I spent most of the Boer War shitting my breeches as a stretcher bearer. The only thing those buggers do better than music is shoot. Without them the concert wouldn't be worth a cardboard boot.'

Maybe Mr Hankin thought his newspaper gave the family enough publicity, because he never again asked my granpa for his opinion on anything, even though the prison warders did the same thing at every concert for the duration of the war. Mrs Boxall, who was the town's correspondent on matters cultural, could always be relied on to devote most of her column, 'Clippings from a Cultured Garden by Fiona Boxall', to my performance. For days after it appeared my mother was in a state of dazed euphoria and I was conscripted to deliver a bunch of roses to the library twice a week for a month.

In the process of keeping faith with my mother, Doc instilled in me an abiding love for music. What my clumsy hands could never play I could hear quite clearly in my head. A love of music was, among his many gifts to me, perhaps the most important of them all, and he continued to teach me even after his calm and gentle life was thrown into turmoil, and the joy of being alone with him on the high cliffs and kranses was stolen from my childhood.

TEN

I had been enrolled at the local school when the new term began at the end of January. Six was the starting age for Grade One, but after a few days it was clear that my year spent in a mixed-age class at boarding school had put me well ahead of the rest of the kids. I was pushed up to Grade Three where I easily held my own against kids two years older than me. Doing the Judge's arithmetic, my early grounding in reading, a comprehensive understanding of Afrikaans in a classroom of English-speaking kids coming without enthusiasm to the language for the first time, and Doc's demand from our first day that I write up my field notes all gave me a hugely unfair advantage. I might possibly have been elevated even further but for the embarrassment it would have caused.

I quickly earned a reputation, rather unjustly, for being clever. Doc had persuaded me to drop my camouflage and not to play dumb. 'To be smart is not a sin. But to be smart and not use it, that, Peekay, is a sin. Absoloodle!' I had needed little encouragement. Under his direction my mind was constantly hungry, and I soon found the school work tedious and simplistic. Doc became my real teacher and school was simply time spent between eight and one o'clock when I would rush from the classroom to his cottage hidden in the cactus garden.

His thorny garden was a never-ending source of delight. It was half an acre on the more or less flat top of a small hill which overlooked the town and valley. A ten-minute climb to solitude, up a little dirt and rock road that led nowhere else. His cactus garden may well have been the best private collection of cacti and succulents in the world. I, who grew to be an expert on cacti, have never seen a better one.

Doc's cottage had three rooms and a lean-to kitchen. The three rooms were called the music room, the book room and the whisky room. Each having its specified purpose, music, study and drinking himself to sleep. For in all things, even in drunkenness, Doc had a tidy mind.

In the first year we spent together I never once witnessed him drunk, though when I arrived just after dawn for my music lesson I often had to wake him, whereupon he would stumble outside to retch and cough. Then he would come to sit beside the Steinway, his blue eyes red-rimmed and dulled from the previous night's whisky, his long fingers wrapped around the enamel mug of bitter black coffee I had made him on the Primus. Doc never talked about drinking. All he would sometimes say as I set my music out on the big Steinway was, 'Pianissimo, Peekay, the wolves were howling in my head last night.' I would look through my music for something soft and easy on the nerves. Perhaps this is why, as I grew older and more proficient, I seemed more attracted to playing Chopin. There is a great deal less fortissimo in a Chopin *étude* than in Liszt or Brahms and Doc's early morning hangovers may, over that first year, have somehow inclined me to softer music.

It was the cactus garden which testified to 'his problem with Doctor Bottle', as my mother would call any person who ever held strong drink to their lips. Bordering both sides of the path for a hundred yards through the cactus garden were embedded Johnny Walker bottles, their square bases shining in the sun like parallel silver snakes winding around the cactus and aloe and blazing orange and pink portulaca. Each bottle represented an attempt to obviate some private torture. Doc made no apology for his drinking. He seldom even mentioned it and when he did it was always blamed quietly and politely on the wolves, which I imagined slavering away, great red tongues lolling, gnashing teeth chomping up Doc's brains.

It was at sunset on a Saturday afternoon late in January 1941, a little more than a year after Doc and I had first met on the hill behind the rose garden. We'd spent the day in the hills and had almost arrived back at Doc's cottage. We'd found a patch of *Senecio serpens* high up in a dry kloof, growing over the tailings of an old digging. It was a nice find although blue chalksticks, as they are commonly called, are not too rare unless they flower in an unusual colour. We had decided to plant them in the cactus garden and wait until they flowered again. That was the magic of the cactus garden, some succulents can play dumb; a common blue chalkstick can turn from a Cinderella into a princess in front of your very eyes. I was the first to notice the army van with the white-stencilled Military Police on its hood. The van was parked directly in front of the whisky bottle path which led to the cottage, hidden from view amongst the tall cactus. Two men leaned against the front mudguard smoking, their red-banded khaki caps resting on the hood of the van which had been turned to face down the hill. Doc was explaining the differences between the genus *Senecio serpens* and the lighter-coloured *Glottiphyllym uncatum*, banging his long hiking stick into the ground as he walked and getting generally excited as he did when his mind was absorbed in esoteric botanical detail.

The two men saw us approach, and dropping their cigarettes ground them underfoot. Clearing their throats almost simultaneously, they reached for their caps, carefully placed them back on their heads the way men do when they are about to undertake an unpleasant duty. Both wore khaki bush shirts, shorts, brown boots, puttees and khaki stockings, though one of them wore the polished Sam Browne belt of an officer while the other, a sergeant, wore a white webbing one. The officer stepped right in front of Doc who stopped and looked up in surprise. Doc was taller than the officer by at least a foot, so the military man was obliged to look up at him. He had a thin black pencil moustache just like Pik Botha, and although he was not standing to attention his body seemed permanently rigid. From the top pocket of his tunic he removed a piece of paper which he held up.

'Good afternoon, sir. You are Karl Von Vollensteen, Professor Karl Von Vollensteen?' he asked in a sententious voice.

'Ja, this is me,' Doc said, surprised that anyone would question so obvious a fact.

The officer cleared his throat and proceeded to read from the paper he held in front of him. 'Under the Aliens Act of 1939 and by the authority vested in me by the Provost Marshal of the South African Armed Forces, I arrest you. You are charged with conspiracy to undermine the security of a nation at war.' He handed the paper to Doc. 'You will have to come with me, sir. The civilian police, under the direction of military security, will search your premises and you will be detained at Barberton prison until your case can be heard.'

To my surprise Doc made no protest. His face was sad as he looked down at the officer and handed him back the piece of paper without even glancing at it. He raised his head to look over the officer and past where the sergeant was standing next to the van, his gaze following the line of the cactus garden. He turned slowly, his eyes filled with pain, taking in the hills, the marvellous aloe-dotted hills, his garden of Eden for twenty years in the Africa he so savagely loved. Finally he turned to look over the town, across the valley to the sun beginning to dip behind the escarpment.

'The stupidity. Already the stupidity begins again,' he said softly, then turning to me he patted my shoulder. 'You must plant the *Senecio serpens* to get the morning sun, they like that.' He removed his bush hat and absent-mindedly put it on the roof of the van. He got his red bandanna from his overalls and slowly wiped his face and sniffed into it and pushed his nose around before returning it to the pocket of his overalls. Then he lifted his bush hat from the roof of the van and put it on my head. I looked up at him in surprise, Doc didn't play that sort of childish game. But his eyes were sad and his voice soft, barely above a whisper. 'So, now you are the boss of the cactus garden, Peekay.' I wanted to cry and I think Doc wanted to as well. But we didn't. We both knew enough not to show our feelings in front of the military.

Turning to the officer, Doc said, 'You will please allow me first to shave and change my clothes. A man must go to prison in his best clothes.'

The officer rolled his eyes heavenwards. From the number of cigarette butts on the ground they had been waiting for some time and he obviously wanted to get going. 'Orright, professor, but make it snappy.' Turning to the sergeant in an official manner he rapped, 'Sergeant! Escort the prisoner to his house for kit change and ablutions.'

We walked slowly down the whisky bottle path and Doc dropped his canvas shoulder bag on the open verandah. I followed him into the dark little cottage. 'Do not light the lamps, Peekay, the light is soft and we will soon be gone.' I followed him to the lean-to kitchen where he placed an enamel basin on the hard earth floor and poured water into it from a jug. I took the jug and refilled it from the rainwater tank behind the cottage. Doc's cottage, isolated from the town by the small hill, had no running water. He stripped down in the lean-to kitchen and using a loofah washed himself from head to toe. I brought him the fresh jug of water and, stepping out of the lean-to into the garden, he stood beside a tall cactus and poured it over his head, giving the cactus the benefit of the over-flow. Then he wiped himself briskly with an almost threadbare towel. He was brown all over, for we often lay on a rock in the hills to sun ourselves after a swim in a mountain creek. His thin body was hard and sinewy and the snowy-white hair on his chest seemed incongruous. I had seen my granpa nude and while he too was a thin man, he didn't have the same hard-as-nails look.

The sergeant had grown impatient waiting around the kitchen and had wandered into the music room where he was playing chopsticks on the Steinway. Doc seemed not to hear as he shaved carefully, stropping his cut-throat razor for ages until it was perfect. Then he dressed slowly in his white linen suit and black boots. Finally he placed a spare shirt and his shaving things in a sugar bag, and walking through to the book room he selected a large book from the very top shelf of one of the bookshelves which he had constructed from bricks and pineboard planks. 'Put it also in the bag, Peekay.' I took the large leather-bound volume from him and looked at the spine. It was an old book whose maroon leather binding was scuffed and mottled with rough brown leather spots showing through the once smooth and polished cover. The title embossed on the spine was hard to read as the gold had mostly worn away leaving only the pale embossing. It read, '*Cactaceae. Afrika und Amerika. K. J. Von Vollensteen.*' I opened the heavy book to find that it was written in German. I walked into the whisky room where Doc had left the sugar bag, and using the edge of the blanket on the small, hard bed I wiped the dust from the cover of the book and put it in the bag. On the packing case dresser next to the bed was half a bottle of Johnny Walker and this too I put in the bag. Then heaving it over my shoulder I joined Doc who was standing at the front door. He removed his panama hat from a hook on the wall and picked up his silver-handled walking stick leaning in the corner behind the door. 'We are ready, sir,' he said, turning slowly to the sergeant a few feet away in the music room.

The sergeant rose from the piano stool. 'That's a blêrrie good peeana you got there, professor. Once in the bioscope I saw this fillim star dance on the top of a peeana just like this one, only it was all white. I think it was Greeta Garbo but I'm not sure.' He took a last look around the cottage,

'Okay man, let's go.' He took the sugar bag from my shoulder and looked into it. 'Hey, what's this? You can't take whisky where you going, are you stupid or something?' I started to apologise, but he checked me with his hand and grinned. 'If you like we can have a quick spot now, *oubaas*?' he said to Doc. 'Who knows when you'll get another chance hey?' He gave him a conspiratorial wink and uncorked the bottle. Raising it to his lips, he took a long drag of whisky. He winced as he withdrew the bottle from his mouth, then wiped his mouth with the back of his hand and the top of the bottle with the palm of his hand. 'Lekker, man, that's blêrrie good whisky! No use leaving it lying around hey?' He handed the bottle to Doc who raised his hand in refusal. 'C'mon don't be stupid, man. It's going to be a long time between drinks, better make the most of it.' He held it towards Doc after taking another long swig. In two goes he had reduced the whisky to less than a quarter of a bottle. Doc took the bottle of Johnny Walker and held it briefly to his lips without opening his mouth before handing it back. The sergeant shrugged. 'Suit yourself, man, all the more for me, it's blêrrie good whisky. Who knows? Tomorrow maybe we're all dead.' He took another long swig and walked over to the piano. 'In this fillim this man was playing the peeana like at a funeral, then a drunk tipped some whisky on it and suddenly it was playing like mad.' He tipped the remaining whisky over the keys of the Steinway. Doc, who had been standing passively waiting, seemed to come alive. He raised his stick and rushed at the sergeant.

'*Schweinhund* Do not defile the instrument of Beethoven, Brahms, Bach and Liszt!' He brought his cane down hard onto the sergeant's wrist and the bottle fell from his hand to smash on the cement floor. Gripping his wrist, the sergeant danced in agony amongst the broken glass. Doc, using the sleeve of his linen jacket, ran his arms across the keys in an attempt to wipe them and sent the piano into a glissando. Then he turned and walked towards the front door.

'You fucking Nazi bastard!' the sergeant yelled. I hurried after Doc and he caught up with us on the path outside the cottage. 'I'll show you, you child fucker!' He was trying to remove a pair of handcuffs from his belt as he ran. 'Stop! You're under military arrest!' But Doc, his head held high, simply continued down the path towards the van. The sergeant grabbed Doc's arm and clicked a handcuff around his compliant wrist. Doc seemed hardly to notice and just kept walking, obliging the sergeant to hang onto the other handcuff as though he were being dragged along like a prisoner. He took a swinging kick at Doc, knocking his legs from under him and bringing the old man to his knees on the path. In his fury and humiliation he aimed a second kick just as, screaming, I flung myself at his legs. The army boot intended for Doc's ribs caught me under the chin knocking me unconscious.

I awoke in Barberton Hospital with a man in a white coat shining a torch into my eyes. My head was ringing as though voices came from the other end of a long tunnel. 'Well, thank God for that, he's regained consciousness,' I heard him say.

'Thank you, Jesus,' I heard my mother say in a weepy voice. I looked around to see her seated at the side of the bed. She looked pale and worried and her hair hung in wisps around her eyes for she had come out without her hat and still wore her pink sewing smock. My granpa was also there, sitting on a chair at the opposite side of the bed. I tried to talk but found it impossible and my jaw hurt like billy-o. I managed a weak grunt without opening my mouth, but that was all. My mouth tasted of blood and, running my swollen tongue around my palate, I realised that several of my teeth were missing.

The doctor spoke to me. 'Now son, I want you to tell me how many fingers I'm holding up in front of you.' He held up two and I held up two fingers. 'Again.' He held up four fingers and I too held up four. He repeated this with several combinations before he finally said, 'Well, that's something anyway, he doesn't appear to have concussion. We'll have to X-ray the jaw, though I think it's probably broken.' He turned to my mother and granpa. 'The boy is in a lot of pain, we'll be taking him into theatre almost immediately, we may need to wire his jaw and there are several broken teeth which we will have to clean up. He'll be sedated when he comes out so there isn't any point in your staying.'

They both rose and my mother leaned over and kissed me on the forehead. 'We'll see you tomorrow morning, darling. You be a brave boy now!' My granpa touched me lightly on the shoulder. 'There's a good lad,' he said.

I watched them leave the emergency ward where I appeared to be the only emergency, as the other three beds were unoccupied. My jaw ached a great deal and while I think I may have been crying, I only recall being terribly concerned for Doc.

It turned out my jaw had been broken. They wired the top jaw to the bottom one in the closed mouth position so I was unable to talk. I couldn't enquire about him. Adults decide what they want kids to know and all my mother would say when she came to visit was, 'You've had a terrible shock, darling, you mustn't think about what happened.'

In fact, that was all I could think about. Doc was the most important person in my life and the thought of him lying in a dark cell probably dying was almost unbearable. I managed to communicate to a junior nurse called Marie, who had taken to calling me her little *skattebol*, that I wanted paper and a pencil. She brought a pad and a pencil and in running writing I wrote, 'What's happened to Professor Von Vollensteen?' She read the note and her eyes grew large.

'Ag no, man! Sister says we can't tell you nothing.' She held out her hand for the pad and pencil but I quickly tucked it under the quilt. 'Give it to me back! Please, I'll get into trouble with Sister!' I shook my head, which hurt. 'I'll tell on you, you hear!' But I knew she wouldn't. I felt less vulnerable with the pad and pencil beside me. I tore a single sheet from the small pad and brought it out from under the bedclothes. Placing it on the cabinet beside my bed, I leaned over and wrote, 'My name is not skattebol, it is PEEKAY.' I didn't much like the endearment as I didn't see myself as a fluffy ball which is a name you give to really small kids. I tore the bit I'd written on from the sheet of paper and handed it to her. She read it slowly then walked to the end of the bed.

'That's not what it says here,' Marie said, looking down at the progress chart which hung from the foot of the bed. 'Don't you know your proper name then?' she teased. 'It's wrong,' I scribbled, tearing off a second note and holding it out to her. 'Sis, man! You don't even know your own name. I never heard of a name like Peekay, where'd you get a silly name like that?' On the remaining scrap of paper I wrote, 'I just got it.'

Marie took a sharp breath. 'Anyway, it's a rotten name for a hero who tackled a German spy when he was trying to escape.' Her eyes grew big again and she moved her spotty face close to mine. 'It says in the paper you even maybe going to get a medal!' She drew back suddenly, alarmed that she'd told me too much. 'Don't you tell Sister I told you, you hear.' She brought a finger up to her lips, 'I promise I'll call you Peekay if you promise to stay *stom*.' I nodded my head, though I wondered how she thought I could tell anyone. The tears began to roll down my cheeks. I hadn't wanted them to, they just came because of the news about Doc. I could hear his voice when the officer had handed him the piece of paper. 'The stupidity. Already the stupidity begins again.'

'Don't cry, Peekay. Sister'll know I told you if you cry,' Marie said, distressed. I knuckled the tears from my eyes and then she bathed my face with a wet flannel. 'I don't really think Peekay is a silly name,' she said gently. 'Who showed you how to write so good? I went to school up to fourteen and even I can't write so good as you.'

After three days alone in the ward I was moved onto the

verandah where there were eight beds all occupied. Except for the fact that I still couldn't talk, I was much better. I had walked into the ward with the sister and with the exception of two old men who were asleep, all the others had applauded and said things like, 'Well done, son!' One man said that I was a proper patriot. As soon as Sister left the ward I wrote on a piece of paper as big as I could, 'What happened to Professor Von Vollensteen?' I jumped out of bed and took it over to the bed nearest me and gave it to the man in it. He read it and handed it back to me.

'You mean the German spy? Sorry, son, we're not supposed to tell you,' he winked at the others, 'we got strict orders.' The others all nodded. 'Mind you, you're a brave little bugger, I have to say that for you.' The other men seemed to agree with him.

My mother came to the hospital in the mornings when Pastor Mulvery was able to bring her. She sat with me while he went around the hospital to witness for the Lord. But first he came in to see me, and he'd flash his lightning smile which prevented his two front teeth from escaping and held my hand in his damp, warm grasp for ages until it felt as though it wanted to jump out of his soft grip and run away and hide. In his soft woman's voice he said, 'We're all praying that this terrible ordeal will make you accept Jesus into your heart.' Then, still holding my hand, he knelt beside the bed and my mother also knelt on the other side and Pastor Mulvery would pray out aloud. When he prayed his voice rose even higher and he became quite excited.

He would start with a few random 'Hallelujahs' and my mother would respond with 'Praise His name! Praise His precious name!' And Pastor Mulvery would say, 'Lord, we are gathered here in Your precious name to pray for this poor child.' 'Amen,' my mother would say. 'In his terrible affliction, show him the path to salvation. Oh precious Redeemer who died on the cross so we might be free.' 'Hallelujah, praise the Lord,' my mother would answer.

'Son, open your heart to Jesus, accept Him into your life. Lord, do not condemn him to the terrible fires of hell, grant him everlasting life with your glorious salvation.' 'Hallelujah, blessed be His name!' 'Bring your sin to Jesus, son, lay it at His feet so that He may grant you His precious redemption. Precious Jesus, answer our prayers, open his young heart, let him see you in all your glory. Lord, we pray for this child's soul, we earnestly beseech you to bring him from darkness to the light, from the inky black of the stone tomb on Golgotha into the glorious morning of the resurrection of our sweet Jesus Christ!' 'Yes Jesus! Precious Jesus!' my mother would be saying on her side of the bed. And so it would go every morning.

Not long after I'd first met Doc, we were sitting on our rock on the hill behind the rose garden and I had asked him why I was a sinner and what I had done to be condemmed to eternal hell fire unless I was born again.

He sat for a long time looking over the valley and then he said, 'Peekay, God is too busy making the sun come up and go down and watching so the moon floats just right in the sky to be concerned with such rubbish. Only man wants always God should be there to condemn this one and save that one. Always it is man who wants to make heaven and hell. God is too busy training the bees to make honey and every morning opening up all the new flowers for business.' He paused and smiled. 'In Mexico there is a cactus that even sometimes you would think God forgets. But no my friend, this is not so. On a full moon in the desert every one hundred years he remembers and he opens up a single flower to bloom. And if you should be there and you see this beautiful cactus blossom painted silver by the moon and laughing up at the stars, this, Peekay, is heaven.' He looked at me, his deep blue eyes sharp and penetrating. 'This is the faith in God the cactus has.' We had sat for a while before he spoke again. 'It is better just to get on with the business of living and minding your own business and maybe, if God likes the way you do things, he may just let you flower for a day or a night. But don't go pestering and begging and telling Him all your stupid little sins, that way you will spoil His day. Absoloodle.'

I still sometimes got a bit scared about going to hell and I used to think quite a lot about being born again. But my heart didn't want to open up and receive the Lord. All the people I knew who had opened up their hearts to Jesus struck me as a pretty pathetic lot, not bad, not good, just nothing. I couldn't afford to be just nothing when I was aiming to be the welterweight champion of the world. I guess my mother was right when she said if I kept rejecting the Lord and hardening my heart one day He might just go away and leave me to it. That's what must have happened because after a while it got a lot easier and I didn't worry as much. I decided I liked Doc's God a lot more than my mother's and Pastor Mulvery's and Pik Botha's and all the people who loved Jesus at the Apostolic Faith Mission. Jesus, who was God's dearly beloved son, seemed to be in charge of things there. He seemed to be very keen on saving souls and had actually died for their sins, but I couldn't help feeling it may have been a bit of a waste. Still, they seemed pretty grateful because they spoke a lot more about Jesus than about God. Jesus was definitely number one at the Apostolic Faith Mission.

Later I was to learn that there was a third party involved called the Holy Ghost who spoke in tongues of invisible fire and he gave people a thing called 'the gift of tongues'. When he did this, people would jump up in prayer meetings and wave their arms around and shake a lot with their eyes closed. They never seemed to bump into anything either, it was quite uncanny. And they'd babble away and sing, using strange words. I'd try to do it afterwards but it never sounded right. It was a gift all right.

A visiting pastor from the Assembly of God Church in America told us once when we were having a revival week that he had definite proof that a woman who had never been out of her small town in America spoke in Swahili when the Holy Ghost entered into her. There was a missionary from Africa who understood Swahili present in the same small church in America and she'd understood every word. He didn't tell us what she said, but he said there were lots of cases like this and that he'd personally witnessed quite a few. I had listened from then on but nobody in the Apostolic Faith Mission ever spoke Zulu or Shangaan. Maybe Zulu and Shangaan weren't exotic enough for the Holy Ghost. I wondered what was so special about Swahili.

Pastor Mulvery got up from beside the hospital bed and gave me a flash smile and said that Jesus loved me anyway. Then he trotted off with the Bible under one arm and a handful of tracts to visit all the other patients and my mother called him a precious man and stayed with me.

After I got the pad I wrote her a long note asking her about Doc. She took it and without reading it, asked, 'Is this about the Professor?' Her lips were drawn tight as I nodded. Then she scrunched the note in her hand. 'I don't want you ever to mention his name again, do you hear? He is an evil man who used you to cover up the terrible things he was doing and then he nearly killed you.' There were sudden tears in her eyes. 'The doctor says, if he had caught you on the side of the head he would have killed you! Another three inches and you would have been dead. You've been through a terrible experience and I've prayed and prayed the Lord will make you forget it so you are not scarred for life.' She wiped her eyes and blew her nose.

'No! No!' I forced myself to say. What came out was sort of two squeaks from the back of my throat which forced their way past my bruised and swollen tongue and out of my clamped mouth. I started to cry silently without wanting to in front of my mother. They were blaming Doc for what had happened to me and I was the only one who knew the truth and I couldn't help him. It was my fault anyway. If I hadn't put the bottle of Johnny Walker in his sugar bag this never would have happened. Doc, whom I loved so dearly, had become another Pisskop victim. This time it was much worse than a nervous breakdown.

My mother had stopped sniffing when she saw my tears. 'You poor little mite, you've been through a terrible time. We'll never talk about it again. Mrs Boxall from the library has asked to come and see you but the doctor and I have agreed that you're not well enough to have visitors.' She opened her bag and withdrew a green folded card. 'Now I have some good news for you. Your report card came and you came first in your class. Your granpa and I are very proud of you.' She beamed at me, her tears forgotten. 'They've put you up another two classes, you're going to be in with the ten-year-olds. Fancy that, seven and in with the ten-year-olds!' She handed the report card to me and through my tears I took it and tore it into four pieces. For a long time my mother said nothing, looking down at the pieces of green cardboard in my lap. Finally she gave a deep sigh. I hated her sighs the most because they made me feel terribly guilty. 'The Lord has blessed you with a good brain. I pray every day that you will take Him into your heart and use your fine mind to glorify His precious name.' She gathered the pieces up and dropped them into her handbag, giving me a sort of squiffy smile. 'I'm sure it can be mended, you are just not your old cheerful self at present, are you?' But her eyes weren't smiling as she spoke.

That afternoon I wrote a note to Mrs Boxall at the library. All it said was, 'Please come! In the afternoon,' and I signed it. I also wrote a note for Marie asking her if she would take the note to Mrs Boxall at the Barberton public library. Marie had switched mid-week to night duty and came on at six p.m. with our dinner. I handed her the note. She read it and quickly hid it in the pocket of her white starched junior nurse's uniform. She picked up my dinner tray from the trolley and brought it over to me.

'I'll only do it if it's got nothing to do with that spy,' she whispered as she put my tray down in front of me. I handed her the second note. She gave me a suspicious look as she took it. 'I got to read it first before I say I'll do it.' She read the note and seemed assured by its contents. 'I've got my day off tomorrow, I'll do it then. Now promise you'll eat your pumpkin, you left it last night and also your peas.' She seated herself on the side of the bed and, taking up a teaspoon, she filled it with pumpkin and put it through the hole in the corner of my mouth. I had lost four top and bottom teeth on the same side where the sergeant's boot had landed, and Marie called it my 'feeding hole'. She was the best of anyone at getting the mashed food they were beginning to give me through the hole without making my gums bleed.

I spent the rest of the evening writing for Mrs Boxall a long, detailed description of what had happened. Doc, when I presented him with my botanical notes, would always stress that a botanist is concerned with detail. 'Observation is what makes a scientist,' he said. 'It is only by seeing things in minute detail that we learn their secrets. Others can walk past a plant for a whole life and never even notice the colour of its blossoms, but the botanist knows every beat of its heart and turning of petal.' And so I wrote it all down just the way it happened, even the swear-words, and then I hid the three sheets of paper in my pillowslip. Mrs Boxall came the very next afternoon. In her string bag she carried a new *William* book by Richmal Crompton, a book called *Flowers from the banks of the Zambesi* by Revd William Barton of the London Missionary Society and three copies of *National Geographic*. 'You are such a precocious child, Peekay, I hope they suit your catholic taste.' Like Doc, Mrs Boxall never talked down to me. With the result that I didn't always understand her and wondered what the Catholics might have to do with my taste.

I withdrew my notes from inside the pillow and handed them to Mrs Boxall. 'Well now, pray, what have we here?' she said, taking the three pages and reaching into her bag for her glasses. She read for a long time and then read the three pages again before looking up at me. 'Remarkable! You are a remarkable child. This comes just in time. A military court is being convened next week and things are looking pretty grim for our professor, my dear. The whole jolly town is up in arms about him. People are seeing Jerries in their chamberpots.' She chuckled at her own joke. 'I tried to see him in prison but those dreadful Boers said only authorised people could see him. If a librarian isn't an authorised person then who is, I ask you? But the stupid warder at the gate wouldn't budge. I've started a petition in the library but so far I only have twelve signatures and three of them are Boers and we all know where their sympathies lie, do we not? That dreadful little man, Georgie Hankin, has threatened to say some perfectly ghastly things about me in *Goldfields News* and has told me privately that, if I persist, he can't have a Nazi-sympathiser writing a column in his newspaper. Honestly, you'd think it was *The Times* of London the way he carries on about that dreadful little rag!' She paused, dug once more into her string bag and withdrew a copy of the *Goldfields News*. Taking up almost half the front page was Doc's picture of me sitting on the rock. Above the picture in huge black letters it said, THE BOY HE TRIED TO KILL! Just above the headline and below the masthead was written Special Spy Edition. Under the picture the caption read, Like Abraham's biblical sacrifice of Isaac, the innocent boy waits on the rock. No doubt Georgie Hankin, who as usual had it all wrong, saw this as his finest professional hour.

Doc's arrest had occurred just in time for the weekly edition which appeared on a Monday. It carried the original news of the arrest and this special two-page mid-week edition, using precious rationed newsprint, was an attempt by Mr Hankin to achieve immortality in his profession. The reason Mrs Boxall hadn't been able to visit me was because Dr Simpson, in resisting Georgie and his photographer's attempts to come and see me, had banned all visitors. She was surprised that I hadn't seen the earlier paper and promised to bring it the following afternoon, though as a trained librarian she had little trouble verbally reproducing the essence and the flavour of Monday's big story.

The essence of the story reported in the *News* was that the Provost officer and his sergeant had waited most of the afternoon for Doc to arrive. When he appeared with a small boy in tow, he was in a dishevelled state and it was obvious to the two military policemen that he had been drinking. The sergeant, on the orders of the officer, escorted him back to his cottage to allow him to clean up. Whereupon, when his back was turned, Doc attacked the sergeant with a heavy metal-topped walking stick and attempted to run for the hills. It was pointed out that Doc knew the hills well and would easily be able to conceal himself indefinitely in one of the hundreds of disused mine shafts dotted all through the mountains. He would then make his way across the mountains to Lourenço Marques, the nearest neutral territory.

The story had gone on to say that the sergeant was stunned from the blows he had received and it looked as though Doc would make good his escape had it not been for me who had bravely tackled him. Hearing my scream, the officer had rushed down the path just in time to see Doc take a vicious kick at my head. The officer arrested the suspected spy at the point of his pistol.

The editorial went on to point out that Doc was a noted photographer, and that under the guise of photographing cactus he had undoubtedly taken pictures of likely enemy landing places and established landmarks and mine shafts for storing food and weapons for enemy spies infiltrating South Africa from Portuguese territory. The paper pointed out that there were no pictures to be found of such places, confirming that they had already reached the enemy and that no clever spy would leave such incriminating evidence around. Fortuitously, inside the expensive German Leica camera the spy had used that very afternoon was exposed film of a hole in the mountainside, with the ore tailings dug from the mine heaped directly outside the shaft making it an ideal defensive position. In Doc's notepad had been found a compass bearing and exact location of the disused mine. There had also been several pictures of a succulent, which proved how cunning and careful to cover up Doc had been.

The picture was, of course, the site where we had found *Senecio serpens*, the blue chalksticks. The remainder of the exposed pictures on Doc's film had been of the succulent. Doc, as he had taught me to do, always established the location of a find, the direction of the prevailing winds, by studying the bush and larger plants in the immediate area, the soil conditions and the surrounding rock types.

To the rumour-happy folk of Barberton it was all very feasible and few of them paused long enough to examine the evidence or to question the town's fifteen-year relationship with Doc. Mrs Boxall said people were going around saying, 'Once a Jerry always a Jerry!' satisfied that this covered a multitude of sins. 'Goodness, Peekay, I'd suspect my dear old father before I'd suspect the professor. He doesn't have a patriotic bone in his body unless it's for Africa and has something to do with cactus.' She folded my notes carefully and placed them in her handbag. 'Oh dear, I nearly forgot, I brought you a bag of gob-stoppers. Oh my goodness!' she said in an alarmed voice. 'I'd quite forgotten about your jaw, what an idiot I am.' She dropped the rock-hard candy into her bag and clipped it shut and leaned over and touched me on the chin. 'Chin up, old chap, we've got all the evidence we need to get our mutual friend out of trouble. I'll get back tomorrow with the news.' She was gone, her sensible brogue shoes clattering on the polished cement floor, her back straight as a ramrod and her bobbed head held high. I could hear her still clattering down the verandah long after she was out of sight.

For the first time in a week I felt happy. Mrs Boxall was not the sort to be trifled with and I had every confidence that she'd sort things out. She was Doc's friend and mine as well and as Doc had so often said, 'This woman, she is not a fool, Peekay.'

But I didn't see Mrs Boxall the next day. Somehow my mother had heard of her visit and had seen Dr Simpson who brought down a ban on visitors again. I had begun to make semi-intelligent sounds through my wired jaw and Marie, after a few trial sessions, had little trouble understanding me. She said she had a little brother who was a bit wonky in the head and I sounded a lot like him, which made it easy for her to understand me. It was nice to talk to someone again and it was Marie who told me about my mother's visit to Dr Simpson which she overheard while she was in the dispensary. My mother said nothing to me the morning after she had visited the doctor and I was once again cut off without any news. Marie also told me that I would be going home on Tuesday and she was quite sad about it. She was fifteen years old and came from a farm in the valley. She only got one weekend a month off to go home. She lived in the nurses' home while all the other juniors lived in town. She wasn't very pretty or very clever and she had pimples, which she called her 'terrible spots', so she didn't have any friends. I told her I was her friend and if she liked she could come into the hills with me. She seemed a bit worried about that and said girls weren't supposed to go climbing hills, but she'd like to come anyway.

On the Monday evening she came into the ward and put a large brown paper bag on the bed. She brought a finger to her lips, signalling for me to say nothing. 'Mrs Boxall brought it to the nurses' home, she says it's the latest on you know what,' she whispered, thrilled to be a part of the conspiracy but also frightened. Though later when she was feeding me, she said, 'I did nothing wrong, did I? I just brought in this brown paper packet, that's all. It's only polite to do people a favour, isn't it?'

I had looked into the paper bag which, at first glance, seemed to contain nothing but bananas, but under the bananas was a tightly folded newspaper and a letter from Mrs Boxall. After lights out I stuffed both into my pyjama jacket and walked down the corridor to the lavatories. Taking the letter out, I began to read. It was written in Mrs Boxall's neat librarian's hand.

Dear Peekay,

Much news from the war zone. I have been to see Mr Andrews. He is the lawyer who comes into the library and only takes out books on birds. He read your notes and he said, 'By Jove! This places a different complexion on everything.' He seemed very hopeful that he could get to the military judge when he arrives from Pretoria next Wednesday. He agrees with me your notes are excellent. 'Too good,' he said, 'who will believe a seven-year-old can express himself in such detail?'

Well, my dear, that's the problem he thinks we may have. He knows about your inability to speak. But he's hit on a clever plan. He wants you to take an intelligence test, a written test in front of the judge so the judge can make up his own mind. Mr Andrews has been to see your mother but she won't hear of your having anything to do with the case. But she did say she'd pray about it so all is not lost. It's a bit of a problem really, but we're not beaten yet. I'm sure God is on our side and not on the side of Georgie Hankin or the military. British justice will come through in the end, even if we have to write personally to Mr Winston Churchill.

Can you come and see me when you get out of hospital? Keep your chin up!

Yours sincerely,
Fiona Boxall
Librarian

I wondered what sort of test the judge would give me. What if I failed and let Doc down? What if the Lord didn't give my mother permission for me to see the judge?

But the Lord, with a little help from Mr Andrews who came from one of the oldest and most important families in town, came out in favour of my being a witness at the hearing. The lawyer had pointed out that it was very much in my mother's interests to clear our family name as the prattle tongues in town might well accuse her of neglect for having allowed me to roam the hills with a German spy.

I was released from hospital on Tuesday and on the following morning Mrs Boxall called round in Charlie, her little Austin Seven, to pick me up and take me down to the magistrates' court where the military tribunal was to be held. Mr Andrews was waiting for us and so, to my surprise, was Marie.

'She seems to be the only one who can understand you, Peekay, so we've brought her along as interpreter. It was my idea and a good one, even if I say so myself,' Mrs Boxall declared. Marie was dressed in a freshly starched nurse's uniform and looked even more scared than I felt.

Mr Andrews left us and we had to wait a long while, sitting on a bench in the waiting room. Finally, he came back and said the judge would see us privately in the magistrates' chambers and, depending on how things went, I wouldn't be required as a witness.

None of this made very much sense to me but we had to walk down a long corridor of cork lino that smelt of floor wax. A lady with a trolley full of teacups went rattling past us and she stared at me. I was not yet used to people seeing me with my jaw wired up. I looked into every open door in the hope that I might see Doc. We finally reached a door with Magistrate in gold lettering on a square of polished wood screwed to the door. Mr Andrews knocked on it softly and a voice said 'Come!' and we followed him in. Sitting behind a desk was a man wearing a proper uniform with tie and polished leather Sam Browne belt. He stood up when we entered and I could see he wore long pants and a revolver at his side. Mr Andrews introduced him to us as Colonel de Villiers. There were four chairs arranged in front of the desk and we all sat down. My notes were on the desk on top of a file that was tied with purple tape. Colonel de Villiers put on a pair of gold-rimmed spectacles which slid down his nose as he looked up so he looked over the top of them as he spoke.

'Well now, young man, Mr Andrews here tells me that you are bright enough to have written these notes.' he tapped my notes with his forefinger. 'How old are you?'

'Seven, sir,' I rasped at the back of my throat. The colonel, Mr Andrews and Mrs Boxall turned to look at Marie. Her mouth opened but nothing came out. Her whole face appeared to be frozen in terror, then two big tears squeezed out of her eyes. She tried again but still nothing came out. I held up seven fingers to the colonel who looked stern and cleared his throat.

'I see, seven. Well, you write very well for a seven-year-old. I think someone must have helped you, don't you?' I looked at Marie who was sniffing into a hankie Mrs Boxall had handed her. I shook my head. 'Umph!' the colonel grunted and looked at Mr Andrews. 'These alleged swear-words the sergeant is claimed to have said, they would seem an unlikely part of the vocabulary of a seven-year-old child who, you tell me, has a religious background. I am also a little surprised at his knowledge of Latin, *Senecio serpens* and *Glottiphyllym uncatum* seem a little esoteric for a small boy who, I imagine, like all small boys, is more interested in getting his mouth around a sucker than a Latin noun.'

Mrs Boxall said, 'The professor is an amateur botanist of considerable ability and the child has been trained by him to take punctilious notes. Besides, he has almost perfect recall.'

'Hmm . . . a bit too perfect if you ask me, madam,' the colonel said, as though talking to himself. I could see Mrs Boxall bristle.

'He did it all himself, I seen him do it in the hospital,' Marie said suddenly, her voice quaking with terror.

'Well that's one good thing, little Miss Florence Nightingale has found her voice,' the colonel said. 'Perhaps we can get on with the interview now?' He turned to me. 'Son, I want you to tell me the whole story again, just as it happened.' I repeated the story although Marie had no chance of pronouncing the Latin names of the two succulents which I then referred to as, 'blue chalksticks and another succulent genus which I can write for you, if you want?' The colonel pushed a piece of paper across the desk and I wrote the Latin names on it. 'Extraordinary, it seems I owe you an apology, madam,' he said, dipping his head at Mrs Boxall. When we got to the swear-words Marie refused to say them. 'Please, sir, I can't say them words, I've never said words like that in my whole life,' she said fearfully but with absolute resolve.

The colonel would cut in every once in a while and ask me questions such as, 'What was the colour of the sergeant's cap and belt?' They were all questions which involved some minor piece of detailing, but I had no trouble answering them.

When I was finished, he told Marie that she had done an excellent job and she blushed crimson and the pimples stood out on her face. Then he turned to Mr Andrews.

'The child's statement coincides almost precisely with that of the prisoner. We have already determined that neither has been in a position to compare notes nor to have a third party co-ordinate a defence. Mrs Boxall did try to see him but was not allowed to do so. The prisoner has been visited and interviewed only by military personnel and I am satisfied that the incident took place as the boy has alleged. I am quite sure the court will find for the defendant in all matters except one. I will ask that the charges of assault to a minor and attempted escape be withdrawn. Quite obviously the striking of the Provost sergeant was under severe emotional provocation and the court is likely to look upon it as such. Both the army and the prison reports state that the prisoner smelt heavily of whisky but we can quite easily ascertain whether his coat sleeve is stained.'

He pulled at the purple tape on the file and opened it up. Inside were two folded copies of the *Goldfields News*, the picture of me sitting on the rock and a number of Doc's other photographs and also one of his small spiral-bound notepads. The colonel held up one of the newspapers. 'Really, this kind of hysterical nonsense makes it very difficult for us. The trial of aliens is distressing enough without having the general population turning the butcher, the baker and the music maker into enemies of the State. The only charge Professor Von Vollensteen faces is a technical one, that of not having registered as an alien.' He rose from his chair and smiled briefly at me. 'I only wish I could be here to have a chat with you when your jaw is better, young man. I am also beginning to form a healthy respect for the teachings of your professor.' He shook Mrs Boxall and Mr Andrews by the hand and said something privately to him, then Mr Andrews hustled us out of the room.

When we got back to the waiting room Mr Hankin of the *Goldfields News* was waiting. Mr Andrews spoke to him and he nodded towards the colonel's office. Mr Hankin rose and walked towards the office. 'I think Mr Hankin's career as a spy catcher is about to come to a sticky end,' Mrs Boxall said to me and then started to laugh. 'We won, Peekay, we won!' she said triumphantly.

But we hadn't won. While Doc was acquitted of all the charges just as the colonel said he would be, he was charged with being an unregistered alien and the court ordered him to be detained in a concentration camp for the duration of the war. The *Goldfields News* headline read, NO SPY BUT STILL A GERMAN! It was a year before Mrs Boxall agreed to resume her column, 'Clippings from a Cultured Garden by Fiona Boxall'.

ELEVEN

Doc was to be kept in custody at the Barberton prison until arrangements could be made to send him to a concentration camp somewhere in the highveld. Two days after Doc had been sentenced I went to the library to take a bunch of roses from my mother to Mrs Boxall. Mr Andrews had explained to my mother how my evidence had saved Doc from a severe sentence, one that might well have killed a man of his age. He had also persuaded her that we had nothing to be ashamed of and that he only wished his two sons, now at boarding school in Johannesburg, had had the benefit of a man as remarkable as the professor. My mother decided that the Lord had guided her in the matter and that His will had been quite clearly wrought through me. The roses to Mrs Boxall were her sign that the librarian's trespass into the hospital to see me had been forgiven.

Mrs Boxall seemed excited when she saw me come through the door. 'I'm so fearfully glad you came, Peekay, I have a letter for you.' I handed her the roses. 'How very nice of your mother.' She placed them on the book-sorting table and withdrew into her tiny office to return with a small blue envelope which she handed to me. The envelope was sealed and I opened it carefully pulling back the flap at the back, the glue giving way reluctantly. 'Do hurry, Peekay, I can't bear the suspense,' Mrs Boxall said, looking over my shoulder. I withdrew a single sheet of cheap exercise paper and opened it. Doc's neat hand covered the page. 'Oh dear, I'm such an awful nosy parker! May I read it with you?' Besides Hoppie's note, it was the only letter I had ever received and the first one sealed in an envelope. I would have preferred to read it alone but of course I couldn't possibly say so and I nodded my agreement.

Dear Peekay,

What a mess we are in. Me in this place where they tear down a man's dignity and you with a broken jaw. But things could be worse. I could be a black man and that would be trouble and half. Absolute.

I have been placed under open arrest, it means I can go anywhere in the prison grounds and my cell is not locked. Best of all, it means I can have visitors. Will you come and see me?

Ask Mrs Boxall to telephone the people here and make arrangements. There is also good news about the Steinway. The Kommandant is going to allow me to have it in the prison hall. This is good news, ja?

I do not think of myself as a German. What is a German? To say a man is a German what is that? Does it tell you if he is a good man? Or a bad man? No, my friend, it tells you nothing about a man to say he is German. A man must think what he is inside, what he is on the outside, how can this matter?

Also, because I am German, I am well treated by the warders. This also is stupid. Have you planted the Senecio serpens? No of course not, I am getting old and think only of my own welfare. Perhaps Mrs Boxall will take the books in the cottage and put them in the library? In the meantime I am treated well and whisky is getting easier not to have. Please come soon.

Your friend, Doc.

'We will call the prison at once,' Mrs Boxall said, inviting me into her office.

The superintendent of Barberton prison, Kommandant

Jaapie Van Zyl, told Mrs Boxall that Colonel de Villiers had said Professor Von Vollensteen should be allowed access to the boy within the normal rules of the prison. He added that he had heard of my bravery and wanted to meet me himself. That if Mrs Boxall cared to have me bring Doc library books this would be permitted. The professor was a musician and a scholar and Barberton prison was honoured to have him.

Mrs Boxall selected three botanical books she knew to be among Doc's favourites and I set out with a note from her to visit Doc in prison.

I arrived at the gates of the prison which were made of wrought iron and locked with a huge chain and padlock. It was the biggest lock I had ever seen, nearly twice the size of a grown-up's hand. I wondered how big the key would have to be to open it. The gate seemed about twelve feet high and along the top there were pipes welded every two feet or so. They were about three feet long, bent inward at a thirty-degree slant threaded with strands of barbed wire six inches apart and set into huge blocks of blue granite. Without thinking I identified the components of the rock, mainly felspar and quartz, quarried in the Barberton district so in addition it contained a fair amount of mica. After a year with Doc it had become second nature to identify almost anything that didn't move and I was an expert at the geology of the district.

I decided that escape from inside the wall would be impossible. Set high up to the side of the gate was a church bell and from it, hanging almost to the ground, was a rope. A sign fixed onto the wall said, Ring for attention. My heart beat wildly as I tugged on the rope and the noise from the bell seemed deafening as it cracked the silence. Almost immediately, a warder carrying a rifle slung over his shoulder came out of guard house some twenty feet from the gate and walked towards me. His highly polished black boots made a scrunching sound on the white gravel drive-way. I handed my note to him through the bars of the gate and he opened it suspiciously. He looked at the note for a bit and then looked up at me.

'*Praat jy* Afrikaans?' he asked.

I nodded my head, indicating to him that I understood Afrikaans. The swelling in my tongue had subsided and while my voice had very little volume and sounded a bit gravelly I could talk quite clearly through my wired-up mouth. The young guard looked relieved and started to talk in Afrikaans. He asked me to read the note as he didn't have much English, coming from the North Western Transvaal where only the taal is spoken. 'It says that I am here to visit Professor Von Vollensteen and have permission from Kommandant Van Zyl,' I told him.

'I will get on the telephone and ask. Better wait here, you hear.' He walked over to the guard house and I could see him talking on the phone. He was quite young and looked nervous. Finally he replaced the receiver and stuck his head out of the door. 'Kom!' he beckoned to me. But the gate was locked and he shook his head in exasperation and disappeared to return with a very large key on a huge ring. To my surprise the gates opened smoothly and closed with a clang as he locked them behind me.

The young warder told me to report to the office in the administration block and pointed it out to me. '*Totsiens* and thanks for reading the note, you are a good *kêrel*,' he said.

The area between the gate and the administration block was completely bare. Lawn stretched from either side of the gravel driveway for about five feet and thereafter the square turned into a parade ground of sun-hardened red clay. The strip of living green on either side of the pathway was a brilliant though incongruous contrast to the baked earth of the parade ground and the dead blue-grey walls and buildings. I could see a warder's head in the window of a little tower built onto and jutting out from the wall. There was a stretch of walkway for fifty feet on either side of the tower. Two guards with rifles slung over their shoulders paced up and down this walkway. I seemed to be the only person on the ground below them and I wondered how, on my way out, they'd know I wasn't a prisoner trying to escape. Maybe they'd give me a white flag to carry or something.

It was one of the longest walks of my life. I could sense the oppression of the place, the terrible silence. Without trees, no cicadas hummed the air to life. No birds punctuated the stillness. My bare feet on the gravel made an exaggerated sound. There were tiny dark windows arranged three storeys high. Each was divided by two vertical steel bars. I imagined hundreds of eyes hungrily devouring my freedom as they watched from the prison darkness.

The door of the administration block was open, and after hesitating I put my head around it. Inside was a small hallway that had the same wax polish smell of the magistrates' courts. Three benches, arranged like church pews, filled half the hallway and there was a window with bars set into a wall. Through the bars I could see an office. I walked into the hallway and sat on the front bench and waited.

I don't know how long I sat there, but it seemed to be a very long time. I could see two men in uniform pass the grille window occasionally, but they never looked out. I could hear them talking on the phone. After I'd been there for ages and ages I heard the voice of a man on the phone behind the grille, he was shouting in Afrikaans and seemed very angry.

'He hasn't arrived, you domkop! Are you sure you directed him to this building? We can't have a blêrrie kid walking around the prison. It's been almost half an hour and there's no sign of him. We'll have to look for him now and it's all your blêrrie fault!' I could hear the receiver being slammed back into its cradle. 'Kom!' I heard the voice say to someone else and a moment later a door opened and a big man followed by another big man who looked younger than the first one came out.

The big man saw me as he entered the hallway. 'Jesus Christ! Where have you been?' he shouted at me.

'I been here, I been here all the time, Meneer,' I rasped.

'Well, why didn't you make yourself known then?' he asked in a slightly mollified voice, possibly because he had noticed my wired jaw.

I pointed to the two notices on the wall behind the benches. 'It says on that notice, Wait here and on that other one it says, Silence,' I replied fearfully.

The younger of the two men suddenly laughed. 'I think the kid won the first round, lieutenant,' he said.

'Okay, man, I admit you got me there fair and square,' the older one chuckled. 'Kom, we must take down your name and things.'

They led me into the office and after taking my name, address and age the older one made a phone call and asked to speak to the Kommandant. Then he put the phone down. 'The Kommandant wants to see you but he's doing an inspection now, we have to wait twenty minutes.' He turned to the younger warder. 'Klipkop, get Peekay here a cup of tea and a biscuit.' I wondered how someone could be called 'Klipkop'. In Afrikaans it means stone head. But when I looked at the tall, blond man, his rawboned features looked as though they could well have been carved out of stone.

Klipkop rose and held out his hand. 'Seeing we're going to be here for a while we might as well introduce ourselves. Oudendaal, Johannes Oudendaal,' he said formally in the Afrikaans manner, giving his surname first then repeating it attached to his Christian name. 'This is Lieutenant Smit.' He indicated the older warder, who stretched out his hand without looking at me and I took it briefly, blushing with embarrassment. I wondered whether Captain Smit was related to Jackhammer Smit, maybe his brother? But I didn't have the courage to ask. After all, Smit is a pretty common Afrikaans name. If he was, I hoped he was a better type than the miner. 'Come, I'll show you where we make tea,' Klipkop said. 'There's a Kaffir who makes it but if we want a cup in between we make it ourselves, it's very handy. Every week we put in a shilling for milk and sugar and biscuits, but the authorities supply tea. You got to watch the Kaffir, or the black bastard pinches everything. I'm telling you, man, this place is full of thieves.'

I followed him into a small kitchen behind the office and he put water into an electric jug and plugged it in. 'Peekay, that's a name I haven't heard before.'

'It's just a name I gave myself. Now it's my real name,' I said.

'Ja, I know man, it's the same with me. They call me Klipkop because I box and can take any amount of head punches. Now I sometimes find it hard to remember my born name.'

For a moment I was stunned. 'You box?' I asked.

'Ag ja, man. In this place if you want to get on you have to box, but I like it anyway. On the weekend we travel all over the place to fight, it's much better than rugby, man.' He took three mugs down from a cupboard above the small sink. 'Lieutenant Smit is the boxing coach, he used to be a heavyweight.' He paused as he spooned a heaped tablespoon full of tea from a much used tea caddy into the pot. 'But all the easy stuff is over now, man. Next month I have my first professional fight. There's good money in the fight game. I've got a nooi in Sabie and we're thinking of getting married.' He poured the water from the electric jug into the tin teapot and then stirred it with the tablespoon before placing the lid on the pot. 'Do you box, Peekay?' He asked the question to be polite and did not expect my reaction.

My heart was pounding as I spoke. 'No, but can you teach me please, Meneer Oudendaal?'

He looked at me in surprise and must have seen the pleading in my eyes. 'First your jaw has got to get better, but I think you're a bit young anyway. Lieutenant Smit teaches also the warders' kids but I think the youngest in the junior squad is already ten years.'

'I can be ten. I'm ten in class already. I could be ten in

boxing easily and my jaw will be better in eight weeks,' I begged.

'Hey, whoa! Not so fast! Ten is ten. On the form we wrote you were seven years old only.'

'If you fight first with the head and then with the heart, you can be ten years old,' I said.

'Magtig, you're a hard one to understand, Peekay. You'll have to ask Lieutenant Smit, he's the boss. But if you ask me, I don't think you've got a snowball's hope in hell.'

'Will you at least ask him for me?' I rasped. The excitement made me over-project so that my throat was strained.

'I'll ask him, man, but I already told you what he'll say.' He picked up the pot and poured tea into the three enamel mugs, added milk, three teaspoons of sugar and stirred them all. He went to the cupboard and took out a tin and prised it open. 'That blêrrie Kaffir! We had nearly a quarter of a packet of Marie biscuits in here, now they all gone. It's time that black bastard went back into a work gang. Take your cup and bring the milk, Peekay. If you come again, next time we'll have biscuits.'

'Please, Meneer Oudendaal, you won't forget to ask the lieutenant? You see, I've got to start boxing because I have to become the welterweight champion of the world.'

I said it without thinking. It was more a thought expressed aloud than a statement. Klipkop whistled. 'Well you're right, man, with an ambition like that you've got to get started early.' He paused, two steaming cups in one hand, the teapot with the sugar bowl balanced where the teapot lid would normally have been in the other. 'Me, I'll be happy if I can beat the lieutenant's brother in Nelspruit next month.' He turned and looked over his shoulder at me. 'You can call me Klipkop if you like, I won't mind, man.'

I followed him back into the office where Lieutenant Smit was working on some papers. Klipkop put a mug of tea down in front of him. 'Peekay wants to ask you something, lieutenant,' he said and turned to me. 'Ask him, man.'

Lieutenant Smit hadn't looked up from his papers but he gave a short grunt. 'Please, sir, will you teach me how to box?' I asked, my voice down to a tiny squeak.

He still didn't look at me but instead lifted the tea to his lips, and first blowing the steam from the surface took a sip from the mug. 'You are too young, Peekay. In three years come back, then we will see.' He was taller than me even when he was sitting down and now he looked down at me. 'We read about you in the paper. You have lots of guts, that's a good start but you are not even big for seven like a Boer kid.' He ruffled my hair. 'Soon you will be ten, just you watch.'

At that moment an African came into the room. He was quite old and looked very thin, wearing the coarse knee-length grey canvas pants and shirt of a prisoner. In his hand he held the teapot lid. 'I have come to make tea, baas, but the pot she is not here,' he said slowly in Afrikaans. He stood with his head bowed. In two bounds Klipkop had reached him, and grabbing him by the front of his canvas shirt he lifted the African off his feet and gave him a tremendous swipe across the face. The blow landed with a loud, flat sound and the black man's face seemed to squash in slow motion as Klipkop's huge hand landed on the side of his nose and mouth. Klipkop released his grip and the man fell at his feet, whimpering.

'You black bastard! You stole the Marie biscuits. Not just one, you piece of dog shit, you stole them all!' He gave him a kick in the rump.

'No baas! Please baas! I not stole biscuit. I good boy baas,' the old man pleaded and still holding the teapot lid he locked his free arm around Klipkop's ankles.

The warder turned to Lieutenant Smit. 'Please, Lieutenant, can't we transfer this black bastard to the stone quarry? First he steals sugar, now the Marie biscuits.' He looked down at the whimpering African at his feet. Blood from the prisoner's nose had dripped onto the shiny toe of his boot. Klipkop kicked him loose, sending the black man flying against the wall where he hit the back of his head with a thud, the teapot lid clattering to the floor at his side. 'He's bleeding on me, the filthy black shit house is bleeding all over my boots!' He thrust one foot towards the dazed African slumped against the wall. 'Lick it off, Kaffir, make quick!' The stunned man bent over the proffered boot and licked the blood from the toe cap, then, without being told, did the same with the other boot, at the same time holding his hand up to his nose to prevent further blood spilling on the warder's boots. 'Now wipe your filthy black spit off my boots, you black bastard, I don't want foot and mouth disease!' Lieutenant Smit, who hadn't even looked up, grinned at the joke. The African removed his canvas shirt, and trying to sniff back the blood commenced to wipe Klipkop's boots with it. 'On the floor also,' the warder said, pointing to several scarlet drops of blood on the floor. The black man wiped the drops of blood from the green linoleum floor. 'Now get up and clear out, you bastard!' The African scrambled to his feet and Klipkop gave him a flying kick which sent him sprawling again. Crawling on all fours, his shirt clutched in one hand, the black prisoner fled from the room.

Klipkop examined his hand. 'They got heads made of blêrrie cannon balls.' He grinned. 'I'm learning, man, notice I didn't hit him this time with my fist.' He turned to me. 'Always remember, when you hit a Kaffir stay away from his head. You can break your fist on their heads, just like that. Hit him in the face, that's orright, but never on the head, man.' He made a fist and rubbed it into the palm of his hand. 'I got a big fight coming up, I can't afford a broken fist from a stinking Kaffir's head.'

Lieutenant Smit hadn't said a word. He took another sip from his tea. 'We can't send him to the quarry, man. He's had rheumatic fever, he'd die in a week. Besides he is the first Kaffir we've had who can make proper coffee and tea.' He pointed at the cup in front of him. 'Not like this shit. I told you not to stir it and to warm the pot first.' He turned to look at Klipkop, with just the hint of a smile on his face. 'Next time, man, ask before you hit. I ate the blêrrie Marie biscuits, I never had breakfast this morning so I ate them.'

Klipkop's mouth fell open and then he grinned. 'Okay, so I hit him because he steals the sugar, what's the difference?'

The phone rang and Lieutenant Smit picked it up and listened for a moment. 'Right,' he said into the receiver and replaced it. He turned to me. 'The Kommandant is back, come on, son.'

Grabbing Mrs Boxall's books I followed the lieutenant up a set of stairs to the second floor. We entered a small outer office where a lady sat behind a desk typing on a big black machine which had Remington Corona in gold letters on its back. 'Go right in, Lieutenant Smit, the Kommandant is waiting for you,' she said, smiling at me.

We entered a large office, dark brown and filled with dead animals. A kudu head was mounted directly behind the Kommandant's desk with a sable antelope head beside it, the elegant curved horns touching the wall. There were gemsbok and eland head to complete the display of larger antelope and next to them, in a cluster of five heads, were the smaller variety of buck: grey duiker, klipspringer, steenbok, reebok, and springbok. I turned to face the wall behind me, for it too was covered in trophies. This time a large black-maned lion looked down at me, mouth in the full roar position. Next to it were a leopard and a cheetah. All the carnivores were on one side of the door while on the other were their most common prey, a zebra and a black wildebeest. Below these, fixed to brackets on the wall, were a Boer Mauser and a British Lee-Metford. Immediately below these two Boer War rifles was a long-shafted Zulu throwing assegai. The rest of the wall space was taken up with small framed pictures, mostly of hunting parties standing over dead animals.

The room was furnished with two heavy leather club chairs and a large matching sofa and on the polished floorboards were a zebra and a lion skin. Directly behind the Kommandant's head and below the kudu and sable antelope hung two large portraits. One was of King George and the other of President Paul Kruger, the last president of the defeated Boer Republic. The picture of the Boer president was in an elegant oval walnut frame. King George looked to be the sort of official photograph in a cheap gilt frame issued to public institutions and requiring mandatory display.

Kommandant Van Zyl rose from behind his desk, which was really a large ball and claw dining room table with a sheet of glass covering its surface. There was nothing on the table except the pad on which he appeared to be writing, his fountain pen and an ashtray.

'Good morning, Smit. Sit down, please.' He turned to look down at me. 'So this is the boy, eh?' He walked out from behind his desk and stuck out a huge hand. 'Good morning, Peekay.' He was even bigger than Lieutenant Smit and his tummy stuck out in front of him even more than Harry Crown's. Like the Lieutenant and Klipkop, he wore the grey military-style uniform of a prison warder. The only differences were four stars and a crown on his shoulder tabs and a small tab of blue velvet inserted into the top of his lapels. I shook his hand shyly, not quite knowing what to say.

'Sit, son.' He pointed to the remaining leather chair. I pushed myself up into the large chair. By sitting on the edge I could make my feet almost reach the ground. Kommandant Van Zyl sat down heavily on the sofa.

'So, you want to see our professor?'

I nodded my head, 'Yes please, sir.'

The Kommandant adjusted himself on the sofa, his body soaking up most of it. 'The law says he must be detained and I must follow the law, but inside this place, *I* am the law. In here he can come and go as he pleases provided he stays within the gates. Also he can have visitors in official visiting hours.' He looked at me and smiled. 'I have decided to make an exception in your case. You can come any time you want, only not Sundays,' he paused and looked at me again, 'how do you like that, hey? Two old *maats* together again.'

'Thank you, Meneer Van Zyl,' I said.

'Ag man it's nothing.' He looked at Lieutenant Smit as though he felt the need to explain his decision. 'A friendship between a man and a boy is not a thing to be broken. This boy has no father, I know what that is like, man. My father died with the Carolina burghers at Spion Kop when I was the same age.'

'Yessir,' Lieutenant Smit said, looking down at his hands which were crossed in his lap.

'Make out a permanent pass for the boy so he can come any time except Sunday, you hear?'

'Ja, Kommandant.' Smit looked at the larger man. 'What about the professor's peeano?'

Kommandant Van Zyl slapped his hand on his thigh. 'I clean forgot. Thank you, Smit.' He turned to me. 'We are going to let the professor have his peeano here, there are already many musicians amongst us. Everybody thinks Boere are not cultured, but I'm telling you man, when it comes to music we leave everyone for dead. For us it is an honour to have a man such as him in our prison community. Magtig! A real professor of music, here, in Barberton prison. *Wonderlik*!'

'Thank you for letting me come to see him, Meneer.'

'The boy has nice manners. I like that,' he said to Lieutenant Smit. 'It's nothing. You can come any time, you hear.' He hesitated for a moment. 'Peekay, we need just a small favour. On Monday, about one o'clock, we will be having a nice little surprise for the town folk in the market square. I already telephoned the mayor but I can't trust him to tell people. Will you inform Mrs Boxall who telephoned about you and who, I understand, is also a friend of the professor? Ask her to tell everyone, you hear.' I nodded and he seemed pleased. 'Dankie, Peekay, I think we will like each other a lot. Now Lieutenant Smit is going to take you to see the professor. I see you have some books for him.' He stretched his hand out. 'Show me.' I jumped down from the big chair and handed the books to him. He opened the top one and leafed through it for a few moments. 'Plants, I don't know much about plants. Animals, that's my speciality, you can ask me anything about animals, you name it,' he brought his hands up as though he were squinting down the barrel of a rifle, pulled an imaginary trigger and made a small explosive sound, 'I've shot it.' He lowered the imaginary rifle and grinned at me. He had two gold teeth. 'I love wild animals,' he said. His hands returned to the books which he handed back to me, and his face wore a look of benign satisfaction as he scanned the trophies around the walls.

Lieutenant Smit cleared his throat loudly and the Kommandant turned back to us. 'Well it's been nice to meet you, Peekay.' He patted me briefly on the shoulder. 'If you want anything you just come and see me, you hear?'

It was like the time I had to decide whether to offer to do the Judge's arithmetic. Like then, I was doing pretty well. Why risk it? If I got on the wrong side of the lieutenant, I stood to lose everything, even the chance of becoming a boxer once I turned ten.

'Please, Meneer Van Zyl. Could I learn to box here?'

The Kommandant had already risen from the sofa, preparing to dismiss us. 'You want to box?' he looked at me. 'That's the lieutenant's department.'

'I already told the boy he must wait until he is ten, then maybe,' Smit said, trying not to sound terse.

'When you're seven it's a long time to wait till you're ten. That's nearly half your life,' the Kommandant said.

'We train at five-thirty in the morning. Unless he lived here, how could he get here?'

'I will get here, I promise. I will never miss, not even once. Please, Meneer Smit?'

Lieutenant Smit looked down at his boots for a long time. 'We can try when your jaw is fixed. But I must have a note from your mother to say it's okay to teach you.' He looked up, appealing directly to the Kommandant. 'He is too small, Kommandant.'

'He will grow, Smit, as I recall you and your younger brother started very young. Is he still fighting?'

'Yes, sir, his next fight is against Oudendaal.'

'That's right, the Lowveld heavyweight title next Saturday, you must get me tickets, lieutenant.'

'Yessir, your secretary has them, sir.'

Kommandant Van Zyl ushered us to the door. 'All the best, Peekay.'

When we reached the bottom of the stairs Smit stopped, and getting down on his haunches he grabbed me by the front of the shirt. He had said nothing when we left the Kommandant's office, but I was too good at listening to silence not to know I was in real trouble. I closed my eyes, waiting for the clout across the head that must inevitably come. I hadn't been hit for a year except for a few hidings from my mother which you couldn't really call hidings after what I'd been through. But the memory of a skull-stunning blow across the head was still very much a part of my experience. To my surprise the blow didn't come and I opened my eyes again to look straight into Lieutenant Smit's angry face. 'I'm telling you flat, don't do that to me again, you hear? When I tell you something I mean it, man!' He shook me hard, expecting me to cry; instead I held his gaze. 'Who you looking at? You trying to be cheeky?'

'Please, Meneer, I saw your brother fight in Gravelotte last year. That's when I decided.'

A look of amazement crossed Smit's face. 'You were there? *Wragdig*? You saw that fight?'

I nodded. 'He fought Hoppie Groenewald . . . Kid Louis,' I corrected. Lieutenant Smit released his grip on the front of my shirt.

'I was there also. Magtig! That was a fight and a half. You saw it? Honest?' He rose from his haunches and suddenly his eyes grew wide. 'The kid with Hoppie Groenewald! I remember now. We thought you was his kid.'

We had reached the office again. Klipkop was on the floor doing push-ups and broke his sequence and stood up rather foolishly as we entered. 'You know the fight in Gravelotte my brother had against Groenewald the welterweight last year?' Klipkop nodded. 'Peekay saw that fight, he is a personal friend of Groenewald.'

The warder laughed. 'I lost a fiver on that fight. Who would have expected a welter to beat a light-heavy?'

'I'm telling you, Groenewald isn't just an ordinary welter. You mark my words, if he comes out of this war he's going to be South African champ, you can put money on it,' Smit said. 'He'd take you with one arm behind his back, man.'

Klipkop grinned, 'That'll be the frosty Friday. No way, man! I'm going to do the same to your brother on Saturday as he did.'

'Don't be so blêrrie sure of yourself, Oudendaal. Jackhammer Smit is no pushover, this time he'll be fit. Don't count your blêrrie chickens before they hatch!'

Smit turned to me suddenly. 'Okay, I changed my mind, you on the squad. But no fighting for two years, you hear? Just training and learning your punches and technique, you understand me?'

I nodded, overjoyed. My eyes brimmed with tears. I had taken the first step to becoming the welterweight champion of the world.

'Klipkop, take Peekay to see the professor. I'll make a phone call and you can meet him in the warders' mess.' He turned to me. 'Come back when you're finished and I'll have your permanent pass ready for you.'

We left the administration block and passed through another building. 'This is the gymnasium for the prison officers,' Klipkop said. We walked over to the punching bag and the boxing ring set up at one end of the large room. Large leather balls lay on the floor and Klipkop bent down and scooped one up in his hand. 'Here, Peekay, hold on to this.' I put both my hands out and he flipped the ball lightly into them and suddenly I was sitting on the floor with Klipkop laughing over me. 'It's a medicine ball and it weighs fifteen pounds. When you can throw one of these over my head you'll be strong enough to begin to box.' I got up, feeling very foolish, then I bent down and tried to pick the large brown leather ball up. Using all my strength I managed to lift it but was happy to let it drop again. 'Not bad, Peekay,' Klipkop said with a grin. We were standing next to the ring and I liked the smell of the canvas and the sweat. I wondered how I could possibly wait two years before I climbed into the ring to face a real opponent.

We left the gymnasium and crossed the huge indoor courtyard, an area half the size of a football field which I had seen from the top of the hill on my first morning in Barberton. The prison blocks rose up on every side of the square where two old lags were raking its neat gravel surface so all the tiny rake lines ran diagonally across the quad. 'It's Friday, diagonal lines. I like Monday best when they make a big star in the middle,' Klipkop said. I wasn't sure what he meant but I was soon to learn that each day had a different rake pattern. It was how the prisoners knew what day of the week it was.

'Where are all the prisoners, Klipkop?' I asked. The two old lags doing the raking were the only humans I had seen since leaving the administration building.

'Ag man, they're all out in work gangs. Most work on farms, some at the quarries and some at the saw mills at Francinos Rust. The people who hire them must call for their gangs at four o'clock in the morning and they got to be back here by six o'clock at night. What you see around here in the day time is just old lags, too old to work hard like that black bastard who makes our tea. Also the murderers, they not allowed to come out of their cells, even to eat. But we don't keep them long, man. It's not good to have murderers around, the other Kaffir prisoners get very restless.' He grinned, 'The warders don't like them around also, so we hang them jolly quick smart, I'm telling you.'

'What about the white prisoners, do they also work in the gangs?'

Klipkop looked surprised. 'No blêrrie fear! Gangs is not a white man's work. Mostly white men are only here in transit to Pretoria. They don't have to work so hard, because they not here for long. If they real hard cases, like that guy who murdered his wife and three children in Noordkaap, we just locked him up till the district judge sentenced him, then we put him on the train to Pretoria. If you lucky you get sent along as a guard, you get a day off in Pretoria and ten and sixpence expenses.'

We had crossed the gravel quad and passed though a narrow archway which led to the back of the prison. A long corrugated-iron shed stretched from the main building and smoke rose from three chimneys along its length. 'Kitchens. The warders' mess is on the other side,' Klipkop said.

Doc was overjoyed to see me and he hugged me and patted me on the head and his sharp blue eyes went watery. 'Now I see you I can sleep again. Let me see your jaw? Tut-tut-tut, I wish only I could have taken the kick, then you would be okay. Yes, I think so? Peekay, why are the peace lovers always the first to suffer in the war? Can you talk?' I had never seen him so worked up and his words tumbled out so that I had no chance of getting a word in.

'My jaw is not so bad. They are going to take the wire out in six weeks, maybe even four, but I have learned to talk with my mouth shut.'

Doc laughed. 'You and I, Peekay, even when they cement our mouths, we find a way to talk.' He was still patting me on the head as though to reassure himself that it was really me.

I handed him the books from Mrs Boxall and he held them briefly before putting them on the table beside him.

'She is a goot woman, not so stupid either. You and she, Peekay, eleven out of ten for brains. Absolute. Also Mr Andrews. I do not think they would listen to a poor old German professor of music on his own. German measles was in the air and only you and Mrs Boxall don't catch a big dose, ja?' He chuckled at his sad little joke.

'I can come and visit you as much as I like,' I said happily.

Doc looked bemused. 'Without the hills it will not be the same, what can I teach you here, my friend?'

'Lots of things, like out of books and things. And I could go into the mountains and find things and bring them here and then we could talk about them.'

Doc gave me one of his proper grins. 'You are right, Peekay. A man is only free when he is free in his heart. We will be friends like always. Absoloodle. But also one more thing, they are going to let me have the Steinway here. You can continue your lessons. You must tell your mother this, I think she will be happy. On Monday they are letting me come with them to get it. If they move it wrong it can be damaged. I will see my cactus garden one last time. Maybe also you can be there, Peekay?'

Dr Simpson had said that another week's recuperation was in order. My granpa had given me a big wink and said, 'Who are we to argue?'

'I'll be waiting for you, I've already planted the *Senecio serpens*, just like you said, facing east.'

Doc looked pleased, but then a worried expression crossed his face. 'Peekay, on Monday is happening a stupid thing. It is not my decision, but please you must trust me, that is why I want you to be there. I think Kommandant Van Zyl wants to be a schmarty pantz with some people in this town. I am too old for such silly games, you will help me, please?'

'Kommandant Van Zyl said I was to tell Mrs Boxall everyone has to be in the market square at one o'clock, but he didn't say what it was all about.'

Just then Klipkop emerged from the door leading to the

kitchen carrying a small plate of roast potatoes. 'Here, have some,' he said offering me the plate. I pointed to my wired mouth and he laughed, 'Sorry man, I clean forgot.' He offered the plate to Doc who shook his head.

'Monday, Peekay. Be so kind as to be at the cactus garden at twelve o'clock, then I will explain. Also, tomorrow maybe find for me Beethoven Symphony Number Five, you will see on the cover is printed my name and Berlin 1925. Inside I have marked the score. That is the one I want.' I knew where to look, for the music Doc played only to himself was kept under the seat of his own piano stool. I found it strange that he would ask me to find it. After all he knew perfectly well where it was. 'Peekay, put what's above the score in my water flask, the key for the piano stool lid you will find under the pot on the stoep where grows the *Aloe saponarie*.' He said all this in a perfectly straight voice in English. Klipkop appeared either not to understand or to be disinterested. I looked quizzically at Doc but he put his forefinger to his lips and indicated the warder with his eyes.

A hooter sounded somewhere in the prison. 'Lunchtime, Peekay, we must get back to the lieutenant and the professor must go to lunch.' Klipkop pushed the last potato into his mouth. 'You can stay if you want and have lunch with the prison warders.'

'I have to get home for lunch, thank you, Mr Oudendaal. What is the time, please?'

'That was the twelve o'clock hooter. Just call me Klipkop, okay?' I nodded, I was becoming accustomed to calling adults by their Christian names. I would have to run all the way home as my mother would expect me back from the library by now. I wasn't at all sure how she would take the news of my potential comings and goings to the Barberton prison, nor how I would break the news to her. This more immediate preoccupation made me forget Doc's curious instructions.

After Sunday school the next day I went to the cactus

garden. Dum and Dee had the afternoon off on Sundays and had excitedly agreed to come with me to clean things up a bit for Doc's return the following day. They took brooms and feather dusters and other cleaning things in two galvanised iron buckets which they carried on their heads, chatting away happily about how they would clean my friend's house like it had never been cleaned before. There wasn't much they could do on their half-day off as they hadn't yet learned to speak Swazi. While I didn't think of it at the time, they must have felt isolated from their own kind. On the farm they had been at the centre of things. Quite important really, by comparison with the farm workers, certainly a notch up the social ladder. Here they were two lonely little girls who, outside our home, could make no contact and who knew no other people. We were their family and they were as cloistered as nuns in a convent.

When we arrived at the cactus garden they set to, delighted that they owned every inch of the task without supervision from anyone. I went straight to the large terracotta pot on the stoep of Doc's cottage where *Aloe saponarie*, also known as Soap Aloe, was growing. It has spots of lighter green and rust on its thick leaves.

It was with some difficulty that I pushed the large terracotta pot aside to reveal the key to Doc's piano stool. I hurried to the stool and opened it. The recess was almost a foot deep and it was packed with sheets of music and handwritten music manuscript. There was also a bunch of programmes tied with tape, though at the time I didn't know what they were. The top one had Doc's name on it and the rest was written in German. I dug down quite deeply into the manuscripts and sheet music without finding Beethoven's Fifth Symphony. Then, lifting another batch of paper, I revealed a bottle of Johnny Walker Scotch. I lifted the bottle and directly under it was the piece of music for which Doc had asked.

On Friday afternoon after lunch I had gone to see Mrs

Boxall in the library to give her the Kommandant's message.

'Whatever do you think they're up to, Peekay?' she had said, a worried look on her face. 'Do you think it has anything to do with the professor?'

'I don't think so. At twelve o'clock they are going to fetch the Steinway and take it to the prison. Doc asked me to be there to help him.'

'My God! He's going to give a concert! The professor is going to give a concert in the market square. How thrilling, how perfectly thrilling!' I had never seen her so excited.

It was suddenly also clear to me. 'I don't think he's very happy about it. He said Mr Van Zyl was trying to be a smarty pants with the people of the town. That he would need my help.'

Mrs Boxall, in her excitement, appeared not to have heard me. 'I once checked up on our professor, he turned out to be terribly famous.' Her eyes shone. 'There's something dark and very mysterious about it all, if you ask me. Why would a famous European pianist give it all up and bury himself in a tiny dorp in Africa where he lives on the smell of an oil rag giving lessons to little girls?'

'I think he just likes collecting things like cactus and aloes and climbing in the mountains,' I said, though she didn't appear to be listening. She had her elbow on the desk, chin cupped in her hand, and was obviously deep in thought.

'Peekay, did he ask you to do anything? I mean when he said he needed your help?'

'He asked me to get out Beethoven's Fifth Symphony with his name on it and Berlin on the cover.'

'Hip hip hooray! Jolly good show! Beethoven, eh? What a treat we're in for. I heard the Fifth for the first time when I was a gal and we'd travelled up to London to hear the brilliant young Artur Rubinstein play at the Albert Hall.' Mrs Boxall clasped her hands and looked up at the ceiling fan turning fitfully above her head. 'Oh bliss! Oh blissful bliss!'

'He also said I must put what is above the sheet music into his water flask.'

'Whatever can he mean?' she said absently. It was obvious her mind was on Doc's concert in the market square and her duty as the town's cultural representative was clear. This was no time to attempt to solve one of Doc's conundrums. 'Peekay, you'll have to excuse me, my dear. I think we're going to have to close early today. I have such a lot of phoning to do. One o'clock, are you sure that's the time Mr Van Zyl said?' I nodded and prepared to leave. 'You will thank your dear mother for my lovely roses. I shall write her a nice note next week.' She had already started her telephoning and as I went out of the door of the library I heard her say, 'Barbara, you'll never guess!'

Now I stood holding Doc's music, staring down at the bottle of Johnny Walker. Doc only ever drank in his room, why would he keep a bottle in his piano stool? If Klipkop hadn't walked in at the moment he was about to tell me, everything would have been clear. I reached into my pocket for Doc's note and read it again, maybe there was a clue I'd missed. I kept coming back to the last words, . . . *and whisky is getting easier not to have.* Had I been older it wouldn't have been a puzzle at all, but seven-year-olds are not very good at puzzles and usually know nothing about the drinking habits of grown-ups.

I wasn't at all sure I was doing the right thing but the bottle was directly above the musical score Doc wanted and it was the only item in the piano stool which you could pour into a water flask. I was more than a little conscious that when I had last interfered with Doc's whisky, the repercussions had been enormous. I took the water flask and the bottle of Johnny Walker into the cactus garden where I dug a hole in the ground and planted the flask with its neck protruding. I must say it was a good plan and I spilled hardly any. After that I planted the bottle upside down. It was to be the last Johnny Walker bottle to be planted in Doc's cactus garden.

I returned the flask to the piano stool, placing Doc's musical score over it. Then I locked the seat and put the key in my pocket.

I was waiting at Doc's cottage by nine a.m. on Monday morning. Dee and Dum had cleaned everything and the place was spotless. The Steinway shone like a mirror, from a fresh coat of beeswax. The girls had spent an hour cleaning the whisky from the keys. Seated on the two piano stools, they had giggled fit to burst at the cacophony they made. I don't believe they'd ever had a more enjoyable afternoon. They continued to clean Doc's cottage every Sunday afternoon for the next four years, until I'm sure they believed it was their sabbatical home.

I passed the time waiting for Doc separating succulents and generally clearing weeds from a small part of the garden. After a couple of hours I heard the low whine of a truck and the less agonised sound of a light van as they made their way up the steep road to the cottage.

The black prison flat-top was a Diamond T. The van, coming along behind it, waited a little way down the road while the truck turned to face downhill again. On the back were six black prisoners and two warders carrying rifles. The driver and third warder sat in front. I recognised one of the warders as the young one who had let me into the prison on the previous Friday and I said hello. He jumped down from the back of the truck and stuck his hand out. 'Gert Marais, *hoe gaan dit*?' I shook his hand and replied that I was well and, in the Afrikaans manner, enquired formally about his health. Just then the van drew up and I could see that Klipkop was driving and Lieutenant Smit was beside him. They stopped in front of the lorry and Klipkop jumped out. Walking to the rear of the van he unlocked it. To my surprise Doc stepped out. He was dressed in a clean white shirt, blue tie and his white linen suit. The place where his knee had torn through the trouser leg when the sergeant's kick brought him to the ground had been mended, the suit had been washed and pressed and his boots shone. I had never seen him looking so posh. Lieutenant Smit and Klipkop both greeted me like an old friend.

I could see Doc was agitated and when Klipkop and Lieutenant Smit moved towards the house he turned to me urgently. 'We must talk, Peekay, today is a very difficult thing for me to do.' We followed the two warders into the cottage and Doc pointed to the Steinway and the stool. He was too preoccupied to notice the clean up and while I felt a little disappointed I said nothing.

Cleanliness wasn't something I regarded too highly myself. Two of the other warders came in, leaving Gert and one other warder to mind the prisoners. Together with Doc they discussed how the Steinway might be safely moved.

Klipkop went to call the prisoners in and Doc turned to Lieutenant Smit and asked if he could go and look at his garden, as he couldn't bear to see the piano being moved. Smit laughed and added that it was necessary to have a warder along. 'I know Gert Marais. Can he come please?' I asked. Lieutenant Smit shrugged his shoulders and signalled for Gert to come with us.

'I can't have you two escaping into the hills, now can I?' he said jokingly. But I was to learn that Lieutenant Smit was a careful man and liked to play things by the book. Gert couldn't speak English which meant Doc and I could talk without the danger of being overheard.

We walked in the garden, following the Johnny Walker bottles as they meandered through the tall cactus and aloe. For a long time Doc said nothing, stopping to look at plants and bending down to examine succulents which grew close to the ground. It was as though he was trying to memorise the garden, to etch it on a plate in his mind so the memory of it would sustain him in his prison cell. At last we stopped and sat on a natural outcrop of red rock with our backs to the town below and looking up into the hills. Gert stood some little way away chewing a piece of grass, his rifle slung carelessly over his shoulder. He seemed happy to be away from his superiors.

Finally Doc started to talk. 'Peekay, these domkopfs want I should do a recital in the town today. I have not played a concert since sixteen years, now I must play again. Peekay, I cannot do this, but I must.'

I looked up at Doc and I could see that he was terribly distressed. 'You don't have to, Doc. They can't force you!' I said defiantly but without too much conviction. My short experience with authority of any kind had shown me that they always won, they could always force you.

Doc turned to look at me. 'Peekay, I love you more than my life. If I don't play today they will not let you come to see me.' I could feel the despair in his voice as he continued softly, 'I do not think I could bear that.' I hugged him and he patted my head and we sat there and looked at the hills dotted with the aloes in bloom and at the blue and purple mountains beyond them. At last he spoke again. 'It was in Berlin in 1925. I had been ill for some months and I was coming back to the concert circuit with a concert at the Berlin Opera House. I had chosen to play –' he turned to me – 'the score you found in my piano stool. Beethoven's Symphony Number Five is great music but it is kind to a good musician, the great master was a piano player himself and it is not full of clever tricks or passages which try to be schmarty pantz with the piano player. That night I played the great master goot, better than ever until the third movement. Suddenly, who knows from where it comes, comes panic. In my fingers comes panic, in my head comes panic and in my heart comes panic. Thirty years of discipline were not enough. The panic swallowed me and I could not play this music I have played maybe a thousand times when I practise and forty times in concert. Nothing. It was all gone. Just the coughing in the crowd, then the murmuring, then the booing, then the concert master leading me from the stage.' Doc sat, his head bowed, his hands loosely on his knees. 'I have never played in front of an audience again, not since this time in Berlin. Every night for sixteen years I have played the music, the same music and always in the third movement it is the same, the music in my fingers and my head and my heart will not proceed. It is then the wolves howl in my head and only whisky will make them quiet again. Today, in one hour, I must play that music again. I must face the audience or, my friend, I lose you.'

I cannot pretend to have understood the depth of Doc's personal dilemma. I was too young, too inexperienced to understand his pain and humiliation. But I knew he was hurting inside and I knew there was nothing I could do to stop it. 'I will be there with you, Doc. I will turn the pages for you.'

Doc took out his bandanna and blew his nose. 'You are goot friend, Peekay.' He gave one of his old chuckles and rubbed a hand through my hair and then examined one of my hands. My kneecaps and hands were dirty from weeding between the cactus. 'Better wash in the tank if you are going to be my partner, we must look our best. Ja, this is true, the audience has been waiting sixteen years.' He rose and took me by the hand. 'Come, Peekay, we go now.'

On the journey into town Doc and I sat in the front of the van with Lieutenant Smit. Klipkop drove the truck while Gert sat in the back of the van. The Steinway had been loaded onto the flat-top and roped. Even so, five prisoners were arranged around it to hold it firmly in place on pain of death, while one sat with Doc's piano stool between his legs.

About half a mile from the market square the Diamond T stopped and the two warders herded the six blacks off the truck. One of them climbed back on while the other started to march the prisoners out of town towards the prison. We entered the top of Crown Street about three hundred yards from the market square. The main street was deserted, as quiet as a Sunday afternoon. 'Jesus Christ, I hope this doesn't backfire on the Kommandant,' Lieutenant Smit said, almost as though speaking to himself. We had been travelling behind the truck and now we moved ahead of it. I noticed all the shops were closed, even Goodhead's Bottle Store and the Savoy Café, which never closed for lunch. We turned the corner into the square and my mouth dropped open.

The market square was packed with hundreds of people who had started to cheer as they saw us. A warder signalled us to a space which had been kept clear under a large flamboyant tree. Lieutenant Smit told Gert to stay with the van but not to show his rifle. Then he jumped out, and walking in front of the Diamond T he guided it into a roped-off section in the centre of the square.

Several warders scrambled up a stepladder onto the flat-top and untied the ropes securing the Steinway. One placed Doc's piano stool in place while another, an electrician from the prison, rigged up a microphone.

The moment we saw the crowd, Doc began to shake. I was half sitting on his knee and I could feel him quivering. 'Peekay, did you do what I said about the water flask?' he asked in a tight voice.

'It is in the piano stool, Doc.'

'Peekay, you must take it and when I ask, you must hand it to me, you understand?' I nodded.

When we drew to a halt under the large flamboyant tree the Kommandant was waiting for us. He opened the van door and Doc got out, very unsteady on his feet.

Kommandant Van Zyl took him by the elbow and held him firmly. 'Now then, Professor, remember you are a German, a member of a glorious fighting race. We of the South African Prison Service are on your side, you must show these Rooineks what is real culture, man!'

Doc looked round fearfully to see if I was by his side. 'Do not forget the flask, Peekay,' he said. We walked to the centre of the square, Doc holding tightly onto my hand and being steadied by the Kommandant.

The excitement of the crowd could be felt around us. Nothing like this had happened on a dull Monday since war was declared. We reached the flat-top to find that some twenty rows of chairs had been placed behind the ropes on either side of it. The chairs must have come out of the shops and offices, for no two matched, but they formed a ringside audience of the best people in town. Mrs Boxall was in the front row. She was dressed in her best hat and gloves as were most of the other town matrons considered of social rank. At the back end of the lorry, in three rows of identical chairs, sat the prison warders and their wives, the men in uniform and the women wearing their Sunday best. It was obvious they were very pleased with themselves.

Doc had pulled himself together a little by the time we reached the truck and he and I climbed the stepladder onto the flat-top without assistance.

The Kommandant, helped up by Klipkop, climbed the stepladder onto the flat-top. Klipkop then walked over to the microphone. 'Testing one, two, three, four,' his voice boomed from the four corners of the market square. Satisfied, he climbed down again to join Lieutenant Smit on the ground. The Kommandant moved over and stood in front of the microphone.

'*Dames en Here*, ladies and gentlemen,' he began. But from then on he spoke in English. 'As you all know from reading the newspaper, there has been a very big fuss made about one of our most distinguished citizens, Professor Karl Von Vollensteen, a professor of music from across the seas. The good professor, who has lived in this town for fifteen years and has taught many of your young daughters to play the peeano, was born in Germany. It is for this alone that he is being put under my custody.' Several pockets of people in the crowd had started to boo and someone shouted, 'Once a Jerry, always a Jerry!' which brought about a little spasmodic laughter and clapping. The Kommandant held up his hand. 'I am a Boer, not a Britisher. We Boers know what it is like to be robbed of our rights!'

Considerably more booing started and the same voice in the crowd shouted, 'Put a sock in it, Jaapie!'

The Kommandant, as though replying to the heckler, continued. 'No it is true, I must say it, you took our freedom and now you are taking the professor's!'

This time the booing started in earnest and suddenly Mr O'Grady-Smith, the mayor, stood up and shouted up at the Kommandant, 'Get on with it, man, or we'll have a riot.'

The Kommandant turned angrily on the mayor, oblivious of the microphone in front of him. 'Don't you blêrrie tell me to get on with it! Jes because you the mayor of this dorp you think you can boss people around, hey?'

The booing stopped, for Mr O'Grady-Smith was no more popular than the Kommandant. He was also a very fat man and at least ten inches shorter than the Kommandant. He strode from his seat, and with the help of a couple of town councillors mounted the stepladder and walked over to the microphone. Standing on tiptoes he shouted into the loudspeaker, 'It's high time we moved the jail and the nest of Nazis who run it out of Barberton. This town is loyal to King George and the British Empire. God save the King!'

Most of the crowd clapped and cheered and whistled and Mr O'Grady-Smith turned and looked up at the Kommandant, a smug, self-righteous expression on his face.

From where I stood next to Doc on the flat-top I could see about a dozen men making their way through the crowd towards us. 'Some men are coming,' I said to Lieutenant Smit, who was now standing beside the stepladder with Klipkop to discourage any further townsfolk from emulating the mayor. They quickly mounted the flat-top, pulled up the ladder and placed the microphone next to the Steinway so that the bottom half of the flat-top was clear. Without any ceremony, the mayor and the Kommandant were hastily pushed to the top end to stand beside the seated Doc and me.

There was a good ten feet between the truck and the first row of seats behind the ropes. This was to allow the more important citizens a clear view of Doc at the piano. The attackers crossed this strip of no man's land and swarmed onto the back of the flat-top. Lieutenant Smit and Klipkop held the high ground which evened things out considerably while the other warders took the clearing between the lorry and the seats. The flat-top and the apron around it were filled with fighting men and the screams of the ladies as they tried to back away from the brawl. The Kommandant ventured out from behind the Steinway and received a punch on the nose. Fat Mr O'Grady-Smith was crouched on all fours halfway under the piano, trying to look invisible.

Only Mrs Boxall stood her ground and was waving desperately in our direction and, I suddenly realised, at me. 'Jump down, Peekay, run for it, jump, jump!' she screamed.

Just then Doc tugged me on the sleeve. 'The flask, Peekay.' His hand was outstretched. I handed the flask of whisky to him and he unscrewed the cap and took a slug and handed it back to me. 'When I make my head like so, you must turn the page.' He turned to the score in front of him and paged quickly to the beginning of the fortissimo movement, which in Beethoven's Fifth occurs at the end of the second movement. Then he started to play. The microphone had been knocked down and its head now rested over the upright section of the piano. It picked up the music, which now thundered across the square.

Almost immediately the crowd grew quiet, and the fighting stopped. The flat-top cleared and the men around the apron slipped back into the crowd. The mayor squeezed out from under the Steinway, he and the Kommandant were helped down the replaced stepladder. Even the sobbing ladies soon grew quiet.

On and on Doc played, through the second into the third movement and, hardly pausing, into the fourth, his head nodding every time he wanted the page turned. It was a faultless performance as he brought the recital to a thunderous close.

Intellectually the audience had probably understood very little of it. It was not, after all, their kind of music. But emotionally they would remember Doc's performance for the rest of their lives. Mrs Boxall was weeping and clutching her hands to her breast and the other ladies also pretended to be swept away with it all.

Lieutenant Smit shouted at several of the warders who began to clear a way for the truck. Lifting the microphone off the back, he shouted for Klipkop to get into the truck and drive away, then he jumped into the passenger side of the cabin as the big Diamond T started to move. Doc, who had been bowing to the crowd, fell back onto his seat. With a flourish of the keyboard he began to play Beethoven's Moonlight Sonata.

I had never seen him as happy. He played all the way back to the prison, not stopping when we got to the gates and reaching the final bars as we drew up outside the administration building. Then he took a long swig from the flask and rose from the piano and looked out over the prison walls to his beloved hills.

I quickly opened the piano stool and put the flask into it together with the score. I locked it and slipped the key into my pocket.

Doc rubbed his hand through my hair. 'No more wolves. Absoloodle,' he said quietly, and then he looked up at the hills again.

TWELVE

Dee or Dum woke me up at a quarter to five every morning with coffee and a rusk. Shortly after five I strapped my leather book bag to my shoulders and was off at a trot to the prison some three miles down the road.

I was let in the gates without equivocation, as regular as the milkman and just as harmless. The guards, with an hour and a half to go before the nightshift ended, waved from the walkway on the wall. They were weary from the boredom of guard duty, and I was the first tangible sign after the grey dawn that the long night was almost over.

I learned that the greatest camouflage of all is consistency. If you do something often enough and at the same time in the same way, you become invisible. One of the shadows. Every recidivist knows this. In prison, to be successful, plans have to be laid long term. Habits have to be established little by little, each day or week or month or even year, a minute progression towards the ultimate goal. When a routine is finally set, authorities no longer see it for what it is, a deception; but accept it for what it isn't: an authorised routine. The prisoner enjoys the advantage over his keeper of continuity. Warders change, get promoted, move elsewhere. But old lags, those prisoners who remain inside with long sentences, have the advantage of time to plan. In prison, the old lag is the real authority. The warder unwittingly depends on the old lags to run the prison system, for it is they who restrain the younger prisoners who lack the patience to go along with the system or who see violence as the only solution to getting what they want. A prison without this secondary system of authority can be a dangerous and unpredictable place.

I found myself a part of this shadow world, brought into it with great patience over a long period by an old, toothless lag known as Geel Piet. Translated from Afrikaans, his name simply meant Yellow Peter. In fact, it was more than simply a name. Geel Piet was a half-caste, or a Cape Coloured, neither black nor white, treated as a black man but aspiring in his soul to be a white one. Geel Piet was the limbo man of Africa, despised by both sides. He was also a recidivist, an incorrigible criminal who freely admitted that it was hopeless for him on the outside. Geel Piet was the old lag who exerted the most influence in the shadow world of the prison.

My prison day began in the gymnasium at five-thirty a.m. where the boxing squad, under the direction of Lieutenant Smit, assembled for callisthenics. There were twenty of us altogether and this included four other kids between eleven and fifteen. Seniority went by weight, with Klipkop, who had defeated Jackhammer Smit on points over ten rounds and was now the Lowveld heavyweight champion, the most senior, down to myself at the very bottom of the ladder.

Lieutenant Smit stood in the boxing ring with a whistle in his mouth and to a series of whistles we would perform a routine of exercises familiar to everyone. These were interspersed with push-ups and sit-ups at any interval Lieutenant Smit wanted them. Each session of push-ups and sit-ups was of longer duration than the previous one. Lieutenant Smit was a big believer in push-ups to strengthen the arms and the shoulders and sit-ups to strengthen the gut muscles. He also liked fighters, and contended that the Boer made a better fighter than boxer and that most prison warders were naturally aggressive and better equipped to be fighters. He said toughness and determination overcame skill in the ring. The boxers from Barberton prison were known throughout the lowveld and as far as Pietersburg and Pretoria as tough men to take on.

Lieutenant Smit was true to his word and for the first two years he would not allow me to step into the ring. 'When you can throw a medicine ball over Klipkop's head, then you will be ready,' he said. The first of my goals was set, and for the fifteen minutes after callisthenics, when all the other boxers were paired off with sparring partners, I worked until I could no longer lift my arms.

After a five-minute shower I reported to the prison hall for my piano lesson with Doc, and at seven-thirty we would both go into breakfast at the warders' mess.

Doc had a special status in the prison. While he lived in a cell, he could come and go as he pleased, he ate in the warders' mess, and wasn't required to do any special work. 'You just play the peeano, professor,' Kommandant Van Zyl had said, 'that's your job, you hear?'

Doc often wandered into the gymnasium to watch the squad going through its paces. He knew that I yearned to box, to stand up against another person in the ring. While he made it clear that he didn't understand why I should have such a need, he respected my ambition and soothed my impatience with musical analogies. 'In music you must first do the exercises, always first the exercises. If you do the exercises goot then you have the foundations. You cannot build a good musician on a bad foundation. I think with this boxing business it is the same. Ja, I think this is true.'

And so I did all the things required of a boxer and practised on the punching bag until the whole armoury of punches was as familiar to me as the piano scales. That old punching bag took a terrible hiding on a daily basis over those first two years. I would imagine it cowering as it saw me approach, sometimes even whimpering. 'Not too many of those deadly uppercuts today, Peekay!' Or, 'Oh no! Not the right cross. I can't take any more right crosses.' I'm telling you, man, that big old punching bag learned to respect me all right.

But it was the speedball which I grew to love. Gert, the

257

young warder who spoke no English, was also on the boxing squad and we'd become firm friends. He'd modified an old punching ball in the prison workshop so that it stood low enough for me to reach.

I can remember the first day when, after many weeks of practice on the speedball, I achieved a continuity of rhythm, the ball a blur in front of my boxing gloves. I imagine Fred Astaire or Bojangles must have felt the same way when they got their first complete tapdance sequence from their taps.

After several weeks Lieutenant Smit walked over to watch me. My heart pounded as I concentrated on keeping the speedball flurried, a blurred, rhythmic tat-tat-tat-tat of leather on leather. 'You're fast, Peekay. That's good,' he said and then walked away. Two years later when I mastered a difficult passage in a Chopin prelude, the thrill was minor compared to Lieutenant Smit's praise. They had been the first words he had specifically directed at me in the six months I had been on his squad.

Doc's Steinway was kept in the prison hall, a fairly large room with a sprung wooden floor used mostly for tiekiedraai dancing and other events in the lives of prison officers and their families. There was also an upright French Mignon piano, for Doc's Steinway was not to be used except to play classical music. This was an express order from Kommandant Van Zyl, who pointed out that a peeano of such superior qualities should not be expected to play tiekiedraai or to accompany the banjo or accordion. Naturally his wishes were respected and the Steinway became a symbol of something very superior which, in the eyes of the prison officers and their families, elevated them and gave them a special social status. Doc and I, the only two people who played on the Steinway, were included in this status. While my own playing was elementary and far from competent, it was respected as proper music and was referred to as my gift. The fact that the great German professor of music gave me lessons was the only confirmation needed that I must be a budding genius. Doc was kind enough never to contradict this opinion. While being the most honest person I have ever known, he was not a fool. He quickly learned that every small advantage in the prison system was mental capital in the bank, but it was a shame that his brilliance as a teacher was wasted on such inferior clay.

I visited the cactus garden most days on my return from school and every Sunday after church I went with Dee and Dum to clean Doc's cottage and work in the garden. Doc and I discussed the progress of the cactus garden in detail from a chart prepared by him of every succulent and cactus species in the garden. Considering there were several thousand, it was an intellectual task of some brilliance. In correcting the chart, which took me some weeks, I found that he had only made eleven errors. Taking a small patch of garden at a time from the chart, I reported on its progress. Doc made notes on the comings and goings of blossoms and instructed me when to thin or separate plants. The separated plants I put in a hessian bag and brought it to the prison where Doc had started a second cactus garden. Sometimes insects ate a cactus bloom and I'd capture a specimen in a matchbox and bring it to Doc for identification. If it was within my capacity to do anything about them, he instructed me in their elimination. This was rare. Doc believed all creatures had a place in the system and, in the end, everything sorted itself out. It was only when an insect appeared in such numbers that it was likely to disrupt the ecology of the garden that he instructed me to act. He would liken this to a locust plague which, though a natural thing, was a riotous act of nature which should be contained. In these cases he supplied the know-how, Mrs Boxall or my granpa supplied the materials and Dee and Dum supplied the labour. Usually the enemy was overcome. The girls saw this as part of their Sunday outing and took great pride in their work. They enjoyed the business of working with the soil, though I dare say so much effort on something as silly as a cactus must have left them bemused.

Marie, the little nurse from the hospital, had been invited home soon after my jaw incident and had become firm friends with my mother. She loved needlework and would sit for hours chatting away to my mother and doing buttonholes and making shoulder pads and bits and pieces. It seemed certain she would soon fall into the clutches of the Lord.

Being a farm girl she understood Dee and Dum and to my surprise only bossed them about a little. She taught them to cook a number of new dishes, including pumpkin scones and cornbread and they soon became my favourites. I took her to see Doc's cottage one Sunday afternoon; the two black girls were silent for most of the way. When we arrived at the cottage, Marie started to tell them what to do; their faces grew longer and longer as the afternoon progressed. At last even I saw the mistake I had made, and Marie, much to the delight of Dee and Dum, wasn't invited again. I think they both liked Marie a lot, but there are certain things between women that musn't be tampered with. Doc's house wasn't his any more, it belonged to Dum and Dee, and Marie's imperious instructions were those of an intruder, or even a guest who had forgotten her manners.

Marie brought sweet potatoes for me from her farm, and fresh eggs, sometimes even a leg of pork, a churn of farm butter or several pounds of home-cured bacon. She always brought a large bunch of cured tobacco leaf for my granpa. He smoked a Rhodesian blend called African Drum and hated the sharp, raw, unblended tobacco from Marie's farm, though he was much too polite to tell her. He would hang it by the stems from the ceiling of the garden shed. Occasionally he added a couple of large leaves to a forty-four-gallon drum filled with rainwater which stood directly outside the shed. The tobacco-infused water was used for aphides on the roses. But the water required only a tincture of tobacco, and the supply hanging from the ceiling grew alarmingly. Eventually it was to become one of the most important factors in my rise within the prison system.

For the first year Geel Piet, the half-caste, was a part of morning piano practice, for he was always in the hall on his knees, polishing the floor. After a short while he became entirely invisible, a shadow in the background who greeted Doc and myself with, '*Goeie Môre, Baas en Klein Baas.*' He followed this with a toothless smile and then a soft cackle as though the day was perfect and he couldn't think of any place he'd rather be. Doc, who was no racist, and I who had mixed with servants all my life, both returned his greeting. It was forbidden to talk to any of the non-European prisoners and our careless replies must have been a great encouragement to the old man.

Geel Piet was small and battered-looking. His left eye hung lower than his right and the bottom eyelid drooped, showing more of the eye than one would normally see. Both eyes were permanently bloodshot and somewhat weepy. His nose had been completely flattened and his deep yellow face was criss-crossed with scars. A section of his bottom lip had been cut away, leaving a purple wedge of scar tissue to droop in a line of permanent disappointment from the corner of his mouth. He stood around five foot two inches on his buckled legs, for they were more than simply bandy, the result of having been broken several times and no doubt carelessly mended. Had he been able to straighten them he might well have been four or five inches taller. In the process of surviving, Geel Piet had achieved an outward appearance which would have made it near impossible for him to last for very long outside the jail system. He had worn out his luck in the outside world, if indeed he'd ever had any. Born in District Six, the notorious coloured township in Cape Town, Geel Piet had been in and out of jail for forty of his fifty-five years. He took pride in the fact that he knew the working, at an intimate level, of every major prison in South Africa, and he was the grandmaster in the art of camouflage. Should a warder beat him for whatever imagined reason, Geel Piet bore no animosity, no hate. He had long since transcended both, and regarded a beating as self-inflicted because it resulted from some piece of carelessness. Geel Piet had no sense of morality, no sense of right or wrong. He existed for only one reason, to survive the system and to beat it. To gain more from it than he was entitled to. He had long since realised that, for him anyway, freedom was an illusion. He had accumulated years of sentences, he wasn't quite sure or no longer cared how many, and was realist enough to know that he was unlikely to survive the system at his age and with his deteriorating health.

After all the years of incarceration he was a polished performer, no less a maestro at his profession than Doc was at his. Perhaps more so, for as a procurer Geel Piet was a genius.

Geel Piet ran the prison black market, in tobacco, sugar, salt and dagga (cannabis). In the end, he controlled the mail coming and going from the prison and thus the money brought in. He also had an encyclopaedic knowledge of boxing and a rare gift for spotting errors of style and weakness in performance. My desire to become a boxer was all too apparent, but it is a sixth sense to men who have to survive on their wits, and who have to sniff the air before every move and wager everything on a chance observation or a cunning guess, that told him I was an easy mark.

It took just over a year for Geel Piet to ingratiate himself to the point where I would unknowingly begin to serve him. Our entire relationship was built upon small conversations eked out over weeks until an understanding formed which eventually led to the conspiracy which made me present him with a leaf of tobacco.

I had been culling a patch of *Euphorbia pseudocactus*, a cactus-like plant which grows close to the ground and is extremely thorny. It has a habit of spreading quickly under ideal conditions and it had started to invade territory in the cactus garden which didn't rightly belong to it. Because of the thorns I had put Doc's cutting in a galvanised bucket which I'd brought from the garden shed at home. Almost without thinking I had lined the bottom of the bucket with a large tobacco leaf which was covered by the thorny cactus for Doc's prison garden. Something must have made me do it: perhaps Geel Piet, somehow, with his patience and snatches of seemingly unconnected dialogue. Tobacco is, after all, the greatest luxury and the most essential commodity in the prison system. With the war on, the normal shortage behind the walls had become severe, so that it was more highly prized than ever.

I was never searched as I entered the prison, although on this particular day, carrying a bucket rather than a bag, a mildly curious guard wanted to know what was in the bucket and had come on over to take a look. In fact I had not been worried, having entirely forgotten about the tobacco leaf. 'Funny how he likes all these ugly plants, hey?' the guard said, for Doc's cactus garden was directly outside the warders' mess and was the butt of many a joke, most of them about cactus being just the sort of plant for a prison. 'If the prisoners revolt we'll all hide in the professor's garden, those blêrrie Kaffirs wouldn't be game to try to get us out.'

I had taken the bucket through to the hall after the squad workout and as usual Geel Piet, who was becoming more and more useful and who, over the ensuing year would assume the place of personal servant to Doc, took the bucket with the cuttings to Doc's garden. He had returned with it, his permanently broken face wreathed with smiles. 'I will help you to be a great boxer,' he simply said. And that was how it all got started.

I broached the subject of the tobacco to my granpa when I returned home that afternoon after school. I did not really think about the moral issue involved. After a year of going in and out of the prison each weekday I had come to understand the system. Morality was suspended, war existed between two sides and even aged eight I could see the odds were heavily biased towards one of them. The prison warders were an extension of the kids at the hostel: a brutal force confronting a defenceless one where crimes supposed or otherwise were being paid for. The idea of committing further petty crime in this sort of atmosphere and being brutally, often savagely punished was bizarre and quite unreal. Doc and I were not a part of either side, we were an audience who would, from time to time, make a decision to enter the play. While we couldn't change the plot, we could relieve the actors of their tedium.

My granpa was generally suspicious of unquestioning moral rectitude, preferring to judge each item as it came to him; as prepared to have Inkosi-Inkosikazi cure his gallstones as he was to give the Boers credit for being musicians and good shots. We sat on one of the steps leading up to a terrace. Between much tamping, tapping and lighting of pipe and staring into the distance over the paint-faded and rust-stained roof, and after ascertaining that I was never searched, he decided that the prisoners should have the tobacco.

'Poor black buggers, it's worse for them than it was in England in the seventeenth century. Most of them are in for crimes that deserve no more than a tongue lashing.'

He was wrong. Barberton was a heavy-security prison and most of the prisoners, except for the politicals, had committed crimes that were worthy of formal punishment in any society. It was the administration of the prisoners' life that was the real crime, and it was not unusual for a prisoner to be beaten to death for a comparatively minor infringement of prison rules. Such occasions were discussed among the warders quietly, almost secretly, but with an inner glee.

I think my granpa was partly influenced by the thought that the mounting stock of tobacco leaves from Marie's farm would start to dissipate and that in some small way he too was fighting the sort of injustice he abhorred. He carefully instructed me in the use of tobacco-infused water for insect control, and gave me a note to Doc explaining how it was done. The plan was for Doc to set up his own drum beside the cactus garden and infuse it with two tobacco leaves at rare intervals. In the event of a single load of tobacco entering the prison being discovered, Doc, a non-smoker, could quite easily explain its destination.

Doc had requested to remain in Barberton prison rather than be transported to an internment camp in the highveld. The thought of being away from his beloved mountains, his cactus garden and his piano, was more than he could bear, and I'm sure our friendship also played a large part in his reluctance to leave Barberton. Kommandant Van Zyl, who had come to regard Doc as the personal property of the prison and a constant thorn in the side of the English-speaking town, was more than happy to co-operate. I think in the end the military authorities must have given up trying to extricate him from the civil prison system, and Doc spent the remainder of the war under the benign supervision of the Kommandant.

Of course, Doc was co-conspirator in what became a sophisticated smuggling system. Being in the prison constantly he was there when the work gangs returned at night and left again at dawn. He was forced to see an aspect of Africa he had never witnessed. Doc was a man who preferred not to take sides in any issue other than one of the intellect. Rather than face the dilemma of black and white confrontation and the pre-ordained decision of white superiority, he had chosen to avoid it altogether by not having servants or any dependence on Black Africa. But he was also a compassionate and fair-minded man and the unthinking brutality of the warders offended him deeply. Both of us lacked the wisdom or the knowledge of the baser side of men, though I probably had more experience of this than Doc did. We saw the brutality around us not as a matter of taking an emotional side, or of good versus evil, but as the nature of evil itself, where good and bad do not come into play. We were simply intellectually forced to take the side of the prisoners. Man brutalised thinks only of his survival. Geel Piet was as ruthless as his oppressors and of necessity a great deal more cunning. The power the tobacco and the other things which later came into the prison gave him was enormous, and he used it to ensure his own survival and to serve his own ends as ruthlessly and as carelessly as the warders used their superiority.

As it turned out he spoke English passably, but had chosen Afrikaans to make his mark with me, knowing that Doc would then not be in a position to understand what he was saying and therefore to see through his long and carefully planned campaign. His next conquest after me was to be Doc. He became the perfect servant to him, a humble man who strove to anticipate Doc's every need while never intruding into the world Doc and I shared as expatriates of an orderly social environment.

Geel Piet successfully contrived to get into the gymnasium while the squad was working out. At first he was a familiar shadow, hardly noticed, polishing the floor or cleaning the windows. Then gradually over a year he became the laundry boy, picking up the sweaty shorts and jockstraps and the boxing boots in the shower room and returning them the next day freshly laundered and polished. By the time I could throw a medicine ball over Klipkop's head, Geel Piet had established himself as an authority on boxing. The lieutenant gave him the job of supervising the progress of the kids in the squad, only occasionally taking over when he felt it necessary to establish his superiority by deliberately contradicting an instruction from Geel Piet to one of us.

The standard of the young boxers improved measurably under Geel Piet's direction for, despite his background, the old lag was a maker of boxers. When he hadn't been in prison he'd worked in gymnasiums, and somewhere in the dim past had been the coloured lightweight champion of the Cape Province. He had a way of teaching kids that made even the Boer kids respect him, though at first it was only their fear of Lieutenant Smit that prevented them from refusing to be coached by a blêrrie yellow Kaffir.

266

From the first day Lieutenant Smit agreed that I could begin to box I was under Geel Piet's direction and he treated me like new clay. From day one Geel Piet concentrated on defence. 'If a man can't hit you, he can't hurt you,' he'd say. 'The boxer who takes chances gets hit and gets hurt. Box, never fight, fighting is for heavyweights and domkops.'

It wasn't what I had been waiting for two years to learn. But Doc persuaded me Geel Piet was right, and the logic, even to an eight-year-old, was irrefutable.

It was some weeks before I was allowed to get into the ring with an eleven-year-old from the squad. The boy's nickname was Snotnose, Snotnose Bronkhorst, because there was always a snolly bomb hovering from one or both of his nostrils. He was a big kid and a bully but he had only been with the squad for a few weeks and he lacked any real know-how. He had pushed me away from the punching ball, and I had tripped over a rubber mat and fallen. Picking myself up I had squared up to him, when Lieutenant Smit, seeming not to have noticed the incident, said he wanted to see us in the ring. My heart thumped as I realised that the moment had come.

We climbed into the ring and it was Hoppie and Jackhammer Smit all over again, in size if not in skill. But to my satisfaction I had absorbed a great deal over the past two years and even more over the six weeks Geel Piet had been coaching me. Snotnose chased me all over the ring, taking wild swipes, any of which, had they landed, would have lifted me over the ropes. Over a period of three minutes I managed to make him miss with every blow while never even looking like landing one myself. After three minutes Lieutenant Smit blew his whistle for the sparring session to stop.

I noticed for the first time that most of the squad had gathered around the ring and when the whistle blew they all clapped. It was one of the great moments of my life.

Peekay had completed his two-year apprenticeship. From

now on it was all the way to the welterweight championship of the world.

I turned to walk to my corner before climbing out of the ring, and sensing something was wrong I ducked just as a huge fist whistled through the air where my head had been a second before. Without thinking I brought my right up in an uppercut, using all the weight of my body behind the blow. It caught Snotnose Bronkhorst in the centre of the solar plexus and I could feel my glove sinking deep into the relaxed muscles of his stomach, forcing the air from his ribcage. He staggered for a moment and then, clutching his stomach, crumbled in agony onto the canvas, the wind completely knocked out of him. The cheers and laughter from the ringside bewildered me. Looking over the heads of the squad I saw Geel Piet, unseen by any of them, dancing a jig in the background, his toothless mouth and funny lip stretched wide in uncontained delight.

Throwing caution to the winds he yelled, 'We have one, we have a boxer!' The coloured man's intrusion into the general hilarity caused a sudden silence around the ring.

Lieutenant Smit advanced slowly towards Geel Piet. With a sudden explosion Smit's fist slammed into his face. The little man dropped to the floor, blood spurting from his flattened nose.

'When I want an opinion from a fucking Kaffir on who is a boxer around here, I'll ask for it, you hear?' Then, absently massaging the knuckles of his right hand, Smit turned back to the squad. 'But the yellow bastard is right,' he said. 'Get into the showers now, make haste. Bronkhorst, you are a domkop,' he added as Snotnose rose shakily to his feet.

I was still standing in the ring, a little bewildered at the fracas I had caused. I watched Geel Piet crab-crawl along the gym floor, making for the doorway. When he reached it he got unsteadily to his feet and looked directly at me. Then he grinned, and without raising his hands gave a furtive thumbs-up sign, a movement so slight it would have gone unnoticed to a casual observer. To my amazement, the expression on his battered face was one of happiness.

On my way to school that morning Snotnose Bronkhorst sprang from behind a tree and gave me a proper hiding, although I managed to get him with a right cross that snapped his head back as well as a solid uppercut in the balls which made him release me so that I could run for it.

It had been my experience that the Snotnoses of this world were a plentiful breed and I thought it might be a good idea to learn street fighting as well as boxing. Geel Piet, I felt sure, would show me how to fight dirty as well.

But I was wrong. Perhaps I was the first human clay Geel Piet had been responsible for shaping into a boxer, but it was more likely pride; he was a purist and he knew the corruption that turns a boxer into a fighter and a fighter into a street brawler.

'Small boss, if I teach you these things a street fighter knows, you will lose your speed and you will lose your caution and when you lose your caution you will lose your skill.' His face split into a grotesque smile. 'It will take longer to win as a boxer, but you will stay pretty.'

I was disappointed. Being tough was one of the ambitions I had set for myself. Being pretty certainly wasn't on my list of priorities! How could you be tough if you had to bob in and out like a blowfly? 'Please, Geel Piet,' I begged, 'just teach me one really rotten dirty trick.' After some days of nagging he agreed.

'If I teach you one, then you must promise not to ask again, you hear?'

'It's got to be a proper one, the worst in the book, you've got to promise that too?'

'Okay man, I will teach you the Sailor's Salute. It is the best dirty trick there is. But you got to know timing also to get it right. A boxer can know this trick and still be a boxer.'

'Promise it's the worst one of all?'

'Ja, man, I'm telling you for sure. It is so rotten the police

269

use it all the time so they can say in the charge book they never laid hands on you. Its other name besides the Sailor's Salute is the Liverpool Kiss.' He held the flat of his hand three inches from his brow and with a short, lightning-fast jerk of his head his forehead smacked loudly onto the hand. 'Only you do this against the other person's head, like so.' He drew me towards him and in slow motion demonstrated the head-to-head blow. Even in slow motion he nearly took my head off and my eyes filled with tears. It was the head butt Jackhammer Smit had used to floor Hoppie, and now I knew why Hoppie had gone down so suddenly.

'Do it to me also,' Geel Piet said, patting his forehead with the butt of his hand. I did so and received a second severe blow to the head. I was beginning to have misgivings about street fighting. It sure wasn't like fighting a punching bag.

But over the next few weeks I perfected the Liverpool Kiss. The quick grab of the punchbag and a lightning butt to the imagined head of an opponent. Every now and again Geel Piet allowed me to practise on him and he grinned when I got it right. 'Once you got it, you got it for life. But only use it quick and as a surprise. If you get it right you kiss your opponent to sleep with just one little tap, no problems, man.'

School had one disadvantage. I was two classes higher than my age group and so friends were hard to make. The kids of my own age thought of me as a sort of freak and in fact, with my early school background and now my prison experience, I was a lot tougher than any of them. Doc and the jaw incident had made me somewhat of a celebrity but I kept mostly to myself, being a shy kid and the smallest in my class. I acquired a reputation for superiority without having to earn it and so was left pretty much alone. I wasn't aggressive, and when a challenge came from a boy called John Hopkins and his partner Geoffrey Scruby, supposedly the two toughest kids in my class, I tried to avoid the fight they demanded, mostly because I was arrogant enough to believe that my status as future world welterweight champion made it inappropriate for me to be a street fighter. The Judge and even the jury had been so much tougher than these two that it never occurred to me actually to be frightened of them. The English-speaking kids at school had no idea of my boxing or prison background, as the small contingent of Afrikaans kids in the school seldom mixed with the English and almost never spoke with them, other than to challenge them to fight. The two ten-year-olds badgered me for some days and so I took the problem to Geel Piet, who immediately understood my dilemma.

'Small boss, it is always like this. This is what you must do. You must make them feel you are scared. Tell them, no way man. Tell them you don't want to fight. Let them get more and more cheeky, more and more brave. Even let them push you around. But always make sure this happens when everyone is watching. Then after a few days they will demand to fight you and they will name a time and a place. Try to look scared when you agree. You understand?' Geel Piet held me by the shoulders and looked me straight in the eyes. 'More fights are lost by underestimating your opponent than by any other way. Always remember, small baas, surprise is everything.'

It happened just as he said, a constant badgering during break, then a few pushes in front of everyone. Protests from me that I didn't want to fight. Finally a demand that I be behind the bioscope after school where I could choose either of them to fight.

When I got to the small yard behind the town cinema where all the official school fights took place, it was packed, with at least fifty kids crowded around John Hopkins and Geoffrey Scruby. All of them were English-speaking with the exception of Snotnose Bronkhorst, who had somehow got wind of the fight. To my surprise he stepped up to me and said in Afrikaans, 'I'm here to be your second, these are all Rooineks, you can never tell what they'll do.'

I looked at him in surprise. 'I'm also a Rooinek.'

'Yes I know man, but you're a Boer Rooinek, that's different.'

I elected to fight Hopkins who seemed delighted as he was the bigger of my two tormentors and had not expected to be chosen.

The kids formed a ring and Snotnose, who didn't know a lot of English, simply said, 'Okay! Make quiet! Fight!'

Hopkins threw a haymaker at me and missed by miles and I landed a hard blow to his ribs. He looked surprised and shook his head and came rushing in again swinging at my head. I ducked in under his punch and caught him hard on the nose. He stopped dead in his tracks and brought his hand up to his face. I hit him with a left and then a right to the solar plexus and to my astonishment he started to cry.

'All over!' Snotnose held up my hand as Hopkins, sniffing and thoroughly humbled, walked back into the crowd. I pointed to Geoffrey Scruby. 'Your turn now, Scruby,' I said, feeling a rush of adrenalin as I saw his fear.

'I'm sorry, Peekay,' he said softly. I had won. Just as Geel Piet said. Suddenly the crowd loved me. And I liked the feeling a lot.

Then Snotnose stepped up.

'Does any of you blêrrie Rooineks want to fight him?' he asked. There was complete silence and nobody stirred, not even the bigger kids. 'You're all yellow, you hear!' he snarled, then he turned slowly and looked at me with a grin on his face. I grinned back. He seemed an unlikely ally but he had stood by me. 'Okay then, I will,' he said. There was a murmur of apprehension through the crowd. They were clearly shocked at the idea, I must say I was pretty shocked myself.

'It's not fair. You're much bigger than him,' Geoffrey Scruby said. 'And older,' someone else shouted.

'Shurrup, man, or I fight you.' Snotnose walked up to

Scruby and stabbed him in the chest with his forefinger. Then he turned and squared up to me.

It had been four months since we'd first met in the ring and he'd learned a fair bit about boxing in the meantime. I tried to stay out of his way, dancing around him, making him miss. But he hit me a couple of times and it hurt like blazes. I was connecting more often than he was, aiming my blows carefully, but I knew it was only a matter of time. *First with your head then with your heart, first with your head then with your heart,* Hoppie's words drummed through my brain as I tried to stay alive. Snotnose had tried to come in close on one or two occasions, but soon learned that this evened things up. At close range I was much the better boxer. So he stood his distance and picked his shots, knowing that a big punch had to get through sooner or later. All I could do was to try to make him miss. The kids, now on my side, were yelling their heads off trying to reach me with their encouragment. But I think they all knew the Boer was too tough and that the outcome was inevitable.

'Come closer, Boer bastard. Are you scared or something,' I taunted. Snotnose stopped in his tracks and his eyes grew wide. With a roar of indignation he bore down on me. I stepped aside at the last second and he missed knocking me over. As he turned to come back at me his head was lowered so it was on a level with mine. He had his back to the bioscope wall and I had mine to the crowd. I stepped in, and using both hands grabbed him by the shirtfront and gave him a perfectly timed Liverpool Kiss. The blow was so perfect I felt nothing. Snotnose simply sat on his bum, completely dazed. He just sat there in the dirt quite unable to comprehend what had happened. The crowd hadn't seen it either. They were behind me and my hands flying up to grab his shirtfront must have looked like a two-fisted attack. Forever afterwards it was retold that way; 'Then Peekay said, "Come closer you, Boer bastard," and with two dazzling punches to the jaw he knocked Snotnose Bronkhorst out.'

To my surprise Snotnose started to sniff and then got up unsteadily and made his way through the crowd and down the side of the building. He stopped halfway down the alley and shouted in Afrikaans, 'I'll get you back for this, you Rooinek bastard!' The English kids jeered as he walked away, but I knew better. One doesn't allow a Boer to lose face and expect to get away with it. Though, to my amazement, even Snotnose came to believe that he had been punched.

After the fight with Hopkins and Snotnose Bronkhorst my status at school improved immeasurably. While there were no more than sixty Afrikaans pupils, the sons and daughters of Noordkaap miners, farmers, men who worked in the saw mills at Francinos Rust and the warders' kids, they tended to be bigger than the English kids and much more aggressive. Most of the English boys had at some time or another suffered at the hands of one of the Boers. I was seen as being the one kid who had successfully fought back and won. A single victorious ship on an ocean of defeat.

Occasionally a Boer boy of roughly my size would cross the lines to challenge me and after school the back of the bioscope building would be packed with kids. The Boer kids on one side and the English on the other with my opponent and myself sandwiched in between. The prison guys formed a clique of their own, not sure where they belonged but seemingly glad when I won. Geel Piet was a good coach and as I was never matched with one of the prison kids, my superior boxing skill allowed me to win. Whereupon a bigger Boer kid would challenge one of the English boys of roughly the same size and usually manage to beat him, which restored the racial status quo.

The prison kids explained that it was acceptable to be beaten by me as I was a sort of honorary Boer who spoke the taal and was also one of them. That came first. Even Snotnose left me alone unless we were sparring in the gym when he would go all out to try and hurt me.

This position of semi-neutrality had a great many advantages. In times of war there always has to be a go-between, someone whom both sides are prepared to trust. I was accepted by everyone as a brain and so I ended up doing the negotiation between the Boers and the English, often sorting out differences, arranging sides for rugby or *kleilat*, marble contests and *bok-bok*, an exceedingly rough game based on strength and endurance which the Boers, despite having fewer boys to choose from, usually won.

With some forty kids of my own age I was now undisputed leader, a situation I must confess I found to my liking. Being somebody after being nobody for so long was a heady experience but I also found it, on occasion, a bit onerous. Fights had to be settled, bullying stopped and the small kids set straight when they did things wrong. And then there was the tobacco crisis.

The tobacco crop on Marie's farm failed. This left a period of three months when the curing shed was empty. Marie kept apologising for this, as though it were somehow her fault: the more my granpa protested that he didn't mind the more guilty she seemed to become. By this time Geel Piet had become undisputed quartermaster for the prison. To tobacco we had added sugar, salt and a letter writing business which was getting news in and out of the prison to and from all over South Africa. Postal orders would come in from outside contacts. Prisoners would order sugar, salt and tobacco and Geel Piet would add thirty per cent to the groceries and charge threepence a cigarette. Tobacco was by far the greatest luxury because it was rationed due to the war. It was, of course, unavailable to the casual purchaser and impossible for an eight-year-old to buy under any circumstances. The little I brought in leaf form was carefully rolled into slim cigarettes. A single cigarette in a week of hard labour was a luxury beyond the imagination of the average prisoner. Somehow I understood how such a small thing as a cigarette, a tablespoon of sugar or a teaspoon of salt made the difference between hope and despair. A prisoner with a cigarette safely stashed in a used

.303 cartridge case up his anus considered himself rich. These cartridge cases were highly prized, they were after all, in conjunction with his anus, the only private storage space a prisoner had. We kids gathered them from the rifle range at the army camp and they were the only item which Geel Piet actually gave away; as the prisoner's pantry they were essential to his business.

Letters were becoming a big thing at the prison and Doc wrote most of them as Geel Piet dictated to him. The little man could remember the contents of entire letters, together with the addresses of a dozen or more black prisoners at a time. Doc would write them at night. He would then write out a sheet of music theory for my homework and attach the letters to the back of it. Any search would have quickly revealed them but Doc was not a naturally cunning man and I think in his mind he regarded my music book as somehow, like the Steinway, above the possibility of question.

The letters were much of a muchness, men not accustomed to writing are apt, in any language, to reduce their words to simple formalities such as telling their families they were all right and enquiring after the health and welfare of the wife and kids, all the small, important human things that make us all, in the end, exactly the same. Some would include a request for money, although most knew this to be impossible and were too proud to impose such a burden on their families. It was not unusual for a family not to know that a husband had been arrested or where he was detained. He had simply disappeared and was often sent to a prison some distance from the place of his arrest. To trace him without the co-operation of the police was nearly impossible and so the letters provided a vital link in the spiritual welfare of the prisoners.

Mrs Boxall acted as post mistress and I must say she ran a pretty slick operation. The letters would be dropped in after school. Using the large square stamp used for marking the inside covers of books and which said: BARBERTON

MUNICIPAL LIBRARY, de Villiers St, Barberton, we stamped a blank envelope, attached a postage stamp to it and included it in the original letter with instructions to the receiver to use it as the return envelope. We also wrote the name of the sender on the inside of the return envelope. This was done because we often received letters which started, *Dear Husband* and carried no other identification. Finally Mrs Boxall or I would address the outgoing envelope and send it off.

She explained these elaborate precautions to me. 'The world is full of sticky beaks. If we get a lot of letters addressed to the library in primitive handwriting, the post master just might smell a rat. I've been sending our overdue notices to country members for years which include return addressed envelopes using the library rubber stamp, he won't suspect a thing.' And he didn't. The system worked perfectly and returned letters were taken into the prison and locked away in Doc's piano stool, to which only he and I had a key, though I'm sure Geel Piet could have picked the lock any time he chose to do so.

The money prisoners received from outside was generally in the form of a postal order for two shillings. As all incoming mail was opened by Mrs Boxall, she cashed the postal orders and put the money back into the envelopes and wrote the names of the recipient on the front. I pasted the envelope back together using the large pot of library glue and a slip of rice paper to cover the slit where the envelope had been carefully opened using Mrs Boxall's letter knife. The knife had a handle striped red and white like a barber's pole, and on the blade on one side was written, Have you written to your sweetheart? and on the other, A souvenir from Brighton 1924. I used to wonder who had Mrs Boxall for a sweetheart, but I think I already knew it was nobody.

And so a regular mail system in and out of the prison was established with Mrs Boxall cheerfully paying for the stamps and stationery. She would often sit and read a letter to one of the prisoners from a wife, written by someone who could write in English, and as she read it to me the tears would roll down her cheeks. The letters were mostly three or four lines, often in a huge, uncontrolled childlike hand.

My Husband Mafuni Tokasi,

How are you? The children are well. We have no money only this. The baas says we must go from this place. There is no work and no food. The youngest is now two years. He looks same like you. We have no other place to go.

Your wife Buyani

A postal order for two shillings in the letter meant that the whole family might not have eaten for two days or more. Mrs Boxall would wipe her eyes and say her conscience was quite clear and even if she was arrested she knew she was jolly well doing the right thing. She badgered friends and people coming into the library for clothes and these she sent off to needy families, even sometimes sending off a postal order of her own to a prisoner's family. She referred to prisoners as 'Innocents, the meat in the ghastly sandwich between an uncaring society and a vengeful State'. Her code for these families simply became the word 'sandwich'. 'We need more clothes for the sandwiches,' or 'Here's a poor sandwich for whom we'll have to find half a crown.' She kept a forty-four-gallon drum in the library which had a six-inch wide slot running almost the width of its lid like a huge money box. On the side was written: Cast-off clothes for the Sandwich Fund. People would bring lots of stuff and no one ever asked what the Sandwich Fund was.

'People feel they ought to know, so they don't dare ask,' she would say. She once told me that the sandwich was named after the Earl of Sandwich, who was a terrible gambler and because he was always so busy gambling he had no time to take meals. To overcome the problem his butler had made him two hunks of bread with something in between them. These were the first sandwiches. 'If anyone ever asks we'll say it's the famous Earl of Sandwich Fund for the poor. That ought to shut them up, don't you think, Peekay?'

Eventually someone must have asked, because the Earl of Sandwich Fund became the most social of all the war effort funds in Barberton. Even more important than knitting socks for prisoners of war. At the Easter and Christmas fête held in Coronation Park, Mrs Boxall and I ran a sandwich stand where cakes and other delicacies donated by the town's leading families were sold. My mother sent pumpkin scones baked by Dee and Dum who were also allowed to work on the stand. Mother made two identical pinnies and caps for them and they worked from dawn until dusk laying out cakes on the trestle tables and cutting and buttering bread and making sandwiches.

Because I was on the boxing squad and regarded as one of the prison kids, the wives of the warders baked for days for the sandwich stand and gloated when their cakes and cookies were the first to go. Boer baking was generally superior to that of the town's leading socialites. The rather snobbish Earl of Sandwich Fund sandwich stand earned enough to pay for the entire mailing system and to send money and clothing to a great many destitute families.

When the tobacco crisis came we solved it through the Earl of Sandwich Fund. Mrs Boxall sent a note to the headmaster of our school requesting that children bring in cigarette butts from home. She even managed to get the butts from the sergeants' mess at the army camp. Everyone assumed the re-cycled tobacco was going to the prisoners of war as Mrs Boxall simply referred to them as prisoners. Some kids brought half-packets of unsmoked cigarettes from a parent's precious ration, a sacrifice to the war effort. I took half a packet of smokes to Geel Piet, who thought all his Christmases had come at once. The bags of butts were taken to Doc's cottage where Dee and Dum, their noses masked by a dish towel, spent Sunday afternoon shredding the week's tobacco supply. Geel Piet never had it so good. When the new crop came from Marie's farm, it was with some dismay that he was forced to switch back to straight tobacco leaf.

What I didn't know was that little by little the prisoners had pieced it all together and I had been given the credit for everything. I was enormously surprised, when one day I passed a gang of prisoners who were digging a large flower bed in the town hall gardens, to hear the chanter who was calling the rhythm so the picks all rose in unison and fell together, change his song at my approach.

'See who comes towards us now,' he sang. 'Tell us, tell us,' the rest of the work gang chanted back. 'It is he who is called the Tadpole Angel,' the leader sang. 'We salute him, we salute him,' they chorused.

I glanced around me to see whom they were singing about, but there was no one to be seen. The warder, who recognised me, obviously didn't know Zulu. He called out to me, 'How things going, man?' and I replied, 'Very good, thanks.' The warder, who was bored, obviously wanted me to stop for a chat.

'He who is a mighty fighter and friend of the yellow man,' the leader continued. 'The Tadpole Angel, the Tadpole Angel,' the chorus replied, their picks lifting on the first Tadpole Angel and coming down on the second. I realised with a shock that they were talking about me.

'I hear the lieutenant is going to let you fight in the under twelve division in the Lowveld Championships in Nelspruit this weekend.'

'Ja, I'll be the smallest, but he thinks I'll be okay.'

'We thank him for the tobacco, the sugar and the salt and for the letters and the things he sends to our people far away.' 'From our hearts, from our hearts,' came the chorus.

'Nine is not very old, man, eleven can be blêrrie big with a Boer kid.'

I shrugged my shoulders. 'I am ten in two weeks.' I was trying to hide my embarrassment at the salutation going on around us.

'Ja, man, and the kid you fight will be most likely twelve in two weeks,' he said gloomily.

'I have to go, I'm late for the library.' I wanted only to get away from the chanting of the prison gang.

'You'll be okay, man, I seen you sparring, you fast as buggery.' He looked at me closely and grinned, 'You is a funny bloke, Peekay. Now why you blushing like mad suddenly, hey?'

'He is the sweet water we drink and the dark clouds that come at last to break the drought,' the leader sang. Up came the picks, 'Tadpole Angel.' Down they went in perfect unison, 'Tadpole Angel. We salute him, we salute him.' I started to run towards the library and broke out in a sweat, my embarrassment consuming me.

I tackled Geel Piet about the matter the next morning and he admitted that this was my name. 'It is a great compliment, small baas. For them you are a true angel.'

Doc was listening, as Geel Piet and I now spoke in English when we were with him. 'Ja, and for you we are all angels, Geel Piet.' He chuckled. 'You are a rich man I think, ja?'

Geel Piet made no attempt to deny it. 'Big baas, it is always like so in a prison. If I am discovered I will be killed, so I must have something for risking my life. Thirty per cent is not so much, in Pretoria and Johannesburg it is fifty per cent, in Robben Island and Pollsmoor it is sixty per cent.'

'I think you are a skelm, Geel Piet, but we will say no more.' Doc, like Mrs Boxall, had come to realise how important the letters were and how the small amount of contraband made life bearable for men who were shown no compassion and whose diet of mealie meal and a watery stew of mostly cabbage and carrots with an occasional bit of gristle floating on the surface was only just sufficient to sustain them though not sufficient for the brutally hard work on the farms or the saw mills or the granite quarries. He had also come to accept the role Geel Piet played in the distribution system, knowing that without it chaos would ensue. 'Inside all people there is love, also the need to take care of the other man who is his brother. Inside everyone is a savage, but there is also happening tenderness and compassion.' Doc sighed and took out his bandanna and wiped his face as though trying to wipe the prison atmosphere from his skin. 'When man is brutalised in such a place like this always he is looking for small signs. The smallest sign that someone is worried for him is like a fire on the dark mountain. When a man knows somebody cares he keeps some small place, a corner maybe of his soul clean and lit.'

While the food allocated for each prisoner was insufficient to keep a man doing hard physical labour, whoever hired a gang was expected to supply a meal at noon. It was this meal which kept the prisoners alive, for the regulations required it to be a vegetable and meat stew consisting of eight ounces of meat per prisoner and a pound of cooked mealie pap. I sometimes heard the warders discuss a scam whereby they tried to get a contractor to cut the rations in half, pay the warder ten shillings and save himself ten shillings. This only worked when gangs were hired for short periods, otherwise the men soon grew too weak to work. It was a big risk. Lieutenant Smit rotated warders so they had a different gang each week and couldn't set up a scam. The prison authorities depended on this one good meal a day from outside so they could cut rations on the inside. Although, I must say, Geel Piet told me this story and so it is not necessarily the entire truth. If a warder was caught in a scam he was not only dismissed but drafted into the army. Nobody in the boxing squad ever tried a scam, they were all Lieutenant Smit's men and, even more than the good musicians, were considered special, seldom having to go out with gangs and mostly getting guard duty on the day shift.

While no more than a quarter of the prisoners were Zulus, they held the highest status in the prison. Work songs were mostly composed in Zulu and it was always a Zulu who called the time and set the working pace. Zulu is a poetic language and while many songs are traditional, the ability to create spontaneous new lyrics to capture a recent incident or pass information on was almost always handled by a Zulu prisoner whose gift for poetry was greatly respected.

Even among the old lags this method of passing on information was used. When a warder spoke an African language in this part of the world it was seldom Zulu, more likely to be Shona, Shangaan or Swazi and even these would only be spoken by warders who came from farms. Townsfolk do not learn an indigenous African language other than Afrikaans and sometimes a language developed for use in the mines, known as Fanagalo, which is a mixture of several African languages as well as Afrikaans and English.

I asked Geel Piet why the word 'Angel' was prefaced with the word 'Tadpole'. At first he seemed not to know, or at least pretended not to, but I understood enough of Zulu naming to know that nothing is accidental and a name is chosen carefully so that it is a good description of status or of some characteristic which unmistakably belongs to the recipient.

For instance, Klipkop did not know that his nickname was 'Donkey Prick'. This came about from his habit of using a long rubber truncheon which he used with the least excuse. Most warders used their fists on prisoners. Their logic for doing so was quite simple, punishment administered with the fist was unofficial or, as the warders called it, friendly persuasion, while the truncheon was used when reports needed to be made. Klipkop was the exception, as heavyweight champion of the Lowveld he had to take good care of his hands, so he took to using the donkey prick for casual punishment. As he was also complaints officer it didn't much matter. 'A man like me can't afford to break a pinkie or something on some stinking black bastard's kop,' he would explain defensively, for even outside the prison a man was expected to use his fists on a Kaffir, reserving the sjambok for serious misdemeanours.

I recall walking down a long winding passage in the interior of the prison administration building where half a dozen old lags could always be found on their knees, their kneecaps swathed in polish rags, as they shone an already immaculate corridor floor. Long before we even sighted them I could hear one of them sing out, 'Work hard and keep your heads down, Donkey Prick is coming,' and back would come the chorus, 'Donkey Prick, Donkey Prick.' As we passed, each prisoner would stop polishing briefly, and bringing his hands together in a gesture of humility would smile and say, 'Good morning baas, good morning small baas.'

Knowing there was some reason for 'Tadpole' before 'Angel' I persisted in questioning Geel Piet about it. 'It is like this, small baas. The professor is known as *Amasele* (the Frog), because he plays his peeano at night when the prison is quiet. To the Zulus the frog makes always the loudest music at night, much louder than the cricket or the owl. So it is simple, you see. You are the small boy of the frog, which makes you a Tadpole.' It was a perfect piece of Zulu naming logic.

THIRTEEN

While Geel Piet was growing rich and even seemed to be getting a little pot belly, he had also become indispensable to the boxing squad. He maintained the gym, organised the laundry and even had the blue and yellow boxing singlets and white trunks made in the prison workshop. But most importantly his knowledge of boxing was encyclopaedic and he was a demanding and resourceful coach. The squad kids had been turned into clever boxers, our natural aggression combined with real skill. From the under fifteen division down to the under twelve, the Barberton Blues hadn't lost a fight in two years.

How I got my first real fight was a matter of sheer luck. The championships in Nelspruit were in early August, only days before my tenth birthday, and I had tried to persuade anyone who would listen that ten was almost eleven and that one year wasn't much to have to forfeit. But Lieutenant Smit wasn't the sort of man who changed his mind and nobody, least of all me, was willing to petition him on my behalf. In fact the two under twelves, Snotnose Bronkhorst and Fonnie Kruger, were almost twelve and therefore two years my senior, and being Boer kids were much bigger.

Geel Piet claimed he saw intelligence and speed in me that more than made up for my lack of size. He was a fanatic about footwork. 'You must learn to box with your feet, small baas. A good boxer is like a dancer, he is still pretty to watch even if you look only at his feet.' He taught me how to position myself so the full weight of my body was thrown behind a punch, and despite my size and my speed my punches were capable of gaining respect from a bigger opponent. 'If they do not respect your punch they simply keep going until they knock you down, man. A boxer must have respect.'

I longed to have a real fight against an unknown opponent. In two years I had never missed a day of boxing and I had worked with all my heart and soul for the moment when I could climb into a boxing ring with real people watching and an opponent whose every blow, unlike those of my sparring partners, could not be anticipated.

On the Monday of the week of the championships Snotnose didn't turn up at the gym. After the session Lieutenant Smit called Geel Piet over and they talked earnestly for quite a time, every so often looking in my direction. Finally Geel Piet came over to me. He was trying hard to keep the smile off his face. 'Ag man, I'm a heppy man today, small baas. You want to know why?'

'They going to let you out of jail?' I said.

He laughed, 'No, never no more. I'm heppy here, man. I got my own stable of boxers, I got a good scam going. I will die heppy in this place.'

'What then?'

He bent down so his face was only inches from my own. His breath smelt foul. 'You got your first fight, man! Small baas, Bronkhorst he is sick with the yellow disease, you got his place.'

I couldn't believe my ears. Snotnose had jaundice which had been going around school. I went to hug Geel Piet, but he quickly sidestepped. 'No, no small baas, the lieutenant will come over and beat me.' He grinned. 'Today this black bastard is too heppy to have his nose busted. Better go over quick, man, and thank the lieutenant. Make quick or maybe he changes his mind, hey?'

I ran over to where Lieutenant Smit was talking to Klipkop and stood and waited. They ignored me for a long time and then the lieutenant said in a brusque voice, 'What is it, Peekay?'

'Thank you for the fight, Lieutenant Smit,' I stammered. 'I will try my hardest.'

He massaged his knuckles. 'That won't be enough, you're going to get your head knocked in, but it will do you good. Nobody should win their first fight.' He turned and walked away.

Geel Piet told me to bring my tackies in the next morning so they could be properly cleaned for me to wear at the fight. Using a piece of string he measured my chest and my waist. When I got home after school I told Dee and Dum my tackies should be put next to my school satchel so I wouldn't forget them, as Geel Piet needed to clean them. Dum got up quietly from where she was sitting on the floor at my feet while I drank a cup of coffee. She returned a few moments later with my tackies. They had been scrubbed and were spotless. 'Who does this yellow man think he is?' she asked. 'Does he think we let our baas go around in dirty things?' She and Dee were clearly hurt. I had to go to some lengths to explain that Geel Piet did all the things for the boxers and that now I was one of the squad he would do the same for me. 'He will not wash your clothes or clean your tackies,' Dee said. 'It is a woman's work and we will look after the clothes of him who belongs to our own kraal,' Dum added.

I wasn't at all sure how my mother would take the news of my inclusion in the squad. Boxing was never mentioned, and as far as she was concerned my early morning journey to the jail was in order to take piano lessons. She had been very busy of late with a commission from a Johannesburg shop to make three ball gowns and her Singer machine could be heard whirring away late at night. I knocked and entered the sewing room. It seemed full of a plum-coloured taffeta evening gown which was almost finished. My mother rose and held it against her body and she looked just how I imagined Cinderella must have looked when she went to the ball. The neckline plunged in a deep vee-line and the sleeves were puffed. The skirt billowed from the narrow waist and as she moved, the taffeta caught the light and rustled in a most expensive and provocative way.

'Such an extravagance, I can't imagine where they found the material for this in the middle of the war.' She kicked at the skirt and it billowed out to reveal a second layer of net in a peacock blue.

'You look beautiful,' I said, not thinking to flatter her.

My mother laughed, and reaching for a cloth-padded hanger proceeded to hang the dress up on a rod protruding from the wall. Even away from her body the dress had a life of its own, filling the small sewing room with glamour. 'That's the trouble with the things of the devil, they are often sorely tempting and very pretty,' she said with a sigh.

I had forgotten for a moment that dances were very high on the Lord's banned list. My heart sank. If dancing was frowned upon by the Lord, what would he think of a boxing match? I immediately consoled myself with the knowledge that, as far as I knew, God was a man, and therefore He'd obviously like boxing a lot better than dancing.

'You've come about the boxing, haven't you?' my mother said, resuming her seat at the sewing machine.

'Yes, Mother.' I was unable to conceal the surprise in my voice.

'Yes well, Lieutenant Smit, a very nice man, came to see me this morning, though I'm not at all sure I liked what he had to say. I've spoken to your grandfather about it and I made it the subject of my quiet time with the Lord after lunch. I have to tell you He gave me no clear guidance on the matter, though your grandfather seems to think it can't do you any harm.' Her head jerked back in a sudden gesture of annoyance. 'Oh, how I do wish you'd stick to the piano. It's quite clearly the Lord's wish that you do so or He wouldn't have made it possible for you to learn under such trying circumstances. Lieutenant Smit seems to think you have a natural talent as a boxer which is more than the professor has admitted about your music.'

'Doc has said my Chopin is coming along extra good,' I said, mimicking him ever so slightly.

My mother was sewing a press stud onto what looked like a cummerbund for the taffeta dress, and she now looked up at me. 'I do wish you wouldn't call him by that silly name. Heaven knows this town has few enough nice people and, after all, he is a real professor of music and merits your respect. His being German is simply unfortunate. I suppose we'd all talk German with a funny accent if Hitler won the war. You'll have to sleep on Friday afternoon if you're going to be up that late on Saturday night.'

I jumped with joy. 'Thank you, thank you, thank you,' I cried and gave her a hug and a kiss.

'I'm not at all sure the Lord approves,' she said, but I could see she was glad I kissed her. 'Run along now.'

On Friday morning, after callisthenics, Lieutenant Smit called us all together around the ring. 'I want to tell you first a few things,' he said. He turned to the five kids standing to one side with Geel Piet. 'The rules for under fifteen says, you get knocked down, you out. No use getting up, man, you finished and *klaar*. So don't get knocked down, hey.' He indicated Klipkop who was standing on his right. 'Sergeant Oudendaal is a semi-pro so is not allowed to fight, so Gert will fight in the heavyweight division and Sergeant Oudendaal and me will be your seconds. You do as you told, man, and no monkey business, you hear? Don't go thinking you know better. You all know the rules, the most clean blows landed wins, that's how Geel Piet here taught you. The rest of you in the weight divisions just fight your normal fight, if you need to change tactics I'll tell you, man.' He was turning to leave the ring when his eye caught something at his feet. He stooped down and picked up a small blue singlet, on the front of which in yellow were the letters BB, standing for Barberton Blues. He turned the singlet around to face us; on the back, written in neat cut-out letters, we saw PEEKAY. 'Welcome, Peekay,' he said and everyone clapped. 'Welcome to the Barberton

Blues.' There was a roaring in my head and my throat ached as I choked back the tears. Lieutenant Smit bent down again and picked up a pair of blue shorts with a yellow stripe down the side, and bundling the shorts and singlet together he threw them at me. They parted company in mid-air and my left hand shot out to grab the singlet while my right fetched the shorts out of the air. 'The little bugger is fast and uses both hands well. I only wish he carried another fifteen pounds,' he said as he climbed from the ring.

I showed Doc my singlet and shorts and he seemed very pleased for me and I told him about the three rounds. 'Do you think you can go three rounds with Mr Chopin, Peekay?' he asked. I nodded, determined to show Doc that his precious music was not taking a backseat, although I suspect he knew that my mind was more on staying on my feet and not getting knocked down than on the *étude* with which I was trying to come to grips. Out of the corner of my eye I saw Geel Piet enter. I knew that if he wanted to he would come in unnoticed, that he had worked out the exact angle to enter so he was seen without disturbing anyone. It was unusual for him to come into the hall at this time. I always put the day's mail in the piano seat and later, when he came in to polish the Steinway, he would retrieve it. We had decided the three of us should never be seen together near the postbox. I glanced over to where he stood pretending to clean a window, a bucket at his feet. Finally Doc noticed him and raised his hand for me to stop.

'You must not come when we practise, that is the rule,' he admonished. The battered little man quickly picked up the bucket and trotted towards us. Doc looked annoyed. 'What is it?'

'Please, baas, it is very important, baas.' Geel Piet put down the bucket and withdrew a parcel wrapped in a piece of cloth. 'The people have put money together and in the bootmaker's we have made for the small baas a present.'

He opened the cloth to reveal a pair of boxing boots. I gasped. They were beautiful, the black leather brought to a soft sheen and the soles the bluish white of raw new leather. 'It is from all the people, a present for the Onoshobishobi Ingelosi, it is from all of us so you will fight a mighty fight tomorrow, small baas.'

I leapt from the piano stool, unable to contain my delight. 'It is why I asked you for the tackies, small boss.' He gave me a big, toothless smile. 'It was to know the size.'

I quickly pulled my school boots off and put the boxing boots on. The leather was soft and pliant and the boots felt light as a feather and fitted perfectly. 'Geel Piet, they are the nicest present anyone ever gave me, honest.'

'They are from all the people, it is their way to thank you.'

Without warning he dropped to his knees, and using the cloth in which the boxing boots had been wrapped he started to polish the floor around my feet. Some instinct in him which never rested had sensed danger. A good five seconds elapsed before the warder actually stood at the entrance to the hall.

He was a new sergeant whom we'd only met once in the mess. His name was Borman and he had been transferred down to the lowveld from Pretoria Central because of his wife's asthma.

He stood, one hand holding the door frame. 'Professor, the Kommandant wants to see you, report to administration after breakfast you hear?' He turned to go, then caught sight of Geel Piet. 'Kom hier, Kaffir!' he rapped.

The little man jumped up and ran across the hall. 'Ja baas, I come baas,' he cried.

'What you doing in this place?' the warder demanded.

Doc bent down and picked up one of my school boots. 'The boy got some kak on his boots, he come to clean them.' He appeared to be scrutinising the sole of one of my boots. 'Ja this is so,' Doc said, waving the boot at the warder and then pointing to where Geel Piet had been cleaning the floor. 'Also some was on the floor when he walked in.'

Sergeant Borman grinned. 'Next time make the black bastard lick it clean, he is used to eating shit.' He turned to Geel Piet, 'That's right isn't it, Kaffir? You all eat each other's shit, don't you?'

Geel Piet had his head bowed and was standing to attention, though his thin, bandy legs, crossed with scars and blobbed with black scar tissue from past bush sores, didn't actually come together at the knees. 'No, baas,' he said softly. There was no fear in his voice, only a sort of resignation. He seemed to know what would happen next.

The warder reached out and grabbed him by his canvas shirt. 'When I say so, you say yes, understand? Now, do you eat shit, Kaffir?'

'Yes, baas,' Geel Piet replied.

'Loud! Say it loud, you shit-eating bastard!'

'YES BAAS!'

'Yes baas what?'

'Yes baas, we eat each other's shit!'

The sergeant from Pretoria turned to us. 'There you are, Professor. I told you they eat each other's shit. Next time make him lick it up, it will be a proper treat for him.' He turned and walked away.

Geel Piet came padding over to us, his bare feet making hardly any sound on the sprung wooden floor. 'Thank you, big baas,' he said with a grin. 'He is right, man, in prison we all eat shit.' He turned to me as he picked up the bucket. 'Your feet, small baas, box with your feet, punch clean so it is a scoring shot. No clinches, that way a bigger boxer can push you over. Good luck, small baas, the people are with you.'

'Thank you, Geel Piet, tell the people I thank them.'

'Ag man, it is nothing, the people love you, you are fighting for them.' He was gone.

Doc cleared his throat to break the silence. 'Maybe now we can play Chopin, yes?'

I gave him a big hug. 'That sure was quick thinking, Doc.'

He chuckled. 'Not so bad for a brokink-down old piano player, ja?' He frowned suddenly. 'I wonder what wants the Kommandant?'

We were to leave for Nelspruit, a distance of some forty miles, at eight a.m. the following morning. Though I avoided having to rest on Friday afternoon, I had been ordered to bed at six o'clock. I woke as usual just before dawn and lay in bed trying to imagine the day ahead. What if I was beaten first off? How would I hide my despair? With seven Eastern Transvaal teams competing, I had to win twice to get to the final. I had never boxed six rounds in my life, and even if I got through them I would have to box another three in the finals! What if I lost concentration and the other kid pushed me over? Even if I was winning, I'd lose because I'd hit the canvas!

I couldn't stand the 'What ifs' any longer and I quickly got out of bed and dressed and ran through the garden. In a little more than ten minutes I was on top of the hill sitting on our rock.

It was early spring and the dawn wind was cold, I shivered a little as I watched the light bleed into the valley and merge with the darkened town below me, smudging the darkness until the roofs and streets and trees were rubbed clean. The jacaranda trees were not yet in bloom but patches of bright red from spring-flowering flamboyant trees already dotted the town. I tried to think how Granpa Chook would have looked at the situation. He would have taken things in his stride, just like any other day. While Granpa Chook was a less important mentor now, he remained a sort of check-point in my life. A reference on how to behave in a tight spot. I thought of Hoppie too. If only Hoppie could have been there to see me. 'First with your head and then with your heart, Peekay.' I could almost hear his cheerful and reassuring voice.

After a while I felt much calmer. I made my way back

down the hill as the sun began to rise. Some of the aloes, mostly the taller *Aloe ferox*, were showing early bloom. I watched as a ray of sunlight caught a tiny jewelled honey-sucker as it hovered around a spray of orange aloe blossom. Its long hooked needle beak probed for nectar, the tiny bird's wings beating so fast they held it suspended in one spot, too fast even to make a blur in the surrounding air. I imagined being able to punch that fast, my opponent retelling the fight to someone else. 'I was still thinking about throwing a right when the welterweight champion of the world hit me three hundred times on the chin.' Even to me it sounded improbable.

When I got back to the house Dee and Dum had prepared breakfast, brown kaffircorn porridge, fried eggs and bacon. On the kitchen table stood my school lunch tin. After their day spent as purveyors of sandwiches to the Earl of Sandwich Fund at the Easter fête they regarded themselves as world authorities on the sandwich and my school lunch was always a bit of a surprise. Grated carrot and jam was one of the combinations that would crop up once in a while, or avocado pear and peanut butter. I had drawn the line at onion and papaya, and gooseberry jam and Marmite was another variety struck off their culinary repertoire.

I wondered briefly what they'd packed to sustain me, hopefully for nine rounds of boxing, but refrained from looking. Until, unable to contain themselves, they opened the tin to show me six pumpkin scones neatly wrapped in greaseproof paper. 'We baked them last night, your favourite!' Dum said and I could see they were both very pleased with themselves.

I packed all my stuff into my school satchel, including my beautiful boxing boots which Dee had given another polish, even though they were spotless. At half-past seven I had already said my farewells to my granpa and my mother and was sitting on the front wall waiting for the blue prison light utility which was to pick me up. I could have gone to the prison but Gert said, 'No problems, it's only a few minutes out of our way, save the energy for the ring!' Gert wasn't like the other warders. Indeed all the kids thought he was the best thing since sliced bread. He liked to help people and he once told me he only hit Kaffirs if they really did wrong. 'A Kaffir hurts also, maybe not like a white man, 'cause they more like monkeys, but they hurt also when you hit them.'

After breakfast when I had gone to bid my granpa goodbye I put the question to him about being knocked down so that even if I was winning the fight I would lose it. The usual tamping and puffing and lighting up took place. Finally, squinting into a haze of blue smoke he answered.

'I think you'd best do what I did in the Boer War.'

'What was that?' I asked anxiously.

'Why lad, run away as much as possible.'

That was the trouble with my granpa, the advice he gave when you needed it most wasn't always very useful.

I saw the blue prison ute coming up the hill with Gert at the wheel. Next to him someone sat reading a newspaper, I couldn't see who it was. Gert stopped outside the gate. 'Jump in the back with the other kids, Peekay,' he said cheerfully. I climbed into the back of the ute, helped by one of the others. It was an exciting business all right as Gert changed gears and we pulled away. A fourteen-year-old called Bokkie de Beer was in charge and he told me no one was allowed to stand up. All the other kids were giggling and splurting into their hands as they looked at me.

'What's so funny?' I shouted above the sound of the wind and the roar of the engine. Bokkie de Beer pointed to the rear window of the driver's cabin. I followed his hand and there, framed in the window, wearing his unmistakable panama hat, was the back of Doc's head. I couldn't believe my eyes and all the kids fell about laughing at my astonishment. I just couldn't believe my good fortune.

It was the first time since my arrival by train three years earlier that I had left the small town. It was a perfectly clear, early spring morning as we travelled across the valley towards a row of distant hills. The thornveld and the flat-topped acacia had already broken into electric green leaf. In a month they would be a mass of tiny pom-poms that turned the valley into a sea of yellow and pink.

The road from Barberton was tarred all the way and by nine-thirty we'd reached Nelspruit. My wind-blown skin felt tight around the eyes and cheeks, and I was glad to get out of the back of the ute when we drew to a halt in a parking lot behind the town hall. I rushed to Doc's side to open the door for him. His blue eyes were shining and I think he was almost as excited as I was.

'We are together outside again, Peekay. It is goot, ja? Absoloodle.'

'How did you escape?' I asked clumsily.

He chuckled. 'With the permission of the Kommandant. That's what he wished to see me about after breakfast yesterday.' He saw me frown, we both knew the way of the prison system where nothing is given unless something is taken in return. Doc shrugged. 'It is not so much he wants. He wants only I should play a little Chopin when the brigadier comes from Pretoria next month.'

I knew how Doc felt about playing in public. He refused to play at any of the town concerts and had long since retired as a musician. While he overcame his fear when he triumphed at the Beethoven lunchtime recital in the market square, Doc was a perfectionist and it gave him great pain not to meet the standards he demanded for himself. When I told him Mrs Boxall had said there was no one in Barberton who didn't think he was the greatest pianist they had ever heard, he had replied, 'You must thank Madame Boxall for her kindness, but I am too old and too weak to inflict badly played Beethoven and Mozart on myself.'

'You should have said no!' I said.

'Tch-tch, Peekay, then I would not see you in your début. One day I will say, I was there when the welterweight champion of the world made his boxing début. Absoloodle!'

'You still shouldn't have.'

'Beethoven yes, Mozart yes, Brahms yes, but Chopin I can still play enough not to tear myself to little bits. I will play Chopin to this Mr Brigadier. That is not so hard, ja.'

We entered the town hall through a back door and walked down a corridor until we reached a room which said Barberton *Bloue* on a piece of paper stuck on the door. The room smelt of dust and sweat, even though nobody had changed yet. Lieutenant Smit was standing against the far wall and next to him stood Klipkop.

'This is where you will change today, but not all at once, hey?' The room tittered. 'This morning are the preliminary fights for the kids and this afternoon for the weight divisions. Tonight, starting six o'clock, the finals. Nobody leaves the town hall and if I catch anyone drinking a beer, I'm warning you now, there'll be trouble. We come here to win and that is what we going to do! Okay, so what's our motto?'

'One for all and all for one,' we all shouted. Doc put his hand on my shoulder and I felt very proud. 'I wish Geel Piet was with us,' I whispered. The room emptied and Klipkop shouted for the kids to stay behind. Doc, who was in charge of first aid, left to fetch the towels and the first-aid kit from the parking lot but promised to be right back.

Klipkop grinned. 'Today, man, I'm Geel Piet.'

'Does that mean we can hit you and you can't hit back?' Bokkie de Beer said cheekily, and we all laughed.

Klipkop smiled. 'I will look after you and the lieutenant and me will be your seconds. You can all get changed now and I'll fetch you in fifteen minutes. Don't nobody go nowhere, you hear?'

I found a corner and took my boots from my book satchel and put them on first. All the kids crowded around. 'Where'd you get those, man?' Bokkie de Beer exclaimed. I had been too excited to think up an explanation.

'My, my granpa made them,' I stammered.

'Boy, you lucky having a bootmaker for your granpa,' Fonnie Kruger said.

'Well, he's not really a bootmaker, more a sort of gardener.'

'Well he's blêrrie clever, that's all I can say,' Bokkie de Beer said enviously and the other kids seemed to agree with him.

I rolled my grey school socks down so they made a collar just above the boots. Then I put my lovely blue singlet on and the blue boxing shorts with the yellow stripe down the side. Geel Piet had sized the waist perfectly but the length was wishful thinking. The bottoms of the shorts went way past my knees. When I stood up the other four kids broke up. Maatie Snyman and Nels Stekhoven even rolled on the floor. I guess I must have looked pretty funny with my sparrow legs sticking out, but I also felt terribly proud.

Fonnie Kruger and myself were the first of the Barberton Blues to fight as we were in the under twelves, the most junior division. We waited for Klipkop and followed him into the town hall. Kids from other major towns in the Eastern Transvaal were standing in groups with adults and they too were changed and ready. I looked around wondering whom among them I would have to fight.

Doc entered the hall and moved over to me. We sat on two chairs, slightly away, but within easy beckoning distance from the others. Doc held my hand and I think he was more nervous than I was. He had taken out his bandanna and was wiping his brow. 'I think examinations in the conservatorium in Leipzig when I was so big as you was not so bad as this, ja. Absoloodle.'

'I'll be okay, Doc. I'll dance and everything, just like Geel Piet says. Lieutenant Smit says I'm blêrrie fast, you'll see they won't hit me, for sure.'

'It's nice of you to say this, Peekay. But what happens when comes one big Boer and connects?'

I grinned, trying to make him feel better. I repeated Hoppie's comment. 'Ag man, the bigger they are the harder they fall.' I felt pretty corny saying it and I knew now why

Hoppie had said it to me. He must have felt pretty corny too.

Doc groaned and buried his head in his red bandanna. 'Peekay, I want you should be very careful. In that ring are not nice people.' Just then Klipkop called me over and Doc squeezed my hand. 'You must use your feet to run away, Peekay. In my head I can hear only Wagner. No Mozart, only Wagner.'

Klipkop and Lieutenant Smit were standing with a large bald man with a big tummy who wore long white pants and a white singlet. A few feet from them stood two adults and a kid. The kid was quite a bit bigger than I though not as big as Snotnose. He wore a red singlet and in white on the front was the word Sabie. That was the town where Klipkop had his nooi, to whom he had recently become engaged.

The big man in the singlet looked at me and then at Lieutenant Smit. 'He is not very big. Are you sure you want him to fight?'

The lieutenant nodded. 'It will be good for him.'

The big man looked at the boy from Sabie and then looked doubtfully back at me. He turned to Lieutenant Smit. 'His opponent is eight inches taller and has probably got five inches more reach, man.'

'If I think he's getting hurt I'll pull him out.'

'I blêrrie well hope you know what you doing, man,' the big man said, shaking his head. The two men from Sabie were grinning and I could hear what they were saying inside their heads. They were glad their kid was going to get an easy fight first up.

Klipkop turned to me. 'This is Meneer de Klerk, Peekay. He is the referee and also the judge. He just came down from Pretoria last night.'

'Good morning, Meneer,' I said, sticking out my hand. The referee took it and shook it lightly.

'You got nice manners, son,' he said. Behind his back I could see one of the men pushing the kid from Sabie so he would do the same thing. Meneer de Klerk turned and indicated a large wooden crate on the floor below the boxing ring. Inside the crate were at least fifty pairs of boxing gloves. 'I want ten-ounce gloves. I don't want to see no kid hurt. Pick your gloves and then show them to me, you understand.'

'We got our own gloves,' Lieutenant Smit said.

'Then bring them, let me see.'

'Us also,' said one of the men from Sabie and stepped forward holding out a pair of gloves.

Meneer de Klerk examined both sets of gloves and declared them suitable. 'Okay, glove up. We on in five minutes.' He turned to a man sitting at a table directly beside the ring. 'Five minutes, you hear?' The man nodded and consulted a large pocket watch in front of him. He also had a bell and was obviously the timekeeper.

Klipkop and Lieutenant Smit both worked on lacing me up. I felt very important as neither of them had ever actually supervised any aspect of my boxing before.

'Remember, Peekay, boxing is a percentage game. Just make sure you hit him clean and more times than he hits you. No clinches, in clinches he can throw you off your feet. Stay out of the corners, stay off the ropes.'

The man at the table rang the bell and we walked over to the ring. Klipkop helped me through the ropes and then he and the lieutenant climbed in after me. There was a proper stool in the corner and Lieutenant Smit told me to sit on it. I felt a bit silly because the kid from Sabie was standing up and punching into the air and I was sitting like a little kid on a chamberpot.

'Right! Both in the middle,' Meneer de Klerk called and climbed into the ring. 'What's your names?'

'Du Toit, Meneer.'

'Peekay, Meneer.'

'I want a clean fight, you hear? No clinches. When I say break, you break. No hitting below the waist or behind the head. One knock down and the fight is over. You understand, Peekay? Du Toit?'

'Ja, Meneer,' we both said.

'Right, when you hear the bell you come into the centre of the ring, touch gloves and start boxing. Good luck.'

I walked back to my corner and on Lieutenant Smit's instructions sat down. Because it was the first fight of the day, all the teams were gathered around the ring and there were even some people from the town watching. It was my first boxing crowd and my heart was beating. Du Toit was standing in his corner and he too was looking around. I don't think either of us wanted to make eye contact. Seen from my stool he seemed very big, but I had waited too long for this moment to be afraid.

The bell rang. 'Box him, Peekay, you hear,' Klipkop said as I jumped from the stool.

We touched gloves in the middle of the ring, and as he pulled away I darted in and snapped a left and a right to Du Toit's jaw. His eyes widened in surprise. I could see that the punches hadn't hurt him, but nevertheless my early aggression had caught him unawares and he looked surprised.

He was a good boxer and didn't lose his composure but circled around me. He threw a straight left which went over my shoulder and flew past my ear. I went in under the arm with a quick uppercut and caught him hard in the ribs. I heard him wince so I knew I'd hit him hard. He caught me with a right on the shoulder and spun me around. I anticipated the left coming at me and ducked under it and got another good body blow on exactly the same spot as before. His arms wrapped around me and I was in a clinch, which I wasn't supposed to be in. I hit him furiously in the ribs with both hands, but my blows were too close to be effective and I knew he could hold me as long as he liked.

'Break!' I heard the ref say, and as Du Toit's arms slackened I got right out of the way. For the rest of the round I let him chase me. I was much the faster boxer and had much better foot work. Towards the end of the round

I could see by the way he set his feet which punch was going to come next. Just as the bell went I got inside with a short right and clipped him neatly on the point of the chin.

I had heard nothing during the fight and now realised that the crowd was making quite a noise and that my name was being shouted in encouragement. At the end of the round there was a lot of clapping and one or two whistles.

'You done good, Peekay,' Klipkop said. Lieutenant Smit wiped my face with a towel. 'He's missing with the right cross, but not by much. Watch it, man. If that kid finds his range he's going to hurt you bad. Keep your chin buried in your shoulder, that way if he gets one through you'll take most of it on the shoulder.'

The bell went for the second round and I let Du Toit chase me around the ring. I think he must have been told to try to get me into a corner because he would work me carefully towards one but at the last moment I'd feint left and duck out right and his right cross would miss by miles. But then I did it once too often and he caught me with a left uppercut in the gut and had it not been for the ropes behind me I might have gone down. He knew he'd hurt me and in his anxiety to capitalise was telegraphing his blows, trying for the big hit. All I could do was duck until I could use my feet to get out of trouble.

To my surprise, in the second half of the round he seemed to be tiring. He'd thrown a lot of punches, most of them landing on my gloves, though he did hit me a good body blow that hurt like hell. I began to move in quickly and pick him off. Towards the end of the round the crowd was beginning to laugh as I seemed to be able to hit him almost at will. A look of desperation had crept onto his face. I don't think I was hurting him much but I was making him very tired and very frustrated, just the way Geel Piet had said it must be done. The bell went and I was sure I had won the round.

'You don't have to hit him again to win,' Lieutenant Smit said. 'Just stay out of his way, you hear? Just counter punch, no attack. You going to win this clear, man, unless he cops you a lucky one.'

'You do like the lieutenant says, Peekay. You just stay out of trouble,' Klipkop added with a grin.

The bell went for the final round and we went into the centre of the ring and touched gloves. Du Toit must have had instructions to nail me because he kept rushing me, throwing wild punches. I'd nail him with a straight left or a right hook as he passed, but I was careful not to get set to throw a big punch. The crowd was laughing as I made him miss and I was beginning to feel pretty good. I had out-boxed him and hadn't been hurt, the bell would go any moment and I'd won. The right cross came at me and I couldn't move out of the way. It smashed into my shoulder and into my face and I felt as though I had walked into a telegraph pole. I felt myself going and grabbed at the ropes behind me to stop myself falling. The next blow came but I managed to get my head out of the way, then Du Toit threw another right and it just grazed my face. But my legs felt okay and my head had cleared. I ducked under a straight right and danced out of the way just as the bell went.

'Phew!'

Doc was at the ringside jumping up and down. 'Eleven out of ten. Absoloodle!' he yelled at me. It was the happiest moment of my life.

I had started to move back to my corner when Meneer de Klerk called us both into the centre of the ring. We shook hands and I thanked Du Toit for the fight but I think he knew he'd lost as his eyes brimmed with tears and he didn't reply. 'You got nice manners, you been taught right, Peekay,' Meneer de Klerk said again. Then he took us both by the hand and said: 'The winner three rounds to nothing is Gentleman Peekay!' He held my hand up and the crowd clapped and laughed at my new name. The Barberton Blues all yelled and whistled.

'That was good,' Lieutenant Smit said. 'But it's early times, you were lucky, man, you got a palooka. When I tell you to stay out of the way you stay out of the way, you hear? That right cross nearly brained you, man. Two like that early in the next bout and we throw in the towel, you understand!'

I nodded, and tried to look contrite. As Klipkop pulled the big mitts off my hands I suddenly felt light, as though I was going to float away. It was a wonderful feeling. It was the power of one stirring in me. Nothing Lieutenant Smit said could dampen my spirits. I jumped down from the ring feeling ten feet tall.

Doc gave me a big hug and then he held both my hands and we did a little jig which made me feel a bit silly but he was very happy. 'Peekay, I am very proud today! Absoloodle!' Then he stopped and reached into his pocket for his red bandanna and sniffed into it. He looked up, his blue eyes all watery. 'Such a dancer, already. Absoloodle.' I had never heard him say so many absoloodles before.

Fonnie Kruger won his fight against a kid from Boxburg and so did Maatie Snyman in the under thirteens, Nels Stekhoven in the under fourteens, and Bokkie de Beer in the under fifteens. I'm telling you, we were a pretty proud lot in the Barberton Blues, every one of us had advanced to the semis. Fonnie Kruger and I were both in the under twelve division, if we got through the semis we'd be in the final together. But our hopes were soon dashed. There was a kid from Lydenburg called Kroon who was the biggest eleven-year-old I had ever seen. He was at least a foot higher than me and twice as wide. He wasn't a boxer, but he polished off a kid from Nelspruit in the first round when he sat him on the canvas after about one minute. We instantly dubbed him Killer Kroon. We all got scared just looking at him and Bokkie said he was glad he was fighting in the under fifteen division and not in the under twelve.

Fonnie Kruger got Killer Kroon in the semis and managed to go one round before he was sat on his pants, seconds after the second round had begun. I think he was glad that it was all over, Killer Kroon had closed his right eye. 'It's like boxing a blêrrie gorilla,' he said when he climbed down from the ring.

Just before lunch I entered the ring again to fight a kid from Kaapmuiden. He was a square-built, nuggety sort of bloke and very strong around the shoulders but not a lot taller than me. It was the first time I had stood up to another boxer whose chin level wasn't above my head. It was a good fight and my speed saved me from taking the weight of his blows. He hit hard and straight, but I was able to move away as the punch came so the sting had gone out of it. Nevertheless he landed quite a lot of punches and was scoring well. Before the final round began Lieutenant Smit wiped my face.

'You're not doing enough to make certain of this fight. Watch his straight left, he keeps dropping his right glove after he's thrown the left. Get in under the blow and work him with both hands to the body. I want to make certain you got enough points.'

We touched gloves for the final round and Lieutenant Smit was quite right. The kid, whose name was Geldenhuis, threw his left and then curiously dropped his right. I went in underneath and got five or six good blows to the body before he pushed me away. The final bell went and the crowd chanted, 'Gentleman Peekay! Gentleman Peekay!' They were all Afrikaners and the English word obviously amused them. I thanked Geldenhuis who also thanked me. Then Meneer de Klerk announced for the second time that day, 'The winner in two out of three rounds, Gentleman Peekay!' The crowd laughed and clapped and the Barberton Blues went wild.

Doc could hardly contain himself. 'Not even one scratch, black eyes not even one. Perfect, you should play Chopin so good as this, ja?' He laughed and handed me a towel. 'Lieutenant Smit says you must have a shower and change into your clothes again. Tonight, six o'clock we fight again.'

He suddenly grew serious. 'Peekay, in the finals is a big Boer, you must dance very goot, in him is too much Wagner. You must box like a Mozart piano concerto, fast and light with perfect timing, ja?'

Doc found a small antechamber leading off the corridor in which there was a leather couch. After lunch he made me lie down. I was anxious to watch the adult preliminary fights and succumbed with ill grace. Despite the heat he threw a prison blanket over me, and to my surprise I fell asleep. It was five o'clock when he came to fetch me and I felt a little stiff and sore. He made me have a warm shower before I changed into my boxing things again. By the time we got back into the town hall it was almost six o'clock and the preliminaries were over. Bokkie de Beer said five of the Barberton Blues were through to the finals, including Gert who had had an easy and a hard fight, but was okay. That made nine of the fourteen Barberton Blues in the finals. I went over to Gert to congratulate him and he seemed pleased.

'Ag it wasn't too hard, Peekay. I think I got lucky. But like you, man, I got a Boer in the finals that's as big as a mountain, a super heavyweight. He won both his fights on knockouts in the first.'

'You got the speed, speed is everything,' I quoted Geel Piet.

'Not if he gets me in a corner,' Gert said solemnly.

'Then stay out of corners, man!' I said flippantly, but the advice was meant as much for myself as it was for him.

'You on soon, I've got my money on you, Peekay. You can do it, I'm telling you.' But I could hear him talking in his head and he was very, very worried about me.

Fonnie Kruger came over and said that Lieutenant Smit wanted me.

Lieutenant Smit and Klipkop were in earnest conversation with Meneer de Klerk and seemed not to notice my arrival. I stood and waited for them.

'The Boer kid has thirty, maybe forty pounds on yours.

I don't like it. I don't like it one bit,' the referee was saying, shaking his head.

'You saw him in the other two fights. He hardly got touched, our kid's a good boxer,' Klipkop said.

'He's better than that. He's the best I've seen in a long time. But he's a midget compared to Kroon. Kroon dropped both his opponents in the first. That's a bad kid. I work with young boxers every day, I'm telling you, this kid is not a sportsman.' Meneer de Klerk threw his hands open in a gesture of reconciliation. 'There's plenty of time, he's only ten. Let the boy grow a bit, wait till next year. He's champion material, too good to spoil with a mismatch.'

I could see a hesitant look cross Lieutenant Smit's face. The voices going on inside his head were confused. My heart was going boom, boom, boom and I couldn't swallow, there was a huge aching lump in my throat. Then he cocked his head and squinted at the bald referee. 'I make you this promise, Meneer de Klerk. If my boy even looks like being hurt we throw in the towel. You don't know Peekay. That kid has worked three years for this fight. In three years he hasn't missed one training session. For two years he just fought the bag and the ball. I can't pull him out without giving him a chance.'

'I'll give him one round, Smit. If he even looks like being hit in the first round I'm giving the fight to Kroon on a TKO, you understand?'

Lieutenant Smit nodded his head, 'Ja, okay, you the ref, man.' He turned and saw me and I grinned at him as though to indicate I'd just arrived. They had to give me a go. I had to fight Kroon. Kroon was no bigger to me than Jackhammer Smit was to Hoppie. I could take him, I knew I could take him. 'We got to glove up now, Peekay,' Lieutenant Smit said as he took a glove from Klipkop and slipped it over my left hand.

I climbed into the ring and sat on the little stool and Killer Kroon also sat on his. When he sat down he didn't look as though he was on the potty. He stared directly at me. Shit he was big! He had a grin on his face and I could hear his conversation to himself, 'I'm going to knock this little bugger out first round.'

'You got to catch me first, you bastard,' I said to myself. But I could feel his hugeness growing and beginning to fill the ring.

With the arrival of the townspeople for the finals, the town hall was at least half full. I had looked down on a bigger crowd when I played Chopin at the Barberton concert, but a boxing crowd is different, much more raw or something. I remembered Doc's words, 'You must box like a Mozart piano concerto.' In my head I could hear the way Doc would play a Mozart concerto, no arpeggio, fast and straight, the timing perfect. It made sense to box Killer Kroon in the same way.

'Never mind his head, Peekay. You just keep landing them to the body. Quick punches in and out with both hands. Scoring shots. Stay out of reach and don't let him get you against the ropes, not even once. You box him in the middle of the ring. Make him work, make him chase you all the time, you hear?'

I listened to them carefully, but I knew the real answer came from Geel Piet. That I had to box with my feet. I had no idea what sort of a boxer Killer Kroon was. His first opponent had lasted less than a minute and Fonnie went down a few seconds into the second round but had spent all of the first back-pedalling.

As I just sat there waiting, Kroon stared at me with an evil grin and I began to feel very small and a little bewildered. The feeling of being in front of the Judge came back to me and the ring became the dormitory and the audience the jury.

I closed my eyes and counted from ten to one. I stood on a rock just below the full moon, the roar of the falls in my ears. The river and the gorge and the African veld stretched out below me in the silver light. I was a young Zulu warrior who had killed his first lion and I could feel the lion skin skirt around my hips, the tail of the lion wrapped around my waist. I took a deep breath and jumped the first of the falls into a pool lashed with white spray and thunder, rose to the surface and was swept to the rim of the second, plunged downwards and rose again to be swept to the edge of the third pool where I fell again, rising to the surface at the bottom of the falls where the water danced with silver and the first of the stepping stones shone wet in the moon-light. I crossed the ten stones to the other side and opened my eyes and looked directly at Kroon. Killer Kroon saw something in my eyes which made him turn away and not look at me again.

The referee called us up, and taking us by the wrists he held our hands in the air, introducing me first. 'On my left, Dames and Here . . . Gentleman Peekay of the Barberton Blues.' The crowd gave me a big hand, although this was mixed with laughter as they saw my size next to Killer Kroon. 'On my right, from Lydenburg Martinus Kroon.' The crowd had already chosen sides and with the exception of the Lydenburg squad the clapping was only polite. I went back and sat on my stool. It was the first fight of the finals and anticipation made the crowd enthusiastic even though it was the most junior fight of the night.

The bell went for the first round and I sprang from my stool while Killer Kroon got up slowly, almost disdainfully. We moved to the centre of the ring, and he threw a left at my head which only came up to below his shoulder. I could see it coming for miles and let it pass my ear. He followed with a right and I ducked under the punch. It was almost the same opening Du Toit had used and I followed it the same way with a left and a right under Kroon's heart. I got some body behind the two punches which I drove in hard but he didn't even seem to notice. I danced quickly out of the way and a clumsy uppercut with his left missed my chin by six inches. The crowd winced at the ferocity of the punch even though it was all show and no blow.

I stayed in the centre of the ring, moving around Kroon

who threw four more punches and missed. He threw another right which parted my hair but the punch was too hard, throwing him off balance. I moved in fast and hit the same spot under the heart with a left and right combination which I repeated. Four good short punches with plenty of shoulder behind them. But I'd been too greedy getting the extra two punches home, his huge arms locked around me and, lifting me bodily, he threw me away from him. I was sent spinning across the ring, my legs working like pistons to keep me on my feet. I bounced into the ropes, and grabbed the middle one with both arms to steady myself. I was wide open as the straight right came at me. It should have been an uppercut, I was against the ropes and would not have been able to move out of the way of a punch coming up at me. To put everything he had into the punch, Killer Kroon had pulled his shoulder back just a fraction too far. It allowed me a split second to move my head to the right. Instead of sending me bye-bye-birdie, the blow caught my ear and it felt like a branding iron had been pushed into the side of my head. But I'd taken worse from the Judge and I feinted left and moved off the ropes under his right arm. He turned quickly but my feet were already in position and he walked into a perfectly timed right cross, coming at him with the full weight of my body behind it. The punch had landed flush on the point of his chin and his head snapped back. I knew I had hurt him. It was the best punch I had ever thrown by far. Gert said later, had I been nearer to Killer Kroon's size, he'd have been out for a week.

Kroon shook his head in bewilderment. He was hurt and he was mad and he came looking for me. I stayed out of his way, taking a straight left on the shoulder moving away, and managed two more good punches to the spot under his heart when he telegraphed another right cross. The spot under his heart had developed a red patch. The bell went for the end of round one, and as I returned to my corner I could see a grin on Meneer de Klerk's face.

Doc was standing outside the ring in my corner as Lieutenant Smit and Klipkop climbed in to attend to me. He had his bandanna in both hands and was twisting it round and round with the tears falling down his cheeks.

'You done good,' Klipkop said with a huge grin. Lieutenant Smit said nothing at first but smeared Vaseline over the ear where Kroon had glanced his big hit off me. He covered my good ear with his hand.

'Can you hear me, Peekay?' He spoke from the side I'd been hit.

'Ja, Lieutenant, I hear you good,' I replied.

'If a thick ear is all we get out of this fight we'll be blêrrie lucky.' He turned to Klipkop. 'Give him another half-glass of water. Rinse only, don't swallow.' He looked directly at me. 'Now listen good, Peekay. It looks like this gorilla's only got four punches. Straight right, straight left, right cross and left uppercut. He's a fighter and he's never needed any more than those, every one is a good punch and he throws them well except the left uppercut is a bit clumsy and he tries to hit too hard with the right cross so you can see it coming. You done good to move under it and hit him under the heart. That's a damn good punch. He's very strong but if you can get in enough of those they're going to count in the end and you'll slow him down for the third. Keep moving, you must keep moving, you hear? Make him work, he's not as fit as you, make him work and keep hitting him on that spot under the heart, okay?'

I had never heard Lieutenant Smit talk so fast, and listening to what he wasn't saying I could see he now thought I had a chance. 'No more attack, counter punch, you hear? Only counter punch.' I nodded and the bell went for the second round.

Kroon came storming out of his corner and I could see from the look in his eyes that he wanted to finish the fight. For the first half of the round I ducked and weaved and back-pedalled and moved him around. He must have thrown fifty punches without landing even one. The crowd was beginning to laugh as he repeatedly missed and he was becoming frustrated. Towards the second half of the round he slowed down just a little and his right cross wasn't coming quite so fast. He was breathing heavily and to my surprise I could smell his sweat. A kid's sweat doesn't smell until he's about Bokkie de Beer's size, but I could smell Killer Kroon's sweat all right, plain as anything. I moved up a little closer and started coming in under the right cross again, to land on the same spot under the heart time and time again. I couldn't believe his lack of imagination. The right cross came at me regular as clockwork and I moved under it and landed two and sometimes four punches to the spot under his heart. His breathing was getting heavier and heavier and he grunted as I landed a left and a right and I realised that my punches to the heart were beginning to hurt him. I was getting pretty tired myself when the bell sounded for the end of the second round.

The crowd stood and clapped. As I returned to my corner I looked towards Doc. He had the bandanna in his mouth and was chewing on it.

'He's going to try and finish you this round, Peekay. You got both rounds, you miles ahead on points. He is going to try to put you down.' Lieutenant Smit's usually calm voice was gone and he was breathing hard. 'Stay away, man. I don't care if you don't land a blêrrie punch, just run away, keep clear, you hear? Keep clear, you got this fight won. Magtig! You boxing good!' His eyes were shining as he spoke.

The bell for the final round went and we met in the centre of the ring and touched gloves. Killer Kroon was still breathing hard and his chest was heaving. As we moved away he said, 'I'm going to kill you, you blêrrie Rooinek.'

Geel Piet said you always had to answer back, so they know you're not afraid. 'Come and get me, you Boer bastard!' I shot back at him. He rushed at me and I stepped aside but his swinging arm caught me as he passed and knocked me off my feet. It wasn't a punch, it was the inside of his arm, but it sat me down. I couldn't believe it had happened. One knockdown and you lose the fight! I had lost the fight! I had opened my mouth to talk, lost my concentration and lost the fight! I couldn't believe it was me sitting on the canvas. There was a roaring in my ears and a terrible despair in my heart.

'No knockdown, continue to box!' I heard Meneer de Klerk shout as though in a dream. I was coming to my feet but it felt as though I was underwater. The thought of defeat had drowned my senses. Killer Kroon rushed in and that clumsy left uppercut just missed my chin. This time he should have used the right cross as I couldn't move upwards to my feet and sideways at the same time. A right cross would have caught me flush on the chin and finished me for keeps. Instead I simply moved my head backwards and the uppercut whizzed safely past the point of my chin. I was back on my toes and dancing out of reach, moving around him. The stupid bastard couldn't box for toffee. No way was he going to get a second chance at me.

I was making him miss pretty easily and began to realise that there was something wrong with him. His breath was coming in rasps and his chest was heaving, his punches had lost their zing. I moved up and hit him as hard as I could with a two-fisted attack to the spot under his heart and his hands fell to his sides. His gloves came around my waist but there was hardly any strength left in him and he leaned heavily on me, his gloves working up and down my waist. The thumb of his glove must have caught the elastic band of my boxing shorts for they slipped neatly over my hips and fell to my ankles. I didn't know what to do. I couldn't step backwards for fear of falling, anyway his arms and weight made it impossible to move. So I just stood there and hit him again and again as he draped his arms over me, my bare arse pointed at the crowd. Then he gave me a last desperate push and I tripped over the shorts caught around my ankles and fell down. I tried to pull my pants up with my boxing gloves but without success. The crowd was convulsed with laughter and Killer Kroon was standing over me with his hands on his knees, head hanging. He was rasping and wheezing and trying to take in air.

'No knockdown!' Meneer de Klerk shouted. 'Get back to your corner, Kroon!' He grabbed me by the wrist and jerked me to my feet and then pulled my pants up. I had been covering my snake with my gloves. In those days nobody wore underpants and I was bare-arsed and fancy free in front of everyone. But I didn't care a damn, the only thing that mattered was Killer Kroon in the ring with me. I would have fought him with no clothes on if necessary. Meneer de Klerk wiped my gloves on his pants. 'Box on,' he said. I turned to face Killer Kroon's corner. He was standing with his back to me and his chest was still heaving. Suddenly a towel lofted over his head and landed at my feet. I couldn't believe my eyes, Kroon's corner was throwing in the towel, the fight was over! Meneer de Klerk moved quickly over to me, and with a huge grin on his face held my hand aloft. 'Winner on a technical knockout, Gentleman Peekay!' he announced. The crowd stood up for the second time and shouted and cheered and Lieutenant Smit and Klipkop jumped into the ring. Klipkop lifted me up and held me high above his shoulders and turned around in the ring and everyone went wild.

Meneer de Klerk had moved over to Kroon's corner and now he came back to the centre of the ring and held his hand up for silence. The timekeeper rang his bell until the crowd quietened down. Klipkop put me down again. 'The Lydenburg squad want me to say that Martinus Kroon retired because of an asthma attack.' A section of the crowd started to boo and there was general laughter. 'More like a Rooinek attack!' someone shouted. The bald referee held up his hand once more. 'I just want you to know that I had the fight scored two rounds to none for Gentleman Peekay and I also had him ahead on points in the third round. The technical knockout stands. Let me tell you something, this boy is going to be a great boxer, just remember where you saw him first.' The crowd whistled and stomped and cheered again and Lieutenant Smit held my hand up and then we left the ring. Doc was crying and I had to sit down and hold his hand for a bit and then we went together to the showers. But first Doc and I shared the last two pumpkin scones.

'I think Geel Piet and the people will be very happy tonight,' Doc said as he handed me a towel. 'I go to get you a soft drink? What colour do you want?'

'But we haven't got any money,' I said.

'That's what you think, Mister Schmarty Pantz!' Doc fished into the pocket of his white linen suit and produced two half-crowns.

'Five shillings! Where'd you get that?' I said in amazement.

He grinned slyly. 'I am making this bet with a nice man from Lydenburg.'

'A bet! You bet on me? What if I'd lost? If I'd lost you couldn't have paid him!'

Doc dropped the coins back into his coat pocket with a clink and then scratched his nose with his forefinger. 'You couldn't lose, you was playing Mozart,' he said.

I asked for an American cream soda. It was the drink Hoppie had bought me in the café at Gravelotte after we'd changed the tackies at the Patels' shop and it was still my favourite. It was also the closest I could come to sharing my win with Hoppie. If Geel Piet and Hoppie could have been there, everything would have been perfect. Not that it wasn't perfect. But more perfect.

FOURTEEN

By the time we got to the last fight of the evening, the Barberton Blues had won five of the eight finals and only the heavyweight division remained. Naturally it was the event from which the crowd expected the most and they were not disappointed. Gert was matched with a giant of a man called Potgieter, a railway fettler from Kaapmuiden who was six foot seven and a half and weighed two hundred and eighty-nine pounds. Gert was no lightweight and at six foot one he weighed two hundred and twenty.

Potgieter was a better boxer than he first appeared and in the first round he had Gert hanging on twice, but Gert won the round by landing more clean punches. In the heavyweight division a knockdown did not mean the end of the fight and in the second round Potgieter, way behind on points, connected with an uppercut under the heart which doubled Gert up like a collapsed mattress before he dropped to the canvas. The bell went at the count of five but it looked all over for him anyway.

To our surprise he came out for the final round and started hitting Potgieter almost at will. The big man knew he was behind on points so he dropped his defence, confident he could take anything Gert dished out. Gert dished out plenty and there was blood all over the giant's face and one eye was completely closed. He smiled throughout the fight, a grotesque, dangerous-looking smile from a mouth that was missing the front teeth. Gert's straight left and right were working like pistons into a face that was moving relentlessly forward. Potgieter chopped his way to within range of Gert and finally managed to trap him in a corner. The uppercut seemed to be in slow motion as it caught Gert on the point of the jaw. The warder was out cold even before his legs had started to buckle and we thought he'd been killed. The referee counted him out and Klipkop and Lieutenant Smit lifted him unconscious from the floor and carried him to his corner. Gert had, as usual, fought with too much heart and not enough head. If only he had known about Mozart.

It was after ten o'clock when we left Nelspruit. We kids huddled together in the back of the utility, sharing two rough prison blankets. The indigo night was pricked with sharp cold stars. We'd spent what energy remained in lavish praise of each other and of the glorious Barberton Blues, and now we were silent and sleepy. Klipkop drove this time, as Gert was not in such good shape and had gone home in the thirty-nine Chevy with Lieutenant Smit.

Bokkie, Fonnie, Nels and Maatie were soon sleeping fitfully. Jolts woke them momentarily, their dulled eyes opening for a minute before heavy lids shut them down again. I was enormously tired as well, but couldn't doze off. In my mind each of my three fights kept repeating themselves. I played them back in sequence as though they were scenes on a loop of film which I was able to edit in my imagination, snipping here, joining there, remaking the fights, seeing them in my mind as they should have been.

I didn't know it then, but this ability totally to recall a fight scenario made me a lot more dangerous when I met an opponent for the second time. In the years ahead I also taught myself to fight as a southpaw, so I could switch if necessary in the middle of a fight, as though it were entirely natural for me to do so.

It was nearly midnight when the ute stopped outside our house. Everything was in darkness. I crept around the back because the kitchen door was never locked. A candle stub burned on the kitchen table and on the floor, each rolled in a blanket, lay Dum and Dee. I tried to tiptoe past but they both shot up into sitting positions, like Egyptian mummies suddenly come to life, the whites of their eyes showing big with alarm.

They were overjoyed at my return and switched on the light to examine me. They burst into tears when they saw my swollen ear and it took some effort to calm them. When I told them that I had won, they showed only polite joy. They clucked and tut-tutted like a pair of old abafazi around a cooking pot and declared they'd be up at dawn to look for poultice weed against the horrible bruises which were undoubtedly concealing themselves all over my body. Despite my protests, for I was almost too tired to stand up, Dum sat me down and washed my face, hands and feet with water from a kettle kept warm on the stove. Dee dried me on a coarse towel and at last I was allowed to totter off to bed.

At Sunday school the next morning Pastor Mulvery noticed my fat ear and gave me a lightning on/off smile showing his escape-attempting front teeth. 'Have you been listening to the devil again, Peekay?' He hee-hawed quite a lot over his clever joke and no doubt repeated it to the Lord later. He always said you had to tell the Lord everything.

I remained unsaved, unborn again, despite the fact that I was officially slated in the minds of every lady in the church as my mother's special prayer burden. I guess if they'd known what was going on in the prison they'd have mounted a whole revival campaign to try and bring me to the Lord. Once I asked in Sunday school if black was equal with white in heaven. The Sunday school teacher, a lady with big breasts and a sharp nose named Mrs Kostler who looked like a fat pigeon, stopped in mid-reply and sent one of the other kids to look for Pastor Mulvery.

'Not exactly, but not exactly not,' Pastor Mulvery said, and then thumbing through Mrs Kostler's Bible he read, '"In my father's house are many mansions, I go to prepare a place for you".' He put the Bible aside. 'Many mansions is the Lord's way of saying that He loves all of mankind but that He recognises there are differences, like black and white. So He has a place for black angels and another place for white angels,' he said smugly. I could see he was pretty pleased with his reply.

A girl called Zoe Prinsloo asked, 'Does that mean we don't have to have dirty kaffirs in our mansion?'

'Ag man, Zoe,' Mrs Kostler cried, 'in heaven nobody is dirty, you hear, not even kaffirs!'

'Will they still work for us?' I asked.

Mrs Kostler looked to Pastor Mulvery for a reply. 'Of course not, nobody works in heaven,' he said, a little impatiently.

'If nobody is dirty and nobody works in heaven and black and white are equal, why then can't they live in the same place as us?'

Pastor Mulvery gave a deep sigh. 'Because they are black and it wouldn't be right, that's all. The Lord knows more about such things than we do, man. We mustn't question the wisdom of the Lord. When you are born again you'll understand His infinite wisdom and you won't ask such silly questions.' I knew Mrs Kostler would report all this back at the next ladies' prayer meeting and I'd have to face another session with my mother. It wasn't easy being a sinner.

She would send me to my room and come and sit on my bed and sigh quite a lot. Then she would say, 'I'm very disappointed in you, son-boy. Mrs Kostler says that you were questioning the word of God. Why do you mock the Lord so? You are not too young for His wrath. "I am not mocked," sayeth the Lord. I pray for your precious soul every day, but you harden your heart and one day the Lord will not proffer up unto you His mercy and His everlasting forgiveness and you will be damned.' She would sigh a few more times. It was the sighs that got to me, I couldn't bear to think I was hurting her so much. But I didn't really know how to stop either. It was natural for me to ask questions. Doc demanded them, had trained my mind to search for truth. To confront that which lacked logic or offended common sense was as natural for me as climbing trees. I was a sleuth in search of the truth and once on the track of biblical malpractice I found it impossible to let a contradiction pass or an assumption go unquestioned.

I would ask for forgiveness and agree to apologise to Mrs Kostler or whoever at the Apostolic Faith Mission I might have offended. But it was never enough. My mother demanded an orgy of confession. She wanted me to renounce my sins, retract my point of view and go down on my knees and beg forgiveness from the Lord. I couldn't do it and so I compounded her disappointment in me.

So she would make me stay in my room and go without supper instead.

I kept a stick of *biltong* under my mattress for these occasions. Marie often brought these hard sticks of dried game home from the farm and Dee and Dum and I, being the only ones without false teeth, were the only ones who could eat it. I would sit in bed reading, cutting off delicious slivers of sun-dried venison with my Joseph Rogers pocket knife. It was Doc's really, but I was minding it for him while he was in prison.

Marie had surrendered to the army of the Lord and in some measure made up for my recalcitrance. Creating born-again Christians for Pentecostals was like scalp hunting for Red Indians. Occasionally there was a really big coup, when a well-known drunk or fornicator or even a three-pack-a-day cigarette smoker was brought trembling to his knees before the Lord. This person then testified in front of the congregation. I'm telling you, some of these past sinners washed in the blood of the Lamb really got carried away when the congregation started to respond. When the halleluja-ing and praise the Lord-ing and spontaneous bursting into song and clapping of hands and sighs of joy were going on, the convert would be crying and sniffing and having a really good time telling about all his really bad deeds. Every time the testimony got really juicy a silence fell on the congregation as they soaked up the last drop of vicarious sin. I have to admit, it was pretty impressive when a repentant drunk was saved. One day you would have to cross the road so as not to go near him and the next, after he was born again, he was called brother, shaken warmly by the hand and loved by everybody. I guess the Lord has to be given credit for that.

But sometimes being born again didn't last and the person who used to be loved was said to have backslid. Backsliding was the worst thing that could happen in the Apostolic Faith Mission. It meant all the spontaneous love had been wasted and that the devil had won. Mind you, this was generally seen as a temporary setback. To the Pentecostals the things of the flesh, tempting as they might be, didn't compensate for the promise of everlasting life. Once you were born again and then became a backslider you challenged this premise and jeopardised the whole glorious presumption of pay now play later. The born-again Christians were all working very hard for their segregated mansions in heaven.

I think I instinctively recognised winners and losers and it seemed to me the members of the Apostolic Faith Mission were to be found more often on the losers' side of life. This was a situation which they seemed to enjoy. 'Blessed are the poor, for they shall see the kingdom of God.' A converted drunk or a sinner who admitted to adultery was such an obvious loser that he just naturally belonged. Backsliding was therefore not easily accepted and a lot of work went into bringing the lost child back to the Lord. The stakes were pretty high. In return for bringing a really lost soul to the Lord you gained a fair amount of real estate in the sky, according to Pastor Mulvery. At least a two-storey mansion set back from the street with trees and green lawns where the soft breezes carried the glissando of harps. Which was a damn sight better than the crackle of hell and the dreadful moans of the everlastingly condemned.

For the drunks who were smart enough to become born

again and then backslide, the Apostolic Faith Mission served as a sort of drying-out clinic where love and reassurance, fresh clothes and a new start could be found from time to time. Really juicy backsliding testimonies filled the church and gave everyone present a precious time with the Lord and Pastor Mulvery a bigger collection plate. Church members put a lot more work and enthusiasm into a bad sinner than someone like Marie who came to them meek as a lamb without any spiritual blemishes, hardly worth a spontaneous halleluja and certainly not worth a good public weep to the glory of the Lord.

Marie's spiritual moment of glory came later when she testified in front of the congregation and told how she had brought an eighty-nine-year-old Boer to the Lord on his death-bed. How he had been afraid to die and when she had brought him to Christ he had closed his eyes and with a soft sigh gone to meet his maker.

I had privately thought this an almost perfect solution. The old man had spent his life as a sinner and then, at the last possible moment, was snatched from the jaws of hell by a pimply-faced girl whose heart was filled with love and compassion. I wondered briefly whether this entitled him to a full heavenly mansion or maybe just the garden shed at the bottom of Marie's garden? Anyway, she got a terrific response from the congregation. Snatching lost souls from the brink of the fiery furnace was pretty high on the list of important conversions and it immediately altered her previous status of sweet girl to that of a capable and resourceful soldier in the army of the Lord.

Like me, Dum and Dee were holding out, although to them the whole business was a bit confusing and their true status was never really known. They had been semi-ordered to be born again by my mother and naturally they had complied. My mother gave them a Shangaan Bible but it was left to me to teach them to read it and we had concentrated more on the Old Testament where the stories of the warriors, drought and famine were much more to their liking. Their favourite was the one about Ruth in the cornfield trying to find enough corn to feed her family after the harvesters had been through the fields. The concept of a white man coming along and forgiving everyone's sins and then getting nailed to a post for his trouble, to Dum and Dee seemed a highly unlikely story. As Dum pointed out, white men never forgive sins, they only punish you for them, especially if you are black. To accept the black man's sins and agree to be responsible and even crucified for them only proved he must have been crazy. Dee then asked, if he'd already done the dying for black people's sins, why was the white man always punishing the black man? I was prepared to agree she had a point and as I also found the miracles very suspect, we just naturally stayed with the Old Testament, which had witchdoctors like Elijah and great leader kings like Moses and fierce and independent generals like Joshua. A book like this made sense and posed all the problems and terrors their own legends told about.

My mother claimed Dee and Dum, along with Marie, on her personal born-again list. There were others, for on Wednesday afternoons she stopped sewing and headed for the hospital with a marked Bible and a bagful of tracts. The tracts had headings such as, Sinner snatched from certain hellfire and The man who talked to God about sin and Salvation: God's precious promise. The one she claimed was the big artillery in the hospital environment was called, Hell is one mortal blink away. She had taken Pastor Mulvery's place after I was released from hospital, and from time to time found worthy sinners lurking behind starched sheets. They were usually fraught with the anxiety of fresh stitches from a hysterectomy or a gall-bladder operation and ripe for the softening-up process. My mother began by enquiring about the operation. She was an expert, perhaps even the world champion, on operations. She seemed to have undergone all the major operations a woman can expect and a few others on the side just to round out her experience. At the drop of a medical complaint she could detail every phase of an operation from the first tiny suspicious pangs of pain to the post-operative depression. My gift for recalling every detail of a fight must have come from her, for she could do the same with operations, even the bits when she was under anaesthetic.

Having determined how long the sinner was likely to be in hospital and therefore how captive as an audience, the spiritual ear bashing began; Marie did the follow-up work for the Lord, keeping the sinner Christwise until the next Wednesday visit. They shared the souls they saved and often witnessed together at the Sunday morning meeting where they basked in the warmth of the spiritual love they received from the congregation. The Lord had a couple of stormtroopers in them, all right. Pastor Mulvery used to refer to them as 'the sisters of redemption', adding that the Lord had touched them in a special way.

Marie was still very conscious of her pimples. One day my mother said enough was enough, if the Lord cared about every sparrow that fell, then surely he cared equally about Marie's pimples. The two of them went down on their knees and exhorted the Lord to cast out the pimple demon. To my complete surprise He did. Within a year Marie's face was as smooth as a baby's bottom, and she turned out to be quite pretty underneath. That was a mighty testimony session, with Marie crying and ruining her new-found prettiness and my mother telling the dramatic story of the Lord's wonderful pimple cure. Pastor Mulvery did a neat little summary afterwards by saying the Lord's rewards are not only in heaven where the big pay-out takes place but also on earth as instanced by the demise of Marie's pimples. My mother's faith and her work with Marie for the Lord had been rewarded personally by Him.

When I first told Doc about the concerted prayer campaign for the removal of Marie's pimples, he suggested that I advise her to eat lots of salad, no fat, and lean meat only, twice a week. Marie tried it, found she liked it better than the stodgy hospital food, and kept to this diet fairly diligently. When I told him of the cure through prayer he declared that some things were too mysterious for words. I thought about it a little more and finally made the connection between the diet and the cure, and I asked him why he hadn't pointed out the possibility of the change in diet making the difference.

'Peekay,' he said, 'in this world are very few things made from logic alone. It is illogical for a man to be too logical. Some things we must just let stand. The mystery is more important than any possible explanation.' He paused for a moment and tapped his fingers on the edge of the keyboard. 'The searcher after truth must search with humanity. Ruthless logic is the sign of a limited mind. The truth can only add to the sum of what you know, while a harmless mystery left unexplored often adds to the meaning of life. When a truth is not so important, it is better left as a mystery.' It was an answer which left me confused for some years, for Doc worshipped the truth and had always demanded it between us at any cost.

Geel Piet had not expected me to win through to the finals in Nelspruit. The most he had hoped for was a berth in the semis. His delight at the Monday morning training session knew no bounds. 'The people are very happy. I'm telling you, since we heard the news they have talked about nothing else, man. The Zulus say you are surely a Zulu chief disguised as a white man, for only a Zulu can fight with this much courage.' He laughed. 'When we heard the news, everybody who had a *stompie* smoked it and the warders could not stop the people singing in the night.'

In fact, one of the warders told Doc and me at breakfast on Monday morning that there had been a strange feeling in the prison on Saturday night and they had alerted off-duty men to be on standby. He said that at about seven o'clock, before any of the warders knew the results, one of the old lags told him I had won. He had only officially been told after midnight, when the news came from the warder on duty at the gates within minutes of the return of Lieutenant Smit to the prison. 'Wragdig, man. Kaffirs are funny that way. Sometimes they just know things without the telephone or anything. I seen it before in Pollsmoor when a prisoner is going to be hanged. The decision is made not even in the jail but they know even before the instructions come to the Kommandant. An old lag once told me they send out their combined energy to find out. I dunno how it works, man, but I'm telling you they blêrrie well know.'

At my piano lesson on Monday, Doc found an excuse for Geel Piet to come into the hall and I played back the three fights blow by blow to him. He nearly died laughing when I told him about my pants falling down. I added that I would get my mother to shorten them and tighten the elastic around the waist. It was Geel Piet who cottoned on to why Killer Kroon had the asthma attack.

'He is not used to boxing three rounds hard. Probably he never even boxed three rounds before, because he always got a TKO decision like the first two fights. Then you come along and he has to chase you all over the place, man, and you keep hitting him under the heart. So what do you think happens? He has to breathe harder and harder, man, and the strain brings on his asthma attack. I had a aunty in Cape Town who couldn't even climb some steps without getting an asthma attack. I'm telling you, it's the truth, man. You found his weakness and you attacked it.' He smiled, 'Hey man, blêrrie lucky he had a bad left hook. When you came in under his right cross he could've done some real damage with a good left hook.'

That morning Lieutenant Smit had made a short speech to us all. 'I'm proud of you all, you hear? Not one boxer let us down, even those of you who lost, you fought good.' He turned to Klipkop. 'Wait until that Potgieter turns professional, man, I'm telling you, you in for a lot of trouble.'

'Let him come,' Klipkop mumbled.

'Gert, you done good. You hit him maybe ten times for every one time he hit you but two hundred and twenty pounds isn't two hundred and eighty pounds. That big ape belongs in the jungle.' We all laughed and then he said, 'I left the smallest for last. The under twelve finals was the best boxing match I have ever seen.' Fonnie Kruger punched me in the ribs and I didn't know how to stop my face burning. 'No, honest man, if you all want a lesson in boxing then watch Peekay.' He paused and looked directly at Geel Piet standing twenty paces behind us. 'Geel Piet, you just a yellow Kaffir, but I got to hand it to you, you a good coach.'

We all looked round to see Geel Piet cover his face with both hands and dance from one foot to another as though he were standing on hot coals.

'Don't think you can get cheeky now, you hear?' Lieutenant Smit said. But there was a hint of amusement in his voice.

Geel Piet pulled his hands down over his face as though wiping away the expression concealed under them. 'No, baas, thank you, baas. This yellow Kaffir is a very happy man, baas.'

The prison photographer came into the gym and Lieutenant Smit announced we were going to have our picture taken but not our fingerprints. We all laughed and the photographer lined us up, fussing around until he had got it just right. There was an explosion of light as he took the picture, and then he said he wanted to take another for luck. Lieutenant Smit looked about him as Doc entered the hall. 'Come Professor, come stand here,' he invited and then to everyone's surprise he beckoned to Geel Piet. 'You too, Kaffir,' he said gruffly.

Klipkop stepped out of the photographer's former arrangement. 'No way, man! I'm not having my photo taken with a blêrrie Kaffir!'

Lieutenant Smit brought his hand up to his mouth and blew a couple of breathy notes down the centre of his closed fist. 'That's okay, Sergeant Oudendaal,' he said pleasantly. 'Anybody else also want to step out?'

Geel Piet stepped out of where he was standing on the

edge of the group. 'I am too ugly for a heppy snap, baas,' he grinned.

'Get back, Kaffir!' Lieutenant Smit commanded.

Geel Piet returned to the edge of the group, whereupon the remainder of the adult boxers stepped out of the group with the exception of Gert, then Bokkie de Beer moved away followed by the other kids. I could see they were real scared. Only Doc, Gert, Geel Piet and myself were left when Lieutenant Smit stepped back into the picture. 'Okay man, take the snap!' he commanded.

The photograph captured the exact moment when I understood with conviction that racism is a primary force of evil designed to destroy good men.

We were all given a large ten by eight inch photograph of the Barberton Blues and the photographer gave Doc, Gert and me a copy of the second photograph. The lieutenant refused his copy which I begged from the photographer and gave to Geel Piet privately. He kept it in the piano stool and looked at it every day when he collected the prisoners' mail.

Some weeks later Lieutenant Smit was promoted to captain and some people even started to talk about him as the next Kommandant. He called me aside after training session one morning and asked if I would return the second photo and get Doc's copy back as well. I had no option but to obey, and Gert did the same. Lieutenant Smit tore them up but forgot about the extra copy. He obtained the plate from the prison photographer and destroyed this also. A man cannot be careful enough about his career and the second photograph had been aberrant to his normal behaviour. He had no intention of living to regret it.

Between Doc and Mrs Boxall, my education was in fairly safe hands. Mrs Boxall consulted with Doc by note and they decided on my serious reading. She was the expert on English literature and he on the sciences, music and Latin. The Barberton library, apart from containing Doc's own botanical collection, had also been the recipient of two surprisingly good private collections and Mrs Boxall said it was choked with intellectual goodies for a growing mind. Both Doc and Mrs Boxall were natural teachers and enthusiasts who never lost patience when my young mind couldn't keep up. Doc set exams and Mrs Boxall conducted them in the library. I had an exam on Tuesday and Friday every week and I grew to love this time spent with Mrs Boxall, who often violently disagreed with a conclusion reached by Doc. I was the carrier of debate notes and some of the intellectual arguments went on for weeks at a time. I was never excluded and I learned the value of debate and of having a point of view I was prepared to defend.

The three of us had been playing chess for some time. Doc and Mrs Boxall each had a board and Gert had made one more, turning the chess figures on the lathe in the prison workshop and doing the wood inlay for the board by hand. It was not as good as Doc's ivory set but Doc said it was very well made and original. The two boards were set up, one with my game and the other with Mrs Boxall's. Every morning I gave Doc Mrs Boxall's move and he positioned it on the board and made his reply which I took back to her. We set ten minutes aside at the end of the lesson to play. At first that was enough for Doc to beat me but as the months and years went by, a game would often last a week.

I had never beaten Doc in four years and in two years Mrs Boxall only managed it once. It was the game the Russian Lenchinakov played when he beat the American Arnold Green in 1931 and she had studied it for three weeks. Even so she was lucky to pull it off. On her eighth move Doc realised she wasn't playing her usual game. 'Ask Madame Boxall who is playing for her this game?' he instructed me. But it was already too late, he had walked into an audacious trap set so early in the game that he had not suspected she was capable of such a move.

When I brought her the news that Doc had conceded the game she jumped up from behind her desk and rubbed her hands gleefully together, a huge grin on her face. 'By golly, it feels dashed good to beat the pompous old Teuton,' she exclaimed. 'Tell him not to be a bad sport, all's fair in love and war!'

Two of me were emerging, a small boy approaching eleven who climbed trees, used a catapult, drove a billycart and led an eager gang in kleilat and other games against the Afrikaner kids, and a somewhat precocious child who often left the teachers at school in despair, unable to cope with my answers or even tolerate the fact that I was already well in advance of anything they had to teach. They simply awarded me first place in class every term and got on with the business of teaching the other kids.

In my tenth year a new teacher, Miss Bornstein, arrived at the school. She taught the senior class, getting them ready for the emotional leap into high school and while I was still two classes below the seniors she had summoned me to her classroom after school one Friday afternoon.

'Hello, Peekay, come in,' she said as I knocked on the door. She was seated at her table reading a book.

'Good afternoon, miss,' I said, entering a little fearfully. She looked up and smiled and my head began to zing as though I'd been clocked a straight right between the eyes by Snotnose. Miss Bornstein was the most beautiful person I had ever seen. She had long black hair and the biggest green eyes you've ever seen and a large mouth that shone with red lipstick. Her skin was lightly tanned and without a single blemish. At ten you are not supposed to be sexually attracted, but every nerve in my body cried out to be a closer part of this beautiful woman. She was dazzling and when she smiled her teeth were even and perfectly white. Except for the fact that she was not as willowy as the C to C cigarette lady painted on the clockface of the railway café in Tzaneen, she could have been the living version.

'They tell me you're rather clever, Peekay.'

'No miss,' I said without false modesty. Despite the fact that I was accepted as the brightest child in the school, both

Doc and Mrs Boxall had been careful to disabuse me of such a notion. 'Cleverness is a false presumption,' Doc had explained. 'It is like being a natural skater, you are so busy doing tricks to impress that you do not see where the thin ice is and before you know, poof! You are in deep, ice-cold water frozen like a dead herring. Intelligence is a harder gift, for this you must work, you must practise it, challenge it and maybe towards the end of your life you will master it. Cleverness is the shadow whereas intelligence is the substance.'

Miss Bornstein tried me on Latin vocabulary and then on my Latin verbs. It was pretty simple stuff but as Latin was only taught in high school in South Africa she seemed impressed. She then made me sit at a desk and handed me the book she had been reading. 'Do as many of these as you can in ten minutes,' she instructed.

The book had thirty pages and was full of little drawings and sentences with missing words and trick questions where you had to pick the answer from several choices. It was like old home work for me. This was Doc's personal territory and he had a great many books on logic and thinking, as he would call it, out of the square. Miss Bornstein's book was for beginners and I finished the whole thing in under five minutes.

I had to wait while she marked the answers. After the first page she looked up and chewed on the end of her pencil and then tapped it against her beautiful white teeth, her long, polished red nails holding the pencil lightly so that it bounced making a rat-tat-tat-tat sound. Then, using it to point at me, she said, 'I wouldn't say you were stupid, Peekay.' She turned to the last page and marked it, I guess because the book was supposed to go from easy to hard. She looked up again. 'No, I wouldn't say that at all.'

After that she made me read a book out loud and do a writing test and then she opened her suitcase, brought out a chess board and set it up. 'You open,' she said. I used one of Doc's favourite openings and she whistled through her teeth as she studied it. After an hour I conceded the game. Doc said it was the thing to do when you were going to stalemate anyway. It made your opponent less wary and therefore gave you an advantage next time. 'But only do this in a friendly match,' he cautioned. 'Chess is war and in war nothing can be predicted except death.'

Miss Bornstein looked up at me, a flicker of annoyance crossing her face. 'Don't ever do that again!' she said. 'When I play chess I'm your opponent and not to be patronised like some silly woman!'

I blushed furiously. 'I'm sorry, miss,' I said, mortified and wondering what the word meant.

'Miss Bornstein please, Peekay. "Miss" sounds just like any other kid who doesn't know any better. Samantha Bornstein. You may call me Sam in private, if you like. I think you and I are going to see quite a lot of each other.'

The idea of calling this beautiful creature by her Christian name was unthinkable. And by a boy's name, a common boy's name like Sam, plainly impossible.

Miss Bornstein thanked me for coming and said that on Monday I was to report to her class. 'Though I can't for the life of me think what we're going to do with you, but at least you'll make a worthy chess opponent,' she said, with a throatiness in her voice that made my chest feel tight.

I told Doc about the whole incident on Monday morning and at the end he asked two questions. 'Tell me, Peekay, how bad in love are you?'

I told him that I didn't know much about love but it was like being hit in the head with a really good punch.

'I think maybe you in love bad, Peekay. About women I don't know so much, but I know this, I think it is not so smart to tell Madame Boxall. I will think about this. Maybe Geel Piet can help also?' We left it at that for the time being.

'Next question, please! Madame Bornstein, she plays chess maybe better than Madame Boxall?'

I told Doc that Miss Bornstein was a good chess player and had I not used one of his sneakiest openings she would most likely have beaten me. 'She's much more cunning than Mrs Boxall,' I concluded.

'Hurrumph! Cunning? This is goot,' he grunted and opened the book at my music lesson. At the end of the practice he handed me a hastily scrawled note. 'Please, with my compliments, to give this to your Madame Bornstein and tomorrow you bring the reply if you please.' I knew better than to open the note.

'Please, Doc, don't tell her I'm in love with her,' I pleaded.

Doc looked askance. 'This I would never do, Peekay. Absoloodle. To be in love is a very private business.'

With Lieutenant Smit's promotion to captain, Sergeant Borman became the new lieutenant. This was not a popular promotion, though it was not unexpected. Borman had been sucking up to the Kommandant ever since he'd come down from Pretoria. He let it be known that his wife's asthma had curtailed a promising career at Pretoria Central, where to survive a warder had to be tougher and smarter than the hard case rapists, grievous bodily harms, thugs, thieves and con merchants. A sergeant under these conditions, he hinted, was easily the equivalent of lieutenant in a small-time prison such as Barberton. He demonstrated at every opportunity that he was tougher and harder than any of the other warders. A glance as he passed was sufficient to get him going.

'Who you looking at, Kaffir? You trying to be cheeky, hey?'

'No baas, no inkosi, I not cheeky, I not look.'

'Don't tell me you not cheeky. I know what you thinking, Kaffir! On the outside you all gentle Jesus and on the inside you a black devil, you hear.'

'No, inkosi. Inside same like outside.'

'That will be the blêrrie day, Kaffir. Come here. Come!' The prisoner would hasten towards Borman and stand head bowed to ragged attention. 'Look me straight in the eyes, Kaffir.'

'No baas. I not look you.'

'Look, you black bastard! When I tell you to look, you look, you hear?' The prisoner would lift terror-stricken eyes to meet those of the sergeant. 'Ja, it's true, man, inside is filth.' He would hit the African with a hard punch into the gut, doubling him over. 'Stand up, you black bastard, we got to get the filth out, we-got-to-get-it-out!' He would hit the prisoner again and again in the same spot. 'Vomit out the filth, make clean inside!'

Most Africans from the lowveld have weak stomachs from having been infected with Bilharzia. The larvae, found in river water, enter the system through the skin and eventually attack the liver and the kidneys. Three or four hard punches in the gut will generally cause severe vomiting and great pain.

Borman would look at the vomit on the floor and over the prisoner's hands as the man tried physically to hold back the contents of his gut. 'Ag sis! Now look what you done now! Why did you make dirty on the nice clean floor?' The donkey prick would come down hard across the prisoner's neck. 'Because you a fucking animal, that's why.' He would continue to hit the prisoner until the prisoner collapsed.

Making an unnecessary mess was a major prison offence and entitled a warder to use the donkey prick in an official capacity. Borman took great pride in the fact that he could legitimise an interrogation within three or four minutes from the time he started to taunt a prisoner. The English equivalent of the name the prisoners gave him was, 'Shit for Brains'. When he was anywhere near you would hear the chant go out, 'Move away, move away, here comes Shit for Brains. Here comes he whose mother threw away her child, kept the placenta, and called it Shit for Brains.'

Lieutenant Borman was too old to belong to the boxing squad, but he often talked big about the fighter he had once been. Gert said that a man who talks about how tough he is is probably yellow. But, while the warders didn't like

Borman, they respected him for being a professional. He spoke Fanagalo pretty well and since most prisoners learn to speak this African lingua franca, he used the African way of frightening the soul with word pictures. It was not uncommon for a prisoner to be reduced by him to a state of abject terror without physical torture. If there was any trouble in the prison, the Kommandant soon learned to put Sergeant Borman in charge. It was this facility to terrorise the prisoners, both physically and mentally, that had made him the Kommandant's choice to take over when Lieutenant Smit was promoted.

Lieutenant Borman deeply resented the freedom Geel Piet had achieved in the gymnasium under Captain Smit. 'Give a lag a blêrrie pinkie and before you know it they eaten your whole hand off up your shoulder,' he would insist. Geel Piet was careful to keep out of his way. When Borman entered the gym, unless he was in the ring actually coaching one of the kids, Geel Piet would quietly slip away. Lieutenant Borman's eyes would follow him as he crept out. 'He will get me. One day, for sure, he will get me. All I can say is I hope I come out the other side alive,' the battered little coloured man confided in me.

Captain Smit would watch Geel Piet leave the gymnasium when Borman entered, but he remained silent. Borman was not overly impressed with Doc or myself. He saw the unholy alliance of Doc, Geel Piet and myself as a basic breakdown of the system. Because he was a professional, he was quick to realise that such a break in the normal discipline of the prison could lead to other things. As a sergeant his influence did not carry to the Kommandant. But as a lieutenant his power increased enormously.

Had it not been for the Kommandant's desire to keep Doc sweet for the bi-annual visit of the inspector of prisons, Lieutenant Borman would almost certainly have had his way and our freedom within the prison would have been severely curtailed.

The Kommandant was a man who saw things in simple

terms. Doc at his Steinway was the cultural component of the Inspector's visit. A braaivleis and tiekiedraai, the fun; a boxing and shooting match, the physical; showing the Kommandant as a man of culture who was nevertheless a fun-loving disciplinarian. He had no intention of allowing Lieutenant Borman to disrupt his careful plan. Nevertheless, it was apparent to us that Borman was patient and relentless, determined to find something which would lead to our destruction.

The war in Europe was rapidly drawing to a close. The Allies had crossed the Rhine and were moving towards Berlin. Doc was terribly excited. After four years' incarceration he had a deep need for the soft green hills, the wind-swept mountains and the wooded kloofs. We would talk about walking all the way to saddle back mountain on the border of Swaziland and tears would come into his eyes. It was as though, now that the prisoner years were almost over, he dared to think for the first time of freedom. He would look over the prison walls to the green hills beyond and his voice would tremble. 'The years of hate are nearly over, it is soon time to love again, time to climb high with the sun on the back until a person can reach up and touch nearly the sky.'

Doc's second book on the cacti of Southern Africa had been written while he was in prison. This one was in English, each page edited by Mrs Boxall who in the end had come to confess that there was more to the jolly old cactus than she could possibly have imagined. Doc now talked of making the photographic plates and Mrs Boxall went to see Jimmy Winter at the chemist to get him to put aside one spool of precious rationed film each month until she had three dozen waiting for Doc on his release. Jimmy Winter was an artist who, when he wasn't running his chemist shop, loved to paint the hills. Before Doc went to prison he would sometimes come across him in some lonely spot high up on a mountain top painting away.

By the time the Allies had crossed the Rhine, precious

few music lessons were taking place. We spent most of the hour discussing our plans for Doc's release. He made me describe the cactus garden and the rate of growth of each plant and he talked happily about the extensions he would need to accommodate the stuff we would find waiting for us in the hills. Also, all the photos we needed for his book.

Like me, Miss Bornstein had never managed to beat Doc at chess. So she introduced her grandfather, Mr Isaac Bornstein, who was referred to as Old Mr Bornstein. Old Mr Bornstein turned out to be a match for Doc and the two of them were having a mighty go at each other, with Doc clucking and shaking his head as he read Old Mr Bornstein's latest move. 'Such a German, but very clever, ja this move is goot.' He would move over to the board which rested on top of the upright piano, make Old Mr Bornstein's move and think for a while and then make his own. '. . . But not so clever as me, Mr Schmarty Pantz Isaac!'

To Doc's surprise Mrs Boxall had accepted Miss Bornstein quite happily and the two of them were really making a go of the Sandwich Fund, which was sending out weekly bundles to prisoners' families, as well as food parcels. They discussed the time when, with the war over, it would be necessary to come clean, but decided the end of the war wouldn't bring about the end of human need and they'd find some excuse to continue.

Doc, Geel Piet and I had discussed the matter of my love for Miss Bornstein and, I must say, neither of them was a lot of help. Between the three of us we knew very little about women. Geel Piet never had a mother, or at least he could never remember having one. His aunty, the one with asthma who couldn't climb up steps, had taken him in with her nine kids and then when she got sick and couldn't manage he had gone to an orphanage and at the age of ten had been thrown onto the streets.

Doc had been a bachelor, though evidently not a very promiscuous one. He spoke with horror of the big-bosomed

Frauleins who demanded to see him after concerts and came to the conservatorium with invitations to dinner or afternoon tea. Sometimes, when they were very persistent and he could no longer politely refuse, he went, only to find his hostess, with a very revealing *décolletage*, the only other guest. These moments of terror had scared him off women, seemingly forever.

Geel Piet was quick to point out that his adult experience with women was entirely inappropriate and had no relevance to my predicament. The two of them finally decided that regular bunches of roses from my granpa's garden was all that was needed. The rest would take care of itself.

I was not quite sure what the rest was. 'I think maybe just let the roses do the talking, Peekay,' Doc advised and Geel Piet had added that he'd heard somewhere that lots of roses sent to a lady always did the trick. I wondered for some time what the trick was until Bokkie de Beer told me. I was unable to imagine myself doing the trick with Miss Bornstein.

Mr Isaac offered to motor out to the prison to visit Doc, but this had been turned down by Doc who wouldn't even let Mrs Boxall come to see him. Doc was a proud man and he was determined to meet his peers on equal terms. The prison put him at a distinct disadvantage and made him an object of sympathy. He could not bear such an idea. But now that the war was drawing to a close he talked often of visiting Herr Isaac, which was his name for Mr Isaac, and of the grand games of chess which awaited the two of them.

Mr Isaac Bornstein had arrived from Germany in 1936. He had escaped the Holocaust and had come to live with his family. Miss Bornstein's father had come to South Africa as a young man in 1918. The Bornsteins were the only Jews in Barberton where he was in partnership with Mr Andrews as the town's only firm of solicitors. Miss Bornstein, who had been lecturing at the university in Johannesburg, had returned home because her mother was dying of cancer.

I heard all this from Mrs Boxall who, it turned out, had known Miss Bornstein 'since she was a gel' and didn't mind at all when she discovered I was in love with her. 'She'll make someone a fine wife and if she's prepared to wait until after you're the world champion, then the two of you will make a fine couple.' Mrs Boxall knew that nothing, not even marriage to Miss Bornstein, was allowed to stand in the way of my being welterweight champion of the world. In the meantime I started the barrage of roses, which my granpa would select for me each Friday.

To my surprise my granpa seemed much more informed on the subject of being in love than Doc and Geel Piet and he examined me closely on the quality of my love. His had been of the highest quality involving the building of an entire rose garden with roses and even trees imported from England. When I said that I was not prepared to give up being world welterweight champion for Miss Bornstein, amid a lot of tapping and tamping and staring into space over the rusty roof, he announced that the quality of my love was certainly worth a dozen long-stemmed roses a week but fell short of a whole garden. I accepted this verdict although I knew it was impossible to love anybody more than I loved Miss Bornstein.

The Kommandant had long since accepted that Hitler wasn't going to win the war and together with most of the warders had joined the Nelspruit chapter of the Oxwagon Guard, a neo-Nazi group dedicated to the restoration of independence for the Afrikaner people. The Oxwagon Guard was very similar to the Ku Klux Klan only it included the English in with Jews and Kaffirs as the corrupters of pure Afrikanerdom. The war had helped them to grow into a powerful secret society which would one day become the covert rulers of South Africa and the major influence in declaring it a republic. I heard all this from Snotnose whose father was a member. He went away on weekends to a training camp where they sat around a big bonfire and sang songs and plotted the downfall of the Smuts government.

He also told me that the Kommandant was only a *veldkornet* and that Lieutenant Borman was the boss of the Barberton chapter. During the day the Kommandant could do anything he liked to Lieutenant Borman but at night, outside the prison, the warder from Pretoria was the boss. His wife didn't have asthma at all, Lieutenant Borman had been sent down from Pretoria by 'them' to get the Oxwagon Guard started. Bokkie de Beer said all this was true and that he'd swear it on a stack of Bibles. He'd heard his ma and pa talking about it in the kitchen at home when he was supposed to be asleep.

I could understand their hatred for the English and the Kaffirs. After all there were those twenty-six thousand women and children still to pay for. And Boers just hate Kaffirs anyway. Dingane, the King of the Zulus, had murdered Piet Retief and all his men after he'd given his word he wouldn't. So there was that to pay for as well. But why the Jews? I hadn't heard of any nasty business between the Jews and the Boers and no one I asked seemed to have either. I'd only known two Jews in my whole life, I was in love with one of them and Harry Crown was the other. I even decided that when I grew up, I'd be a Jew. At one stage I thought that maybe I had been left on the doorstep as a baby by a wandering Jew and my mother had found me and decided not to tell me. This, I felt certain, explained my headless snake and the absence of a father. But when I asked my mother she seemed pretty shocked at the idea and told me that the Lord was not at all pleased with the Jews. That they had been scattered to the four corners of the earth because they hadn't recognised Him when He came along and had nailed him to the cross. She was quite adamant that I hadn't been found on the doorstep and that my circumcision was a simple matter of hygiene.

I'd read about circumcision in the Bible; when King Herod heard about Jesus being born he sent his soldiers to kill all the babies who were circumcised. When I asked in Sunday school what being circumcised meant, Mrs Kostler pouted and replied that it wasn't something I should know about at my age.

'But it's in the Bible, so it can't be nasty, can it?' I protested. So, as usual, she sent me to Pastor Mulvery who agreed that I should wait to find out. It was Geel Piet who finally told me, at the same time pointing out in the showers that I was in fact circumcised. It was then that my Jewish theory started to develop. If it hadn't been for the fact that my mother was a born-again Christian and couldn't tell a lie, I'm not so sure I would have believed her rather pathetic explanation about hygiene. Perhaps she asked the Lord for special permission to tell a lie so as not to hurt my feelings.

Snotnose couldn't tell me why the Oxwagon Guard hated the Jews, but Bokkie de Beer said it was because they killed Jesus. Well, all I could think was, the Boers had mighty long memories and it was news to me that the Boers were around at the time of Jesus. But then my mother told me the Lord also allowed people to be born-again in other churches, except in the Catholic Church, which was the instrument of the devil. She said there were even born-again Christians in the Dutch Reformed Church. This immediately explained everything. The Boers had simply gone along with the rest of Christianity in condemning the Jews by adding a hate straight from the Bible to the existing hate for the English and the Kaffirs. That way they were bound to get the Lord on their side. It was a neat trick all right, but I for one wasn't falling for it. Quite plainly the Oxwagon Guard was the next threat now that Adolf Hitler had been disposed of, or nearly anyway. News of Germany's imminent collapse was coming through on the wireless daily.

The Kommandant promised Doc he would be released the day peace was declared in Europe, whether his papers were in order or not. We were already into the first days of summer, and Doc and I had talked about being out of prison in time for the firebells, the exquisite little orange lilies no bigger than a two-shilling piece, flecked with specks of pure gold, which bloomed throughout the hills and mountains after the bushfires. Doc was disappointed when the firebells came and went and VE day had not arrived.

We had already arranged for a new depository for the tobacco leaves, sugar and salt and, of course, the precious mail. These were placed in a watering can made of a four-gallon paraffin tin which had been fashioned originally for Doc's cactus garden. The homemade watering can had been doctored by Geel Piet. A false bottom had been inserted leaving a space which was cunningly fitted with a lid to look like the real bottom. Filled with water the homemade watering can looked perfectly normal, and would even work if it became necessary to appear to be watering plants. It was left standing in Doc's cactus garden and on my way to breakfast I would simply pass through the garden and put the mail and whatever I'd brought into the false bottom of the can. It was natural enough for me to go to the warders' mess via Doc's cactus garden as I often brought new plants for the garden. The warders almost never came this way and habitually used the passage in the interior of the building to get to the mess. We had been using this method for some months as the idea was to make it routine before Doc left and the piano stool with him. The Kommandant understood Doc's need for his cactus garden and decided it would remain as a memorial to Doc's stay, also allowing that Geel Piet could maintain it. As I would be continuing on with the boxing squad, the new system was nicely designed to work without Doc.

The writing of the letters proved to be a more difficult task. Geel Piet wrote with great difficulty at a very elementary level. Without Doc to take dictation, the prisoners would be unable to get messages to their families and contacts. This was solved when Geel Piet and I approached Captain Smit to ask if, for half an hour after boxing, I could give Geel Piet a lesson to improve his reading and writing. Captain Smit was reluctant to agree at first but finally gave his consent.

A strange relationship had grown up between the captain and the little coloured man. They only spoke to each other on the subject of boxing and Captain Smit would occasionally belittle a suggestion from Geel Piet to one of the boxers, but you could see that he respected Geel Piet's judgement and it was only to show who was the boss of the boxing squad. In the months which followed my win against Killer Kroon I continued to enter the ring against bigger, stronger and older opponents, yet had never lost a fight. Captain Smit saw in me the consummate skill Geel Piet had as a coach and secretly admired him for it.

I knew this because Bokkie de Beer said Captain Smit had told his pa that I would be the South African champion one day, '. . . because, man, he is getting the right coaching from the very beginning.'

Under the guise of learning how to read and write, Geel Piet would stare into a school book and dictate the prisoners' letters to me. His facility for remembering names and addresses was quite remarkable. He claimed it was easy for him, he could remember the names of the horses and their odds for every Johannesburg maiden handicap since 1918.

We had the new system up and running well before VE day and while it wasn't quite as foolproof or as convenient as the piano stool, it worked well enough. Geel Piet was too old a lag not to maintain absolute caution and he would never let me get careless or less mindful of the risks involved. For instance, on rainy days I would bring nothing to the prison as the idea of my taking the outside path in the rain to the warders' mess rather than through the interior passage would seem both silly and, to an alert warder like Borman, suspicious. Nor would the drops be made every day or on the same days. Geel Piet was smart enough to know that little boys are not consistent and so he created this random pattern for my drops even allowing that on some dry days I would take the interior passage to the mess as well. While the system was clumsy and not as convenient as the old one, it was very fortunate that Doc was smart enough to initiate it some time before he left.

One morning, shortly after he had been promoted to lieutenant, Borman wandered into the hall while we were practising. This was simply not done. The Kommandant's orders were that we should not be disturbed during our morning session, two geniuses at work, so to speak. Lieutenant Borman walked over to us, his boots making a hollow sound on the sprung floor. I continued to play until his footsteps ceased as he came to a halt just behind me.

'Good morning, Lieutenant Borman,' we both said together.

'Morning,' Borman said in a superior and disinterested way. He was carrying a cane not unlike the one Mevrou had carried and with it he tapped the leg of the piano stool. 'Stan 'up, man,' he said to me. I rose, and he bent down on his knees and with his index finger and thumb stretched he measured the width of the seat. 'A bit deep, hey, maybe something lives inside this seat?' He got down on all fours and put his head under the seat. 'Maybe a false bottom, hey?' He tapped the bottom of the piano stool which gave off a hollow sound. 'Very inter-res-ting, very clever too.' Doc rose from his stool, inserted the key into my stool and raised the lid. Lieutenant Borman started to rise. Halfway up he could see that the seat was filled with sheets of music. Remaining in a crouched position he stared at Doc and me for what seemed like a long time. 'You think this is funny, hey? You think this is playing a funny joke on a person?'

'No, Lieutenant,' Doc said, his voice surprisingly even. 'I think only you should ask before you look. Inside lives only Klavier Meister Chopin.' He opened the lid of his own stool, 'And here lives also Herr Beethoven, Brahms, Mozart and Bach and maybe are visiting also some others, perhaps Haydn, Liszt and Tchaikovsky, but not Strauss, definitely not Strauss. Like you, my dear Lieutenant, Strauss is not welcome when I am teaching.'

Lieutenant Borman rose to his full height. He was a big

man with a roll of gut just beginning to spill over his belt, and was used to looking down at people, but Doc's six foot seven left him five inches short as the two men stared at each other. The lieutenant was the first to drop his eyes from the gaze of Doc's incredibly steady blue eyes. He laid the cane on top of the Steinway and hitched his pants up. 'You think I don't blêrrie know things is going on? You think I'm a blêrrie fool or something, hey? I got time, I got plenty of time, you hear?' He picked up the cane then brought it up fast and down hard against the open lid of my piano stool, the blow knocking the lid back into place. The sound of the cane against the leather top echoed through the hall. He turned slowly to face Doc again, pointed the cane at Doc so that it touched him lightly on the breast bone as though it were a rapier. 'Next time you try to be cheeky you come off secon' bes'. I'm telling you now, you kraut bastard, I'm finish an' klaar with you both!' He turned and stormed out, his heavy military boots crashing and echoing through the empty hall.

'Phew!' I sighed as I closed the lid of Doc's piano stool and sat down weakly on my own. Doc also sat down, reached over to the Chopin Nocturne No. 5 in F sharp major on the Steinway music rack and commenced to fan himself with it. He was silent for a while, seemingly lost in thought, then said softly, 'Soon come the hills and the mountains.'

FIFTEEN

We were reasonably safe for the month after the piano stool incident as the inspector of prisons was due to arrive and Lieutenant Borman had the job of seeing that the place was spick and span, with fresh whitewash everywhere you looked. Much to Doc's annoyance even the stones bordering his cactus garden were whitewashed. He was prepared to accept whisky bottles outlining his paths but painting real stones seemed to him an insult against nature. Fresh gravel was brought into the inner courtyard together with several loads of finely crushed iron pyrites and mica with which a large letter 'B' was formed in the centre. The darker colour and sheen from the mica and pyrites mix made the letter shimmer against the almost white gravel. The 'B' of course stood for Barberton. This was the lieutenant's idea and he spent hours supervising the old lags sweeping and raking, until it was perfect. I must hand it to him, it did look very nice. Gert said the Kommandant was particularly pleased and Borman was up to his eyeballs in his good books. The prison corridors smelt of polish and the cells of Jeyes Fluid disinfectant. Windowledges were painted prison blue and everywhere you went smelt of new paint. But it was done early so the smell would have gone by the time the brigadier arrived. New canvas uniforms were issued to the old lags to be worn only during the visit. This was because they were doing all the painting and cleaning and their old patched and worn uniforms had paint on them and would give the game away. The Kommandant wanted the brigadier to think that everything was normal and that he could have popped in any old time and found things just the same. After the inspection, the lags handed back their new uniforms and wore their old patched and worn clothes until they finally fell apart.

Captain Smit had arranged the usual boxing exhibition and for weeks the Kommandant spent most of his mornings, as he did before every inspection, practising his pistol shooting on the pistol range behind the warders' mess.

The rapidly approaching VE day was a matter of concern to the Kommandant. If it arrived before the brigadier's visit then the truly cultural part of the programme would disappear with the release of Doc. He had tried to elicit a promise from Doc that, should this occur, he would return to the prison and play for the inspector. But Doc had not spent over four years in prison for nothing and he had learned the rules of prison life where everything is in return for something else. The *Goldfields News* had already printed a picture of the Kommandant above a piece by him saying that Doc was in prison because he was a German and that the moment Germany surrendered Doc would be released. The Kommandant couldn't go back on his word without losing face. This he would not allow to happen. Doc's price for staying over, if necessary, caused an uproar among the warders but as far as the Kommandant was concerned no price was too high for a smooth visit. Doc asked if he could give a concert for all the prisoners.

On Sundays, being God's day, the prisoners did not go out in work gangs. Instead they were locked in their cells and fifty at a time were allowed in the exercise pen, a high-walled enclosure of brick and cement about the size of two tennis courts. This was done tribe by tribe, each tribal group allotted ninety minutes. First the Zulus, followed by the Swazis, then the Ndebele, Sotho and Tsonga. The Boers had long understood the antipathy each tribe has for the other, and by keeping the tribes separated in prison they maintained the traditional tensions between them. This was thought to lessen the chances of a mass uprising or a prison strike.

Doc told me how each Sunday he would take a position in the guard tower overlooking the exercise pen to listen to them. Each tribe would use much of the ninety minutes allotted to them singing together, and he soon learned which tribal song each tribe liked best. He had written out the music for it, and then he had composed a piano concerto which represented, in melody terms, each of these songs. Doc said that he had never heard such magnificent harmony. Most of the songs were very beautiful and even though he did not understand the words, he could hear in them the people's longing for their homes, their people, the comfort of their fires, and the lowing of the cattle in the evening. He would sigh and say that his concerto could never capture the beauty of the original voices. He called it 'Concerto of the Great Southland'. It was this which he hoped to play to all the prisoners as his tribute to them before he left the prison.

The idea was for Doc to play the concerto through first, each movement in effect being one or more of a particular tribe's songs. Then on the second time through the tribe whose movement it was would sing the song to Doc's accompaniment on the Steinway. In this way each of the tribes represented in the prison would participate in the concert.

Once the Kommandant had agreed that the concert could go ahead, a great deal had to be done. No rehearsal was possible of course, but through Geel Piet each of the tribes was told which song was needed and the exact time it should take to sing. At night Doc would play the various songs fortissimo with all the hall windows open so the sound carried to the cell blocks. The warders claimed you could hear the cockroaches scratching as the prisoners strained to hear the music.

Because Doc would be at the piano, he decided I should conduct. This I would do in the simplest possible sense, signalling the piano breaks and the pianissimo as well as the fortissimo to the choir. After some weeks I was quite good at taking my directions from Doc and we went through the concerto during morning practice until I knew what every shake and nod of his head meant. Geel Piet had also taken basic instructions back to the prisoners so supposedly they knew what my hand signals would mean. Had Doc proposed that I assume the role of conductor in front of a white audience I could not have done so, but such is the nature of white supremacy in South Africa that I thought little of standing up in front of three hundred and fifty black prisoners and directing them.

Geel Piet informed me of the mounting excitement among the inmates. For several weeks the warders had an easy time, they simply had to threaten an inmate with non-attendance at the concert to get him to comply with any instruction. When the news spread that the Tadpole Angel would be directing the people in the singing indaba, it was immediately assumed the concert had a mystical significance and I had chosen this time to meet all of the people. Work time was used as practice and farmers and the people at the saw mills who hired gangs spoke of singing from dawn until dusk. Even the dreaded quarries rang with the songs of the tribal work gangs. Concerto of the Great Southland was being wrought into being, a musical jigsaw where, on the big night, all the pieces would be brought together under the magic spell cast by the Tadpole Angel.

Lieutenant Borman had tried his best to prevent the concert from taking place, but Captain Smit seemed to have decided that it was a good idea, perhaps for no other reason than that the concert was opposed by Lieutenant Borman. The two men had never liked each other and Captain Smit, who was not a member of the Oxwagon Guard, was said to have been bitterly opposed to the elevation of Borman to lieutenant.

The concert was to take place on the parade ground, and a special platform had been built in the carpentry shop to

349

raise the Steinway above the level of the prisoners. It was proposed that each tribe would form a semi-circle around the platform with ten feet separating each group. Two warders carrying sjamboks would be stationed in this corridor to stop any monkey business. A double shift issued with extra ammunition would be on guard duty on the walkways along the wall, and throughout the concert spotlights would be trained on the prisoners.

The concert was scheduled for Monday May 7th, 1945 and all the warders had been placed on full alert. Prisoners were never paraded at night and rumours were rife of tribal fights and vendettas being settled in the dark, as well as of an attempted prison break by the Zulus. The warders, whipped up by Lieutenant Borman, grew increasingly edgy as the concert night drew closer.

Lieutenant Borman had taken to wearing a Sam Browne belt across his shoulder with revolver with its holster unclipped on his hip and he lost no opportunity of telling anyone who was prepared to listen that trouble, more trouble than any of the warders could handle, was on its way. 'Give a black prisoner a pinkie and he eats your whole arm off at the shoulder, I'm telling you, man.' He said it so often that it became a joke around the prison and some of the warders started to refer to him behind his back as Pinkie Borman. He even tried to have the concert aborted at the last minute, claiming that it was against prison regulations to assemble more than fifty prisoners in one place at the same time. Captain Smit had demanded that he show him the standing instructions but he couldn't find them, claiming he knew them from Pretoria.

It was difficult to get my mother to agree to me staying up late for the concert. After consulting the Lord and receiving a note from Miss Bornstein which assured her that my school career would not be affected by one late night during the week she gave her permission.

Doc asked me how I would be dressed as conductor. The choice was limited: khaki shirts and shorts, and a pair of black boots with plain grey school socks were the entire contents of my wardrobe. Then Geel Piet suggested that I should be dressed in my boxing uniform, wearing the boots the people had made for me. Doc thought this was a splendid idea and I must say I quite liked it myself. Doc decided it would be awkward for me to wear boxing gloves as it would make it difficult for me to conduct. Geel Piet seemed disappointed and later came back with the suggestion that I should wear gloves and then just before the concert proper began, remove them. He seemed awfully keen on the idea and assured me that it wouldn't be showing off one little bit.

Thus, on the night of the concert, all the myths Geel Piet had so carefully nurtured among the prisoners about the Tadpole Angel would harmonise in my appearance as their leader, uniting all the tribes in the great singing indaba.

In any other society Geel Piet would have been a great promoter. He knew how to set the warp so as to weave a complex pattern which appealed to the imagination of the people. The Tadpole Angel would appear to the people dressed as a great fighter who would lead them in their tribal songs, crossing over the barriers of race and tribe. Was he not already a slayer of giants? Was he not the spirit of the great chief who bound Zulu with the Swazi and the Ndebele and the Tsonga and the Sotho so that they all sat on one mat in a great singing indaba? The one who touched the pencil and letters went out to the families of the people and returned with news of loved ones, who caused children to be warm in winter and wives to have dresses and food for hungry infants? Did he not bring tobacco and sugar and salt into the prison, making it disappear when he entered and reappear when there was no risk? How otherwise could he do this thing for four years without being caught by the Boers?

As with Mrs Boxall's Earl of Sandwich Fund, Doc's wonderful Concerto of the Great Southland was appropriated by the prisoners as being my work and my doing. Geel

Piet's clever entrepreneurial mind had seen that it would be more appropriate if it was presented in this way.

The night of Doc's concert arrived. The moment I passed through the gates I knew something in the prison was different. The feeling of despair was not in the air. The sad chattering which was in my mind the instant I stepped within the prison grounds had ceased. The thoughts of the people were calm. I felt a thrill of excitement. Tonight was going to be special.

A full moon had risen just above the dark shadow of the hills behind the prison walls and the parade ground was flooded with moonlight. Doc's Steinway stood sharply outlined on the platform with its top already propped up. The scene had a silence of its own, like looking into a Dali painting. I stood for a moment, for even at my age with my limited grasp of logistics and the law of human probability, this concert seemed a remarkable thing.

As I stood looking at the Steinway etched in the moonlight, the floodlights, bright and sudden as a burst from a welding gun, came on. When my eyes had adjusted to the harsh, raw light I could see that around the platform in a semi-circle on the hard ground, whitewashed lines denoted the area for each tribe. A dozen warders carrying sjamboks came out of the main building and walked towards the piano, their boots making a scrunching sound on the gravel footpath.

I crossed the parade ground, entered a side door and made my way to the hall where Doc would be waiting for me. He was sitting at the Mignon upright, absently tapping at the keys. He looked up as I entered. 'Geel Piet is late, he should be already here now,' he said, his voice tetchy. Doc had grown very reliant on Geel Piet and he regarded him as an essential part of the entire operation. Without him working with the prisoners, a concert still fraught with the potential for unrehearsed disaster would have had no chance of succeeding.

'He'll be here any minute, you'll see,' I said to cheer him

up. 'I'll save time and go and get my gloves.' I hurried from the hall and walked down the passageway towards the gym. An old lag was coming towards me carrying a two-gallon coffee pot, another followed him with a tray of mugs and a tin of brown sugar. They were taking coffee to the warders on duty in the parade ground. 'Have you seen Geel Piet?' I asked one. I spoke in Shangaan for I could see from the cicatrisation on his cheeks that he was of the Tsonga tribe. 'No baas, we have not seen this one,' he said humbly. As I departed I heard him say to the lag behind him, 'See how the Tadpole Angel speaks the languages of all the tribes, is he not the chosen leader of the people?'

When I reached the gymnasium I switched on the lights in the gym and the shower room. The lights above the boxing ring were on the wall opposite and the ring was in semi-darkness, but there was enough light for me to see into the box containing the boxing gloves and I quickly selected one of two pairs I liked to use. I went to the showers where I undressed and put on my boxing singlet, shorts, socks and boots, then I loosely tied the laces of the gloves together and slung them around my neck for Doc to lace up for me later.

I returned to find Doc still alone in the hall, the expression of concern showing clearly on his face as he absent-mindedly gloved me up. 'It is too late to wait longer, we must go now, I will tell Geel Piet I am very cross because this happens.'

The door I'd used to enter the building couldn't be opened from the inside, so we left the hall and walked down the long passage into the main administration building which led out to the parade ground. We passed through the small hallway where I had first entered the prison four years earlier. The lights were out in what was then Lieutenant Smit's office but which was now occupied by Lieutenant Borman. I allowed Doc to walk ahead and moved over to the service window and peered for a moment into the darkened office. In the half light I could see where Klipkop sat and next to him the larger desk which was Lieutenant Borman's. My eyes wandered around the room and stopped when they rested on a thin strip of light showing under the door of the interrogation room which led off from the main office. The door must have been slightly ajar, because I heard the unmistakable thud of a blow and a sudden sharp groan such as men make when they receive a hard punch to the solar plexus. It was not an unusual occurrence but it seemed inappropriate on this full moon night of the playing of the Concerto of the Great Southland.

The prisoners were already seated in their marked off sections when we arrived, the warders walking up and down the corridors striking their sjamboks against the sides of their legs and looking business-like. The prisoners avoided looking at them, almost as though they were not there. Talking was not allowed, but as we passed I could see the people smiling and a low murmur swept over the seated prisoners as Doc and I stepped onto the platform.

The Kommandant arrived shortly after us and stood on the platform to address the prisoners. Lieutenant Borman was to have done the translation into Fanagalo but appeared not to have arrived. The Kommandant was clearly annoyed by this and after a few minutes during which he looked at his watch repeatedly, he started to speak in Afrikaans.

'Listen to me, you hear,' he said and I quickly translated into Zulu. He looked surprised. 'Can you translate, Peekay?' I nodded. 'Okay, then I will speak and stop after every sentence so you can translate.'

The Kommandant was uncomfortable talking to the prisoners and he spoke too loudly and too harshly. 'This concert is a gift to you all from the professor who is not a dirty criminal like all of you, you hear! I don't know why an important person like him wants to make a concert for Kaffirs, not only Kaffirs, but criminals as well. But that's what he wants so you got it because I am a man of my word. I just want you to know it won't happen again and

354

I don't want any trouble, you hear, you just listen to the peeano and you sing then we march you back to your cells.' He turned to me, snorting nervously through his nostrils. 'That's all. You tell them what I said now.'

I said the Kommandant welcomed them and that the professor welcomed them and thanked them for coming to his great singing indaba. He hoped that they would sing each tribe better than the other so they would be proud. They should watch my hands, and I took my boxing gloves off to demonstrate the hand movements. When I had finished the sea of faces in front of me were smiling fit to burst and then spontaneously they started to clap. 'You done a good job, Peekay,' the Kommandant said, pleased at this spontaneous response to his speech.

Doc played the Concerto for the Great Southland through entirely and the prisoners listened quietly with nods of approval as they heard the melodies of their own tribal songs. At the end they all clapped furiously.

I then stood up and showed them how I would bring each tribe into their part and stop them by fading their voices out or simply ending a song or a passage with a downward stroke of the hands, a slicing gesture. I asked them to raise their hands if they understood and a sea of hands rose.

Doc played the prelude which was a musical medley of each of the melodies and then I brought in the Sotho singers. Their voices melded into the night as though they had caused the early summer air to vibrate with a deep harmony before they broke into song. It was the most beautiful male singing I had ever heard. They seemed instinctively to understand what was required of them and followed every gesture as though anticipating it. They were followed by the Ndebele who carried a more strident melody and whose voices rose deep and true, repeating the thread of the song carried by a single high-pitched male voice, chasing the single voice, sometimes even catching it to surround it and nourish it with beautiful harmony before allowing it to

355

escape once more to carry the song forward again. The Swazis followed as beautiful as any, then the Shangaan. Each tribe sounded different, seemingly building on the tribe before, each separated by a common refrain which was hauntingly African and seemed somehow to be a mixture of all. The Zulus took the last part which rose in power and majesty as they sang the victory song of the great Shaka, using the flats of their hands to bang on the ground as the mighty Zulu impi had done with their feet, until the parade ground appeared to shake. The other tribes soon got the rhythm and they too hit the ground to add to the effect. The concerto lasted for half an hour, the last part being the by now familiar refrain which all the tribes hummed in a glorious finale. Never had a composer's work had a stranger debut and never a greater one. Eventually the composition would be played by philharmonic and symphony orchestras around the world, accompanied by some of the world's most famous choirs, but it would never sound better than it did under the African moon in the prison yard when three hundred and fifty black inmates lost themselves in their pride and love for their tribal lands.

Doc rose from the Steinway and turned to the mass of black faces. He was crying unashamedly and fumbling for his bandanna and many of the Africans were weeping with him. Then without warning came a roar of approval from the people that would have been impossible to stop. Doc would later tell me that it was the greatest moment of his life, but what they were saying was 'Onoshobishobi Ingelosi! Onoshobishobi Ingelosi!' Tadpole Angel! Tadpole Angel! chanted over and over again.

The Kommandant looked worried and some of the warders had started to slap the sjamboks against the ground. Onoshobishobi Ingelosi! Onoshobishobi Ingelosi! Doc had risen from his seat to take a bow and I jumped up onto it and started to wave my hands to indicate that the chanting must stop. Almost instantly there was silence. Doc looked up surprised, not sure what had happened. I said,

'The great music wizard and I thank the people for singing, you are all men who tonight have brought honour to your tribes and you have brought great honour also to the great musical wizard and to me.' I would have lacked the maturity to make such a speech in English but the African tongue is gracious and by its very nature fits such words easily. 'You must go quietly now in the names of your wives and your children, for the Boers grow restless.' My voice was a thin piping sound in the night.

Suddenly a shower of stars sprayed across the sky above the town and then another and another, single red and green stars that burst high, cascades that danced in the heavens. The prisoners looked up in awe, some even covering their heads against the magic. A warder came hurrying up to the Kommandant, whispered in his ear and the Kommandant turned towards Doc and then extended his hand. 'You are free to go, Professor. The war in Europe is over. The Germans have surrendered.' He pointed in the direction of the town. 'See the fireworks, the blêrrie Rooineks are already celebrating.' A final cascade of stars burst against the dark sky and the black men cried out in awe; they had never seen such a happening before.

Was this not the final sign? Even the heavens spoke for the Tadpole Angel, spoke for all to see. The myth of the Tadpole Angel was complete. Now it could only grow and shape as legends are wont to do. Nothing I would ever do could change things. I had crossed the line to where only the greatest of the medicine men have ever been, perhaps even further, for not even the greatest were known by all the tribes and honoured by all of the people. I had become a myth.

Each tribe rose when they were commanded to do so and marched silently away until the parade ground was empty but for the guards who manned the walls, and the Kommandant.

'Magtig! I have never seen such a thing in all my life, man,' the Kommandant said, shaking his head. He turned

357

to Doc, 'Your music was beautiful, man, the most beautiful I have ever heard and such singing we will never hear again. Peekay, someday you will make a great Kommandant. I have never seen such command of black men. It is as though you are some kind of witchdoctor, hey?'

Quite suddenly there was a single voice in the night as though from the direction of the gymnasium, 'Onoshobi-shobi Ingelosi!' I heard it just the once and the sad voices in my head began chattering; the trouble in this place had returned.

Doc was overwhelmed by the news of the German surrender and the excitement of the concert, and he sat on the piano stool for a long time sniffling into his bandanna. The Kommandant bade us goodnight and the floodlights had once more been switched off so that the moon, which had risen high in the sky, ruled the night again. Then I remembered Geel Piet. I turned to Doc who looked up at me at the same time, we were thinking the same thing.

'Geel Piet never came. I cannot understand it. He would not have stayed away,' Doc said. I could see he felt guilty for not having thought about his absence sooner.

There was a scrunch of footsteps on gravel and soon Gert appeared out of the darkness. 'Captain Smit says it's late and school tomorrow, so I must drive you home now, Peekay.'

I was surprised, for I had expected to walk home as always. 'I'll go and get changed and take the gloves back,' I said, and I left Doc sitting on the piano stool, staring at his hands.

'It was a wonderful concert, Professor,' I heard Gert say in his halting English as I ran into the dark towards the gymnasium. I entered the side door to the gym and switched on the light, moving past the wooden horse and the medicine balls and giving the punching bag a straight left and a right hook. The big wooden box in which we kept the gloves was just to the side of the ring. I had tied the laces of my gloves together after the concert and had strung them around my neck as before. I secretly felt this made me seem more like a fighter. Now I took the gloves off and threw them towards the box from halfway across the gym. It was almost a good shot with one glove landing inside the wooden box while the other hung over the rim. I moved over to drop the glove in and suddenly, with a certainty I knew always to trust, became aware that something was terribly wrong. I ran over to the wall opposite and turned the ring light on. For a split second the sudden blaze of light blinded me; then I saw the body in the centre of the ring.

Geel Piet lay face down, as though he had fallen, his arms stretched out to either side of him. His head lay in a pool of blood where he had haemorrhaged from the nose and mouth. Without thinking I jumped into the ring screaming, although I could hear no sound coming from me. I fell to my knees beside him and started to shake him, then I rose and took him by one of his arms and tried to pull him to his feet. I began bawling at him, 'Get up, please get up! If you'll get up you'll be alive again!' But the little yellow man's body just flopped at the end of his arm and his head bounced in the pool of blood which splattered in an explosion of colour around his face. Inside me the loneliness bird cackled: 'He's dead . . . he's dead! He'll never be alive again!' I kept pulling him and trying to make him come alive. 'Please Geel Piet! Please get up, if you can get up you'll be alive again! It's true! I promise it's true! Please!'

There was a trail of blood as I pulled him across the ring. And then I saw that in his other hand he held the picture of Captain Smit, Doc, Gert, myself and himself. The corner of the photograph covering Captain Smit's head was soaked in blood. I dropped his hand and fell over his body and sobbed and sobbed. Then I felt myself being lifted from Geel Piet's body by Captain Smit, who held me like a baby in his arms and rocked me as I sobbed uncontrollably into his chest. 'Shhhh, don't cry, champ, don't cry,' he whispered as he rocked and rocked me. 'Shhhh. I will avenge you, this I promise. Don't cry, champ, don't cry, little brother.'

The festivities in honour of the inspector of prisons were held on the following Saturday night. Doc tried to get out of playing; the death of Geel Piet had upset him dreadfully and the idea of returning to the prison, even for the concert, filled him with apprehension. The Kommandant didn't quite see it the same way, Geel Piet was simply another Kaffir. 'No man! Fair is fair! I gave you your Kaffir concert, now I want my brigadier concert! I'm a fair man, and I kept my word. I let you leave the prison the morning after Germany surrendered. A man's word is his word.'

Doc's return to his cottage had been an emotional business. Dee and Dum had scrubbed and polished and his home had never been as clean and neat. Gert dropped Doc at the bottom of the hill as the roadway to the cottage had eroded over the four years he'd been away and it wasn't a good idea to try to drive to the top. Gert reported the road would not allow the truck to return the Steinway; the very next day Klipkop sent a prison gang to repair the road. They worked on it furiously so that it would be ready on the day after the concert for the piano to be returned.

Doc had mentioned on his way home that his first job would be to extend the cactus garden. Gert told Captain Smit who instructed the warder ganger that, after they'd completed the road repairs, the work gang should construct the new terraces Doc required.

Mrs Boxall had ordered groceries from H. C. Duncan, the town's leading grocery shop, and had made sure that the municipal ratcatcher had been up to the cottage to check the outside lavatory hole to see that no snakes or anything else had made their home down there in the past four years. He had dropped a bucket of chlorine pellets down the hole and for the first week you had to hold your nose against the sharp fumes when you entered. When Dee and Dum unpacked the box of groceries from H. C. Duncan they found that Mrs Boxall had included a parcel of her own which contained one of those really soft rolls of toilet paper. Goodness knows where she found it, because only the hard kind had been available since the war. Dee and Dum held the roll against their cheeks and exclaimed at its softness, marvelling that paper such as this could be used for such a silly purpose. I must say they had a point, Doc would have agreed, for he only ever used the *Goldfields News*.

Mrs Boxall also gave me a bottle of Johnny Walker for Doc which she said Mr Goodhead of the Barberton Bottle Store had been fearfully sweet and let her have. After my jaw incident and all the mentions I'd heard of the demon drink down at the Apostolic Faith Mission I wasn't at all sure that Mrs Boxall was doing the right thing. I carried the whisky up to the cottage convinced that at any moment the Lord might send a bolt of lightning out of the clear blue sky to strike the bottle from my hand and possibly take me along with it. If God could part the Red Sea then striking a bottle of Johnny Walker with a bolt from the blue seemed like a simple enough thing for Him to do.

For several weeks before Doc's release Mrs Boxall had been sending the boy from the library to the cottage with his bike basket filled with Doc's books. She referred to these books as not really the town's property but simply 'borrowed for the duration'. When Doc returned to his cottage on the morning after the people's concert he found it exactly as it had been some four years before, with only the Steinway missing. He told me some weeks later that he sat down on the stoep and wept and wept because his friends had all been so lovely to him.

After school on the first day of Doc's freedom I found him in his cactus garden cutting a dead trunk from a patch of halfmens; their proper name is *Pachypodium namaquanum* and they stand about seven feet tall and look like large, prickly elephant trunks sticking out of the ground.

I made coffee and we sat on the stoep for a while. Neither of us had mentioned Geel Piet, both unwilling to share our individual grief. After a while Doc brought up the loss by saying, 'No more letters for the people. No more anything.' Then we talked about the garden for a while and Doc pointed to an overgrown hedge of krans aloe which he had originally used as a windbreak and which was now beginning to intrude into the garden. 'We are being invaded by *Aloe arborescens*. I will attack soon, ja in one week.' I could see he loved the idea of making plans again, of being free to decide the divisions of the days and the weeks ahead.

He rose from his stool to refill his coffee mug and groaned. I looked up in alarm to see him trying to conceal his pain with a smile. 'Ja, I am a domkopf, Peekay. This morning I climb the hill to our rock but such a small climb has made me very stiff. It is four years since, and my muscles are soft and my lungs soon grow tired. It will take maybe a month, maybe more before we can go into the hills again.' He walked stiffly towards the kitchen where I had left the coffee pot, and for the first time I saw that Doc had become an old man.

He spent most of Thursday and all of Friday in the cactus garden, content to be on his own. He planned an excursion to visit Mrs Boxall at the library on Saturday morning – the day after school broke up for the June holidays and the day of the Kommandant's concert. He had instructed me to ask her if this would be convenient. Mrs Boxall was in quite a tizz when I told her that Doc would be coming to see her. I also told my granpa of Doc's visit to the library and early on Saturday morning he cut two dozen long-stemmed pink and red roses for Doc to give to Mrs Boxall. 'He can't go giving her a bunch of cactus flowers now, can he?' he declared a little smugly. My granpa was a rose man and saw no virtue whatsoever in a cactus garden.

We arrived at the library just as the clock on the magistrate's court tower struck nine. The library was closed and the library boy was sitting on the step outside. 'The missus, she be come soon,' he said. Doc started to stride up and down the footpath, stopping to hook his finger into the front of his celluloid collar and to clear his throat. Then I saw Charlie, Mrs Boxall's little navy blue Austin Seven, coming down the road towards us. It was making a dreadful racket and was obviously quite sick but Doc seemed not to hear it approaching. 'Here she comes!' I yelled, and thrust the bunch of roses at him. He jumped visibly and grabbed the flowers with both hands. Charlie lurched to a halt outside the library and the engine died with a clunking sound. Mrs Boxall stuck her head out of the window and spoke to me.

'Come along, Peekay, give a gel a hand, there's a good chap,' she said cheerily. In my anxiety for Doc I didn't move immediately. 'Come along, Peekay, open the door, you're not a Boer you know.' I hurried to open the door of the Austin. 'Now that the war is over we can all go back to having nice manners,' Mrs Boxall said, stepping out of Charlie. I realised she was grateful for the opportunity to chide me so as to cover the first few moments of her reunion with Doc. She looked up at Doc and gave him her best smile. Doc thrust the roses at her. 'And here's the man with the nicest manners of all,' she said, burying her nose into the pink and red blossoms and breathing deeply. 'There's nothing quite as charming as roses, don't you think?' She cradled them in her arm like the Queen and stretched her hand out towards Doc. 'Roses say so much without having to say anything at all.' Doc immediately clicked his heels together, almost knocking himself over in the process, then he bowed stiffly and, taking her hand, lifted it high above her head and kissed it lightly.

'Madame Boxall,' he said.

'Oh dear, I have missed you, Professor. It is so very nice to have you back.' I thought for a moment that she might cry, but instead she buried her head in the roses again and then looked up brightly. 'A cup of tea for Peekay and me and for you, Professor, I have some fresh ground Kenya coffee. Peekay, bring my basket from Charlie.' She handed the roses back to Doc and reached into her handbag for the keys to the library. 'I've baked a lovely Madeira cake, it's in the tin beside the basket, do be sure to bring it along, Peekay.'

Once we were inside it was like old times. The four and a bit years slipped away and it was the same old Doc and Mrs Boxall. Doc spoke with some consternation of the prospect of returning to the prison that evening to fulfil his obligation to play for the brigadier and Mrs Boxall volunteered to drive us over. Doc, to my enormous surprise, then suggested that she might like to attend the concert and she seemed thrilled at the idea. We phoned Captain Smit who said that Mrs Boxall was most welcome, that any friend of Doc's was a friend of his.

We then talked for the first time about Geel Piet. Mrs Boxall had never met him but he was almost as real to her as he had been to Doc and me. Doc lamented the fact that the Sandwich Fund was effectively finished and to our surprise Mrs Boxall would hear of no such thing. 'Just a temporary hiccup, we can't have Geel Piet thinking we're a bunch of milk sops. I have a plan.' She gazed at us steadily. 'I'm not prepared to reveal it yet, not even to the two of you. But I can tell you this much. I had proposed taking the train to Pretoria but now, by golly, Pretoria seems to have come to us.' She wore one of her tough expressions and so we didn't question her any further. 'It's my plan, and if it doesn't work, then only I shall look a proper idiot,' she declared.

On the night of Geel Piet's death, Captain Smit had led me sobbing and hiccuping to the blue prison Plymouth, where Gert was waiting to drive me home. He had told me that I needed a break from training and was not to return to the prison until the boxing exhibition for the brigadier on Saturday night. It was a nice holiday but as prospective welterweight champion of the world, it worried me that I wasn't in training. It hadn't yet occurred to me that I would return to a boxing squad that was now without Geel Piet, and that from now on I would simply be the most junior boxer under Captain Smit's concerned but preoccupied care.

On Saturday night Mrs Boxall picked us up at the bottom of Doc's road. Even though the road was now in splendid repair Charlie, in his present state of health, was not considered capable of climbing it. We arrived at the prison just before seven o'clock and made our way to the hall. Doc's piano recital was to be the first item of the evening: it was the cultural part, it was thought best to get it over with while everyone was still well behaved. After that, the audience would go through into the gym for the boxing exhibition and then back to the hall for the tiekiedraai dancing and braaivlies. The air smelt smoky from the braaivleis fires which had been lit on the parade ground immediately outside the hall. Someone was already playing a piano accordion in the dark, his swaying torso silhouetted by the light from one of the fires.

Mrs Boxall, Doc and I found three seats in the front row so that Doc could get to the Steinway easily. I hadn't seen Gert since he had driven me home four days before and he now made a special point of coming over to me. I excused myself and we moved off into the corner for a chat. Gert told me again how sorry he was about Geel Piet and how it wasn't the same without him on the boxing squad.

'Man, I don't understand, he was only a Kaffir but I miss him a lot,' he confided. He also told me that the brigadier's inspection was an all-time success and that Lieutenant Borman was up to his eyeballs in the Kommandant's good books right up until late that afternoon.

'What happened this afternoon?' I asked, delighted at the suggestion that Lieutenant Borman might have fallen from grace.

'The brigadier stood up and said to us all that he had never seen a prison in better shape. But that also Pretoria had heard of the Kaffir concert.' He paused and his eyes grew wide, 'I'm telling you man, we knew who had told them about it and we thought we were in a lot of trouble.'

He shook his head from side to side. 'But it wasn't like that at all. The brigadier said that it was a piece of proper prison reform and that Barberton led the way and the Kommandant was to be congratulated. Not only were the prison buildings and grounds immaculate and the discipline first class, but also prison reform was taking place that was an example to the rest of the country. You should have seen Pinkie Borman's face, man, he was furious. I nearly wet my pants. Everyone was looking at him with this big smile on their faces, even the Kommandant.'

Snotnose came over and said Doc wanted me. Gert told me he'd see me later in the gym. Doc had decided to play Chopin's Nocturne No. 5, the same piece I had so unsuccessfully been coming to grips with for some weeks. I knew the music well enough to turn the pages for him and that's why he had sent for me. Doc had agreed to play two pieces for the concert. When I had enquired about the second piece he had said it was to be a surprise and that after the Chopin nocturne I was to return to my seat beside Mrs Boxall.

The hall was almost full, and the warders and their wives and guests from the town had all taken their seats when the Kommandant walked to the front of the hall and stood beside the Steinway.

'Dames and Here,' he began, 'it gives me much pleasure to welcome you all to this concert in honour of our good friend Brigadier Joubert, Transvaal Inspector of Prisons. The brigadier this very afternoon said nice things about Barberton prison and I just want to say to all my men that I am proud of you. Now it is our turn to say nice things about the brigadier who is a good kêrel and also a good revolver shot as some of us saw at the pistol range this afternoon. We thank him for his visit and,' the Kommandant grinned, 'for going so easy on us.' The audience laughed and he continued, 'No, seriously man, it is men like Brigadier Joubert who make the South African Prison service a place where good men can hold their heads up high.' He paused and seemed to be examining the large gold signet ring on his hand before looking up again. 'The concert we held for the black prisoners last week, the brigadier was kind enough to say, was a good example of prison reform. It was just a little idea I had and it worked. But the brigadier is a man of *big* ideas that work, a big man who gives us inspiration and strength to continue.' I could feel Mrs Boxall's arm trembling against my own and I turned to see her trying very hard not to laugh. 'He is a man of the Church, a God-fearing man and a man dedicated to the prison service.' The audience broke out in spontaneous applause and the Kommandant let it go on for a moment before holding his hand up. 'He is also a cultured man, which brings me to our first item on the programme for tonight.' He cleared his throat and looked around. 'All of you know that we have had in this prison as our guest,' one or two titters issued from the audience and the Kommandant went on, 'no, I mean it, man, as our honoured guest for the past four years, a man who is a musical genius. This is the last time we will hear him play for us. Last week he helped us with the prisoners' concert and tonight he is giving a personal one just for us in Brigadier Joubert's honour. I ask you now to welcome Professor Von Vollensteen.' Doc rose and did a small bow to the audience and gave me a nod and with the applause continuing we moved over to the Steinway.

Doc lost no time getting started and the Kommandant was still on his way to his seat when the first notes of the Chopin nocturne filled the hall. At first the music was wonderfully relaxed, deceptively simple and straightforward and then, as the recital continued, the melody line became more and more ornamental.

Doc's finger technique was remarkable as the delicate filigree writing for the right hand came into play. In the middle section the music became more and more complex, fast and urgent, leading to a long crescendo and frenzied climax where Doc could shake his head a lot and bang furiously at the keys which he knew the audience would like. The nocturne ended with an elegant descent in steps towards a rustling, almost muted final chord.

Doc had chosen well. Chopin's Nocturne No. 5 is not difficult music to understand and it is very beautiful. The audience stood up, clapped and seemed very pleased. Doc rose and took a bow and nodded for me to return to my seat next to Mrs Boxall. Then he removed several sheets of music from inside his piano stool and fixed them carefully to the music rack. He turned to the audience and cleared his throat.

'Ladies and gentleman. Tonight I would like to dedicate this next piece of music, which I have played once only before, to a friend, a very good friend. I have named this music by his name and it is for him. I give you, "Requiem for Geel Piet"!'

Without further ado Doc sat down at the Steinway and commenced to play the Concerto of the Great Southland which he had now renamed. The melodies of the tribal songs seemed to take over the hall, as the Ndebele song followed the Sotho with its more strident rhythm, Doc's left hand taking the part of the solo high-pitched voice and the right chasing it as the singers themselves had done. The Swazi melody followed and then the Shangaan, each separated by the haunting refrain that carried a hint of each, yet acted to lead away from the one and into the other. Finally came the victory song of the great Shaka and the Steinway seemed to build the drama of the magnificent Zulu impi, the chords crashing as they marched into battle. The requiem closed with a muted and very beautiful compilation of the songs of the tribes. The music seemed to swell as all around us from the cells beyond the hall the voices came as the tribes completed the requiem. Geel Piet, who had had no tribe, whose blood was the mixture of all the people of Southern Africa – the white tribe, the Bushman, the Hottentot, the Cape Malay and the black tribal blood of Africa itself – was celebrated in death by all the tribes.

He was the new man of Southern Africa, the result of three hundred years of torture, treachery, racism and slaughter in the name of one colour or another.

There was a special kind of silence as the performance ended. To our own was joined the silence of the listeners beyond the hall. We had all been a part of the lament for Africa. Requiem for Geel Piet was a lament for all of us, the tears shed for South Africa itself.

During the applause Brigadier Joubert, the Inspector of Prisons, rose from his seat and moved to the front of the hall. He raised his hands for silence and the hall grew quiet again. Taking a khaki handkerchief from his trouser pocket he slowly wiped his eyes and began to speak very emotionally.

'Tonight, dames and here, we have heard a work of true genius. Whoever this Geel Piet was, we know from his name that he was an Afrikaner who is honoured by this music. He was also the spirit of Africa and as Afrikaners we should all honour him and his death.' He folded the handkerchief neatly and put it back into the pocket of his tunic. 'All I can say is that he must have been a great man for the professor to write a piece of music just for him. I now ask you all to stand and to bring your hands together once again for the professor.' I saw that Captain Smit had a big smile on his face and was clapping madly. Even the Kommandant seemed to have decided to ignore the irony, he was clapping for all he was worth. I think he must have seen a colonel's insignia on the lapels of his uniform in the very near future.

Doc stood with his head bowed throughout the brigadier's speech and I could see that he had his bandanna out and was doing one of his sniffs into it. I knew he was crying for Geel Piet. But I also knew Geel Piet would have found this moment very funny.

'Ag, man,' he would have said, 'why must a man always wait until he is dead for such a clever joke to heppen?'

Then the warders, wives and guests moved into the gym

to watch the boxing exhibition. The chairs were being cleared from the hall to get ready for the Boere music and tiekiedraai which, with the braaivleis, were the highlight of the evening.

Captain Smit had worked out a routine for the boxing exhibition which was pretty clever. All the boxers were seated in a row facing the ring and he was in the ring with a whistle round his neck, acting as referee. When the audience had filled the gym he blew his whistle and I climbed into the ring with Snotnose. We shook hands and Captain Smit blew his whistle again and Snotnose and I started to box. The idea was that after every round, one of the boxers would step down and another would replace him. As the youngest I stepped out first and Fonnie Kruger came in and boxed the next round with Snotnose. Then Maatie Snyman replaced Snotnose and fought Fonnie and then Fonnie stepped down and Nels Stekhoven came in and so on right up to the heavyweights, where Klipkop fought Gert and then as a joke I stepped in and fought the final round with Klipkop. It was a good way to entertain the crowd, as every boxer ended up fighting someone lighter and heavier than himself and we fought as hard as we could to give them a good show. It all went like clockwork and not a word was spoken by Captain Smit who just blew his whistle to start and stop a round. When I stepped into the ring with Klipkop the crowd cheered like mad and someone said, 'Murder da bum, Peekay!' and everybody laughed. I danced around Klipkop and gave him a terrible time, punching him in the solar plexus. He also attempted to take my head off with huge uppercuts, always missing by a mile. The crowd enjoyed it a lot and finally Captain Smit blew his whistle and held my hand up and there was a lot of cheering.

Afterwards, as the crowd was leaving, I went over to Doc and Mrs Boxall to tell them that I had to change and would see them at the braaivleis. Mrs Boxall said that she wanted to have a word with the inspector chappie and that she'd be obliged if Doc would go with her for moral support, so they'd see me later. As I turned to go she called me back.

'Peekay, I must say I've never been too keen on your boxing. But you do seem to be rather good at it and I do believe you will be a welterweight champion of the world some day. Jolly well done is all I can say!'

'A champion already. Absoloodle!' Doc added.

We were all in the showers changing when Klipkop came in. 'Captain Smit wants you all to come back into the gym when you finished. Make quick, you must all be there in the next ten minutes. When you get into the gym the lights will be off. Only the lights above the ring will be on.' He had changed hurriedly as he spoke and now he fumbled with his shirt buttons and then sat down and pulled on his socks and shoes. 'Sit in the dark and be very quiet. Not near the door but on the far side of the ring, you hear?' We all nodded and he hurried from the room.

We hadn't been seated long in the darkened gym when one of the double doors opened spilling a shaft of light from the passage into the gymnasium. Caught in the light were Captain Smit, Klipkop and, standing between them, Lieutenant Borman. The door swung back into place and we could only dimly see the three men walking towards the ring while they would not have been able to see us. Then they appeared suddenly in the circle of light illuminating the ring.

'Climb in, Borman, up into the ring,' Captain Smit said.

'What you doing man, what's happening?' we heard Lieutenant Borman say.

'Just climb in, we'll tell you in a minute. Everything will be made clear in a minute,' Captain Smit said. Borman climbed up into the ring and Captain Smit and Klipkop followed. A pair of boxing gloves hung from the posts of each of the two boxers' corners and in one of the neutral corners lay what appeared to be a piece of rolled up canvas. Like Captain Smit, Lieutenant Borman was wearing civilian clothes, an open neck shirt and long pants. Captain Smit leaned into the ropes and removed his shoes, leaving his socks on.

'Take off your shoes, please, lieutenant,' Klipkop said politely.

'Hey man, what's going on here?' Borman said, with just a hint of apprehension in his voice. 'I'm not going to fight, man. I don't want to fight nobody. What's going on?'

'Take off your shoes, please lieutenant,' Klipkop repeated. Captain Smit picked up his shoes and placed them neatly beside a corner post.

'I got no quarrel with you, Smit. I never done anything personally to you. Why do you want to fight me?'

'Take off your shoes or am I going to have to take them off for you, lieutenant?' Klipkop asked calmly.

'Keep you hands off me, you hear,' Borman snarled. 'I am your superior, Oudendaal! You show me respect or you on report, you hear?' He seemed to gain courage from the sound of his voice, shaking his finger as he shouted at Klipkop. Klipkop sighed, shook his head slowly and started to move towards Lieutenant Borman. Borman hurriedly pulled one shoe off and dropped it on the canvas, then removed the other and placed them both in the neutral corner right next to the rolled up piece of canvas.

From the moment Captain Smit had stepped into the ring he had remained silent, and I could sense this was beginning to unnerve Borman. Klipkop lifted the gloves from the post nearest to the lieutenant and walked over to him.

'Give me your hand, please sir,' he said in a matter of fact sort of voice.

Lieutenant Borman immediately folded his arms, tucking his hands under his armpits. 'No man! No way! You can't make me fight, man. Let Smit tell me first what I done.' Captain Smit had retrieved the gloves in his corner; placing one between his legs, he slipped his hand into the other. 'Jus' tell me, you hear!' Borman shouted. Captain Smit looked up from the glove straight at Borman. Keeping his eyes fixed on the lieutenant he slowly pulled the glove from his fist and dropped it, then opened his knees so that the second glove also fell onto the canvas. He walked over to the neutral corner and picked up the object lying there. We could now see, for sure, that it was a roll of canvas. He held the roll up to his chin so that it unrolled. My heart gave an enormous leap. The canvas sheet Captain Smit was holding was covered with dry blood. Borman pulled back in horror but then, as quickly, recovered himself.

'What's this, man? I never saw that before in my whole life.'

Captain Smit said nothing but began to roll the canvas up again. I had been terrified, when I climbed into the ring earlier, that I might see signs of Geel Piet's blood, but the old canvas had been removed and the ring re-covered. The sight of Captain Smit holding part of the old blood-stained canvas brought back the shock I had felt, and without realising it I began to sob. Suddenly a large, hard hand covered my mouth and Gert's arm came around my shoulder and drew me into him.

Captain Smit put the canvas back in the corner and retrieved the boxing gloves. Klipkop pulled Borman's arms open and slipped his gloves on. This time the lieutenant made no move to stop Klipkop who laced up the gloves.

'I don't know what you talking about, you hear! I swear I was at home the night the Kaffir died. I can prove it! I had to go home because my wife had an asthma attack. Everybody saw I wasn't at the Kaffir concert. That's because I was at home, I got called on the telephone, my wife had a bad attack and I had to go home. You're mad, I'm telling you, you mad, I never done it. I never killed that Kaffir!'

Klipkop finished tying Captain Smit's gloves and he walked to the centre of the ring. 'No butting, no kicking, fight like a man,' Klipkop said, and climbed out of the ring leaving Smit and Borman to fight.

Captain Smit started across the ring towards Lieutenant Borman, but Borman held up his glove open-handed. 'Look. I admit I phoned Pretoria about the Kaffir concert, I admit that. Orright you got me on that. I thought I was right, I done my duty, that's all. You can't blame me for that. I done what I thought was right.'

Captain Smit brushed the open glove aside with a left and drove a hard right into the soft roll of gut that spilt over Borman's belt. The lieutenant doubled up, clasping at his stomach with both hands trying to catch his breath. Smit stood over him waiting. Without warning, Borman suddenly smashed his gloved fist into Captain Smit's balls. The captain staggered back, grabbing at his genitals, and then he sank to his knees. Borman was on him in a flash, and catching him on the side of the jaw he sent Captain Smit crashing to the canvas. Borman shouted, 'You Kaffirboetie, you nigger lover, don't fuck with me you hear, man!' He kicked Captain Smit in the ribs just as Klipkop, who had climbed back into the ring, reached him and brought his arms around him. But Borman's blood was up, he was a big man, and he jerked free just as Captain Smit was attempting to rise. He caught Smit another solid blow to the side of the head, putting him back on the canvas. Klipkop tried to hold Lieutenant Borman again.

'I killed the bastard, you hear!' Borman shouted. 'I killed that yellow nigger. He wouldn't tell me who gave him the letters, who brought the letters in. I caught him red handed, two letters, man, red handed! Two fucking letters in his pocket. He wouldn't tell me. I broke every bone in his face. I jammed the fucking donkey prick up his arse till he shit his entrails, but he wouldn't tell me! The black bastard wouldn't talk!' There were flecks of foam at the corners of Borman's mouth and he began to sob.

Captain Smit had dragged himself to his feet and stood facing Borman, who was no longer trying to get out of the bear hug Klipkop held him in. Bringing his gloves up, Smit signalled to Borman to come and fight. Klipkop released his grip and Borman rushed at Smit, walking into a straight left from Smit that stopped him in his tracks. Borman charged in again and Captain Smit stopped him again, repeating the straight left into the face. It was obvious that Borman had never been a boxer. A trickle of blood ran from his nose and he brought his arm up to wipe it. A smear of blood covered the top of his arm and he stared down in horror at it. 'Shit, I'm bleeding!' he cried. 'Jesus Christ, I'm bleeding!'

Then Captain Smit stepped up and smashed his glove into Borman's face. The blow seemed to flatten Borman's nose and he dropped to the canvas. Covering his face with his gloves, he wailed, 'Don't hit me, please don't hit me!'

Captain Smit signalled to Klipkop to get Borman back onto his feet. Klipkop got his arms under Borman's armpits but the man refused to get up. The blood from his nose had stained his white shirt and his eyes were wide with terror. Klipkop let him go and he dropped to the ground; then, crawling on all fours towards Captain Smit, Borman held Smit around the legs. 'Please don't hit me, Captain. I don't understand, why you doing this to me? It was only a Kaffir, a dirty stinking yellow man, why you hitting a white man over a Kaffir?'

Captain Smit kicked his legs free of Borman's embrace. 'You can't even fight, you low bastard. You can't even stand up and fight like man!' It was the first time Smit had spoken since they'd entered the ring. He turned and extended his hands to Klipkop who unlaced and removed the gloves. Then Smit went over to the neutral corner, picked up the canvas roll and unrolled it beside the sobbing officer. Klipkop grabbed Borman by the legs and Captain Smit grabbed him around the wrists and they lifted him and placed him on the blood-stained canvas and rolled it around him. 'This Kaffir's blood will haunt you till you die,' Captain Smit said. He picked up his shoes and then he and Klipkop climbed from the ring. Klipkop moved over to the wall and reaching for the switch plunged the gymnasium into darkness.

In the darkness from the direction of the swing doors

there came a sudden shout, '*Abantu bingelela* Onoshobi-shobi Ingelosi!' The people salute the Tadpole Angel! The door opened slightly and in the shaft of light it threw we saw a black figure slip quickly out of the gymnasium. The people knew. The curse was fixed. Lieutenant Borman was dead meat.

When I got outside, the tiekiedraai dancing was already going full swing with someone on the Mignon hammering out the Boeremusiek accompanied by the man with the piano accordion and a banjo player. Outside, on the parade ground, warders and their wives stood around the barbecue fires now burnt down to glowing embers, homemade sausages known as boerewors were held over the fires and the sizzle of the fat dropping from the sausage skins made the embers flare in the dark.

Doc and Mrs Boxall were nowhere to be seen. I watched the guy beating the Mignon half to death, thankful he wasn't using Doc's Steinway, when I felt a tap on my shoulder. 'Howzit?' It was Gert. 'How you getting home?' he enquired. 'Maybe I can borrow the Plymouth and take you all.' I explained that Mrs Boxall had brought us in her old crock which made a fearful racket and I was doubtful that it had long to live. 'You know where the professor and that lady is don't you?' Not waiting for my reply, he said: 'I seen them going into the administration building with the brigadier and the Kommandant.'

Gert was amazing like that; he always seemed to know what was going on. 'Maybe the professor will get a medal or something for the Kaffir concert.' Then he giggled, 'Jesus! I hope the brigadier never finds out that Geel Piet was only a broken down old lag.' He punched me lightly on the shoulder, 'Sorry man, about shutting your mouth back there.' I hung my head, the memory of the blood-stained canvas still too sharp in my mind for me to chance looking at him.

'You did right,' I said softly.

'So long, Peekay, I'd better kick the dust,' Gert said.

At last Doc and Mrs Boxall came out. I ran up to them and I could see Mrs Boxall was excited.

'By Jove, Peekay, miracles will never cease. I do believe we've done it!' she exclaimed.

'Done what?' I asked.

'Have done what?' she corrected automatically. 'We have been given permission to start a letter writing service. Isn't that simply grand news? The brigadier says that every prisoner may send and receive one letter a month. It's the first time it has happened in South Africa and it's going on trial for six months.' She grabbed me by the hand and Doc by the other and we danced around in a circle to the sound of the tiekiedraai music coming from the hall. 'You're going to be needed because you speak three African languages as well as English and Afrikaans. Every Sunday morning after church we'll come out for two hours and take dictation from the prisoners. I say, it's a real victory for the forces of good. The brigadier was most impressed when I told him that it would be done under the auspices of the Earl of Sandwich Fund,' she stopped, puffed from the dancing, and then giggled. 'The Kommandant assured the brigadier that the Earl of Sandwich Fund was a very respected organisation with worldwide contacts and that all the warders' wives baked for it at the Christmas and Easter show.' We all started to laugh. Doc finally said, 'Madame Boxall, you are absoloodle the best. For this I give you eleven out of ten.'

She did a small curtsey. 'Why thank you, kind sir!' She gave Doc one of her extra special smiles. We hung around for a while longer just so we wouldn't seem rude and finally made our way to the car. As we approached we could hear soft grunting sounds and then we saw that a pair of boots was sticking out from under Charlie. Gert got up sheepishly and wiped his grease-blackened hands on the sides of his khaki shorts. He bowed awkwardly to Mrs Boxall.

'Does Mevrou speak Afrikaans?' he asked me.

I shook my head. 'I'll translate, if you like?'

Gert nodded. 'Tell her she's got more power now, you only had three cylinders firing,' he spoke fast, swallowing his words as he fought his shyness, 'but you still got a bad knock in the diff.' He turned to Mrs Boxall. 'If you can get it here tomorrow, maybe just after you been to church, I'll borrow the Plymouth and drive you home and I'll fix the car up for you.' I introduced Gert to Mrs Boxall and translated what he'd said. Mrs Boxall was very grateful and called Gert 'A dear, sweet boy,' which I didn't translate but I think he understood because he seemed very embarrassed.

'Oh dear, I have no idea what a knock in the diff is. Is it something very bad?'

'It's the differential, I think it's pretty bad,' I replied without consulting Gert.

Pulling up his socks which were already pulled up Gert stammered, 'Good night, Missis,' in English and then walked quickly away into the dark.

We zoomed away and Mrs Boxall had no trouble driving up the Sheba road hill. The difference in Charlie was amazing now that we were driving on all cylinders. We dropped Doc off at the bottom of his hill. I think the new four-cylinder Charlie could've made it easily but Mrs Boxall had never been invited by Doc to his cottage and she said as she drove me home, 'This wasn't the right time' – whatever that was supposed to mean.

SIXTEEN

Mrs Boxall promised to talk to my mother about the new letter writing arrangements in the prison. These were to take place on a Sunday morning and I had some real doubts about being allowed to partake in them. Sundays were difficult for me, it was a day filled with taboos, beginning with Sunday school and church in the morning and ending with evening service, which consisted of a short message from Pastor Mulvery and then 'a precious time', when the congregation witnessed for the Lord. I wasn't allowed to do anything except the Lord's work on a Sunday, but as I wasn't a born-again Christian any of the Lord's work I might do, like reading the Shangaan Bible to Dee and Dum, wasn't creating any bricks for my mansion in the sky. Reading the Bible was regarded as the most superior type of work for the Lord. I was required to read three pages of the New Testament every day and ten pages on Sunday, and I did my compulsory Sunday reading during Pastor Mulvery's Message from the Lord. You'd think if something was called a message from the Lord, it would be a proper message, such as you might give to a person. But Pastor Mulvery's messages rambled all over the place threading bits of the scripture together and frequently leading to wildly unusual conclusions which tended to prove Pastor Mulvery was right while all the gospel scholars since St Paul were wrong. He would call the Catholic Church the 'Catlicks' and they were his special target. He would go to endless trouble to demonstrate that the Catlicks had perverted the Word of God. He would point out that the

Latin scholars who had translated the St James version into English from an original Catlick translation had not understood the original Greek translation of the original Hebrew. As Pastor Mulvery knew no Latin and no Greek and certainly no Hebrew and never gave examples of the corrupted Words of God in Latin or Greek so that I could at least check his accuracy with Doc, he was able to build some pretty impressive arguments against the perfidy of the Catholic Church. I can tell you one thing, you wouldn't have wanted to be a Catlick on a Sunday evening service with Pastor Mulvery delivering one of his messages.

Because reading the Bible on Sunday didn't count for my heavenly brick account, I was expected to find other kinds of good deed stuff. Each Sunday evening my mother would question me closely about this. Sometimes I really had to scrape the bottom of the barrel for things to claim, like praying for Hitler. Which I hadn't done of course, but it sounded good and was unusual enough to throw my mother off the scent.

In fact praying for Hitler created a real crisis at that evening's debate. Marie, who was always there for supper on Sundays, said praying for Hitler wasn't valid coming from me, as it was a case of one sinner praying for another. My mother then debated with her as to whether a sinner praying for a sinner was an okay idea. My granpa said he thought it was time he was excused from the table so that he could go to his room and pray for fewer debates of this sort. My mother then said, as it was Sunday, she was not going to tell him how rude and hurtful his remark had been.

So getting to the prison for two hours every Sunday to take dictation wasn't simply a question of Mrs Boxall asking my mother. A great deal of toing and froing to the Lord would have to take place and my fear was that the Lord was going to be hard put to see that taking dictation from a bunch of criminals was the very best possible use of my indentured Sabbath.

My fears proved to be correct and the scheme had to be

delayed a month while my mother and the Lord came to grips with the small print. A major investigation such as this one would begin by looking for a precedent in the Bible. In this regard I scored a direct hit when I pointed out that St Paul, in his Epistles, had written from prison in Rome. This was just the sort of material my mother liked to take with her when she had a chat with the Lord and so I expected an early reply from Him. My granpa said later that my St Paul research was a stroke of genius. But, it turned out, the Lord wasn't all that satisfied because Paul was a born-again Christian, personally converted on the road to Damascus, and he was in prison under an unjust Roman regime. The prisoners in Barberton prison were criminals being punished by a just regime. The point here was that Paul was doing the Lord's work while I was potentially aiding the devil writing letters from hardened criminals, bound to be up to no good, spreading a network of subterfuge and intrigue throughout South Africa.

To my wife, Umbela,

I send you greetings in my shame. Who is putting food in the mouth of our children? It is hard in this place, but one day I will come to you again. The work is hard but I am strong, I will live to see you again.

Your husband,
Mfulu

I wasn't able to tell my mother how innocent the letters really were because she didn't know about the previous letters or the tobacco, sugar and salt. So for the next week I read the New Testament like mad. There had to be something in there to help me. Pastor Mulvery was always taking bits and pieces of disconnected scripture and putting them together to mean just about anything; surely I could do the same.

I took the problem to Doc but for once he wasn't much help. He pointed out according to the great German Lutheran scholars the prison writings of St Paul probably took place about AD 63. Which was nice to know, but no help whatsoever.

Doc's mind was far too logical for this kind of thing so I took the problem to my granpa who, after my telling opening move with St Paul, seemed anxious to see that the debate was conducted fairly. We sat on the steps of one of the rose terraces, my granpa tapping and tamping and lighting and staring squinty-eyed through the blue tobacco smoke over the rusty roof into the pale blue beyond. After a long time he said, 'All I know about the Bible is that wherever it goes there's trouble. The only time I ever heard of it being useful was when a stretcher bearer I was with at the battle of Dundee told me that he'd once gotten hit by a Mauser bullet in the heart, only he was carrying a Bible in his tunic pocket and the Bible saved his life. He told me that ever since he'd always carried a Bible into battle with him and he felt perfectly safe because God was in his breast pocket. We were out looking for a sergeant of the Worcesters and three troopers who were wounded while out on a reconnaissance and were said to be holed up in a dry *donga*. In truth I think my partner felt perfectly safe because the Boer Mausers were estimated by the British artillery to be accurate to 800 yards and we were at least 1,200 yards from enemy lines. Alas, nobody bothered to tell the Boers about the shortcomings of their brand new German rifle and a Mauser bullet hit him straight between the eyes.' He puffed at his pipe. 'Which goes to prove, you can always depend on British army information not to be accurate, the Boers to be deadly accurate, the Bible to be good for matters of the heart but hopeless for those of the head and finally, that God is in nobody's pocket.' He seemed very pleased with this neat summary which nevertheless wasn't a scrap of help to me.

However, on Sunday night three weeks after Mrs Boxall

had first approached my mother, my granpa elected to play a part in the supper debate. My mother opened by saying the Lord was 'sorely troubled' over the whole issue which had 'weighed heavily upon her'. She liked to use words like 'sorely troubled' and 'weighed heavily' in her debates and I knew they impressed the pants off Marie.

Marie's cousin had lost her husband in a shooting accident leaving her with a small child. My mother had comforted Marie by saying that she would ask the Lord to 'bind up the wounds of her heart and pour in the balm of His comfort. That He would be Husband to the widow and Father to the orphan.' Marie sniffed a bit and said they were the most beautiful words she had ever heard.

My granpa cleared his throat. 'Were there not a couple of chaps who were crucified on either side of Christ, thorough scallywags as I recall?'

'The Word refers to them as thieves who were crucified beside the Lord, though I don't see that they have anything whatsoever to do with the matter,' my mother replied, her irritation thinly disguised. 'I do not recall it saying in the Bible that they wrote home from jail.' I knew that my granpa's opinions on biblical matters, coming as they did from a sinner who had steadfastly refused to accept Christ into his life, were not very highly regarded.

'I seem to remember that Christ forgave one of them, promising him a berth in heaven right there on the spot. Or am I mistaken?'

'Goodness! The Lord does not promise people "berths" in heaven,' my mother said sharply. ' "Verily I say unto you, today shalt thou be with me in paradise", is what the Lord said.'

'It seems to me, from that remark, that Christ has no objections to convicted felons entering the kingdom of God,' he declared.

'Of course he doesn't! That's the whole point. Jesus was sent to save the most miserable sinners amongst us. His compassion is for all of us, His love everlasting and His understanding infinite. Seek His forgiveness and you're saved. You're no longer a murderer or a thief, you're one of the Lord's precious redeemed. The thief on the cross beside Him was saved when he confessed his sins, he was washed by the blood of the Lamb.'

'Hallelujah, praise his precious name,' Marie offered absently.

'And the prisoners here in Barberton. Like him, could they also be saved?'

'You know as well as I do they could,' my mother said primly.

'How?'

'By accepting Christ into their lives, by renouncing the devil and . . . ' my mother stopped and looked straight at my granpa. 'You know very well how.'

'Oh I see. You are going to make it possible?'

'Well, no. The Anglicans and the Dutch Reformed have got the prison ministry and they do absolutely nothing. It's iniquitous. We've prayed a great deal about this, prayed that the Lord would make it possible for the Assembly of God missionaries to have the prison concession so that they can spread his precious word and bring the gospel to those poor unfortunate sinners.'

'Has it not occurred to you that the Lord may have answered your prayers?' my granpa asked.

'What on earth are you talking about?'

'Well, if the lad has direct access to the prisoners, could he not distribute tracts and that sort of thing?'

It was a master stroke. In return for being allowed to take dictation on Sunday at the prison, I was required to take gospel tracts in Sotho and Zulu from the Assembly of God missionaries and give one to each prisoner after he had dictated his letter to me. My mother and Marie had scored another major triumph, first the hospital and now the prison; they were earning recognition as a couple of hardcore fighters in the Lord's army. What's more, my time on a Sunday was counted as first-class work for the Lord.

I don't exactly know how it happened but I did it just the once, then it suddenly got done all the time. One of the prisoners had said that tobacco was sorely missed, and the next week I cut a piece of tobacco leaf exactly the same size as a tract and slipped it inside one. The next thing I knew Dee and Dum were slipping these neatly cut squares of tobacco leaf into every tract, and I would take a whole bunch with me and sort them into their four African languages and put the various piles in the drawer of the desk at which I sat, leaving an 'innocent' pile of Sotho tracts in front of me on the desk. After one of the people had dictated his letter to me I would hand him a tract from the drawer. This was Doc's idea and on two occasions the warder who attended the letter writing sessions absently picked up a tract, looked at it in a cursory manner and then returned it to the pile on the desk.

Letter writing suddenly became very popular and those of the people who didn't have anyone to write to would ask me to write to King Georgie. When I asked them what they wanted to say to the King of England it was almost always the same thing.

Dear King Georgie,

The people are happy because you are our great king. I send greetings to the great warrior across the water.

Daniel Mafutu

After a while a letter to King George was simply a euphemism for a tract. One tract and contents made two cigarettes and were an unimagined luxury. Not only had the Tadpole Angel contrived to continue the supply of tobacco into the prison, but the people no longer had to pay for it and it came together with paper to roll it in. For a generation afterwards, cigarettes in South African prisons were known as 'King Georgies' and some old lags still use this expression today. And of course the mystique which surrounded the Tadpole Angel continued to grow; nothing, it seemed, was impossible for him. More importantly for the Kommandant, the letter writing experiment proved to be a huge success and before the summer was over he had been made a full colonel and also received a commendation from Pretoria for his work in prison reform. The Assembly of God missionaries kept up the supply of tracts and even had them translated into Swazi and Shangaan. When I told Doc that King Georgies now came in Swazi and Shangaan he smiled and said, 'God's ways are mysterious, Peekay. I think because the people cannot read they now send smoke signals up to God.'

It was not long after Geel Piet's death when Lieutenant Borman started to complain of piles. 'Now I'm in administration I sit too much,' he'd say to any person who'd listen. 'I can't eat steak, it hurts too much passing through, man, there's even blood in my shit.' It was true he seemed to be losing weight and Captain Smit advised him to see a doctor. 'It's only piles, my old man was a train driver, he had the same thing.' His wife sewed a special cushion for him which he brought to work and sometimes he'd walk around carrying the cushion in case he suddenly had to sit somewhere.

'It's God's justice,' Gert confided to me, 'Geel Piet wasn't the only one he's used the donkey prick on.' He giggled, 'I hope the bugger can't sit for six months!'

No one said anything but you could see it in their eyes, those of us who had been in the gym that night all knew Borman was under a curse.

Geel Piet had once told me how prisoners could think so hard that, collectively, they could make things happen. Like when they knew I had beaten Killer Kroon hours before anyone brought the official news of my win. How they always knew when there was to be a hanging minutes after a judge had issued the warrant, sometimes hundreds of miles from the location of the prison where the hanging was to take place.

'Ja, it is true, small boss, I have seen it heppen lots of times,' Geel Piet had said gravely. 'Sometimes, when there is enough hate, this thinking can kill. The people will think some person to death. Such a death is always long and hard, because the thinking takes place over a long time. It is the hate; when it boils up there is no stopping it, the person will die because there is no *muti* you can take to stop this hating thing.'

Anyone who is born in rural Africa is superstitious and the warders, who were mostly backwoodsmen, were particularly so. We all watched Borman as he started to shrink. His extended gut remained, but everywhere else the flesh started to fall off him. He seemed to age in front of our eyes and the thinner he became the more vicious he was with the prisoners.

Another prisoner died mysteriously and after a short enquiry Borman was put on a charge and suspended from duty pending the enquiry. Shortly afterwards he experienced a severe rectal haemorrhage and was rushed to Barberton hospital where the surgeon, in an attempt to stop the bleeding caused by a rupture to the wall of the bowel, packed his rectum with giant cotton swabs – a procedure known to be about as excruciatingly painful as it is possible to experience. The doctor's cursory examination revealed the presence of a fungating growth.

Within weeks of leaving prison Doc was fit enough again to head for the hills and we would climb away from the town at first light every Saturday morning. We'd breakfast on hard boiled eggs and yesterday's bread with a thermos of sweet, milky coffee high up on a ridge somewhere or beside a stream. Sometimes we'd make for Lamati Falls, a smallish waterfall ten miles into the hills and we'd wait for the morning sun to whiten the water where it crashed into a deep pool which stayed icy cold throughout the year. Doc was like a small boy, the years seemed to fall away from him as we scampered up the sides of mountains or slid down into deep tropical kloofs, where giant tree ferns and the canopy of yellow-wood turned the brilliant sunlight into twilight and where the soil was moist and smelt both of decay and new life at the same time.

Doc was busy taking the photographs for his new book and sometimes we'd hunt all day for a single perfect specimen. It was good to be working with Doc again. He was an exacting task master who, when we found a specimen to his liking, demanded to know the soil types and the shales, the rocks and the other botanical plants which grew within a radius of fifty feet, the direction of the wind and the hours of sunlight the cactus or aloe he was photographing would receive. Some days we'd communicate all day in Latin and in this way Doc gentled me into Ovid, Cicero, Caesar's conquest of Gaul and Virgil. Mrs Boxall countered this with the English poets. Wordsworth, Masefield and Keats were her favourites, with Byron, Tennyson and Walter de la Mare, if not her favourites, a matter of essential education for a gentleman. I asked Doc about German poets, and he replied that Goethe was the only one in his opinion who could be considered worthy, but that personally he found him a terrible bore and that the Germans put all their poetry into music. He declared I should study the English for their poetry and the Germans for their music.

It was a lopsided sort of a catch-as-catch-can education, added to by Miss Bornstein who had been busy preparing me for a scholarship to a posh private school in Johannesburg. An education well beyond my mother's income as a dressmaker. I was not yet twelve, the minimum required age for entry into a secondary school, and I had languished in standard six for three years during which Miss Bornstein had privately educated me in 'all those things there's never time to learn at school'.

A month before my twelfth birthday I sat for the scholarship exam to the Prince of Wales School, and at the end of the term to my absolute mortification Mr Davis, the headmaster of Barberton school, announced that I had received the highest scholarship marks this school had ever given. That I would be starting as a boarder at the commencement of the first term in 1946. Doc, Mrs Boxall and Miss Bornstein had trained me well, if sometimes a little erratically. I was to find at the Prince of Wales School my knowledge in some things exceeded that of the senior forms and even the masters themselves, while in others I was no better than the brighter chaps in my form. But above all things I had been taught to read for pleasure and for meaning, as both Doc and Mrs Boxall demanded that I exercise my critical faculties in everything I did. At twelve I had already known how to think for at least four years. In teaching me independence of thought they had given me the greatest gift an adult can give to a child, besides love, and they had given me that also.

And so the last summer of my childhood came to an end. I also sat for the Royal College of Music Advanced Exams and passed, although my marks weren't spectacular. I think this was as much as Doc expected from me. He knew I had no special gift for music and what I achieved had been simply out of love for him. For his part he had fulfilled his contract with my mother, for whom my passing the exam was confirmation of my genius. In my mother's mind I had become the logical successor to the young Artur Rubinstein, and it was one of the major disappointments in her life that at boarding school I would elect to play in the jazz band. Jazz was the devil's music and another indication to her that I had hardened my heart against the Lord.

Before Geel Piet died he had been teaching me how to put an eight-punch combination together. I worked solidly all summer on this combination and at the championships held in Boksburg I retained the under twelve title, though this time without effort, even stopping a bigger kid in the second round on a TKO. Killer Kroon had not entered the championship even though he would have been in the division above.

Everyone, even Doc, seemed pleased that I had won a scholarship to the Prince of Wales School in Johannesburg, though I think he was trying very hard to be brave about the break-up in our partnership. Writing for the *Goldfields News*, Mrs Boxall really went to town in her column, 'Clippings from a Cultured Garden', writing about the town's *budding* intellect and its *finest flower* which turned out to be me. News of my pass in the Royal College of Music exams had me declared a *blossoming* musician. In the Afrikaans section of the paper my name appeared as the winner of the Eastern Transvaal under twelve boxing title. My mother declared, 'Our cup runneth over!' but if I would accept the Lord into my heart her joy would be a hundredfold what she was feeling now. But I could see she was pleased, especially when she started to receive invitations to tea from the town's most important families and her dressmaking business picked up so much that she only had time to accept the juiciest invitations.

I kept my apprehension about returning to boarding school to myself; it seemed I would once again be the youngest kid in the school, though this aspect anyway now left me unconcerned. If they had a Judge at the Prince of Wales School, all I could say was he'd better be able to box. In fact, the only question I asked about the school was about boxing. The reply came back that boxing was a school sport and the boxers were under the instruction of Mr Darby White, ex-cruiserweight champion of the British Army.

The final crisis of that last summer of childhood came when the clothing list arrived from the Prince of Wales School. As she read it the tears started to roll down my mother's cheeks. Marie was there on her afternoon off from the hospital so it must have been a Wednesday. My mother read the list aloud. 'Six white shirts with detachable starched collars, long sleeve. Three pairs of long grey flannel trousers (see swatch attached). Six pairs grey school socks, long. One school blazer (see melton sample attached), school blazers or blazer pocket badge and school ties obtainable from John Orrs, 129 Eloff St, Johannesburg. One grey V-neck jersey, long sleeves. Shoes, with school uniform, brown. Shoes, Sunday, black. Blue serge Sunday suit, long trousers.'

'We don't have the money, we simply don't have the money,' she kept repeating.

'Ag man, jong, where's your faith?' Marie said indignantly, not impressed by my mother's tears. 'The Lord will supply everything, just you see. We going to pray right now, go down on our knees and give the precious Lord Jesus Peekay's order. C'mon let's do it now!'

My granpa rose from the table and excused himself but I was obliged to kneel with Marie and my mother. Marie must have reasoned that, as a heathen, my prayers wouldn't have too much impact, because she took the clothing list from my mother and handed it to me. 'We going to pray out loud to the Lord, it's always best when you need something bad to pray out loud. When I tell you, you read out the list, okay?'

I nodded, grateful that I wouldn't have to pray out loud.

'Precious Lord Jesus, we got a real problem this time,' Marie began.

'Praise the Lord, praise His precious name,' my mother said.

'You know how clever Peekay is and how he has won a thing to go to a posh school in Johannesburg for nothing.'

'Precious Saviour, hear thy humble servants,' my mother said, attempting to bring a bit of tone into the whole affair.

'Well we got lots of trouble, man, I mean Lord,' Marie continued, 'the clothing list arrived today and it broke our hearts.'

'Precious Jesus! Blood of the Lamb!'

'The cupboard is bare, there are no clothes for school hanging up in it. What we need, Lord Jesus, Peekay is going to say right now, so please listen good and you talk up, Peekay, so the Lord can hear, you hear? He's going to tell you now, Lord,' Marie prayed, cueing me in.

I must say I'd never been quite as close as this to the Lord before and I was quite nervous. 'Ah, er . . . six white shirts with detachable starched collars, long sleeve,' I read. 'Three pairs of grey flannel trousers (see swatch attached).'

'Show him the swatch, man,' Marie whispered urgently. I didn't know quite what to do so I held the swatch of grey flannel up to the ceiling. After a few moments, when I reasoned the Lord had had a good enough look, I continued, 'Six pairs of grey school woollen socks, long.'

'Only three pairs, man! What about the three pairs you already got for school here?' Marie said in a stage whisper.

'Oh,' I said. 'Only three pairs, please.' My mother had stopped punctuating Marie's remarks and I looked at her. At first I thought she was crying, her face was all squished up and she was holding her hand across her mouth. Then I realised that she was desperately trying not to laugh. I started to giggle.

Without opening her eyes Marie admonished me. 'Peekay, stop it! God will punish you! It's hard enough asking the Lord for you, you not even being born again an' all that! But if you laugh we got no chance.' Her voice became conciliatory. 'Sorry, Lord, he didn't mean it, you got my word for it, it won't happen again. Go on, start reading again, the Lord hasn't got all day you know!'

I went on reading the list and also showed the Lord the swatch of green melton blazer cloth. When I got to the bit about school badges being obtainable from John Orrs, 129 Eloff Street, Johannesburg, Marie whispered again.

'You don't need to give Him the address, He knows where it is.' I finally got to the blue serge suit. 'That's his Sunday suit for going to church, Lord,' she said, to remind the Lord that I was still within his grasp every Sunday. My mother threw in a few more, 'Praise the Lord, praise His precious name's' and the request for the contents of my clothing list was over: The rest was now up to the Precious Redeemer.

Marie's eyes blazed with faith and I could see she was pretty pleased with the way she had asserted herself. There was absolutely no doubt in her mind that the Lord would provide. My mother also seemed considerably cheered up and called for Dum to make tea. I must confess, not being a Christian, I didn't share their confidence. There seemed to me to be a whole heap of clothes in that list and all I had was three pairs of grey socks, two pairs of gym pants and the tackies. These latter items had appeared in a separate list titled 'Sport and Recreation', which included two rugby jerseys, house and school colours, rugby socks, rugby boots, white cricket shirt and shorts form one and two, cricket longs form three onwards. The optional section on this list included cricket boots and white cricket sweater with school colours. It seemed an amazing collection of clothes for one person.

I mentioned the clothing crisis to Doc. Not that he could have helped. Doc, at best, lived hand to mouth with just enough over for an occasional book and film for his Leica camera. But he mentioned it to Mrs Boxall and Mrs Boxall mentioned it to Miss Bornstein and the two women went into action.

Miss Bornstein called me over at the end of class and asked me to copy out the clothing list. I did so and handed it over to her. She read it for a moment. 'What about these swatches, can you get the grey and the green swatch, Peekay? Even if you cut off a little, it's absolutely necessary for me to have them.' I promised to get hold of the swatches somehow, feeling pleased that the matter of my school clothes wasn't singularly in the Lord's hands any longer.

'We don't have very much money,' I said, for the first time in my life realising that money was important. I knew we were poor but it hadn't seemed to matter much. I'd had the occasional penny to spend on nigger balls, large black and extraordinarily hard balls that sucked down into layer

393

after layer of different colours and which would last a good two hours in the mouth. My friends were generous with their sweets so I'd never really felt poor or needed money. I always somehow managed to save up four shillings for Christmas and old Mr McClymont at the drapery shop would give me four ladies' hankies and a man's one as well as a bandanna for Doc. The ladies' hankies would go to my mother, Mrs Boxall and Dee and Dum while the man's was for my granpa. They always looked surprised when they got them, but I don't suppose they were. The only alternative to a handkerchief was a cake of Knights Castile soap and I couldn't see the value in something that wore out after a few baths. When they went to clean Doc's cottage on a Sunday Dee and Dum spread their hankies carefully over the top of their heads in the African fashion, they could never understand why white people would blow the stuff from their noses into such a pretty piece of cloth. Sunday at Doc's cottage was their big outing and they liked to look pretty. When they got there they removed the hankies of course, but they never once used them for blowing into. I think they liked their hankies better than anyone, although I know Doc liked his bandanna which was always a red one.

'There are lots of ways to skin a cat,' Miss Bornstein said. 'This town isn't going to let its *enfant terrible* go to boarding school looking like a ragamuffin.'

Between Miss Bornstein and Mrs Boxall the cloth for my trousers and blazer and blue serge suit just appeared, although I expect old Mr McClymont had a hand in it somewhere. Then Miss Bornstein sprung her surprise. Old Mr Bornstein, who had become Doc's formidable opponent at chess, had been a tailor in Germany. He would cut the cloth and do the hand work if my mother would do the machine work. The suit was easy because 'a suit is a suit, already' but we needed a blazer to make sure that mine was cut and tailored in the same way as those purchased from John Orrs, 129 Eloff St, Johannesburg. Miss Bornstein said children tend to pick on you if you're different and it was important to get everything just right. Mrs Andrews had sent two of her sons to the Prince of Wales School and she still had a school blazer which she gave to Mrs Boxall. Old Mr Bornstein took it apart to see how it was made and did a whole lot of tut-tutting about the poor workmanship. He then cut the blazer to my size and as the badge, which was three ostrich feathers sticking out of a crown, was almost new he cut it carefully around the edges and sewed it onto my new blazer so well that you would have needed a magnifying glass to see where he'd done it. Mrs Boxall sent to Johannesburg for two red, white and green striped school ties which were her special present. All my shirts were cut from a pair of cotton poplin sheets Miss Bornstein said her mother had never used. Old Mr Bornstein knew just how to make the collars so that the starch collars donated by old Mr McClymont fitted perfectly. Marie and her mother knitted me three pairs of socks for Christmas. Only the brown and black shoes remained, and at the prison Christmas party for all the warders Captain Smit handed me a large parcel from the boxing squad. Inside were a pair of new brown shoes and a pair of black ones and a brand new pair of boxing boots. 'Magtig, Peekay, we are all proud of you going to that posh Rooinek school in Johannesburg, just don't get all high and mighty on us all of a sudden when you get back, heh.' Everyone laughed and cheered and I felt the sorrow of leaving people I loved. Even old Snotnose had become a good friend over the years and I would miss them all a lot. The Kommandant stood up and recounted the first day he'd met me and said that I had proved that English and Afrikaner were one people, South Africans. That perhaps with my generation the bitterness would pass. He said I was a leader of men and that even the prisoners respected me for my letter writing. There was some more clapping and, shaking at the knees, I thanked them all. I can't remember what I said but I promised I would never forget them and I never have.

Only one more incident is worth recording in that long, last summer of childhood. My mother and Marie had already testified to the congregation about the Lord's miraculous answer to their prayers. Only the requested V-neck long sleeve mid-grey jersey was missing from my kit, but as it was summer in Johannesburg, my mother knew that the Lord would provide in time for winter. Which He did. Four knitted jerseys were pushed into her hands by separate dear, sweet, Christian ladies less than a fortnight later.

On the same night my mother and Marie also testified that the Lord had once again blessed their work in the hospital. For several weeks they had worked for the salvation of a dear man who was dying of cancer of the rectum – a man still in the prime of his life, struck down by this terrible disease. They told how they had testified to him and had seen him wrestle with the devil, how they had wept for him and pleaded with him to take the Lord Jesus into his heart and how finally, after a massive rectal haemorrhage and with the hours running out, Lieutenant Borman had surrendered his life to the Lord Jesus and had gone to meet His Saviour in paradise.

Lieutenant Borman died knowing what it felt like to have a donkey prick jammed up your arse until your entrails spill out.

SEVENTEEN

It wasn't until I went to boarding school the second time that I learned that survival is a matter of actively making the system work for you rather than attempting merely to survive it.

My partner from the very first day at school was Hymie Levy. Hymie was Jewish of course, which was a very rare occurrence at the Prince of Wales School.

I was wrestling my heavy suitcase off the train at Johannesburg Central Railway Station when he walked towards me.

'Hey you, stop! If you want to build muscles take a Charles Atlas course.' He signalled for the black porter to take my suitcase. 'Howzit? I'm the token Jew. Who are you?'

'Thanks, my name's Peekay,' I said, proffering my hand.

He took it almost absently. 'Hymie ... Hymie Levy, what's your first name, Peekay?'

'It's just Peekay, first and second,' I replied.

Hymie stopped in his tracks. 'Just one name, you're not bullshitting me now are you?'

'Ja, that's right, just one.'

Hymie seemed to be thinking as we continued together down the platform. 'I like that, no complications. Me, I've got the whole catastrophe, Hymie, Solomon, Levy, you can't get more kosher than that, kings and priests, not bad insurance for a kid whose parents escaped the Holocaust by pretending they were Roman Catholics.'

I had no idea what he was talking about but he seemed

a nice sort of a chap. All the Jews I'd ever known were pretty nice. Harry Crown and old Mr Bornstein and of course Miss Bornstein. It seemed a pleasant coincidence that the first kid I should meet from the Prince of Wales School was a Jew.

We were supposed to meet the school sergeant at the station and I was glad to have someone who was so obviously confident along with me. We heard him before we actually saw him. 'Prince of Wales new boys over here! Ahaaat the double!'

'Christ, Peekay, look at that!' Hymie said pointing to a large man wearing a scarlet tunic. Despite ourselves we straightened up a bit and Hymie ran a comb through his dark, brylcreemed hair which was swept up in the pompadour style of the time and ended in a ducktail at the back.

As we drew nearer we could see four other kids who had formed a line in front of the big man who stood to rigid attention, his pace stick clasped under his armpit. The top half of his face was hidden from view under the shiny black peak of a red-banded guardsmans' cap. The only thing that protruded from under the peak was a large waxed moustache. On the right sleeve of his military tunic were three gold sergeant's stripes above which sat a brass crown. His trousers were of black serge with a red stripe running down the sides of each leg leading directly to a pair of highly polished black boots which appeared to be rooted to the platform. A white shirt with celluloid collar and black tie completed his uniform.

Hymie tipped the porter who added our suitcases to a pile already stacked on the platform and we joined the four other boys to stand, more or less at attention, in front of the school sergeant.

I was tired and except for cleaning my teeth and splashing the gritty feel of the train journey from my face I hadn't washed since the morning of the previous day. The Barberton train had left at four o'clock that afternoon, its single

398

school carriage pulled by the coffee pot to Kaapmuiden, where it was shunted onto the school train which would travel through the night to Pretoria and Johannesburg. Several other Barberton boys and girls went to school in Pretoria, while one boy wore the navy blue blazer of St Johns College and another the black and white stripes of Jeppe High, both Johannesburg schools. I was the only one going to the Prince of Wales and, I must say, I had felt constrained and thoroughly out of place in long pants, starched collar, blazer, tie and a strange straw hat called a boater.

It was a big send-off, much bigger than anyone had expected. Of course my mother, Granpa, Marie and Dee and Dum were there, also Doc and Mrs Boxall, Miss Bornstein and old Mr Bornstein and all the kids from the boxing squad, who clapped and howled and whistled when they saw me in my uniform. Snotnose and Bokkie pretended to fall on the ground they were laughing so much, in particular at my straw boater. Gert finally had to tell them to behave, but I could see he also thought I looked pretty funny in my fancy Rooinek school clothes. But the really big surprise came when a prison truck arrived and from it climbed the prison brass band. They set up their stands in the middle of the platform and commenced to play.

'It's the Kommandant's idea, Peekay,' Captain Smit said. 'He wanted to give you a big send off. You know, man, he is very proud of you.' He paused for a moment, 'So am I, I got money on it, you going to be the welterweight champion of the world one day. Don't let that Rooinek school change that, you hear?' He gave me a playful punch on the shoulder. 'You're a proper Boer, little boetie, we all counting a lot on you.'

At last the guard blew his all-aboard whistle and I said goodbye to everyone and climbed into the carriage. Dee and Dum and Marie were all having a bit of a sniffle and my mother would have too if she hadn't thought she ought to set an example for Marie. Doc was burying his nose in his red bandanna and pushing it all over the place. When the guard blew his final whistle and the band struck up with 'Now is the hour for us to say goodbye' nearly everyone started to blub and I was pretty choked up myself.

I recalled how I had last boarded a train to leave a part of my life behind me, how I had fallen over with my clown tackies stuffed with newspaper, and how Hoppie Groenewald had dusted me down and lifted me up the steps, explaining how he too was always falling down the stupid things. 'No worries, little boetie, Hoppie Groenewald will look after you.'

Now here I was, dressed in a starched collar, hand-tailored blazer, long pants and highly polished shoes. Gert had shown me how to polish boots prison-style until you could see your face in them. The coffee pot's chuffa-chuff-chuffing drowned the band, and then the farewell party soon grew so small I could hardly make out Dee and Dum still waving. I looked up to see the hills and in particular the hill behind the rose garden where I had met Doc the day I had gone to grieve for the loss of Nanny. I was once again alone in a railway compartment headed for a new adventure.

After the train left Kaapmuiden I lay awake for a long time in the top bunk of my compartment listening to the wheels saying 'First-with-the-head-and-then-with-the-heart. First-with-the-head-and-then-with-the-heart.' It was as though Hoppie was coming with me on this second train ride into manhood. The night rushed past the window, black light broken only occasionally by a pinpoint as we roared past a cooking fire in an African village.

Every once in a while the train would whistle at something in the dark and I knew the sound would carry for miles across the veld. 'First-with-the-head-and-then-with-the-heart. First-with-the-head-and-then-with-the-heart.' The hectic lickity-clack finally put me to sleep.

Now we were standing in front of this huge old soldier who looked like a recruiting poster for the Great War. With his pacing stick still held under his arm he removed a small spiral-bound note pad from the top lefthand pocket of his tunic and flicked it open. Pulling his head back and squinting down his nose, he looked at each of us in turn. I wondered why he didn't simply lift the peak of his cap so that he could see properly.

'Righto then, my name is Bolter, Mr Bolter to Mrs Bolter if there was a Mrs Bolter which there ain't, thank Gawd! Sarge to you lot. Answer your names as I call them out!' He shouted this information at us as though he were addressing the entire length of the platform. I could see that the five guys around me were just as scared as I was. He glanced down at the pad in his hand. 'De la Cour!' A pale looking kid with curly blond hair stuck his hand up in the air. 'Not your hand, lad! You only raise your hand when you want a pee! Present Sarge! Or just, Sarge!'

'Present, Sarge,' de la Cour said softly.

'Look lively now, lad. Put some Marmite into it!' He glanced briefly at his note pad. 'Atherton!'

'Present, sir!' the kid next to me shouted so that we all jumped.

'Don't call me sir!'

'Present, Sarge,' the blond boy with pale blue eyes said, this time more quietly.

'Atherton? You have a brother at school, in forty-three?'

'My cousin, sir,' Atherton replied.

'Sarge! When I want to be a gentleman I'll bloody well tell you. It's obvious, Atherton, all the brains in your family went to your cousin.'

'Yes, Sarge,' Atherton said, his face a deep beetroot.

'Best fly-half in the school's history, got his colours in form four, let's hope you follow in his footsteps, Mr Atherton. If you do I shall forgive you this one indiscretion. Now look sharp, lad.'

Sergeant Major Bolter consulted the tiny notepad once again. 'Peekay!'

'Present, Sarge!'

'Peekay? No initial, just Peekay? What sort of a name is that, pray tell?'

'It's what I've almost always been called, Sarge.'

'Well I'm afraid that won't do, it's not Christian, lad. A gentleman always has two names at the very least. That is if he isn't a lord. You're not a lord or a duke, are you?'

'No, Sarge. It's just my name. Miss Bornstein wrote to the school and explained.'

Sergeant Major Bolter sighed deeply and bowed slightly towards me with a pretend smile on his face. 'Oh she did, did she now? Well that's settled then, isn't it? I mean if Miss Bornstein asked, we can't quibble over a small matter like a gentleman's Christian name and surname being the one and same, can we?'

'I'm not a gentleman either, Sarge,' I said, my voice trembling slightly. I knew I was in trouble but I thought it might be best to clear up any misconceptions in one hit. The kids around me giggled with the exception of Hymie who gave me a light nudge with his elbow.

The sergeant major's moustaches seemed visibly to bristle as he drew himself up to his full height. 'I'm the only one around here who's allowed not to be a gentleman, lad,' he announced, as though the subject was closed to further discussion.

'Ryder!' A boy with dark hair and piercing blue eyes jumped to a sort of attention.

'Present, Sarge! It's Cunningham-Ryder, Sarge, with a hyphen.'

Sarge looked at him and gave a meaningful sigh. 'And, Mr Cunningham-Ryder with an 'ifin, do we have a Christian name to go with our double-barrelled moniker?'

'Yes, Sarge. George Andrew Sebastian, Sarge.'

'Well now, that's more like it, ain't it, lads? Cunningham-Ryder has three Christian names and two surnames and Peekay here has none. What do you say to that?' The relief I felt at being passed over was short-lived, the bastard was going to have another go.

Levy gave me a small dig with his elbow. 'Perhaps Cunningham-Ryder can give Peekay one of his names, Sarge?' he said. We all turned to look at him, stunned at his audacity.

'What's your name, lad?' Sergeant Major Bolter asked softly, which did nothing to conceal the terrible menace in his voice.

'Levy, Sarge. Hymie Levy, and I'm not a gentleman or a Christian. I'm a Jew. My dad had to pull all sorts of strings to get me in.' He wore an ingenuous expression as he looked directly at the sergeant major.

We all fought back our laughter, but to our surprise Bolter didn't explode. Turning to his notepad, he said, 'Levy, here at the Prince of Wales School everyone is a Christian and a gentleman and that includes both you and Mr Peekay.' He glanced up. 'Johnson!' We all looked over at a small freckle-faced boy with red hair who stood next to Levy with his mouth slightly open. 'Johnson!' Sarge repeated, raising his voice several decibels. The kid with the open mouth had to be Johnson, he was the only as yet un-named one among us, but he remained silent, his terror-stricken gaze fixed on the large man. With a sort of stop-start jerky movement he raised his hand.

'Do we want to do wee-wee, lad?' I could see Sarge was growing impatient with us all.

'No, sir,' Johnson gulped the words out.

'Do not call me sir, you piss-wit!' Sergeant Major Bolter yelled and several people walking along the platform stopped to stare at him. And that's how 'Pissy' Johnson came to get his nickname.

I was enormously impressed with Levy. I had never met a Jewish person my age or someone who couldn't become a Christian even had he wanted to. I knew instantly I liked him. As it transpired Hymie Levy was to become my closest friend, while Paul Atherton, Pissy Johnson and 'Cunning-Spider', which is how Cunningham-Ryder was to become known, were the group with whom I mostly went around.

The school charabanc driven by Sarge had taken us through the sky-scrapered streets out through a place called Hillbrow where we followed a tram down into increasingly quieter suburbs. We left the tram at its terminal and drove into a leafy suburb named Houghton where the houses, set in perfectly manicured lawns and brilliant gardens, were bigger than any I had ever seen. The top of the charabanc brushed against the cool dark oak trees that lined the quiet streets. We passed an occasional nanny wheeling a baby carriage with large wheels that even sported springs. All the nannies wore identical black dresses with a starched white pinny and all the baby carriages seemed to have come from the same factory. I wasn't much for symbols, my life had somehow contrived to be a mixture of people so that social status meant very little to me. Nevertheless I sensed that I was entering a new kind of world with a different set of rules.

We turned into a gateway, through a huge open gate with the crown and three ostrich feathers outlined in its wrought-iron design, and continued down a roadway bordered on each side by giant English oaks. On the way to Wellington House, one of the three boarders' houses at the Prince of Wales School, we passed an emerald green cricket pitch with a rotating hose chit-chit-chittering a jet of water in a large circle around the pitch. On the far boundary, neatly enclosed by a white picket fence, stood a small white pavilion, behind it grew another row of giant oaks and beyond them rose several sets of rugby posts, still further yet the neo-gothic clock tower of the main school rose above the trees. It seemed the perfect place for a posh school but I was not at all sure that it was the perfect place for the future welterweight champion of the world.

Hymie Levy had seated himself beside me on the ride to school and had set about explaining his theory of survival. We were, he decided, odd-bods, he a Jew and me with only one name. Odd-bods, he asserted, were always singled out by plebeians, the worst kind of which were middle-class,

Anglo-South African Protestants, who undoubtedly made up the remainder of the school. I wasn't quite sure whether belonging to the Apostolic Faith Mission qualified me as a Protestant but I had to agree with him that my background was probably different from that of the other guys in the bus. From my previous bout of boarding school I had already learned that being different doesn't pay off. This time I was determined to enter the school environment on my own terms. There wasn't too much I was frightened of and I was fairly confident that I could compete intellectually. It was time to remove my camouflage, all my life I had let others provide for me and while I loved the people who had nurtured and built me intellectually, I felt that emotionally it was time to provide for myself. Everyone on the intellectual side of my life seemed to agree that an exclusive private school education was what I needed, while those on the physical side, mainly the boxing squad, were more than a little dubious about an elitist Rooinek school education. I had been torn between the two, never clearly deciding who I was, changing my camouflage to suit. I had accepted an education at an elitist boarding school while at the same time nurturing my ambition to become the welterweight champion of the world. It didn't take too many brains to figure out that world champion boxers are not spawned within a system designed to educate upper middle-class Christian gentlemen.

I placed less importance on my intelligence than on my prowess as a boxer. If the Prince of Wales School tried to disabuse me of my ambition to be the welterweight champion of the world, then the intellectual nourishment it might furnish as compensation would not be sufficient incentive for me to remain. But I wasn't about to let this happen. No more camouflage for Peekay, I would simply be the best. I hadn't discussed this with either Doc or Miss Bornstein. I was on my own again and I had to do my own thinking, so when Hymie started on about beating the system I knew immediately what he was on about.

He passed me a stick of Spearmint and commenced talking again. 'Now my theory is that to beat any system you have to know it intimately. Rebellion is senseless and being pointedly different only leads to persecution, the only way to control any system is from inside it the way the Jews have always done.'

'It didn't seem to help them with Hitler,' I said. I didn't know much about the Jews in Nazi Germany but Miss Bornstein had told me a little and had added that Old Mr Bornstein actually felt guilty for escaping the Holocaust.

'A-ha, that was different. Hitler's Nazi party presented an impossible problem for the Jews of Germany. After all, you can't undermine a system from within when you're excluded from it in the first place, can you?'

Hymie's point was not well made. I was to learn that he was obsessed with the Holocaust, that it sometimes clouded his otherwise excellent judgement. I could never quite understand why he possessed this obsession, his parents had escaped from Warsaw before the Jews were incarcerated in the ghetto or were even unduly persecuted. Hymie had never known any real racial prejudice, yet he had a strong sense of alienation as well as, it seemed to me at times, of guilt.

Doc had taught me well and I wasn't about to let Hymie get away with a cheap shot like that.

'Every system tends to be mutually exclusive, they're all about keeping someone or something out, by keeping the Jews out of the Nazi party Hitler was acting typically. No system wants to be undermined or abused and therefore it is constantly on guard to exclude those who would destroy it. If, as you say, it is a common Jewish tactic to invade from within then this should have been possible even with the Nazi party. We have to conclude that the Jews failed to defeat Hitler, failed to defeat the system and as a consequence paid a terrible price. It wasn't an exception at all.'

Hymie grinned. 'Hey! You can think. I'm not used to that in a goy. Here, shake a paw.'

I allowed the compliment and shook his hand, although I wasn't quite sure what he meant. 'What's a goy?'

'A Christian, a gentile. Hey, can we be friends, I mean proper friends, Peekay?'

'Sure,' I said, not really meaning it.

'You see, you're different. I know that now. And I'm certainly different, I always have been, but being a Jew at a school like this makes me even more so. I reckon we'll need each other.'

'What for? You mean to beat the system?'

'No, no, to use it. I've got a hunch we'll be a terrific combo.'

I wasn't sure he was right. I still had a problem. While I had all the physical and intellectual equipment needed to succeed within the system, I lacked one thing. Money. The only way I could succeed without money was by being a loner. Friendship with this particular tribe of Christian gentlemen required resources. You were expected to pay your way. The only other way was by ingratiation, but I was damned if that was ever going to happen to me again. Pisskop was still the dark shadow of Peekay, still alive in my mind; come what may, I would never again stoop to conquer.

Added to this was the fact that I was basically a loner. Other than Doc, and when I was small, Granpa Chook, I'd never been in the position of having a partner and I'd never really had a best friend who was my own age. Having an immediate friend in this strange new environment sounded nice, but it also made me feel vulnerable.

'Have you honest and truly only got one name?' Hymie asked suddenly.

'Well sort of, you see I've only ever used one name. One name is me.'

'They won't let you get away with it you know, the system can't handle things like that.'

'It's just going to have to,' I replied, sounding a lot braver than I really was. I longed suddenly to ask Doc what he would advise under the circumstances, though I already knew the answer. He would simply have said that a man has the right to any name he wants to give himself; if a man is saddled with a name he didn't choose, how can he possibly be free for the rest of his life? 'We got to be who we got to be. Absoloodle!' he'd conclude after we had carefully and fully discussed the matter. Doc was not a man to make compromises on important issues such as determining who a person really is in his own mind.

'I bet you're good at sport. Me, I'm rotten,' Hymie said.

'I'm okay.'

'What's your best sport,' Hymie asked, humouring me, 'rugby?'

'No, I box.'

Hymie jerked back in his seat, plainly shocked. 'You what!'

'I'm a boxer.'

'Yeah, that's what I thought you said. Why man, that's positively Neanderthal.'

'You could get badly hurt saying that to the wrong boxer,' I grinned.

Hymie reeled back in mock terror, 'Careful, man, in a court of law a boxer's hands are considered lethal weapons.' He was suddenly serious again. 'I tell you what, I'm a gambler and you're a boxer, that's yet another reason why you and I have to stick together, Peekay.'

'What do you gamble on?' I asked.

Hymie sighed. 'I'm a Jew. People expect Jews to be good with money. So what do Jews do? They oblige. My old man is filthy rich and he'll give me all the money I need. But that's the very problem, you see. I have to make my own, it's an intellectual thing not a greedy thing. I'm not really a gambler, gamblers are stupid, making money is simply a way of keeping myself mentally fit, can you understand that?'

'No.'

'Are you rich, Peekay? I mean your parents?'

'Hell no, I won a scholarship here. My mum's a dress-maker.'

'Well, that's why you don't understand. For me money is like boxing is for you, it's my way of getting even with the world. For a rich Jew money is a weapon, unless I know how to make it on my own I will be defenceless.'

I was suddenly fascinated. It wasn't that Hymie's philosophy was the antithesis of all I'd been taught, although I knew the Lord was against money and definitely in favour of the poor. It was just that, well, Doc and Mrs Boxall, or even Miss Bornstein, had never mentioned money or its importance in the scheme of things. I'd been forced into thinking about money for the first time when the list for my school clothes had arrived and I had already worked out that not having any at a boarding school for the sons of the rich was pretty well going to shape my school career.

'Are you very good at making money?' I asked Hymie.

'About as good as you are at boxing,' he replied.

'You've got yourself a partner, Hymie. Money is something I have to learn about.'

Hymie grinned, 'It's a deal, Peekay. I had a feeling you were a bloody good boxer.'

I was by nature a fairly quiet sort of a guy and had no trouble getting on with things. As a new boy I was at the bottom of the heap but was fortunate enough to be selected as the fag for the head of house, Fred Cooper who was also the second prefect of the entire school and the captain of the First XV Rugby. This immediately gave me some extra status amongst the other new boys all of whom, like me, were allocated to a school or house prefect.

Fagging was hard work and we were on standby for the school and house prefects from first bell at six a.m. until lights out at nine-thirty. No chore was thought too menial and a prefect had only to yell from his study and all the fags within hearing distance would have to come running. Last new boy to arrive did the chore. In addition to this, each fag had a list of duties he was obliged to perform for his personal prefect. He made his bed, shone his shoes, cadet and rugby boots, washed his rugby togs or during the summer blancoed his cricket boots, and if he was an officer in the cadet corps polished his Sam Browne and brasses, laid out his clothes, tidied his study, ran his messages and made trips to the tuck shop on his behalf.

The first tanning I received was for scooping the tiniest dab of cream off the top of a cream bun I was delivering to Fred Cooper. At least it started with the tiniest scoop and then, in an attempt to smooth the scooped part, I took one or two more small scoops on the end of my finger. By the time I arrived at Fred Cooper's study, the bun looked somewhat re-arranged.

'You rotten little bugger! You've been norking my cream bun,' Cooper yelled at me.

'My hand slipped over it and I had to lick it off sort of, sir,' I explained, not quite willing to tell an outright lie.

'Shit! Did you lick my bloody bun, Peekay?'

'No, sir, just my hand.'

'Close the door, boy. We have an excellent way to train slippery hands.' Cooper reached for the cane which hung behind the door. 'How many times do you reckon it slipped?' he asked.

'Not many, sir,' I said fearfully.

'Not many is once or twice or three times, tell me, man?'

'Once?' I said hopefully.

'Right, bend down.' I bent down holding my knees and proffering my arse. Whack! 'That's one for your slippery hand.' Whack! 'That's one for your slippery tongue.' Whack! 'And that's one for your poor memory.' Cooper returned the cane to the back of the door and pointed to the cream bun on his desk. 'Eat it! And go and get me another one with your own money.'

I stood looking at the cream bun with its shiny brown top and cream-filled centre. This was my first major crisis. 'I . . . I don't have any money, sir.'

Cooper turned back to his book. 'Use those slippery fingers of yours to find some,' he said, dismissing me.

I left his study holding the offending cream bun gingerly in my hand. Pocket money was drawn every Wednesday after lunch and every Saturday morning, but as I hadn't been given any for the term, the fact that it was Tuesday meant two things: none of the other fags would have any money this late in the week and even if I could borrow some I had no possibility of paying it back.

My arse stung like hell, but I hardly noticed it in my anxiety. Hymie Levy was waiting at the end of the corridor which led to the sixth form studies.

'Christ, Peekay, I could hear it from here, that bastard sure blasted arse!'

'I'm in deep shit,' I told him. 'I've got to buy Cooper another cream bun and I haven't got any money.'

Hymie shrugged, 'Easy man, I'll give it to you.' Then he pointed to the bun in my hand, 'What's that? That's a cream bun!'

I explained to him what had happened. 'Sorry, but I can only accept a loan if you'll let me do something to pay it off,' I added.

'Don't be stupid, Peekay. Pay me tomorrow after pocket money.'

It was the first time I had had to admit that I had no money whatsoever.

'You mean nothing? No money at all?' Hymie was clearly astonished. He dug into the change pocket of his grey flannels and produced a two-shilling piece. 'Here, take it, you can pay me back when you leave school.'

'Bullshit, Hymie, that's in five years.'

Hymie grinned, 'I'm a Jew, remember, we're supposed never to forget.'

'You're also a pain in the arse, Levy. Keep your two bob, I only need threepence anyway. Bugger it! I'll go and throw myself on Cooper's mercy.'

'What, and get your bum blasted again? Give us that

bun. Here, hold this.' He carefully lifted the top half of the bun and handed it to me. Then, using his forefinger, he spread the cream from the centre of the botton half of the bun to the edges, piling the cream high on the edges. He held out his hand for the top and replaced it onto the bottom half, squeezing lightly with his forefinger and thumb to force both halves together. As he did this the cream squirted out of the sides as natural looking as you please. He handed the fully restored cream bun back to me, a satisfied grin on his mug.

'Gee thanks, Hymie. I owe you man,' I said, relief flooding over me.

'Don't thank me, Peekay. It took two thousand years of persecution by bastards like Cooper to make me smart, I really ought to thank him.'

It was the first time we'd beaten the system, although of course it was Hymie who had really done so. After I'd given Cooper his 'new' bun, we retired behind the bogs and laughed our heads off. Then Hymie took out his miniature chess set and we battled it out for the next hour. We were evenly matched players; his cunning was matched by my years of memorising all Doc's games plus my having a reasonable grasp of the niceties of the game. We were in the school first chess team right from the start, which wasn't earth shattering news, the Christian gentlemen were not exactly breaking down the doors to join the chess club.

Boxing presented a problem. It wasn't a major sport at school and therefore not compulsory. Only about twenty boys out of the six hundred in the school took part. Darby White, the gym master and ex light-heavyweight champion of the British army, had turned six of these twenty into a fairly good boxing team, although I soon learned that we only boxed the Afrikaans schools as the other English schools didn't go in for boxing. No other boxer in the school of any weight had been trained as well as I had been or came close to my skill. Sarge was also very keen on boxing and he and Darby White would work the squad together. While the school team was said to be game, morale was pretty low when I arrived. The school had won only six individual bouts in five years and none in the past two years, let alone a boxing match. The red, white and green ribbon, which were the school colours and which had been tied around the handle of a massive wooden spoon and hung from one of the beams in the gym, were beginning to fade, the spoon having been in permanent residence with the Prince of Wales School so long.

Darby White would sometimes look up at it a little wistfully and say, 'I don't expect ever to win the schools trophy but I'd just like to lose that dirty great wooden ladle for just one year.'

I told Hymie about this and he immediately became interested. Hymie's interest in sports was zero, but he couldn't resist an intellectual challenge. 'How good are the other chaps in the squad?' he asked. I was forced to admit that they were pretty average. The kids in the prison squad back home could have taken them with one arm tied behind their backs. 'How good a coach is Darby White?' Darby White wasn't Geel Piet but he knew his boxing and he was certainly as good as Captain Smit.

'I think he's lost his enthusiasm, but he seems to know his onions,' I replied.

'You need a manager and I know just the chap,' Hymie said. That was the nice part about Hymie, he never bragged but he was absolutely certain of his superiority. It crapped a lot of people off, but Hymie had prepared himself for a life where the slings and arrows were fairly frequent and he didn't seem to give a damn whether or not he was liked. 'Persecution is the major reason for a Jew to exist. If it didn't happen we'd soon be as intellectually inferior as you lot,' he'd say.

I asked Hymie how he proposed to turn possibly the weakest school boxing team in the world into a winning combination. He looked at me and for once the slightly cynical grin left the corners of his mouth. 'We need only one winner for a start. One guy you can rely on to win. The rest is easy, the rest is only good management. When men can be made to hope, then they can be made to win.' He placed his hands one on each of my shoulders. 'How many fights have you won in the ring, Peekay?'

'Thirty-four,' I replied.

'How many have you lost?'

'Well . . . none,' I said, a little embarrassed.

'You'll do nicely. There's nothing a gambler likes better than a certainty.'

'This is the highveld, the standard is much higher than in the lowveld where I've done all my boxing, sooner or later every boxer gets beaten.'

'Sure, sure, but let's do all we can to delay that moment as long as possible. Peekay, I smell money in that boxing team.'

'You mean by becoming an integral part of the system, me boxing and you managing, and then making it work for us?'

'I love a fast learner,' Hymie said.

When Darby White and Sarge saw me work out I could see they were enormously impressed. 'Where'd you learn to box, son?' Darby White asked.

Without thinking I answered, 'In prison, sir.'

It was a reply Darby White would never grow tired of recounting. To my often acute embarrassment it became his favourite boxing story and given the slightest opportunity, he'd recount it to the coaches from the other schools.

Sarge was second in command of the boxing squad and acted with Darby White as a second or alone when Darby was refereeing a fight. As a young guardsman with the Coldstream Guards he'd been quite a useful amateur in his day. Later he'd worked as a second under the famous English trainer Dutch Holland of the Thomas à Becket Gymnasium in south London. Dutch Holland was the best cut-man in England and Sarge claimed to have learned the art of stemming an eye bleed from him. A cut eye would usually stop a fight in school boxing, which wasn't always fair as the better boxer could lose on a TKO when he was ahead on points. Sarge could work miracles with a cut-stick, cotton wool swabs, adrenalin and vaseline. In fact, his special skill as a cut-man was one of the weapons Hymie was to use in his campaign to lift the boxing squad out of last place in the schools competition.

Hymie had himself elected as the manager of the boxing squad by the simple expedient of volunteering for the job. No first form boy had previously held this job. The managers of the various major sports, cricket, rugby, swimming, shooting and, of course, boxing were invariably chosen from fifth form boys who, while not being sportsmen, were known to be brains, hence these positions came to be known as 'swot spots' and the fifth form boy honoured with a swot spot would invariably become a school prefect in the year following.

However, the swot spot for boxing had become a school joke and was therefore seen as not worthy of a brain. It was considered extremely poor form to apply for it, and Darby White had for the past four years rejected the few applicants on the basis of them not being known brains and therefore simple opportunists. In putting his case for the swot spot in boxing, Hymie pointed out to Darby White that as he was in the school senior chess team he qualified in the brain department and besides, with a first former in the job, Darby could look forward to five years of continuity, with all the advantages of long-term planning.

Hymie's arguments were persuasive. The most telling of them being that we couldn't do any worse than we were doing, so Darby might as well give him a go. Darby White only jingled his balls in his white duck trousers furiously for about two minutes before agreeing. Darby was quite unable to make a decision of any sort without putting both hands into his trouser pockets and giving his balls a tumble, the longer the process the more complicated the decision.

My first fight was as a flyweight, although at one hundred and two pounds I was a very light one and would be fighting a kid who weighed nearly ten pounds more than me. It took place in the school gymnasium a month after the term had begun. Home matches drew little attention from anyone at the school. School spirit did not extend to boxing, it was a recognised fact that we always lost and only the boxing squad and first form boarders, conscripted to watch, would be present to see the tripe walloped out of the Prince of Wales team. These one-sided bouts were privately referred to as 'two-fisted attacks from the hairy backs'. As in: 'Another seven to zero two-fisted attack from the hairy backs.' The malevolence between Afrikaans and English-speaking South Africans continued unabated, with the English still feeling mightily superior. The fact that only Afrikaans schools boxed was further reason to dismiss the boxing team as being somewhat *déclassé* and not worthy of the finer traditions of the school. Darby White in his white ducks and singlet, with his belly spilling over the old tie which held his trousers up, and Sarge in his jazzy hotel doorman's uniform and silly pace stick, were looked upon as a comic opera team by the remainder of the mortar and gowned teaching staff. Nothing was ever said, but you simply knew that those who laboured in the field were not equal to those who laboured in the mind.

While only the handful of Prince of Wales kids attended that first fight the gym was packed with kids from the opposition school, an Afrikaans high school named Help-mekaar, which translated into English means Help each other. Helpmekaar enjoyed a huge reputation in all sport except cricket. Its boxing team was said to be the best in South Africa and had won the South African schools Boxing Championships the year before.

At one hundred and eleven pounds the kid I was fighting was just one pound short of being a bantamweight. I didn't mind as I was used to fighting guys heavier and bigger than me and had fought tougher looking kids than him before.

But Hymie was concerned, this was the first time we were going into business together and at the weigh-in he'd looked worried.

'Ten pounds is a lot to give away, this Geldenhuis guy is supposed to be shit hot.'

'C'mon, Hymie, he's a new boy just like us, how would they know? How's the book going?'

'Great, that's the problem. I've been taking bets in the toilet from the Helpmekaar chaps all night and I've got you at ten to one against four to one on Geldenhuis and they're falling over themselves to bet on their man.'

'That's great, did you tell the first form boarders to bet on me?'

'Ja, they're all pretty excited, but their bets aren't anywhere near enough to cover us if Geldenhuis wins. Christ, Peekay, I must be mad. It's not having all the facts that's pissing me off. We have no form on Geldenhuis, none on you for that matter, we're making book in the dark, that's just plain dumb.'

'We've got to start somewhere. Let's start by trusting each other.'

'No offence, Peekay, but next time first the facts and then the trust.' It was perhaps the most important thing Hymie ever said to me. Hymie was the supreme example of Hoppie's dictum: First with the head and then with the heart. It was to be the basis of our business operations from that time on.

Geldenhuis was solidly built around the shoulders and I knew I'd have to stay away from his right, which he kept throwing straight from the shoulder as he shadow boxed while waiting for the fight to begin.

Geel Piet had warned me that some boxers throw shadow punches before a fight to deceive their opponent into thinking they lead with a left or a right when in actual fact it's the other way around. The idea is to surprise your opponent in the first few seconds and so unsettle him. I studied the big kid and decided there wasn't any subterfuge in his

417

shadow boxing, he was much too confident to bother with any tricks. His leading hand was the left and I noticed he held his right too low, leaving his jaw unprotected. His slightly more open stance suggested that he saw himself as a fighter. In which case he would come out hard and fast hoping to nail me early with a good punch.

For my part I would always 'just sit on the pot', as Geel Piet called sitting quietly on the tiny three-legged corner stool waiting for the fight to begin. 'Tell them nothing, jong,' he had said, 'just sit and watch, watch very carefully. I'm telling you, man, you can tell a lot about a boxer even before he throws a punch, if you watch him carefully.'

The bell for the first round went and after we'd touched gloves the Helpmekaar kid came at me fast. He was hard eyed and I could sense he planned to make short work of the fight. I saw the first straight left coming from a mile off and allowed it to miss the side of my head by a fraction. A near miss with the leading hand often gives a boxer the confidence to try again immediately with a similar punch, thrown even harder than the first it invariably throws the boxer slightly off balance. The second straight left came right on time and as it whistled past my ear his right dropped to the level of his chest leaving his head wide open. I stepped in and with my body slightly turned to maximise the power, the right hook I threw landed flush on the point of his chin. He was already off balance, moving into my punch, and he hit the canvas hard, sprawling on his back. While the blow carried all my strength behind it, it was also a perfectly timed punch and a gasp went up from the Helpmekaar crowd while a wild cheer rose from our first form boarders.

The kid on the canvas sat up as the ref began to count. There was no way I could have knocked him out but he was clearly shaken. Young guys are too proud to stay down for the compulsory eight count and he jumped to his feet glowering at me. The surprise had been on the other foot and I now expected him to move around me for a while, waiting for a chance to use his superior strength to nail me with a few solid blows to the head. First you're going to have to catch me you Boer bastard, I thought. The referee went through the compulsory eight count, then wiped his gloves and told us to box on.

I was so obviously lighter than the other kid and now, looking into his eyes, I suddenly realised that he had regarded the blow as a fluke and had no intention of boxing smart. He moved straight at me again with his right still held too low. He was telegraphing the punch to come by watching the point of my chin. Christ, he's going to try the left lead again. As Geel Piet would say, 'Some fighters you can read better than a book but, ag man, the story has no blêrrie imagination.'

The straight left came hard and missed, merely flicking my ear. I brought my right across his left and hit him on the side of the jaw, only just missing the point. I followed with a left hook into his solar plexus and he sat down hard, the seat of his pants seeming to bounce as he hit the canvas. I cursed myself, you don't get too many chances for a really good right cross in a fight and I hadn't set myself correctly. Nevertheless it was a good punch and the left had dug in just below the ribs where it really hurts.

Geldenhuis was strong and game and was back onto his feet in a second. He waited for the compulsory eight, and as the ref wiped his gloves he warned him that one more knock down meant the fight was over. I knew I'd have to be lucky to get a third crack at him and decided it was time to box, to wear him down jab, jab, jab, waiting for the chance to come under his left lead to land a series of solid punches under his heart. That way, if he wasn't enormously fit, I'd sap his stamina to give me another crack at him in the third and final round. The bell rang for the end of the round and I returned to my corner to find Darby and Sarge grinning from ear to ear.

In the second round I simply boxed him. His style was

exuberant and I waited for him to grow impatient as I kept him at his distance with constant jabs to the face. Towards the end of the round he must have realised that the fight was slipping away and he seemed determined to knock me down, even if it meant taking a couple of punches on the way. He came at me with both hands swinging. I think he expected me to move away so that he could nail me in a corner. But I stood my ground and hit him with a straight left which pushed him back against the ropes. I followed in with Geel Piet's eight-punch combination, two good scoring shots to the head one of which opened a cut above his eye, the next bang on the nose, one more into the cut and the rest neatly placed under his heart. To my surprise, when the bell went for the end of round two, the Helpme-kaar guys gave me a round of applause.

Geldenhuis didn't come out for the third round. The referee had examined the cut above his eye and stopped the fight. I'd won on a TKO, the first win for the Prince of Wales School in two years.

It didn't seem to matter that we lost the other seven fights, though all had lasted the distance. The boxing squad, generally outclassed, hadn't fought with such spirit and determination for years. Sarge was walking around flashing his mouth full of gold teeth and saying in a whisper that carried for yards, 'Bloody marvellous, that ought to show those bloody Boers who's boss.' You'd have thought we had won the match.

The boxing coach from Helpmekaar came over and patted me on the back. 'Who taught you to box, son?' he said in English.

'I learned in Barberton, Meneer,' I replied in Afrikaans.

He looked suddenly smug. 'Magtig. I knew you were too good for an Englishman! I've never seen a kid your age throw an eight-punch combination. Come to think of it, I've never seen any kid throw an eight-punch combination. Who taught you to box, man?'

'Meneer Geel Piet,' I replied.

'Well I wish we had him at Helpmekaar, that's all I can say, man.'

'I don't really think you would have wanted him,' I replied, but he seemed not to hear me.

'You're an Afrikaner, what are you doing in a school like this?' Without waiting for my answer he continued, 'Listen, we could arrange for you to come to Helpmekaar, you'd be with your own people, we can organise a boarding scholarship.'

'I'm English. A Rooinek,' I said quietly. For the first time in my life I felt enormously proud about something. Perhaps it was wrong to be proud, but I'd waited a long time to come to terms with being a Rooinek.

The coach from Helpmekaar looked at me for what seemed like a long time. 'Well you don't box like a Englishman. Don't desert your own kind, son. Englishmen don't talk Afrikaans the way you do, I know, I'm a language teacher as well as a boxing coach.'

'I am English,' I replied in English, 'honestly, sir.'

'Well, Englishman, I doubt that there's a kid in your weight division anywhere in South Africa who could beat you, that is, if this Rooinek school doesn't bugger you up.'

He turned away abruptly, walked over to where Darby White was standing juggling his balls and looking pleased with himself. I could see they were both looking at me and Darby White had a proprietorial grin on his face.

I felt a hand on my shoulder and I turned to see the big kid I'd fought. He wore a large pink elastoplast patch over his left eyebrow. 'Howzit?' He stuck his hand out. 'Jannie Geldenhuis. No hard feelings, okay? You won fair and square, man,' he said in English with a thick Afrikaans accent.

'Thanks for the fight,' I replied in Afrikaans as I shook his hand.

He grinned and seemed pleased that I'd replied in Afrikaans. 'Ag man, I don't think I even hit you once, I've never done that before. It'll teach me a blêrrie good lesson, you looked such a little bugger, I thought I had a easy fight on my hands.'

I smiled at him. 'You're such a big bastard I thought I was going to get a hiding.' Gert had always said that a man should be magnanimous in victory and Jannie Geldenhuis seemed like a nice bloke.

'Ja, that was the blêrrie trouble, man, so did I.' He grinned again. 'Just you wait, man, I'll get you back on the rugby field, what possie you play?'

'Scrum-half. By the way, my name's Peekay.'

'Ja, I already know. Me too, I'm also a scrum-half. *Alles van die beste*, Peekay.' He turned to go and then turned back and rubbed the point of his jaw, 'Jesus, you hit me a beauty in the beginning of the first round!' then he went to join his school mates.

'Ja, so long, Jannie,' I said, pleased it had ended this well.

Hymie walked up just as Geldenhuis departed. 'Howzit? What did the hairy back want, your autograph?'

'Nothing. He just said no hard feelings, he'd see me on the rugger field.'

Hymie grinned, 'I'll say no hard feelings, we're rich!' He frowned suddenly, 'But we've still got to hate the bastards.'

'Shit, Hymie, not after it's over!' I said grinning.

'It may only have been a boxing match to you!' Hymie pointed to the wooden spoon hanging from the beam above our heads. 'To me it's the beginning of getting rid of that! We can only do that by learning to hate.'

I sighed. 'Hymie, you've got to learn there are good Boers and bad Boers, just like everyone else. You can't just lump them all together.'

'The only good Boer is a dead Boer!' Hymie snorted.

'The only good Kaffir is a dead Kaffir is where that came from,' I said, chiding him for his lack of originality.

'Yeah, them too,' he added ruefully.

'Christ, Hymie, you're a Jew! How can you say things like that?'

Hymie laughed, 'I'm a very complicated Jew,' he said.

'Peekay, if we're going to win against those Boers we've got to learn to hate them. Don't you even understand the fundamentals?'

'Bullshit!'

'Yeah, it is. You're right, it is bullshit.' He looked at me and grinned again, 'But for Christ's sake, don't tell the others, we've got them thinking they can win, that the enemy isn't invincible.'

He was the only one on the boxing squad who hadn't congratulated me and I wondered why. I was to learn that Hymie was the world's best persuader, he could pump courage and spirit into a dejected boxer, soothe his battered ego and recover his self-esteem. Hymie smoothed words on and gently massaged them in as though they were a magic balm. But he only used them this way for a pre-determined purpose and only with people he considered less than his equal. A light pat on the back was all I ever got. Hymie considered me his equal and he allowed me to share his superior intellect, which was usually two or three jumps ahead of anyone else.

'Well tell me?'

'Tell you what?' Hymie asked.

'How much? How much did we make?'

Hymie grinned, 'Enough for you to buy Cooper several hundred cream buns if you ever have to again. I reckon we'll get a fiver out of it each.'

'Jesus, Hymie, that's wonderful!'

'It's only the beginning, Peekay. This time we gambled and won. Next time you fight we're going to know the form. We're going to know everything it is possible to know about your opponent. Every time he scratches his bum we're going to analyse why. The making of money should never be left to chance.'

After my solo victory against Helpmekaar, Atherton, Cunning-Spider and Pissy Johnson immediately joined the boxing squad, along with twelve of the other new boys. It soon became apparent that Pissy Johnson was totally unco-ordinated and would never make a boxer, but Atherton and Cunning-Spider were natural athletes and quickly caught on. Hymie called the new boys 'the Wooden Spoon Goons', swore us all into an elaborate brotherhood and elected himself President for Life and me Captain.

Hymie knew the value of a little mystique, the initiation into the Wooden Spoon Goons involved the exchange of everyone's blood except his own. He swore each of us into the brotherhood and then instructed me to swear him in as President for Life. He had personally composed the protocol for the ceremony and when his turn came he handed me a slip of paper to read which went like this: '*Do you, Hymie Solomon Levy, solemnly agree to fight with all your wit and skill and nerve to restore The Prince of Wales School to its former boxing glory?*' This came as somewhat of a surprise to all of us as we had no idea there had been any former glory to restore us to.

'I do,' Hymie said.

'*Do you agree to act selflessly without thought of personal glory or gain as the President for Life of the Wooden Spoon Goons?*' I wondered how he managed to reconcile this with our business arrangments.

'This I do solemnly declare to do,' Hymie said in an impressive flourish of grammatical construction.

'*In consideration for so doing and in the year nineteen hundred and forty-six in the reign of His Gracious Majesty King George the Sixth, I, Peekay, Captain of The Wooden Spoon Goons, declare Hymie Solomon Levy, President for Life.*'

Hymie had confided to me in a rare moment of introspection that in naming him his parents had thrown the whole bloody Polish ghetto at him. 'Why couldn't they have given me just one Goy name, like Derek or Brian or Arthur or something?' It was the only time I ever heard him question his Jewishness.

Later, as we were walking back to Wellington, I ribbed him about the restoring us to our former glory bit in the swearing in ceremony and also mentioned the no personal gain clause in his oath as president for life.

Hymie stopped and turned to face me. With an exaggerated sigh, as though he had seriously come to doubt my sagacity, he said, 'For Chrissake, Peekay, don't you read history? It doesn't matter how much of a crap-up a country makes, by the time it gets into history it's been turned into glorious tradition. It's the same with an institution, you can't go having the school losing on its boxing team generation after generation, history simply doesn't allow for that sort of truth. Of course we've got a glorious tradition, because if we haven't we have now and as Wooden Spoon Goons we're going to have to restore the Prince of Wales to its former glory, whatever the fuck happened in real life.'

'Wow!' as Doc would say. 'No doubtski aboutski, Hymie Levy was the absoloodle best!'

'As for the personal gain, our primary purpose is to restore the school to its former boxing glory, there is no thought of not doing so if we can't make a quid out of it. That's what I mean by no thought of gain. We are not creating a business situation, we are merely exploiting one. Not to do so would be tantamount to sheer neglect, almost criminal if you ask me.'

There had been one strange happening at that first fight against Helpmekaar. Sarge had approached Darby White just before the fight to say that about a dozen blacks, all very neatly dressed and very clean, were standing outside the gymnasium and wanted permission to come in and watch. Darby, with much juggling of his balls, was reluctant. If they were caught on the streets without a note from their employers they would violate the pass laws which put a nine o'clock curfew on all Africans. He didn't want to have a run-in with what he referred to as 'the constabulary', which if you have ever had any dealings with the South African Police Force is a very benign way of describing one of the toughest paramilitary forces in the world.

However, all the blacks showed him notes from their

respective employers and he finally allowed them to stand by the door with Old Jimbo, the boot boy from School House who hadn't missed a fight at the school for twenty years. The boxing coach from Helpmekaar came over and protested and to our surprise Darby replied that the boys, like Old Jimbo, were school servants and welcome to stay.

My fight was first, and after I had been given the decision over Jannie Geldenhuis and the excitement had died down a bit I looked up towards the door. Except for Old Jimbo and a very tall man, the Africans were no longer there. Upon seeing me looking in his direction the tall black man raised his hand in a clenched fist. 'Onoshobishobi Ingelosi!' he shouted and was gone.

'What the hell was that all about?' Sarge said, looking up from cutting the tape on my gloves. 'Sounded like some sorta war cry. Ungrateful blighters, they've all gone 'ome after the first fight.'

It was the first appearance of the people.

At first my black fan club, as it was to become known, was only a dozen or so but when the venue permitted it, it would grow to several hundred and later a great deal more than that. The legend of the Tadpole Angel was spreading.

After a few weeks, it became obvious that my identity had somehow been revealed to the school servants through the same weird osmosis in Africa that makes news penetrate prison walls, travel over mountains and into the townships until it becomes a part of the very air itself. And so a subtle change began to take place. The best cuts of meat appeared on the juniors' table and seconds were always brought first to where I sat. I found that my chores had been taken over. I would go to Fred Cooper's locker to get his rugby gear out for washing or his cricket boots for cleaning, only to find that they'd been done. His Sam Browne and brasses always shone like a mirror and even the laces in his rugby boots were washed. Only the morning chores, such as making Cooper's bed, were left to me, as there were no dormitory servants around first thing in the morning. My own gear was always spotless and back in my locker clean or polished by the time we got back to Wellington from the main school each day for lunch. On one occasion my football jersey had been ripped, I had made a hopeless job attempting to repair it and it concerned me greatly. I knew with certainty that my mother could not afford to replace it. I arrived back at Wellington for lunch to find that it had been neatly machine darned, washed and ironed and was as good as new.

I spoke often to the school servants in their own languages but they never for one moment admitted to anything. They had heard the legend, knew the myth and had simply reacted without needing direction from anyone. In fact, I knew there would be no interested party looking after me, no concerned group of ex-prisoners. Africans don't work like that, each simply acted out his feelings, responding to what he or she felt. The legend of Onoshobishobi Ingelosi was sufficient in itself, it fed off my presence and not because of anything I would consciously do. In fact, despite my desire to do so, there was nothing I could do to stop it. My boxing was the needed proof of my status as a warrior and the fact that I only fought the hated Boer, yet another.

As is so often the case with a legend, every incident has two possible interpretations, the plausible and the one which is moulded to suit the making of the myth. Man is a romantic at heart and will always put aside dull, plodding reason for the excitement of an enigma. As Doc had pointed out, mystery, not logic, is what gives us hope and keeps us believing in a force greater than our own insignificance.

The boarders put my privileged position down to my near fraternal attitude to the school servants, which nicely explained their anxiety to help me. I was, I was beginning to understand, a natural leader, and leaders, I have found, need never explain. In fact the less they explain the more desirable they become as leaders. Except to Doc, I had never been given to explaining myself and this was taken as strength by those who followed me. In truth, my reluctance to share my feelings was born out of my fear as a small child when I had been the only Rooinek in the foreign land of Afrikanerdom. I had survived by passing as unnoticed as possible, by anticipating the next move against me, by being prepared when the shit hit the fan to take it in my stride, pretending not to be hurt or humiliated. I had learned early that silence is better than sycophancy, that silence breeds guilt in other people. That it is fun to persecute a pig because it squeals, no fun at all to beat an animal which does not cry out. I had long since built the walls around my ego which only the most persistent person would ever manage to climb.

EIGHTEEN

I was the youngest kid in the first form but, what with one thing and another, I was clearly seen to have a bright future at the Prince of Wales School. My boxing win had made me a hero amongst the first form boarders who, elated by the financial gain from betting on me, had become devoted fans and who now exaggerated the fight in their constant retelling of it to any of the day boys who cared to listen. The next two matches had been away from the school and these I had also won and the boarders had once again shared in the spoils. Although we didn't have enough information on the two boxers I fought, my opponents were comparatively easy and as both had been beaten by Geldenhuis we took the chance of giving the Afrikaans punters more than attractive odds to back their own fighter, with the result that we turned both matches into nice little earners.

The retelling of these two fights, by Hymie in particular, made them out to be gladiatorial bouts which made the first fight against Jannie Geldenhuis seem like a kissing match. By the time the next home match took place there was standing room only in the school gym and the fifty or so Africans who had turned up were obliged to watch the fight through the large bay windows.

To the delight of the school crowd, I won what turned out to be an easy fight. The other kid was very aggresssive, prepared to take any sort of punishment to get a punch in. He was said to have won his first three fights inside the distance. But he came at me wide open on three occasions in the first round and I sat him on his pants in the middle of the ring three times. Three knockdowns was all it took to win a fight. The school was further vindicated when our light-heavyweight, Danny Polkinhorne, won on points in a brawling but thrilling three rounder.

Hymie and I had started a register on every boxer the school fought against, in every weight division. I would sit with him during a fight and describe the opponent fighting one of our boxers. I would talk about his footwork and his style, his weaknesses or strengths in ring craft, and his personality in the ring. I would point out those boxers who dominated the space they boxed in as if they owned the ring, and those who seemed to be fighting in borrowed space. We would separate the stand-up fighters from the boxers. We would note those who cut easily around the eyes. Hymie would jot down every punch thrown in a fight, how many and what they were. Our notes would end with my summary of the entire fight and of the boxer, noting the punches he liked to throw the most and how many he threw during a fight. Boxers were obliged to weigh in before stepping into the ring and Hymie would record their fighting weight and compare it with the next time they fought. We kept all these records in a big leather-bound accounting book, on the cover of which was embossed in gold: *Levy's Carpet Emporium, 126 Church Street, Pretoria. 'Carpet fit for a Prince'*. In this book, written in Hymie's neat, already mature handwriting, we would add to a boxer's profile every time he fought against the Prince of Wales School.

In a remarkably short time Hymie began to grasp the niceties of boxing. While I could remember the most minute details of almost every fighter, Hymie quickly developed the ability to anticipate with uncanny precision the way a boxer would fight the next time he appeared in the ring. He had an unerring instinct for a boxer's weakness and so we were able to prepare our own boxers to fight an opponent to exploit these. Of course, it also allowed us to set the odds on a fight with a high degree of success. Business was booming, for while the Prince of Wales boxers were still regular losers, the odds we offered meant our losses were well contained and that after a short while we could usually depend on one or two wins to pick up the big money.

After the first year when we had boxed every school twice and I was still unbeaten, it became difficult to get a bet against me. The Afrikaans kids weren't fools and we were forced to offer more and more attractive odds on my opponent to the point where we were taking unnecessary risks and it was beginning to put me under pressure. In a fight against Geldenhuis towards the end of the second year where the odds were twenty to one on Geldenhuis beating me, I only narrowly won on points.

The Afrikaners had wised up. Profits were down. With our juniors beginning to win they could no longer hedge their bets against me by taking shorter odds on some of the other fighters. Hymie decided it was time to quit the bookmaking business.

'It's time to get out, Peekay. There are two important rules of business, knowing when to get in and when to get out. Of the two, knowing when to get out is the most important. We've got bigger fish to fry.'

I'd enjoyed two years of regular pocket money and I didn't relish the prospect of being broke again. 'These fish we are going to fry, what are they?'

'I'm buggered if I know,' Hymie said, 'but something will come along, business is simply a matter of opportunity and money. If you've got the capital, sure as tomorrow is Tuesday, an opportunity will come along.'

We'd built up a considerable bank over the first two years, fifty percent of everything we made went into our capital which was earning interest in the Yeoville branch of Barclays Bank.

That's when I had the idea. 'Hymie, we've got fifty quid in the bank and we're getting two and a half percent on our money, which isn't very much, I mean one pound ten a year, it's nice but it isn't world shattering.'

Hymie laughed, 'There was a time not so long ago . . .'

I cut in, 'Yeah, I know, one pound ten was a lot of money, more than I'd ever owned. But listen, pocket money's on Wednesday and Saturday, by Tuesday and Friday everyone's broke.'

We were sitting on a bench under the oak trees bordering the cricket field and Hymie jumped up in alarm. I could see he was upset and he leaned over me and gripped the back of the bench on either side of me. 'Peekay, are you crazy! Don't you understand? I'm the token Jew around here! What the fuck do you think the Christian gentlemen are going to say? A money lender! Me? Christ Peekay, the whole purpose of my education at this goy school is so that sort of stigma can be removed from my Jewishness. I'm here for the politics and the polish. I've already had several hundred years training in usury!'

'That's all the banks do, isn't it?' I replied. 'If you want a loan from a bank you've got to go cap in hand and they don't even have to earn it in the first place, people just give it to them for a lousy two and a half percent interest and they then turn around and lend it for seven percent, that's nearly two hundred percent profit. That isn't usury?'

'Peekay, you don't understand, when the banks do it it's business, when a Jew does it, it's exploitation!'

'I see, so a Jew can't own a bank?'

'Of course he can. Rothschild, one of the world's most famous banks, is owned by a Jewish family, the Rothschilds are one of France and England's most respected families.'

'Yeah, I know,' I said, 'they started in Frankfurt-on-Main in Germany towards the end of the eighteenth century as money lenders!'

'Christ, Peekay, I don't need to do this, there are other ways to make a quid, you'll see.' Hymie was clearly distressed. 'In the meantime you can borrow from our capital for pocket money.'

'You don't need to do this, but I do. I'm not going to use our capital, I can earn my own way. I'm sorry if I've hurt your sensibilities, Hymie, but I've climbed into the ring twenty-five times in the last two years to support our book-making business, it's your turn now.'

Hymie released the bench and straightened up, clasping his hands behind his back as though he was preparing to give me a lecture.

'Do you know why I really came to the Prince of Wales School, Peekay?' He didn't wait for my answer before continuing. 'Let me tell you. When the Prince of Wales, I mean the then future King, came to Pretoria there was a reception held for him by the Red Cross. My old man supplied the red carpet for the occasion. The deal was free carpet for an invitation. He stood in line and the Prince shook his hand. He never quite got over it. It was as though he'd touched the face of the Almighty. He'd made it. He'd reached the social pinnacle. He was a gentleman at last. A gentleman with a heavy Polish accent, but a gentleman no less. He bought his own carpet back from the Red Cross for a huge sum and carpeted the lounge room at home. I don't think one day of my life went by without at least one mention of the fucking carpet: "A Prince already, with his own feet walked on zat carpet my boy!" ' Hymie mimicked. 'Then he read in the paper that there was a Prince of Wales school in Johannesburg and that the Prince was to lay a wreath at the school's war memorial, he decided that if he had a son he would bring him up as the perfect English gentleman . . . correction, perfect Jewish English gentleman. This school and Oxford to follow, is going to make me the first "respectable" Jew in our family since Moses bawled in the bullrushes. I'll tell you something, Peekay, if he had had to carpet every classroom, all three boarders houses and the school quad to get me in here he'd have thought it was a bargain.'

'What you're saying is that by becoming money lenders we fuck up everything?'

Hymie grinned, 'Yup! That's about it.'

'Well then we'll call it a bank. Look, Hymie, it meets every criterion we've established for a business. There is a known need for our services. The risk factor is small and easy to control, our creditors can hardly default can they? We don't have to borrow capital and the profits are reasonable and regular. As Doc would say: "No doubtski aboutski," it's perfect and it's honest . . . well sort of.'

'What will you do if I say, no?' Hymie asked.

'I'd find it very difficult to come to terms with your answer. Now let me tell *you* a story. The guy who taught me boxing was a Cape Coloured and by any standards a bad bastard. He'd spent more time in prison than out on the street. He was the worst kind of recidivist. By any standards the scum of society. He lied, cheated and robbed. He'd also been beaten up more times than you and I have had hot breakfasts. He was the ultimate loser. That's how the world saw him. That's how they judged him.'

'You're talking about Geel Piet, aren't you?' Hymie said.

'Ja, well Geel Piet was just about the best friend I ever had. He died for me. A warder named Borman rammed a two-foot baton up his arse until he haemorrhaged to death. Geel Piet could have saved himself simply by confessing that it was me who smuggled the prisoners' mail into the prison. But he didn't. I didn't see him as any of the things he was supposed to be. I saw him as one of the best human beings I am ever likely to know. Christ, Hymie, it's not what a man does, it's what a man is that counts!'

We called it the Boarders' Bank, but it simply became known as the Bank and was an immediate success. Interest was at ten percent per week and loans were never extended beyond a fortnight. Which was long enough for any kid to write home for money if he got himself into a financial fix. In the four years we remained at school we didn't incur a single bad debt. The funny thing was that not only the boarders but also the day boys regarded the Bank as a valued institution. Moreover, Hymie's antecedents never entered into it, although the Bank formed the basis of some of his more spectacular future financial ploys. I could say *our* spectacular successes, but Hymie was the real wizard and I remained the sorcerer's apprentice. The Bank also formed the basis for my pocket money; a source of great personal pride to me. I'd solved the major emotional problem confronting my school career and, unencumbered with money problems, was now free to forge ahead.

By the time we had reached form three, the younger boxers were beginning to win on a regular basis and Atherton and Cunning-Spider had each won six of their last seven fights, Atherton as a lightweight and Cunning-Spider as a light-welterweight. Hymie's Wooden Spoon Goons were building a reputation and gaining a whole heap of respect from the Afrikaans schools. The Prince of Wales School was no longer a joke and the Boer War was often won by the English these days. That was the year we finally lost the wooden spoon and the faded green, red and dirty white ribbon was removed and replaced with the colours of another school. Hymie had achieved his first objective which he told the Wooden Spoon Goons was only, 'A small pimple on the great hairy arse of my ambition for the gentlemen Christian boxers.'

In the three years it took to lose the wooden spoon, I earned an exaggerated reputation as a boxer amongst the Afrikaans schools on the Witwatersrand. I started to fill out and by the time I was fourteen I was fighting as a bantamweight. Every fight, at school or away, was attracting the people. A match a hundred miles by bus or train from the school would attract just as many Africans as one at home where the boxing bouts had been moved away from the gym to the school hall. Here the Africans were allowed to sit at the very back of the hall separated from the whites by a wide corridor. During the summer it was popular to have the boxing out of doors, usually with the

435

ring set up on a rugby field. At these times the blacks would be allowed to watch the fights, even those held at the most racist Afrikaans schools, where they were kept well separated from the white spectators. It was at one of these out of town Afrikaans schools that I first heard the word 'apartheid' used to describe the place where the black spectators were allowed to sit and I have often since wondered if I had witnessed the first use of a word which would become universal as an expression of oppression.

The boxing matches at these outdoor venues usually started at six just as the sun was beginning to set and were all over by eight when it was still light enough on the highveld not to need lights over the ring. It was at another of these outdoor fights that we invented the famous 'sun-blinder'. The Prince of Wales boxer simply used the ring so that his opponent could be turned to face into the setting sun which would momentarily blind him. The idea was to work an opponent round and then time a punch just as the hapless boxer moved into the direct line of the late after-noon sun. If a boxer was clever enough on his feet this simple expedient could be made to work half a dozen times during a fight, often earning the extra points required to get the decision. The gentlemen Christians had no compunction about doing this to their opponents, after all this was the Boer War and no quarter was given or expected. Hymie got the idea from a movie he had seen which showed how the Battle of Britain Spitfires had come out of the sun to pounce on unsuspecting German aircraft.

The people would watch the fights in silence until it was my turn to fight and then invariably a soft, almost imperceptible hum would begin, growing in volume and, in the African manner, always in perfect harmony. Then a leader would take up a chant which might go something like this: 'He is the chief who comes in our dreamtime, the caster of spells and the bringer of wisdom.'

'Onoshobishobi Ingelosi!' the people would chorus in reply.

'He can dance in the dew without leaving footprints and stalk the wind until it howls to be free.'

'Onoshobishobi Ingelosi!'

'His blows are like the summer thunder and his lightning strikes his foes!'

'Onoshobishobi Ingelosi!'

'For cunning he matches the thin moon and for wisdom the full, for is he not Lord of the dark and the light, the day and the night?'

'Onoshobishobi Ingelosi! Onoshobishobi Ingelosi!'

'He will win for the people, he will win for all the people, in all the tribes, the people are all his people!'

'He will win, he will win, he will win for the people, Onoshobishobi Ingelosi! Onoshobishobi Ingelosi! Onoshobishobi Ingelosi!!'

Once the fight started there would be not a sound from the black spectators and after I had won the tall black man who had been present at my first fight in the school gym would raise his hand in the fisted salute. 'Onoshobishobi Ingelosi!' he would shout and the blacks would silently leave. I was later to hear that the absolute silence during a fight was so they could not be accused of barracking for me and in so doing incur the wrath of my opponent's people and thus be banned from attending. In fact the absolute silence from the African stands was uncanny and made a contribution to unnerving my opponents.

Hymie was quick to realise the potential of the black audience and in return for admitting them to the boxing matches at the Prince of Wales School they were required to sing. This was thought no hardship, as most Africans love to sing and soon a tradition was born. Hymie also persuaded Darby White to move my fight up so that I was higher on the bill. This meant that the black audience would be able to stay as late as possible while still allowing them time to be home by nine o'clock curfew.

Parents and members of the public began to attend these summer evening fights and the Afrikaans schools were forced to do the same as us to attract white spectators. The fights became popular events, with the African singing a big drawcard leading, as it did, to what was soon regarded as the feature of the entertainment, the chant that preceded my bout.

It is an indication of the enormous dichotomy between white and black that for the first three years no white spectator bothered to ask for a translation of what was being said in the chants. People seemed intrigued by the fact that a small white boy had gathered a huge black following but they simply put this down to my skill as a boxer. The presumption of the white man knows no bounds in Africa. The full story would never come out but somewhere along the line the words Onoshobishobi Ingelosi were translated to mean Tadpole Angel.

The Tadpole Angel quickly became my fighting name among the whites and also, to my extreme mortification, with the kids in the Afrikaans schools. Translated into English it was a dumb name and my embarrassment increased when it was further modified by an anti-following of Afrikaners who referred to me as 'little angel' and even sometimes as 'Mama's little angel.'

Though not large in number, I was conscious of this very vocal group who, like the much larger group of blacks, attended every fight, but who came in the hope that Mama's little angel, the *Kaffirboetie*, would come to a sticky end at the hands of one of their own kind.

By contrast, the people saw the name in only one light. I was fighting for them against the Boer. The tangible evidence of the enemy in the form of the dissident group of Afrikaners only served to increase their fervour. Their numbers multiplied each week and their chants grew more elaborate and beautiful. In fairness it must be said there were whites who were on my side, adult Afrikaners who loved to see me box and didn't give a damn about my being a Rooinek.

The fact that I hadn't been beaten wasn't as big a deal

as it may seem, there were several kids from other schools who enjoyed unblemished records.

My mind was permanently focussed on a single fixed point, the welterweight championship of the world. I thought about it so often, reaffirmed my determination so frequently, that hardly an hour of my life passed when it wasn't in my thoughts. To lose a fight would be a backward step, a hair-line crack in my armour. The only way it was going to happen was for me to come up against a boxer who was a helluva lot better than me. Not just more talented but also a lot better trained.

While I told myself that each win was a small deposit on the ultimate ownership of the world welterweight crown, the enormous need in me to win touched on a whole heap of other responses a fourteen year old can't really work out. It had something to do with rejecting the Lord, with my mother, the Judge, being surrounded by guys who came from wealthy homes, even my headless snake. While I didn't think of it as camouflage, I now know that it was, that I kept myself protected by being out in front. Too far in front to be an easy mark.

Doc and Mrs Boxall had taught me to think. Mrs Boxall in the general sense and Doc in the particular. Doc's life was a constant pre-occupation with minutiae, his eye sought always what lay hidden yet was important, he knew that nature guards her secrets jealously, that acute observation begins with a questioning mind. 'Always to ask questions, ja this is so, maybe the answers come slow, but always they are coming if you wait with your head and your eyes.'

Geel Piet taught me to anticipate the problems likely to occur in any situation and to review the answers to them long before disaster struck. His mind was a network of emergency plans. While small boys are not natural pessimists, he nevertheless taught me the value of a routine which, when practised a thousand times, becomes an automatic reaction to a crisis.

439

Over all this lay Hoppie's dictum: *First with the head and then with the heart.* Winning was something you worked at intellectually, emotion clouds the mind and is its natural enemy. This made for a loneliness which often left me aching to share an emotion but equally afraid that if I did so I would reveal a weakness which could later be used against me. Only Doc was allowed to know all of me with nothing held back.

But even Doc was lost to me when sex lightning struck and puberty arrived in a surge of lust. The superior equipment my mentors had given me and which I had unknowingly used so effectively to perfect my camouflage was suddenly useless. Nothing I had been taught prepared me for the onset of my sexual drive. I found myself more completely a loner than ever, but this time I was trying to keep the lid on an emotional cauldron that threatened to boil over and drown me.

I woke each morning with a rigid tent pole which, in the school tradition, I took to the showers, using my erection as a hook over which to drape my towel. While I joined in with the general hilarity at those of us who had been struck by sex lightning, I knew I was faking it. Buried deep where I hoped he would never surface lay Pisskop and his hatless snake and, while circumcision was too common among the guys at the Prince of Wales to cause embarrassment, my dick was the part of my anatomy that had started all my problems and now it was behaving in a manner over which I had absolutely no control.

Sex had never been discussed at home but among the guys in the boxing squad it was referred to as 'doing it'. Snotnose was said to be *almost* doing it to Sophie Smit, Captain Smit's daughter, having given her tits a feel-up in the dark at a Saturday matinee and, it was hinted, a feel *down there*, as well.

I knew enough about the ways of the Lord to know that if I should find myself in the fortunate position of being able to do it to Sophie, I would be committing a mortal sin.

Though I freely admit, even in my pubescent state with my brains turned to meat loaf, I was aware that the chances of my achieving a supine Sophie were just about non-existent, I knew that the Lord, heavily backed by my mother, wasn't the sort of person who settled for innocence by omission. My case was hopeless. Even for a sinner I was sinning at an alarming rate. Not only in my head but also behind a closed toilet door where I actively fantasised *doing it* to Sophie Smit.

The fact that I wasn't a proper born again Christian somehow made it more important that I practise restraint. It became a test of character which I was failing on a daily, sometimes twice daily, not to mention nightly basis. I tried to keep it down to a minimum, promising myself after each time it happened that I was definitely cured, and this had been the last time my fingers would play a tune on the pork flute. Ha, ha ... some last time! No matter how hard I tried to reform my wicked ways and to concentrate on other things my tent pole would erect at the most awkward times and I would need to sneak off to seek relief.

The trouble was that Hymie seemed not to have been struck by sex lightning at all. He talked dirty in the usual schoolboy way, though never in the same explicit terms as the constanly randy group around him. Not that I was among these big mouth fantasisers, my sex life was clandestine, a furtive business. But what the others claimed out loud they'd like to do with the Vargas girls in *Esquire* magazine was simply a paraphrase of what I felt myself. Cunning-Spider, Paul Atherton and Pissy Johnson were also sex struck though, I felt certain, not as badly as me. Hymie on the other hand seemed to sail through puberty like a bloody eunuch.

I don't want to go on about it; but it was an awkward enough time and, because it disrupted the carefully constructed pattern of my existence, it forced me to think about other aspects of my life.

Hitherto I had never questioned the motives of the adults

around me, nor had I felt any reason to question the conventional wisdom they assumed was correct for me. Now I was beginning to see that the plans for my future were being largely made by other people. That in return for being allowed to dream my boxing dream, I was allowing others to map the road ahead for me. I was perceived as a winner and everyone likes to help a winner. I could sense that I was clever enough to win most of the glittering prizes yet to come and this would inevitably lead to a life of privilege, to doors being opened, barriers lowered, places made for me as I was passed from hand to hand among the rich and the privileged until I melded perfectly, indistinguishable from those few who, in the white man's Africa, have so much power over the many who have none.

Doc had taught me the value of being the odd man out. The man assumes the role of the loner, the thinker and the searching spirit who calls the privileged and the powerful to task. The power of one was the courage to remain separate, to think through to the truth and not to be beguiled by convention or the plausible arguments of those who expect to maintain power, whatever the cost.

At fourteen I had no hope of seeing things quite as clearly as this, but I instinctively understood that power is beguiling and man does not lightly give it up. To maintain it he will bend the truth and warp his values. I was a child of Africa, a white child to be sure, but nevertheless Africa's child. The black breasts which had suckled me, and the dark hands which had bathed and rocked me, left me with a burden of obligation to resist the white power which would be the ultimate gift from those who now trained me.

I saw this same sense of aloneness in Hymie. I sensed his Jewish alienation and I understood the intelligent, clear-eyed pessimism that seemed a part of everything he did. He had inherited loneliness. Despite his need for me, he knew himself ultimately to be on his own. Though we never spoke of it, our friendship was forged on this common knowledge. We had instinctively come together to learn, each from the other, those lessons we needed to use the power within us effectively, to think and act differently from those around us.

To win took on a new meaning. It was still part of my fierce-eyed determination to become the welterweight champion of the world, but in the years to follow winning would become the ultimate camouflage as I trained to be a spiritual terrorist. To achieve this new and barely understood aim, I had to appear to be damn near perfect in everything I did even at the risk of appearing to be a bit of a pain.

Each week I received a letter from Doc, Mrs Boxall and Miss Bornstein. While I wrote home fairly regularly, I think my mother must have been too busy sewing to write very often. Sometimes on the bottom of Doc's letters would appear two inky thumb prints under which Doc would write in his small neat hand, *From Dee and Dum who ask who is washing your clothes and baking rusks for your coffee in the morning?* Dee and Dum continued to make the sojourn to Doc's cottage for the weekly clean-up and he had grown very fond of them. Doc's letters were about the hills and his beloved cacti, and while I had continued my piano under the instruction of the school music master, he never mentioned music in his letters. I think Doc knew I was destined for other things. Mrs Boxall would write all the town gossip, and she said that the Assemblies of God had supplied two young missionaries who could speak four African languages between them to take on the prison letters. She was still in charge, determined that God would not be allowed to interfere with the perfectly lovely business of writing a letter to your loved ones. In one of her letters she had added that the people sadly missed King Georgie and that letter writing had fallen off a fair bit after I had left.

The Earl of Sandwich Fund had started to spread and Mrs Boxall was elected chairwoman of seven different groups which had started prison rehabilitation work among black prisoners in South Africa. Many of these early members of the Sandwich Fund were to become the leaders of the Black Sash movement, a movement among South African women which started in the mid fifties to protest against apartheid and injustice against the black people. It continues as one of the few voices of freedom coming out of this sad land; a voice muted from protest against a regime afraid to hear the just and anguished cries of the people.

Miss Bornstein was determined to develop my intellect and insisted on knowing in some detail exactly which books we were reading, maths we were doing and, in fact, everything. I had written to her about Hymie and she included him in her letters which would consist mostly of pages and pages of questions and discussion points. Finally she would always include in her weekly letter a chess move for each of us from old Mr Bornstein who in the six years we were at school we never managed to beat.

Hymie would groan loudly when the weekly letter arrived plump with questions. He'd hold his hands to the side of his face and rock in an exaggerated manner. 'Oy veh!' he'd say, imitating his granma, 'the only reason I elected to come to this institution for Christian gentlemen was to get away from Jewish women, now I'm at fucking correspondence school with one!' But Miss Bornstein had a way, even at long distance, of involving one's pride and the interest she stimulated in her letters put Hymie and myself far ahead of anyone else in the A class at school.

Hymie was the first to use what became a famous expression throughout the school. We were in 'Mango' Cobett's history class and Mango, an asinine man who taught with a very highbrow bias and was a dreadful snob, was talking about the Crimean War and the Charge of the Light Brigade. Mango carried the nickname because he had an oval-shaped head with fine blond hair which clung to his skull and a sharp blond goatee, the whole assemblage resembled a well-sucked mango pip. Though South African born, he was an avowed anglophile and spoke in a dewy-eyed manner about the bravery of Lord Cardigan in the Charge of the Light Brigade.

From the back of the class where we both sat Hymie interjected, 'According to Miss Bornstein, he demonstrated a lamentable lack of control over the French, he also lacked common sense and a sense of responsibility to his men, sir.'

There was a stunned silence, Mango's mouth was half open and he could hardly believe his ears.

'According to Miss Bornstein, Lord Raglan was also completely out of his depth, in fact, a bumbling old fool,' Hymie added.

Mango Cobett finally regained his voice. 'According to whom, Levy?'

'According to Miss Bornstein of the famous Jewish correspondence school, sir,' I interjected. The classroom broke into an uproar.

'Shut up! Everyone shut up at once!' Mango Cobett yelled. The classroom quickly murmured down into silence. Both Hymie and myself were known as brains and Mango wasn't game enough simply to punish us with a couple of hours' detention without first asserting his superior historical perspective.

'I was unaware that the Jews played a part in the Crimean War. I take it your Miss Bornstein is a history scholar of some distinction, perhaps a better source than *The Invasion of the Crimea* by A. W. Kinglake.' He picked up one of the books which lay on the desk in front of him and held it high, squinting slightly as he read the spine. 'William Blackwood and Sons, Edinburgh and London, 1864. I'd say that was from the horse's mouth, wouldn't you?'

'More like the horse's arse, sir,' Hymie quipped, and the classroom broke up again.

Kinglake's *Invasion of the Crimea* was one of the volumes my granpa had at home along with the complete works of Charles Dickens and I'd read both volumes of Kinglake's account when I was eight. According to Miss Bornstein, Kinglake's account was remarkable but she had also read the Russian and French accounts and now felt the official British version was heavily jingoistic and apt to blame the French and the Turks while allowing that Lord Raglan, the British Commander in Chief, though competent, was somewhat inexperienced and asserting Lord Cardigan to be a man of great sagacity and leadership skills. Miss Bornstein, Hymie and I had been conducting an involved correspondence on the very volumes Mango was quoting from.

'According to Miss Bornstein, A. W. Kinglake was commissioned by the War Office to write the series, which was never a good start. The book has been republished several times and the 1864 version, slightly amended, was the fourth edition. More appeared after the first Boer War when the Transvaal had regained its independence, previously having been shamefully annexed by Britain after gold had fortuitously been discovered. The history was meant to remind the British of their recent glorious past so that they wouldn't dwell too heavily on the trouncing they'd received from a handful of determined farmers who aimed straight and didn't form into a square to fight. According to Miss Bornstein it is rather long on glory and somewhat short on the true facts. The volumes were republished again, just two years before the declaration of the second Boer War. They were, of course, ideally timed and put the British public in the mood for another territorial rape and pillage in the name of Queen and Empire.' Hymie had exactly quoted a passage in one of Miss Bornstein's letters, it was word perfect, even comma perfect.

Mango Cobett's usually deathly pale face had flushed a dark red. 'Are you challenging the integrity of one of the finest historians to come out of the British Isles, Levy?'

'No, sir,' Hymie said. 'Miss Bornstein is.' The class broke into spontaneous laughter again.

'Shut up! Shut up!' Mango yelled. 'I've heard enough!' The class settled down and a flushed Mango Cobett commenced to walk up and down the length of the classroom.

'The Battle of Alma, the first in the Crimea, where the British took the Russian General Menshikov head on, Russians 9,000 dead, British 2,000! Those, gentlemen, are the facts.'

I jumped in. 'According to Miss Bornstein, Lord Raglan lost control of the Battle of Alma almost from the moment it started. He set the frontal attack and then lost control while the French climbed the steep cliffs near the mouth of the river and outflanked Menshikov with very few casualties.'

'Nine thousand Russians, two thousand British!' Mango said emphatically.

'Two thousand dead in three hours!' I retaliated. 'The French lost less than two hundred men.'

'The Russians were peasants without any training and fought in dense columns. Menshikov had scrambled eggs for brains,' Hymie said, to the delight of the classroom.

Mango Cobett pressed on. 'The Battle of Inkerman, Russians 11,000 dead, the British 2,640!' He leaned on the figure forty to emphasize his exact knowledge of the numbers involved.

'According to Miss Bornstein, Lord Raglan exercised no influence on the course of the fighting. The Battle of Inkerman was called the "Soldiers' Battle" because units were committed to the battle piecemeal and the soldiers had to work it out for themselves,' Hymie replied.

'The Russians on the other hand were commanded by General Russian eggs himself,' I said smugly, causing the class to laugh once more.

'That will be enough, Peekay,' Mango said, not too happy about arguing on two fronts. 'We have one more battle to go, the Redan.'

'Ah, the Redan! According to Miss Bornstein . . .'

'Quiet, Levy!' Mango demanded. 'The Russian losses are not known but are thought to be twice that of the British.'

'The British lost five thousand men at the Redan, and again Lord Raglan lost control of the battle,' I said, deter-

447

mined that he should not be allowed to cover up the British losses.

'Lord Raglan was a very sick man and died of cholera ten days after the Redan. He can't be entirely blamed for the huge losses,' Mango retorted.

'You've missed the Charge of the Light Brigade, sir,' Hymie said with a grin.

'Ah yes, Lord Cardigan's Light Brigade, a mistake, a question of a misunderstanding and an ill-drafted order.'

'And under pig's-trotters-for-brains Lord Cardigan, seven hundred mounted troopers charged into the valley of death and four hundred died!'

'I don't like your attitude, Levy, Lord Cardigan was a member of the British aristocracy and is not subject to schoolboy humour. While we're on the subject, Peekay, Menshikov was a respected Russian general and also above your puerile wit. You will both see me outside the masters' common room at the conclusion of school. Your attitude to this history lesson has been reprehensible to say the least.' The bell went for recess and the colour drained back out of Mango Cobett's face. As we were leaving the class he had one last jibe. 'Let me assure you both, England did not conquer half the known world including this country because she placed stupid commanders in the field.'

'According to Miss Bornstein . . .' we both began, and Hymie finished . . . 'that's not true.'

The expression was born. From that moment on, any boy in the Prince of Wales School who disagreed with a statement made by a master would signal his disagreement by prefacing it with, 'According to Miss Bornstein . . .' It caused so much exasperation amongst the teaching staff that it was eventually taken to the head, St John Burnham MA (Oxon), known as Singe 'n Burn, who prided himself on being a liberal educationalist. To the mortification of the masters and in particular Mr Hemming the senior English master, Singe 'n Burn declared the expression, 'A legitimate paraphrase for a dissenting opinion.' And so the expression, 'According to Miss Bornstein,' was officially written into the school vocabulary.

We arrived outside the masters' common room just after three o'clock armed with Miss Bornstein's two letters on the subject of the Crimean War. But Mango refused to continue the argument and simply gave us two hours of detention and a two thousand word essay to write on the Crimean War. He added that the next indiscretion would result in a visit to the head.

Hymie said in disgust, 'I told you history was all bullshit. There goes another generation of Christian gentlemen school boys who will grow up to believe the Charge of the Light Brigade was one of England's finest hours.'

'But it was,' I said.

'It was what?' Hymie said, not sure he'd heard me correctly.

'It was one of England's finest hours. What's important is not whether you win or lose but how you play the game.'

'Bullshit! If the Jews had played that game we'd have been extinct fifteen hundred years ago.'

'You have to be a Christian gentleman to understand,' I kidded him.

'Do me a favour, Peekay, don't just read history, feel it. Try to imagine being an ordinary guy on a half-starved horse, your regiment decimated by cholera, you've got a lance in your hand and are looking into the barrels of the Russian artillery holding the Vorontsov Ridge at Balaclava. Do you know why the English managed to conquer half the globe? Because they were so bloody stupid! Some halfwitted lord jumped up in a general's uniform would simply advance on a position and expend men, he didn't care, they were only yeomen and slum slush, cannon fodder. He just kept sending them in and so help me they kept on going, until eventually he won. You call that bravery? I call that two things, murder and stupidity. The generals murdered their men and the men were too stupid to resist.'

'And too brave, it wasn't just stupidity.'

449

Hymie ignored my interjection. 'History makes it all okay. History forgets the vomit and the shit, the blood and the horses with their guts blown away, the cries of men as they shit their pants and drowned in their own blood. The Charge of the Light Brigade is celebrated because it was the most obviously stupid, most spectacularly stupid, most stupendously stupid sacrifice of men until the brilliant British generals finally topped it for sheer cold-blooded slaughter in the trenches in Flanders and on the cliffs above Gallipoli.'

Hymie changed course suddenly. 'Hitler murdered six million Jews. He had to round them up and rail them to the death camps and the world wept for man's inhumanity to man. But underneath it all there is the feeling that the Jews should have fought, should have resisted, should have died defending their kith and kin, should have died like men. All the women and children and the cobblers and tailors and small shopkeepers who believed that they were Germans and Poles and Hungarians, who believed passionately in logic and order, in Kant and Spinoza, and in minding their own business and never getting involved and most of all, in never volunteering to be stupid, should have turned into a fighting machine that takes pride in dying.

'Because they didn't go chasing a piece of coloured bunting around the place, history may yet judge them cowards.' Hymie sniffed and wiped his nose across the back of his hand. I had never seen him quite as upset and angry before.

'When a British general looking for a new swatch of ribbon for his chest sent men into battle in the eighteenth and nineteenth centuries and then again in the Great War Englishmen volunteered to go. They actually handed themselves over into his care and in return for their trust he was just as careless with their lives as the Jew killers of Auschwitz, Dachau, Treblinka, Belsen and the other death camps were with the lives of my kind. But when it was all over, the world, or the English-speaking world anyway, cheered their Christian gentlemen heads off. More tradition had been made, more regimental bunting to hang in St Paul's and Westminister Abbey. More bullshit.' He sniffed again and grabbed me by the shoulder.

'You know something, Peekay? History stinks and it's bastards like Mango Cobett who add to the putrefaction by believing the crap that's written. Take my word for it, in another thirty years the Germans will claim that only a handful of SS caused the Holocaust unbeknownst to the good burgers who stayed at home and knitted socks for Jewish prisoners of war.'

To Mango Cobett's credit, the detention essays Hymie and I wrote on the Crimean War shared the history prize that year. Miss Bornstein's evidence was too conclusive.

With her weekly letters, some of them up to twenty pages, Miss Bornstein had the happy knack of instigating a line of reasoning which would stimulate us both. We'd rush to the school library to follow its course. By the time we were in form three we were fairly skilled researchers and were given permission to spend Wednesday afternoons at the Johannesburg Public Library.

Form three was a big year for us. It was the year the boxing team lost the wooden spoon and also the year we published, with the help of a typist and the Gestetner machine in Hymie's father's carpet emporium, *The Miss Bornstein School of Correspondence Notes. Results fully guaranteed or your money back. Peekay & H. S. Levy. 5/-.* There were two books, one for form one and the other for form two.

Hymie and I had argued furiously about the price. Five shillings was outrageous when a science textbook cost only two shillings.

'If we charge what it appears to be worth we'd be lucky to get sixpence,' he admitted. 'Good business is when people perceive something to be valuable, and the best way to encourage this perception is by guiding their thinking.'

'You mean by charging outrageously?'

'Now wait a mo, Peekay, that's not quite fair. Value for

money is when the customer is satisfied that he has made the right purchase decision. Or do you disagree?'

I was forced to agree. 'Well then, what are we promising with the *Miss Bornstein School of Correspondence Notes*, for form one and two?'

'The promise is on the cover, but the bloody promise holds good whether we charge them sixpence or ten bob.'

'Not so. A five bob price tag means at least two things: that the information in the notes is important and rare and that by following it, success is guaranteed. The second promise is convenience, all the information they need is between two covers, they don't have to *schlep* through a dozen textbooks, the authors have done all the mental legwork for them. If we charged them sixpence they wouldn't value the book and so it wouldn't work for them.'

'Shouldn't we dress them up a bit? For two bob a copy we could probably afford to have them printed with a hard cover. At least that way the value would be perceived to be better?'

Hymie looked at me in astonishment. 'Peekay, are you mad? Do you want to kill the business in one year?'

'What do you mean?'

Hymie picked up a copy of our textbook and holding it by one corner he shook it violently. The staples in the centre margin gave way and the pages flew apart.

'There you are, look at that! They're rubbish, we'll never get away with this,' I protested.

'Bullshit, they're perfect, they'll only just hang together for one year. If we have them properly printed and bound the guys will sell them at the end of the year to the incoming form. Where would our business be then?'

Hymie was right, despite the price there wasn't a kid in either form who didn't purchase a copy and no one asked to have their money refunded. We were a good business combination with the added advantage of being generally popular; in particular, my ability in the boxing ring and, to a lesser degree, on the rugby field created quite a large following among my peers. Doing business with the Bank when you were broke became the norm for both day boys and boarders, so that every time we went out into another business venture the reception we got was usually pretty good. We referred to this accumulation of goodwill as our 'Image', a word I discovered in an American book on business practice and which had not then gained the currency it enjoys today.

I must say, while Mango Cobett was a bit of a buffoon and a terrible snob, Singe 'n Burn, the head, had taken care to staff the school with liberal thinkers. He was less interested in turning out what he referred to as 'the private school product' than he was in encouraging individuals to emerge. He would refer to his idealised person as a Renaissance man. A boy who delighted in learning for its own sake, the inspired amateur in the gifts of the body and the spirit. The complete man, superior by virtue of his curiosity and the careful nurturing and harvesting of his gifts. A man who was modest and unassuming because he had no need to hide his thoughts or his deeds from others, nor had he the need to seek their approval.

Singe 'n Burn was an Englishman coming to the end of what is usually referred to as a distinguished career. To parents he represented all the values of the English public school system, coming as he did from Winchester where he had been a senior house master. For the board of governors he epitomised a system of privilege which they held in great esteem and desired him to emulate as faithfully as possible.

In his twenty years as headmaster of the Prince of Wales School Singe 'n Burn never quite came to terms with the wealthy South African schoolboy. In a curious way the boys shared the belief in their social superiority with their English public school counterparts, though perhaps the basis for this superiority was different.

In the first instance, like all white South Africans, English and Afrikaans, they believed that God had ordained their superiority as white men. To this was added their proxy

453

Englishness and their absolute belief in the right of wealth and privilege. Perhaps, after all, not so different from their English cousins.

Singe 'n Burn's pupils came to him with minds already narrowed, bigots with their dislike and distrust of the Afrikaner intact. Among them was the unspoken belief that they were the intellectually and culturally superior of South Africa's two white tribes. To this was added their spoken belief that they were of a higher species than the blacks. This corruption of the spirit had taken place in the cradle and the task of driving the racist out of the boy was fruitless. St John Burnham was forced to take in largely shallow minds to be fattened with sufficient information to pass the matriculation exams. Alas, the potential for a Renaissance man to emerge from this intellectual scrubland was severely limited.

Yet for twenty years Singe 'n Burn had kept his dream alive. While most of the boys from the Prince of Wales School were interchangeable with the product of any of the private schools in South Africa, that is, equipped for a society where money and social position were important, he kept for himself just six boys each year. They were the raw material for his Renaissance men, a handful of brilliant boys who were known as St John's People, pronounced 'Sinjun's People'. These boys were selected in form three for special tuition under the direction of Singe 'n Burn, who elected to neglect the many for the precious few. Sinjun's People were the roses amongst the tangle-weed and the school's considerable reputation as a nursery for the country's future leaders had been built on these half-dozen carefully nurtured young minds brought to flower in Sinjun's hothouse.

Brains alone did not qualify a boy to be one of Sinjun's People, though intellect played a significant part in the training to come. 'It is the spirit of the boy, an unselfconscious ability to maintain his status among his peers while remaining true to himself in his beliefs, opinions and ac-

454

tions,' is how Singe 'n Burn would explain it at the first headmaster's assembly at the beginning of each year.

There was always a great deal of speculation in form three and, indeed, among the rest of the school when the election of Sinjun's People took place just prior to the Easter break.

I had prepared myself in my old way for a disappointment and had I not been among the chosen six it would hurt my pride enormously but I knew I would survive. The betting on me being included was pretty high. But I didn't share this general confidence, not for reasons of false modesty, but because of my boxing. While the boxing team had given the school a new status, compared to cricket and rugby it was a sport of small importance. Several of the masters considered it unsuitable for a school of our reputation, and but for Darby and Sarge it would probably have been phased out. I had maintained my position as one of the brains of the school but had never left any doubt that boxing came first in my immediate ambitions. I was certain this would count against me. In my final interview with Singe 'n Burn he had noted that my boxing appeared to come first, ahead of my competence as a musician and as a promising young scholar. 'Your boxing? Is this an obsession with you, Peekay? Where do you propose to take your skill? I must say it seems an unlikely future pastime for a gentleman, even though Lord Byron was said to have been a talented boxer.' When I replied that I intended to be the welterweight champion of the world his eyebrows had shot up and he had looked at me over his steel rimmed spectacles. 'Hmm,' was all he said by way of reply.

Hymie was also among the fifteen candidates to be interviewed by the head. While he was regarded as a powerful intellect Hymie was generally thought to be too brash, and was therefore regarded by most of the schoolboy punters as being a long shot. When I queried him on his interview with Singe 'n Burn, he seemed reluctant to talk about it and so I didn't question him any further.

Sinjun's People were traditionally selected in order of merit, and this provided Hymie with a business opportunity that was to be one of our greatest successes. Apart from doing some of the legwork and sharing in the considerable profit, I played no part in its formation. We called it 'Levy's Remarkable Multiple of One Hundred'. As a punter you could bet two ways, by paying a shilling you could nominate any three successful candidates from the list of fifteen finalists, regardless of order. The winners, for there were certain to be more than one, to share a pot of thirty pounds. Or if you took two bets or more you qualified to enter Levy's Remarkable Multiple of One Hundred which carried a prize of one hundred pounds and required only two successes, the names of the boys in first and second place on the Sinjun's People list.

It was clever stuff, every boy believed he knew at least three certainties and so had an excellent chance to share in the thirty-pound pot. Most punters couldn't resist doubling their bets for a crack at the big money, one hundred pounds if there was only one winner and a guaranteed twenty quid if there were more. Many of the kids, in particular day boys, put ten shillings and a pound on in an effort to get as many combinations right as possible. Even in this haven for little rich boys, a hundred quid represented a fortune. There wasn't a kid in the school who didn't have at least two bets going.

We set up office in the main school bogs for an hour before school and at lunch break every day for a week before the final selection of Sinjun's People. The queue outside the toilet stretched well into the playground and anyone observing the toilets must have wondered whether an outbreak of the runs had struck the school.

Hymie took the money while I acted as pencil man, the guy who wrote down the bets. Tension was high on the last day before the following morning assembly when Sinjun's People were announced. The excitement had helped a little to quell my fears for us both. Hymie, by his own admission, considered himself a doubtful candidate. 'Shit, Peekay, it's obvious, I'm too much of a gunslinger and not enough of a poet to please Singe 'n Burn.' Privately I agreed, his wheeler-dealer reputation and my boxing preference counted heavily against us. In Hymie's case the betting showed this; not once did his name appear in the one/two combination whereas mine did so frequently.

We'd taken bets totalling a staggering one hundred and ninety pounds, win or lose we'd made a neat profit of sixty quid. We'd worked out the odds on someone taking out Levy's Remarkable Multiple of One Hundred and they were small but certainly not impossible, whereas we knew we'd have several winners in the thirty-pound pot. A perfect scam and good business to boot. A guaranteed profit, a number of satisfied winners and the chance to make a huge profit in the event of Levy's Remarkable Multiple of One Hundred not having to pay out. You had to hand it to Hymie, it was copybook stuff.

I could hear my heart beating furiously as I stood next to Hymie in headmaster's assembly the following morning. The hymn chosen before morning prayer was, 'O God our Help in Ages Past', a favourite, although today it seemed to go on for about twenty minutes. The prayer which followed was a long-winded affair about humility in honour and fortitude in times of disappointment. It had obviously been carefully chosen by Singe 'n Burn for the occasion. Then followed a host of trivial school housekeeping notes, including an admonition to stay away from the swimming pool which was being emptied for repainting over the Easter break, and an aside about more boys signing up for their beginner's life saving certificate.

At last Singe 'n Burn cleared his throat for the major business of the day. Standing on the platform in a black gown with purple lining, he had removed his mortarboard so that the light caught his snowy white hair. At a time when short back and sides was the national norm his hair fell almost to his shoulders and a pair of steel-rimmed spectacles sat on the end of his long, impressive nose. St John Burnham MA (Oxon) was the most headmasterly looking headmaster I have ever seen, better even than anything out of a Billy Bunter comic.

The entire school was deadly quiet, apart from the fifteen candidates, there wasn't a boy present who didn't have money resting on the outcome of the next few minutes. Singe 'n Burn cleared his throat and began.

'Each year the school council allows me a very special personal indulgence. I am allowed to choose from the third form those half dozen boys who will become Sinjun's People.' He paused to look up into the stained glass windows at the rear of the hall, as though asking for divine guidance. 'Now, you will all know that I do not take this task lightly. It is, after all, as much a sadness as it is a celebration, for while six are to be chosen, nine who have made it to the finals will be asked to step aside. It is these nine good men and true who make my task an almost impossible one. After all, who is to say I'm right? I feel sure someone else, choosing in my place, might select six boys equally equipped and talented, though different to those I have chosen. All the candidates this year were exceptional young men, all deserve to be included, but alas, there are only six places. My congratulations to you all and a word of solace for those of you who do not become Sinjun's People.' He paused and directed our attention to the nineteen twenty-nine scroll of honour painted in gold leaf on a panel in the centre lefthand side of the hall. 'The name at the very top of that nineteen twenty-nine scroll of honour belongs to the present South African High Commissioner to London, a brilliant diplomat and scholar and the youngest man ever to hold this position. I shouldn't be at all surprised if some day he becomes our prime minister.' He paused again to gain maximum effect for the words to follow. 'This brilliant boy was not elected in his day to be among Sinjun's People.' His eyes seemed to travel across each row as he looked down at us over the tops of his spectacles. 'I had intended to read Rudyard Kipling's great poem "If" to you at this juncture but was reminded that it is a part of your English curriculum this term and therefore well known to you all. I shall spare you a repeat performance. Let me conclude by saying, in my experience the glittering prizes in life come more to those who persevere despite setback and disappointment than they do to the exceptionally gifted who, with the confidence of the talents bestowed upon them, often pursue the tasks leading to success with less determination.' He paused and from inside his gown he produced a sheet of paper.

'The following boys from the third form have been chosen to be Sinjun's People for the remainder of their tenure at the Prince of Wales School. My congratulations to you all.' He glanced down at the piece of paper he was holding and commenced to read: 'Levy H. S., Lyell H. R., Quigley B. J., Minnaar J. R . . .' I had punched Hymie in the ribs when his name came up, but now I could feel my face burning and a huge lump grew in my throat. I was sure I would suffocate . . . 'Eliastam P. J.,' the head paused to clear his throat and then looked up over the assembled boys. Time hung like cobwebs in the air and the paper he'd been holding seemed etched like a white tombstone floating in space.

'And Peekay,' he said finally.

I felt weak in the legs and it took all my strength of will not to start crying on the spot. I had made it. I was the sixth part of Sinjun's People.

Atherton, Cunning-Spider, Pissy Johnson, Hymie and I celebrated by feasting on Perk's pies, cream buns and Pepsi-Cola all that afternoon before Atherton, Cunning-Spider and Pissy Johnson had to leave for the four o'clock roll call. Sinjun's People were not required to attend roll call and as they left playfully cursing us, we looked suitably upset though secretly we felt enormously privileged.

Nine punters had won on the first bet sharing the thirty-pound pot between them. There were no winners on the second bet. Hymie himself had been the wild card, and while some of the punters might have selected him for inclusion in their first bet, none had thought to place him first or second in Levy's Remarkable Multiple of One Hundred. The fact that my name had appeared most often in either the first or second slot meant that most of the bets were not even close. We had cleared one hundred and sixty pounds on the deal.

After the others had left for roll call I turned to Hymie. 'Okay, smartarse, how did you do it?' I said, delicately licking the excess cream squirting from the side of my last cream bun.

'How did I do what?' Hymie said dreamily, upending a Pepsi into his mouth in an attempt to hide his grin.

'You know what I'm talking about! You knew from the betting that your chances of being selected in the number one spot were considered zero. Even I wouldn't have put you there. With you in the number one spot we had to win the big money. How did you do it?'

He removed the Pepsi from his mouth and placed it on the floor beside him. 'It was partly luck, but mostly my usual good judgement,' he said in his unassuming way.

'Christ you're a humble bastard, Levy! Okay, tell me the good judgement part first.'

'Well I guess we should have been happy with a sixty quid profit, with a reasonable chance of winning the big money as well. But there was still an element of luck involved. I had somehow to work out a way whereby the betting was completely honest, but the punter's chance of winning was cut down and ours increased.'

'You greedy bugger, Levy.'

'No, not greedy, I just don't like to gamble, but I do like to win and to win you have to make the odds negligible. Now, you take the horses. There are roughly fifteen horses in a race and over the whole of last year I analysed the results of every race run at Turfontein racecourse. In that entire time the first and second favourites won in correct sequence one hundred and four times in eight hundred and thirty-two races, that means the bookmaker has eight chances of winning to one of losing. That's good, but not good enough.'

'Yeah, sure, but we had sixty quid marked off for a profit anyway. That's a damn good week's work.'

'I know, but the whole thing lacked intellectual excitement. It didn't depend on my wits.'

'Hymie, you can't have it both ways. You want a totally safe scam but you still want to get an intellectual kick from winning.'

'That's what I've told you before. With a Jew making money for its own sake, it is a matter of intellectual survival.'

'Okay, I accept that; so tell me, man, how did you fix it?'

'Fix it!' Hymie exploded. 'Are you calling me a cheat?'

His outburst was totally unexpected and I was shocked. 'Ferchrissake, Hymie, you know what I mean,' I said quickly, trying to hide my embarrassment.

Hymie sighed, 'In the end it's always the same, the gentile believes the dirty Jew is cheating, that's right isn't it?'

'Bullshit, Hymie! That's not what I meant, I'm truly sorry. You know how I feel about you.'

Hymie held my gaze for a long time. 'Yeah, I do,' he said with a grin, 'but thanks for saying it anyway.'

'Well go on,' I said, greatly relieved and anxious to leave the incident and continue the conversation.

Hymie continued. 'It does rather seem like a fix, doesn't it? But all I did was tamper a little with human nature.'

'You'll have to explain that.'

'Well, when you told me about your interview with Singe 'n Burn . . . how he had questioned you about your boxing.'

'I don't understand. What had that to do with setting up the multiple of one hundred bet?'

'Well, you know my theory of a winner. Find one winner and you can build everything around him? Well, you've always been my one winner and with the strong likelihood

461

of your placing in the number one slot for Sinjun's People, Levy's Remarkable Multiple of One Hundred would have been much too risky. It meant the punter had only to get one more correct name to win.'

'But I told you the boxing issue might have eliminated me all together.'

'Not a chance, old buddy! There was never any chance that you wouldn't be chosen, but I was willing to bet that Singe 'n Burn wouldn't be able to resist the temptation to give you your first tutorial.'

'My first tutorial?'

'Christ, Peekay, sometimes you're thick. Singe 'n Burn is a self-confessed liberal thinker, deeply suspicious of the obsessive personality. That's the whole point of his Renaissance man, moderation in all things even in moderation. He was signalling his disapproval by placing you in sixth possie.'

'Jesus, Hymie, you took the trouble to think all that out?'

'Thinking is never any trouble, you should try it sometime.' He grinned suddenly, 'Besides, I might have been wrong, Singe 'n Burn might have just dropped you one slot and you'd still be up there in one of the top two positions. I had to put us completely out of danger. I had to get myself chosen, not just chosen, but elected to the number one slot. You see, even if you were in the number two position and as a rank outsider, a non-contender, I was in the number one slot, that would make it impossible for anyone to get a correct sequence. Nobody in his right mind would combine a hundred to one shot in with a certainty when both places counted together for the win.'

'You've got me. How the hell did you make it happen?'

'Well, I'd figured out how Singe 'n Burn was going to react with you and when you know the man you know the thought process. The opposite to an obsessive personality, in this case yours about boxing, is a well-adjusted one. The epitome of a well-adjusted personality is modesty and a willingness to sacrifice your own ambition for the greater good of the whole. What was it that Christ said? "No greater love hath a man than he lay down his life for a friend".' Hymie gave a little laugh, 'So when Singe 'n Burn discovered personal sacrifice together with generosity of spirit to be a fundamental part of my character, I knew I had the number one possie in the bag.'

'And just how did you prove this to him? I mean, those two personality traits are not exactly obvious in you,' I added with a tinge of sarcasm.

Hymie turned to me, an embarrassed look on his face. 'I don't think you're going to like this next bit much. We were talking about the importance of friendship and I brought up my friendship with you. Singe 'n Burn then asked me about your obsession with boxing.' He paused, 'Are you sure you want me to go on?'

'I think I know where this is leading, but I can't stop it now, go on.'

'Well, I told him about your childhood, your last boarding school, the prison, although I promise I didn't tell him about the Tadpole Angel, just Geel Piet and the boxing, just some of the stuff you told me.'

'Jesus, Hymie, that was confidential.'

'Yeah, I know, I mean I knew it was, but you'd never actually told me not to tell anyone.' Hymie paused, 'Christ, Peekay, you've got nothing to be ashamed of.'

'I've never been ashamed of anything in my life, except when I was made to feel that way the first time I went to boarding school. It's . . . well, it's just that I don't want any Christian gentleman feeling sorry for me because my mum hasn't two bob to her name.'

Hymie jumped to his feet and grabbed me by my blazer lapels. 'You bloody fool! They'd do anything to be like you. So would I. To have done the things you've done, led the life you've led. Believe me, being rich in a Jewish household isn't a lot of fun. Everything is overdone. Too much love, too much money, too much food, too much care, too much reminding you that you're different, that you're Jewish. I've been bored since I was five years old! Bored by the predictability of being born into a wealthy middle-class Jewish home. You can have my twelve bedrooms and six bathrooms. I'll swap you my old man's five cars and three chauffeurs for a fortnight with Doc.'

I suddenly realised that I was making far more of a meal over his indiscretion with my past than he had made when he thought I had accused him of cheating.

'Okay, we're quits, you smooth-talking bastard,' I said, grinning. 'Now, get on with the story. How, for instance, did telling him all this talk him into giving you the number one spot?'

'I simply told him that I was a Jew, which I suppose he knew already but it didn't hurt to remind him. That my father was enormously rich. That I had enjoyed and would continue to enjoy every possible privilege. That I would be sent to Oxford where I would read law and well blah, blah, blah. The future for me was all sewn up.'

'So?'

'This is the worst part. I told him that if I was selected to Sinjun's People and you were not, that I wished to forfeit my spot in your favour.' He looked at me querulously, waiting for my anger.

I was silent. I knew with a sudden certainty that Hymie, after hearing the results of my interview with Singe 'n Burn, had grown concerned that my boxing obsession would eliminate me from Sinjun's People. That he'd ridden to the rescue, prepared to sacrifice any chances he might have had to ensure my inclusion. In the process he had read Singe 'n Burn brilliantly and had capitalised handsomely on the situation.

'You'd have done that anyway, wouldn't you? You'd have been prepared to give up your chances even if the scam hadn't been there.'

'Hell no! No bloody fear!' he said in alarm. 'Christ, Peekay, it's a dog-eat-dog world, where would the Jews be if all of a sudden they started making sacrifices for the bloody Christians!'

'Thanks, Hymie,' I said.

'Don't insult my intelligence, Peekay. If you're trying to tell me I wasn't doing all this for mercenary motives I resent it. Don't you think I'm capable of thinking up a ploy as good as this one turned out to be?'

'On the contrary, you had it figured out so that whatever happened you influenced the game.'

Hymie blushed, which I'd never seen him do before. 'No point in leaving things to chance; much too risky,' he said with a deprecating grin.

'Christ, the number one spot always belonged to you anyway.'

'You're right,' he said. 'Look, why don't we take a tenner each for the holidays?' He handed me a ten-pound note. 'I'll put the rest in the bank, I've got big plans for next term we'll talk about after the holidays.'

NINETEEN

Going home at the end of each term was like sloughing a skin. The joy of a small town lies in its unchanging nature. Except for Doc, Mrs Boxall, Miss Bornstein, old Mr Bornstein, the guys at the prison and of course, my mother, Granpa, Marie and especially Dum and Dee, people would look up when you entered a shop and enquire casually, 'Goodness, hols again, Peekay? How's life in the big city? Are you playing in the Easter concert? What can I do for you?' They'd say this almost in one breath, not because they were bored and felt compelled to be polite, but mostly because time has a sameness in a small town, which the coming and going of people doesn't disturb. I liked the idea of nothing ever changing in Barberton, it gave me a sense of belonging. Now that the war was over and the military camp no longer a part of the town's economy, Barberton settled back into its favourite old scuffed leather armchair and went to sleep again. Even the prison warders seemed to fit into the community more easily and for the last two concerts they had remained while 'God save the King' was played, though Mrs Boxall reported that they still protested in their own way by not standing to attention. This made Mr Hankin, of the *Goldfields News* mad as usual, but it rated a paragraph, not a leader or the entire editorial like the good old days.

Mrs Boxall had become a firm favourite at the prison. The Kommandant, who had become a colonel because of Doc's concert, decided he liked prison reform and had allowed her to start a Sunday morning school for the prisoners. She had negotiated with the Kommandant to reward progress with King Georgies. The Pentecostal missionaries, who had agreed to do the teaching in return for a fifteen-minute sermon every Sunday, disagreed violently with the distribution of tobacco to students who excelled. Their God was neither a consumer of strong drink nor a user of tobacco. They were forced to conclude that God worked in mysterious ways when attendance and scholastic effort increased markedly with the introduction of King Georgies as an incentive. A prisoner would study for every limited moment he had during the week for the reward of one cigarette. With the result, many blacks left prison able to read, write and do simple arithmetic. Mr Bornstein, Miss Bornstein's father, had converted the Earl of Sandwich Fund into the Sandwich Foundation and already one little old lady had left it a bequest of two thousand pounds. The letter writing sessions still continued, and during the holidays I'd take over from the missionaries and Marie's father's tobacco leaf would once again be fitted into the folds of the tracts and given out with every letter. In fact during every school holiday letters to King George, which of course we never posted, became very popular again. The Tadpole Angel was back in town and Gert used to swear that trouble in the prison was almost non-existent during these periods.

Gert, with encouragement from Mrs Boxall, had tackled English and now spoke it fairly well. He'd become very attached to Doc and Mrs Boxall and made sure that the repairs around Doc's cottage or Mrs Boxall's house were done and that Charlie's motor was kept going. Every time I'd get home it would be the same thing, 'I'm telling you, man, only chewing gum and axle grease is holding that old *tjorrie* together, one day I'm just going to have to take it to a cliff top, say a prayer and push it over. Only it won't be able to make it up the hill in the first place!' But under Gert's concerned and tender care Charlie kept going.

Klipkop had been transferred to Pretoria and Gert, to his

enormous surprise, had been given the job of assistant to Captain Smit. As a consequence he had earned his corporal's stripes. He was now the prison heavyweight and would be fighting for the vacant title at the next championships. The giant Potgieter, who had continued to beat Gert in the final of the two subsequent championships after Gert's original defeat in Nelspruit, had turned professional.

The Lowveld Championships had been expanded and were now known as the Eastern Transvaal Championships, bringing in some of the bigger towns and making it tougher for the Barberton Blues. As they always occurred during the December school holidays, it was important to Captain Smit that I take part as a member of the Blues.

Regular boxing against the Afrikaans schools during term had made me a much better boxer, although I personally longed for the magic of Geel Piet, who knew how to make me think better in the ring. Whereas Darby White and Sarge, like Captain Smit, were honest carpenters, Geel Piet had been an artist and I missed his uncanny understanding of how to exploit my personality in the ring.

I felt I wasn't growing as a boxer. Yehudi Menuhin once said that playing the violin is like singing through your limbs; Geel Piet had had the ability to make boxing seem the same, each punch the result of perfect timing, continuity, controlled emotion and intelligence. If I was to become the welterweight champion of the world, I knew I'd soon have to find a coach who thought beyond schoolboy boxing.

The holidays were packed. I'd be at the prison at five-thirty a.m. for boxing, and Captain Smit would make me go three rounds with two of the other kids. Mostly with Snotnose and Jaapie, both heavier than me but really the only two boxers who could box well enough to push me. Both would itch to have a go, both were fighters in the Smit tradition, and both were very tough. It called for all my ringcraft to stay out of trouble. Halfway through the second round, Captain Smit would blow his whistle and one of them would step down and the other come in. This meant each of them only boxed one and a half rounds and so they'd go flat out, prepared to take a few punches to get a good one in. Captain Smit was convinced that it was the only way to increase my speed and keep me sharp.

After an hour and a half in the prison gym I'd head for Doc's cottage, where either Dee or Dum, who took it turn about, would have delivered breakfast. By the time I arrived at eight, the coffee would be made and a loaf of fresh bread would be on the table, together with eggs and bacon, plopping away on the back of the stove waiting for me to arrive. Doc was, after all, still a German and he expected me to be exactly on egg and bacon time. The girls loved the holidays and they'd spoil me rotten, with baking and fussing and generally cooking up a storm. Doc always claimed he put on several pounds when I was around.

Doc and I would sit outside on his stoep for breakfast and we'd plan the weekend hike. This usually meant repeating an old trail. Doc would bring out his notepad and we'd discuss the last time we'd done the planned walk, which might have been five years before. We'd discuss every specimen we'd found then and sometimes even leave the table to check the progress of some long forgotten succulent we had collected. Doc was still tied to the Steinway and his little girl students during the week, so our long walks had to take place over the weekend. Though I'm sure, after a while, he'd have had it no other way, the planning and the discussion over his notes became just as important to him as the excursions themselves. At nine he'd give me a piano lesson, shaking his head at the bad habits I'd acquired under the direction of Mr Mollip, the Prince of Wales School music master. 'This Mr Muddleup, you are sure he teaches pianoforte?' he would say, shaking his head. 'I think maybe the banjo yes?' He would spend the rest of the holidays getting me back into some sort of musical shape.

The first time I played St Louis blues for Doc I had expected to shock him out of his pants. In fact it was meant as a joke. Instead he nodded quietly. 'Ja, that is goot.' I turned to look at him in surprise. 'But to play black, the music must come from your soul not out from your head, Peekay.' He indicated that I should rise from the piano stool, and seated in my place he played the piece in the same haunting way as Hymie's seventy-eight of Errol Garner.

'Bloody hell, Doc, where'd you learn to do that!' It was the first time I'd sworn in Doc's presence but he seemed not to notice. 'Okey-dokey, Mr Schmarty-Pantz, who is a person called W. C. Handy?'

'He sounds like a lavatory brush,' I said flippantly.

'Mr W. C. Handy wrote this music, and now you want to play it without heart and even without knowing who is the composer! Would you do this to Beethoven or Bach? No, I think not. But now Mr Schmarty-Pantz thinks to play the black man's music is easy.'

'Sorry, Doc, it was only a joke. I only wanted to shock you.'

'Then to shock me you must play me bad music, not play me good music badly,' he said softly.

I was the one who had been shocked and Doc had in the process taught me once again to do my research and my thinking before I did my judging. 'Where'd you learn to play like that, Doc?'

Doc laughed. 'So long ago, ja, when I write my first book on cactus in North America, I was in New Orleans. I had no money so I played fifteen minutes classical every night in a fancy cathouse, the Golden Slipper. Ja, this is the name of that place. After I play comes every night a jazz band and soon we talk and so on and so forth and they think the German professor is very funny, but not my music, the rich people who come to this cathouse, they don't understand Mr Beethoven and Chopin and Brahms. But the black men, they understood. I teach them a little of this and a little of that and they teach me a little of that and a little of this,' he touched the keys and played a couple of bars of blues music. 'It was here I meet Mr W. C. Handy and later also Mr Willie Smith.'

'You met Willie Smith!' I yelled at him. 'The Willie Smith?'

'Ja, I think there is only one.'

'Doc, please, please teach me how to play jazz piano.'

Doc laughed, and affecting his version of an American accent replied, 'Not on your sweet-tootin' nelly, Peekay.'

'Please, Doc!'

He shook his head. 'I cannot teach you what I cannot feel. Peekay, you must understand this. It is not possible for a man to touch the heart of the negro man's music when he cannot feel it through his fingers.'

Doc had just explained to me why I would never amount to much musically. What Geel Piet knew I had as a boxer, Doc knew I lacked as a musician.

I would leave Doc at eleven o'clock and by a quarter past I had arrived at Miss Bornstein's house. Mr Bornstein who, as I mentioned before, was a lawyer in partnership with Mr Andrews, had a big white double-storey house designed in the Cape Dutch style. A huge bouganvillaea creeper cascaded purple bloom over one side of the house, its mass of purple blossom stark and beautiful against the wall so gleaming white that it hurt to look at it in the near noon sun. The next impression the eye met was of the sweeping lawns which smelt of cut grass and never seemed to lose their wet green look even in the late summer when every other lawn seemed strawed and faded from the heat. There were other things in the garden, trees and tropical shrubs and a bed of deep red canna. And of course all the usual junk like roses and things. But all I seem to remember is the dramatic splash of the deep purple bouganvillea against the blinding white of the house, the green, perfectly manicured lawns and the chit-chit-chit of the hose spitting stingy jets of water somewhere in the garden.

I'd spend the first half-hour or less, depending only on whether I could hold out that long, playing a game of chess with old Mr Bornstein. He would always checkmate me with the same words: 'Not so shameful. Tomorrow maybe, if God spares us, you will win.' God spared us but I never won.

A houseboy in a white starched coat would then bring me a glass of milk and two chocolate biscuits, my favourite. Then the lesson would begin. We'd work until two o'clock when the same boy brought in a jug of orange juice and a plate of polony and tomato sandwiches, also my favourite.

Miss Bornstein was determined that I should win a Rhodes scholarship and go to Oxford, and the work we did was far in excess of anything I needed to know to pass my matriculation. With her pushing me, particularly in Latin and Greek, by weekly letter and during the school holidays and with the tuition reserved for Sinjun's People I was probably getting as fine an education as it was possible for anyone of my age to absorb.

After orange juice and sandwiches I was free. Some days I'd spend the afternoon with Mrs Boxall or help Granpa in the garden or play a little snooker down at the Impala Hotel with John Hopkins and Geoffrey Scruby and some of the other guys all of whom, like me, were going to boarding school. They'd drink a couple of beers and smoke a little and we'd all generally act a bit tough with each other, though I was always in training and neither smoked nor drank.

I was beginning to understand how intellect separates men. For common ground we would talk rugby and cricket and girls. Daily we destroyed the reputations of the girls who'd been in class with us in primary school and who were now supposedly screwing like rattlesnakes. We never quite worked out with whom, it was always supposed to be someone older than ourselves, like Paul Everingham and Bob Goodhead who were in form six at Jeppe High and both had their school colours for rugby and cricket.

Puberty had taken a fierce and urgent grip on all of us so that the fantasy of fucking was never more than an unuttered sentence away. But my mind, when it wasn't on sex, was different. I guess it had always been, but now the dichotomy was beginning to show. I didn't feel superior, there was nothing to be superior about, my mind simply seemed to gaze over different intellectual landscapes. I dare say had I not been a boxer and rugby player and greatly respected for the former, the rest of the chaps in Barberton would have dismissed me as a brain and a bit of a loner.

I found Doc, Mrs Boxall, Miss Bornstein and old Mr Bornstein a source of stimulation, but the adult mind has lost much of its craziness, its zany quality and I missed the verbal jousting that Hymie supplied in our day-to-day relationship at school. In fact, when I got back to school after the holidays, it would take me a couple of days to get my verbal riposte sharp and my timing right again.

'Christ, Peekay, your brain's addled by too much deep and meaningful discussion about the weather and the crops and whether the locusts will come again this year!' Hymie would tease. Atherton, Pissy and Cunning-Spider also shared an intelligence which would readily mix into a really good verbal over an abstract point simply for the love of argument itself.

Hymie would contend that anything, no matter how banal, could be raised to the level of intelligent debate if the minds which attended to it were good enough. He told the story of the little cobbler in a shtetl in Russia who was spreading honey on a piece of bread when the bread fell to the floor. To his amazement the bread fell right side up. 'How can this be?' he said, and with the slice of bread in his hand he ran to consult the rabbi and the village elders. 'We are Jews in Russia, how can it be that I spread honey on my bread and when it fell to the floor it landed right side up? Since when did luck such as this come to a Jew?' The rabbi and the elders pondered the point for several days, consulting the Torah frequently. Finally they called the little cobbler to the synagogue. The rabbi pronounced the verdict, 'The answer my boy is quite clear, you honeyed your bread on the wrong side.'

We had all cawed and moaned at the story but Hymie,

as usual, had made his point, good conversational debate was an end in itself and talking for the love of conversation is what makes us human.

That Easter holiday Doc and I had planned an overnight hike to a waterfall we knew about some twelve miles past Saddleback Pass. As waterfalls go it wasn't a major one but it tumbled down through an area of rainforest which, in our only previous visit, we'd come across too late to explore properly. The cliffs rising above the forest looked interesting and Doc was sure we'd find succulents and several species of dwarf aloe in the rocky crags and ledges. I had been concerned when Doc had suggested the hike, it was a good twenty miles across the mountains and Doc was over eighty. Just how far over no one knew and while he was as lean as a twist of liquorice and tough as a mountain goat it was a hard day's march by any standards, and in the notes he had made on our previous trip nearly eight years earlier, he'd noted that the hike had been an exhausting one.

He had answered my protests with typical Doc logic. 'Peekay, if not now it will be never again. Our work here is unfinished, the topography, see I have made a drawing here in my notes, suggests limestone in the cliffs. If this is true it is rare, almost impossible, some geological freak happenings maybe?'

Doc knew he'd stirred my need for adventure, and the prospect of finding something that shouldn't be there allowed me to brush my concern aside and agree that we should undertake the trip.

Doc had managed to postpone his little girls for Friday and we set out at dawn with our blanket rolls, billy cans and enough food for two days, as well as a hurricane lamp, Doc's eight-battery Eveready torch, rope, a small hammer and a dozen homemade metal spikes hooked at the ends to secure the rope if necessary. Gert had made these for Doc in the prison metal shop soon after he'd left prison and they'd been invaluable for scrambling up rock faces now that Doc wasn't as young a mountain goat as he pretended to be.

By the time the sun rose over the escarpment and filled the de Kaap valley, we had climbed the foothills and were into the mountains proper. The aloe and thorn scrub were replaced by scree and tussock grass, turning to rocky crags where the wind can be cold even on a hot day. We often saw an eagle high above us seemingly drifting without purpose, carried by the currents of air. With a stop for lunch of cheese and cream crackers, washed down by a billy of sweet black tea, we crossed Saddleback Pass in the early afternoon and started the climb down the other side. By late afternoon we'd reached the peculiar formation of mountain cliffs rising above the deep kloof of rainforest Doc had noted in his diary.

We made camp beside a mountain brook flowing from the waterfall which dropped like a bridal veil down the far edge of the cliffs above us. I had chosen our campsite on the edge of the rainforest where an overhanging rock protected us from the wind. It can get bitterly cold during the night in the mountains and we set about collecting firewood before we lost the light. High above us we first heard and then saw a troop of baboons climbing the strange cliff face and running along the white ledges eroded into the face of the rock. Their urgent barking echoed down into the kloof where we'd made our camp.

Doc put his field glasses onto the cliff. 'It's too much shadow now, but I think tomorrow we find up there for sure something.'

Darkness comes quickly in the mountains and less than an hour after we'd arrived the sun had set, throwing the deep kloof into shadow. Even though there was still some light I got the fire for supper going, the dry branches crackling and popping with plenty of smoke to ward off the mosquitoes which always seem to come from nowhere moments after sunset. I set about making our supper while Doc washed at the stream. Chopping an onion and two tomatoes into a billy can, I then upended a can of bully beef into the billy, mashing it all together with my hunting knife, ready for when the fire would glow down so that it would cook slowly. I'd already trapped two large sweet potatoes under the unmade fire so that we'd be able to pluck them out of the cooking embers later for dessert. The rainforest grew dark first, the clear outlines of the giant tree ferns smudged and then blackened into darkness while high up in a yellow wood tree a couple of green loeries called out one last time before they called it a day. Next the valley on the edge of the forest where we'd camped dimmed down for the night, closing out the light, blurring rock and bush and tree. Finally the sky on the high ridge above us pulled a dark sheet over us and pinned it with stars. The distant sound of falling water from the falls seemed to emphasise the silence. Doc spoke quietly in the night. 'No one has written a great symphony or even a concerto about Africa. Why is this so?'

He hadn't expected an answer and I waited for him to continue.

'The music of Africa is too wild, too free, too accustomed to death for romance. Africa is too crude a stage for the small scratching of the violin, too majestic for the piano. Africa is only right for drums. The drum carries its rhythm but does not steal its music. Timpani is the background, the music of Africa is in the voices of the people. They are its instruments, more subtle, more beautiful, infinitely more noble than the scratching, thumping, banging and blowing of brass and wind and vellum, strings and keyboard.'

'What about Requiem for Geel Piet?' I asked.

Doc chuckled. 'For twenty years I have tried to compose ten or even five minutes of music, good music for the great Southland. And then, after twenty years of failure, I find it in the chain gangs, in the rhythm of a pick and the sweat of black backs and the vicious crack of the sjambok and the almost noiseless thud of the donkey prick. The voice music is not the keening of despair but the expression of a

476

certainty that Africa will live and the spirit will survive brutality. The music of Africa is in the soul and its instruments are in the voices of its people. Such a domkop, Peekay. All the time it is waiting absoloodle under my long German nose. Requiem for Geel Piet is not my music, it is the music of the people. The necklace is only mine because I strung the beads.'

I handed Doc a steaming plate of bully beef. Then, using a short stick, I rolled the two sweet potatoes from the embers to cool a little for later. We ate in silence. Doc never took food for granted and would chew for ages before swallowing. I added a couple of logs to build the fire up again and then walked down to the stream to wash the plates and fill the billy.

After I'd made coffee and poured a tablespoon of condensed milk into the tin mug just the way Doc liked it, I placed the steaming cup next to him and sliced open his sweet potato. Steam rose from its fat, succulent belly and to this too I added condensed milk as a special treat. The mosquitoes, kept at bay by the early smoke from the fire, were out in force again. I rubbed Citronella oil over my arms and legs and handed the bottle to Doc. The oil smelt pretty bad, but it was a damn sight better than being bitten half to death. We'd been going since four-fifteen in the morning and were exhausted. Too tired to wash the mugs, I wrapped myself in my blanket. Checking first to see that Doc lay well clear of the fire, I curled up under the overhang of the rock so that my blanket wouldn't be wet with dew in the morning and went to sleep.

I awoke at dawn, and keeping my blanket wrapped around me I built the fire up again. The valley was shrouded in mist and the rainforest which began not twenty yards from our camp site was invisible. Minutes after the sun hit the valley the mist would vanish, but until it did the cold would remain. My hands were freezing as I filled the billy from the stream for coffee. Doc was snoring again, tightly wrapped in his blanket, and I let him sleep on until I'd made his coffee and blown a generous tablespoon's worth of condensed milk into it. I did the same for myself and the steaming mug soon warmed my hands. I didn't wake Doc; I knew the smell of the fresh-brewed coffee would do that for me. Doc loved coffee more than I think he loved his cactus garden and almost as much as Beethoven and J. S. Bach. Pretty soon his nostrils began to twitch, and grunting to himself he sat up in the blanket and knuckled his eyes open. High up through the mist we could hear the barking of the baboons; the sun must have reached them and they were moving on.

Doc gripped the mug I gave him in both hands, then looking up in the direction of the cliffs invisible above him in the mist he said, 'Today will be different, Peekay.' The barking of the baboons echoed down the misty valley. 'Ja, for sure and absoloodle, today we find something.' Taking a careful sip of coffee, 'I hope you sleep good, Peekay?' he asked.

I cooked two sausages and a couple of rashers of bacon and then split the sausages down the centre and laid them on two slices of bread, topped them with bacon and sandwiched them with two more thick slices of bread. I handed one of the crude sandwiches to Doc and ate the other myself, holding it to my mouth with both hands.

While we were having a second cup of coffee the sun was beginning to dazzle its way through the mist and seemingly in minutes the valley was filled with sunshine. A few patches of mist hung near the floor of the rainforest, but they too were soon gone. Above us the strange-looking cliffs looked less foreboding in the bright morning light and I scanned them to see how we might set about the climb.

In a mist-shrouded landscape, sounds are always exaggerated. Now, with the mist gone, the morning settled down into all its reassuring components, the chatter of birds, running water, the urgent whirr of a grasshopper and in fact the generally busy noises of the mountain day coming fully to life. I walked over to a small clump of bushes and

478

was in the half squat position with my pants around my ankles when two plump bush partridges whirred from the underbrush directly beside me. I rose, my pants still around my ankles, and squinting down the barrel of an imaginary shotgun, I let them have it, first with the left and then pulling carefully around to get the second bird with the right barrel. I then watched, laughing, as they disappeared like a couple of hurricane fighters over a small ridge beyond me.

After washing I cleaned up camp and stowed our stuff under the overhanging rock, sprinkling our blanket rolls with Citronella oil. If anything approached, particularly a scorpion looking for a nice warm place to nestle, the unfamiliar smell of the oil would drive it away.

Doc slung the rope around his neck and hung his eight-battery Eveready torch from his belt. I took a small climber's rucksack with water bottle, trowel for digging footholds, hammer, metal spikes, paraffin lamp and Doc's field glasses. The climb didn't look too bad, buttresses of rock led to long ridges eroded into the face of the rock, as though the cliff face itself were made from a composition of hard and soft rock. It was these seemingly soft, white striations of rock which had first caught Doc's interest and which he was pretty sure would be dolomite or some sort of limestone. The torch and the paraffin lamp were a giveaway. Doc, always a romantic, was hoping we'd find a cave in the cliff face, a prospect which naturally appealed to me enormously.

We climbed for an hour, the going not too hard. Doc, despite his age, was a skilled mountaineer who took no chances and whereas I might have made it to the first ridge of eroded rock perhaps a hundred foot from the ground in half the time it took us, our progress was sure and the way back carefully mapped out in our minds. Getting down a steep face can often be more difficult than getting up it. The first ridge of eroded rock proved Doc's theory to be right, the material was dolomite which had been worn away by tens of thousands of years of wind and rain to make deep ledges with overhangs cut into the cliff face. We followed the ledge until we found a way back onto the cliff face, and continued to climb. It took us another hour to get another hundred feet up the cliff to yet another ledge. This one, more exposed to the wind, had been cut deeper into the rock and we could smell where the baboons had settled for the night. Another fifty feet up the face and we came to a third ridge, deeper yet again. Walking along this ridge we found it gouged deeper and deeper into the cliff face until it came to a sudden end. We'd reached a blind alley; there seemed to be no way of getting back onto the face so that we could climb higher.

By now we'd been going almost three hours and the sun, beating onto the face of the cliff, was hot. Doc's khaki shirt was wet with perspiration and I suggested we sit down for a drink and a rest. The ridge we were sitting on was, I judged, about a hundred feet from the top of the cliff but it appeared impossible to go any further. Down below us we could see the canopy of the rainforest, with one old yellow wood tree, its branches stretching clear to the sky fifty feet above the canopy of the forest and no more than a hundred feet below where we were sitting. Doc said it could well be a thousand years old. The cliff face was shaped in a wide arc and on our right, about a hundred feet below us, the waterfall gushed from the rock face, more a fine, misty spray than a gush really, but sufficient to feed the stream we'd camped beside.

Doc took his notebook from the rucksack and turned to a crude sketch he'd made of the cliff from the ground level the previous afternoon. 'Ja, we are sitting now in the deepest ledge, above is harder rock and not so deep striations.' He sighed, clearly puzzled. Doc didn't like to be wrong about his observations which he would only have permitted himself to voice after a great deal of careful consideration. 'Well Peekay, we found dolomite and also there is water, but no cave. This is very strange. You can see the waterfall comes straight from the cliff, the stream must run deep inside the face of the cliff. There should be caves. Ja, this is so, absoloodle.'

I walked back to the wall at the end of the ledge and peeked over the edge, hoping to find a small ledge which would take us further across the face. About three feet below me a small ridge of rock, no more than six inches wide, ran for two or three yards and then took a slight turn so I was unable to see whether it continued. I swung my body over the edge of the ledge, dangling my feet until they reached the narrow ridge of rock. With my stomach against the cliff I edged my way along it. I'd hardly moved more than three feet when I found myself looking directly into a hole in the cliff, about two feet wide and three feet high. I was able to look some ten feet down the tunnel before it turned to darkness. It was quite clearly an entrance to a cave, and not simply a tunnel worn into the rock. A fire bush grew from a crack in the rock to the right of the opening to conceal it from being seen from below. Suddenly a bat flew out of the tunnel, blurred past me, and I heard the unmistakable squeak of bats deep in the rock face. I was certain I had found a cave.

'I've found it! We've found our cave!' I yelled. My voice, hugely magnified, echoed down the valley. It would take very little effort to lift myself up into the hole, but holes have a habit of containing surprises infinitely worse than a few hundred harmless bats. So I edged back to where Doc was waiting. Helping me back up onto the ledge, Doc too was excited. 'So, I am right, Peekay,' he said triumphantly. I explained that if we could secure a rope handrail it would be possible for him to follow me into the cave.

We discussed a way of doing this for some time. Then, hammering a couple of spikes into the floor of the ledge, we secured one end of the rope through the eyes of the spikes, both of us pulling on the rope to make sure the spikes were firmly bedded into the rock. Next we tied the rope to my waist and I tucked three spikes, the hammer and Doc's torch into the back of my belt where I could reach back and get them comfortably. Doc paid out the rope as I slid backwards, down onto the thin lip of rock below the ledge. Had I fallen it was unlikely Doc would have been able to haul me back again but I was very sure on my feet and unconcerned by heights. In less than thirty seconds I was in front of the cave entrance. I lifted myself through the hole with comparative ease and commenced to crawl along the narrow tunnel which continued in a slightly upward direction for about twenty feet then widened out. I untied the rope from around my waist and removed the long silver torch from my belt. The daylight had disappeared by the time I'd crawled to the end of the tunnel so I switched on the powerful Eveready to find that the tunnel led into a cave which appeared to be about fifteen feet long and equally wide, while being high enough for me to stand upright.

The cave smelt powerfully of baboon and bats. As I played the torch around the walls I could see hundreds of bats hanging from the roof and the walls. I returned down the narrow passage to the cliff face, and sticking my head out yelled at Doc that I'd found a big cave. My voice echoed down the valley as the barking of the baboons had done the previous evening and again that morning.

'It's not too hard, Doc. I'll hammer a couple of spikes into the tunnel wall and tie the rope and you can use it as a handrail to come across.' I set about this task, drawing the rope tight so that it made a firm handrail from the ledge into the mouth of the tunnel. Doc was a fearless old coot and dropping himself backwards onto the rock ridge and holding the rope he quickly edged across the cliff face to the mouth of the tunnel. I pulled him in and now he was lying on his belly looking into the dark tunnel.

'Wunderbar, Peekay, a cave. How big? A big one, yes?' he panted.

'You'll have to crawl, it's slightly upwards. Follow the torch, it's only about twenty feet in.'

The cave was not high enough for Doc to stand upright so he squatted holding the torch while I lit the hurricane lamp which he'd brought with him in the rucksack strapped to his back.

I placed the lamp in the middle of the cave where it threw a dim but adequate light and Doc started to examine the walls with the torch beam.

The floor was covered with bat shit. 'It should smell worse than this.' Doc took out a box of matches and struck one on the side of his pants. The match flared, momentarily lighting his face. 'A wind! In here is a wind, from some place else there is coming a wind.' Doc was right, the flame from the match was flickering and then went out. He shone his torch into the left corner of the cave where a sharp buttress of rock protruded. The torch light played on the rock and as Doc swept the beam to the top of the buttress the light disappeared into a void. We realised that there was an opening beyond it from which came the unmistakable sound of water dripping. We both moved round the back of the rock to discover the opening about four feet above the ground which reached to the ceiling. Doc lit the opening for me to scramble through and he passed the lantern to me and then the torch before following. As he dropped to the ground I swung the powerful torch into the black void.

'Holy Molenski!' The torch showed a huge chamber, from the floor and the ceiling of which grew stalactite and stalagmite. The roof of the cave must have been at least forty feet high and the snowy white calcareous structures falling from it, some of which had reached the ground, looked like an illustration from a child's fairy tale. Pools of infinitely still water on parts of the cave floor mirrored the grotesque shapes, creating an enchanted world which appeared to be carved in crystal.

I handed the torch back to Doc and took up the lantern as we moved forward to explore. Doc kept stopping to train his torch on one or another of the beautiful crystal columns. 'Absoloodle, absoloodle wunderbar!' he kept repeating. It was certainly the most amazing natural phenomenon I had ever witnessed and I followed Doc as we explored the huge chamber. We found several fissures in the walls, none of which were wide enough to climb through; we traced the source of the water to a point high in the ceiling from which a constant drip of water fell. Doc pointed out that this drip was too rapid for the formation of stalactites. The gradual movement of water seeping through rock collects a load of calcium carbonate, when it finally squeezes through to the ceiling of the cave and reaches the air it sheds its load of calcium carbonate and an infinitely small part of a stalactite is formed. Each drop adds its minute contribution. He pointed to a massive stalactite to our right. 'Perhaps three hundred thousand years, maybe more.' Doc's voice was filled with awe. On the far wall, some sixty feet into the cave, a ledge of rock protruded about fifteen feet from the floor. Above it hung huge spikes of stalactite and clumps of glittering crystals, while directly under the ledge, like grotesque legs to a giant table, stalagmites had grown. A buttress of crystal stalagmite had grown to the one side of the platform to resemble steps leading up to it, so the entire effect was like a magnificent slab held high by crystal shafts with huge spikes of crystallised light suspended above it.

'Look, Doc, it's like Merlin's altar in the crystal cave!'

Doc sucked in his breath, 'Ja, in such a place went Merlin for sure.' He pointed to the throne, 'To lie on this altar and in a hundred and fifty thousand years maybe the body would be a part of this cave. A part of the crystal cave of Africa. Imagine only this, Peekay.'

I grinned, 'Can you hold off for a while, please Doc, I still need you here.' The thought of Doc dying had never entered my head. I often thought of him growing old, unable to do the things we'd done in the past; but I never thought of him as disappearing, not being there, not being a part of my life. I understood death, it happened at any time. It was a brutal accident like the death of Granpa Chook or Geel Piet, or Big Hettie's flyweight. Even Big Hettie's death could be explained in that she was freakishly big and thus fell into the category of unexpected death. Doc did not fall into any of the criteria I had set aside in my mind for death. Doc was calm and reason and order and the kind of death I knew had no part in the expectations for our relationship.

He had walked ahead up to the crystal-like speleothems which formed the steps to the platform. Climbing these, his boots made a scrunching noise on the hard calcium deposits, and soon he stood on the platform. Suddenly, without warning, he squatted and then stretched out full length, so his body was lost from my sight.

'Ah, come on, Doc! That's not funny,' I said, suddenly a little scared. Doc's torch shone upwards, lighting the stalactites falling from the ceiling above him so that they looked like crystal bolts of lightning frozen in place above him. It was the most frightening and magnificent effect I have ever seen.

Doc's voice came back to me, sounding serene. 'It is beautiful, Peekay, we must never tell any person about the crystal cave of Africa.'

'C'mon, Doc, you're giving me the creeps,' I answered, not fully taking in what he had said.

Doc stood up, shining the torch straight into my eyes so that I was blinded by the light. 'You must promise me, Peekay. It is very important. You must promise, please?' He withdrew the torch from my face and in the fuzziness the temporary blinding had created he looked just like Merlin, standing between huge spikes of crystal on the platform ten feet above me.

'Doc, please come down. I promise, now please come down.'

'Ja, I come. Remember you have promised, Peekay.' He made his way down from the platform carefully and I ran to give him a hand. He was breathing heavily, and as I helped him down I could feel the excitement in the old man.

We made our way back to the bat cave and Doc shone the Eveready back into the chamber. 'Peekay, we have found a place in Africa no man has ever seen, the purest magic cave, the crystal cave of Africa.'

'Come on, Doc, let's skedaddle, what's the time?' He fished into his trouser pocket for his hunter and shone the torch on its face. 'Half clock ten,' he said. Doc always told the time in this funny manner.

'We've got to go. If we get back to camp by noon it'll be dark by the time we get home.' Fortunately most of the way home was downhill and we knew we would gain a couple of hours on the way back. I calculated it would be around eight that evening before we would be home. Walking the foothills in the dark wouldn't be much fun and Doc would be exhausted. My anxiety to get going had taken the edge off my excitement. Doc grabbed me by the arm, he was still shaking. 'Remember, Peekay, this is our cave, the crystal cave belongs only to you and to me.'

'Okay, Doc, I promise. I already promised. Now let's get the hell out of here.' It wasn't at all like Doc to be so insistent, anyway he knew he could trust me implicitly. The cave had had a tremendous effect on him and I knew he'd want us to come back, though I doubted that he'd be able to make such a tough climb for much longer. I'd cut the rope we'd taken into the cave but had left the rope handrail intact for Doc to use getting out. Once we were back on the ledge I began to retrieve the two metal spikes, as we'd already lost two by having to leave them embedded in the tunnel wall.

'No, leave them, Peekay,' Doc said suddenly, 'there is no time.' It was unlike Doc, who was always very careful about equipment. We'd account for everything before moving on from a camp site or where we had been collecting specimens. It was the first time he had ever been devious and I realised how emotionally charged he had become over the crystal cave; the old bugger was determined to come back.

We arrived back in the foothills above the town just as a giant moon was coming up over the escarpment, flooding the de Kaap valley in silver light. It was a full moon again and that was always a difficult time for me. It had been a full moon when Granpa Chook died and while the memory of that funny old rooster had dimmed, when the moon was full memories came galloping through the silver night to sadden me. It had also been a full moon when Geel Piet had died.

I was right, this would be the last big trek with Doc, who was at the point of collapse by the time we finally reached his cottage. I laid him on top of his bed and removed his boots. He had two large blisters, one under each big toe, so I threaded a needle and cotton and ran a loop of cotton through each blister which I then tied, leaving them overnight to drain the fluid. It was a technique Doc had shown me years before and I knew that by morning the blisters would have flattened and there would be no pain. I washed his face and put Vaseline over a cut under his eye and threw an army blanket over him. He was a tough old blighter and in the morning I was pretty sure he'd be okay.

'Ours. The crystal cave. Africa. You, me, Peekay,' he mumbled and then seemed to drift off into sleep. I waited until his breathing was deep and even before leaving for home. On the way the moon was so bright that one could see the purple blossom of the jacaranda trees. I was saddened at the thought of never again being with him in the high mountains. Each time I came back from school Doc seemed a little more frail. We had found the crystal cave of Africa but would I see it only once? Perhaps I would return, perhaps not. When you share things, as Doc and I had done, somehow it seemed wrong to halve the secret by returning alone. I thought of the rope rotting and perhaps in a hundred years they'd find the holes where the spikes had long since rusted out and observe the rust stains in the dolomite. They'd search and find minute metal fragments which they'd analyse, and then propound all sorts of theories that would have nothing to do with a six foot seven inch German professor of music and the future welterweight boxing champion of the world.

TWENTY

The second term of form three began with a new aspect of school life. Singe 'n Burn's tutorials three times a week were quite unlike school. We talked for an hour and from it would come at least three hours of reading and preparation for the next tutorial. The headmaster had a wide grasp of subject and he was quick to discover where a boy's special aptitudes lay. These he would cultivate carefully while at the same time balancing the mental menu with the discipline of tackling subjects which, though less interesting, he thought essential to a well-rounded education. Sinjun's People seldom met as a group and once chosen they were never mentioned again in the activity of the Prince of Wales School. No attempt was ever made to make any one of us seem special or especially important, although a powerful struggle between the six took place in the normal course of school, with each one of Sinjun's People competing fiercely in the classroom for honours. All this, combined with boxing and rugby football, left me very little time to myself.

Hymie had also revealed his big plan. By now he was so intimately involved with me as a boxer as well as a friend that he acted quite unselfconsciously as my manager. In two and a bit years Hymie had acquired a remarkable expertise on boxing and he too was aware that we'd reached the limitations of both Darby White and Sarge and needed to take the next step in my training.

'Who's the best professional boxing trainer in South Africa?' he'd asked one afternoon shortly after our return to school.

'You already know the answer to that; Solly Goldman.'

'Well, I went to see him during the holidays. We're working out for him when he gets back from a trip to England in six weeks. If he likes what he sees, he'll take you on.'

'Jesus, Hymie, that's wonderful! How'd you get him to agree? Solly Goldman only handles professionals.'

For once Hymie wasn't ready with a flip answer. He looked down at the back of his hands as he answered. 'We're going to pay him. We've got enough money in the bank to pay him for a year then we'll think of something else.' Hymie looked up at me. 'Now I know what you're going to say; but as far as I'm concerned my money is yours, you'd do the same for me.'

'It's not on, Hymie. Thank you, but it's simply not on. There are two reasons. The first you already know about, no hand-outs, not under any circumstances, friendship notwithstanding. The second is more practical, that's our business capital, the first rule of business is never to eat into your capital, you above all people know that!'

'Look, we'd still keep the Bank, I can borrow money from my old man to keep the float going. You don't have to take a hand-out. You can buy back your share of the float capital from the profits and you can take a salary as pocket money, you'll see, it will work out.'

'Hymie, there's nothing in the world I want more than Solly Goldman's expertise, but I can't do it. It's got something to do with an incident in my life when I was five years old and I've promised myself I would never again forfeit my independence, never again find myself in a position where I wasn't in control of my life.'

Hymie looked hurt and I couldn't blame him, in a sense I was rejecting his friendship and his trust. But the wounds entrenched by the Judge and Nazi stormtroopers had left adhesions on my psyche as a constant reminder to me that I was on my own.

'Okay, Peekay, have it your way, man.' Then Hymie

grinned. 'If I think up a scam and your share makes enough money to pay Goldman, will you be in it?'

I grinned, relieved that he had accepted my objection. 'That's business, that's different! But only if I play my part and the whole thing's kosher.'

'Shake a paw, partner,' Hymie grinned. 'This one is going to be an intellectual masterpiece!'

Atherton, Cunning-Spider and I had been a combination on the rugby field from form one. I was a natural scrum-half with Atherton, following in the footsteps of his famous cousin, developing into a brilliant fly-half while Cunning-Spider was a centre with a lot of style. Hugh Lyell and Jean Minnaar, both Sinjun's People, were also on the team. While I was still technically under fourteen I elected to play in the under fifteen team to keep the combination together. Pissy Johnson, who seemed to grow bigger every term, was a front row forward and, of course, Hymie only became interested because most of the Wooden Spoon Goons were in the team. The under fifteen team in any school is the nursery for the first fifteen and so the players in it are always carefully watched by the rugby masters who regarded this particular team as one with great promise.

Hymie, as usual, analysed the teams against whom we played and, like his boxing notes, we had a pretty good idea of their game plan and capability before taking the field against them.

As he had done in his swot spot in boxing, Hymie made us think and behave like winners. 'Winners make their own luck but winners are also lucky,' he said.

In the under thirteens and fourteens, when we had played Helpmekaar, the Afrikaans school where I had boxed my first bout to beat Jannie Geldenhuis, the much bigger Helpmekaar forwards had made mincemeat of us and the stronger, bigger backs had run us off our feet. Geldenhuis, playing scrum-half opposite me, had thoroughly enjoyed his revenge on each of these four occasions. In the last under fourteen match there they'd beaten us narrowly, as we left the field he'd given me an unnecessarily patronising pat on the back. 'In the ring is one thing, on the rugby field is another. Rugby is more important than boxing, man.' We'd met five times in the ring and while he was always a tough opponent, on each occasion I'd beaten him; he had a right to try and get even. We would play each school twice during a season and so in our personal score it was me with five boxing wins, Helpmekaar four rugby wins. Hymie, in particular, was anxious to change these rugby statistics when we met in the under fifteens. While the Helpmekaar team were still bigger than we were, things had evened out a bit in size. Hymie was convinced we could beat them. 'Look at the statistics, Peekay, in the under thirteens they beat us twenty to nil and again fifteen nil, last year it was nine nil and ten three and we scored a try to two free kicks and a drop goal. Statistically we have to take them this year.'

I had my doubts, Helpmekaar with four wins to their credit in the preceding two years had a right to be confident. 'Hymie, they're Boers, they'd rather die than lose to an English school, it's not simply a matter of statistics!'

'Ja, I know, that's what we're going to have to fix.'

On the Wednesday afternoon two weeks prior to the match, when we were meant to be studying at the Johannesburg library, Hymie drew me aside. 'Will you come to Helpmekaar with me this afternoon to see Jannie Geldenhuis, don't ask any questions, just say, yes . . . it's important.'

Sitting on the top deck of the Parktown bus he outlined his plan. 'There are nearly twelve hundred kids at Helpmekaar and six hundred at our school, if we can get most of them to place a bet on Helpmekaar winning against our under fifteens we could really clean up, we'd have your Solly Goldman money.'

'Christ, Hymie, we're back to straight gambling! You're crazy, this isn't like those first boxing matches when we took a few bets in the toilet before the fight. There I was a surprise factor in that scam, the punters from the other schools didn't know we had a boxer who could fight. This is just the opposite, they know how good we are and what's more we've never beaten them! This whole thing contradicts our business philosophy.'

'You know what your problem is, Peekay? You worry too much.'

'With you as a friend, that's hardly bloody surprising. I hope you've got a plan?'

Hymie opened his hands expansively. 'Does a bird fly? Of course I've got a plan, but I may have to tapdance a little when we get there so please excuse me if I don't explain it to you in detail. But I promise you our business philosophy is intact.'

'Hymie, listen! Picking up a dozen punters in the shit house is one thing; taking on a whole bloody Afrikaans school is another. You don't know these buggers like I do, these guys don't gamble, the Afrikaans are very religious, you know.'

'Greed, my dear Peekay, transcends religion. Did not the Roman soldiers gamble for Christ's garments at Golgotha? Besides, when those Helpmekaar guys see the odds I'm offering, their little Boer hands won't be able to get a kitchen knife to their money boxes fast enough.'

'Hymie, I hope this whole thing's kosher. If it turns out to be a con and they find out, we're dead meat!' Hymie had taught us all the Jewish word 'kosher' and it had become the generic term for something being legitimate.

Hymie smiled. 'I've racked my brains, in fact I'm rather ashamed of myself, but even with my considerable intellect, there is no way of ensuring the outcome other than to pay them off, which is patently impossible. We simply have to beat them on the day. Believe me, it's as kosher as my granma's chicken soup.' He turned to me and gave me his most disarming smile. 'Peekay, I know you've got a considerable rep with these Boers, no way I'm going to spoil that. You're the only Rooinek Christian gentleman they respect,' he paused. 'Just get it into your head that we can beat the bastards!'

'I hope you didn't mean you'd pay them off if you could find a way?'

'No, of course not, I was only kidding. The nicest part of a scam is the brains part. Anyone can learn to cheat.'

We reached the top of the hill and arrived at the Helpmekaar gates just as school was getting out. A sea of brown blazers piped with yellow braid engulfed our two green ones. Remarks were flying left, right and centre and things were getting decidedly uncomfortable.

'What now?' I whispered to Hymie.

'We just wait here, you'll see,' he replied.

Just then a voice cut through the sea of brown blazers, 'Peekay, howzit?' It was Jannie Geldenhuis. 'Sorry I'm late, man, I had to see one of the masters. Come with me.' He extended his hand in the Boer manner and we shook it in turn and then followed him through the gates.

'Magtig, I thought we were going to be lynched,' I said to Jannie in Afrikaans.

'No way, man, they all know you here, you a sort of hero.'

We had reached the school toilets where a couple of guys about our own age were having a quiet smoke. Jannie asked them politely to leave and they kicked at the ground with the toe cap of their shoes, then deciding to obey, killed their cigarettes by pinching the heads off and put the unused stompies in their blazer pockets for use later.

Hymie said he'd accept odds of three to one on the Prince of Wales School winning.

Geldenhuis gasped. 'You're crazy, man! We already beat you four games to nil!'

'Those are the odds,' Hymie said quietly.

'That's blêrrie terrific for the punters,' Geldenhuis said, 'but what about us? We . . . you'll be cleaned out! Fifteen percent of nothing is nothing, and I'll end up with my arse kicked by twelve hundred bloody angry Helpmekaar punters.'

Geldenhuis was not just a pretty face, I observed. Hymie'd gone crackers! Helpmekaar had to be favoured to win. Three to one odds was suicide.

'Okay, Geldenhuis ... Peekay and I will give you a written guarantee that we'll honour our debts if the Prince of Wales loses.' He reached into the inside pocket of his blazer and handed me a square of folded paper. I opened it to see that it was a guarantee by the Bank to pay in the event of a Helpmekaar win. There was a place at the bottom for two signatures. Hymie had already signed as one of them.

'Sign it and give it to him,' Hymie said casually.

I made a rough calculation in my head. Assuming two thirds of the punters bet against us at an average of two shillings a bet, we stood to lose around three hundred and seventy pounds. If we sold the Bank to a syndicate and our rights to Miss Bornstein's *Famous Correspondence School Notes* and took all our savings we could just make it.

I breathed a sigh of relief, if it had been more than our total assets I would have had to turn Hymie down in front of Geldenhuis, causing us both no end of embarrassment. I borrowed Hymie's Parker 51 and holding the guarantee against the toilet wall I signed it. But I can tell you I was not happy; Hymie Solomon Levy was going to be in a lot of shit when we were alone again.

Geldenhuis took the guarantee from me, read it and pulled out a small leather wallet from his pocket, as he opened it to stow the guarantee I noticed it contained no money.

'Okay, Geldenhuis, twenty percent of the winnings or fifty quid now, it's your choice,' Hymie said.

Like me before Hymie had entered my life, Jannie Geldenhuis had probably never seen a ten-pound note in his life, much less fifty. Eight pounds a week was the average white workers' wage, Helpmekaar was not a private school and his parents were probably battling to make ends meet.

Hymie had read his man correctly. 'I'll take the fifty pounds now,' Geldenhuis said.

Jannie Geldenhuis must have believed we couldn't win, Hymie was offering him fifty quid against a potential of seventy-five.

Hymie pulled out his wallet and opened it. 'Just a second!' Geldenhuis said suddenly. He withdrew his wallet again and took the guarantee from it and proffered it to Hymie. 'I got a condition of my own, without it we got no deal, man.'

We both looked at Geldenhuis with surprise. 'What's the condition, Jannie?' I asked.

'Well, first of all, I'm only agreeing to set up the Helpmekaar side of the betting because you're in this, Peekay.' He jabbed his finger in Hymie's direction. 'I don't do business with a Jewboy!'

'Hey, now wait a minute!' I was suddenly angry, 'Hymie and I are in this together, no Hymie, no deal!' I turned to Hymie, 'C'mon, let's piss off.'

Hymie put his hand up in a conciliatory manner. 'Now hang on a sec. Take it easy. We're a partnership, if Jannie here wants to deal with you that's fine.' He had moved so as to unsight Geldenhuis and gave me a knowing wink, then turned again so that Geldenhuis could see him and removed five ten-pound notes from his wallet. 'Here, Peekay, you pay the man.'

Before I could take the money, Geldenhuis said, 'That's not the condition.' The beginnings of a smile played at the corners of his mouth.

I was still angry. 'So what's the condition, Geldenhuis?'

'Fight me!'

He must have seen the surprise in my face. 'What here? Now?'

'I just turned featherweight, you still easy a bantamweight, I want a last chance to get even.'

'And if he says no?' Hymie asked.

Still looking directly at me Geldenhuis said: 'No deal! You can stick your fifty quid up your Jewboy arse! What do you reckon, Peekay? Box me three rounds here in the gym?'

'Christ, and to think I liked you, Geldenhuis. You're on! But I haven't got any gear.'

'I already thought of that, I got stuff for you.' Geldenhuis paused and then shrugged his shoulders, 'Hey, no hard feelings, man. You a Rooinek, I'm a Boer, I won't be happy till I beat you,' he said simply.

'You may be a long time unhappy, man! Where do I change?'

'Who's going to referee?' Hymie asked.

Jannie Geldenhuis pointed to Witwatersrand University campus which was only a couple of hundred yards from the school. 'We got a guy from Wits just in case you said yes.'

Geldenhuis put the guarantee back into his wallet and I turned to follow him out of the toilets, but Hymie stood his ground.

'Just a moment, Geldenhuis!'

We turned to face Hymie who held the five ten-pound notes up in his hand, just the hint of a smile played over his face.

'I bet you fifty quid Peekay smacks your arse!'

Geldenhuis stood, his arms held stiffly as though at attention, he was rigid with anger. Hymie had outfoxed him and avenged himself at the same time.

'You got your bet, Jew!' he spat.

Geldenhuis took us over to the shower block and pointed to a brown paper bag on a bench. 'Everything's there, I'll see you in the gym.' He turned and walked away, presumably to change elsewhere.

'Christ, what a turn up for the books,' Hymie said.

The gear fitted well enough and the boxing boots were nicely worn. We left the showers and walked down a long corridor towards the gym. I entered ahead of Hymie.

Suddenly the hall resounded with clapping and whistling, it was packed to the rafters with Helpmekaar guys.

'Holy shit!' I exclaimed, turning to Hymie.

Hymie glanced at the grinning faces looking at us. 'Keep calm, pretend you're not surprised, we don't want him to have the psychological advantage.' Hymie, as usual, was thinking on his feet. We climbed up into the ring and Hymie gloved me up. Geldenhuis was already in his corner throwing punches into the air. As usual I sat on the pot and waited.

The referee, a chap in his mid-twenties, called us into the centre of the ring. 'Okay, boxers, shake hands! Break when I say break. A knock down takes a compulsory count of eight, I don't start counting until you're in a neutral corner. Three warnings on a foul and the fight goes against you.'

Neither of us were listening to him. 'This time I get you Rooinek,' Jannie Geldenhuis said out of the corner of his mouth.

'This fight comes to you with the compliments of the Jewboy, Boer bastard!' I spat back.

'Ready timekeeper? Seconds out of the ring!' The bell went and we danced towards each other. I could see Geldenhuis meant business, he had five defeats to avenge and his eyes were hard. Fighting in the enemy camp in front of a hostile crowd I wasn't about to let him have the satisfaction. He was a naturally aggressive fighter and I wasn't going to give him the opportunity of landing a few good punches early so I spent the first half of round one on the back foot using the ring and staying clear of the ropes. Later Hymie told me the Helpmekaar kids were yelling their heads off but it was as though I was fighting in a vacuum, my concentration was complete. Geldenhuis threw a lot of leather but most of it landed on my arms and gloves, though he did score with two punches. A beautiful uppercut as he caught me briefly on the ropes and a right under the heart. Both punches hurt like hell. It was sheer luck that I hadn't had any lunch. Sinjun had had me for a tutorial which had gone on an extra half hour and so I'd missed lunch. I was willing to bet Geldenhuis hadn't eaten since morning.

I caught Geldenhuis a beautiful punch on the jaw which stopped him in his tracks. He had come at me with a careless left lead and I brought my right hand across his lead to hit him hard on the side of the jaw. Jannie was a sucker for repeating a mistake and later in the round he led again with a sloppy left. This time I came under the blow and caught him with everything I had under the heart. I could see his eyes boggle and he staggered back into the ropes where I hit him with a left right combination in the gut, expecting his gloves to open so that I could get an uppercut to the jaw. Instead, anticipating the uppercut, he defended his head, leaving his gut exposed. In went the Geel Piet eight-punch combination and he grabbed at the ropes just as the bell went. The first round was mine.

Hymie had noticed the same thing as I had, Geldenhuis had developed a peculiar habit, in order to set himself for a left hook, he held his right elbow high, opening up his rib cage, and I'd given him a lot of punishment in the area right under the heart. The eight-punch combo was just what I needed to soften him up for later in the fight. As Geel Piet would say, 'If you hit them enough in between the heart and the belt the legs will soon melt.'

To my surprise, in the second round he continued to be the aggressor. I'd never seen him fight better. His punches were crisp and finding their mark disconcertingly often. In the middle of the round I changed to a southpaw stance. This confused him enough to get me through the round with no more punishment. And while I'd put a lot of hard work into his body he'd won the round, I felt sure. When a fighter gets set and is able to move his opponent into the corners, he can do a lot of harm and look very good.

I hated to lose the second round, it gives your opponent the psychological advantage, knowing he's going into the last round with his tail up. Besides, it gives the referee a chance to call a draw if the final round isn't convincing.

The extra weight Jannie had gained had increased his strength and he had seemed to take in his stride the punishment I'd given him.

Jannie knew he had to make the final round look good, and I knew I had to make it look great. As a fighter he had the edge over a boxer, the aggressor moving relentlessly forward is a crowd pleaser and a partisan crowd is apt to forget the winner is the guy who lands the most clean punches. I hoped the ref was good enough to call it correctly but with a home crowd like this a close decision in my favour would get us lynched.

Jannie began the final round by circling me, boxing clever. I had switched back from a southpaw stance and he was no match for me as a boxer, provided I stayed in the centre of the ring and off the ropes. I held him off easily enough. He kept moving in close, trying to throw the left hook to the head, the punch he'd decided would take me out. I could have kept him off with a straight right, just jabbing away and scoring, but I felt I was fast enough to keep my head out of the way of his vicious left hook which, every time he threw it, lifted his right elbow and made a delicious target for me to plant a hard left uppercut under his heart. To a percentage boxer like me this was money in the bank.

Geldenhuis threw another hard left hook which caught me a glancing blow on the side of the head. I didn't even have to look, the right elbow would be way up in the air and I drove a left hook in as hard as I could. The light suddenly left his eyes, Geel Piet was right as usual, his head had gone.

I changed onto the front foot and into attack. The sudden onslaught caught Geldenhuis completely by surprise and gaps in his defence opened up everywhere. His concept of me as a boxer who worked mostly off the back foot was so completely fixed in his mind that he was unable to respond to the fighter who now brought the fight to him, hitting him seemingly at will. He dropped his defences as he reached out too soon for a clinch and I caught him on the point of the jaw with a right cross which knocked him into the ropes, leaving his midriff exposed as his hands shot up into the air. I moved in with another of Geel Piet's eight-punch combinations, all of them clean, hard punches even though they were thrown at short range. He pulled me into a clinch and the ref separated us. I'd taken the stuffing out of him and thirty seconds later he missed with a right and the left that followed and I hit him with the best punch I had thrown in my life, a right uppercut which packed everything I had behind it and caught him perfectly under the point of the chin.

It was the first absolute knockout I'd ever achieved. Jannie Geldenhuis went down like a sack of potatoes and lay sprawled on the canvas. I retired quickly to a neutral corner; while he hadn't moved I fully expected him to take the eight count before getting up. The ref stood over him counting; at seven Geldenhuis managed to get up onto his elbow but that was all. At ten he slumped back onto the canvas.

The ref moved over and held my hand up. The audience was clearly stunned. After their initial shock, and as Jannie got to his feet, they stood up and gave me a really big round of applause. Hymie jumped into the ring and held my arm up again, which was unnecessary. Jannie Geldenhuis helped by his seconds climbed through the ropes without coming over.

I grinned. 'Christ Hymie, what a preliminary for getting the punters ready to bet on a game of rugby.'

'Couldn't be better if I'd set it up myself,' he said.

We climbed from the ropes and the Helpmekaar chaps made way for us as we walked towards the door. 'Promise me something, Hymie.'

'Yeah, sure, what is it?'

'Promise me you didn't set this all up?'

'Are you crazy! What about that anti-semitic bastard?'

'You got your revenge, that was the quickest fifty quid anybody ever had.' We had reached the privacy of the showers and Hymie started to giggle. Soon we were thumping each other on the back and howling with laughter.

On the way back in the bus I turned to Hymie. 'You haven't answered my question.'

'What question?'

'Was today a set-up?'

Hymie looked down at his hands, 'Technically no. But when you bring the right elements together you're entitled to expect a predictable outcome.'

'I ought to bust your teeth, Hymie Solomon Levy! I ought to do it right now!'

We repeated the attractive odds at the Prince of Wales and as we had expected the gentlemen Christians bet heavily on Helpmekaar to win. School spirit was one thing but money was quite another. Only the Wellington House boarders, Darby and Sarge and the under fifteen team itself bet on the Prince of Wales School. Setting the odds up as he had done had the result of inspiring the under fifteens enormously. The David and Goliath syndrome was operating, Hymie's psychology was perfect, by the day of the game we really thought we could win. At Helpmekaar it was hoped it would have a different effect, for while the Afrikaans punters bet heavily on their team to win, the team itself should have felt a little uneasy. Why would we make the Prince of Wales School the favourite, when virtually the same team we were fielding had been beaten on four previous occasions? Like ours, their team contained a number of boxers in its ranks and they'd seen how we had improved out of sight in the ring, to the point where we had drawn the last boxing tournament with them. If we could do it in boxing. . . ? Hymie and I were known not to be fools.

Hymie's poison, we hoped, was working.

Despite being only an under fifteens match, the game drew the biggest crowd of the season. The punters from both schools were out in full and Hymie was still taking bets when the two teams were lined up on the field. He had even got the school pipe major to play 'Scotland the Brave' out in the middle before we ran on. It was grand stuff.

The ref blew his whistle and Atherton kicked off, a short kick which landed in the middle of their forwards. Pissy Johnson, by some miracle, got there first and bowled over the Helpmekaar forward who caught the ball. A loose scrum formed but the ball wouldn't come out and the ref blew his whistle for a set scrum.

It was our loose head and, despite a big push from Helpmekaar, the ball came to me quite cleanly. We were halfway between the halfway mark and their twenty-five and Atherton was standing almost on the halfway line directly behind me. I knew he was going to go for the drop kick which, even for him, seemed a bit ambitious. I flipped the ball back at him as their flankers broke away and seemingly with time to spare he put the ball straight through the posts for four points. It was the best drop kick I had ever seen from him and it set the tone of the match.

Shortly afterwards we scored a converted try and just before half-time they landed a free kick. At half-time it was nine three, but their heavier pack was taking its toll and we were exhausted.

In the second half they closed down the game and eventually scored by pushing our lighter pack over the line. It was nine to eight with ten minutes to go and I could see our forwards were dead on their feet. It was just a matter of time before they scored. Somehow we hung on, tackling everything in sight.

Hymie had the pipe major on the sideline and he was blasting away, but we were too tired to care or even hear him. Geldenhuis had given me a torrid time and was over anxious to get at me. On two occasions during these last minutes of the game when they were camped on our line I'd dummied a pass from the scrum and his over-eagerness to get to me put him off-side and gave us a free kick. These two relieving kicks alone may well have saved us.

With two minutes to go we packed down for a scrum on

our five yard line. It was our loose head but they were pushing us hard towards the line. Somehow we managed to ruck the ball. I dummied a pass to our fullback and Geldenhuis hesitated for a fraction of a second, enough time for me to move down the blind side. I drew their wing and passed to Atherton who'd come round with me. He cut inside, drew their fly-half and kicked the ball across field towards the far corner posts. Lyell, our right winger, beat the full-back to the ball and scored in the corner. The Prince of Wales School went beserk, despite the fact that they'd all lost their money. Atherton failed to convert the try but we'd won twelve to eight.

When all the bets were counted and we'd paid the faithful handful who'd bet against Helpmekaar we were left with four hundred and eighty-seven pounds, fifteen shillings and sixpence. Of the eighteen hundred kids in the two schools almost every one of them had a bet on the outcome. It was the mightiest scam of all time and my share paid Solly Goldman for the next three and a half years.

Hymie broke out a fiver for a party in the team dressing room and sent Geldenhuis and the Helpmekaar team a case of Pepsi and four dozen cream buns. He opened a cream bun and placed a tenner in it and put it on top of the pile of buns going to Helpmekaar dressing room. 'That will teach the hairy back to do business with a Jewboy,' he laughed.

The Solly Goldman Gym in Sauer Street was just like any gym you've read about. It smelt of sweat, chalk, liniment and hope. Solly ran his gym colour blind, the way gyms are run the world over. His only concession to apartheid was a locker room for non-Europeans. The rest depended on your skill as a boxer. The Johannesburg police turned a blind eye to Solly's personal race integration programme. The police commissioner, Kruger, was a boxing man, and to boxing men black isn't black in the ring. Too many great black boxers existed in the world and a man jabbing a pair of twelve ounce gloves into your face wasn't a dirty Kaffir, he was a boxer, if only for the duration of the fight.

While a number of amateurs worked out in the gym, none of them was instructed by Solly, who had his work cut out handling the pros. Boxing was becoming a big time sport in the African townships surrounding Johannesburg and Solly had a regular stable of black fighters he trained in return for a percentage of the purse. Black and white boxers were not allowed to fight in public for the same title but they'd spar together and sometimes the sparring would get out of hand when a white or a black guy, but it was mostly the white boxers, decided to have a go. Solly would let it go for a couple of rounds, particularly when it looked as though the white man was getting a bit of a drubbing.

The first time Hymie and I appeared, Solly put me in with a young pro bantamweight who hadn't been out of the amateur ranks very long. After two rounds he stopped the sparring session.

'Who taught you to box, Peekay?'

I told him about Geel Piet without giving him the exact details.

'Next time you see him, my boy, you give him my compliments.'

'He's dead, Solly.'

Solly cocked his bald head to one side. 'Well he didn't die in vain, my son, he's given you an almost perfect grounding, you use the ring like a wizard.'

'Thank you,' I said, not quite knowing what else to say. Solly Goldman was the best and I found his over-generous compliments unnerving.

'Thank me later, my boy, there's a lot of work to get through. You need a little more starch in your left hand and your right is no great shakes niver. Like all amateurs you're looking for points, you hold your hands too bleedin' high. You're fast enough to drop 'em a little and give yourself more punching power. We'll get you onto weights and build up your upper body. It would also be very comforting indeed to know you also packed a good left right combination. Before I'm through with you, my son, you're going to be the only amateur boxer in South Africa who can put a thirteen-punch combo together. That's the show stopper, that's the one man band that starts with a bleedin' mouf organ and ends with a big bass drum.'

I was amazed that Solly Goldman, a cockney Jew from London, could read so much into my boxing after watching me for only two rounds. But he was true to his word. By the Christmas holidays I was a vastly improved boxer with a lot more power in both hands. We fought as usual in the Eastern Transvaal Championships that December and Captain Smit couldn't believe the difference. The championships were in Barberton and it seemed the whole town turned out to see me box. My mother stayed at home but my granpa had a ringside seat with Doc, Mrs Boxall, Miss Bornstein and old Mr Bornstein. Miss Bornstein told me later that old Mr Bornstein winced every time I threw a punch, while Doc, by now a seasoned campaigner, pretended to take it all in his stride.

I was awarded the trophy for best boxer in the tournament, and afterwards my granpa and I walked home while Mrs Boxall drove Doc to his cottage. We reached the front gate and my granpa patted me on the shoulder. 'I've never been so proud in my life, son,' he said and then, to cover his embarrassment, reached into his white linen jacket for his pipe.

I had been home a week. The train from Johannesburg arrived at Nelspruit at nine am on the previous Saturday morning. Usually I would then go on to Kaapmuiden and wait until mid-afternoon for the coffee pot to Barberton which would crawl exhausted into town about eight in the evening. But to my delight Gert was waiting for me at Nelspruit.

'Ag man, we had to put in some papers here about a white drunk and disorderly who attacked a prison gang with a pick handle so Captain Smit said take the car and pick up Peekay at the same time.' He extended his hand, 'How goes it, man?'

On the road back to Barberton, Gert told me that Doc had been in a storm in the hills and had caught pneumonia and spent a week in hospital. 'He's looking old, Peekay. I reckon he'll be making his peace pretty soon.'

I was stunned. 'He's a tough old bugger, he'll be okay I'm telling you,' I said, more to give myself comfort than as a reply.

'Ja, he's tough all right, but the old bugger must be eighty-five, maybe more, he can't last forever, man.'

'Well, he's still climbing into the hills, that's something at least.'

'Not since he was sick, he talks about it, about when you get back, but I dunno, man, I reckon he's finish and klaar. I told him I'll send a gang any time to work in the cactus garden but he says he can still manage. But I dunno, man.'

I said nothing. A huge lump grew in my throat and the road in front of me blurred. The thought of Doc not being there when I returned home from school was too distressing even to contemplate.

'Those two abafazi at your house look after him like he's a chief. They spend all their spare time over at his place and they bring food every day and now they even shave him.'

Doc was the most independent person I'd ever known and I knew at once that Gert wasn't imagining things. If Dee and Dum had to shave him his hands must have become very shaky.

I had bought Dee and Dum a Singer hand machine and they'd turned their sewing into a regular little business making cotton shifts for many of the local house servants. My mother and Marie had shown them how to cut out and how to make buttonholes and hem by hand and they were going great guns. I had learned by accident that Dee and Dum were using their small earnings from sewing to look after Doc who could no longer take in his little girls for

507

music lessons. When I could after that, I would send them money for him. The Bank was a regular source of income and I could generally manage a pound a week and what with one or two other scams Hymie and I had going, between the girls and me, Doc was okay.

Realising that my mother would expect me home on the coffee pot, I asked Gert to drop me off at the bottom of Doc's road. Hiding my suitcase under some bushes I climbed up to the cottage. He was sitting in the shade on the stoep in his favourite riempie chair and I thought he must be asleep. But he looked up and saw me approaching and rose from his chair a little stiffly, one hand on the small of his back. His six foot seven frame almost touched the rafters of the verandah and he seemed to be swaying slightly as his arms went out to me. I ran up to him and he put his hands on my shoulders and then I could no longer contain myself and I grabbed him fiercely.

'Please, Doc, please don't die,' I sobbed.

Doc and I seldom showed emotion, our love each for the other was so fierce that it burned like a flame inside of us. But now I was suddenly overcome, Gert's conversation on the way over mixed with the emotion of seeing him standing with his arms outstretched to me, frail as a wisp of smoke, was too much.

His hand came round and patted me on the back. 'Absoloodle! We have no time to die, Peekay, the hills are still green and waiting, it is not yet time for the crystal cave of Africa.'

I pulled away from him and he sat down in his chair. Still sniffing I wiped my eyes with the back of my hand. 'You've been sick, Doc. Gert told me you've been sick?'

'Just a bad cold, Peekay. It was nothing.'

'It was pneumonia!'

'Ja this is true, but some pneumonia is big, some is small, this was a *pickaninny*, a very small pneumonia for sure and absoloodle.' He rose again from the chair. 'Come I make coffee, Peekay.'

508

'Marie will tell me how bad it was.'

Doc threw up his hands. 'Marie! Such a person! "Professor you must give your life to Jesus, there is not much time. You must choose between the eternal damnation of hellfire or the love of Jesus Christ." I think maybe I stay a little longer here, miss, I say to this Marie. I think she was quite a lot disappointed. Ja, I think so,' Doc said, chuckling as he poured a mug of strong black coffee for me, holding the coffee pot in both hands to stop himself shaking.

We sat on the verandah sipping our coffee in big tin mugs, Doc's only half full so that he wouldn't spill it. He was up to all his tricks to hide his frailty. We said very little, I could see Doc was happy I was back and I felt I would give him strength. We talked about the crystal cave of Africa, which Doc now regarded as our greatest discovery.

'It is good we are together again, Peekay. On Christmas Day I will be eighty-seven years old.'

'Doc, you've got to live until I'm welterweight champion of the world, you've got to make it until you're at least ninety-four or five!'

Doc chuckled at the urgency in my voice and rose slowly from his chair. 'Come, I show you *Pachypodium namaquanum*. It grows so big, maybe we have the world champion here also.'

As we walked together into the cactus garden, Doc still tall and straight as *Pachypodium namaquanum* himself, there seemed to be a little more spring in his step. 'Next week we will go into the mountains, Peekay, it has been too long.'

We did, mostly skirting the foothills and taking the easy paths, but Doc seemed to gain strength and was much better by the time I returned to school in mid-January.

TWENTY-ONE

Nineteen forty-eight was a great year in South Africa's history. Princess Elizabeth had recently toured and we'd all stood beside the road and waved flags and caught a glimpse of our future Queen as she rode past in a long, black, open Rolls-Royce.

It was the year South Africa got white bread, an event which excited a lot more people than catching a glimpse of the future Queen of England.

History will tell of how the election of the Nationalist Party, who still hold power in South Africa forty years later, was the turning point when the Afrikaner once again became the dominant force in the country. History is bound to treat this event with great pontification, showing how the struggle between the two white tribes of Africa reached its climax. In fact the turning point came, not because of an ideological clash between white and white, but because the Nationalists promised to bring back white bread to replace the healthier wholewheat loaf which had been introduced during the war. An already overfed white minority elected to vote on its stomach. Within a week of being elected, the Nationalists kept their promise and white South Africans derived great satisfaction from knowing that for once they had a new government which kept its word. Meanwhile, the black South Africans prepared to bend their backs to the sjambok and for the invention of a new game where they voluntarily fell on their heads from the third storey of police headquarters to the pavement below. It was curious that the whites, renowned for their sporting prowess, never learned how to play this game and there isn't a single instance of a white South African becoming proficient at it. Nobody ever got their Springbok blazer for this new national game, even though a lot of very good heads played it with great courage.

Hymie, in a grim pun, said the election of the Nationalists to power was one of the crummiest moments in the history of any people.

Nineteen forty-eight was the year South Africa lost all hope of joining the brotherhood of man. Yet the black man held his humiliation and his anger at bay. It was not until nineteen fifty-two, four years later, that Chief Lutuli of the African Congress and his counterpart, Dr Monty Naicker of the Indian Congress, led the black and coloured people in the first defiance campaign where the words, 'Mayibuye Afrika!' became the cry of the black man asking for an equal share of justice and dignity for himself and his family.

Private schools have a habit of carrying on regardless, oblivious of social or political change. Had it not been for a boxing incident which led to the establishment of a Saturday night school for Africans, the Prince of Wales School would certainly have remained smugly wrapped in its cocoon of privilege and white supremacy.

The incident happened during the ten-day Easter break in nineteen forty-nine. Hymie's parents decided to spend Jewish passover with relatives in Durban. Hymie elected to stay home and invited me to spend the short holidays with him. I wrote to Mrs Boxall who wrote back to say Doc was well so I agreed. The cook and the rest of the staff would take care of us and one of the chauffeurs would drive us the forty miles from Pretoria to Johannesburg every day to work out in Solly Goldman's gym.

Solly protested but we insisted he be paid extra for the holidays. Hymie's entrepreneurial sense extended to all things. He'd go to Barclays Bank in Yeoville on Saturday morning and demand a brand new five-pound note. Keeping it unfolded he'd place it beside the week's entry in a large leather-bound ledger. On Sunday morning, after I'd worked out we'd go into Solly's ramshackle office and Hymie would open the ledger where he had written in his neat, precise hand: *Paid to S. Goldman five pounds for services rendered.* He would make Solly sign the ledger and remove the five-pound note from the page. Then they'd shake hands solemnly like a couple of little old men, whereupon Solly would get his revenge by stuffing the pristine five-pound note carelessly into the back pocket of his dirty grey flannels.

Solly was a very natty street dresser but in the gym he always wore a sweatshirt and the same old grey flannels, tied around the waist with a frayed brown striped tie.

'Why do you go to all that trouble when he just shoves it into his back pocket?' I once asked Hymie.

'So he'll stick it carelessly into his back pocket. Every week my stupid ritual and his defiance reminds him not to take us for granted. Every time he sticks it into his back pocket like that I know he won't.'

On the third day of the Easter holidays Solly asked whether he could see Hymie and me in his office. He pointed to two old cane upright chairs and, pushing a pile of papers out of the way, sat on the corner of a desk covered to a depth of six inches in evenly distributed paper. In addition to boxing bills, unopened letters and general paper clutter, there was a bronze cup about ten inches high green with verdigris, a telephone and a large desk blotter added to the mess. The telephone sat on top of the desk blotter which was covered with coffee rings and hundreds of names and numbers. If anyone had ever replaced the top layer of blotting paper Solly's gym would have ground to a halt.

'You've had an offer of a fight for Peekay in Sophiatown next Saturday night. It's not my decision, mind, but it can't do the lad no 'arm.'

'Sophiatown! You mean the black township?'

'Yeah, I'll admit it's a bit unusual, it's a young black bantam who's just turned pro.'

'Solly, are you crazy? Peekay's an amateur, he can't fight a pro!'

'The black kid's not from up here, he isn't registered in the Transvaal yet. Technically he's an amateur here. Anyway, if the fight takes place in a native township, who the hell's going to know?'

'You should know better than that, Solly.'

Ignoring Hymie's remark, Solly appealed directly to me, 'This fight would do you a lot of good, sharpen you up nicely for the South African Schools Championships an' all.'

'Christ, Solly, you're off your rocker!' Hymie continued. 'You find a professional bantamweight, probably in his twenties, and you want to put him against Peekay who's fifteen years old?'

'That's just the point, my son. Peekay wouldn't be mismatched, the black kid is only just sixteen. Three professional fights. Would I mismatch Peekay? Don't insult my intelligence.'

'Hey, hang on, wait a minute both of you.' I turned to Solly, 'There's more to this isn't there? First we're fighting a black man in a black township, that's not allowed for a start, then an amateur is fighting a pro . . .'

'An unregistered pro,' Solly interjected.

'You haven't answered my question, Solly,' I repeated.

'It's not what you're thinking, Peekay, there's no money in it, there would be no purse for the fight.'

'What about the book?' Hymie asked.

'No betting niver, Gawd's onna!' Solly folded his hands on the desk in front of him and stared down at the untidy blotter.

'We're waiting, Solly,' Hymie said.

'It's Nguni, he wants the fight . . . Mr Nguni.'

'Who's he when he's at home?' I asked.

'He's a black fight promoter. Owns the game in the black townships.'

'So what's that to us?' I asked.

Solly looked up at me. 'He reckons if 'e was to match you with this Mandoma bloke it would be a t'riffic fight, that's all.'

'If you'll come clean with the real reason you want this fight we could discuss it. What is it, Solly?' I asked again.

Solly threw his hands up. 'Okay, it's business. Mr Nguni brings in the blacks, I train 'em, we share in the action. When you've got fifteen percent of fifty black fighters on the black township circuit it's a nice little earner. I don't honestly know why 'e wants this fight, I admit it don't make a lotta sense.'

Hymie spoke as though he was thinking aloud. 'The black guy is squeezing you and now you're putting the hard word on us. I can understand that. But even if he is making book, and you say he isn't, that's not a big enough reason. He could lose his boxing promoter's licence if he got caught.'

'Hymie's right, Solly. There has to be a better reason. Nguni is either a fool or he's taking an enormous risk for a reason we don't know about. Either way, we wouldn't want to get involved. By the way this Mandoma, is he a Zulu? I had a nanny named Mandoma.'

'Buggered if I know, until they earn me a quid they're just black monkeys wearing boxing gloves,' Solly said absently.

Hymie's chauffeur was waiting in the Buick which was parked on a vacant lot a block away. As we walked to the car Hymie kept shaking his head. 'I don't get it; this Nguni guy would have to be crazy to take the risk of putting on a fight between a nigger pro and an amateur white guy in a black township. The cops would have him on about ten counts. I mean what's the angle? A fifteen-year-old schoolboy boxer and a sixteen-year-old black bantamweight is not exactly big time, even in a black township.'

'You haven't figured it out have you?' I said quietly.

'No, not yet, but I will.'

'Don't bother, it's got something to do with the people.'

Hymie spun around and grabbed me, 'You're right, Pee-kay. The Tadpole Angel!'

We turned into the vacant lot to find the Buick shining like a great black beetle among the cut down forty-four gallon drums half filled with solid tar, piles of bricks and the accumulated debris that seems to furnish vacant city blocks. The chauffeur was talking with a tall, well-dressed African and stepped forward as he saw us approaching.

'Well, we're going to know what the scam is in about thirty seconds. Look who's here, Hymie.' The tall black man straightened slightly as we came up. He was the tall African who always led the people in the chant to the Tadpole Angel.

'This man he want speak you, baas,' the chauffeur said to me.

'I see you,' I said in Zulu to the African who towered above me.

'I see you, Inkosi,' he replied and shook my extended hand lightly, barely touching it. Politeness required that we talk about other things before coming to the reason he wanted to speak to me. This is the Zulu way.

'The weather has been hot and the rains have not come, where I come from the crops will be thirsty.'

'It is so also in my place, the herd boys will need to drive the cattle far from the kraal to find grazing and the river will be dry but for a few water holes.'

'What's he saying?' Hymie chipped in.

'Nothing yet, we're still talking about the weather.'

'Your kraal is a far place from here?'

'Many, many miles, Inkosi, my kraal is near Ulundi in Zululand.' The royal homesteads of three out of the four great Zulu kings, Dingane, Mpande and Cetshwayo, had been near Ulundi and the chances were that the tall man in front of me was a high-born Zulu.

'It is a long way from your wives and children, it is not good to be away from them.'

'It is the custom, Inkosi. For the white man's pound the

black man must leave his family. These are hard times and I have few cattle and land.'

The time had come to introduce myself. 'I am Peekay,' I said softly, extending my hand for a second time.

'I know this, Inkosi. I am Nguni.' We shook hands a second time, this time first in the conventional manner and then by slipping the hand over the corresponding thumb to grip it in a kind of salute which is a traditional African handshake.

'I see you, Nguni.'

'I see you, Peekay.' It was audacious of Nguni to call me by my name but I didn't mind. I felt as though he had known me a long time anyway.

'Is it about the business of the boxing in Sophiatown?'

'It is so,' Nguni confirmed softly.

'Can we speak in English so my friend can share this talk?'

Nguni laughed, showing a brilliant smile. 'My English she is not so good,' he said in English.

Nguni's English turned out to be very good and Hymie seemed relieved that he could share in the conversation.

'It's about the Sophiatown business,' I said to him.

'Ask him, no wait on, I'll ask him myself . . .'

'Hymie, this is Mr Nguni,' I turned to Nguni. 'This is my best friend, Hymie Levy.'

'How do you do,' Nguni said to Hymie, instinctively not extending his hand but bowing his head slightly instead.

'Howzit!' Hymie said, not yet used to the idea of meeting a black man on equal terms. 'Why did you ask Mr Goldman if you could arrange a fight with Peekay?'

Nguni looked surprised. 'It is always so in boxing, to ask the trainer?'

'I'm the manager, it is me you have to ask.'

Nguni threw back his head and laughed. 'We knew this thing, but also if your trainer he say this thing cannot happen I do not think you will listen?'

'What did you offer him to make him agree?'

'It is not necessary, he has boxing business same like me.'

'How many boxers have you got, Mr Nguni?'

'All,' Nguni replied simply.

'You're not bullshitting me, you control all township boxers?'

Nguni turned to me and said in Zulu, 'Your friend has no respect, Inkosi.'

'I apologise for him, Nguni. He acts only like a white man from the city.' I turned to Hymie. 'Turn it up.'

Hymie shook his head. 'Sorry, Mr Nguni, no hard feelings hey? This fight you want . . . it's just that it doesn't bloody well make sense.'

Nguni turned to me and spoke in Zulu. 'I will have to explain it in Zulu, this man I think he does not understand the ways of the people.'

'Mr Nguni's going to explain the reason to me in Zulu, it's evidently pretty complicated,' I said to Hymie.

'You are Onoshobishobi Ingelosi,' Nguni began, 'this is very powerful among the people. The people see you box only against the Boer and always you are winning also. The people think you are a great chief of their tribe, the Sotho think this, the Shangaan think this, the Zulu also, all the people,' he paused, 'I think this also. It is witnessed that you can make the stars fall from the heavens.'

'It is not true, Nguni. I am not a chief of the people,' I said quickly.

'Who is to say what is true and what is not true. The people know these things, it is not for you to say, Inkosi.'

'It's about the Tadpole Angel, we were right,' I said to Hymie.

'There is a woman who has thrown the bones and made a fire to read the smoke,' Nguni said suddenly. 'The bones say Onoshobishobi Ingelosi who is a chief must fight him who is also a chief among the people.'

'A witchdoctor? She said this?'

'This is so, Inkosi.'

'This chief. Who is this chief I must fight?'

'He is the great great grandson of Cetshwayo.'

'Pssh! Many such Zulus exist. Cetshwayo has surely many, many great great grandsons.'

'He is the one,' Nguni said quietly. The Zulus do not inherit titles but it is known who has the blood. 'One day he will be a chief.'

'Why is it necessary to fight this person who will one day be a chief?'

'The people must see if the spirit is still with you. You are a man now, the people knew the spirit of a great chief was in the small one, but now they must know if it is still in the man.'

'You mean if I lose to him who will be a chief, then I will no longer be Onoshobishobi Ingelosi?'

'This is so, Inkosi. The woman says this is in the bones and in the smoke.'

'Then I will lose,' I said suddenly. 'That way the legend will be dead.'

Nguni shrugged his shoulders. 'It is not for me to say, Inkosi. You will only lose if you are not Onoshobishobi Ingelosi.'

'But if you can arrange the fight it will be good for you as a promoter?'

Nguni looked down at the palms of his open hands which were almost yellow, the colour of Sunlight soap. 'This is true but it is expected I should do this thing. Have I not led the people to all your fights?'

'This is true, you are the one,' I said, ashamed of myself.

'Then you will fight?'

'First we must talk to Hymie, he is my brother in this matter.'

'I understand, it is right that it should be so.'

Hymie was clearly impatient to get a translation and when I told him what had been said he shook his head. 'Christ, it's witchcraft, Peekay. This is nineteen forty-nine!'

'Ja, I know, but it might as well be eighteen forty-nine. Some things don't change.'

'So what do we do?' he asked.

'We fight, we have no choice.'

'I don't understand? Why?'

'It's difficult for you, but the people believe in the Tadpole Angel. I've never said this before, but it's a symbol, a symbol of hope. There is a story amongst all the tribes that a chief will rise who is not of them but who will unite them against the oppressors.'

'It is so, Mr Levy,' Nguni said.

'And this is the test to see if you're kosher?'

I laughed despite myself. 'Hymie, I didn't start this, it just happened. I don't want it any more than you. If the young Zulu chief Mandoma gives me a hiding, it's all over. But I can't walk away without the fight, that would make a fool of the people all these years. I couldn't do that.'

'What a shit of a possie to be in, but it's not a good enough reason to throw the fight.'

'You know me better than that, Hymie.' I turned to Nguni and offered him my hand, 'Mr Nguni, tell the people I will fight this one who will be a chief.'

'I will tell the people,' he said.

I set about preparing for the fight with Mandoma the Zulu bantamweight with all the vigour and purpose I could command. While I longed to be rid of the concept involving the Tadpole Angel it was quite impossible for me to bring myself to the point where I would throw the fight. I had steeled myself to win so often that, in my mind, a single loss in the ring would have meant that I would not become the welterweight champion of the world. A childish concept perhaps, but nonetheless one which was bound with steel wire through my resolve. I had even taught myself never to consider the consequences of losing a fight. Too much cross-referencing of consequence robs the will of its single-minded concentration to win. While this fanatical resolve never to be beaten may have been a sign of immaturity, the sophistication I brought to the task of winning I was to see adopted by sports psychiatrists throughout the world in later years. The mental exercises adopted, first behind the Iron Curtain and then worldwide, in an attempt to win that endless cold war called the Olympic Games or any of the other master race events, were all familiar to me.

The greatest difficulty confronting me with the Mandoma fight was information. We knew nothing about the Zulu bantamweight. I always felt awkward going into a fight with an unknown opponent. It was like entering a dark room having been told to beware of the trap doors. If you know everything there is to know about an opponent your mind will do the fighting for you, triggering the body mechanism to do the things it needs to do a fraction faster. It is this fraction that makes for a winner.

The power of one is above all things the power to believe in yourself, often well beyond any latent ability you may have previously demonstrated. The mind is the athlete; the body is simply the means it uses to run faster or longer, jump higher, shoot straighter, kick better, swim harder, hit further or box better. Hoppie's dictum to me: 'First with the head and then with heart' was more than simply mixing brains with guts. It meant thinking well beyond the powers of normal concentration and then daring your courage to follow your thoughts.

Saturday arrived. The fight was to take place in a ring set up in an African school soccer field in Sophiatown. We arrived about four-thirty on the outskirts where Mr Nguni was waiting for us.

The roads were dusty and it had been a hot day. Dust clung to the whitewashed walls of shanties and shops and everywhere there were advertising signs, for Gold Seal Cooking Lard, Blue Light Paraffin, Primus Stoves, Drum Tobacco and Sunlight Soap. There were a few trucks on the road and we saw one native taxi and several buses crowded to the point of bulging, though hundreds of people were on bicycles. The chauffeur kept an almost constant hand on the horn, which only seemed to add to the sense of excitement. As we drew closer to the school, people were lining the dusty narrow streets which seemed to weave haphazardly in among shanties built from every conceivable kind of material. Mr Nguni requested I turn my window down so the people could see me. Blushing, I complied. 'You are very famous in this place, Peekay. The people have come for many, many miles to see you.'

'Why are they all women and children?' Hymie asked.

'It is the men who will see the fight. The women they have come to see the Onoshobishobi Ingelosi.'

'Christ, I had no idea. You're more famous than Johnny Ralph, Peekay.' Johnny Ralph was the reigning heavyweight champion of South Africa and a household name among whites.

Mr Nguni laughed. 'Johnny Ralph, they do not know who is this boxer in Sophiatown.'

'Mr Nguni,' I said, 'you must tell the people I am not a chief. I have no power. You must tell them that the Onoshobishobi Ingelosi is only a name, a name I was given at the prison in Barberton. It was for nothing.'

Mr Nguni turned to me in the back seat. He was clearly shocked. 'I cannot do this thing, Inkosi. It is not for me to say who is Onoshobishobi Ingelosi. Tonight we will see, we cannot change this thing, it is in the bones and in the smoke.' He turned back to the chauffeur to give a direction.

'Shit! He believes it himself,' Hymie said out of the corner of his mouth.

We turned into the school grounds and were met by a sea of Africans. The Buick was forced to inch its way through the crowd. It was an hour and a half before the fight and the soccer ground was totally full, with only a narrow aisle leading to the ring in the centre. There must have been ten thousand spectators with more pouring through the school gates.

'I thought you said it would be a fight in a school,' Hymie said to Mr Nguni. 'I thought you meant a school hall or something. The whole of Africa has come to see the bloody fight! What if there's trouble, a riot or something?'

'No, no! No trouble here, Mr Levy. The woman, she will speak to the people.'

'You mean the witchdoctor?' I asked.

'It is she, Peekay, she will speak to the people.'

Hymie grinned nervously, 'It's got to be the first time a witch-doctor has ever announced a fight. Are you sure you've told me everything there is to know about you, Peekay?'

I grabbed him by the shirtfront, 'Don't *you* start now!'

We were taken to a shower block to change. Solly Goldman was waiting for us. 'They're doing it kosher orright, they've got Natkin Patel, the Indian referee from Durban to handle the fight. Blimey! 'Ave you see the crowd?'

I changed and we walked along to the school hall for the weigh in. Hymie looked at the scales, they'd been borrowed from a local trader and were the kind on which bags of mealie meal are usually weighed. 'What's the bloody difference, we're going to fight him anyway, even if he's over the limit,' Hymie said.

'It is very important, Mr Levy. The people must know everything is correct,' Mr Nguni said.

Standing in the middle of the school hall beside the scales were a dozen or so Africans all neatly dressed in suits and ties. Though the suit parts were not always of the same parentage, they were clean and pressed. Standing to one side was Gideon Mandoma, the Zulu bantamweight I was to fight.

I broke away from Solly and Hymie and walked over to him and extended my hand. 'I see you, Gideon Mandoma,' I said in Zulu.

Gideon Mandoma took my hand, barely shaking it. He did not look up as he replied, 'I see you, Peekay.'

'I hear you come from the Tugela River Valley. It is where my nanny came from when I was a small infant, her name was Mary Mandoma, was she from the same chief's kraal perhaps?'

Gideon Mandoma looked up at me, his eyes wide, a shocked expression on his face. 'The one you are asking about is my mother. She is dead now five years.' He pointed a finger at me. 'You are the one of the night water?'

It was my turn to be shocked. I stood in front of the Zulu fighter completely stunned. I was going to fight Nanny's son, the infant she had had to leave to look after me. It was I who had stolen the milk from her breasts when she had been hired to be first my wet nurse and then my nanny.

Gideon was the first to recover. 'They say you are a chief, but must prove you have the spirit of Onoshobishobi Ingelosi. I know I am a chief and have the spirit of Cetshwayo and before that of Mpande, Dingane and even of Shaka the king of all the kings.' His eyes grew suddenly hard. He had waited a long time and now he would fight the one who had taken his mother from him so that he had not known her until he was six years old. It was not meant to be like this, but for him there was now an added reason to win. To the Zulu there is no such thing as coincidence. I knew this would be a certain and powerful sign for him. Gideon Mandoma had a reason greater than my own to win. For the first time in my boxing career I was afraid. I knew Mandoma could beat me.

We weighed in in front of Solly, Mr Nguni, Natkin Patel the Indian referee and the other Africans. Both of us made it into the bantamweight limit, though I had five pounds to spare and Gideon was right on the limit.

The sun was setting as we walked out to the ring and already the air smelt of wood smoke and coal fires. It was still bloody hot and I'd been drinking water all day. I wondered about Mandoma, if he'd been right on the limit he'd have stayed off liquids, and we were fighting a six rounder, my first ever. It was the compromise Solly had reached with Mr Nguni, the difference between the three rounds of an amateur fight and the ten of a professional. It struck me that if I could keep him moving around the ring, the black fighter might just dehydrate enough to weaken in the last two rounds.

An old woman wearing a tired looking fur coat over a shapeless dress was haranguing the crowd from the ring. Her high-pitched voice carried to where we were standing on the steps of the school building. As she came to the end of her talk the crowd responded in thunderous applause. Two men entered the ring and lifted her and two others standing outside the ring took her from them.

'It is time. We must go now, please,' Mr Nguni said, and he led us down the narrow human corridor to the ring, following a rubber electrical cord which connected with a microphone. Gideon Mandoma and his seconds had preceded us by a few yards and the whole football field thundered to the roar of the crowd. We entered the ring almost together, though from opposite sides, and the human roar increased. Hymie and Solly were my seconds and Hymie moved over to the black fighter's corner to check the glove-up, while a large Zulu in a mismatched suit with the jacket straining at its single brown button came over to do the same for us. I could feel the sweat running down from my armpits as Solly taped my hands and gloved me up.

Mr Nguni held his arms up and slowly the crowd grew silent. The microphone on a stand had been lifted into the ring and his voice echoed around the field as he addressed the crowd. First he introduced the referee, pointing out that he was an Indian who had come from Durban especially for the fight. The point of his neutrality was not lost on the crowd who gave Natkin Patel a big hand.

Mr Nguni then told the crowd that they all knew why this fight had been arranged. It was not for him to talk about it anymore. The talking would now be between the two spirits and the stronger would win and the people would know what they could think. The crowd was completely hushed as he spoke. He then introduced Gideon

Mandoma who, arms held high, moved to the centre of the ring to huge applause. Mr Nguni held his hands up for silence and then asked the crowd to sing 'Nkosi Sikelel' i Afrika', the African national anthem.

Ten thousand voices sang in perfect harmony and I shall forever remember the beauty of the moment. The yearning and love Africans put into this anthem is a hugely emotional experience. I was hard put to keep my concentration. Gideon Mandoma had the perfect reason to win the fight and now had been given the greatest inspiration any boxer ever had.

I was having trouble keeping the steel trap in my mind closed. Images of Nanny swept through my head. A sweet, dark woman who gave me unstintingly of her love, who never once mentioned the child torn from her when her breasts were still firm with milk. Gideon Mandoma had a right to hate me and hate is a good friend in a fight.

Next Mr Nguni called me to the centre of the ring and, to my surprise, the applause was just as thunderous. As I stood there he began the chant of the Tadpole Angel, his voice ringing out to the silent crowd. When it came time to respond with the chorus 'Onoshobishobi Ingelosi . . . shobi . . . shobi . . . Ingelosi', ten thousand voices rolled like thunder. I stood in the centre of the ring, the tears rolling down my cheeks. It was perhaps the greatest single moment of my life. The people wanted to know. This was not a fight between black and white, it was a testing of the spirit, the spirit of Africa itself. Two kids, not fully grown, on a hot summer evening that smelt of wood smoke and sweat, would decide if there was hope for white and black and coloured, for the people of the great Southland.

'Mayibuye Afrika!' Mr Nguni shouted.

'Mayibuye Afrika! Afrika! Afrika! Come back, Africa! Come back, Africa!' the crowd thundered back.

Handing the microphone carefully through the ropes, Mr Nguni left the ring and Natkin Patel called us over. He had deep pock marks over his face which was almost precisely the colour of good curry, silly as that comparison sounds. His steel-grey hair was brylcreamed flat across his head, the parting absolutely straight with not a single hair crossing the shiny road of his scalp. He was dressed in a white shirt, cream flannels and white tackies and looked more like a cricketer than a boxing referee. We both looked down at the ground as he spoke.

'You are listening to me, please. When I am shouting break you must break, at once. When a knockdown is coming I am counting to eight, then I wipe your gloves also and then you continue. No heads, no elbows, you must fight clean or, by golly, I am giving you penalty points. Good luck, boys.' He patted us both lightly on the shoulders. 'Shake hands, when the bell is sounding please to come out fighting.' Our gloves touched lightly though neither of us looked at the other.

I walked back to my corner and sat down. The bell rang. 'Go get him, Peekay,' I heard Hymie say as he pulled the stool out of my corner. I jumped up towards a blur of brown coming towards me across the ring.

Mandoma was coming at me fast, throwing everything. His punches landed on my arms and my gloves, he had come at me so quickly that he was able to keep me in my corner and I was forced to pull him into a clinch. The ref called for us to break as I managed to swing him around; the sun was in a perfect position, low and dying fast. He turned right into it, blinded for the split second it took for me to put a hard straight left bang on the nose. It was a good punch and a trickle of blood ran from one nostril. I would be bloody lucky to pull that stunt again, the sun wouldn't last more than another round and he'd probably wised up already. Mandoma was enormously aggressive, prepared to waste a dozen blows to break through my defence. Towards the end of the first round he caught me under the heart and I thought I was gone. He packed a left hook like a charging rhino. I was keeping him away by jabbing my left at him. They were all scoring shots but none

526

of them were hurting him. The bastard was terribly strong. I spent the first round looking for bad habits, but apart from the fact that he was throwing too much leather it was going to be difficult to fight him on the back foot. The bell went for the end of round one and already I was sweating profusely.

'Take a look at Mandoma, he's leaking,' Hymie said.

'Christ he hits hard, I'm going to have to keep him moving, keep him off balance.'

'Only for the first four rounds. Look at him.' Hymie was right, Mandoma was in a lather of sweat and with the sun so low it seemed even hotter than before.

'Watch and see if he drinks in round four,' I said to Solly as the bell went for round two.

'Just box him, my son, keep him moving, coming to you,' Solly said quietly.

Mandoma came at me just as hard in the second round, and while I took most of his punches on the gloves and arms, I realised that if he kept it up like this he'd hurt my arms and weaken me that way. I needed to make him miss more but he was fast as blazes and I had all my work cut out staying out of his way. I landed enough good punches to be ahead on points at the end of the second round, but there wasn't much in it and I was using every bit of ringcraft I knew to stay out of trouble.

We came out for the third and again he came at me with the leading hand and crossed over with a right hook that caught me on the side of the jaw. Quite suddenly I was on the canvas, sprawling on my back. I could see two of Mandoma as he retired to the neutral corner and then the ref began to count. I knew I'd been hit hard but felt nothing, my head was ringing and I was using all my concentration to hear the count. At six my eyes suddenly cleared and at eight I was back on my feet. It had been a beautiful punch and I knew I couldn't take too many others like it and survive. Patel wiped my gloves and made me count the three fingers he held up to me, and then six. It was all valuable time and my head had stopped ringing. Finally, he told us to box on.

Mandoma was after blood and came in too fast and carelessly. This alone saved me. If he'd waited to get set for another big punch he would have taken me. He wanted the knockout and his eyes were telegraphing his punches. Halfway through the round I was feeling strong again and I began to work to the old plan. Ignoring his head I went for the body, under the heart, in the soft area under the rib cage and into the solar plexus. He'd throw a wild left hook or a right uppercut and I'd follow in with two or three hard blows to the spot. Nothing fancy, but I could feel my knuckles digging deep. If I could stay away from the big punch and if he kept sending me a letter every time he prepared to throw a punch, I'd eventually get him. I'd been in against fighters most of my life, Mandoma had a bigger punch than any I'd been in the ring with before, and he was bloody fast. But I thought he was becoming predictable as most fighters do.

Had it been the usual three round fight the decision may well have gone to Mandoma. By the fourth round he had started to slow down. He'd been chasing me for three rounds and throwing a lot of leather, the heat had to get to him. But he hadn't taken water, just rinsing and spitting. So I kept going low and hard and toward the end of the fourth round I heard him grunt as I got three solid punches home. It was beginning to go like clockwork. Mandoma pulled me into a clinch and on the break hit me with a beautiful left lead. I thought I'd run into a train. I went down, my arse actually bouncing on the canvas. I couldn't believe it, I shook my head but it wouldn't clear. At the count of eight I was only just able to stand. Mandoma had me, one half decent punch and I was history.

The ref asked me if I was all right and when I nodded he wiped my gloves and told me to box on, this time not asking for a concussion count. I knew I had to hang on until the end of the round. Patel wouldn't stand for more than two knockdowns. That is, if I could have gotten up a third time. 'Dance, klein baas, your feet, you must dance, only your feet can keep you out of trouble,' I could hear Geel Piet clear as anything. To my enormous relief the bell went for the end of the fourth.

'He's got a huge punch in both hands, lad, but he's slowing. I want you to box him close so he can't put a big one in, keep working at his body, he has to be feeling it.'

'You could have fooled me,' I panted. But my strength was coming back. I rinsed and spat, the water cool and delicious to my mouth.

'Christ, he's taking water!' Hymie said. 'The bastard's taking water!'

The first twenty seconds of the fifth round were the hardest yet. Mandoma threw everything at me, but I wove and ducked, back-pedalled and kept out of the way. He threw a left lead and I crossed over with a right, catching him under the eye and opening it up. His nose was still bleeding and while I hadn't hit him much in the head, I'd kept the nose bleeding with a regular jab right on the button. Nothing influences a referee more than a liberal splash of blood. Mandoma threw another left hook, telegraphing it from a yard away and I moved in and had him on the ropes with an orthodox straight left followed by a straight right to the head. Two copybook punches which, when timed correctly, carry a lot of zap.

The black fighter's hands came up to defend his head and I moved in close as his gut area opened up and in went a Geel Piet eight, right where the water he had swallowed would be. I knew the pain and the nausea would be terrible and he gave a loud gasp as the flurry of punches went home, and tried to chop my gloves away with his own. I was ready with a right hook which caught him flush on the jaw, coming up with all my strength behind it. While his punches had bounced me off my feet, mine bounced him hard against the ropes and then he sunk to his knees, both his gloves resting on the canvas. Blood from his nose dripped onto the grey canvas as I retired to a neutral corner.

At eight he rose, but I could see he felt bad and I moved in and began to pick him off. I could have come in swinging and tried to finish him, but a fighter like Mandoma digs deep for his courage and can always find that one last big punch. I was almost certain that he was a spent force and wouldn't recover between rounds fast enough. I'd get him in the final round. The bell went and I got to my corner to be met by Hymie and Solly, both shouting at me.

'Ferchrissake, why didn't you finish him off,' Hymie screamed. 'His gut, his gut is gone, you could have taken him, now he's got bleedin' time to recover,' Solly said.

'He only needs one more big punch and he can take me out,' I protested. I was following a Geel Piet plan and not a Solly Goldman plan. Geel Piet would have wanted me to box him off his feet, not punch him. 'You must always go safety first, klein baas, box, box, box, never fight.'

Solly regained his composure. 'You're right, son. I'm glad one of us is still thinking.' Whether he believed it or not, he knew he had to restore my concentration and was aware that in his excitement he'd acted foolishly.

The bell went for the final round. Mandoma, desperate for strength, had taken water again. For the first minute of the last round he came hard, but his timing was out and he wasn't putting his punches together properly. I stayed away from him. Flicking lightly at his cut eye. Keeping the blood coming, waiting for the chance to move in. He hit me with a right cross which, had it come earlier in the fight, would have put me down. Now it lacked authority. It was time to move in. I worked him into his own corner and went to work under his heart. Three solid punches before he managed to pull me into a clinch. He was too spent to stay out of trouble. After each break I'd move him back into a corner and set to work on his body. I couldn't believe he could still be standing. I'd never hit anyone as often or as hard. But the bastard wouldn't go down. I had to put him on the canvas again. I started to hit the black fighter hard on the nose and his gloves went up and opened him up down below. The Geel Piet eight became the Solly Goldman thirteen, the first time I had ever got a thirteen combination together perfectly. Mandoma gave a sort of a gurgle and then a sigh and fell. He was totally exhausted, his eyes were open looking at me but his body could no longer respond and he was unable to get his head off the canvas. He'd been boxed off his feet. His heart hadn't died it just couldn't hold him up on its own. Mandoma was the greatest natural fighter I had ever seen.

I had never been as exhausted in my life. Not only had I never boxed six rounds before, I'd never taken as much punishment. I tried to walk with dignity to the neutral corner as Natkin Patel started to count Mandoma out.

For the first time in the fight I heard the crowd, who were going absolutely wild.

'Onoshobishobi ... shobi ... shobi ... Ingelosi!' the chorus rolled like thunder across the football field. On and on it went until the microphone was pushed back into the ring and Gideon Mandoma's seconds had helped him to his corner. I walked over to see if he was all right and to shake his hand.

'You are the great chief, you are him who is Onoshobishobi Ingelosi,' Mandoma said, and standing on still trembling legs he held up my hand. The crowd went wild.

'It is you who are a chief, your spirit is still with you, we will be brothers, Gideon Mandoma.'

'I see you, Peekay. We have taken the milk from the same mother's breast, we are brothers.' I held up his hand and the crowd roared their applause.

Mr Nguni was back at the microphone and after some trouble got the crowd to quiet down. I had returned to my corner and was sitting on the pot while Solly was rubbing me down and Hymie held a fresh towel to drape over me.

'We have seen what we have seen. You must all go to your homes, tell the people that the spirit within the

Onoshobishobi Ingelosi lives also in the man. You have seen it with your own eyes and it is so,' he said simply. He turned and called Gideon Mandoma and me over and we stood next to him with our arms around each other. 'We have seen the spirits fight, in this we are all brothers,' Mr Nguni said and the roar of the black crowd closed the proceedings.

I touched Gideon on the shoulder and returned to my corner. It was just beginning to move into darker twilight and the smell of wood smoke and coal fires came to me again. In the distance a train whistled, cutting through the hubbub of the departing crowd. All around us black faces were grinning and some would stretch out and touch me lightly as though I were a talisman. But most looked at me and I could see that they believed. The legend was cast deeper and would spread further. I wondered if it would ever end. I suddenly realised that every bone in my body felt as though it had been broken.

With my arm around Hymie's shoulders for support we walked through the corridor of black bodies on our way back to the school. Black hands touched me, wiping sweat from my body and wiping it onto their faces.

'There you are, what did I tell you, lads, didn't I say it would be a t'riffic fight?' Solly said as we entered the school. 'Blimey! Twice there I thought you was gone, my son. It's good to know you can take a punch. Lemme tell you, I never seen an amateur throw a perfect thirteen-punch combination before. It was worth comin' just for that.'

'Cut it out, Solly, can't you see Peekay's hurting,' Hymie cut in.

'Not as much as the swartzer, my boy,' Solly said.

When we got to the shower block I sat down and started to cry. It was as though I saw the years ahead. The pain in my body had somehow sharpened the focus of my mind. I saw South Africa. I saw what would come. Something had happened to me; Hymie was talking but it was as though his voice were in an echo chamber. No, not an echo chamber; in the crystal cave of Africa. His voice echoed across the tops of the rainforest, down the valley just as the barking baboons had done. 'I've found it, Doc. I've found the power of one!' Hymie's voice was saying. The cave about me was shining crystal, the crystal became my pain and the pain sharpened as the light grew more intense. My concentration focused down to a pinpoint. The sadness I felt was overwhelming; sadness for the great Southland. In the whiteness, in the light, was a sound, as if the light and the sound were one. It was the great drum and the voices of the people. They came together as an echo. 'Mayibuye Afrika! Afrika! Afrika!' Come back, Africa! Africa! Africa! My life, whatever it was to become, was bound to this thing; there was no escaping it, I was a part of the crystal cave of Africa. And in the pain and confusion I wept, I could see only destruction and confusion and the drum beat; boom, boom, boom, and the light began to fade and Doc entered the cave, his hair white as snow, tall as ever, 'You must try, Peekay. You must try. Absoloodle!'

Hymie put his arm around me. 'There's more to this Onoshobishobi Ingelosi than I know about, isn't there, Peekay?'

'Christ, I dunno. I just don't know,' I sobbed.

'Don't worry, Peekay, no one can hurt you. No bastard can hurt you while I'm alive!'

'Doc's dead!' I heard my voice saying as though it were totally divorced from my body.

That evening when we returned to Hymie's place in Pretoria there was a message to call Mrs Boxall.

'Peekay, we have sad news, the professor has disappeared! Gert, and all the warders not on duty, and half the men in town are in the hills looking for him, but he's been gone two days. Now they say there's little chance of finding him alive!' Her voice faltered and then broke as she began to sob. The line from Barberton was crackling, fading in and out and Mrs Boxall's sobs grew and receded. 'Please come home, Peekay, please come quickly, you're sure to find him, you went so many places together,' she wept.

Hymie forced me to sleep. 'We'll wake you at two a.m. and a chauffeur can drive you the two hundred miles to Barberton, you'll arrive by sun-up.'

I knew where to find Doc. I knew that somehow he had done the impossible and had reached the crystal cave of Africa. Doc would be lying on the platform, his arms across his chest. In one hundred thousand years people would find the cave again and would climb up to the magic platform and they'd say, 'What a strange coincidence, that looks just like the shape of a man made of crystal. A very tall, thin man.' And then I cried myself to sleep.

TWENTY-TWO

No one, not even I, knew Doc's religion, but after a week where I had visited all our old haunts (except one) with various teams of men, it was decided that a church ceremony should take place. Marie came forward and claimed that Doc had found Christ while he was in hospital with pneumonia and my mother was ecstatic. Pastor Mulvery claimed the right to hold a burial service sans Doc's mortal remains. I didn't protest. Marie had convinced herself that Doc had said yes to Jesus and she had notched him up as one of her most important salvations. I don't think Doc would have minded too much, besides, his love for the great Southland was complete in the most beautiful eternity he could conceive of, not dust and ashes but a wonderful pagan burial that would make him a living part of his beloved Africa. His spirit would dwell in the crystal cave of Africa looking out across the rainforest down the misty valley and over distant mountains which smudged blue as a child's crayon drawing.

Doc's death left me completely numb. I went through the motions but it was as though I had lost my centre of gravity. Everything seemed topsy-turvy, people would speak to me but I wouldn't hear them. Their mouths opened like goldfish in a bowl, but nothing came out. Their movements seemed exaggerated as though by walking up to me they were growing bigger from the same spot, their feet not moving but their bodies just elasticising cartoon-like to where I stood. The pain was all inside, deep and dull and I knew it was this that made me feel numb. I felt I would never be quite the same again, that I could never love as much again. I kept telling myself that I knew Doc was going to die, that Doc had been telling me himself for months, but I knew nothing about this sort of death. Death was violent and ugly like Granpa Chook and Geel Piet, or even macabre like Big Hettie. Death, as I had come to know it in Africa had no gently slipping awayness about it, no dignity. And so I felt Doc had cheated, he'd just gone, he disappeared, he had made death happen rather than have it happen. I felt cheated, even angry. Why hadn't he waited for me? Why hadn't he told me so that I could have taken him to the crystal cave? But secretly I knew that I couldn't have done it, I would have clung to the last thread of life in him. I also knew that he would have known this. But it didn't help the numbness. It didn't take away the need, the dull permanent ache under my heart on the exact spot where you work on another boxer till he runs out of steam. That was it precisely: the bell had gone but I couldn't find the strength and the will to come out for the next round on my own.

Pastor Mulvery said a lot of things about it being the end of Doc's travail and his vale of tears. He had called Doc a great piano player and gardener. 'The Lord Jesus has given our beloved professor a garden in heaven filled with the fragrance of pansies and sweet peas where he can play his music for a choir of angels.'

The regulars in the congregation must have thought it was one of his better descriptions of the born again hereafter and they peppered Pastor Mulvery's eulogy with 'Praise the Lord' and 'Blessed be His glorious name'. I heard it all, but it didn't make any sense, it had nothing to do with Doc. Absoloodle not.

'Oh, dear, oh goodness, dearie me. Our dear, dear professor would most certainly have chosen eternal hellfire in preference to an eternity spent in a bed of pansies and sweet peas, playing for a choir of angels,' said Mrs Boxall, having been exposed to Pastor Mulvery and the workings of the Apostolic Faith Mission for the first time.

The aloe was in bloom on the hillside above the rose garden and early on the day of the service I had climbed to our rock and cried for a while until the sun came up over the valley. On the way down I gathered several candelabra of aloe blossom which I put in a large copper vase I found in the back room of the church. When I entered the church later to attend the funeral it had been removed and an arrangement of pink and orange gladioli had been put in its place.

Even old Mr Bornstein, wearing a hat throughout, attended the service with Miss Bornstein. Miss Bornstein's shiny lipstick and long red nails looked strangely out of place in a church which taught that make-up of any sort, except for face powder, was a sin. I once heard long painted nails described by a lady witnessing for the Lord as the devil's talons dripping with the blood of sinners. Miss Bornstein looked beautiful among the scrubbed, plain-faced women, with their greying hair pulled back and held by cheap celluloid clips, their hats stuck with sprigs of linen flowers, some small attempt at adornment. I could see them stealing glances at her, at her perfect complexion, magnificent shining, almost purple black hair, green eyes and brilliant sinful lips and nails. They would spit it all back in righteous vituperation when next they gaggled around a cup of tea to tell each other they had seen sin in the flesh, the devil himself sitting among them.

Outside the church after the service, as there was no Doc in a coffin to look solemn about, the regulars were able to congratulate Marie for her spectacular conversion. Even my mother got a bit of gratuitous praise for her original foresight in bringing Doc into focus as a potential candidate for salvation.

All the warders who knew Doc, including Captain Smit and the Kommandant came to pay their respects. Afterwards Captain Smit invited me back to the prison where the boxing team was having a wake. This turned out to be a jolly affair, more like a braaivleis and singsong and I tried

537

hard to be cheerful, for I suspect it was held as a gesture and as a bit of a cheer-up for me. Doc would have approved much more of this than of the sanctimonious burial service.

Gert took me to one side. When I'd arrived back to help in the search for Doc, I'd taken over from him. He had barely slept for three days and had been exhausted. 'Tell me, man, how come we never found him? You know every place he went.'

'Ja, it's funny that, but you know Doc, Gert. He probably had a place in an old mine shaft that only he knew about, someplace he found years ago before he met me.'

Gert looked at me directly. 'No man, no way. You and him was too close. I reckon you know but, ag man, you right, I wouldn't tell also if it was me.' Gert was a naturally quiet person who didn't miss much; he'd just been promoted to sergeant and everyone said he was going places.

Doc left everything he owned to me, including the Steinway. He left a small insurance policy worth about twenty pounds to Dee and Dum. My mother had the Steinway moved to the lounge at home where it practically filled the room so that the two chairs which matched the sofa had to be put on the back verandah. A jolly good idea because that's where everyone sat anyway. Except for church ladies and town people coming for fittings, we never had proper visitors of the kind that got sat uncomfortably in the front room, so the back stoep was perfect for the old ball and claw brocade chairs, which after forty years of being stuck in the parlour saw some real 'bottom work' at last.

At first I think my granpa was a bit hurt about the banished chairs. His beautiful wife, for whom the rose garden had been created, had originally bought the furniture. But by the time I was back for the holidays again one of the chairs was permanently claimed as his and had several small burn holes in the upholstery where bits of glowing tobacco ash had fallen from the bowl of his pipe to burn through the faded brocade.

Doc's cottage was well away from any other European houses on a small *koppie*, and his will read to me by young Mr Bornstein showed that he owned the whole of the small hill. I moved Dee and Dum in as caretakers, although it was really intended as their home. The tiny three-room cottage with lean-to kitchen was a veritable mansion after the small brick room next to the rose nursery which they had shared. They had both been terribly distressed at Doc's death. Doc had asked them to pack food for three days and not to speak to anyone about his departure. When he hadn't returned on the fourth day Dee had gone to see Mrs Boxall who had raised the alarm. True to her word, Dee had simply told Mrs Boxall that Doc hadn't returned from the hills the previous evening as his bed had not been slept in and the ash in the tiny potbelly stove was cold. They had both confessed to me about Doc requesting food for three days, which meant that when Mrs Boxall had called me, Doc had actually been gone four days. When I had known with absolute certainty after the fight with Gideon Mandoma that Doc was dead, he had been out three days. It would have taken him two days to reach the crystal cave of Africa, whereupon he would have rested and then, sometime on the third day, climbed the cliff. Doc was a methodical man, he would have planned everything meticulously to the last ounce of his energy. Marie told me that while he was in hospital he had complained each night of being unable to sleep and they had given him a sleeping pill. Doc would never have taken a pill, which he termed 'putting bad chemicals in the blood'. I knew that he would now have the sleeping pills with him. Doc never did anything carelessly and he wasn't going to be any different in planning his death.

It was Dee and Dum keeping faith with Doc which prevented the search parties from going further into the hills. In one day a frail old man recovering from pneumonia could not have travelled far into the foothills, least of all across the Saddleback Range. I knew Doc better than that; he would have planned it, knowing his chances for success.

I waited until the day before I was due to return to school and the furore of Doc's death was beginning to die down a little so that I would be allowed to go into the hills alone. Telling my mother at supper the previous evening that I was going for a last ramble in memory of Doc, I left home before dawn. I knew there was still something Doc needed: if it had not been so he would have left some sort of message for me. Together with Dee and Dum, I searched the cottage and the cactus garden in vain. Doc wanted me to perform some last duty, I felt quite sure about this; and in any case, I needed to perform some sort of ritual of my own to mark Doc's passing. I packed a can of sardines, a couple of oranges and filled my old school lunch tin with a tomato, two boiled eggs and a couple of leftover cold potatoes, and with a bottle of water and a torch, I set off. To avoid suspicion I didn't take rope as I was certain I could climb the cliff without it.

Pausing only at sunrise to drink and to eat a potato, by mid-morning I had arrived at our old campsite on the edge of the rainforest. Above me the cliff loomed, now suddenly meaning so much more to me. Doc, as I had expected, had used the site again. There had been no rain for the last ten days and the ash in the fire hole I'd dug was still fresh and powdery. To make certain, I went to the spot where I had buried our rubbish and dug it up. Sure enough a second bully beef tin and the wrapping from a packet of Bakers Pretty Polly Crackers had been added. Doc loved the dry, tasteless crackers and always bought the same brand.

Half an hour later I was standing on the shelf which led to the cave. At first there seemed to be no sign of Doc having been there and my heart beat furiously. What if Doc hadn't made it? What if he had fallen trying to scale the cliff and lay somewhere in the thick rainforest which grew at its base? I fought back the panic, for I knew I would have to find him and somehow get him up the cliff and into the cave and onto the platform. A task which would take me two days, if I could achieve it at all.

I also knew that if Doc lay in the crystal cave of Africa he would not have wanted me to enter. Doc was a man of great sensitivity and the idea of subjecting me to the sight of his corpse on the platform would be unthinkable. He would have left me instructions outside the cave, in daylight; that's where his message would be. I began to search the shelf inch by inch. Doc had trained me to observe and I knew he would expect me to make the kind of detailed examination of the shelf which would be beyond the casual searcher so that if he had hidden something it would not be apparent to any but a trained eye.

I searched for half an hour but the limestone shelf had been worn out of the cliff face by a hundred thousand years of wind, rain and water erosion, the hollowed-out shelf was smooth and regular and there were no cracks in the dolomitic rock. I began to doubt. Doc might have intended to leave me a message but been on the point of collapse when he finally made it up to the shelf, saving every ounce of strength for the task of reaching the platform.

And then I saw it. A dark stripe of some sort of mineral sediment, long since dry, had stained a small part of the shelf. I ran my hand over the stained rock and received a sudden sharp prick. I pulled my hand back and looked at it; a tiny drop of blood formed on my palm. Sticking out of the middle of the dark patch no more than an eighth of an inch, was the point of the blade of Doc's Joseph Rogers pocket knife.

Doc had discovered that the dark sedimented patch was softer than the rock surrounding it and he had gouged a hole into the centre of it using the pocket knife. He had then mixed the sand which came out of the hole with a little water from his water bottle and, first inserting the knife with the tip of the blade only just showing, he had repacked the granules of sand to mend invisibly where he had buried the knife.

It was typical of Doc; he trusted his training of me so much that he knew he could make the hiding place difficult for others to find, and that I would find it. I scraped the dirt away from the point of the blade and dislodged the small knife. Around its handle, tied with cotton thread, was a note.

The hole appeared deeper than I had first suspected, deeper and wider, and behind the knife was Doc's gold hunter. With the tip of the knife I pulled the fob chain out and then the beautiful old gold pocket watch. I stuffed the watch and chain into my trouser pocket and with clumsy, trembling hands picked at the cotton thread tying the note to the black bone handle of the knife.

It was a page torn from one of Doc's small field notepads and margin to margin from the top to the bottom of one side of the page were musical notes, minute in size but exact, a precisely written piece of music. I turned the page. In Doc's neat handwriting was a short note centred on the page.

My dear Peekay,

In all the world no man has such a friend as you. Last night is come some music to my head, when it is coming I know it is time for me to go. Maybe, who can say, it is the music for Africa? Maybe only it is my music to you? Not so good as Mozart, never like Mr Beethoven or like Mr Brahms, but maybe better than a Chopin nocturne. Such a little piece of music for such a long life. I am such domkopf. But not such domkopf that I don't let you be my friend. for this I am having eleven out of ten. I must go into the crystal cave of Africa now. You must not follow until it is your time also. Maybe in one hundred thousand years we will meet again.

Goodbye, Mr Schmarty-Pantz welterweight champion of the world.

Your friend,
Doc

I had done my crying for Doc and the note gave me comfort. Doc was safe and where he wanted to be and his secret would be kept forever. I entered the tunnel leading to the outer cave. Testing the rope handrail we'd built for Doc's entry to the cave the first time, I found it still strong. He would not have had a great deal of difficulty getting into the narrow entrance. It took me only a few minutes to work the steel hook out of the tunnel wall and to remove the rope.

I returned to the cliff shelf and removed the second spike and put the two spikes and the rope into my rucksack. In a very few years the small holes the spikes had made would be eroded from the rock face, leaving no trace of man. Only the baboons or an occasional leopard would visit the outer cave, but neither would enter the dark, damp inner crystal cave of Africa. Doc would be safe for the hundred thousand years it would take to turn him into crystal, forever a part of Africa.

I was home again just as the moon was rising over the valley. The pain, the deep dull pain under my heart had lifted. Sadness remained, but I was now proud that Doc had achieved what he wanted to do. And we would always be bound together, he was very much a part of me. He had found a small, frightened and confused little boy and had given him confidence and music and learning and a love for Africa and taught me not to fear things. Now I didn't know where the boy began and Doc ended. I had been given all the gifts he had. Now that Doc was resting right I knew we could never be separated from each other.

The coffee pot left at four the next day to connect with the all-night sleeper from Kaapmuiden to Johannesburg.

That last morning at home I walked into the front room and opened the Steinway and started to practise Doc's music, which I'd earlier transcribed onto three sheets of music manuscript. After I picked at the notes for an hour, the melody began to form. It was a nocturne with a recurring musical phrase running through it. Very beautiful, it was unmistakably African, with a sadness and yearning for something that seems to be in the music of all of the people. The musical phrasing and the recurring melody were somehow familiar, like something I'd heard in a dream or the dreamtime or which simply races unknown through your blood. And then I realised what it was. It was the chant to the Tadpole Angel.

I stopped bewildered. Doc had never heard the chant which had started only after I had gone to boarding school. I played the music again; it was no coincidence, the chant was clearly a part of the music, it ran through the nocturne repeating itself in a dozen variations but always there: clear, unmistakable, wild, beautiful. Onoshobishobi Ingelosi . . . shobi . . . shobi . . . Ingelosi, the piano notes enunciated as clearly as if the people themselves were singing it.

It was getting late and it was time to say my goodbyes to Mrs Boxall, old Mr Bornstein and Miss Bornstein. Gert had promised to pick me up and run us down to the station in the prison's new Chevy which meant my mother and my granpa didn't have to rely on Pastor Mulvery, whose anxious-to-escape front teeth and unctuous presence I found increasingly depressing, and I was glad that he wouldn't add to the awkwardness I always felt at departures.

I put Doc's music between the pages of a slim volume of poetry by Wilfred Owen which Mrs Boxall had given me. 'Not as soppy as Rupert Brooke, but a better war poet I feel sure,' she had said.

Leaving home with the knowledge that when I returned it would be to a place which no longer meant Doc made this parting almost unbearably sad for me. My mother tried to chat brightly, but she wasn't much of a bright chatterer and my granpa just tapped and tamped and puffed and turned and looked up at the mountains and said, 'The cumulus nimbus is building up, could be a storm tonight, just as the Frensman are in loose bud.' Frensman was a deep red long-stemmed rose and unless the petals were still in tight bud the storm would damage them. Gert, who at the best of times didn't have too much small talk, added to my sense of foreboding and made the waiting for the coffee pot to pull out almost unbearably long. I put my hand into the pocket of a new pair of grey flannel slacks, made for me by old Mr Bornstein, and took out Doc's hunter. I was about to click it open when I was conscious of my stupidity and quickly slipped the beautiful old watch back into my pocket. My haste in doing so immediately pointed to my guilt. I thought I might have escaped detection but after a couple of minutes, when my mother had turned to talk to my granpa, Gert whispered, 'So you found him, hey? I'm blêrrie glad, Peekay.' I ignored his remark, pretending not to hear him, and I knew Gert would remain silent.

A whistle warned of our departure and the small crowd on the platform became animated, as happens when an over-extended farewell is suddenly terminated. It occurred in our group too, each of us secretly glad that the waiting was over. 'Look after yourself, son boy,' my mother said, offering the side of her powdered cheek.

'There's a good lad,' puff, puff, my granpa shook my hand. As I looked into his face I realised that his blue eyes had become a little rheumy and that the skin around his cheeks and mouth stretched tightly, as happens with thin men when they begin to grow old.

Gert gripped my hand in the traditional excessively firm Afrikaner manner. 'All the best, Peekay, see you in July, man.' He jumped into a boxing stance, it was a small physical joke to hide his awkwardness. 'Keep your hands up, you hear.' He grinned and leaned forward so that only I could hear, 'No more fighting Kaffirs you hear, their heads is too hard, man.'

The coffee pot gave a blast of steam whistle, loud enough to belong to a much bigger, more important train. The people in the third-class Blacks Only carriage yelled and screamed with delight, five or six heads and a dozen arms to each carriage window waving bandannas and generally making the most of the farewell occasion, as the little train slowly left the platform. I continued to wave until the train had passed the long bend which took the platform from sight. With a conscious sigh of relief I leaned back into the green leather seat. I knew I'd have the compartment to myself until Kaapmuiden, and I cherished the idea of being on my own. It had been a long week since I had fought Gideon Mandoma.

Hymie was full of news when we got back to school. He'd worked out a formal business arrangement with Mr Nguni and now there were twenty young black boxers training at Solly's gym, as well as three black boxing officials who would be trained in the handling of boxers and would eventually sit for their referee's tickets.

Gideon Mandoma and three other young fighters were separated from the other blacks to do their workouts with me on Wednesday afternoons and before church on Sunday morning. Gideon soon became more than just a good sparring partner. He laughed a lot and had a quick wit which delighted me. His English wasn't strong and at first we mostly spoke in Zulu, until after a workout some three weeks into the term he patted me on the shoulder with his glove. 'No more Zulu. Peekay, your Zulu comes from my mother's breast now my English must come from your fists. You must teach me English.' He propped and slowly stroked his hair in a backward movement the way Hymie would do it, lightly touching it as though preening in front of a mirror. 'I have one good English words from Hymie.' He mimicked the way Hymie spat words out: 'Cheeky bloody Kaffir!' Gideon threw back his head and laughed happily. 'This English I understand very good.'

It was then that I hit on the idea. 'We're going to start a school for Solly's black boxers,' I announced to Hymie on the tram back to school after training.

'Christ, Peekay, isn't that going a bit far? Educate the black bastards and before you know where you are they'll want to take over the country.'

'It's as much theirs as it is ours. More actually,' I said, surprised at his outburst.

'You're perfectly right, but can't we let them take a little longer to find out? Keep the buggers in the dark as long as possible?'

'Hymie, what are you saying? I thought you were a liberal thinker?'

Hymie laughed. 'First and foremost I'm a pragmatist but there's bound to be a quid in it somewhere, although I'm buggered if I can see where. How do you propose going about it, integrate the Prince of Wales School?'

'C'mon, Hymie, take this seriously. If we go to Singe 'n Burn and put it to him as two Renaissance men and give him a whole line of bullshit about liberalism blah, blah, blah, I'm sure he'll be in it. We could have the black school in one of the classrooms on a Saturday night.'

'Already I like it! One lesson a week shouldn't pose too much of a threat to white civilisation as we know it on the southern tip of Africa.'

'Well, what do you reckon?'

'Off hand I can't think of a way to make any money out of it but as Karl Marx, or was it Christ, said: "Man does not live by bread alone". Okay, whatever you say.'

'Great! Because you have to open the subject with Singe 'n Burn by telling him that as a Jew you know what it's like to be an oppressed people.'

Hymie thought for a moment. 'Fine, nothing to it, I simply go in and ask Singe 'n Burn to open a black school in this citadel of white privilege, pointing out to him that as an expertly oppressed person for roughly nineteen hundred years . . .'

'Good, I'll make an appointment to see him after school tomorrow.'

Singe 'n Burn proved more difficult than we had anticipated. He was not at all sure of the attitude the Nationalist government might take to one of the country's most famous English-speaking private schools becoming the cradle of black adult learning.

There were, of course, black schools and some very good ones. But most Africans left school before they reached high school and a great many more after only two or three years of the most basic education. Some, perhaps a majority, never made it to school at all. If, in later years, they wished to learn to read and write, then no adult school facilities existed for them.

We seemed to have reached a stalemate, with Singe 'n Burn promising to put the issue to the school governors, where it was almost certain to be defeated. Their idea of Christian gentleman did not include the brotherhood of man, if it meant lowering the colour bar.

Our arguments had been sound but our politics naive. In South Africa, when a black skin is involved, politics and social justice have very little in common.

'We've been a couple of schmucks to think he'd buy it straight off like that, we're going to have to make the bastard feel guilty, it always works with a Renaissance man,' Hymie said. We were sitting in the prefects' common room which was seldom used by the other prefects after school and was a nice private place to talk or work.

'I thought we'd already made him feel guilty?'

'Guilty in the mind, intellectual guilt yes. But guilty so it hurts inside, that's different. Jews are expert at soul guilt. Let me illustrate what I mean. Until we fought in Sophiatown, the only black people I knew well were Mary, our cook, and Jefferson, the butler. And, of course, the various other nameless servants who pretended to work around the place. The afternoon of the fight was the first time I had ever been close to African people. I mean actually experienced them as people, not just servants or faithful family retainers, but as people with problems. I mean just like other ordinary people. I haven't told you before, but the effect was shattering. I found myself liking them. More than that, I understood for the very first time how the persecuted Jew must have felt. When they sang for you, not just for Gideon, that was understandable, but for you also, the generosity of spirit made me ashamed of my white skin. That's the sort of guilt I mean.'

'Christ, Hymie, you didn't tell me any of this.'

'So what's to tell? You can't tell it, you have to feel it. That's what Singe 'n Burn needs. He needs to feel not what he is denying but whom he is denying. We're going to introduce him to Gideon.'

'You had ten thousand Africans singing Sikelel' i Afrika to experience, do you think Gideon can convince him on his own? He's the only tone deaf Zulu ever born.' It was true, Gideon had a singing voice like a rusty rasp on hardwood.

'No, of course not. But by the time we're finished with that cheeky black bastard he's going to sound like Othello.'

Hymie and I composed a speech for Gideon Mandoma which, I must say, was pretty terrific. The idea was that Gideon would learn it in Zulu and I'd translate it into English as though hearing it for the first time. Singe 'n Burn would be so knocked out by the language, the poetry and the brilliance that he would realise the black man was not just a hewer of wood and a drawer of water, nor even a noble savage, but someone who had all the brilliant potential even to become one of Sinjun's People.

We trained Gideon in the speech and, dressed in a white shirt, neatly patched pair of pants from an old suit and with his old black shoes shining, we presented ourselves at Singe 'n Burn's study. I must say he was very gracious and we all sat in his big old leather armchairs and Miss Perkins, his secretary, brought us tea and Marie biscuits. We'd anticipated the offer of tea and had practised Gideon in the balancing of a cup on his knee so he looked pretty suave and at home. But I knew on the inside he'd be all tom-toms and flutter.

I explained to Singe 'n Burn that Gideon's English wasn't sufficiently fluent for him to conduct a conversation and that I would act as interpreter. I think the fact that one of Sinjun's People could conduct the interview in Zulu impressed the old boy no end.

Gideon, as we had rehearsed it, began in English. His beautiful white teeth flashing in one of his best smiles: 'Excuse for my English, sir, she is not so good for tell this thing in my heart.'

The head nodded sympathetically. I could see the plan beginning to work already. Gideon cleared his throat and then began in Zulu. After each carefully rehearsed sentence I translated in my best voice, keeping it low and dramatic.

'I do not come from a nation of slaves, but I have been made a slave. I come from a people who are brave men, but I am made to weep. I, who am to become a chief, have become what no man ought to be, a man without rights and without a future.' I paused dramatically before continuing, 'I am seventeen summers, I have killed a lion and sat on the mat of the high chief, but I have been given my place. That place is not a seat at the white man's table, and that place is not a voice in the white man's indaba.' I could see Singe 'n Burn was beginning to feel uncomfortable. He wouldn't know what hit him by the time we were through. Talk about guilt, old Singe hadn't seen anything yet.

To my surprise Gideon suddenly stopped following the script. 'My bondage is not of the white man's making. My bondage is not forced upon me by the white man's sjambok. My bondage is in my own brain. Here in my head I carry the Zulu pride of my ancestors but I also carry no learning. My stupidity is my bondage, it is the instrument of the black man's misery and despair. If the white man would give me his rights and the same voice, I would not be able to use them, I would still be in bondage. I would still be a servant, a black Kaffir, an inferior human, because I would not know how to use these rights, how to make my voice felt amongst the people. Please, sir, my mind cries for knowledge. I wish to cup knowledge in my hand and drink it as one drinks water by the side of a stream. I am naked without knowledge. I am a nothing without learning. Please, sir, give me this knowledge, give me this learning, so that I too can be a man.'

Gideon's words had been so easily put that I had no trouble making an almost perfect translation and his flow was hardly interrupted. The tears rolled down his cheeks and he made no effort to wipe them away. I realised suddenly that for a Zulu to cry is a great shame, but he couldn't wipe away his tears with the cup and saucer balanced on his knee. I leaned forward and removed the cup and looked over at Hymie, not daring to look at Singe 'n Burn. I could see Hymie was annoyed that I'd removed Gideon's cup, the tears were the best part, the clincher. Othello had nothing on Hymie's cheeky black bastard.

'The tears are not for myself, they are for the people, Inkosi,' Gideon said softly, wiping them away with the back of his hand. I sneaked a look at Singe 'n Burn and saw his eyes had grown misty and he too was struggling with his emotions.

'Remarkable, quite remarkable.' Then turning to Hymie and me, he said: 'This young man shall have his school and I charge you both to give of your best.'

We'd won! Singe 'n Burn, the senior house master from Winchester School and trustee of the great private school tradition to the colonies, Renaissance man and liberal thinker, had been made to touch the heart and feel the soul of black Africa.

Hymie was the first to react. 'Can the school supply exercise books and stationery, sir?' Singe 'n Burn nodded.

'See Miss Perkins for a stationery authority, Levy. Your students must be properly equipped.'

'Thank you, sir,' I said then turned to Gideon to tell him the news. Gideon broke into a giant smile.

'Many boy, same like me, we thank you, Inkosi.' Singe 'n Burn acknowledged Gideon with a nod of his head. It was plain he was enchanted with the young Zulu chief.

The school began with the black boxers from Solly's gym its only pupils. Within a month, local chauffeurs, cooks and houseboys had swelled the ranks and Pissy Johnson, Cunning-Spider and Atherton, as well as two guys from School House who could speak Sotho, were roped in to teach on Saturday nights.

Even before the head's agreement we had despatched a long letter to Miss Bornstein asking her how we should best go about teaching language and numbers to adult Africans; she had responded with a superb set of teaching notes and several textbooks which enabled Hymie and me to prepare a complete curriculum which I was able to translate into Sotho, Zulu, Shangaan as well as Fanagalo.

With Singe 'n Burn's approval we also set about teaching the curriculum to the newly elected Sinjun's People so that the night school could be carried on after Hymie and I matriculated at the end of the year.

After only a few weeks the results were astonishing. Students, loaded down with homework after Saturday night's four-hour teaching session, would return with everything done, anxious for more. Word of the school spread among the Prince of Wales School boys and soon collections of nursery rhymes, primers and all sorts of textbooks were brought in and we had more volunteers than we could cope with. Then Hymie, loath to waste any free resource, hit on a one-to-one teaching method where every black student had a personal white tutor. All our black students would be taught collectively in the school hall for the first hour after which they would break away into a corner of a classroom with their personal tutors. Every tutor worked to a set of notes supplied by us and was required to stick to Miss Bornstein's outlines.

Progress was much faster than it would have been for any white students in a conventional classroom situation. Hymie, not content with our first curriculum, worked and worked on the notes, ironing out the errors and getting them perfect.

Some four months later we were visited by a reporter and photographer from the *Rand Daily Mail* and in the following Wednesday morning edition we had a full page write-up, which also contained a picture of Hymie, Gideon and me.

The article, very exaggerated, told a cocked-up version of the fight I had with Gideon and how Hymie and I had opened a school for boxers which continued to grow, giving the impression we had become a major black education resource. It was full of inaccuracies but nevertheless it caused some real excitement in the school. Singe 'n Burn called Hymie and me into his study and admonished us for not checking with him before speaking to a reporter. He suggested it was altogether a rather silly thing to have done in the light of the political situation, where black schools were forbidden in white urban areas.

Coming out of the head's office, Hymie shrugged his shoulders. 'Any publicity is good publicity, I guess.'

'I hope you're right, I reckon we goofed.'

'Yeah, so do I,' he said softly.

The following Saturday night the police raided us. The doors of the hall were suddenly blocked by khaki-uniformed police both white and African. A police lieutenant wearing a Sam Browne belt and a holstered revolver jumped up onto the stage and blew his whistle loudly.

'This is a police raid, everybody remain seated and nobody will get hurt, you hear!' He stood on the stage, his legs apart, with his hand on his revolver holster as though daring one of us to move. 'Who is in charge here?'

'*Ons is*,' I said in Afrikaans, indicating Hymie and myself.

The police officer continued in English. 'Why is there no adult in charge?'

'The class is run by the boys,' I said.

'You mean white kids teach these blêrrie Kaffirs?'

'That's right.' I was beginning to gain courage after my initial surprise.

'Ag sis, man, are you telling me you teaching blêrrie stinking Kaffirs their ABC's? Don't you have anything better to do with your time on a Saturday night?'

'Have you got a search warrant?' Hymie asked.

'Who're you, man?' the policeman asked.

'You answer my question first,' Hymie said in an even voice.

'Hey, you being cheeky?'

'He merely asked if you have a search warrant, officer,' I said. The policeman suddenly realised that we were not intimidated. In fact he was wrong, we were both scared to death.

'And what if I heven't?' he challenged.

'Then you're trespassing and I must ask you to leave at once,' I said.

'You're only a blêrrie kid, who you think you talking to, hey?'

'If you haven't got a warrant to enter this school then piss off!' Hymie spat at the officer.

To my surprise the police officer suddenly grinned. Then stroking his nose with his forefinger and thumb he said, 'You're the Jewboy, hey.' He turned towards me. 'And you the boxer who fights Kaffirs.' He pointed at the Africans seated silently in front of us. 'Let me see the Kaffir you fought, man.'

Without being asked to do so Gideon rose from his chair. 'Come here, Joe Louis, come and stand next to the Jewboy and the Kaffirboetie.'

The officer called a black policeman over from the doorway, and as he waited for him to come onto the stage, he undid the shiny brass button holding the flap of his khaki tunic pocket and withdrew a piece of paper which he extended in our direction. 'Here, Jewboy, read it for yourself.' Hymie moved over and accepted the paper which was obviously a warrant to enter and search the premises. The lieutenant turned to the black policeman at his side. 'Tell the black bastards that they must all show their pass books and a pass from their employer to stay out after nine o'clock curfew.'

I turned to the white policeman. 'It isn't nine o'clock yet, Lieutenant. No one's broken curfew.'

He grinned. 'Ja I know, man, but it will be when I'm finished here and any black bastard without a pass is arrested.'

'This warrant is for St Johns College,' Hymie said suddenly. 'Look, see it says St Johns College, Houghton. That's the school about a mile down the road!'

'Don't play silly-buggers with me, you hear? Or you three will spend the night in a cell down at Central.'

Hymie walked over to the white police officer. 'Read it for yourself. It says St Johns College, Houghton. That's not us. Now will you kindly leave!'

'This is the right place, this is the place in the newspaper, I'm telling you, man! St Johns, that school, does it also teach Kaffirs?' I could see he was suddenly confused.

'You'll have to ask them that yourself, officer,' I said, not trusting myself to look at Hymie.

The police officer folded the warrant and put it back in his pocket. 'I should arrest you for obstructing the police in their duty, you know it's only a technical error, man. They got it wrong when they was looking on the map. This is the school, I'm telling you!'

'That's not what it says on your piece of paper, I really must ask you to leave, officer,' Hymie said, playing the situation for all it was worth.

'Okay, Jewboy, but don't think you seen the last of me. I know a comminist when I see one.' He pointed to me. 'You too, you and your Kaffir friend. I can smell a comminist a mile off.'

He left with his men and we could hear their boots on the cobblestones as they crossed the school quad.

'Holy Molenski! That was close,' I said. 'What happens now?'

Gideon grinned, a lopsided sort of smile, 'I think it is finish . . . the school is finish.'

'Not on your fucking life!' Hymie said. 'I'll get my old man's lawyers if they try doing that again.'

Gideon gave a wry laugh. 'You will be safe but we will go to jail, it is always like so. You are very clever and the magic of the Onoshobishobi Ingelosi is make the change for the school name on the paper. But the police they are bad people, they will not give up so easy, but also I think the big baas for headmaster he will make finish with this school.'

'Over our dead bodies,' Hymie said. 'I'm telling you, he'll fight for the night school.'

But he didn't. The next Monday the two of us were called to Singe 'n Burn's office to be confronted by an officer of the South African police force.

'This is Captain Swanepoel of the Johannesburg Central Police Station, he wishes to ask you a few questions,' Singe 'n Burn said sternly. 'It seems your report to me on the weekend doesn't quite respond with the one submitted by the police officer who attended your class on Saturday night. I urge you to tell the complete truth to Captain Swanepoel.'

'We told you precisely what happened, sir,' I said to the head.

'With respect, the officer in charge of the visit is trained to report correctly, you can take my word for that,' the police captain said.

'Well then, in that case there will be no difference in our versions, Captain Swanepoel. I mean if we both told the truth,' Hymie said softly.

'The truth? What is the truth? In my experience the truth goes out the window when emotions come in. Emotions always tell a story different, you take my word for that, Headmaster,' Captain Swanepoel replied.

'Captain, both these boys have been trained to observe a situation with some dispassion, even though it be one in which they are involved.'

'Ja, I mean no disrespect, Headmaster, but I must take the written evidence of an adult police officer against two young boys who were very excited at the time.'

'Perhaps Captain Swanepoel can tell us where our evidence differs, sir?' I asked.

'Well, yes, of course.' The head cleared his throat. 'According to Captain Swanepoel you did not co-operate with the officer in charge of the visit and you were abusive in the extreme.'

'We were not given the opportunity to co-operate, sir. The officer was both abusive and bullying and referred to me as a Kaffirboetie, Levy as the Jewboy, and to Gideon Mandoma as a blêrrie stinking Kaffir.' I looked up to see the beginnings of a smirk on Captain Swanepoel's face.

'This is not possible, a police officer of the South African Police Force is trained to be respectful to the public,' he turned to Singe 'n Burn. 'People make things up all the time, things the police are supposed to say.'

'Are you calling us liars, Captain?' I said.

Swanepoel ignored my question. 'It says here that you used abusive language to the officer in charge of the investigation?'

'Yes, I told him to piss off,' Hymie said, 'but you have yet to answer Peekay's question, Captain.'

'I will answer it later, son, don't you worry about that,' Swanepoel shot back. 'Is what you said not abusive language?'

'Levy was extremely provoked and as the officer had no right to be on the premises the remark was not unjustified, sir,' I replied.

'I didn't ask you and he didn't answer my question.' He

pointed his finger at Hymie. 'I'm asking you again, is what you said not abusive language?'

'Put like that, yes, but . . .'

'No but, man, you admit you were abusive to the officer then?'

'I admit I told him to piss off, Captain,' Hymie replied.

'Then we are in agreement. The first fact we challenge turns out to be correct, why must I not believe this report is a correct statement of what happened?'

'I say, that's not fair rules of debate, Captain Swanepoel,' Singe 'n Burn demanded.

Captain Swanepoel turned to face the headmaster. 'I am a police officer, not a school teacher, I look at the evidence, I do not play games.'

'We have forty-two Africans as well as our own chaps who will confirm what we've said,' I protested. I'd heard the warders interrogate prisoners and they would use the same technique as Swanepoel was now using on us.

'Ah yes, forty-two hostile witnesses. Africans do not have the same idea about truth as a white man. As for the other white boys, we are reluctant to take evidence from juveniles.'

'You still haven't answered my question, Captain,' Hymie said, his teeth clenched.

'You know something, son, sooner or later your type of person comes before the police again. I will remember your face.'

'*Please*! Answer our question, sir!' Hymie shouted.

Swanepoel laughed, 'When we meet again, I will answer it then, you hear?'

'What happens to this report, Captain Swanepoel?' Singe 'n Burn asked.

The police captain sighed. 'Because of the technical error in the search warrant I must very reluctantly withdraw this report.'

'May I please have it, Captain Swanepoel?' I asked.

Swanepoel laughed again. 'The South African Police do not give souvenirs, if you want some souvenirs, go to the Easter show.'

'I'm delighted to hear that's the last of it,' Singe 'n Burn said, obviously relieved.

'No, Headmaster, it is only the beginning. You can consider yourself very lucky we got the wrong school name on the search warrant because today I have come here as a friend. If we come again next Saturday night and we find that this wonderful school you have here is teaching black communists then we will be forced to make some very unfortunate conclusions.'

'I really do protest, sir!' Singe 'n Burn was suddenly angry.

Captain Swanepoel grinned. 'These days it is not very hard to find a black communist.' He looked at Hymie. 'Or even a white one,' then at me, 'even more than one. When blacks want suddenly to have education you can take it from me, they up to no good, somebody else or something else is behind it.'

'Are you telling us to close down the night school, Captain?'

'Headmaster, the law in this matter is not clear yet, but teaching black people in a white school will not be allowed in the new Group Areas Act. You can see my position, Headmaster. I must tell you also my duty in this matter is very clear. Next time we will not make a mistake with the search warrant. And when we come we will find something.' He paused and looked again at us, 'We always find something.'

He rose and extended his hand to Singe 'n Burn. The headmaster did not take it, instead he gripped the side of his desk and leaned forward slightly. 'We will not be intimidated by the police, Captain Swanepoel. We have not broken the law and as far as I know this is still a free and democratic country.'

Captain Swanepoel shrugged and stooped down to retrieve his cap from the floor by his chair. 'I am sorry you will not co-operate with the police, sir.' He adjusted his cap, then turned back to face the headmaster, touching the peak lightly in a casual salute. 'Good afternoon, sir.' Without a look at Hymie or me he turned and left, closing the door quietly behind him.

'Shit, what now?' Hymie said under his breath.

'What was that, Levy?'

'Nothing, sir.'

The light from the window backlit Singe 'n Burn's snowy hair and he looked frail as he continued to grip the desk, swaying slightly as though the motion kept him from disintegrating into a million tiny bits which would silently float away on the dusty beam of sunlight.

'Bravo, sir,' Hymie said.

He shook his head slowly, 'We are beaten.'

'But you just said . . . ?'

'Sheer bravado, my boy. We will have your school on Saturday and Captain Swanepoel will officially raid the Prince of Wales School, after which the board of governors will meet and their conclusion is foregone.' He looked up. 'Nevertheless, we will open next Saturday evening, a Pyrrhic victory to be sure, but there is an important principle at stake.'

We left the head's office on a thorough downer. 'Fuck the Pyrrhic victory, the principle and the principal as well!' Hymie exploded, once we were out of earshot.

'We'll have to let Gideon and the other boxers know. It's only fair that they decide for themselves whether they'll come.'

'Yeah, I suppose,' Hymie said morosely. 'What about the others?'

'Forget it, they won't come. Last Saturday was enough, there's no principle involved for them, just another opportunity taken away, another door closed. They spend their lives being screwed by the system. Would you turn up if you knew you were almost certain to be arrested, thrown in jail, lose your job and be branded as a communist?'

'I'm beginning to realise how lucky I am to have a white skin.' Hymie was taking it worse than I was. I had been around this kind of intimidation all my life and I knew Captain Swanepoel could have been a lot more difficult had he chosen to be.

'What are we going to do, Peekay?'

I laughed, 'You really are a city slicker aren't you, you still think the police are there to protect you from the big bad wolf? After Saturday night this whole scenario was predictable. The Nationalists don't see it as a kindergarten for adult blacks, to them we are starting a black revolution in the heartland of white privilege.'

'You can't be serious. Our dumb school for boxers and house boys?'

'From little acorns mighty oak trees grow. The Nats are not stupid. You should know; the Jews made that mistake before with the Nazis, they thought of them as a bunch of thugs whom they could buy off. Have you seen the educational qualifications the Nationalist government has for its cabinet? It's probably the best educated cabinet in the world. Racism does not diminish with brains, it's a disease, a sickness, it may incubate in ignorance but it doesn't necessarily disappear with the gaining of wisdom!'

'Are you telling me you knew all along this was going to happen?'

'No, of course not. I thought we had a chance, you were right to be somewhat cynical at the beginning, but it was worth a try.'

'But just now in the head's office ... you seemed so disappointed?'

'Christ, Hymie, I'm not saying I wanted it to happen! I was angry and bitterly disappointed. Disappointed that I was right.'

'You're a complicated bastard, Peekay. I'm supposed to be the realist in this partnership. What do we do now?'

'Well Saturday's out for a start, no point in putting the boxers at jeopardy, not for a Pyrrhic victory anyway.'

'Well, at least we can teach them after boxing.'

'No way. That Swanepoel bastard will be watching us like a hawk.'

'I feel so bloody helpless.' Hymie looked at me and shrugged, 'You know, before our visit to Sophiatown I couldn't have given a damn. Yeah, sure, I'd probably have gone along with you on the school, like you've gone along with me on some of our scams. But after the fight, seeing those people, it's different somehow. I begin to have a concept of the people, of what it means to be oppressed, of what it must have meant to be a Jew in Hitler's Germany.' It was the first time I'd seen Hymie confused. He'd come up against something that couldn't be resolved with money or influence. 'It was such a small thing they wanted and we failed. I mean, those poor blighters wanted so badly to learn, just to read and write and do a few sums. It was the least we could do.' Hymie was almost crying from rage.

'So, that's what we're going to continue to do. I didn't spend four years with Geel Piet without learning how to beat the system.'

'What do you mean, Peekay?'

'Correspondence school. Miss Bornstein's Correspondence School!'

'Peekay! You're a genius! We've already got the whole course in three African languages, as well as Fanagalo. It's in the bag, old chap, we'll guinea-pig the whole thing. We'll make it free for the class who have just been expelled, then with Mr Nguni's help and for a small sum, yet to be determined, we'll sell a correspondence course for blacks throughout South Africa. We'll even send one to Captain Swanepoel and tell him to jam it up his arse so that every time he farts he sounds intelligent!'

Miss Bornstein's Correspondence School would one day become the biggest of its kind in the southern hemisphere, with Miss Bornstein as actual principal. Mr Nguni simply let it be known that the course came from the Tadpole Angel who wanted the people to take pride in learning to read and write and do sums. It would turn out to be one of the more important elements in his financial and political empire in the years to come.

TWENTY-THREE

Nineteen fifty-one was the year I won the South African Schools featherweight title, and the Prince of Wales School won the schools championship for the third year running. Darby and Sarge were heroes and both had become welcome members of the masters' common room. Success of any sort seems to break down social barriers. We all sat for our matriculation, although a first-class pass for Sinjun's People was a foregone conclusion. Atherton was selected for the South African schoolboy rugby team to tour Argentina and Cunning-Spider had made it into the Transvaal Schools cricket team. Pissy Johnson, with a lot of coaching from Hymie and me, felt confident that he'd get the marks in his matric to study medicine. He had become an expert at fixing cuts in the ring and from this small beginning his ambition to be a doctor had blossomed.

I had, by all accounts, a brilliant school career, getting my colours in rugby and three times for boxing as well as being head prefect and a company commander in the school cadet corps. While my music hadn't really progressed, I was still by school standards considered amongst the more superior musicians.

In Sinjun's terms, I was well on my way to being a Renaissance man. In my own terms I felt less successful. I had survived the system but that was in many ways the problem. I seemed to be losing control of my own life, forfeiting my individuality for the glittering prizes and the accolades of my peers. The need to win had become everything, the head had become more important than the heart, Hoppie's advice had worked too well.

I had supported myself at school with the Bank and the various scams Hymie and I had developed. But what had been intellectual amusement for Hymie was deadly serious for me. I needed the money not only to survive but as a means of dignity. Hymie and I had become inseparable friends and with the death of Doc he was certainly the most important person in my life. But I knew deep down that Hymie had been chosen because he could help me survive the system. I was a user. It had become a habit; winner that I seemed to be, I had become a mental mendicant.

I was conscious also of the price I paid. That in return people took strength from me. Hymie, Miss Bornstein, Mrs Boxall all needed me as a focal point, I was required to perform for them in return for their unstinting help and love. The concept of the Tadpole Angel which I had tried to set aside would not leave me. After the Mandoma fight the black crowds at my boxing matches had become enormous and at the South African Schools Championships the police had been called to disperse the chanting crowd outside the Johannesburg Drill Hall. I knew that eventually something more was expected of me. All my life I'd been pushed around. By the Judge. By the Lord. By the concept of the Tadpole Angel. In my own way I had fought and in return had been given Doc and Hoppie and Geel Piet as my mentors. The point of all this was difficult to understand. Perhaps, after all, life is like this. But I felt that I needed to take one independent action that would put my life back under my own control. It was as though I needed to lose but hadn't developed the mechanism to do so. I only had one problem with this; I hadn't any idea how to go about doing so.

The only totally independent thing in my life was my ambition to become the welterweight champion of the world. It was the only thing that couldn't be manipulated.

I either had it in me or I hadn't. It was the thing those who loved me, with the exception of Captain Smit and Gert, couldn't understand. It was the one thing in my life that seemed to make sense to me. In this single action there was no corruption of the spirit.

In the last week of term Singe 'n Burn accompanied me to my interview with the Rhodes scholarship board. I had sat for two scholarships. One to Witwatersrand University and another to the University of Stellenbosch, an Afrikaans-speaking university with a brilliant law school. But, more than anything, I wanted to go to Oxford. I felt I was unlikely to compromise this desire, come what may. Hymie's family had already agreed to pay for me to go, but even as a loan I found this unacceptable. Unacceptable to me, to the memory of Doc, to Mrs Boxall, Miss Bornstein, Captain Smit, Gert, Hoppie Groenewald, Big Hettie and most of all, to Geel Piet, who had never in his life experienced a hand extended to him in help.

Even my mother, convinced that the temporal things of life were secondary and who had given the Lord the entire credit for making my education possible, had sat behind a sewing machine from dawn until dusk to support me as much as she was able.

I was a man now, I was through with taking. I felt the rest was up to me. If I didn't know what the next step in my life was to be, I felt that I might set it in motion by acting independently of the help that was always so generously extended to me by others.

Hymie, the gambler and businessman, reckoned the odds on my winning one of three Rhodes scholarships for South Africa were less then even. As the time for my interview grew close he grew more and more distraught. He sensed my need to act independently and that to some large degree the Rhodes scholarship would achieve this aim. At the same time he wanted to cushion me from the disappointment if I lost. It was not unknown, but highly unusual to be awarded a Rhodes scholarship straight from school. Rhodes scholars were almost always chosen after an initial degree at university, when the student had already confirmed a brilliant school career with an equally brilliant first degree taken in conjunction with a sporting and cultural contribution in the university environment.

'Christ, Peekay, in my old man's terms the fees to Oxford are petty cash. We'd be together like always and come back home and eventually open a practice together. You can start looking after the people and I'll make us a squillion dollars. It's all so easy. Why do you have to make it so bloody difficult?'

'Well, for a start I'm going to be welterweight champion of the world. If I took your dad's money, I'd have to use all my time to justify it at university.'

'You don't have to justify it, you can do both!' Hymie yelled.

'You know me better than that. Let me tell you something stupid, Hymie. If I had to choose between becoming welterweight champion of the world and taking a law degree at Oxford, the boxing would win.'

He looked stunned. 'Why? You're not the sort of guy who wants to be famous that way. In fact, you're exactly the opposite.'

'It's got to do with something which happened when I was very young. I can't explain it, it's just got to be that way.'

'Peekay, the money you'll make as a professional, even a world champion, will be nothing compared to the two of us together in a law practice.'

'It's not something I can explain. I've worked for this since I was six. It has nothing to do with the importance of being the welterweight champion of the world.' I chuckled inwardly. How the hell could I explain to him that I was doing it, in part, for a dead chicken!

'Look, Peekay, you're only just a lightweight, it will be two, maybe three years before you become a welterweight, you can take your degree, or a good part of it anyway, and then go on with your boxing career. I'll help you. We'll even make a lot of dough out of it.'

The interview with the selection board was a fairly harrowing experience, the first hour taken up with the board talking to Singe 'n Burn while I cooled my heels in the waiting room of University House. The waiting was the worst part. The selection committee was comprised of three fairly elderly men who simply started to chat with me. One of them, a thin man with round steel-rimmed glasses which slid down to the tip of his very long nose and whose hair was parted precisely in the middle and slicked down with brilliantine, looked like Ichabod Crane. He peered at me over the top of his glasses and quoted the first line of three verses from Ovid, then asked me to complete them. I had to laugh, it was stuff I'd learned from Doc when I was nine.

'Not bad, not at all bad, only one small mistake.'

'Please, sir, I disagree,' I replied, my heart in my mouth. The three poems had been among Doc's favourites and I knew them intimately. I was certain I'd not made a mistake.

'Bravo, young man!' Ichabod said. 'You're quite correct and, besides, you had the courage to say so.' He pulled his glasses back to the top of his nose and wrote something down on a tablet of lined bright yellow paper.

The three examiners looked positively musty with learning and not at all like sporting types. But, after they'd chatted to me seemingly about this and that, they fixed on my boxing. Why, they wanted to know, was I obsessed with boxing? My submission showed me to be a brilliant student, a very talented musician, a good rugby player and a brilliant boxer. One of them read from the submission, 'Has the ambition to become a professional boxer and to win the welterweight championship of the world!' I could see he was quite taken aback.

'Surely a boy of your obvious intelligence, or according to your headmaster, brilliance, must see that a vocation as a professional pugilist is not compatible with reading law at Oxford?'

'Lord Byron was a pugilist, sir. No one doubted his intellectual integrity,' I answered. He grunted and wrote something down on the pad in front of him. Ichabod Crane had a slight smile on his face.

'Ah, I do not recall whether Byron was an Oxford man!' he said, which caused his two colleagues to laugh.

'Your point is well made, Mr ... er, Peekay, but as I recall he was an amateur.'

'There is considerable evidence that he fought on occasions for a wager which today would make him a professional, sir.'

'Be that as it may, a small wager on the side amongst friends is hardly the same thing, is it?'

'No, sir,' I replied, unwilling to press my luck any further by pointing out that quite large sums of money were involved.

At the end of the interview I was asked to wait with Singe 'n Burn in the waiting room. The head seemed even more nervous than me and made me repeat every word of the interview. When I got to the bit about Byron he was delighted. 'Excellent!' he said, clapping his hands, but then when I told him about Byron fighting for a wager and the somewhat brusque reply I had received, he frowned. 'That's Lewis of Natal University, a man who doesn't care to be contradicted.' When I concluded my account he simply said, 'Well done, Peekay, you have acquitted yourself well.'

We were then ushered back in and it was Ichabod Crane who announced that I had been listed in the last five candidates and would be required to sit for the Oxford University entrance examinations.

'The Prince of Wales School which you attend has an enviable reputation, and if you are an example of its product, the least I can say for myself and my colleagues, is that we have been impressed.' They then stood up and shook hands with us both.

Singe 'n Burn was elated, we were over the major hurdle.

They had taken my schoolboy candidature seriously. Several days later I sat with Hymie for the Oxford University entrance examinations the results of which would be announced before the Rhodes scholarships.

I arrived home for the Christmas holidays to find my picture was on the front page of the *Goldfields News*. Mr Hankin, frustrated newspaperman to the last, had used the picture Doc had taken of me sitting on our rock the first day we had met on the hill behind the rose garden. Despite the fact that every one in town knew who I was, above it a banner headline read: BOY ON A ROCK FOR OXFORD! I recalled with a touch of bitterness the stupid old fart's last use of this picture on the front page, when he accused Doc of being a Nazi spy and of breaking my jaw.

I found myself a local hero once again. As far as the town was concerned my elevation to Rhodes scholarship status was all over bar the shouting. In the month it took for the results of the Oxford entrance examinations to come through, Miss Bornstein became a nervous wreck.

Down at the prison they were much more impressed with Solly's thirteen-punch combination. If they could have chosen between a scholarship to Oxford, a place they'd never heard of anyway, or a thirteen combo, there is little doubt they'd have plumped for the latter. Once again I won the Eastern Transvaal featherweight title and also best boxer of the championships. With this, my fourth successive win, Captain Smit, in what he later described as one of the great moments in his life, was able to claim the trophy permanently for the Barberton Blues.

My examination results arrived in late January and stated that I had received a distinction in all subjects. Miss Bornstein was beside herself and it was such big news around the place that old Mr Bornstein contrived to lose the first ever game of chess to me while denying hotly that he had purposely done so. Four days later a letter arrived from the Rhodes scholarship committee.

Dear Mr 'Peekay',

*On behalf of the selection committee for Rhodes Schol-
arships for the year 1951, we regret to inform you that
your application has been unsuccessful.*

*I have been asked by the selection committee to com-
mend you for the manner in which you conducted yourself during your interview and for the results you achieved
in the required examination.*

*It is the earnest opinion of the committee that, having
completed your first degree, you should apply again.*

Yours faithfully,
L. J. Fisher
Secretary to the Committee

The people around me had become accustomed to my
winning, it was a habit they shared, an indulgence they
took for granted. I could see they were shocked and bitterly
disappointed that, having done their part, I had somehow
failed them. Miss Bornstein and Mrs Boxall were distraught
beyond belief, having quickly convinced themselves of some
sort of plot. My mother, after shedding a few tears, soon
concluded that the Lord had decided it was not His will for
me and that, if only I would accept Him into my heart and
into my life, His purpose for me would become clear. Two
days later she announced at the dinner table that the Lord
had guided her quite clearly and that I should give up
boxing as it displeased him. When I had done so, I would
be guided in the Lord's special plans for me.

When I replied that boxing was too important to me, she
had burst into sudden tears. 'That is the devil in you talking,
God is not mocked!' she shouted, leaving the table with her
face buried in her table napkin.

'There, there. There's a good lad,' my granpa soothed.

The following day a letter arrived from Singe 'n Burn in
which he said that he was confident I would ride through

the disappointment and that I had the internal fortitude to grow stronger from the experience. He added that the true Renaissance man accepted defeat as the ingredient which made eventual success worth striving for, blah, blah, blah. He then added that he had received a letter from Professor Stonehouse of Witwatersrand University who, it turned out, was Ichabod Crane. In it Stonehouse had remarked that the committee had been visited by a Captain Swanepoel who had not been complimentary about the school and its activities and in particular my implication in these activities. He wanted to assure Singe 'n Burn that should he hear otherwise, this involvement by the police did not affect his judgement nor did it, he felt sure, affect that of his colleagues. Stonehouse concluded by saying that my application for a scholarship to Witwatersrand had been accepted and that he hoped the headmaster would be able to influence me to accept.

The following week the second scholarship, to Stellenbosch, was confirmed and I received an invitation to apply to Natal University. But I knew, in the minds of those who loved me, that this would be accepting the crumbs from the rich man's table. They were emotionally involved with Oxford and no other place, no matter how grand, would have satisfied their expectations for me and rewarded them for the parts they had played.

Only my granpa seemed unconcerned. He'd said nothing when the letter from the committee had arrived, except of course, 'There's a good lad.' I found him later in the garden grafting rose stock and we sat out of the blazing December sun in the dark shade of one of the big old English oaks. As usual he took ten minutes to tap and tamp and strike and eventually puff up a blue haze around his head. I'd given him a tin of Erinmore which I'd bought in Johannesburg and the honey-treated tobacco smoke smelt delicious as it swirled around his head.

'My brother Arthur went to Oxford, he was the clever one in our family. Like you he won scholarships, first to grammar school and then to Oxford.' He puffed and looked over the roof which still hadn't been painted. 'In my time not too many grammar school boys made it through to the dreaming spires of Oxford and Cambridge.'

'What happened to him, Granpa?'

The old man puffed at his pipe and stared out into space for ages, puff, puff, puff. 'I don't know what went wrong, lad. He rose to be Lord Chief Justice of Appeal and was completely crippled by arthritis by the time he was forty. A miserable life really, made a lot of money and a lot of misery for himself and everyone else. According to my sister Jessie, he died rich and lonely.' He puffed on his pipe a little longer. 'Funny thing about Arthur, he never could get things in their right perspective.'

Hymie had sent a telegram every week demanding to know if the results had come out and asking me to phone him, reverse charges, when they did. I called him from Mrs Boxall's office in the library.

'Hard luck, Peekay, so close, so bloody close!' There was a click on the phone and then a woman's voice. 'Operator here, please do not swear on the public telephone,' the phone clicked again. 'Christ! Who was that?' Hymie said on the other end. The phone clicked again and went dead. I dialled the exchange.

'Operator, I was cut off.'

'Peekay, this is Doris Engelbrecht!' Doris was a woman in her mid twenties, a Marie 'tonsillectomy' convert who now taught Sunday school at the Apostolic Faith Mission. 'I am supposed to cut off calls that contain obscene language. Your party in Pretoria used filthy language and has taken the Lord's name in vain. I can't allow it on the public telephone even if he is paying reverse charges.'

'I'm sorry, Doris, he just talks like that, he means no harm, it's just his way.'

'Ag sis, Peekay, how can you know such a person? You who are so clever and all and whose mother is a very high up born-again Christian?'

'Doris, you're not supposed to be listening, telephone calls are meant to be private.'

'It says in the book I must not allow people to use obscene language on the telephone. How can I not allow them when I don't hear them?'

There seemed to be no ready answer to this. 'Doris, if you get me my party in Pretoria, I'll tell him not to use bad language.'

'Tell him also to wash his mouth out with Lifebuoy soap!' Doris said.

The phone rang a couple of minutes later. I grabbed it and before Hymie could speak said, 'Watch your mouth, Levy. Doris the born-again Christian is monitoring you.'

There was only the slightest pause on the phone. 'What's your favourite chocolates, Doris?' Hymie asked. There was silence on the other end. 'Black Magic or one of those big three-pound boxes with the picture of an English cottage on the outside showing all the flowers in the garden, you know, with a big pink ribbon?' The silence continued. 'I just want to say I'm sorry for my language, language like that can upset certain parties.'

Doris's voice cut in sharply. 'Tell the party on the other end I will not be tempted by the devil, Peekay!'

'Ag man, Doris, my friend has a chocolate factory, it is just a way of saying sorry,' I coaxed.

'A box so big you can't pick it up with one hand, Doris,' Hymie said.

'The box with the garden and the pink ribbon, then,' Doris piped in a small voice.

'Okay, then you've got to promise not to listen any more, Doris,' I said.

'Only if you promise on the Lord's name that your friend won't swear some more,' she said, a trace of warning still in her voice.

'Thanks, Doris,' we both said. The phone clicked and Doris was gone.

574

'For Christ's sake, don't forget to send the chocolates, Hymie. I've got to live in this town.'

'Is it safe to talk now?' Hymie said.

'Of course! You have the word of a born-again Christian!'

'No I won't forget, we keep a roomful of obscenely large boxes of chocolate at the carpet emporium. My dad calls them his "sweeteners"; every customer gets a box when a salesman determines it's time to close the sale. My dad claims his entire carpet empire is built on chocolate.' Hymie laughed, 'He even calls the salesmen his chocolate soldiers!'

His voice changed abruptly. 'The offer still stands, old mate. You don't have to take the money, it's just a loan. Now that you've passed the Oxford entrance examination and all.'

'Hymie, we've been through that! You promised you wouldn't bring it up again.'

'Cripes, Peekay, what are you going to do?'

I told him about the three scholarships I'd been offered and the paragraph in the letter which encouraged me to apply again when I had obtained my first degree.

Hymie was silent for a moment. 'Got it! We'll go together to whatever university you choose and then we'll take the last two years at Oxford. You're only just seventeen and I'm just eighteen, we've got lots of time!'

It was my turn to be silent. 'You've forgotten one thing,' I said finally.

Hymie was quick as a flash. 'Of course I haven't, we'll go to Witwatersrand and Solly can continue to train you and the old combo will stay together.'

'It sounds great, Hymie, but you've already been accepted for Oxford. This doesn't fit in at all with your plans.'

'Plans! Plans are meant to be broken. This is a much better idea.'

But I knew it wasn't.

'Let me think, Hymie. I just need a few days to think things out.' I knew quite suddenly that I would have to visit the crystal cave of Africa, that I had to 'speak' with Doc. Doc was still a very real part of my life and I had come to think of the crystal cave of Africa as the place I would be closest to him.

'Call me, reverse charge, in a week, you promise now. So long, Peekay.'

The next morning I packed a rucksack and left before dawn for the cave. By mid-morning I had climbed to the shelf next to the cave. I had no desire to enter; Doc's spirit was everywhere, I was as close as I needed to be.

The shelf faced west and caught the late afternoon sun so that now I sat in shadow, the smooth dolomite surface still cold from the night. I closed my eyes as Inkosi-Inkosikazi had shown me how to do so many years ago.

Now there came the sudden roar of water in my head and then I saw the three waterfalls. I was standing again in the moonlight on an outcrop of rock directly above the falling water. Far below me the river rushed, tumbling into a narrow gorge. Just before the river entered the gorge an apron of green water spread from the base of the last of the falls and across its centre, a small boy's jump separating them, were the ten black stepping stones, their smooth wet surfaces only inches above the swirling current.

I took a deep breath and launched myself from the rock; the cool air mixed with spray rushed past my face. I hit the pool at the bottom of the first waterfall, the sound of the splash drowned in the roar of the water. I surfaced to be swept over the second of the falls and then again over the third, landing in the deep pool of swirling green water. I fought my way to the surface and struck out towards the first of the black stones. Pulling myself up onto it, I hurriedly jumped from one stone to another, finally leaping for the pebbly beach beyond. I felt my toes and the ball of my foot touch the smooth round river pebbles, and as I landed I found myself inside the crystal cave of Africa.

The cave was illuminated as though by soft sunlight and I had no trouble seeing around me. It was more magnificent than I had ever imagined, the stalactites suspended in every imaginable colour, some hanging thirty feet from the ceiling. I walked towards Doc's platform skirting the mirror-still pools of water reflecting the grotesque and beautiful stone icicles. A ray of sunlight, as sharply defined as if it were painted in a Raphael skyscape, fell onto the platform. I looked up to see a perfectly round hole in the ceiling through which the sun shone as though predestined for this precise hour of this precise day. The beam of light shone through the crystalline structures above the platform and spilt down the steps leading up to it. Slowly I climbed the rough, natural steps until finally, standing on the top step, I looked down onto the platform where Doc lay at my feet.

Doc lay as I had imagined he would, fingers extended, arms bent at the elbows and crossed at the wrists across his breast, his legs straight, like the effigy of a medieval knight at rest on a gothic tomb in a quiet corner of a great cathedral. He was made of pure crystal, the soft sunlight reflected from the effigy dancing at the edges. Doc's sculptured face was surrounded by burnished light.

I told him of my fear of losing control of my destiny, how, because I had camouflaged myself so well, I seemed now to be shaped and directed too much by the needs of others. How the power of one within me was being dissipated even though their purposes for me were not corrupt or ill-intentioned. On the contrary, their deeds came swaddled in the innocence of love. I was becoming powerless as those around me plundered my spirit with the gift of themselves.

It was as though there was a voice inside me explaining me to myself: I had become an expert at camouflage. My precocity allowed me, chameleon-like, to be to each what they required me to be. To Doc a companion, to Mrs Boxall an enchantment, to the people a champion, to Captain Smit a fulfilment, to Miss Bornstein a bright lint in a dull warp, to Hymie a foil, to Singe 'n Burn a product and to my peers an idealised school boy, a winner and a great guy.

I was a poor boy among rich ones and in my mind the status they gained by the simple expedient of being wealthy was only leavened by my superior performance in every other expectation. I had come to identify with my camouflage to the point where the masquerade became more important than the truth. While this posturing was so finely tuned it was no longer deliberate, it had nevertheless been born out of a compulsion to hide. As a small child I had discovered that only two places are available to those who wish to remain concealed. The choices are to be a non-entity or an exception. You either disappear into a plebeian background or move forward to where most others fear to follow.

My camouflage, begun so many years before under the persecution of the Judge, was now threatening to become the complete man. It was time to slough the mottled and cunningly contrived outer skin to emerge as myself, to face the risk of exposure, to regain the power of one. I had reached the point where to find myself was essential.

I was not conscious of how long I had been sitting cross-legged on the shelf but slowly my eyes focused and the soft blur of blue in front of them sharpened into the mountains to the west. In the rainforest below me I heard the cry of a red loerie. My legs were stiff and my ankles sore where they had been crossed. I felt an overwhelming sense of freedom . . . the same sense of being free that I had felt when the big, black, hissing train had pulled out of the platform, away from the hostel, Mevrou and the Judge. When Hoppie had sat opposite me and we had first shared an adventure and a green sucker between us.

I had come back from the dreamtime in the crystal cave of Africa with a certainty that I would be tested once more before the power of one would become mine alone. When my destiny would be in my own hands.

I continued to sit completely still as Doc had taught me to do when observing any living thing. 'Still like rock, Peekay, past the itch and the scratch and the pain, where the concentration sees with a diamond-sharp light.' And so I sat perfectly still, emerging slowly from the cocoon of the trance I had been in. In my mind I asked Doc for a sign.

At that moment, sitting still as a rock on the shelf directly outside the crystal cave of Africa, I had no doubts, nor was I troubled by the intellectual absurdity of the request for a sign, a confirmation in a physical sense of the message I felt so clearly within me.

At first it was hardly a movement at all, less even than the flicker of an eyelid, a slight blurring of light. Then the head of the black mamba rose above the edge of the shelf two feet from where I sat. Its flat anthracite head froze inches above the shelf. Its forked tongue, as though possessing a life of its own, flicked and trembled the air for vibrations. The huge snake rose, periscoping above the shelf, moving forward until its head was no more than six inches from my face. I could see its eyes, black tektites without movement set above jaws of injected death. Its head moved in slow motion from side to side, sweeping across my sightline. If it struck I would have fifteen minutes to live . . . enough time to enter the cave and lie beside Doc before my nervous system collapsed. The mamba's head moved below my line of sight and then came to rest on the toe of my boot. I could feel the pressure of its body as it slid over the boot and along the shelf to disappear over the cliff's far edge. The snake could only have come out of the cave. Doc had sent me a sign. I knew what I was required to do.

Slowly the numbness left my body and I felt the rush of adrenalin as it hit my bloodstream, leaving me trembling. I waited until the shaking had ceased before I dropped down to the tiny ledge and worked my body flat against the cliff wall until I stood facing into the opening to the cave. The floor of the tunnel leading to the cave was covered with sand worn from the walls by the erosion of the wind. I could clearly see where the snake had entered and then returned, no doubt having fed on the hapless bats asleep inside. Doc had sent me the sign I wanted.

I carefully worked my way back to the ledge, shouldered my small rucksack and started to climb down the cliff. The snake was unlikely to be on my path. Fat from eating bats, it would find a place to sleep under the safety of a rock where it was unlikely to be disturbed.

Once I had recovered from my fear, I found the snake an entirely appropriate, even perhaps a magnificent symbol. The black mamba, the most deadly snake in the world, takes one partner for life. If its partner is killed the second snake will often wait for the killer to return, prepared to die in order to take revenge. Not naturally aggressive, it will nevertheless defend its young, raising itself onto the last few inches of its tail and striking sideways in a whipping action. As most humans instinctively raise their arms in panic to defend their eyes the mamba fangs most often strike into the top of the upper arm. The journey to the heart is swift and the outcome deadly certain.

There was a great deal of consternation from everyone concerned when I announced that I wanted to take a year off between school and university and that I would go up to Northern Rhodesia to work in the copper mines. It was as though all who loved me, even the boxers, felt that if I broke the continuity of my life, the spell which bound our relationship would be broken.

Gert's brother had visited him at Christmas from the Copperbelt and had talked of the shortage of white labour in the mines of both the Copperbelt and the Congo. The Korean War had just started and copper prices had soared. He told of diamond drillers making two hundred pounds a week and young grizzly men making a hundred after they were paid their copper bonus.

Northern Rhodesia was a British colony across the Zambesi, it was far away from the people who held me so dearly within the thrall of their ambitions. It was away from the legend of the Tadpole Angel. It was even away from boxing. I saw it as an opportunity to come to terms with myself and to build my body to the size of a welterweight. The hard underground work would toughen me, while twelve months away from the ring would do me no harm. I had been boxing since I was seven years old and had fought one hundred and sixteen amateur fights. My instincts, which always served me well, told me it was time for a rest.

Gert's brother, Danie, worked as a diamond driller, the elite corps among the Copperbelt miners. Most of the diamond drillers were Afrikaners from Johannesburg attracted by the huge copper bonus white mine workers were being paid. They were so named because the cutting edge of the drill bits were studded with industrial quality diamonds to make them hard enough to cut through the rock. Danie worked in a mine near Ndda, in the centre of the Copperbelt. He said he could get me a job as a grizzly man at the Rhoan Antelope Mine owned by Anglo American in the small mining town of Luanshya. A grizzly man worked with high explosives and was the next highest paid job on the mine.

The four-day trip by train left South Africa at Beitbridge and travelled across Southern Rhodesia to Victoria Falls where I crossed the Zambesi into Northern Rhodesia. Southern Rhodesia is not unlike the Eastern and Northern Transvaal but across the great Zambesi the country changes to flat grassland and equatorial forest. The trees which covered vast areas of the country were unlike any I had seen before, for they carried their autumnal colouring all through summer. Leaves of brilliant reds and yellows and even mauves and purple, all the colours expected of a northern hemisphere autumn. A passenger who sat beside me told me of giant edible mushrooms that appear in the forest overnight and grow two feet tall with a canopy three feet across. A mushroom weighing thirty pounds. I'd been around long enough not to take everything I heard as gospel, but in the months to come I would see Africans selling these huge mushrooms at the side of the road, simply cutting off the amount the purchaser required. Giant, brilliantly coloured moths with a wingspan ten inches across also bred on the wet, leafy floor of the forest.

Northern Rhodesia felt different and the Africans, like most from central Africa, were truly black, their faces seemingly flatter and their build smaller than the lighter milk chocolate brown of the Zulu or the Shangaan. They spoke Swahili, and it was with some consternation that I realised it was a language I did not speak and that I was cut off from the African people for the first time in my life. In the mines they talked a language known as Ki-swahili which was not unlike Fanagalo, but like all languages designed for a working purpose, it was limited and stunted. Africans raw from their villages in the bush were recruited to the mines where they were taught this mine language so that they could take instructions from their white bosses and, in many cases, talk to each other. A work gang often contained black miners from half a dozen different tribes, each with a different language.

At four o'clock in the afternoon on the fourth day we finally pulled into the sleepy town of Ndola. Ndola was really only a small community made up of miners' families and tradespeople who lived off the giant copper mines. The remainder of the town's people were British colonial service administration officers and their families. It made for an uneasy white dichotomy. The mining families seldom mixed socially with the civil service families established at a separate end of the town. Ndola was thirty miles or so from Luanshya but the end of the railroad as far as passenger trains were concerned.

Gert's brother met me at the station where the air was filled with the babble of confused and frightened blacks. White mine officers feigned indifference while blue uniformed black mine policeman filled with self-importance and professional impatience herded and pushed hundreds of Africans from the train. Too late now to turn back, they had been harvested from the bush like wild tsamma melons.

For the past two days and nights the train had stopped at small sidings with no more than a tin shed and a small clearing to separate them from the rest of the bush. Here small groups of perhaps a dozen Africans wrapped in blankets would be herded onto the train by a black recruiting officer. The whites of their eyes showed their fear and confusion as they were bundled aboard the hissing, steam-belching monster, jeered at by those who had earlier been gathered up and who were by now, with arms resting casually on the sills of carriage windows, accustomed to the clickity-clack of momentum and the wonderment of the snake which runs on an iron road.

Now they were almost at the end of their journey. I watched as the black mine police tried to get them roughly into line. They came only because drought and a great locust plague had destroyed their crops and the grazing for their cattle. Driven from their villages as indentured labour for the mines, they would work for a year so they could send money to keep their starving women and children alive. The fear these poor creatures felt the first time they were plummeted into the bowels of the earth was a source of great mirth to the initiated black miners as well as to many of the whites.

Gert's brother noticed me looking at the poor buggers. 'Ag man, they like a monkey when they first come. They can't even climb a ladder and when you show them a mirror they go almost white when they see the big ape looking back at them. It's very funny man, I'm telling you.' He picked up my suitcase and I followed him over to a green Bedford utility. 'I just come off shift so I'll drive you to Luanshya, I telephoned the mess there yesterday and they know you coming. Tomorrow you got to report to the mine recruiting office for a medical and then you go sign on for the school of mines for three months. I got to warn you, man, they got a Welsh bastard there called Thomas, watch out for him. If you get out of the school of mines and get your blasting licence you go onto grizzlies for six months, three if you lucky. But the money is good.'

'Why only six months or even three?' I asked as we pulled out of the station.

'I didn't want to tell you before, but if you on grizzlies much longer the odds is cut down.'

'The odds?'

'Ja man, the odds of getting badly injured or killed.' Gert laughed. 'They don't pay you that kind of money for nothing, you know.'

'Does everyone go onto grizzlies?'

'Ja, all the young guys, if you over twenty-two your reactions not fast enough. Only young guys are fast enough or,' he grinned, 'mad enough to do it!'

'Christ, it doesn't look as though I've got a lot of choice!'

Gert's brother laughed again. 'None. All young guys got to be grizzly men, nobody else will do it. On the Rand it's not even allowed. Moving ore through a grizzly is the best way, but it's also the most dangerous. The miner's union on the Rand won't have a bar of it and grizzlies are banned anywhere in South Africa, but here in Northern Rhodesia they don't care, man. As long as they get the muck out they happy.' He paused as he made a turn, heading the ute onto a corrugated dirt road leading out of town. 'But you make blêrrie good money and if you careful you'll be orright.'

I laughed. 'Don't worry, Danie, I'll be bloody careful!'

He looked at me, his hands vibrating on the steering wheel as we hit a particularly badly rutted strip. 'That's the blêrrie trouble, a grizzly man comes on night shift, eleven to seven, he got the job to pull all the ore out of a stope. That's my job as a diamond driller, I drill the stope all day and you got to pull the muck out through the grizzly at night. If you too careful and you don't get enough muck through the grizzly so I got an empty stope to work with, you in a lot of trouble man!' He gave me a knowing grin. 'You do that a few times and you can collect your ticket.

The diamond driller is king and you fuck up his stope you don't work in the mines no more, man.'

I remained silent. I hadn't any idea what he was talking about, but I gathered that whatever a grizzly man did he was under all sorts of pressure. And pressure creates accidents.

'That's one good thing about Thomas in the school of mines, he makes things so blêrrie bad in your training that if you make it and get your blasting licence you got a good chance of staying alive on a grizzly.'

Danie left me at the mine mess where I had a room reserved for a month before I moved into a hut of my own in one of the single men's compounds surrounding the mess.

'I'll try to visit sometimes, you hear. But up here it's not so easy, each mining town is on its own and you will work night shift and me always day so it's no use for me to come over. If it gets very bad you can call me.' He scribbled the name of his mine and a phone number on a piece of paper. 'Just leave a message for me at the mine office, I'll come as soon as I can.' He extended his hand. He was a big bloke, six foot two or three and he had the usual Afrikaner gorilla grip.

I thanked him for his help. 'Ag man, Peekay, any friend of my little boetie is a friend of mine. Gert says you a real man and will one day be a world champion, I'm glad to help.' He paused. 'There's boxing up here also, but nobody as good as you. Some of the Kaffirs is okay, they will be quite good to practise on, these blêrrie apes has got heads so hard they'd wear out a diamond drill. So long, Peekay, all the best, hey.' I watched as the ute accelerated, skidding its wheels before moving away in a cloud of dust.

Apart from the smelter and mine administration offices the small mining town of Luanshya consisted of two parts. The town itself, which contained the married mine officials and their families, school teachers, shop owners, and colonial administration, most of whom were police, and a quite separate area for single men of several hundred small circular huts known by the South African term 'rondavels'.

Each of these rondavels had a corrugated iron roof and walls and floor of cement. A square flyscreen verandah, six feet wide and fifteen feet in length, was attached to each hut. While this stoep was a flimsy affair intended to keep mosquitoes out and let a breeze in, the door to the hut was made of sheet iron, almost impossible to break down if locked from the inside. Two small windows on either side of the hut were barred. There was nothing friendly or homely about these huts except perhaps for a large ceiling fan which sometimes, on a blazing hot day after a nightshift working a grizzly, stirred the air enough to induce a fitful sleep.

The rondavel contained a bed and mattress, a wardrobe, a table and two chairs. In the centre of this untidy army of huts was the mess, where for a few pounds a month you ate. The block I was to live in contained men from forty-two countries, many of whom had a dubious past and a doubtful future in the country from which they originated. While there were a few grizzly men like myself, young guys who were fast and fit enough to work the tungsten steel grizzly bars without killing themselves, most of the miners were in their thirties, some even older. They were without exception tough, hard men who had come for the money. Few were traditional miners, many were drunks and criminals, some of them ex-Nazis on the run, some mercenaries who had just kept moving when the war ended, waiting for another to happen though not prepared to don a uniform for formal affairs such as the one gathering momentum in Korea. Some were card sharps, con men and thieves who, while working in the mines in order to remain in town, had come for the after-hours action.

I learned that the normal courtesies did not apply, and not to ask a man where he came from or to inquire into his past. He might tell you when he became soulfully or sentimentally drunk, but most of the crud, as the compound men were called by the town's people, had learned to keep their mouths shut, drunk or sober. I also quickly learned to keep my hut shut on a Saturday night, when the week after I'd been allocated one I narrowly avoided being pack raped. In a town with no women, other than a handful of married dames, a seventeen-year-old boy was a grand sexual opportunity for a drunken group of Germans, Russians, French Algerians and Slavs. Had I not been rescued by Rasputin, a giant Georgian who almost never spoke, I would have been bum bait for sure. While the town itself was policed, the crud compound was on mine property and largely left alone unless a stabbing took place or a drunken brawl got out of hand.

Every six weeks a Belgian DC–3 would land on the small airstrip a mile out of town near number nine shaft. To the cheers of the waiting crud it would disgorge twenty-five whores from Brussels via the Belgian Congo where they had already spent a lucrative week in the copper mines of Katanga province. A couple of weeks on their backs would set them up for a year at home. Indeed many of them were young housewives putting together the deposit for a home or shop girls earning a dowry. Europe was short of men and a girl had to have a little more than a respectable background if she hoped to marry. Two easily explained weeks away on holiday and a pair of constantly opening legs was all it took to consolidate a proposal for marriage with the deposit, ostensibly from the bride's parents, on a nice little cottage in the suburbs of Antwerp. Some of the ladies were professional whores, because that's what some of the crud wanted. A good whore knows how to get drunk with a man, give him what he wants and rob him of a week's wages without disturbing his anonymity or touching his heart. A man on the run finds compassion or love or even pretended innocence his greatest source of emotional danger.

The crud would wait from dawn on the day the whore flight came in, chaffing each other about getting the fresh meat and the prettiest women, cursing the bloody frog crud across the Congo border for having first go, telling each other that it was a well-established fact that frog crud have tiny pricks and that's why the women went there first. They would tell each other with winks and guffaws that, had it been the other way around, the bloody frogs would have ended up getting it for nothing because the whores wouldn't have known they'd been on the job. The whores were known as French letters because the frog crud had first dipped their pens in and then sent them by airmail across the border. The Congo miners were a mixed lot just like the Copperbelt, though the majority were Belgian who spoke French. But the distinction escaped most of the crud. 'If he speaks French he's a frog. So who's going to argue?'

My new life began in the school of mines, a school conducted mostly underground on day shift at number nine shaft which stood on the edge of town. It was run by two large Welshmen who, it was claimed, played together in the front row for Cardiff before the war. Dai Thomas and Gareth Jones were a remarkable duo with Thomas working underground with the class and Jones, an ex-school teacher and the mine technical officer, taking the two-hour theoretical class before our eight-hour underground shift began.

The combination was worked to extract the maximum agony out of the three months spent in their care. Jones would feed Thomas the weaknesses of each member of the class and Thomas would exploit these for all he was worth when we arrived underground. They saw themselves as being in the practical business of showing men how to stay alive underground and they damn near killed them in the process.

At seventeen I was the youngest and also physically the smallest of as tough a collection of reluctant students as ever assembled to learn anything. We had all come for the money and not for the career, but the Northern Rhodesian Department of Mines required that all miners obtain their blasting licence, a process which required that we learn not only how to use dynamite but that we were trained as lashers, timber men, drillers and pipe fitters. The first two months were physically the hardest of my life. At one hundred and thirty pounds I was not designed for the kind of work required. This was not South Africa and Thomas demanded that the men under him do all the work normally done by African miners. The back-breaking labour of drilling and lashing a freshly blasted haulage could bring grown men to total exhaustion and, many a time, to the point of mutiny. Thomas was remorseless. Lashing was the process of removing blasted rock by hand and shovel and loading it into underground trucks. This we performed six hours a day, every day for the first month, often in narrow haulages a thousand feet underground in temperatures of a hundred degrees. The eight-hour underground shift allowed half an hour for lunch and a five-minute water break every hour. Years of boxing had conditioned my arms and upper body and I quickly learned the rhythm of working a blunt-nosed, long-handled miner's shovel. But by the end of the shift I was buckling at the knees and blubbing from exhaustion. Thomas heckled the men with invective, constantly trying to provoke a fight, trying to make a man lose his head and have a go at him. One or two tried and apart from receiving a thrashing were expelled from the school, their chance at the big money gone forever. I longed to take Thomas on. No one knew I was a boxer and when I was not too exhausted and could dream a little, I fantasised about him throwing punches at me, missing hopelessly and finally falling exhausted on the ground having been made a monkey of in front of the crud. In my daydream I would leave him grovelling on the ground while I quietly picked up my long-handled shovel and continued lashing the end without saying a word. Just the knowledge that I could probably manage to do this in real life kept me going when he baited me, sometimes without let-up for an hour at a time.

'Okay shit for brains, you're so fucking smart, how much gelignite is required to blast a twelve hole end?' In the first week I had read the textbooks Gareth Jones had issued to us from cover to cover, and Thomas soon discovered I knew the answers to the simple questions he threw at us when we went underground each day. He didn't like a smartarse in his class and seemed determined to get me. He would ask questions which appeared in the books weeks ahead of our learning them, but I usually knew the answer. The rest of the crud were not known for their brains and reading isn't generally a strong point among such men. I knew I couldn't goof the answer just to satisfy Thomas' need to put me in my place. The crud derived enormous pleasure from my getting the answers right and therefore, in their minds, getting the better of Thomas.

'Six foot drills or nine, sir?' I'd ask.

'You being a smartarse, boyo?'

'No sir, but it would make a difference wouldn't it?'

'Of course, you half-wit, of course it would make a difference!'

'Well, that's why I asked, Mr Thomas.'

Caught in his own verbal trap. Thomas would answer angrily, 'We don't use too many nine-foot Jackhammer drills, now do we?'

'If the rock is a bit cakey we do, sir,' I answered.

Thomas would jump up in glee. 'There's precious little cakey rock in a fucking copper mine, boyo!'

'In that case eighteen pounds, sir,' I would answer smoothly. The men around me would wear smiles as big as water melon slices.

'Correct!' Thomas would yell. 'But don't you be a smartarse with me, boyo, or you'll be lashing ends until your arms fall off and you have to use your shoulder stumps to pick your nose.'

'Yes, sir,' I'd say, but I knew he would have the last say, moving me over to a badly blasted end where the ore had broken in large lumps too big for a shovel so that I had to break and lift the rock all day until I collapsed from exhaustion.

'No malingering, boyo, back on the job in five minutes or you're fined a quid.' In the school of mines we were paid a token salary which just covered the cost of the hut and our mess bill with a couple of quid over for essentials. If, by the end of the month, you were down five pounds it made things tough.

I told myself that nothing Thomas said or did could wear me down. I convinced myself that the hard work was why I'd come, and indeed, after two months in the school of mines my body had never been harder and I knew the muscle bulk would soon begin to follow. While I kept a speedball and a punching bag in my hut where it wouldn't be noticed and worked out every day with weights in the club gym as well as doing five or six miles of road work three times a week, I made no attempt to join the boxing club.

Sport was the one thing both miners and good citizens shared and the club, heavily subsidised by the mines, was the social centre of the small town. The club affected all the traditions and mannerly ways anglophile institutions of this sort demand from lower middle-class members who find themselves fortuitously thrust into the upper echelons of a colonial backwater society, and it solved the problem of having to accommodate the multi-national crud by building a separate bar for them. This was in a separate building from the club, with its own entrance where men could come without being seen by the town establishment, mine officials and the more acceptable of the miners' families.

The crud bar, as it was known, contained a fifty-foot bar counter, cement floor and white lavatory tiles six feet up the walls. It also featured swing doors like a Western saloon. The bar room itself was empty and permitted standing room only. Outside was a beer garden with a hundred tables or so, each one sporting a permanent tin umbrella welded into the centre of a steel table which, in turn, was bolted onto the painted green cement yard. The chairs too were made of steel, their legs permanently bolted to the cement. Each table and six chairs were painted a different colour so that from a distance it all looked very gay. Above the tables, suspended like tall washing lines, were strings of coloured lights which at night gave a weird sort of green and mauve cast to everything.

Three barmen, all Germans, all called Fritz and all fat, worked the bar like an ordinance office. Each Fritz operated his third of the bar and behind him was a complete stock of liquor and a cash register. He never left his own territory to pour a drink, draw a beer or make change. Each Fritz was known by a number, Fritz One, Fritz Two and Fritz Three. Each had a crud following whom he came to regard as regular to his part of the bar. The Fritzs boasted there wasn't a drink in the world they didn't have or couldn't make. But mostly they served brandy, beer, rum and vodka, in that order. If you did your drinking standing in the bar you could get your liquor served by the measure and your beer by the glass. But if you wished to sit outside, you got a jug of beer or bought a full bottle of spirits, unless you wanted to keep fighting your way back into the bar for single serves. No Fritz was ever known to move from behind the long bar. The crud bar stayed open from seven a.m. until midnight when one Fritz would hose it out, removing at the same time the crud too inebriated to leave on their own.

During the day, until three o'clock when the day shift ended, the three Fritz wives, each one as big as her husband, worked the crud bar. They were known as Mrs Fritz collectively and remained un-numbered. Husband and wife, it seemed, never got together and it was a source of constant wonder among the crud that the Fritzs between them boasted fifteen fat blond children. The joke going around was that when the Fritzs left the crud bar they were going to buy the whole red light district in Hamburg.

At the end of three months, only eleven of the eighteen men who joined the school of mines with me remained. We were eligible to take our blasting licence, choosing either the international or Northern Rhodesian version. Thomas, in a rare show of kindness, suggested that I sit for the international, as he hadn't had a student pass the international in seven years.

'If you pass you'll be the youngest ever, which would be a feather in Mr Jones' cap, and I might even take a pat on the back myself, boyo.' The rugby season had begun and Thomas had discovered, too late to be of any use to me, that I could play and in the trials looked like I could make the first team of which he and Jones were selectors.

The examination was held at the office of the Department of Mines in Ndola. It consisted of a half hour written examination and an hour of verbals. This was because many of the men were not much good at writing but could answer most of the questions put to them directly.

Most of the guys with me were frightened to the point of paralysis. If you failed you returned to the school for another month, and failure after that and you were out of the mines. I had been coaching them for the last month and had come to be known as Professor Peekay. On the bus into Ndola I fired endless questions at them.

All but a huge Boer from the Orange Free State obtained their blasting licence. The Boer, a likeable enough bloke but thick as mahogany, was out forever, but cheered himself up with the knowledge that he had been accepted as a stoker on Northern Rhodesian Railways. Thomas and Jones had followed us to Ndola by car and after the morning's examination we'd all repaired to Ndola's only hotel, where just about everyone got very drunk and ended up telling Thomas what a good old bastard he was. I had passed the international licence and must have consumed a gallon of lemon squash just responding to the toasts the men kept proposing to Thomas, Jones and Professor Peekay. The more drunk they became the more effusive, until towards the end Thomas had become a certain candidate for sainthood and they all swore that they would protect me against all comers and that there was nothing I couldn't ask them for.

My life as a grizzly man commenced the next day when I went underground for the first time on my own, on the eleven to seven shift.

The workings of a grizzly need to be briefly explained. Imagine if you will, a funnel pointing downwards towards the ground. The top bit of the funnel before it narrows down to the spout is the stope, which is, in fact, a huge underground hole. The spout from it is used for getting the rock, blasted off the sides of the hole, out of the hole. This spout is sixty feet long and leads directly to a main haulage. The bottom of the funnel spout is fitted with a steel door worked with compressed air. Halfway down it, that is thirty foot from the main haulage and the same distance from the beginning of the stope, a set of six tungsten steel bars are fitted across the funnel spout with a narrow walkway cut sideways into the rock leading to it. These six tungsten bars are known as a grizzly. The reason for this name being that tungsten bars were made in Canada, hence 'grizzly bars'. The ore drilled and blasted from the sides of the stope by the diamond drillers is funnelled down the spout at the bottom of the stope and comes rushing down, with the smaller bits falling through the grizzly bars, filling the bottom half of the funnel spout. The bigger bits fall onto the bars and need to be blasted through them into a suitable size for loading onto the trucks in the main haulage. Underground trains pull up to the compressed air door and operators standing on the main haulage open the door at the end of the funnel and fill the trucks with ore. It's really a very simple operation but also a very dangerous one. The grizzly man works the bars which are directly under the mouth of the stope which is capable of disgorging rocks the size of small motor cars without warning.

The grizzly man works in the dark; his miner's lamp attached to his hard hat with the battery clipped to his webbing belt is the only source of light. He has five Africans to help him lash the rock through the grizzly bars and to prepare mud for the explosives. Occasionally he will get the muck flowing from the stope and it will continue to run all night, with only an occasional blast or a little work on the bars with long crowbars to keep it going. But mostly it's gut-wrenching work laying charges and working ore through the bars, sometimes as many as forty or fifty blasts a night until a powder headache caused by the sweet, sickly smelling gelignite sticks threatens to tear your head off your shoulders. Only diamond drillers, who use more gelignite than grizzly men, get worse powder headaches, sometimes being reduced to a state of unconsciousness or temporary insanity by the terrible pain.

A grizzly man works on the actual bars which are about six inches thick and two feet apart. Safety rules require that he be attached to a twenty-foot chain which clips to the back of his webbing belt. But the chain, like so many safety procedures, is a Catch 22: if he slips and falls through the bars into the bottom half of the funnel his back will snap like a piece of celery as his fall is broken by the chain some fifteen feet below the bars. If he doesn't break his back and the muck starts to run, the ore coming through the bars would tear him into mince. A good grizzly man takes his chances on the bars without a safety chain and learns, even in the dark, to be as agile as a monkey, jumping from bar to bar all night carrying a five-foot steel crowbar in his hands.

Grizzly men always work the same grizzly, knowing their lives depend on their intimate knowledge of the character of the stope and the funnel. Each grizzly has a personality of its own and a good grizzly man can read his grizzly as though his mind is tuned into the very rock it's made from. A slight leaking of pebble in a hang up and he knows to run for safety as a hundred tons of rock is about to come down directly over his head. The wrong pitch in an echo from the stope and he knows a single rock may come hurtling through to smash him off the bars. His reactions are as fine tuned as those of a top racing car driver, and his adrenalin pumps all night. At the end of a shift a grizzly man will have lost four or five pounds in weight and will be in a state of total exhaustion. At the end of three months he is taken off grizzlies for a spell of two months, before he is allowed to return. While the money was enormous, most grizzly men elected not to return and took a lower-paid job as a pipe fitter, timber man or ganger.

One particular job on the grizzly led to the final unnerving of even the most courageous of men. Some time during most shifts and often three or four times the rock would become blocked at the mouth of the stope. That is, at the very top of the funnel some thirty feet above the grizzly bars. In mining terms this was known as a hang-up or a bunch of grapes. Rocks of every size jammed the mouth of the stope. The safety procedure required to dislodge the rock and get the stope flowing again was to make up a parcel of gelignite. This is then tied to the end of a thirty-foot bamboo pole. The sticks of explosive are then wrapped with cordtex, which is explosive made into a cord which looks like white electrical flex. The idea is to push the parcel of gelignite against the rocks jamming the mouth of the stope. Then to light the fuse attached to the end of the cordtex which has been trailed from the parcel of gelignite to the level of the grizzly. Whereupon, if you're very lucky, the blast against the hang-up hopefully dislodges the rocks, causing the mouth of the stope to open again and the muck to flow.

But life on a grizzly isn't meant to be easy, and dynamite or gelignite, when it is not sealed with a mud pack, blasts outwards away from the rock, taking the line of least resistance. Blasting a hang-up with the bamboo pole technique is seldom successful. The pressure on the grizzly man is enormous, he must get the muck flowing and, using the bamboo pole technique he could blast away unsuccessfully all night. He is paid by the truck load, and if he doesn't empty his stope the diamond driller will lose his day shift, which often results in a grizzly man losing a couple of teeth. Apart from all this the grizzly man's pride is involved. A grizzly man who leaves a grizzly hung up is the lowest form of life in a mine. As Thomas would say, 'It's just not fuckin' done, boyo!'

After unsuccessfully trying to bring a hang-up down with a bamboo pole bomb, the grizzly man fills the front of his thick woollen miner's shirt with mud and a gelignite bomb strung with cordtex, and scales the sheer face of the funnel until he reaches the hang-up. This is the dangerous part, if the hang-up comes down while he is fixing the explosive against it, the grizzly man is dead, thrown sixty feet down through the bars to be buried under fifty tons of rock. Fighting the panic of being totally committed with nowhere to go, you find a jamming point between the rocks and insert the gelignite bomb. Then you wind the cordtex around it and let enough cordtex fall to the grizzly below so that you can attach a fuse to it. Finally you seal the bomb with mud to make it airtight so that the blast will go inwards into the rock. Having set it and packed it you then have to come down again, each precarious step up and down the sheer face of the funnel a gamble that the hang-up will hold. Back at the grizzly level you connect the cordtex to a fuse, signal the African to blow the warning hooter, light the fuse with a cheesa stick, a flare the size of a thick pencil which, once lit, cannot be extinguished. Then you have thirty seconds to retire into the safety tunnel before the blast goes off.

If the hang-up still doesn't come down you are forced up again, aware that with the added blast it could be teetering and on the point of crashing down. You soon learn to make only one trip up the funnel laying several blasts across the face of the hang-up and stringing them together with cordtex. This means you spend ten or fifteen minutes up against the hang-up with each second increasing the tension and the danger. But this way, when the four or five bombs go off simultaneously, you have a good chance of bringing the hang-up down. It all depends on nerve . . . yours. If you have the nerve to stay up the funnel for fifteen or twenty minutes, carefully laying a blast pattern and sealing each bomb with mud, it takes a very big hang-up to defeat you. In the year I was to work grizzlies, five of the twenty grizzly men working the mine were killed when a hang-up gave way while they were up the funnel laying charges against it.

Mine rules did not permit grizzly men to climb up into the mouth of the stope: caught doing it meant instant dismissal. But because you were forced to at least twice during a shift, the shift boss would stay away from the grizzly levels so that he wouldn't catch you. Everyone's copper bonus depended on the grizzly man getting the ore out of the stope. No shift boss would police the rules when he knew that the bamboo pole technique was so ineffectual that a hang-up might remain all night and not a ton of ore would be moved out of the stope.

When I wasn't shitting myself I took a perverse pride in being a successful grizzly man. I was the youngest in the mine with one of the best ore tallies. The diamond driller who worked the stope above my grizzly was an Afrikaner called Botha whom I never met as he worked day shift and I worked nights. The diamond drillers were the underground elite and never spoke to the grizzly men personally, the work was too dangerous and a driller didn't want the responsibility of knowing who was working his stope. But if you kept your ore tally up and his stope empty, he would send you a case of brandy at the end of each month.

A case of brandy from your diamond driller was the badge of honour every grizzly man worked for: in the crazy crud world of the Central African copper mines it became an approbation even more important than money.

I gave the brandy to Rasputin, the giant Georgian who lived in the hut next to me. Rasputin worked as a timber man on the same night shift as I did and we cycled to number seven shaft about three miles out of town where we both worked. From the night he had saved my rear end virginity, we had been friends, our friendship based less on words than on the things we shared. Rasputin spoke very little English and rather than learn any more he simply didn't talk. He'd sit on my stoep or I on his and we'd play chess. He was a good enough player to keep me interested and if I lost concentration he would sometimes take a game. Often we would simply sit and I would read a book or he'd play his collection of Tchaikovsky symphonies and concertos on his new portable record player. He never played anything but Tchaikovsky and would sit with a huge block of native timber in one hand and a kindling axe in the other, and without ever releasing the block of wood he would chip away until three hours later it became a perfect ball. Rasputin was almost as tall as Doc had been but he was twice as broad, even bigger than the Afrikaners, and the axe would have weighed five pounds. The act of carving the block of wood into a ball was one which took almost unimaginable strength. When Rasputin wasn't carving a ball he was sharpening the axe. He would work away to the music, going through the entire repertoire of concertos and of the three symphonies. Sometimes silent tears would roll down his cheeks and spill into his shaggy beard. These he never bothered to wipe away, but he simply continued to carve at the block of wood, occasionally putting down the axe long enough to pick up a tin mug filled with VSOP brandy which he would half empty in one gulp and then refill to the brim. When Tchaikovsky came to an end, which meant sitting through all three of his piano concertos and his violin concerto and at least three symphonies, mostly his number one in G minor, two in C minor and always ending with his sixth, the grand and brilliant Pathétique, a bottle of Botha's brandy would be empty and the wooden ball would be complete.

Rasputin would carefully pack away the record player, dust the records and slip them into their jackets and lay them on top of a towel in an old suitcase. Then he would take the wooden ball and add it to a pile on the floor inside his hut. There must have been six or seven hundred of these about the size of a bowling ball, stacked in separate heaps of about one hundred each, one ball added each day. Some of the older ones had turned a lovely silver grey colour and others bore beautiful markings from the native timber he used. Each ball was identically sized and beautifully made, you could pick up two carved months apart and their perfect roundness and size were so close the eye couldn't pick out the difference, each ball a testimony to his enormous skill and strength. His hut smelled of the sap of young timber, not unlike the smell of a forest. Rasputin would step into his hut and take a deep breath, inhaling the sappy odour of the uncured native timber.

'Smell like Roosha, Peekay.' I often wondered if in his native Russia he had once lived among the birch forests of the Taiga, but I could think of no way of asking him.

I became fascinated by the beautifully carved balls and found that I could hold the axe in position to work a piece of wood for no more than three minutes before the hand holding the wood would no longer function and the pain in my right wrist from holding the axe became unbearable. I realised that the exercise involved would strengthen my arms, wrists and even my hands for boxing, so I purchased a smaller and lighter axe and Rasputin sharpened it for me until it was like a razor. The idea that I wished to emulate him gave the huge bear of a man great pleasure. We'd sit on his verandah whittling away, listening to Mr Tchaikovsky, Rasputin drinking brandy and shedding tears which fell like drops of liquid silver down his cheeks to disappear into his huge black beard.

Eventually I worked out that the wooden balls were Rasputin's calendar, one ball for each day he had spent in the mines. By my reckoning he had been there about three years.

We would meet after our shift came up at seven a.m. and cycle back to the mess for breakfast. Rasputin would always be showered and waiting for me as my cage came up from underground, somehow he managed to finish his shift early and get up to the surface before the grizzly men.

600

'Much muck move, Peekay. You good boy,' he would say without fail as I stepped out of the cage. Then he would take my miner's lamp from me and put it on charge in the battery room so that I could go straight to the shaft office, check my ore tally, sign off and quickly get to the showers. When I emerged from the change rooms twenty minutes later he would be standing outside in the morning sunlight with my bicycle, ready for a quick getaway.

I'd been off grizzlies for only a week after having done my three months, when the mine captain called me into his office and asked me to volunteer to go back on. I was supposed to be rested with a main haulage job such as bossing a gang of lashers but three grizzly men had been badly injured and the mine had no replacements coming out of the school of mines. The incentive was to double my copper bonus for the period I was back on grizzlies. It seems Botha the diamond driller had been screaming about the new grizzly man on his stope and wanted me back. The money and the compliment were too much for me. Youth has a strong sense of its own immortality and I was no different from most. I found myself back at my grizzly platform for another three months. At the end of the month two cases of brandy arrived from Botha which made Rasputin completely independent of the crud bar. He was so proud of me he started to cry.

Lashing a case of brandy to the carrier on each of our bikes we pushed them the three miles to town, the twenty-four bottles in each case clinking merrily as we steered the bikes over the corrugated dirt road. When we arrived at the crud compound he put the cases in his hut and emerged moments later carrying an ancient twelve-bore shotgun.

'Tonight Rooshan stew!' he announced. Rasputin's rabbit stew was his highest compliment and I must say it really was delicious, a thick broth flavoured with strange herbs he gathered in the wild and delicious chunks of pink rabbit meat served with tiny whole onions and potatoes. I watched as he headed for the bush, not even waiting to have his breakfast at the mess.

I rose at four in the afternoon as usual. From Rasputin's hut came the delicious smell of the rabbit stew. I knew he would call me in about five-thirty to eat and so I headed off to the shower block to do my ablutions. We would eat and then attend a movie at the club. It was Wednesday night and Wednesday was always a Western. Rasputin loved Westerns with a passion. We would arrive early and sit in the front row, Rasputin with a bottle of brandy and his mug, ready to shout and scream and wave his fists at the baddies on the screen. He would weep when the hero was in a tight spot about to be burnt by Indian braves or tortured by malicious outlaws. Finally, when the film reached its climax and the hero emerged unscathed and triumphant with the girl, he would stand up and bang his mug against the empty brandy bottle and shout his approbation in Russian. Nobody seemed to mind, Rasputin was a part of the Wednesday Western and he'd always buy sweets and ice cream at the interval for all the kids. It became a tradition to yell and scream and pretend to cry at all the places Rasputin did and a grand time was had by all.

At five-thirty I heard his bellow, 'Peekay, you come!'

Rasputin had placed two bowls on the table and beside them were two large spoons. Arranged in a jam tin in the centre of the table were wild flowers he had gathered when he was out rabbit hunting and beside the flowers rested a round loaf of fresh bread. The flowers were a nice homely touch and the stew in a large pot on his single electric burner smelt wonderful. Rasputin poured it straight from the pot into the bowls, the delicious broth came steaming up at me. He dipped into the pot with a fork, stabbing chunks of pink rabbit meat and placing them in my bowl. Finally he produced a bottle of lemonade for me and, filling his tin mug with brandy, we tucked in, tearing huge hunks of bread from the loaf and slurping hungrily at the delicious stew. Neither of us said a word until it was all eaten and we'd had a second helping.

'Russian stew very delicious, Rasputin,' I said finally, rubbing my tummy to emphasise my satisfaction.

Rasputin looked pleased, even a little embarrassed at the compliment. He rose from the table, and walking over to the wardrobe withdrew from it the ancient twelve-bore shotgun. Pretending to aim at an imaginary rabbit in the distance he squinted down the barrel. 'Ho, ho, Peekay, rabbit go meow meow, me go boom boom, rabbit kaput!' he laughed uproariously and put the shotgun back into his cupboard.

I had never eaten a cat before but I knew there was no way I would be able to refuse Rasputin next time he paid me his supreme compliment and went rabbit hunting again. I quietly prayed that I wouldn't do anything in the future that would please him too much. I wondered silently which of the town families was wondering what had happened to their cat.

TWENTY-FOUR

It is the human experience, particularly true of the young, that all routine no matter how bizarre soon becomes normal procedure. Just as the survivors of the Nazi concentration camps talk of the routines imposed and followed which measured the days of horror until they seemed the normal passages of life, working a grizzly became a job as unexceptional as any other. Boldness, at first a stranger to be treated with caution, soon becomes a friend, then partner and finally is taken for granted, as is the daily relationship between two married people.

There comes a stage when the nervous system adjusts to accommodate the new environment, in which a former state of anxiety becomes one of calm, and situations which formerly brought a rush of adrenalin through the blood leave it calmly going about the business of supplying the heart.

A good grizzly man attracts a good black gang. Africans straight from the bush instinctively understand the group security a confident leader brings. As the months went by and my grizzly remained accident free and I unscathed, those blacks who worked regularly with me would seldom stay away sick, preferring to shiver through a bout of malaria rather than to take a chance of losing their place to another black anxious to work in a juju, or mystically protected gang.

When a grizzly man blew himself up it was not unusual for him to take his number one boy with him. The number one is the most experienced mine boy in the gang, usually a second timer. Better paid than the rest of the crew, he acts as black leader as well as right-hand man to the grizzly man. It is he who handles the charges and prepares the mud packs to bed down the explosives. If an accident occurs he is generally working close to his grizzly man. Knowing this, a good grizzly man will generally dismiss his number one to the safety shaft, to man the blast warning siren before he lights the fuse, and a good number one will repay his grizzly man by building the mystique of the grizzly man in the eyes of the bush Africans who make up the rest of the gang.

Once a gang has been associated with an accident on the grizzly level, they become bad juju in their own eyes and in the eyes of the other black miners. It was inconceivable to these primitive bush Africans that a superior white man should die and that a thoroughly expendable black one should live. The gods had, quite obviously, made a mistake. The 'stick lightning' had been meant for them, the mark of death was upon them if they remained in the mines.

Black miners did not understand or believe in the concept of increasing odds and would have been quite unable to grasp the simple logic which dictated that the longer I remained working grizzlies the more likely I was to come unstuck. The superstition which held them to me is understandable in a simple mind; the fact that I began to half believe it was not.

With the exception of a week's break after my first three months on grizzlies, I had been working for nine months. While I knew that simply by requesting to do so I could be relieved, I hung on. Botha's two cases of the best South African brandy continued to arrive for Rasputin at the end of every month and the fact that the ore tally pulled from my grizzly almost always headed the night's tally list did important things for my ego, though I would probably not have admitted this even to myself. Even in this unlikely environment I still hadn't conquered the need to be the best. Though the odds had grown well beyond simple foolishness, I convinced myself that my brains (ha-ha) were the difference, that I knew how to survive a grizzly because I could read it better and was less likely to make emotional decisions under pressure. Which was, of course, a load of codswallop.

I had reached the point where Fats Greer, who drove the number seven shaft hoist and who also acted as the mine's part-time insurance agent refused to give me cover. 'For fuck's sake, Peekay, the all-time record for a grizzly stand is eleven months and the bastard who had it is pushing up daisies. Stop being a smartarse.

But I was through doing what other people wanted and I told myself that if the copper bonus held and I could stay on grizzlies for a year I would have earned enough to put myself through Oxford. No more emotional handouts for me. I could pay my own way! My whole life had been a testament to using the human resources around me, to winning against the odds. If I understood the system as I felt I did, I was no longer willing to pay the emotional price it demanded from me. If this was only in my own mind, well, every man is an island and at the same time also Robinson Crusoe, you're on your own and must learn to fend for yourself. The year of despair I had spent as a five-year-old, in the hands of the Judge, had tainted everything I had subsequently done. My childlike notion of camouflage to avoid being emotionally besieged had persisted. In my mind, although I'm certain at the time I would not have been able to articulate the idea, the mines represented a return to fear of that first boarding school. But this time it was I who would win. The grizzly I worked would be the Judge, but this time I would not be broken. I had come to the mines to find out who the hell I really was.

It is curious that in the retelling of a dangerous situation the explanation is often made to include a premonition of the disaster. Whereas, in truth, most accidents strike like a viper of lightning from an apparently clear blue sky. It is as though human beings like to pump up the importance of a near escape or even a catastrophe by placing the hand of destiny at the helm of calamity.

The day before the grizzly got me I dreamed I was bent over a routine charge to light the fuse. A normal length of fuse is designed to take two minutes to reach the dynamite charge but for a routine explosion of rock resting on the grizzly bars a good grizzly man will cut the fuse to a burn-through of thirty seconds, which is enough time to get into the safety shaft. During a single underground shift on a hard night when the muck refuses to run, a grizzly man can make forty or fifty separate rock blasts. With a saving of ninety seconds for most of these he can easily cull an extra hour's tally from the shift. In ore terms this can make a considerable difference to the night's final tally.

In my dream I held the lighted cheesa stick to the fuse, waiting for the familiar kick of sparks to indicate that it was alight. But the fuse turned instead into the black mamba of the crystal cave of Africa: it rose as it had done outside the cave, its head weaving and its darting tongue becoming the spluttering sparks of the lighted fuse. Mesmerised, I was unable to move until I realised it was too late. I jabbed the cheesa stick at the head of the snake as it struck. The lighted stick of sulphur blended with the explosion as I was blown to smithereens.

I awoke, my heart pounding furiously. Grizzly men often talked of the dreams: 'When the dreams come it's time to quit.' I had not dreamed before and now I was afraid: the grizzlies had started to invade my subconscious. That night I told the shift boss I wanted off and gave him a week's notice. He didn't question me but simply nodded and said, 'You earned it, Peekay, we'll give you a soft option, maybe lashing on a main haulage hey?' I thanked him but he suddenly looked alarmed. 'Shit! Who's going to tell Botha, he thinks you're Jesus Christ.' He grinned. 'Someone else can tell the sonovabitch, that's the day shift's job.' While I had received two cases of brandy regularly for the past five months, I had not met Botha. As I mentioned, it was a tradition that a diamond driller and his grizzly man didn't meet. Nobody seemed to know quite why this was, but like most time-worn behaviour it had turned into a superstition and both men would go to some pains never to meet while they worked in conjunction with each other.

'Rasputin will miss the brandy,' I said, conscious that now that I had made the decision to quit, a weight had lifted from my mind.

The shift boss laughed. 'You can bloody well tell him that!' Rasputin was the best timber man in the mine, but the scourge of shift bosses whom he wouldn't allow near his work site when he was building a bulkend or timbering a new haulage. But they had all come to accept Rasputin: what he did, he did well, without taking unnecessary chances with his gang. That was the first rule of mining, the rest was simply the niceties of deferring to authority, a concept the huge Georgian seemed not to understand.

There was nothing exceptional about the first part of the shift following my talk with the shift boss. I stopped to rest my gang as usual between three and four in the morning, the time known everywhere men work underground as 'dead man's hour'. It is the time when the human pulse is said to regulate by running slow and the circadian rhythm to falter. It is the time, old timers insist, when the bad accidents happen. To work through dead man's hour would be sorely to tempt fate. While we are meant to be rational humans there lurks in each of us a covert superstition which probably began when man worshipped rocks and trees and which we ignore at our own peril. For the grizzly man, better the hour saved by cutting fuses short than one used when death stalks the dark underground tunnels at the same time every night.

At four-fifteen I completed laying the mud pack over a routine charge, cutting the fuse short as usual. I had inserted it under the mud-covered gelignite and took the lighted cheesa stick from the number one boy, whom I called Elijah because he liked to light the cheesa stick himself, forfeiting his chance to retire to the safety of the escape shaft. He waited with me until the fuse began to splutter. With the cheesa stick Elijah handed me I touched the notched and splayed end I'd cut to reveal the granules of black gunpowder which ran through the body of the fuse. Nothing happened. No flare as the gunpowder caught, no familiar splutter as it tore down the centre of the fuse. Even before I could question the reason, the vision of the black mamba filled my mind's eye, 'Christ! It can't be. It's a running fuse!' A running fuse is when a fuse burns inwards and appears from the outside to be inert while in fact it is moving just as quickly towards the charge of gelignite. It is extremely rare, most grizzly men have never seen one, or if they have, haven't lived to tell the story.

I grabbed Elijah by his shirt collar and propelled him towards the safety shaft, tackling him the last few feet into the shaft as I dived for safety a split second before the charge went off. The explosion roared fifteen feet from where we lay. Had the snake not returned to me in my dream I might have persisted with the shortened fuse. Three seconds longer and Elijah of the burning bush and I would have been history.

Rising to his knees and dusting his hands on the seat of his trousers, Elijah started to babble with excitement as the rest of the gang came running towards us. He told them how a devil fuse which did not light had set off the charge, but how I had known of its magic and thwarted its evil intention by pulling him to safety. The gang listened with open-mouthed astonishment. Then each in turn came over to me and touched my arm, dropping their eyes as they did so. Once again I had confirmed my magical status, was this not yet more proof that their collective safety was assured? The Tadpole Angel was back at work again.

I am forced to admit, I too felt hugely elated by the experience, enchanted with the meaning of the dream. I kept asking myself whether I would otherwise have recognised a running fuse? It was a mining occurrence so rare Thomas hadn't even mentioned its possibility in the school of mines. I had seen it noted briefly before being dismissed as extremely unusual in one of the numerous textbooks we'd been issued, a textbook possibly only I, amongst the class, would have taken the trouble to read.

Instead of seeing the near disaster as a real life warning, I became so elated I decided to withdraw my notice to quit grizzlies. I felt a tremendous sense of my own destiny, of the rightness of the path I had chosen. I had gambled and won, my slate was wiped clean, the accident designed to happen had been thwarted, the original odds were once again restored. I would see this old bitch grizzly through until the fifteenth of February, one week over eleven months, to the day. Screw Fats Greer, I'd make it a new record.

I admit to the unsoundness of my reasoning, but it wasn't all stupidity. The pay for a soft option job on a main haulage was less than half the amount I was receiving each month working a grizzly. With my double copper bonus as well as my tally bonus I could add another forty percent to this as well. Giving all this up would mean staying on at the mines another three months and by doing so missing the commencement term at Oxford.

Feeling good all over, I walked up to the grizzly, and standing on the bars shone my lamp up at the hang-up which had developed at the mouth of the stope. It looked unsafe, a bunch of grapes where the loosening of one small rock might bring the lot down. Fifty tons of rock could be held suspended above my head by a mere pebble. The old bitch was playing with me, teasing me, my ears strained to hear her talk . . . a creak, a moan, the echoed clatter of a single pebble . . . so I might read the constraint of the rock avalanche poised above my head.

It came at last, the sudden sharp, erratic clatter of a single rock as it broke free from the hang-up to ricochet against the steeply funnelled rock sides leading from the stope. One, two, it would take three bounces before landing on the grizzly bar furtherest from where I stood. My intimate, almost instinctive knowledge brought about from working more than two thousand hours on this one grizzly told me the rock was about the size of a large grapefruit and that it almost certainly preceded the collapse of the hang-up.

I moved fast, leaping instinctively across the bars towards the protection of the safety shaft. Above me the hang-up groaned momentarily, a second or two's warning before the roaring avalanche followed. My feet had already left the bars in the final leap to safety when the single rock hit the grizzly and, bouncing erratically off the tungsten steel bar, flew through the air to hit me in the stomach.

The roar of the rock breaking free reached my ears before I was knocked unconscious through the bars, to fall sixty feet down the almost empty shaft.

The fall should have killed me. The ten tons of rock which followed me through the bars should also have done so. I had been unconscious the moment the rock struck me and had fallen through the bars like a sack of potatoes, bouncing against one wall of the down shaft. My hard hat had miraculously stayed on and prevented my head from being smashed in as I landed in about three feet of fine shale at the bottom of the grizzly. The shale had been the result of the huge rock I had blasted through the bars with the running fuse. I had been conscious at the time of using too much gelignite but the grizzly shaft below the bars had been empty and a good grizzly man tries to put a buffer of fine shale against the pneumatic steel doors to protect them from the effect of bigger rocks smashing against them. I had landed in this soft bed of shale and sand, my body rolling and finally wedging under a narrow shelf of rock where the side of the shaft had been carelessly blasted. Ten tons of rock from the hang-up had followed me through the bars, covering my body and building up over me though, miraculously, in pieces big enough to allow some air to reach me.

I lay unconscious under the shelf, covered by several tons of rock. What happened over the next seven hours I have pieced together from talking with my gang and the rescue team.

Elijah was shocked beyond belief. His elation of a few minutes before had turned to complete dismay. Yet he hadn't panicked and had sounded the blast warning hooter ... five prolonged blasts each interspersed with fifteen seconds of silence, then a minute break and a repeat of the same pattern three times. There was no mistaking the disaster message. The rest of the gang huddled together in the safety shaft, too shocked to respond, their lives suddenly shattered with the certainty in their minds of their own death should they remain even to help with the rescue. For them their luck had run out, their white talisman was dead. It was time to get to the surface, hand in the copper discs which hung around their necks and get back to the jungle where in the bright tropical sunlight it was more difficult for death, who saw better in the dark, to find them.

Rasputin, working on the main haulage half a mile away, was the first white man to hear the disaster warning. He sent his number one boy to alert the underground shift boss, and he headed for my grizzly. Frantic with concern he nevertheless loaded an empty truck with bulkhead timber and instructed his gang to push it to the area of the accident. If it was a grizzly disaster, Rasputin knew the huge slabs of native timber would be needed for any rescue attempt.

News of a disaster in the mines spreads seemingly by osmosis. Grizzly men who were working the sixteen hundred feet level with me would close down their grizzlies and bring their gangs in to help. I'd done it myself on three occasions and I knew what it was like when the rescue crews finally pulled the smashed and broken, even sometimes the separated parts of a body from the blood splattered rock and placed it in a canvas body bag. I had even seen blood leaking from the pneumatic doors closing the bottom of a grizzly shaft and had waited the six hours it had taken finally to get to the body which lay only a few feet away, as I did now.

It was an unspoken rule that the grizzly men helped in any rescue attempt. They were the personal witnesses to the death with which they had learned to live every time they climbed the sixty feet of vertical ladder shaft to a grizzly level. The generally unsuccessful rescue attempt was a grim ritual they felt forced to play a part in, out of respect for a dead brother.

Rescue procedure is dictated by the environment. A stope and the grizzly below it are a live thing and have to be silenced before a rescue attempt can be made. The shaft directly above the grizzly bars has to be timbered up, the old bitch silenced. Huge bulkend timbers, capable of holding back rocks crashing from the stope, were used for this task. Shoring up the grizzly shaft was in itself a dangerous task, particularly as timbermen are not adept at reading a grizzly. The job was complicated by the twenty tons or so of rock which rested on the bars when the hang-up had come down. This would need to be manhandled into the air escape and safety shaft, while the pieces too large to lift would remain on the bars where they acted as some sort of protection should the bulkend timbers give way.

It was Rasputin's task to build the bulkhead that shored up the shaft above the grizzly. The ten foot by ten inch raw native timber slabs, known as ten-by-tens, weighed well over three hundred pounds each and had to be manually pulled up the sixty-foot entry shaft to the grizzly level. By the time the rescue crew arrived from the surface, the giant Georgian had already exhausted his own crew and the crews from the three other grizzlies were working turnabout to haul the heavy raw timber.

Rasputin worked in a cold, controlled fury, though with no unnecessary movement or wasted energy, speaking quietly to the blacks to keep them from panic, he'd even managed to get my crew back to work. He knew that rescue was a long process made dangerous by hastily contrived directions and the terrible infection of fear. From the grizzly level he directed the removal of the manageable rock which lay on the tungsten bars. When the rescue captain arrived on the grizzly level, panting from the exertion of climbing the ladders up the entry shaft, Rasputin was waiting for him at the top.

'No come here, Peekay he mine, I fix!' He glared at the rescue captain, opening and closing his huge fists.

The light from the captain's white hat shone into Rasputin's eyes and held the fury and cold determination. Rasputin was taking no chances; handing the rescue operation over to the mine captain wasn't going to happen. 'Okay, Ruski, I'll send a rigger and an electrician up to give you lights and a rock hoist, you just carry on.'

'You send Zoran the Croat, I work him.' He turned back to the grizzly. Later the rescue captain, a man named McCormack, a decent sort of guy and a very experienced miner, would tell how he knew, looking into the crazed eyes of the Russian, that the giant would have snapped his neck like a chicken bone and thrown him back down the entry shaft had he taken a step towards the grizzly. He felt a lot better about not examining the accident site when the electrician returned after setting up the lights to report that the rescue was futile, there was absolutely no chance of my having survived.

Rasputin had allowed the rigger, a Yugoslav simply known as Zoran, to remain and had demanded that his own gang, only just rested from hauling timbers, be sent up to him. Maintaining his furious though measured pace, he timbered up the shaft above the grizzly. Three hours passed before it was safe to enter the shaft where I lay buried.

Rasputin, his woollen miner's vest and the shirt over it soaked with perspiration, paused only briefly to drink a canteen of water before allowing himself to be lowered by the hoist the Yugo had rigged to the rock covering me nearly fifty feet below. Working with great grunts he started to fill the hoist basket, giving a short, sharp whistle each time the basket was ready to be hauled up.

With Rasputin safely down the shaft McCormack and the remainder of the rescue crew, together with the three grizzly men, had crowded into the grizzly area. The white men worked with the blacks to empty the basket and pass the rock along fire-bucket style to the air escape shaft. The Russian's work proved to be a model rescue operation and McCormack set up the oxygen tent and the transfusion apparatus he knew the mine medic would want when eventually he arrived.

McCormack would have liked to have sent an African down every ten minutes, about the time it took to exhaust a man lifting rocks, some of which weighed as much as fifty pounds. He knew Rasputin would not allow this. An African careless or inexperienced might cause a rock slide, impacting the rock which lay over me even further. Until he actually lifted my body and held my chest to his ear, Rasputin was not going to accept my death.

Men, especially miners, who live in the constant shadow of death do not stand mute-voiced and solemn for hours at the scene of an accident. The look one sees on the gawking faces of people surrounding a road accident victim is not the same as the one worn by miners. Miners carry their grief in an outwardly matter of fact way, each man a silent repository of his own feelings, each grizzly man knowing his name may well be on the next card in a stacked deck.

Mick Spilleen, known of course, as Mickey Spillane, an illiterate Irishman who had been in the school of mines with me and who had only just volunteered to come back onto grizzlies in an attempt to pay his gambling debts, was the first to start the betting. 'The Ruski won't make it, I'm tellin' you now, lads.'

'I reckon he will, man,' someone else said, probably Van Wyck the Afrikaner. Suddenly every one was in on the betting. Even Elijah, who had refused to leave the grizzly level when my gang had been relieved, was allowed to put five pounds, a week's wages, on the Russian getting to my body before he collapsed. Mickey then offered odds of fifty to one on my being alive and this time only the little African took the bet, putting another week's wages on the talisman who had kept them all alive over almost nine months. Most of the men bet against Rasputin lasting the distance and the bets between the dozen or so whites present amounted to nearly two thousand pounds. When, years later, I told Hymie of the incident, asking him how he would have bet, he had laughed, 'The Irishman was right, only I'd have offered two hundred to one against your making it. But I would have shortened the odds on the Russian.'

Rasputin's tremendous energy was beginning to give out. He was digging deep for the strength to keep going, his breathing laboured and rasping. When the basket was filled he could no longer summon up the breath to whistle. Zoran, watching from the top, would start to lift the basket, whereupon the giant would stoop down, his huge hands raw and bleeding, clasping his knees. Once he threw up, and once he removed his torn shirt and miner's vest and tearing strips from the shirt, bound his bloody hands. But always as the bucket lowered he was ready to start loading again. Several of the men had offered to replace him but he'd simply shaken his head. 'Nyet, nyet!' he gasped. Soon the flinted edges of the broken rock he was lifting cut into his chest and stomach. His dirt-covered torso, caught in the light from the single electric bulb burning directly above him, glistened with blood and raw exposed flesh, his stomach muscles pumping red. The men above watched fascinated, waiting for the moment when the giant would collapse.

'He's done for, I'm tellin' you now, half a ton more and he's history,' Mickey whispered, even though there was no chance of the Russian hearing him or even understanding his heavy brogue. What they were witnessing was a great feat of strength and they told each other they would one day tell their grandchildren of this night.

It must have been about this time when Rasputin heard me groan, though how he would have done so over his rasping breath was a miracle. He gave a sharp agonised cry and threw himself at the rock in the area from which the sound had come. No longer bothering about the basket he tore the rock aside, frantically stacking it behind him. He worked, 'possessed by the devil himself', Mickey later claimed. Rasputin was finding strength to continue from beyond the realm of normal human consciousness, his breath coming in short animal snorts, like a pig sniffing for truffles. The blood streamed from his chest and stomach, soaking the top of his pants down to the knees while the ragged bandages were ripped from hands reduced to raw slabs of meat.

When he finally reached me, wedged miraculously under the narrow though protective ledge, my body was soaked in blood, as it turned out, from large sections of skin which had been removed in the fall. Rasputin lifted my unconscious body to his chest and placed his ear to my heart.

'Peekay he live!' he wailed. Slowly he sunk to the ground, his legs no longer able to hold him.

We sat in a nest of rock like the one the loneliness bird laid deep inside me, my head resting in the giant's blood-soaked lap. He'd severed his index finger at the first knuckle and as he tenderly stroked my forehead the blood from the stump ran down my brow and filled the cups made by my closed eyes. The hollows soon filled, then ran from the overflowing bowl down my cheeks. Rasputin tried to stop the flow, wiping at it with the stump of his severed finger, unaware of the real source of the blood. 'Peekay! Rasputin find Peekay, Rasputin make rabbit stew,' he sobbed.

Later Mickey Spillane would claim that when they got to us there were tears of real blood coming from the giant's eyes, but by that time he was already dead.

*

I spent a week in hospital, most of it being treated for shock. The skin had been scraped from a large part of my body and I was badly bruised, but not a single bone was broken. When I regained consciousness and heard of Rasputin's death I wept and then begged that they delay the burial until I could attend his funeral. In a hot climate in a town without a mortuary it wasn't possible and the huge Georgian had been buried for three days when they released me from the cottage hospital. While I looked a mess with both eyes blackened and the skin on each side of my face purple with scab, I was in excellent shape. My first task was to go to the general store in Luanshya and order a tombstone for Rasputin, a black granite slab which would have to come from Bulawayo more than six hundred miles to the south and would take several weeks. On it would be written simply *RASPUTIN, maker of excellent rabbit stew, who gave his life for his friend*. I then went to the small cemetery where he lay under a mound of red clay. On top of the clay was a single wreath of battered gladioli. We were almost at the beginning of the rainy season and it had rained a little the previous night and the heavy drops of tropical rain had kicked up the red clay so that the pink and orange petals, opaque from being wet, were stained with mud. Rasputin loved wild flowers as Doc had loved aloe: why is it that the ubiquitous gladioli always crowds everything else out? I dropped painfully to my haunches as the scab on the side of my leg stretched, and read the mud-splashed card on the wreath. *RIP. The management, Rhoan Antelope Mine*. That was all. I had taken Rasputin's old shotgun with me and now I rose, and lifting the old gun to my shoulder I fired both barrels over his grave. It was a pointless gesture, I guess, and the kick of the gun into my bruised shoulder made me hop around in pain. But it was just the sort of thing which could happen in a Wednesday matinee Western and of which I could see Rasputin thoroughly approving.

The following day I returned to the grave, having loaded

all Rasputin's wooden balls into the back of a borrowed utility. With a long-handled lasher's shovel I flattened the mound and buried the shotgun next to him; then I built a pyramid over the grave using all the wooden balls. When I was finished it stood five foot tall. Taking careful measurements I had the welding shop at number nine shaft make me a pyramid-shaped containing frame with small bars running parallel every four inches across the sides, so that the balls, while being clearly seen, could not be removed. The metal frame was completed in two days and together with the help of Zoran the Yugo I rigged a hoist over Rasputin's grave and dropped it neatly over the wooden balls, seating the corners into a cement footing.

It made a very impressive tombstone and when his headstone arrived Rasputin's grave would be the pride of the tiny cemetery.

Together with Zoran, who could speak a little Russian, we went through Rasputin's papers. There wasn't very much to tell of his past; Norwegian seaman's papers bearing his name, a Russian passport and his discharge papers from the Russian navy which indicated he'd been a stoker. Finally we found a sheet of paper on which a woman's name, similar to the one in his passport, was written. It was followed by an address in Russia. Zoran had said that a slight difference in surname was common in Russia and I gathered he meant that this was a feminine version of the male surname. Rasputin's bank account came to nearly seven thousand pounds and I arranged to send this to the name on the slip of paper, after taking Zoran with me and convincing the district magistrate that this was Rasputin's closest kin. A wife, a sister or a mother? But at least someone, somewhere, other than me, who would remember him for the good fortune he had brought them.

I had been visited in hospital by Fats Greer, the part-time insurance agent. He pushed a piece of paper in front of me. 'Sign here, Peekay,' he said, his pudgy finger indicating a blank line on the sheet of paper. I signed. 'I need two cheques for twenty pounds each, don't date them.' To my surprise he produced my cheque book. 'Elijah, your number one boy, delivered your *chorla* bag to the mine captain after your accident. I took the liberty of using the keys in it.' I nodded still a bit dazed and not really knowing what was happening; as far as I knew he had refused to cover me for the last two months on grizzlies. I signed the cheques and asked him what it was all about. 'I'll tell you when you feel a little better.' He grinned, 'The crazy Ruski gave you more than his life, son.' A week later I was to learn that Rasputin had a long-standing insurance policy with Fats Greer for a thousand pounds and had made me the benefactor. Fats also handed me a cheque for five hundred pounds, 'What's this for?'

'Your accident compo,' he replied. 'Check your cheque butts, you never missed a premium.' He walked away whistling to himself.

It meant that I had no need to return to the mines for a further three months. As Solly Goldman would have put it, 'You're home and hosed, my son!' With the money I had saved and Rasputin's legacy I had sufficient funds for three years at Oxford. I also had enough left over to travel to London once a week for training by the famous Dutch Holland. Holland didn't usually take amateurs but Hymie had sweet talked him into allowing me to show my stuff. If he liked what he saw, he'd take me into the professional ranks under his care.

I had three weeks' sick leave after coming out of hospital and I knew that the best way to get rid of my bruises was to work my body. I put in a lot of road. I also rigged an extra heavy homemade canvas punchbag the mine sailmaker had made for me, hanging it from a rafter Zoran had reinforced on the verandah of my rondavel. Beside it hung the speed-ball and the lighter punching bag I had brought from South Africa and on which I had worked out every day I had been at the mines.

Speed was something I couldn't afford to lose and while

the work in the mines had built up my body so that I was by now almost a welterweight, I didn't want to forgo speed for the extra power I had gained. The year away from boxing had been good for me. While I hadn't talked about it to anyone even in the letters I wrote, the flame that lit my ambition to be welterweight champion of the world burned as fiercely as ever and had never left me for even one single moment of any one day.

In fact, when I regained consciousness in the hospital I thought that I had been fighting for the world championship and that I had been knocked out. The disappointment I felt was enormous, and when I was fully conscious and aware of what had happened I comforted myself with the knowledge that I now knew what it felt like to lose the world championship, it now only remained for me to experience winning it.

I sweated out the aches and pains over three hard training sessions a day. Within a fortnight the scabs were beginning to flake off, leaving large blotches of new pink skin all over my body which made me look a little like an albino who'd been passed backwards through a meatgrinder. My head had also been shaved to get at a cut on my skull which had turned out to be pretty superficial and had only required five stitches. As Solly Goldman would say, I looked a proper Charlie. The mine required that I complete a final shift, though not on a grizzly, so that I could sign all my papers and be passed as completely fit again. This was so that I couldn't sue them at some later date for some real or imagined after effect.

I spent the last week of my sick leave writing home, to Miss Bornstein and Mrs Boxall and of course to Hymie who had written to me weekly from Oxford. I also wrote to Gert and to Gideon Mandoma who was already beginning to write quite well himself. Finally I wrote to Singe 'n Burn whose retirement from the Prince of Wales School coincided almost exactly with my own from the mines. They had all written regularly with Miss Bornstein and Mrs

Boxall keeping up with Hymie and Singe 'n Burn, to my constant surprise, wrote every six weeks or so. After his initial disappointment over my refusal to take a scholarship to a South African university he had become imbued with the idea that I should make it to Oxford under my own steam and had arranged for me to be accepted at Magdalen College with Hymie. I knew this final letter telling them all that I'd made it would be a big event for them. I was back on track and all would be forgiven. The prodigal son had returned. I even wondered if old Mr Bornstein might let me win another game of chess.

There had been almost a full case of brandy left in Rasputin's hut and I decided to take it up to the crud bar on the Saturday before my final work day on Monday. I left it this late, not wishing to be seen much in public. I was quite well known around town because I played scrum-half for the Luanshya rugby team and had been selected on three occasions to play for the Copperbelt. It embarrassed me to be made a fuss of and so I kept pretty much to myself.

I intended to go to the crud bar just after three o'clock when Fritz One, Two and Three came on duty. The idea of going earlier when the Mrs Fritzs were doing the morning shift and being fussed over by the three fat fraus was too much to contemplate.

I planned to ask Fritz whoever to raffle off the case of brandy and to use the proceeds to buy ice cream for the kids at the Wednesday matinee in memory of Rasputin. I figured the brandy would more than likely raise enough money to pay for ice cream for several weeks. It was something I felt sure Rasputin would have liked.

I had attended the last two Wednesday matinees, sitting in the same place Rasputin and I had sat. The kids had come in as usual and sat all around me. I groaned and moaned and shouted and generally carried on a treat in all the places the big Russian would have done. At first the kids did not respond but I persisted and soon they fell into the familiar mood and we all had a good time. Except at the end of the first Wednesday I began to cry which had spoilt it a bit for them. As usual during interval I bought ice creams all round and the kids went along with the new game, knowing full well what I was attempting to do. When, at the third Wednesday matinee after Rasputin's death, I told them I would be leaving, two small boys had approached me.

'Don't you worry about Ruski's grave and the wooden balls and all, we'll look after them for you, Peekay,' the larger of the two assured me.

'Yes, for ever and ever!' the smaller added.

Rasputin's affairs were finally in the only hands he would have personally trusted. 'You'll have to paint the metal pyramid frame every year or it will rust away after a while,' I said.

'What colour?' the bigger one asked.

'Red, of course!' the smaller answered.

'Yes, red, that would do nicely,' I said.

'You see, I told you! Russians like red,' the small boy said in triumph.

I lugged the case of brandy up to the crud bar. It was early yet and only a handful of men were there. On the few occasions I had been in the bar I had done my drinking with Fritz Three and I now walked over to his section of the long bar and explained my purpose.

'Ja, for sure, we do this, but you must make ze book,' Fritz Three replied emphatically, as though the idea had been his all along. Without my asking he made up a large lemon squash with soda and a dash of bitters the way I liked it.

'No, no, I don't want to bet, just a raffle, Fritz Three.'

'Ja raffle! you make ze book, come I show you.' He raised the bar panel to let me in behind the bar, and lifting the case of brandy he indicated that I should follow him into a back room which turned out to be an office. From a drawer he withdrew a staple gun, a roll of adding machine paper about two inches wide, an old Croxley fountain pen repaired with an inky piece of sticking plaster, scissors, an ink pad and rubber stamp. Working quickly he cut off a four-inch length of paper and wrote the number one at each end of the strip, doing this until he had twenty slips of paper marked from one to twenty which he then stamped on the righthand side with the rubber stamp which read Luanshya Club and stapled the opposite end to make a neat little book of raffle tickets.

'Now we have one raffle book, ja? You make like this for five hundred tickets ... Okey dokey?' I nodded and then told him that I wanted to buy two more bottles of brandy to complete the case. 'No, Fritz buy!' he said, jabbing his finger at his chest. 'Ruski he my fren.' He left me in the office and returned to his bar.

I worked happily making tickets for an hour or so, creating a sophisticated version by using a large pin to punch a perforation line down the centre of each book I completed so the bit the customer retained could be parted easily. The noise in the bar grew steadily as more and more men came in. Making the raffle tickets was routine work and I was soon lost in thought, oblivious to the noise outside.

A soft, though urgent whistle cut through my day dreaming. I looked up to see the large shape of Fritz Three filling the doorway. I was immediately aware that there was silence in the crud bar.

The fat German seemed agitated, his mouth working wordlessly and one hand hooking the air in an urgent gesture for me to approach.

'What's wrong, Fritz?' He winced at the sound of my voice.

'Shh! You will be quiet please, we have here some trouble, ja.' I rose and walked quietly towards him. 'Botha! Botha, the diamond driller, he got powder headache and he go mad.' He stabbed his forefinger over his shoulder. 'If he find you he vill kill you!' he whispered hoarsely.

'Shit Fritz, Botha's my diamond driller, he wouldn't hurt me,' I whispered back.

Fritz Three grabbed me by the shirtfront. 'He does this before. All men must bugger off from crud bar when Botha drink the brandy, until he is kaput and falls on the floor. Ja, this is when I call the hospital. If he catch you, he kill you, Peekay.' He pointed to the window. 'Please you will jump now.'

I moved over to the window and attempted to open it, but it had been nailed shut. Suddenly the snake was back in my mind's eye, its diamond-shaped head with tiny darting tongue flicking faster than I could blink. I turned back at the sound of a cry of panic from Fritz Three to see his fat body jerked backwards into the bar beyond. A huge man, almost the size of Rasputin, rushed forward crashing his forehead against the top of the doorway. He let out a roar of astonished pain and blood ran from his head as he stooped to enter. His eyes were puffed and swollen and shot with blood. From his nostrils ran a thick trickle of yellow mucus.

'*Kom hier jou fokker!*' he roared as he came at me with both hands, bending forward slightly as though he were about to catch a trapped rabbit.

'It's me, Botha! It's Peekay, your grizzly man!' I shouted back at him.

The huge man seemed not to hear me. 'I kill you! I kill you, you bastard!' His sleeves were rolled up almost to the top of the shoulder in the Afrikaans manner and as he lunged at me I saw the tattoo.

Under normal circumstances I would have easily avoided his clumsy lunge but the shock of recognition caused me to freeze on the spot. Tattooed high up on Botha's left arm was a jagged, badly etched swastika. I had seen this tattoo before . . . on the Judge.

Botha, the Judge now grown into a crazed giant of a man, grabbed my shirtfront with one massive hand, and with the other he grabbed the back of my belt. He lifted me from the ground and moving through the door he threw me over the long bar into the bar room beyond.

I landed on all fours, but managed to break my fall with the butt of both hands. An anger so cold and fierce possessed me that I felt my mind would have to be torn from it, like a finger torn from dry ice. My concentration was so complete that the edges of the room disappeared and the huge form of the Judge as he climbed over the bar came into such sharp focus that, at ten feet, I could see the individual hairs on his day-old stubble.

'First with the head and then with the heart, that way small can beat big.' It was Hoppie's voice that I heard in my head and my resolve became a solid force, a pure, clean feeling, totally controlled by my head.

'Jaapie Botha come! Come, man, come, I've been waiting for you for most of my life.' There was a menacing growl in my voice I had not heard there before.

Fritz Three, back behind the safety of the long bar, screamed at me. 'He been sniff gelignite, he crazy! Run, Peekay. That Boer kill you!'

The Judge dropped from the bar and with an angry roar charged towards me. A powder headache as severe as his could cause temporary insanity and I knew he was capable of killing. I stepped to the side and hit him with a left uppercut hard on the nose, seating the punch deep, aware that the crude explosion of pain into the swollen sinus tissue would be devastating. A man my size would certainly have passed out from the blow. Bellowing like a wounded animal, the Judge turned to face me again, blood and mucus running from his nose.

I had waited a long time for this moment; I knew exactly what to do. The Judge was the bull and I was the matador, it was I who would shape the fight. I knew suddenly that all of Geel Piet's footwork had been designed for this moment; it was time for the 'klein baas' to dance.

The Judge was a man of around twenty-five but he had already let himself go around the middle and his brandy gut hung over his belt. Years of working on a farm and then in the mines had built up his bulk and he was probably at the height of his physical strength. But, looking at him, I knew his condition was poor. With his sinuses already severely blocked I would try to work on his mouth. If I could make him swallow enough blood as well as lead him into frequent charges, he'd soon be winded. My hands were strong from carving Rasputin's balls and the skin and knuckles were hardened from the canvas punching bag I had worked with my bare fists. The Judge charged repeatedly and each time he came at me I stepped in with a lightning punch and hit him on the nose or in the mouth. Soon he was spitting a lot of blood, his chest heaving deeply as he tried to regain his breath. The salty blood would be mixing with the brandy in his stomach by now. Later I would put a Geel Piet eight right into the nexus of the solar plexus, where all the nerve ends came together.

He was beginning to move more slowly, trying to get me into a corner where he could crush me. I let him work me until he had my back right into the corner then I lifted my hands up as if I was going to plead for mercy. His punch came from ten miles away, I ducked and weaved out of the corner as his huge fist smashed into the wall. His knuckles split, the bones in his wrist smashing through the skin, splattering blood all over the tiles as his wrist and hand broke.

The cold rage inside me cocooned me into a circle of concentration, centred on the Judge and myself. Like a Goya painting, only the action in the centre mattered; the rest was blurred peripheral belonging to another place and another time. I was unaware that the space behind the bar had filled, a couple of hundred miners were standing three deep along the sixty-foot counter. The Judge turned suddenly and lumbered towards the bar. Men pushed back in fear and collided with shelves and bottles of spirit which rained down on them. The Judge grabbed a half empty bottle of brandy from the counter which no one had thought to remove. He smashed it on the edge of the bar, sending a spray of brandy into his face, some of it going into his eyes and blinding him. The Geel Piet eight went into the blinded man's gut and I finished it off with an uppercut into his pulped and smashed nose. By the time he swung the broken bottle I was clear again.

The Judge, as though in slow motion, fell to his knees and threw up onto the floor. The fight had been going nearly twenty minutes and I hadn't said a word, my fury concentrated in both my hands. My knuckles were raw and bleeding from hitting him, but I felt nothing.

As he sat there in his own vomit a small child's voice cried out from somewhere deep inside my body, 'You killed Granpa Chook!'

The Judge rose slowly to his feet using the broken bottle to push himself up off the floor. His face was a bloody mess, blood dripped from his broken hand and wrist, the front of his shirt stuck to his chest and stomach, soaked with brandy, blood and vomit. He lifted his head and looked up at me, through his broken lips he whispered the single word, 'Pisskop.' Using his remaining strength he hurled the broken bottle at me missing me by several inches. His useless broken hand and wrist hung at his side and he swayed unsteadily on his feet. The Solly Goldman thirteen went in, each punch deep and hard into the Judge's gut. The hurl of vomit travelled three feet before it splashed to the floor as the Judge collapsed unconscious.

My head exploded. The roar in my head was all white light. It was time for the heart. I was onto his body in a flash, straddling his torso. The snot and blood ran from his nose as his head rested on his right arm just above the broken wrist. His left arm with the swastika tattoo faced me. I was unaware of having gone to my shorts but Doc's Joseph Rogers pocket knife was open in my hand, the blade small but razor sharp. It struck high up on the arm where the mamba strikes and sliced through the epidermis above the ragged swastika, the blade cutting a square about four inches across and three down, then I crossed the square from corner to corner to make an X in a cross of St Andrew and then again from centre to centre to make the cross of St George, cutting deep almost to the muscle. The blood, before it started to run down his arm, made a perfect Union Jack. Across the jagged blue lines of the swastika I cut P. K. Then, smearing my hand into the mess on his shirtfront, I rubbed it into the Union Jack and into the initials, knowing it would set up a massive infection and cause the keloid to build up on the arm. Nothing would ever remove the wide band of scar tissue which would form to make up the flag and the initials which cancelled the swastika. I wiped my hands and the blade of Doc's knife on the back of the Judge's shirt and rose to my feet. Closing the blade of Doc's Joseph Rogers I returned it to the pocket of my blood-splattered shorts. 'Rasputin thanks you for the brandy, Botha,' I said, suddenly calm.

I became aware of the men behind the bar. They hadn't moved and were silent, their eyes following me, as I walked slowly towards the Western style saloon doors and then out of the crud bar. Outside, high above me, a full moon, pale as skimmed milk, floated in a day sky. I felt clean, all the bone-beaked loneliness birds banished, their rocky nests turned to river stones. Cool, clear water bubbled over them, streams in the desert.

BRYCE COURTENAY

Tandia

Half Indian, half African and beautiful, Tandia is just a
teenager when she is brutally attacked and violated by
the South African police.

Desperately afraid, consumed by hatred for the white
man, Tandia at last finds refuge in a brothel deep in the
veldt. There, she learns to use her brilliant mind and
extraordinary looks as weapons for the battles that lie
ahead: she trains as a terrorist.

Then Tandia meets a man with a past as strange as
her own. An Oxford undergraduate, Peekay is also the
challenger for the world welterweight boxing
championship – and a white man. And in a land where
mixed relationships are outlawed, their growing love
can only have the most explosive consequences . . .

THOMAS HARRIS

The Silence of the Lambs

'*The Silence of the Lambs* is razor-sharp entertainment,
beautifully constructed and brilliantly written. It takes
us to places in the mind where few writers have the
talent or sheer nerve to venture. I confess it, I'm
addicted.'   Clive Barker

A killer is attacking women across the United States.
His methods are horrifying, his motives unknown.
Only Dr Hannibal Lecter, a homicidal genius
incarcerated in a hospital for the criminally insane, can
help Clarice Starling, FBI trainee, to prevent the murder
of another young woman.

'A virtual textbook on the craft of suspense, a
masterwork of sheer momentum that rockets seamlessly
towards its climax.'   *Washington Post*

'It's marvellous, the best I've read for a very long time.
Thank heavens for a novel with a real plot at last,
subtle, horrific and splendid. It is infinitely superior to
any novel published this year.'   Roald Dahl

KIM WOZENCRAFT

Rush

A PROBLEM WITH DRUGS

Pasadena, Texas. Somewhere between suburb and city, it's a place with a problem.

Kristen Cates never dreamt of being a cop. Fresh out of high school and bored, it beats night school and waiting tables. It's real.

She meets Jim Raynor the day she is hired as a narc. Jim says she's a natural. Made for it.

But undercover narcotics means playing the part. And Kristen's lover-partner soon shows her how to bend the rules to be more effective. Shooting up with the junkies. Splitting down with the dealers. Making the buys to frame the convictions. Snorting dope, faking cases, stealing evidence, perjury – it's all in the line of duty.

Before she knows it, Kristen's hooked. And not to the job.

'Convincingly critical of a justice system that wastes the lives of both cops and defendants.'   *Vanity Fair*

ALAN ALDRIDGE

The Gnole

Fungle is a Gnole: an intelligent, mole-like creature
living in the wilds of the Smoky Mountains. Fearing the
ominous signs of human encroachment – razed trees,
bulldozed land, blasted mountains – and given special
urgency by a mission to stop a powerful demon getting
hold of a device that can destroy the earth, Fungle
embarks on a daunting quest: find the device before the
demon *or* humans can get hold of it and turn the world
into a wasteland.

Packed with dazzling escapes and quirky characters,
The Gnole is an old English fairy tale told to a rock and
roll beat. It's an urban *Wind in the Willows*, its's Bilbo
Takes Manhattan; it's the ultimate collision of cultures.

The Ecology Movement has never had a mascot – until
now.

A List of Film and TV Tie-In Titles
Available from Mandarin

While every effort is made to keep prices low. it is sometimes necessary to increase prices at short notice. Mandarin Paperbacks reserves the right to show new retail prices on covers which may differ from those previously advertised in the text or elsewhere.

The prices shown below were correct at the time of going to press.

☐	7493 0942 3	**The Silence of the Lambs**	Thomas Harris	£4.99
☐	7493 1416 8	**Wayne's World**	Myers & Ruzan	£4.99
☐	7493 1345 5	**Batman Returns**	Craig Shaw Gardner	£3.99
☐	7493 3601 3	**Rush**	Kim Wozencraft	£3.99
☐	7493 9801 9	**The Commitments**	Roddy Doyle	£4.99
☐	7493 1334 X	**Northern Exposure**	Ellis Weiner	£3.99
☐	7493 0626 2	**Murder Squad**	Tate & Wyre	£4.99
☐	7493 0277 1	**The Bill (Volume 1)**	John Burke	£3.50
☐	7493 0278 X	**The Bill (Volume 2)**	John Burke	£3.50
☐	7493 0002 7	**The Bill (Volume 3)**	John Burke	£3.50
☐	7493 0374 3	**The Bill (Volume 4)**	John Burke	£2.99
☐	7493 0842 7	**The Bill (Volume 5)**	John Burke	£3.50
☐	7493 1178 9	**The Bill (Volume 6)**	John Burke	£3.50

All these books are available at your bookshop or newsagent, or can be ordered direct from the publisher. Just tick the titles you want and fill in the form below.

Mandarin Paperbacks, Cash Sales Department. PO Box 11, Falmouth. Cornwall TR10 9EN.

Please send cheque or postal order. no currency, for purchase price quoted and allow the following for postage and packing

UK including BFPO £1.00 for the first book, 50p for the second and 30p for each additional book ordered to a maximum charge of £3.00.

Overseas including Eire £2 for the first book. £1.00 for the second and 50p for each additional book thereafter.

NAME (Block letters) ....

ADDRESS...

....

☐ I enclose my remittance for ....

☐ I wish to pay by Access/Visa Card Number

Expiry Date